KU-766-208

KATARZYNA BONDA

Conspiracy of Blood

HODDER &
STOUGHTON

First published in Great Britain in 2022 by Hodder & Stoughton
An Hachette UK company

1

Copyright © Katarzyna Bonda 2022
Translation Copyright © Filip Sporczyk 2022

The right of Katarzyna Bonda to be identified as the Author of the Work has been
asserted by her in accordance with the Copyright, Designs and Patents Act 1988.

All rights reserved. No part of this publication may be reproduced, stored in a
retrieval system, or transmitted, in any form or by any means without the prior
written permission of the publisher, nor be otherwise circulated in any form of
binding or cover other than that in which it is published and without a similar
condition being imposed on the subsequent purchaser.

All characters in this publication are fictitious and any resemblance to real persons,
living or dead, is purely coincidental.

A CIP catalogue record for this title is available from the British Library

Hardback ISBN 978 1 473 63049 9
Trade Paperback ISBN 978 1 473 63050 5
eBook ISBN 978 1 473 63051 2

Typeset in Plantin Light by Manipal Technologies Limited

Printed and bound in Great Britain by Clays Ltd, Elcograf S.p.A.

Hodder & Stoughton policy is to use papers that are natural, renewable and
recyclable products and made from wood grown in sustainable forests. The logging
and manufacturing processes are expected to conform to the environmental
regulations of the country of origin.

Hodder & Stoughton Ltd
Carmelite House
50 Victoria Embankment
London EC4Y 0DZ

www.hodder.co.uk

Conspiracy of Blood

Also by Katarzyna Bonda

Girl at Midnight

In memory of my grandmother, Katarzyna,
murdered in 1946
in the purge of Orthodox villages in Podlasie.

For my mother – Nina,
orphaned when she was six.
As tribute to her fortitude,
which I have inherited in my genes.
With love

According to Empedocles, all matter is composed of four elements, or 'roots': air, earth, fire and water. These elements are eternal, for that which exists does not come into being, nor does it perish; it is unchanging. Change does exist, for that which is mortal cannot come into being, nor be destroyed by death. There are merely mixtures and combinations of these mixtures.

Famous snake charmers use spectacled cobras. Before the audience, the terrifying snakes become docile, heeding the magical power of the charmer. The trick is rather simple: the snakes have been defanged or have had their mouths sewn shut. Sometimes the charmers immunise themselves against snake venom by repeatedly injecting themselves small quantities thereof. There are instances, though, when a charmer is not protected by anything more than his knowledge of the psyche of the spectacled cobra and his mastery of snake charming. At times, the *fakir*, too certain of his own skills, pays the ultimate price for the illusory power over the snake – the price of his life.

V.J. Stanek, *Wielki atlas zwierząt*

You're a 'local' if the ashes of your ancestors have been buried in local earth.

Background

Sasza Załuska

Sasza Załuska is a psychological profiler with a history of alcohol abuse. For years she lived in England with her daughter Karolina, hiding from her past. Before she left Poland, Sasza used to work as an undercover cop, investigating a man suspected to be the Red Spider – a diabolical serial killer targeting young women, whose calling card is the fact that he paints pictures of his victims. During the investigation, Sasza made a rookie mistake and grew emotionally attached to Łukasz Polak, the man she was supposed to keep under observation. At some point, he found out who Sasza really was and, out of desperation, took her prisoner. Unable to find a way to escape, as a last resort Sasza decided to seduce her captor in the hope of gaining his trust. As soon as Polak let his guard down, Sasza called for help. Before the anti-terrorist unit managed to storm the flat the Red Spider was keeping her in, Polak, determined not to be taken alive, set fire to the apartment. Sasza was saved by firefighters, but sank into a coma. When she regained consciousness weeks later, she learned two things – that Łukasz Polak was dead, and that she was carrying his child. At that point, Sasza decided to turn her life around. She left the police, quit drinking, and moved to England, not returning to her home country until many years later.

Podlasie

The north-eastern border of Poland, or Podlasie as the region is called in Polish, is a beautiful, fascinating land – home to the last primordial forest in Europe and hundreds of historical monuments and places of remembrance. It is a highly diverse region with a rich history and a stunning heritage. It is also a melting pot of cultures and religions with a dark and difficult past. As a place where the fighting during World War Two was especially fierce, it is a region where the scars to the psyche of the local populace run deep, and the memories of crimes committed in the past still divide people.

Two major religious communities dominate the area – the Catholics and the Orthodox. The former are mostly Poles, while the latter include Belarusians and Ukrainians. Because of the difficult history between the two groups, parts of both have radicalised, and in recent years far-right nationalistic movements have dominated the political scene of the region. Tensions between the two groups are common, and tend to revolve around the historical injustices and terrible atrocities committed by roving bands of deserters who refused to acknowledge the cessation of hostilities in the mid-forties, after the war had officially ended. These groups of soldiers-gone-rogue are referred to as the 'Cursed Soldiers'. After they turned their backs on the newly formed communist regime, parts of the guerrilla brigades under the command of Romuald Rajs, *nom de guerre* 'Bury',* went on a bloody rampage across the land of Podlasie, murdering hundreds of innocents – mainly Orthodox Belarusians. Now, nearly eighty years later, those war crimes are still far from forgotten, while their perpetrators are idolised by some Polish nationalists and reviled by the ethnic and religious minorities in Podlasie.

---

* 'Bury' in Polish is 'The Grey' or 'The Dun'.

Prologue

Sopot, May 2014

When, after the third signal, he finally picked up the receiver, she kept quiet, though she should have asked about Zofia.

In the background, she could make out the sound of the TV and the laughter of children. A family reunion, she thought. A tureen of chicken soup on the table, home-made cake on porcelain saucers. The kids, unaware of the things their grandpa, playing the role of Santa Claus each Christmas, did for a living, are running an obstacle course across the apartment. *Tom and Jerry* is blaring from the TV. The adults have to raise their voices to be heard. They toast each other with glasses of pear schnapps. Their guns, clips pulled out and stacked next to boxes of spare ammo, are safely locked in an armoured cabinet.

'Zofia's out,' one of them said. 'Gone to the labour ward.'

Sasza breathed out with relief. When she had left, her handler had already had forty-one years of service behind him, but apparently he was still on duty. His first grandchild had been born after the man had recruited her. She remembered taking notice of the newborn's photo on the desktop of his PC. 'Marcel,' he had beamed, adding, 'his sister's already on her way.' Since that exchange, she had always referred to the officer as 'Gramps'. The moniker had stuck and now everyone was calling him that. For years she hadn't learned his real name. Until yesterday, that is. She counted on Gramps not realising she knew. That would be the first time she would actually have an advantage over him.

'The labour ward?' Sasza smiled. The man wouldn't hang up now. He'd be too curious about what his erstwhile underling wanted. 'What's up with that?'

'I wouldn't know,' he grumbled, falling back on his old routine.

She heard a wheeze in his breath, then a cough, and a crackling noise. He must have excused himself and was now slowly making his way to another room. When he finally closed the door and a silence fell, she felt the need to add something by way of explanation, but he spoke first.

'Telephone books are a thing of the past and I'm not on Facebook, so—' He broke off.

'Guess. You found my number when you mixed me up in that affair with Needles, didn't you?'

'You're not that good.'

'Probably,' she conceded, 'but I have my ways, too.'

'Two more seconds and it'll start recording,' he warned. His voice didn't sound hostile. Bored, more like. 'We'll both get in trouble.'

She hung up and sat down on the floor, cross-legged, lighting a cigarette.

The PC screen flickered and went out. Before it did, Professor Tom Abrams's photo filled the desktop. Her PhD supervisor. They still had to discuss the last seminar. She hadn't contacted him for a while and Abrams was getting worried. He had been trying to catch her on Skype for the last couple of days, messaging her what seemed like dozens of times. Sasza had been working, but she wanted to finish the last chapter first and only discuss her thesis with him when she was finished. She promised herself she would catch him at the institute tomorrow. She finished her cigarette, got up and doused the butt with water from the tap. Her phone buzzed, playing 'Jism' by Tindersticks. She glanced at the screen. Unlisted number. She picked up before the chorus.

'One question,' she said immediately, the soggy fag still in her hand. 'What was my role in Needles's case? Was Łukasz working for us, too? I have the right to know.'

'I've never lied to you,' Gramps replied. He was composed. His voice was less raspy than earlier. The background hiss was nearly inaudible. He must have used an inhaler before calling her back. 'I had my orders. Besides, that was two questions.'

She breathed in.

'Does Łukasz know?'

'Even I don't know everything,' he started, but quickly trailed off. 'You're a mantis, you know?'

Sasza headed to the fridge and poured herself a glass of milk. She took a sip and waited.

'So the Red Spider was a smokescreen, after all?'

'I've been quite confident that this was the case, but after you left it wasn't that obvious all of a sudden. Polak's aunt, a famous director's wife. One phone call was all it took. You know how it is. How things work. I'd wager it was Sońka, Karp's bootlicker. He was in charge of the clean-up detail. Everything snowballed. The DI made sure the papers were clean. It was out of my hands.'

'Was. He. Working. For. Us.'

'You've had your question already.'

'I'll take that as a "yes",' she sighed. 'You screwed me over.'

'Not how I would have phrased it,' he retorted, 'but if you really have to know, I don't think he was working for us.'

'He's still doing it,' Sasza said. 'You remember that case of the student from Tarnów who disappeared? Lidia Wrona.'

This was a case from three years ago, still unsolved. On the day of her disappearance Lidia Wrona had published an artsy photo on social media. It was easy to find on the web. All you had to do was type in: 'Lidia Wrona, disappearance'. When Sasza had done just that, she froze. The Red Spider's style was present and correct. Top-down perspective. A beautiful, painting-like frame. Contrasting colours, enhanced with Photoshop. Lidia lying on her back, wearing a red dress that looked like a spatter of blood over the lush green of grass.

The police had recently abandoned their last lead and the case had been dismissed, with no one under suspicion.

'We don't know that,' Gramps said after a long pause. 'I can only tell you the Spider didn't work alone. He was never a sexual killer or a psychopathic maniac, like we suspected at first. The network of connections reached high, though. Very high. Higher than you suspect.'

'Politics?'

'If only. It was more of a . . .' he hesitated, 'a higher ideal.'

'Blood and honour?'

'Something of the sort, but not exactly.'

'So it's about money?'

'It's always about money, sweetheart.'

Sasza didn't know what to make of this. 'A higher ideal' could mean anything. She knew that despite official assurances about the Red Spider case being closed, the CBS* was still monitoring it and that as soon as they found anything new, they'd get the investigation back on track.

'Can you get me in?'

'No chance.' He reacted a bit too quickly.

'It's not that I don't want to,' he added.

'I don't drink any more.'

'I know, Sasza.'

She felt a twinge of pain at the sound of her name. He usually always called her by her official aliases: Milena or Thumbelina – or her badge number, 1189. Was this a good time to play the ace up her sleeve? But if she told Gramps she had him exposed, it might spook him. She took a piece of paper and started doodling a flowery mandala on it.

'I had to make a technician cough up some of her own cash for a portable drive so we'd be able to copy data from a suspect's PC,' Gramps continued. 'I knew we'd need something to cover our arses in court. But we had no official funding.'

'Incredible.' Sasza couldn't believe what she was hearing. Did the Polish police really have to worry about things like this? In the twenty-first century?

'That's what I told them,' Gramps agreed. 'Anyway, the search turned up squat. The PC was clean. That must have been the seventh cock-up like that this year, if I'm keeping count. Everyone's constantly a step ahead of us. Two years of working our fingers to the bone for nothing. I'm not sure, but I think someone might have tipped the perp off. Or maybe we were being bullshitted from the get-go. Anyhow, all I got was conjecture and a bunch of names. Famous names. Front-page names. As you can guess, nobody spilled. A few small fry who wanted to squeal suddenly bellied up in jail. "Suicide", of course.'

'And "accidents",' Sasza added. 'Typical.'

'So, as you can see, I haven't really got an argument for expanding the team.'

---

* Central Investigation Bureau of Police in Poland

'I can work for free,' she said. 'I want that profile.'

'Listen, I know you're good, I really do,' he said, 'but it's a top-secret case. Anyway, we've got no body. And you know what they say: no body, no—'

'—crime,' she cut in. '*Ex nihilo nihil fit.* But there's precedent. There have been a few cases when people have been sentenced before the body was found.'

'It's not that I don't trust you,' he said.

She didn't believe him. He was talking to her, though, and he never did anything without a reason. He'd told her much already, knowing that she could read between the lines. She realised he was taking a risk. Gramps was at an impasse. Maybe he was afraid for his position? Or maybe he already knew the high-ups were going to give the case to someone else. Someone who wouldn't have an issue with sweeping it under the rug. But Gramps kept talking. Maybe he suspected Sasza might come in handy soon and maybe they'd finally meet. It crossed her mind that Gramps's openness might have something to do with the recent election of the new prime minister. For the previous government, this case had been a priority and nobody seemed to have skimped on the expenses.

'You can just tell me,' she said.

'I've already said too much.'

'Just between you and me.'

'This is not a private conversation.' He suddenly seemed in a hurry. Was he afraid? Was the line tapped? Surely it was.

'Did you ever think that Łukasz Polak might be innocent?' she asked.

'You'd know that better than me. I didn't sleep with the guy for a week. He's not the father of *my* kid.'

She gritted her teeth for a moment, then went on, 'Maybe we had it wrong?'

'I don't know.'

'What do you think?' She didn't relent. 'I have Karolina now, and if they charged him wrongfully . . .' She paused, threw the soggy cigarette butt in the bin and headed to the window, looking at her own reflection.

'You know how much that means to me,' she went on. 'It would change everything. Not for me, per se, but it would mean the world for my daughter. She's already asking for her father. What am I supposed to tell her? I know you understand. You have children yourself. Grandchildren.'

'It wasn't him,' he croaked. She heard the hiss of the inhaler. Her heart raced. 'Or at least not alone. He wasn't the mastermind, that's for sure. But he did have his fingers in it. If you ask me, he knows who's behind this.'

'Is?' she asked. 'This is still happening? I knew it!'

The photo: lush green grass, like an avocado. Red dress. Lidia's pale, full breasts. Red, curly hair. Dead eyes. The girl could be Sasza's younger sister. The similarity was striking. Why had it dawned on her only now? The hypothesis was far-fetched, but that was her job, wasn't it? She had to take every possibility into account. Even the possibility that the Red Spider had kidnapped her simply because she matched the profile of his victims. It couldn't be just a coincidence. The hairs on the back of her neck stood on end.

'You know who the real Red Spider is, don't you?' she said.

Amazingly, she felt relieved. As if someone had taken a great weight from her shoulders. Could she still trust Gramps, though?

'Ask Polak.' He brushed the question off. 'Maybe you'll get an answer before they bump him off. I don't know about you, but I won't cry for him.'

He hung up. She dialled the number, but a voice told her it was temporarily unavailable. Nonetheless, she added it to her contacts as Kajetan Wróblewski – Gramps.

KOLA

(2000)

The hog was lying on the steel table with its trotters up. Its snout was crooked in a rictus grin, as if mocking its own disembowelled stomach. Mikołaj Nesteruk was just finishing gutting the animal. He shook off bits of intestine into a bucket standing next to the table and then shoved the bucket away with a foot. It spun but didn't topple. Good. He swept the sweat from his brow with a sleeve. He was in no mood for cleaning up. His wife would dress him down for slaughtering pigs in the garage anyway. She could always smell the blood afterwards. Everyone wants to eat meat, but when it comes to slaughter, gutting, and roasting there's suddenly no volunteers.

Back in the day, a man had to be able to slaughter and butcher a hog, a hare or a deer, although preparing a chicken had been a woman's job. An axe should always be kept sharp for that purpose. A dull axe-blade meant a landowner didn't properly care for their homestead, was a layabout, or drank to excess. A properly performed slaughter didn't cause too much pain; if the butcher knew his craft, death came quickly. But those times had gone. Nobody now had the slightest inkling about slaughtering, or about how to butcher a carcass – that you had to hang it on a hook for a while to let the blood out. And catch it all in a bucket without wasting a single drop. There ain't any proper men left in this world, Mikołaj grumbled under his breath.

It would take him a few hours to stuff the pig with buckwheat, lard and offal, get it into a hole in the ground and roast it. The wedding party guests would already be waiting, dressed in their freshly starched shirts and new dresses, for the special bus that would transport them to the restaurant.

Suddenly, there was a loud bang.

Mikołaj froze and listened to the ensuing silence. There was a road nearby. Probably just a flat tyre, he thought, and returned to his work. But the bang was soon followed by three more. Now Mikołaj was sure – gunshots. The forest was too far away; it definitely wasn't a poacher.

He walked to the water bucket and scrubbed his hands clean, then left the garage. The grey light of early morning limited his vision. He headed across the field, towards the road. He looked around. Nothing. But he wasn't the only one who had heard the sound. Lights were on in several houses. When he turned round to go back home, he noticed a silhouette. Someone was running towards him, hunched over.

'Help! Somebody help me!' A man. He fell to the ground and went still.

Mikołaj ran to the dark figure as fast as he could, although that wasn't saying much – he was getting on and couldn't run like he used to.

He reached the man. 'What happened?' he rasped, trying to catch his breath.

'Murder,' the man grated out. He raised his head.

'Petya?' whispered Mikołaj, shocked. He crouched down and pulled apart the lapels of the man's jacket. His shirt was soaked through with a thick, dark fluid.

'Who did this to you?'

'I couldn't see,' the man replied.

This had to be a gut shot. The man was bleeding like a wounded deer. Big-calibre gun, probably. A hunter's weapon? A rifle for hunting deer or bison. Home-made? One bullet had gone straight through the collarbone. The hole was wide enough to fit two fingers. The other rounds were probably still inside. Mikołaj knew what to do. During the war he had dealt with wounds like this. He took his shirt off, tore it into strips and tried to stem the squirting blood. He worked steadily for some time. Sweat dripped from his forehead, stinging his eyes. When he finally dressed the wound, the sun was already casting its first rays across the pinkish sky. The weather was going to be perfect again.

Mikołaj pushed himself to his feet, intending to head towards the buildings. He knew there was a phone at the old mill. The poor sod needed help immediately if he was going to live. That's when the prone man shot out an arm, clutching desperately at Mikołaj's hand.

'Help her, Kola,' he whispered in Belarusian. 'There's a car over there. Larysa is still there. Dead.'

Mikołaj raised his head and looked around. There was no car to be seen.

Gdańsk, 2014

The target moved with a clatter and a gust of air blew it upwards, like a kite. Sasza grabbed the lower right corner of the paper sheet, straightened it and counted the bullet holes. The corner of her mouth rose in a half-smile, but she kept quiet. She hit all her shots. All six in the lower part of the silhouette. Just as planned. The aggressor was incapacitated but alive. She put the revolver on the small felt-covered table and let the spent shells drop to the counter. It was Sasza's first time at a shooting range for eight years. She felt like she was back on her first training sessions – but then again, you never really forget how to ride a bike.

'Impressive,' the instructor praised her. 'What is that, a Glock? Or a Kalashnikov?'

Sasza took off her glasses. The earpieces, squished by the sound-dampening headphones, had been causing her some pain. Chief Inspector Robert Duchnowski was standing with his back to a wall plastered with instructional posters – 'How to incapacitate an aggressor'. He smiled approvingly, thumbs tucked into the pockets of his jeans. In those, and his chequered shirt and leather boots, he looked like someone straight out of a Western flick. At least he had got rid of that horrible braid, Sasza thought. His hair was short now, dishevelled, and, in spite of it having lost its natural deep brown colour and turned steel-grey, Ghost looked younger than when they had met after Needles's murder.

He reached out for a firearm catalogue and clicked his tongue dramatically.

'I'd prefer something better suited to a woman's hand,' Sasza grumbled. 'A little stinger.'

'A Beretta, maybe?' asked Duchnowski.

'Yeah, that'll do. I'll try again from longer range.'

She turned, estimating the distance. She could barely see the target from that far away, let alone the bullseye. She put her glasses back on.

'I counted on you saying that,' she heard him saying.

Sasza shook her head like a mother at a prankish little boy.

'Easily pleased, aren't you?' she retorted.

'Not true, but since you don't want to find out yourself . . .' Ghost smirked, provocatively.

The instructor shot them a grossed-out glance from over the target.

'Ten metres is the standard range,' he told Sasza. He marked the previous hits with a marker pen. 'Twenty-five is the Olympic distance.'

'The customer's always right,' Ghost said, and pressed the green button on the console. The target whizzed all the way to the wall. The instructor fled to his cubicle.

In the next booth, a guy in cargo pants and a ripped vintage T-shirt was spewing shots from a machine gun, Rambo-style. His son, who must have been no more than thirteen, was waiting in line. The guy's wife, covered in colourful tattoos, sporting a clutter of blue-yarn dreadlocks and wearing barely more than a bikini, was listening to the metallic clangour of the spent shells cascading to the floor. She didn't seem at all impressed by the gun range. She was clearly a regular spectator at her hubby's little shooting show. Every now and then she fished in her purse for lip gloss and compulsively applied it to her already lustrous lips. In between, she would drop her eyes and vacantly gaze at the tips of her purple wedge-heeled shoes. Sasza studied her with interest, like an unusual weather phenomenon. For a while, she got lost in thought.

When she came back to the present, a Beretta 950 and a box of ammo were already lying on the table in front of her. She tried the diminutive gun in her hand. It was a perfect fit. Black, with a slightly worn grip. A little beauty, she caught herself thinking. She'd like to keep it. It suited her better than the previous ones. Being back at the shooting range was making her reminisce about the time when gunplay had been her bread and butter. She had always been a natural when it came to sharpshooting. It suited her better than showing off with large-calibre cannons.

'She'd be happy to find a place in your pocket.' Ghost read her mind.

She shook her head. The decision was already made – she'd return to the firm and become a police officer again, focusing on profiling. A good shooting-range score was as important for an officer as a good food hygiene assessment for a restaurant. But other than that formality, she'd never use a gun again – not even for work. Her intellect would be her only weapon.

She loaded the gun and disengaged the safety, bracing in a wide-legged stance and relaxing her upper body. She locked her arms, lined up the sight and the target, and aimed the gun.

'All right, you've got the baddie in your sight. Now, show us what you got,' Ghost encouraged. She could barely hear him. The headphones were doing their job. 'Left circle, three shots. The rest at the right one,' he instructed.

She didn't respond, but followed the order. After the very first shot, she knew it wasn't going well. The lightweight Beretta puffed up a cute little gust of smoke with each shot, but was very unstable. And the more Sasza tried to focus, the more difficulty she had keeping the target in sight. She wanted to get this over with. Eventually the clip was empty. She squeezed the trigger again, just to be sure, then put the firearm back on the table. This time, Ghost examined the target himself.

'It's not all bad,' he said, comfortingly. 'Just take the machine gun now and let's get this over with.'

She took a peek at the sheet and realised that she had actually only missed twice. Both were perfect head-shots. The rest had hit the body, just as Duchnowski had instructed her.

'I killed him,' she sighed.

'You can't make an omelette without breaking a few eggs.' Ghost shrugged. 'I didn't realise you were that good.'

'I haven't shot a gun in years.' The modesty was a facade – she was pretty happy with herself.

'You don't forget that. If you're a fighter, that is,' he said, grinning. 'And *you* are a warrior. Just as I suspected.'

'All-knowing and all-important, as always.'

'That's me, all right.' He beamed.

She grabbed the Kalashnikov. The clip was old and prone to jamming. She broke a nail trying to load the last bullet, but at least her confidence was back. Only an utter knobhead wouldn't be able to hit something with a machine gun, as her ex-boss used to say. Sasza tended to agree with the man. At first, she didn't brace properly and the recoil made her shoot off-target, but she compensated swiftly. Her right shoulder would hurt like hell after that. It went pretty well, all things considered. With relief, she took the headphones off, briefly rubbed the skin behind her ears and tossed her glasses into her bag without looking for the case.

'You can't see a thing without those, can you?' Ghost teased. She didn't respond. He took her silence as confirmation.

'Give me a cigarette, will you?' she asked as they left the building. They shared it for a while. Sasza broke the silence first.

'It went pretty well!' she exclaimed, yanking at Duchnowski's sleeve. 'Come on, you have to give me that.'

He grimaced, though his eyes were smiling.

'Maybe, if you do as well on Monday. I won't be there for you,' he replied, putting out the cigarette with the sole of his shoe. 'You hungry?'

'Are you saying I won't make it without you?' Sasza furrowed her brows. 'And you didn't have the balls to take me where the guys practise?'

She gestured to the building. It was the local gun club, huddled in the middle of a little pine wood. One of the walls boasted a large sign reading: 'Wedding parties, first communions, banquets. Cheap and convenient!' First you shoot a gun or two and then you get shit-faced at the party. Or the other way round, Sasza thought.

'This place was on the way.' Ghost was obviously lying. 'You'll show what you got on Monday and nobody will doubt that you're ready to join the team.'

He wasn't looking at her any more.

'Wait. Wasn't that supposed to be a done deal?' Sasza could smell deception. She bristled. 'So what were all those reports and applications for, then? I won't suck up to anyone.'

'I know,' said Ghost, trying to placate her. 'Though I'd like to see that. How does Sasza Załuska suck up to someone? That could be interesting to watch.'

She laughed. He was the first man in a long while who had made her do that. They had buried the hatchet some time ago, but their conversations still tended to sound like schoolboy banter. He had convinced her to return to the force, reminding her of all the advantages police life could offer. When they had promoted him to chief of the criminal investigations division, he'd booked a spot for her. She was supposed to get his old post. Chief Waligóra had no objections to it. He valued Sasza and sometimes even recommended her to other units. If it hadn't been for Duchnowski's and Waligóra's proposal, Sasza wouldn't even have thought about returning. She had filed the papers, done her basic training in the nearby town of Piła, and then easily passed all her advanced exams.

It's always easier to leave than to return. Leaving is liberating, a bit like diving head-first into the sea. One quick decision and it's done. To return is a bit like climbing up a sheer cliff. In Sasza's case, it meant she had to prove herself all over again, demonstrate her worth.

Ghost wouldn't be Ghost if he hadn't made an additional condition. If she was to earn a place in his team, she had to pass all the trials she had always hated the most: fitness and shooting tests. She had passed the psychological evaluation with flying colours, of course. But that only made her feel the weight of the burden on her back. Waligóra and Duchnowski had vouched for her. She couldn't fail their trust. She knew that, and it was only her natural pride that didn't allow her to voice it. Anyway, either you do something properly, or you don't do it at all – her motto, that. Life has a way of taking you down a peg or two at times, though. You can dream all you want, but sometimes you just have to fall back a few steps and pull yourself together. If something went wrong and they didn't take her in, she wouldn't lose any sleep over it.

All the things she had imagined she would do before she returned to Poland – all the commissions, court analyses and freelance jobs – had quickly fizzled out to nothing. If not for the loan she had got from her family, she wouldn't have been able to make ends meet. In Poland, profilers weren't allowed anywhere near the most important investigations if they weren't working directly for the police. So, she had worked on some cases that paid better and some that paid less, but all those gigs had had one thing in common – they had been easy tasks that didn't require her to employ any more than a small percentage of her true potential. Sasza's talents were being wasted. She hadn't developed at all. She had felt her passion ebb. And, truth be told, she had simply missed the force. She wanted back in and had only realised that after the Staroń case – the last big investigation she had taken part in, which had allowed her the chance to prove herself again. It wasn't about the satisfaction, the adrenaline and the fact that she had been able to do what she loved. What she had always been good at. It was all about settling down.

Sasza wanted to finally put down roots. She wanted to feel the earth beneath her feet without it slipping away. She wanted to be able to look into the future and plan for it. She allowed herself to err. Nobody's perfect. But it was about regaining her honour, too. And there was no position better for that than the one she had lost it in in the first place.

'Let's go. You'll never see me suck up to anyone. Never.'

'Never say never.'

'I've just said it,' she replied, 'so what are you going to do about it?'

Ghost parked in the disabled spot and tucked a disabled sticker behind the windscreen. Sasza looked on with disbelief.

'Really, get a cane or something, at least,' she said.

'You're all the support I need.'

'I'm in no mood to be a part of your stupid show,' she snapped. 'They'll catch you soon enough.'

'Oh, but you're already part of it,' he replied and pushed a CBŚ contractor card – number 0184/2013 – into her hands. She stared at the plastic badge with amusement. The document was a fake. Sasza had never been a member.

'Where did you get my photo?'

'The mugshot database.' She knew he was lying.

'I hope they've got your DNA in there too.'

'Sure, several versions of it.'

She laughed, but kept him pinned with her eyes until he caved and answered truthfully.

'The documents you've submitted, of course. I gave it to the secretary to scan and told her to prepare an ID. It's not even illegal. Kinda.'

'Thank you then, kinda.' She tossed the card into her bag. 'It'll come in handy when I park at the station.'

They stopped at the pedestrian crossing. The traffic was sparse and Sasza wanted to cross on red, but Ghost grabbed her by the arm and made her wait.

'Well, well, aren't you a law-abiding citizen all of a sudden,' she mocked him.

'You got to have principles, I always say.'

'One at least, yeah.'

'Only one. I'm an unrepentant monogamist.'

The light turned green.

It was Saturday. Visiting day. A throng of women carrying paper-wrapped packages and leading children, wearing their best clothes, were waiting at the gate of the Kurkowa Street detention centre. Sasza and Ghost had a couple of things to take care of at the prison, individually. Duchnowski was visiting an informer at the men's wing, and Sasza was seeing a woman. A week before, Marzena 'the Wasp' Koźmińska, one of Poland's most infamous female murderers, had been transferred to Gdańsk prison. Sasza wanted to take advantage of this turn of events and talk to her again. When Koźmińska had been doing time at the Castle, the prison in Grudziądz, she had refused to let Sasza interview her on three different occasions. Now, she was about to testify in the trial of her ex-associate. Sasza suspected she was feeling down, as the man, Rafał Gromek, referred to by the press as the 'Wąbrzeźno Electrician', had already been given parole, was getting his case reviewed, and could hope for an early release. He had married a woman and had a child; he had someone to go back to and the family waiting at the gate scored him some points towards a positive evaluation on his social reintegration sheet.

Marzena, still considered one of the most dangerous inmates in Poland, had no hopes of even getting transferred to a low-security wing. Sasza intended to use all that to her advantage and coerce the prisoner into participating in her research project. Sasza's doctoral thesis was nearly finished. Professor Abrams hadn't even tried to hide his satisfaction with the results of her research, but if she could add Marzena's case, she'd surely get a grant. Sasza loved being the best.

They were led to the man lock, which was monitored by a couple of cameras. The room could house no more than three people at a time. The families of the inmates, waiting for their turn at the gate, screamed obscenities at Sasza and Ghost as the pair overtook them in the queue.

They sat on hard plastic stools without backrests, waiting in silence for the guards to process them. Ghost cracked his knuckles, knowing well enough that Załuska hated the sound it made. She fell for the provocation and snapped her head towards him. The chief inspector sent her an amused look, one brow raised. She couldn't read him.

'What?' she barked.

He dropped his head. She poked him in the gut with a finger and he pretended he was in pain.

'Talk.'

'You hungry?'

'You've already asked,' she said and shrugged. 'I don't know yet. What about it?'

'Maybe we could grab a pizza together later,' he said. 'Or something.'

'Or something?' She inclined her head playfully. 'Are you sucking up to me?'

'I sure am.' He beamed. 'How do you like it?'

She swallowed, blinked and felt herself blushing. That was a surprise. She couldn't control it.

'As soon as I get out of here I have to leave the city,' she whispered. 'I want to finish some stuff before I get to work in earnest. I have to do it now. Tomorrow at ten, to be precise.'

'Ten?' asked Ghost. He couldn't hide his disappointment. 'At ten I'll still be in bed. I intend to finally have a good night's sleep. I've got a really comfy bed, you know, but I've been so snowed under at work that it's pretty much my cross-eyed fat cat's now. And he can't even make proper use of it. Except the pissing, that is.'

He didn't manage to make her smile this time.

'Karo went to Crete with her grandmother,' Sasza continued. 'They send me pictures every day. They're having fun, it seems. I need to shut a certain door once and for all. And it's now or never.'

Ghost played with his car keys. She could see him growing sombre. He had wrongly interpreted her reply as rejection.

'It's personal,' she explained. 'I have to drive right across the country in the evening. To Hajnówka, near the Białowieża Forest. Eight hours, give or take, my GPS tells me. Two days and I'm back. And I'll happily grab dinner with you then, after that damned exam. Maybe. But don't count on me jumping into your bed.'

They stared at each other in silence, then smiled at the same time.

'Denied again,' sighed Ghost, pretending to be hurt. His eyes were sparkling, though.

'I'll get this done in a jiffy,' she said.

Duchnowski reached out a hand. She tensed, trying to calm her racing heart, but as soon as he put his enormous, bony paw on her hand she felt the tips of her ears flushing. He only touched her for the briefest moment, very delicately. As soon as he withdrew his hand, she realised he'd left the 9mm Beretta from the gun club in her palm. She was lost for words.

'I didn't steal it,' Ghost said and giggled. This greying forty-five-year-old had something mischievous in him, like a kid, she thought. There had been a time when she couldn't find anything charming about him. Had he changed that much? Or had *she* undergone some kind of metamorphosis?

'It was my father's. A family heirloom,' he explained. 'I brought it for you.'

'I don't carry,' she protested half-heartedly. 'I don't have to.'

He had obviously been counting on a different reaction. Her lack of excitement clearly dumbfounded him.

'You'll get to practise before the test. So, what's it gonna be?'

'What's it gonna be?'

'It's a gift,' he said with finality. 'An overdue one. Christmas. Kinda.'

'What about the permit?'

'All ready and waiting on my desk,' he said and winked. 'I don't have any ammo, though.'

'I always take my time to get used to new things.' She weighed the Beretta in her hand and then placed it in her lap, her eyes never leaving the weapon. 'When I bought a washing machine I stared at it like an idiot for, like, two weeks before I even turned it on. It's good you don't have ammo. I wouldn't use it, anyway.'

'Not even a little?'

Her lips stretched in a smile and she repeated Duchnowski's words, imitating the timbre of his voice:

'Not even a little. Kinda.'

Ghost opened his other hand and deftly stuck it into her pocket, releasing the handful of bullets he had been hiding from her, like they were candy.

'I was kidding. Seems I'm a bit of a hoarder after all.' He leaned closer to Sasza's ear. She could smell his cologne, his skin and cigarette smoke. It made her head spin. She couldn't focus. When he spoke, she felt his warm breath on her earlobe. He was so close, his lips nearly touching her skin. 'I've removed the evidence, don't you worry. *Nas nye dogonyat.*' 'Not Gonna Get Us'. The title of a pop song, a huge hit.

Sasza snorted with laughter and did her best not to hug the great oak of a man.

'That's so cute,' she squealed.

'I know,' he said proudly. 'That's why you'll be such a great match.'

Now both of them felt awkward. Sasza retreated to a safe distance, tucking the Beretta into her pocket. They both sighed with relief when finally the small window of the guard room opened and they were called to the gate.

The guardsman gave them their papers and ID badges. A while later a woman joined him, introducing herself as a major. Sasza didn't hear her name. She was still too confused by Ghost's behaviour. He had clearly been flirting with her. And what was even worse was that she'd liked it. She dropped her head and took a moment to gather her wits.

The major, the *capo di tutti capi* of the women's prison wing, wore snow-white stockings and her blond hair coiled in plaits, like Helga from the old TV programme '*Allo 'Allo*, which Sasza immediately mentally christened her. Sasza couldn't help imagining the woman in a dominatrix outfit, hefting a whip. She must have looked like a Viking queen in her day, but since then she had gained weight and the only sign of her erstwhile grandeur was the overbearing feeling of discipline she exuded. She was methodically arranging plastic containers on the counter.

'Weapons, gas, mobile phones, please.'

Sasza put the Beretta into one of the boxes, carefully transferring all the ammunition from her pocket. Ghost tossed his Glock in, too. It looked like the guardsman from the men's wing was a little less of a stickler, or maybe the inmate the chief inspector was visiting wasn't as dangerous, because while Sasza was even deprived of her nail file and a pack of plasters, Ghost's warden only lazily pointed to his cowboy-style belt buckle but, astonishingly, didn't make him take it off, instead inviting him to the barred door leading to the men's ward. Meanwhile, Helga scrutinised each and every piece of Sasza's attire.

Ghost was already vanishing down the corridor, assisted by a couple of prison guards, while Helga was still analysing Sasza's biker boots.

'It's not as if I have a hidden knife or something,' Sasza grumbled, but she meekly took off her boots and placed them on the X-ray machine.

'Don't be late!' called Ghost as he rounded the corner. 'Monday, eight o'clock. The next transfer window opens in autumn. But don't worry. In the afternoon we'll celebrate you joining the family. At least I hope I'll be in a condition to celebrate – Wally's organising a late birthday party the day before and he's already bought each guest a pint of Duch Puszczy. Promise you'll be there!'

'We'll see.' Sasza wiggled her toes. She was still standing barefoot, and to say the prison floor was pristine would be a gross overstatement. She turned back to Helga and made an attempt at humour: 'Seems I'm visiting Hannibal Lecter himself, eh?'

'Quite so,' replied Helga, not taking her eyes off the contents of Sasza's bag. She paused the screen of the X-ray machine and pointed to a spike-like object. Sasza fished it out. It was a keyholder. She raised it so the woman could see. Helga snatched it swiftly, turning it this way and that in her fingers as if it could have housed a hidden gun, finally placing it in the deposit box.

'Alcohol, drugs?'

Sasza gave her an ironic look, but if Helga was able to read the expression, she didn't show it, instead continuing her methodical work. She unfastened the strap from Sasza's handbag, wrapped it around her palms and tried it out as a potential suffocation tool. Sasza heard the clanking of the buckle as the woman tightened the strap. Nothing surprised her any more. She'd been to every Polish prison housing murderers, and a search as thorough as this was unprecedented. Even when Helga took out a can of body spray, took the lid off and sprayed a thick cloud of mist, taking a deep sniff and grimacing, the smell apparently not to her liking, Sasza kept still, eyes fixed on the warden in an impassive stare.

'What about this?' asked Helga, pointing to a long, pointy object on the screen.

'That's a pencil. The lead's broken.'

'I won't let you in with that,' barked Helga.

She tossed the pencil into the box. The same went for a lighter, a roll of duct tape, some chewing gum, and a notebook.

'A notebook? Really?' Sasza finally snapped. 'That's a bit over the top, don't you think?'

Helga pointed to the items lying in the box and replied with a straight face: 'Belt: attempted strangulation of an inmate. Lighter, body spray, duct tape, chewing gum: a flamethrower. My colleague is still recovering from her burns. Pencil and notebook: attempted blinding.'

Amused, Sasza took the pencil and jabbed it at the air, pretending to stab someone in the eyeball.

'Like that?'

Helga took the pencil, sharpened it, rubbed the lead vigorously all over a page of the notebook with her finger, swept the excess off and made a gesture of grinding the graphite into her eye.

'Thirteen people since they brought her in,' she said. 'Nobody wants to share a cell with her. All she does is mill around, acting the clown, and then, out of the blue – an assault. Doesn't even matter who she gets hold of.' She dragged a finger across her throat.

Sasza's smirk vanished.

'But she's been doing time for years now. There haven't been any complaints lately, have there? I was close to interviewing her in Grudziądz.'

Helga only shrugged. Her face took on an expression of pity, although it might have also been an attempt at a smile.

'Want me to come with you?'

'No, it's all right.'

'Better if I transfer her to the dangerous inmates' room,' Helga decided.

She took the deposit box and was about to leave, but then she changed her mind mid-stride and asked for the whole handbag. She only allowed Sasza her boots. As Sasza was putting them on, a walkie-talkie crackled. The warden immediately reported her whereabouts.

'An accident at the sewing room,' the speaker spat. 'Senior guard, sector P, to exit number twenty-three, please. We have injured inmates.'

'I'll lead a guest in and will take over asap.'

They headed to the security door.

At the end of a long, windowless corridor there was a flight of stairs, and then a passageway to the next building. That's where they stopped. They could already hear the calls and bawls of agitated inmates. Helga entered a set of numbers on a keypad at the door. The gate clicked but they didn't move. Suddenly a cigarette butt fell from somewhere up high, right in front of Sasza. She picked it up and, ignoring the warden's condemning glare, put it out on the wall and flicked it to the windowsill. Raising her eyes again, she noticed a group of women at the top of the stairs ahead of them. They were of a variety of ages, looks and body types. Some of them had bandages on.

'Ah, there they are. My princesses,' the jailer said softly.

Sasza shot a quick glance at the prisoners. They, in turn, were keeping their eyes fixed on Sasza like bulls ready to charge a matador's red cloak. One of them, the youngest and prettiest, gave a long whistle. And though the insubordinate inmate was immediately pacified with a smack of a baton to her lower back, the rest clearly read it as a signal to attack. Someone snickered mockingly from the second row. Someone else growled angrily. A large, shaggy-haired and sweaty woman stepped to the front of the group. There was a wide bandage wrapped around her arm. The wound must have been fresh; the gauze was soaked through and a thin trickle of blood was making its way down her arm, nearly reaching her elbow. The woman seemed to pay it no heed. She locked her hands behind her neck and rolled her eyes, making obscene movements with her hips.

'Quit showing off, Janet.' The prison guard stuck the tip of her baton under the inmate's chin. 'Nobody's impressed.'

The woman withdrew meekly. Meanwhile, more women were descending the stairs. They couldn't all fit in the passageway, so Helga gestured for them to move closer to her and Sasza. An instant later Sasza was completely surrounded by inmates. They took up the entire space. She could hear them whispering among themselves. Some were pointing at her. Only those lowest in the hierarchy stood immobile, their apathetic faces showing nothing at all.

'Pretty one,' someone called from the back of the throng. 'Why don't we take her with us?'

Sasza tried to ignore the comments, though it wasn't that easy. She knew they were just bored witless and killing time. They didn't really have anything against her. But when she felt someone's hand groping at her crotch, she instinctively took a quick step backwards, face contorted in a grimace of fear. That was clearly what the owner of the groping hand had intended, as the gesture won her a bout of raucous laughter. The large woman with the bandaged arm suddenly appeared out of nowhere, right in front of Sasza.

'Lookie here, pretty princess,' she said and smiled amiably. Sasza suddenly realised just how enormous the woman was. She towered over her. She must have been close to two metres tall. Suddenly, with a theatrical gesture she ripped the dressing from her arm, demonstrating the fresh marks of what looked like self-mutilation. 'They don't give us any free time, the bitches!'

The guardswoman who had led the inmates from the sewing room came to Sasza's rescue.

'Enough, Janet,' she said, wearily. 'Get back in line.'

She signed a document and transferred the herd to Helga, who led the women out to the courtyard. Not one of the inmates seemed to dare to speak, but Sasza knew she would be hearing their whispers for a long while yet. The other guard was nicer. She even smiled a bit. She searched Sasza again, then led her to a small room divided in half by a transparent wall.

Marzena Koźmińska, the killer Sasza had wanted to interview for so long, was already waiting on the other side of the plastic wall. At first glance she didn't look dangerous. She looked normal, like dozens of people you see on the streets every day. Smoking their cigarettes, talking on their phones and pushing their prams. It was hard to guess her age. She looked like your typical, slightly scruffy, auntie, grandma or mother. She might be any of those herself, come to think of it. Thin, shapely, brown-haired, unremarkable. The slightly crossed eyes only made her more appealing. She wore cheap glasses patched with duct tape and had a modest page-boy-style hairdo. Worn slippers and white socks on her feet. The legs of her orange uniform, marking her out as a dangerous inmate, were rolled all the way up to her knees. Her legs were stick-thin, snow-white and clean-shaven.

Sasza wouldn't have pegged her as a murderer if she'd met her anywhere else. Koźmińska didn't resemble the blond-haired redneck she remembered from photos from the investigation that commenced days after she had murdered a high-school student in Warsaw. But it was her. The brains of the gang. The Wasp. The first and only Polish woman sentenced to life without any possibility of parole. She had quit education after high school, but psychological testing pointed to her IQ being very high – close to 178. If she had stayed at school, she would have probably easily graduated from university. She was a talented strategist, a natural leader and a gifted speaker. A diagnosed psychopath, too.

Marzena came from a dysfunctional family. She had been accustomed to aggression and violence since she was a child. That was the only life she knew. Until she was finally caught, crime had just been her way. The death blows hadn't been her doing; in fact she hadn't even touched any of the murder weapons herself, only ever participating in the torturing as a spectator. Always at the back, always taking care that her orders were fulfilled to the letter. The killings had always been committed by men – her lovers or men aspiring to become such. For years she had been too smart to get caught. Investigators said that she must have committed numerous offences, but they could only ever prove a single one. And she had never claimed responsibility.

'I don't agree,' she said now without preamble, grinning at her guest, displaying a gap in place of one of her front teeth.

Sasza sat down on a stool. She didn't know what to do with her hands so she stuck them into the pockets of her jacket. She could feel the pack of R1 cigarettes sitting in the back pocket of her jeans, digging into her buttock. She moved it to her breast pocket. The guard had taken her lighter but the room was a no-smoking zone anyway and the camera's eye didn't leave her for even a moment.

'What don't you agree to?' Sasza didn't intend to play nice. She did feel a slight tingle of unease in her neck, though.

Sasza wasn't here to plead – her plan was to shake Marzena up a bit, make her lose the veneer of calm she hid behind and try to provoke her into taking off the mask of the Wasp. At least for a while. Then she'd think of something else. But first, Sasza had to make sure it was even worth it to expend her energy on the woman.

'I agree to nothing,' Marzena snapped from behind the glass wall. 'I'm innocent.'

'So we're both wasting our time?' Sasza took her hands out of her pockets. She noticed a black smudge on her wrist, rubbed it off and pointed to the bulletproof window cubicle around the woman. 'So why are you inside that?'

Marzena raised her chin defiantly. 'You studied Szymon,' she said. 'She's my good mate.'

'She did pretty well.'

'You paying?'

Sasza shook her head. 'But I can arrange for some coffee and cigarettes for you. Movies, books. Whatever you need. I'm a scientist.'

'Bullshit.'

Sasza flinched.

'You're a cop. I can feel it.'

'Does it matter?'

Marzena sat back more comfortably. She undid the top two buttons of her orange uniform, revealing a green flowery undershirt, tight around her large, shapely breasts. Maybe that had been her secret weapon. Through the deep cleavage, Sasza noticed a scar. From a self-inflicted wound? The bruise looked infected. Revolting.

'You lied to the girls. They're pretty pissed off. They didn't want to talk to the pigs.'

'The situation was different . . .' Sasza began, but thought better of it. She didn't have to explain herself to an inmate.

Marzena pulled out a crumpled photo from a pocket and held it against the window. It showed two women, one of them not very remarkable, the other attractive. Both were slim, tanned and smiling. A man had his arms around them both. He wore a golden Omega watch or at least a pretty good fake. He was handsome, middle-aged. In the foreground, on a table, a bottle of Russian *Igristoje* champagne, a couple of crystal glasses and a half-eaten smoked mackerel partially wrapped in paper.

'That's me.' Marzena pointed to the less attractive woman. Then she slid her finger to the other one. 'This is Monika Zakrzewska. But everyone used to call her Jowita. She's off the grid. You following me?'

Sasza had read Marzena's files and knew about the pretty girl in the photo. She had been working with Marzena in a local whorehouse in Warsaw's Bródno district. They had been friends. One day a white Mercedes, the 'four-eyed' type, model W210, drove up to Monika's mother's house. She took her child and they both got in and the car drove away, never to return. Vanished into thin air. Years later, during the investigation into the murder of the high-school student in Warsaw, her story came up again. One of Marzena's associates had made a deal with the police in exchange for a shorter sentence. He had testified that Marzena used to brag about hiring someone to kill her friend for stealing her boyfriend. Monika's body had never been found.

'Who's that guy?' Sasza pointed to the Pierce Brosnan wannabe in the photo.

'I don't know his name. But I bet he knows who topped Monika. I want you to find that guy and tell him I said hello.'

A silence fell over the room.

'Three teams worked that case,' Sasza said after a long while. 'How am I supposed to crack it on my own, after such a long time?'

'You're a cop, no? You help me, I get you the info you need to get that Nobel prize or whatever they give to psychiatrists.'

Sasza stood up.

'Not gonna fly. And I'm a psychologist. There's a difference.'

For a while, Marzena looked disappointed. A few seconds, no more. Quickly, it turned into anger.

'I know things I haven't told *anyone*,' she hissed, slapping her thighs. She continued, quickly, raising her voice: 'I got that photo only recently. I paid a pretty penny for that scrap of paper. I work in the sewing room here. They pay me eighty *groszy* per rag I make! It's barely enough for smokes and tampons. I mean, I did work there until recently. They ditched me. I'm only going apeshit because I've nothing to lose. I'm not worried about myself. I can bite the dust for all I care. I'm never getting out of here anyway. But I have kids. Alive, out there, outside. Zakrzewska's mother, that old bitch, keeps giving them a hard time. She'll destroy them and I can't do a thing. I want that sow to fuck off. I didn't kill her bitch of a daughter, though God knows I had plenty of opportunities to off that cunt.'

Sasza raised her hand, cutting Marzena off. They sat in silence for a while.

'I'll help you find the man,' the inmate whispered.

'Why do you care?'

''Cause I'm innocent.' Marzena was in control again. Her nonchalant manner was back. 'I've got nothing to do with this. I've done some things, true, but not this.'

Sasza sat down again.

'Stop talking out of your arse and maybe I'll help you.' She smirked. 'What's this really about?'

Marzena was clearly considering whether she should keep up the self-righteous act or just tell the truth.

'I don't count on getting justice,' she said. 'I just want the guy to come and visit. Let him know I have the photo and want to talk. He'll come.'

Sasza couldn't believe her ears. Was the Wasp finally being straight with her?

'So you want me to be your errand boy?'

Marzena shrugged. 'If that's not too much in exchange for the beast's confession for your paper.'

'Words mean nothing,' Sasza retorted. 'How can I be sure you'll talk?'

'You can't,' the Wasp replied, simply. 'In principle, I don't do deals with the devil. But I can give you my word.'

Sasza's chuckle visibly hurt Marzena.

'I've never made a promise I couldn't back up. I got standards.'

'Oh, I bet you do,' Sasza muttered. 'Yet somehow I still don't believe or trust you. I highly doubt that will change.'

Marzena took a deep breath and said: 'Listen up, because I won't repeat myself. If you don't find him, I'll find another way. You're not the only one who wants to rake me for my secrets and make some cash out of it.'

'I'm not doing this for the money,' Sasza protested.

'Aren't you?' The Wasp cocked her head with a sly smile. 'What about the fame and glory? The grants? The back-patting? You don't fool me. Won't a doctorate raise your salary? There's nothing in this life better at making you feel free than money. It's the only thing that counts. If you're rich, they let you be a nutter, a fool . . . or a killer. You're untouchable.'

'So why won't you sell your story? Write a book, sell movie rights. There are dozens of publishers without scruples in Poland. They'll get you a crafty journo with the same outlook on financial matters as yours and they'll happily play their part. Your name will be on the first page above theirs and they won't care. A book like that would be a bestseller. You only got to give it a fancy title. How about "The Bloody Queen's Testament". You'll be famous again,' Sasza taunted.

Marzena missed the irony, taking the mockery as advice.

'I might just do that,' she said, growing calmer, and opened up: 'There isn't a week without someone from the TV knocking at my door. No one's offered the right amount of money, though. Listen, you're here, we both want the same thing. Why don't we make a deal? The price ain't high. At least, I don't think it is. I'm telling the truth. Fuck it, believe me when I say I'd like it to be bullshit. But it isn't. I couldn't care less about who topped Jowita and who's going to take the heat for that. I need money to pay off Jowita's mother. Peace can be bought, you know? If you have the cash.' She stopped and fixed Sasza with a stare. She pointed a finger at her. 'You a mother?'

Sasza nodded reluctantly. Marzena was going to change her tune. She was going to try to make Sasza pity her now. Sasza believed herself to be ready to screen out the performance and focus on the truth.

'My oldest daughter is pregnant. I'll be a grandma. As soon as the neighbours discovered that my children's mother is me, they made their lives hell. As if they're somehow to blame for what I did. I know life's not a walk in the park, but I won't let them destroy my kids' lives like they fucked up mine.'

Sasza couldn't help but feel pity. She wasn't looking at a psychopath any more, but a desperate mother. Locked up in a cage, lashing out because she had never experienced kindness herself. She was only trying to survive. Marzena could be a case for a whole separate research paper. The woman had a soft underbelly and Sasza would have loved to dissect her.

'I'll think about it,' she said.

Marzena shook her head. 'You don't believe me.'

'What did you expect?' Sasza snorted. 'Prisons are full of innocent people.'

The woman was a good actress: her face was a mask of genuine regret. When she spoke, her voice broke.

'But I really didn't kill her. The evidence was all circumstantial. They pinned that kidnapping on me after I killed that student. Yeah, I picked her up from her house, but I didn't kill her. I didn't appeal against the decision. I couldn't afford a lawyer. And now it's too late.'

'What you're expecting me to do is impossible.' Sasza unzipped her jacket. The pack of cigarettes fell to the ground. She caught Marzena's look. The woman was devouring the smokes with her eyes. Sasza pulled one out, playing with it and observing the inmate's reaction out of the corner of her eye. Then, she slid it back into the pack. 'Some investigations remain unsolved, you know,' she said. 'And I'm not a psychic. You don't even know the man's name. Or you don't want to tell me. And besides, what does he have to do with Jowita? And you?'

'If they would let me out, I'd have found that prick. He knows. Maybe he even did it himself.'

Marzena clammed up. There was no trace of the desperate mother any more. She was the Wasp again.

'How did you get that photo?' Sasza asked. 'Who sold it to you? I need a name.'

Marzena didn't reply. She jotted down a court file number on the back of the photograph and then slid it to Sasza through a slit in the window.

'Have a read,' she asked gently. 'You'll be back. I'm very patient. But my children don't have much time. Help them if you can.'

Sasza took the photo. The file number was easy to memorise. The case had been referred to the court in 2001. She flipped the photo and took another look at the three people. The brown-haired man sitting in the middle had to be at least forty, but he was that rare breed of man who would look handsome even in a ripped T-shirt. Monika was clinging to him. The man was glancing at Marzena, though. Or, more accurately, into her cleavage. Marzena was no beauty, but she had charisma. The photo did justice to her magnetism. It also caught the daggers in her eyes. Those two didn't trust each other, but there was something between them. A connection. And it was much stronger than whatever affection was between the gigolo and the disappeared beauty. Monika had been trusting, cute. The perfect trophy for those two predators. Sasza recalled an old saying: three people can keep a secret if two of them are dead. What secret linked those three? She wasn't sure she wanted to know.

'Don't lose it,' said Marzena. 'I don't have a copy. We called him Four-Eyes. He drove that Mercedes. E-class, W210. White, like a wedding limo. The guy would show up every now and then and then vanish. At times he would be away for months. But then he'd come a few times a week. Back in the day, there weren't a lot of people who could afford a car like that. Our customers drove Fiats or got around by tram. We were no call girls.'

Sasza mulled it over. If Marzena was telling the truth, she had just given Sasza the only lead she had. Was she bluffing? What did she want to use her for? Sasza was certain the Wasp would agree to the interview. But she had to give her something in return. Otherwise the woman would just turn around and leave. All right, Sasza would read the file. After all, why not? It may even prove interesting.

'I can't promise anything,' she said and rose.

Marzena shrugged. She had what she wanted. The line was cast, but would she catch the fish she wanted? Nothing was certain. But you have to know when to loosen the line so it doesn't snap. That moment came now. There's nothing worse for a business deal than overselling the product.

'Leave a couple of smokes, will you? They won't confiscate them. I have a deal with the warden.'

The slit beneath the window was too thin to fit the entire pack, so Sasza took the cigarettes out one by one, flattening then with a palm and sliding them through the same way Marzena had handed her the photo. One of the cigarettes broke and the tobacco spilled on the counter. Marzena shot a quick glance at the camera, then carefully collected the spilled contents to the last speck.

'How did you know I was police?' Sasza asked as she prepared to leave.

Marzena, occupied with hiding the smokes in a secret pocket, didn't respond at once but eventually said, 'You've got gunpowder on your fingers.'

Sasza took a look at the spot where the black smudge had been. There was no trace now of the mark left from her visit to the gun range. Marzena laughed bitterly. 'You're a bitch, all right, but you're no pure-breed. One good bluff and you buckle.'

Sasza didn't buy it. The Wasp wasn't one to improvise. She had to have checked her dossier before the meeting. She had done her homework. Better watch out for her. Sasza had never researched such an interesting person.

Hajnówka, 2014

The seamstress was really late now. Another thirty minutes and women were going to start showing up at Iwona Bejnar's flat at 13 Chemiczna Street to bake a *korovai* together. The ingredients for the traditional heart-shaped wedding cake, to be divided between the young couple before the ceremony, and silk ribbons for the wedding braid were all displayed like gallery items on the only table in the cramped, two-room apartment in the slums of Hajnówka, where the twenty-five-year-old bride-to-be had been living with her two older brothers and their mother. They had all been provided by a courier sent by Iwona's fiancé.

The Bejnar family had never had a bread oven. Nevertheless, it had been decided that the traditional women's meeting the day before the wedding would take place at the bride's house. An electric cooker, just like those used to bake pizza, took up roughly half of the space of the larger room. Seeing carriers lugging the thing in, the neighbours had clustered around the entrance to the building, trying to see what riches Piotr Bondaruk had gifted to his future mother-in-law. She had noted the disappointment in their eyes when they had realised it wasn't a new fridge or at least a portable heater. Why would someone living in Hajnówka's Bermuda Triangle need an enormous oven taking up half of the flat? The contraption now stood between the sofa and the shoddy plywood table, obscuring the brand new TV, sensibly covered with a plastic sheet so it wouldn't get messed up during the preparation of the cake.

Aside from the formalised matchmaking and negotiations, or *svaty*, baking the *korovai* was one of the most important rituals of the traditional Belarusian wedding. It was supposed to bring luck, peace, fertility and prosperity to the young couple. For Iwona, that last thing at least was a given. Bondaruk was probably the most influential man in the city and one of the richest people in the region. His company was doing well and he owned real estate all around the province. Nearly half of the inhabitants of Hajnówka and the nearby towns and villages worked in his wood processing plant, manufacturing floorboards and stairs to be exported to Germany and France. A month ago Bondaruk had started negotiations with the Norwegians too. The priests in all four of Hajnówka's Eastern Orthodox churches prayed for the local 'New Forest' floorboards to stand up to the competition from Ikea. There was no one in town who didn't know Bondaruk. There wasn't a family around who didn't benefit from his business, one way or another. Even if it turned out that his hands were dirty, everyone would stand firmly behind him. After all, he was the reason the unemployment rate in the region had fallen by almost two per cent recently. He could have run for mayor if he wanted and would have won without breaking a sweat.

Iwona took a look around the room. Tomorrow, she would leave this hovel for a comfy condo in the recently renovated block on Piłsudskiego, the loveliest street in town, lined with ancient linden trees. Until now, she'd had to fight with her brothers for space. It had its advantages – she had grown to be a bold and resolute woman. That didn't change the fact that her older brothers had usually won their fights, though. No amount of prodding, crying and complaining to their mother had ever helped. Iwona had quickly learned how to cope by using guile and deception. Her personal charm had come in handy too. It had become her weapon of choice. She knew how to use others' weaknesses and would quickly turn them to her advantage to get her way. Bożena, her mother, had never been Iwona's ally in her quarrels with her brothers. She usually just told her to do as they said. Her three sons were the ones who brought home the bacon and as far as she was concerned they had to rest after work, have a hearty dinner and, if they so wished, drink themselves into a stupor.

None of them worked legally. That was the case for most of the inhabitants of the residential project next to the old, now defunct turpentine and chemical plant that had given the street its name. For years, the Bejnar brothers had been beneficiaries of the local social welfare fund. Each one of them had been formally certified as disabled, despite all being large, bull-like, perfectly healthy men. They ran an informal boxing club they had dubbed the 'Wolf Pack' in the basement of the tenement. Only the youngest one, Ryszard, known by the locals as Bison Junior, graduated from vocational school. Not that he ever made use of his education after that. Władysław and Ireneusz, also referred to appropriately as Old Bison and Middle Bison, had said goodbye to education in the second grade of the 'farmyard', as the local agricultural vocational school was known. They had been expelled and blacklisted after blowing up a cabinet of test score-sheets in the principal's office using a military-grade flare. The whole affair had ended in a great fire spreading across the school building. The principal himself had miraculously survived, having been in the toilet next to the school cafeteria after being served *kopytka* and fried cabbage left over from the previous week. Before he had left the toilets, the firefighters had managed to put out the fire, the Bison brothers had been arrested by the police and the crowd of onlookers had started to dissipate.

Since that momentous day, the Bejnar boys had never returned to any educational facility. They didn't treat it as a loss, though, as they had never wanted to become farmers in the first place. They had only been in it for the papers needed to get unemployment pay. Unfortunately for them, it turned out the local employment agency had stripped them of their allowance before they had managed to regain consciousness after the party they had organised on account of their 'permanent holiday'.

They had always taunted their sister for trying to get a bachelor's degree in the local college's administration faculty after graduating from the forestry school in Białowieża. At the same time, they had always been overprotective and treated her as their mascot. The Bison brothers tended to express their love through spectacularly aggressive behaviour; for example, by knocking out their sister's unwanted admirers and setting the homes of her competitors on fire. Rysiek, Władek, and Irek got rid of anyone they thought of as unworthy of a true Polish girl on account of their foreign roots. Their stringent standards meant that Iwona was off-limits for at least seventy per cent of the inhabitants of the entire region. The local populace was composed mainly of Belarusian Poles. 'True-born' Poles were a rarity here, but the Bejnars took pride in being just that.

The Bison brothers loved to celebrate Polish public holidays and be seen doing it. They made their own flags, banners and T-shirts depicting the 'damned soldiers' themselves. They had inherited artistic talents from their grandfather, Grzegorz Rusinuk, who was known to have played – and doped – with Rysiek Riedel, that most celebrated of Polish singers, himself. He had only travelled to Hajnówka for rehab but had ended up staying – he had spent the cash meant for his return ticket on booze as soon as he was released. So, having nothing else to do, he returned to the rehab centre, where he discovered his talent for 'brushwork', as he had called his painting. All his works, even those depicting women, included his self-portrait. For his services to local culture, he had been given the flat on Chemiczna Street, where he had spent most of the rest of his life. In his later years he developed Alzheimer's and was moved to a nursing home. The flat went to his daughter, whom he had never shown any interest in, and her children.

Physically, the Bison brothers were the spitting image of their grandfather, which they liked to remind people of by spray-painting nationalistic graffiti on random walls across Hajnówka. It had to be said they had a knack for it, and the old man, if he had still been alive, would have been proud of them. So, the boys were furious when the locals failed to appreciate their patriotic endeavours and instead called them fascists, skinheads, hooligans or yobs. It was a fact, though, that each time Jagiellonia Białystok played, the Bison brothers would only come home two days later, once the police released them from detention after they had been caught participating in brawls, daubing swastikas on walls, or at least provoking schoolkids to fight them. Iwona had also given in to family pressure and there had been a time when she would accompany her brothers, wearing a hoodie saying, 'Hail to the Heroes!', the traditional pseudo-patriotic slogan. Since she had fallen in love with a Belarusian, she had distanced herself from the Bejnars' nationalist pursuits.

The only place in the flat that Iwona could truly call her own was a little spot by the window. A narrow sofa bed that still

remembered the long-gone time of the national Hajnówka Wood
Processing Plant, a laminated chipboard cabinet and a soft
pouffe covered with fabric in a dreadful colour, where Iwona
kept her underwear. She also had a few hangers in her mother's
wardrobe, and a single bookshelf beneath which she had hung
a theatre play poster depicting Danuta 'Inka' Siedzikówna of
the 5th Wilno Brigade, a Polish national hero and Iwona's idol.
The bookshelf was a little more than a metre long and housed
mainly comedies and romance novels. Though Iwona's mother
had done her best to spoil the notion of love for her, the girl
remained an incurable romantic. Her books contained some
great ideas on how to talk to the opposite sex, so Iwona had
practically learned them all by heart. She had also perfected the
art of batting her eyelashes flirtatiously and playing with the
emotions of men. Among her books was one by Joanna Bator,
as Iwona had been trying to get to grips with the notion of
polyamory, and all of Zygmunt Miłoszewski's crime novels – in
her youth she had been in love with Szacki, their protagonist.
Now, she had decided to throw almost all of her belongings
away, keeping only the poster and her books. None of those
things would be necessary tomorrow. She would take nothing
but her red Samsonite bag (bought by her fiancé, of course).

Iwona glanced at the little mirror hanging on the wall next to a
simple wooden cross, and smiled to herself, satisfied. People were
saying she had never looked better. Not even when she had been
desperately in love with a local hotshot, real name Jurek but better known as Quack, who hadn't even remotely resembled any of
Iwona's favourite book characters but had always worn branded
clothes and had driven a yellow sports bike. She had thought they'd
live happily ever after, but not a week after Quack had proposed the
police had arrested him. Iwona couldn't even visit him in prison, as
the prosecutor was afraid it would affect the case. Quack had been
caught red-handed stealing fast-chargers from a local business and
traces of psychoactive substances had been found in his blood and
in his pocket a stolen iPhone. Quickly, the police learned that the
phone had been stolen from a Catholic priest, but the man himself
had in turn bought it from a fence at the local market known as the
Ruble Mart. The crime itself wasn't so severe, but social pressure

had turned out to be significant enough for Quack to be jailed for three months.

Meanwhile, Iwona, while waitressing at the Leśny Dworek restaurant next to the Belarusian museum, had met Piotr Bondaruk, a regular who popped in for lunch every day at one p.m. Soon after, he started showing up at seven in the evenings too. He would always choose a little table by the window, spread a file of business papers in front of him, and stay until closing, ordering multiple shots of Żubrówka and cold trotters or pickled herring. He would never say a word, just trail Iwona with his eyes as she bustled about the restaurant. She made more from his tips than from her regular pay.

When he had driven Iwona home and then a few days later repeated the favour, people started to talk. A week later she had given them a reason to gossip herself. She had met with Bondaruk on a day off. They met in Hajnowianka, the oldest restaurant in town. Years ago it had been the place to hold a New Year's Eve ball or wedding if you were a member of the local elite. Bondaruk could still remember those times. He had been Iwona's age then. Over time the place had regressed, losing its status and turning into a common den serving watered-down beer that had nothing to do with genuine Dojlidy in spite of being labelled thus.

Bondaruk had an old-school charm about him. He often asked Iwona about her dreams and ambitions. She would tell him about Quack, who had broken her heart (another saying taken straight out of her books), and that she hadn't been in any other serious relationships. She had won Bondaruk over with her straightforwardness and her belief in human goodness. At least that's what he would say in public later. That same night, he took her to the cinema to watch a movie about Jakub Kołas, a Belarusian poet. She had never seen anything as boring, but at least he gave her a handmade wall-rug. which her mother managed to sell the very next day at the Ruble Mart for a few hundred quid to some foreign tourists.

People started saying that the businessman completely fell for the 'Bison girl', and not even two months later, having grown weary of his daily visits to Leśny Dworek restaurant and despite the fact that Iwona had never hidden the fact that she was already betrothed to Quack, he bent the knee and presented Iwona with a little velvet box with a ring inside. Bondaruk declared that he wouldn't stand in her way or rush her, but would instead let her think about it and make an informed decision. No sooner had he said it, though, than he asked about Iwona's prospects in life and put forward his own, incredibly appealing, offer: land for the oldest brother, farmland for the other two, and payment of all of her mother's debts. The little things such as the TV or one of his cars were only the icing on the cake. All the time he kept a calm manner, not asking for anything in return – not even an innocent kiss.

For reasons known only to him, he had chosen Iwona as his latest investment and, for the first time in her life, she felt valued. Truth be told, she hadn't taken long to think before arriving at the conclusion that marrying the older man would solve all her problems. But as far as the rest of the world was concerned, she spent ten days thinking. It was a serious dilemma, after all. Bondaruk was a Belarusian and the Bejnars, who were Catholic, had always taken pride in their patriotic values. Their apartment was adorned with a banner with a nationalist slogan: 'Poland for Poles'. Nearly everyone in the family – although not Iwona – had been in trouble with the law for offences connected with their nationalist ideology. None of the Bison brothers would be happy about having what they would have called a *russkie,* or *katsap,* in the family.

Iwona had told her mother first. Realising all the benefits the marriage would bring to her offspring, in a single evening Bożena convinced the brothers to accept their sister's decision and not stand in her and Bondaruk's way. That same night, she took the old nationalist banner down and burned it in the backyard. Thus, Iwona resolved to finally break up with Quack.

She told him when she went to visit him in prison. He was due to be released in two days' time. The news didn't seem to worry him too much, to Iwona's astonishment. He also didn't accept the cheap ring he had given her previously when she tried to give it back to him.

'It's tombac. Not worth a thing,' he growled. Then he blew his nose into his sleeve and asked: 'Why? Why him, I mean.'

She told him the truth. She couldn't imagine living like that any more, waiting for Quack to get out of prison again and again.

And he would go back to jail, that much was certain. Iwona had had enough of meeting him at dilapidated bus stops or in the shed behind his mum's potato field. She would always love him and only him, she declared. Quack responded that he could understand her point of view but couldn't actually forgive her for a while, as he was 'a bit fucked off'. She cried as he left the visiting room.

He had played the tough guy in front of her, but as soon as he returned to his cell he attempted to hang himself on the door handle. The guards managed to rescue him and decided to keep him in jail for a couple more days. Quack explained to the psychologist that, as his woman had turned out to be a slut, the only option he could see was to honourably off himself. To his mates he declared that he'd have his revenge. People said that he'd set the Bejnars' house or Bondaruk's sawmill on fire after he was released, and the rumour spread like wildfire. The police kept their eyes on him for an entire week. He kept things civil, though, only leaving home twice: first to borrow a few PlayStation games, and then to go to the social welfare centre for his pay. But even when the authorities let him off the hook, the Bison brothers remained on high alert. They called in some mates, goons working for Igor Piątnica, an ex-gunsmith and the alleged boss of the local mob, to keep an eye out for Quack 24/7. Quack hadn't shown his face, though. The rumble of his motorbike's engine, known to everyone around the housing estates, was nowhere to be heard. Iwona spent the next ten nights crying, put half of her romance novels to the torch, and left her waitressing job. On the eleventh day, she accepted Bondaruk's proposal.

She kept Quack's ring, wearing it right next to her new engagement ring, which had a diamond the size of a pea.

'To remind myself of how stupid I was,' she said. 'So that happiness never goes to my head again.'

Her mother had always told her that a woman can only have three meaningful relationships in her life. The rest are just affairs and trivial flings. And that a woman takes her first man out of naivety, the second out of good sense, and only the third one out of love. But that only comes when you're already getting old. Iwona was twenty-five and was already getting to the second stage.

She briefly brushed her hair, with its fringe à la Uma Thurman in *Pulp Fiction*, which she would get extended tomorrow at the local hairdresser's – she'd get a thick black braid made out of real hair, laced with colourful ribbons, that she'd ordered from Ukraine. She'd heard the best wigs in Europe were made there – the stereotypical 'Slavic blond' was the easiest to dye and look after.

'You sell your hair and your arse out of poverty.' Bożena had stripped the myth of its magic. She herself had had to do both years before. She couldn't understand, she had added, why her daughter had to get her hair done at the hairdresser's and pay for it. She never said a thing about Iwona selling herself out now, though, and when Władysław grumbled something about his sister marrying an 'old *katsap*', Bożena immediately booted him out of the flat, ordering him to get some coal.

'What am I supposed to buy coal with?' Władysław spread his arms. 'Business ain't what it used to be.'

'Then why the fuck are you yapping, you mutt?' his mother bellowed. 'As soon as Iwona marries Bondaruk, you'll have all the coal you can carry and then some.'

Iwona smoothed some Vaseline onto her lips. She wouldn't put on any make-up. Piotr was obsessed with traditional notions of beauty. She knew he was a Belarusian activist but, apparently, her ancestry didn't discourage him. That was something of an inconsistency. Everyone has their quirks, decided Iwona. She hadn't noticed any others in him, apart maybe from his age. Not having to use make-up was another advantage; not that she really needed it anyway. Her chocolate-coloured irises practically blended with the pupils of her eyes. Her girlfriends envied her her long, thick eyelashes. And her olive skin didn't need to be covered in foundation to look good. Despite that, she applied a bit of highlighter to her cheeks and glanced at the traditional, colourful, embroidered wedding dress. It was at least three sizes too large for her. She didn't like it, but she knew the rules. It was only a uniform for the day.

The skirt was wrap-around, so she just looped it twice around her waist. They were supposed to give the blouse to a seamstress to tailor; at the moment Iwona looked in it like a slightly more sassy version of a medieval penitent. The ornate white thing hung to her knees like a sack and effectively obscured all her womanly curves all the way up to the rigid collar around her neck. The sleeves would have to be shortened at the elbows. Iwona was a petite woman. She was only 152 centimetres tall and could buy shoes in children's shops. Even in the costume shop at the Belarusian Culture Centre they hadn't been able to find anything her size, so she had agreed to have the outfit Piotr had given her tailored. Apparently, he had been keeping it for his future wife. She didn't want to know who it had been made for in the first place. Or what had happened to the woman. Iwona's soon-to-be spouse was a father to three sons, who had their own children themselves now. He was sixty-six, but this was going to be his first marriage. She could be proud of herself – but she felt the opposite.

The door slammed. Iwona headed to the dark hall. To her despair, it wasn't the seamstress but her friends Anka and Kasia. They both had earbuds in and were swaying to the rhythm of some song. Iwona guessed it had to be the newest hit single – 'Ona tańczy dla mnie'. Both girls were dressed up like Christmas trees. They wore fluorescent, tight-fitting tops. Their airy tunics, bought from the same stand at the Ruble Mart, ended just short of their thighs. To top this off, they both wore leggings – one pair of leopard-print and one snake-print. Plus high heels. Iwona had worn similar clothes until recently. In contrast to the freakishly tall Anka and the chubby Kasia, she had a body to show off. Her legs were her greatest asset and she knew it. Unfortunately, the folk wedding dress she was supposed to wear tomorrow would hide them completely. Even a supermodel would have looked like a Russian doll in that.

Iwona hoped she would be able to wear whatever she liked again after the wedding. Piotr had promised her he wouldn't interfere and had said that she could go to college, work in his company or open her own business if she liked. Or just keep doing nothing. That was the option her friends would have taken. But Iwona didn't want to laze around. She wanted to learn foreign languages, travel and explore new cultures. She would write a blog or even have her own show on local TV. She hadn't told anyone this last one except Piotr. He was friends with a TV director and had promised to help, and had also assured her he would finance both her education and her travels. She believed him. There was only one condition. She had to be loyal, he said, but not as in *faithful*. He promised her to tell her what he had meant by that right after their wedding, as soon as they had their rings on and the priest had doused them in holy water.

'That wedding has to take place,' Iwona's mother said once. She looked at her sons, wagging a finger. 'No surprises, you understand? Otherwise, our arrangement is off the table. And we don't want that to happen, do we?'

The Bison brothers promised to protect their sister, even if nationalist hit squads arrived in town to wreck the ceremony.

'It makes me look fat, doesn't it?' Kasia spread out the long, crimped skirt like a banner. The outfit did nothing to make her look thinner, that was true, but, Iwona thought, she didn't really look like a top model anyway, despite probably thinking so. Outwardly, she only shrugged.

'You won't be wearing a white dress with lots and lots of tulle? Or a veil?' Anka asked, disappointed. She jiggled the colourful ribbons intended for the wedding wreath, swinging them around herself as if shooing off flies. Then she looked at her friend with sympathy. 'Won't you regret it?'

Iwona sighed heavily. What was she supposed to say to that? While she was already at the second stage, her friends still lingered at the first. Their boyfriends, like most young men from Hajnówka, worked in Dublin and only visited twice a year, at Easter and Christmas, over which periods Iwona didn't see Anka and Kasia as they were in bed practically the whole time. After these trips the girls would go to Białystok for morning-after pills. They liked to say that it was cheaper than poisoning yourself with contraceptives all year round. They counted on their boyfriends returning home for good someday, carrying bags of cash. They dreamed of weddings, white dresses and brand new cars they'd drive around town in, showing off. Iwona believed what would happen was something rather more mundane. The boys wouldn't return at all, instead finding themselves new girls abroad, or – even more likely – they'd get caught and thrown in jail for smuggling or tax evasion. She didn't believe the stories they liked to tell about toiling as construction workers. Her own Divine and Lovely Quack, as she had called him during the apogee of their relationship, had liked to spin similar stories. She'd only realised the truth in the prison waiting room. Nobody would fool her like that again.

She spotted her mother through the window. Bożena was heading home, striding vigorously, holding by the arm an elderly lady wearing a headscarf. Amazingly, Bożena didn't have her signature cigarette sticking out from between her lips. Bad news, thought Iwona. The seamstress had been recommended by Piotr and he had asked them to treat the old hag decently.

'Alla is a friend of the family,' he'd said. 'She's practically family herself, actually.'

Practically. Most of his own relatives were dead or dying, the latter thinking of the design of their own gravestones like Iwona thought about the design of her new home.

'He's so old,' Anka hissed, turning to Kasia. 'He could be my grampa.'

'Great-grampa, more like. My gramps isn't even sixty,' Kasia replied, raising her voice to be heard. Suddenly, she tossed the skirt away with a grimace of revulsion. 'You see that? There's cloth moth grubs all over it.'

'Don't touch it!' Iwona crushed one of the bugs between her fingers and put the skirt back on its hanger. Then she turned to her other friend and barked: 'I heard what you said. He may be old, but he treats me well.'

'How are you going to kiss him? He's got a moustache!'

'At least he doesn't wear dentures,' said Kasia. 'Kissing someone without teeth sucks. And believe me, I know. One time my Genek got his teeth kicked in after a party, so I've been there.'

'Wait. But does he? Have his own teeth, I mean,' asked Anka, her face crumpling in a disgusted frown. She waved a hand. 'Better not to know.'

Iwona looked at her friends with pity. 'I won't have to kiss him at all.'

'How so? He's going to be your husband.'

'I won't and that's that.'

'What do you care, anyway?' Kasia turned up the music even more. Another hit. Margaret this time. 'He's rich. You're doing the right thing, Iwona.'

She took out an emery board from her fake Chanel bag and proceeded to file a broken nail. Her gaudy pink nail polish chipped and splintered in large patches, but she didn't seem to care. Halfway done, she fished out a bottle of polish and, without scrubbing off the old layer, applied a thick coat, and waved her hands to dry the nails. She looked like a seal stranded on a beach. With her nails still wet, she pointed to the wedding dress.

'If he's got a rich buddy, I can get one of those too. The older, the better. He'd be gone sooner.'

'And what if Quack comes to the wedding?' Anka asked.

'He won't.' Iwona sent her a chilly gaze, but her friends had already shut up, sitting down on the squeaking sofa. They occupied themselves with peeking under the plastic sheet to check out the TV. Iwona was genuinely surprised that it had taken so little to shut them up.

'If he comes and makes a scene, he's dead,' she heard her mother say coldly from behind her back. That explained her friends' sudden meekness.

The elderly matron Bożena had brought was laying out colourful thread on the old table made from an even older Singer sewing machine pedestal. She took off her florid headscarf and spread it across her shoulders, silently declaring her readiness to take Iwona's measurements. Her white hair was plaited, forming a thin braid affixed around her head with hairpins. Iwona had to forcibly overcome her revulsion. She nodded to the woman, but stood rooted in place, though the lady looked friendly enough. She had next to no wrinkles and her bright green eyes seemed to radiate calmness and sympathy. Unfortunately, she stank. There were dirty black half-moons beneath her longish nails. She probably hadn't bathed for quite some time, and definitely suffered from incontinence. The needle shook in her hand and threading it took what seemed like hours. It was hard to believe she was the greatest expert on embroidery and traditional tailoring in the region. And she seemed mute too. She hadn't said a word since she had entered the apartment.

'What are you standing there for?' Iwona's mother reprimanded her daughter. 'Start changing, on the double.'

Then she dropped into her old, shabby armchair and lit a cigarette. Despite her age, her style resembled that of Iwona's friends. She wore a pink skirt with a bolero, displaying her love handles. Her black, torn tights, paired with white boots she had bought in a second-hand store, did nothing to improve things, but Bożena was sure her apparel made her look younger. She beamed when the girls enthused over her 'awesome style'.

'Miss Alla will take your measurements and the dress will fit perfectly by tomorrow. And when it comes to Quack,' Bożena paused for emphasis and gave each girl a look in turn, 'there's no such person any more. Not for me, at least. And since he doesn't exist, neither he nor anyone like him will ruin your life. I won't let that happen. I liked the sly bastard, I have to admit. He knew how to talk to his mother-in-law. But he had his chance and he ballsed it up. And obviously that's for the better. Otherwise you would have ended up like me. In this hovel.' She gestured around the dank apartment and grew sombre.

The girls giggled nervously. Iwona conquered her disgust, approached the seamstress and handed her the wedding dress. Nobody left when she started taking off her clothes, not even when she stood naked. There was nowhere to go. Two of her brothers were sleeping off a busy night in the kitchen. They had returned from work in the morning and their mother had ordered them to stay out of the way. They'd promised to make themselves scarce as soon as the women came and the ritual of baking the *korovai* began.

The seamstress wrapped up her task in a few minutes. Turned out Iwona shouldn't have been worried about her shakes; the needle danced fluidly and confidently in the woman's arthritic hands. The old woman only nodded by way of goodbye. With a curt gesture, she refused to accept the money Iwona's mother had prepared for her. Having taken the wedding blouse, gown and pinny, she left as quietly as she had entered. The only thing left was the unpleasant smell.

'What a hag,' snorted Kasia, pinching her nose. 'Did he send her? Pretty lame for the beginning of your new life.'

'Shut up, stupid! Those walls are thin as paper!' Bożena rebuked her and gestured for the window to be opened. She herself went to the door, opened it a fraction and started waving a towel, trying to get rid of the stench.

'But the dress won't smell like that tomorrow, I hope,' Anka said. 'People are going to have to congratulate you after the wedding. You know, hugs and kisses.'

'Whatever,' Iwona's mother laughed darkly. She sprayed some air freshener around and lit another cigarette. 'She'll endure it for a day. She'll live like a queen after that. And you'll stay right here.'

At that point they all heard Belarusian chanting. Women bearing cakes, sweets and other delicacies like home-made sausage started pouring into the apartment, ceremonially presenting their gifts to Iwona. Some of them, including some younger ones, wore traditional outfits. One had brought a wreath of wild flowers, which she placed on Iwona's head. The oldest one handed her the Ukrainian braid. It was thick as an arm and at least half a metre long, with a precise, dense weave. It resembled an ear of rye. Hard to believe it was only a hairpiece. The oldest woman recited a solemn speech.

'That Russian?' Kasia whispered in Anka's ear.

'How should I know?'

'It's Belarusian.' Iwona smiled. 'Don't play dumb. You've lived here for ever.'

A while later, the apartment was full to the brim with women Iwona had never seen before. The older ones reminisced about their own weddings. The younger girls, with hair hanging loose or woven into traditional braids, wearing flowery skirts and boots, sang old songs about the appeal of unmarried life. The oldest woman started to knead the dough. Others soon joined her.

When the dough was ready, Iwona was told to form it into figurines – depicting herself and the bridegroom – standing at the foot of a symbolic tree. Each unmarried woman added a little dough twig to the *korovai*. They were supposed to grant the young couple luck and marriage for themselves.

'The moustache! You forgot the moustache!' Kasia called to Iwona, eliciting a round of laughter. She stuck a thin roll of dough to the figurine of the bridegroom. The thing broke in two. The little doll's head rolled across the floor, collecting dust bunnies on its way.

A silence fell over the room. The women all looked to the oldest Belarusian.

'Fuck. My bad,' Kasia sputtered, covering her mouth with a hand. She attempted humour: 'At least yours is still standing! Looking good, doughy girl!'

Nobody laughed. One of the women picked up Bondaruk's head, rinsed it with water and stuck it back on the bridegroom's figurine.

'The man will live long and have many children,' announced the mistress of the ceremony. 'And the *korovai* shall rise and be perfect. I haven't seen a larger one in my life. You'll have a good life, *dzyauchinka*. We just have to make sure it's baked properly. Look inside the oven every now and then, keep the temperature steady.'

Then one of the guests put on a playlist and, hearing the first song, the younger women instantly crowded around the bride-to-be, spinning and dancing.

'Dance! Dance!' they called. 'And cry! And let your mother cry too! Cry for luck!'

But the only thing Iwona did was giggle. The girls spun wildly around the oven. The older women bobbed and stamped their feet to the music's rhythm. Before the playlist ended, the room was filled with the aroma of the baking cake. One of the women took a peek inside the oven and called the others. They swarmed around her.

'Someone's hexed it,' a woman standing close to Iwona whispered, winking at her. They both laughed but the rest kept quiet. A bad omen was a bad omen and nothing to laugh about.

The *korovai* had grown too large and was threatening to burst out of the oven, but the display clearly indicated that the cake still had to bake for another fifteen minutes. Iwona turned to the oldest woman: 'What now?'

'If it were a tiled stove we would have taken it apart to get the cake.'

'Otherwise it's a bad omen, right?'

'The cake has to be pristine.'

One of the women pulled an old-school Nokia phone out of the pocket of her skirt and left in a hurry, talking into it. Iwona shot her mother a baffled look. Bożena rolled her eyes. The guests' unease was beginning to rile her, but the Belarusians had been sent by Piotr – the man who was about to drastically change her family's fortunes – and she couldn't mock them openly. Cinderella had to become a princess first. Bożena hadn't had a chance like that in her life.

'Maybe we take it out in parts?' she suggested hesitantly. 'We can just cut the figurines off. It'll come out in no time.'

'The *korovai* has to stay in one piece. Everyone's going to look at it tomorrow,' the oldest woman replied and added: 'There's only one thing we can do. We have to take the oven apart.'

Iwona's mother rose. 'Over my dead body. This thing cost more than this whole apartment!'

An awkward silence fell over the room. The oldest Belarusian and Bożena gazed at each other for a while.

'It'll burn,' the oldest Belarusian said finally and then repeated it in Polish.

'So we'll bake another one. Smaller. Maybe then it'll fit, even with that ugly mop on top.'

The Belarusian spread her arms, shrugging. 'Your will, Mother, but that's your daughter's life you're playing with. If the cake isn't perfect, she'll be unlucky. A *korovai* is a gift. You don't want to tempt fate.'

'I don't give a flying fuck for your *russkie* superstition!' Bożena exploded. She was over the edge now. 'It's only a piece of cake, for crying out loud!'

A crowd was growing in the entranceway. Someone was pushing themselves in the wrong direction. Several coats fell from the rack. It was chaos.

Then all eyes turned to the door.

A smallish man with a cigarette in the corner of his mouth and a shock of swept-back white hair was standing in the threshold. Despite being at least sixty, he was still devilishly handsome, with deep blue eyes. But his expression was murderous, his jaw clenched in anger.

'I found the bride's father! You'll take the oven apart, won't you? The *korovai* is saved!' called a red-faced woman. It was the one who had made the call on her old Nokia.

If the woman had been expecting elation or accolades, she was disappointed; the only thing she got was Bożena's thunderous fury.

'Get out of my house!'

The women all took a step back, suddenly frightened.

'Beat it!' Bożena repeated, and then shouted even louder: 'I said, get out! Having trouble understanding Polish, *russkie* pigs?'

The women at the back retreated even further, quietly leaving the apartment. The crowd gradually thinned out. The man stood in place, choosing not to comply with his wife's order. He was focused entirely on his daughter. On instinct, Iwona took two steps back.

'It's good she called me,' he said. 'I didn't know about any of this. Everyone in town knew except for the bride's father, it seems. I haven't blessed this marriage, and I most certainly will not.'

'Everyone get the fuck out!' Bożena screeched, hurling flowers, wrapped gifts and pastries at her guests. Finally, she grabbed the oven's power cord and pulled it from its socket. 'Party's over.'

Meanwhile Iwona's father, Dawid Sobczyk, headed over to his daughter, swaying on his feet. He probably hadn't been sober for days. She allowed him to hug her briefly, but quickly pushed herself away and fled to the wall, where she huddled, petrified. She tried gesturing to her mother, but the woman wouldn't look her way, instead focusing fully on her ex with murder in her eyes.

'I won't allow you to marry that old goat,' Dawid announced shakily.

He raised his hand. Something flashed. Panic erupted across the room. Terrified women trampled each other to reach the door. Finally, only Iwona's friends were left. Bożena turned to them. She cursed, but her voice was sweet as honey. 'Nothing to see here. Get lost. Go call my boys, will you? Be quick about it.'

Then, while her husband was briefly distracted, she suddenly dashed towards him, fists flying wildly. Dawid shoved her away and she fell to the floor, her skirt ripped, her white underwear showing through her black tights. The flashing object – a pair of butcher shears – was still clutched tightly in Dawid's hand. He stomped towards his daughter and grabbed her by the arm, locking her in a vice-like grip. Iwona realised how much she had misread the situation. Her father wasn't hungover – he was drunk as a wheelbarrow.

'Do you know who you were going to marry?'

'Leave her alone!' Bożena pleaded. 'Don't hurt her!'

'I'll carve up that old hag too, if I have to,' Dawid said to his daughter, nodding at Bożena. Then he leaned close to Iwona's ear and whispered: 'Bondaruk is the son of a murderer, and a murderer himself. He killed his own wife. I don't care how much money he has. Your mother sold you to a *russkie*. A filthy *katsap*! Get it? The entire city's having a laugh at me now. How much have you sold your child for, you whore?' Dawid twisted back to his wife, pointing the blade at her.

'What are you babbling about, you old fool?' Bożena rose, straightening her skirt. She was back to her normal self again, calm and collected. Her sons were already sneaking through the door, coming to the rescue. The Bison brothers weren't Dawid's blood. Their father – a stoker who'd worked in the lumber mill's boiler room – had died at the age of twenty-nine. He had orphaned three sons and left the young beauty Bożena had been at the time, at exactly Iwona's age, with three kids to feed and not a penny. She had tried everything to keep her family afloat: cleaning, sewing and discreet escort services, the last at the local hotel in Hajnówka.

Both Bożena and the gentlemen she worked for at the hotel valued discretion. Her clients were never local. Dawid Sobczyk had been one such client – a successful engineer from Ełk, visiting Hajnówka once a week for work. He immediately fell for Bożena, promising to take care of her and showering her with gifts – cosmetics, cologne straight from Moscow, or new stockings. He never mentioned marriage, but Bożena didn't really care for that anyway.

'One time's the charm,' she would say. 'I don't need a paper slip to love you.'

When they started to meet in private, Dawid stopped paying for her services. At the time, she thought it a sign of respect. He'd still bring food, various whatnots for the house, or small gifts. Finally, he left his bag and his clothes at her place. He was about to drop his anchor, and Bożena prayed for this to be for ever, afraid that another premature death would break her. When it turned out she was pregnant again, she was over the moon.

'It's most likely going to end in a miscarriage,' the best gynaecologist in town at the time had warned her. 'Don't get your hopes up.'

Hearing that had only made Bożena more determined. She would do everything she could for the unborn baby.

Dawid only visited rarely, but when he did, he was always caring and protective. He had a job in Ełk and couldn't just leave – she understood that. Getting things in order required time and Bożena had always been patient. She believed they had a bright future ahead of them and occupied herself planning their life together, decorating the flat, knitting little clothes for her baby, sewing. She believed the newborn would bring them even closer together. And in the end, she didn't miscarry. Her gynaecologist was surprised when she showed up for a check-up in the sixth month.

'God's will, it seems,' he said. 'But, even if you give birth, it's probably going to be retarded.'

Bożena didn't care about his defeatist prophecies. She would be the oldest young mum in the entire ward. She had no problems during her pregnancy and had never felt more beautiful, or happier, in her life. The birth was easy, natural. Her daughter was born on a Sunday, at nine in the evening. She weighed four kilos. No Down's syndrome or any other issues. Her beloved Dawid came from Ełk the next day, bearing a bouquet of roses, and jars of plum jam so that Bożena's milk would be easier for their daughter to digest. He seemed euphoric. He chose a name for the baby – Iwona. It was so pretty when shortened: Iwuś, Iwek.

Only Bożena's sons remained mistrustful of their stepfather. They were the ones to see through him first. They knew all his tricks because they had been using the same ones themselves. Dawid had lived with them for only a few months, since two weeks before Iwona was born. At that point he stopped bringing money in, but he kept eating and living in Bożena's apartment at her expense. There were no more gifts and no more care. Dawid's flaws began to surface. His great love for booze, for starters. He quickly found new friends in town, with whom he would spend more time than with Bożena. He would tell her he was looking for a job, that he'd like to provide for the family, buy a bigger apartment.

And Bożena believed him. She understood there was no way to work out such things other than over a shot glass. When he asked her for money from her savings so he could bribe an official to get a position at the lumber mill, she gave him the cash without a word. Same went for training, which had supposedly been necessary for him to apply for the post of timber seasoning plant director. She was proud of having such a poised and wise man at her back. Each day after Dawid's meetings with various local VIPs, she would dispose of the empty bottles.

It only occurred to her something was up when the time came to register their daughter's birth. Despite Dawid's promise that they'd go together and that Iwona would get his surname, when the day came he didn't even get up; he was unconscious and utterly hammered. Later, he would say it was because he had been so overwhelmed by having a child. Bożena had to put off the registration.

One day, a man in a suit knocked at Bożena's door, demanding she pay off a debt. For Dawid's wife. Otherwise, he would pull strings and make town hall take away Bożena's apartment and boot her and the kids out. All that meant exactly three things: one – her perfect lover had lied about being divorced; two – he had lost his job and was spending the cash he did have, from loans, on booze, which was why he was now being hounded by creditors; and three – he was an alcoholic. He had been hiding at her place, lying low to avoid being pursued about his debts.

Bożena finally came to her senses and put all the pieces of the puzzle together. All the stories Dawid had been feeding her were just that – stories. She made the only logical decision. It hadn't been easy at first – she still had feelings for the man, after all. Thankfully, that was now in the past. After her sobering realisation, Bożena went to town hall, filled in the papers, gave Iwona her own surname, and marked the father as 'unknown'. Then she packed up Dawid's stuff and left it outside the apartment. There wasn't much. One half-empty bag and a couple of bottles of booze.

This was too much for Dawid. From that moment on, he would do his best to turn her life into a living hell. He would show up at her apartment without warning and, with the help of her sons, she would have to throw him out. Bożena would never get close to anybody again. She liked to say her supply of love had run dry, even though it wasn't entirely true. The man just couldn't accept that, in his eyes, she had taken his daughter from him. That everyone in town knew he was Iwona's father did nothing to improve the situation.

Now, Bożena hoped to distract him. She spoke slowly, calmly, pretending she wanted to negotiate.

'Piotr didn't have a wife. Iwona will be his first. Besides, what can you do? She's an adult.'

'Everybody knows that Łarysa, his Belarusian wife, disappeared,' Dawid said. 'He nearly went to prison for that. And Mariola, the butcher's daughter?'

'And why should anyone believe you?' Bożena retorted with a grim laugh. 'A thief and a drunkard. A grifter, no less. Don't listen to him, Iwona. I regret every day I spent with this man.'

'You bitch!' Dawid took a swing at his ex but missed, lost his balance and fell. He thrashed, trying to get up again.

Iwona stared scornfully at her drunk father. She felt ashamed of him. 'What Belarusian wife?' she asked. 'What's that all about?'

'You don't know?' He was on his feet again. He frowned. 'The whole town was put on high alert. He shot her in the face on the road to Białystok. Ask him. Maybe he'll tell you what he did with the body. He's a *katsap*! A vile old *russkie*. The worst of the worst.'

He didn't get to finish. The Bison boys grabbed him like a sack of spuds and threw him unceremoniously out of the flat. The shears Dawid had been threatening the women with turned out to be completely dull. But it had to be said, they did at least look threatening. Ireneusz slid them into his boot as a trophy.

'Get lost, Pops. You're not welcome here,' he said, swinging a kick at Dawid's head before the man could put up a block. 'Stupid old fart. I swear to God, Mum, I can't get my head around how you fell for this muppet.'

Bożena went outside to talk to her sons. Curious neighbours flocked to the scene. Accompanied by jeers and sneers, they all chased the aggressor from the block.

When everyone else had left the room, Iwona collapsed on the old sofa with a heavy sigh. This was her family, her life. She'd never be able to escape. How would it work? Where could she run? Move a few blocks away and Dad would show up and keep pestering her. Mum would still boss her around like a child. Her brothers would keep 'rescuing' her, beating the living crap out of any boy who came near. All with good intentions, of course. But she had no say in any of it. Did anyone ever ask for her opinion?

And who the hell was Łarysa? What had her father been talking about? Iwona glanced at the oven and thought she was going to miss out on luck and happiness again. The *korovai* was flat as a pancake and completely burnt.

She opened the oven door and took a piece from the top. It was the bridegroom figurine. She bit off the head, which wasn't completely blackened and was actually sweet and soft. If everything had gone as planned, the cake would have been glorious. Iwona burst into tears. The one constant in her life. All her dreams and goals, almost within reach, but never achievable.

Suddenly, a creaking noise. The door to the wardrobe opened and Kasia's head stuck out, covered by Iwona's wedding dress. She had thrown it over herself to hide and now looked like the Groke from the Moomins. Iwona burst out in uncontrollable laughter. She had an idea for how to turn her luck around.

The sound of a text message woke Sasza up. She blinked, unable temporarily to recall where she was. The ceiling was fitted with plaster panels intended to look palatial. A glance at the wall, decorated with a colossal Minotaur head, jogged her memory. She was at the Bison Motel. Late the previous night, at the end of her long drive from Gdańsk, she had taken the only room they had left. The honeymoon suite.

Sasza had turned her computer on and rapidly written a good chunk of her thesis chapter on the Wasp. She'd also jotted down a list of bonus questions she'd ask the woman if they met again. She'd hit the hay at five in the morning, exhausted, but satisfied with having made such good progress. She felt like Sisyphus, she thought. The stone's on the summit. It didn't bother her that it would roll down the slope any moment now and she'd have to start all over again.

Sasza glanced at her ancient Delbana wristwatch. It was a quarter past ten. She should have been at Ciszynia already, in the director's office. The psychiatrist hadn't tried to sound affable over the phone. On the contrary, he had done everything in his power to discourage her and had only agreed to her visit when she told him she was with the police. Field operations, she said. With no choice left, the man had reluctantly set up a meeting for Saturday. It was scheduled to last an hour but Sasza suspected she would only get half of that. It didn't matter. She only needed the answer to a single question. As soon as she got it, she'd know if she'd have to grab her daughter and flee the country or if she could finally enjoy a calmer spell in her life, crowned with her return to the force.

'Damn it!'

Sasza pulled her trousers on in a hurry. The sun poked its nose into the room through a crack in the curtains. She felt as if she had sand under her eyelids, and her mouth was parched after all the cigarettes she had smoked as she wrote. She'd forgotten her toothbrush. Of course. Rummaging through her bag, she finally pulled out a crumpled shirt, but then decided on a white polo shirt, a navy blue blazer and a light scarf instead. Her go-to 'classy' outfit. It made a good impression, whatever the occasion; and more importantly, it didn't require ironing. She brushed her hair and collected various bits and bobs, throwing them into her bag, packed up the laptop and cleaned her teeth with a finger. Ready to leave. She stopped at the reception desk to check out. The receptionist took his time. Sasza glanced at her mobile.

Three texts. All from Duchnowski. Encouraged by yesterday's lucky streak, he was trying flirting again. In his peculiar style – rough and awkward. She left two sexist remarks unanswered, but 'watch out for beefalo' made her smile a bit.

Not listening to the receptionist, who was assuring her that the motel had the only buffet serving salted pork lard with onions and brine pickles in town, Sasza rushed out. She swallowed, remembering she hadn't had anything to eat since yesterday's visit to the shooting range. She promised herself she would try the local speciality next time.

Ciszynia private psychiatric hospital was huddled in the heart of a birch forest neighbouring the convent of the Order of Saint Clare at Lipowa Street. It was surrounded by a wooden fence covered in motifs designed like traditional Belarusian embroidery.

Sasza drove up the cobbled road to the car park. Crossing the gate leading to the main building, she passed a black limo that was racing away so fast it nearly crashed into her white Fiat Uno. The driver – a fat bald guy with an absurdly bushy moustache – waved her on, irritated. Sasza raised a hand to apologise. She couldn't see the face of the passenger – the rear windows were tinted – but she thought it had to be a local VIP.

She parked awkwardly, taking up two spaces, but she didn't care. Aside from a van sporting a logo of a chainsaw cutting through a log, the car park was empty. Sasza spilled the contents of her handbag on her Uno's bonnet. The silence was broken by the clangour of bells calling the faithful to pray at the nearby church. She found the document case at the very bottom of her bag and breathed out with relief. For a while, she'd been afraid she had driven across the country without the papers and that they wouldn't just refuse to let her in but that she'd be totally screwed if she got caught by a patrol on her way back. She took her ID and slid it into her pocket, just in case. The rest she tossed back into the bag. She looked around.

Residents were lounging in a small park that surrounded the building. Most of them occupied benches placed along meandering alleys, but a few, in pairs, were strolling around a pond. A girl wearing a flowery dress was idling next to a fountain, sitting in an uncomfortable-looking position. The wind ruffled her bright blond hair. That was when Sasza noticed the painter, half-hidden behind a thicket of bushes. He stood in front of an easel, his back turned to her. She couldn't see his face, but her heart immediately started beating like crazy. She took a step back, putting on her glasses. A short blond man, legs slightly bent outwards at the knees, like a cowboy's. A blue hoodie. He was staring attentively at the girl, who twisted into an even weirder stance. It took Sasza a while to realise the girl was posing. The man crouched over a basket, snatched a couple of paints and mixed them on the palette. Sasza could discern his profile now. A pointy nose, heavy jaw, deep-set eyes. Not him. Only similar. She sighed with relief and headed to the building.

The facility was quiet. Not a patient in sight. It was also squeaky clean, as if someone had sprayed every possible surface with polish. You could see your own reflection in the floor. It didn't smell like a hospital. No sweat or any of the other human secretion smells characteristic of state-run facilities. It was also overbearingly silent.

There was a woman in a white uniform sitting behind the reception desk. She didn't resemble Nurse Ratched. She gave Sasza a kind look and offered her a guest ID badge and Sasza headed briskly down a long corridor. There was no one around aside from her and the nurse on reception. The unsettling quiet was broken only by the sharp tick-tocking of her hobnailed boots. For a moment Sasza doubted the hospital was open. The expansive, modern spaces felt desolate. It seemed there were no patients except those back outside in the park. Maybe this was a terminal care ward.

'Where can I find the director's office?' she called back to the receptionist, disconcerted, when she reached a turn in the corridor and encountered only a little fern and an information board.

'A bit farther down the corridor. First door to the right,' the receptionist replied. 'But the director has left. Only the vice-director is in.'

Sasza turned and strode back towards the desk.

'I had an appointment. I drove across the country to meet the ward head.'

'Director,' the woman corrected, suddenly losing her amicable bearing. Her eyes grew alert, wary. 'This is a private facility. Not a state hospital. We only accept patients directed here by courts or prosecutors. Name?'

'Załuska.' Sasza glanced at her watch. It was still quarter past ten. The watch's arms had frozen in that position a good while ago, it seemed. 'What's the time?'

'Three minutes past noon,' the nurse replied automatically, keeping her eyes on the documents she was leafing through. The guestbook's pages whirled in her fingers like images in a cartoon. Finally, they stopped. Sasza leaned over the counter and spotted her own name with an annotation saying 'Police – private'.

'The director waited for you until half past eleven. I think he was a bit angry. He came just for you but he's gone now. You must have passed him on your way. His driver was here just a while ago,' she said.

Suddenly the entire hall was reverberating with the roar of what sounded like a vacuum cleaner and Sasza couldn't hear the nurse any more. She turned her head and saw exactly why this place was so clean. A hulking, industrial-grade floor cleaning machine was passing her. The man behind the steering wheel wore a uniform and a baseball cap. He scoured away all traces of Sasza's feet up to the little fern and back, vanished round the corner and then turned the machine off. Sasza observed the show with disbelief.

Only supermarkets or really big companies could afford machines like that. Ciszynia had to have a pretty inflated budget if it could maintain a professional floor-scrubbing machine and a post for a driver.

'Shit,' Sasza breathed, then turned back to the receptionist. 'God damn it.'

'You came from Warsaw?'

'Worse.' Sasza smiled apologetically. 'Gdańsk. I got here very late last night and I overslept. I know it sounds pathetic, but my watch died.'

The nurse's alertness transformed into genuine sympathy. 'Come back Monday. I'll tell the boss you came.'

Sasza leaned against the counter, meeting the woman's brown eyes. She spoke slowly, accenting each syllable.

'On Monday I have to be back in Gdańsk. I have an exam at the shooting range at eight in the morning. I have to speak to the director right now.'

The nurse just shook her head. Her distrust was back.

'I'm sorry.'

'This is a small town,' Sasza pushed on. 'Where does he live?'

'I can't tell you that. You have to understand.'

Anxiousness was now creeping into the woman's eyes.

'Give me his number then. An email maybe.'

'It's on the website. But he won't read it until Monday. He won't come back today or tomorrow.'

Sasza withdrew, propping her hands on her hips.

'Are you giving me the brush-off?'

'No, not at all,' the nurse scoffed. She jotted down an email address on a piece of paper, adding a telephone number below.

Sasza sat down in a chair, holding the slip, and dialled the number. The phone on the receptionist's desk rang. The woman stared at the blinking light but didn't pick up. Sasza laughed bitterly and hung up. The phone stopped ringing.

'Clever,' she growled, getting up and heading to the door. 'Thanks for the help. Have a nice weekend.'

The receptionist hesitated but, after a while, she left her post and followed Sasza. She caught up with her in the door.

'The vice-director is in. She came in to see a patient. Maybe she'll have the director's mobile? If you can convince her to give it up.' She spread her arms helplessly and added: 'But if you go to see her, it's at your own risk.'

'Where?'

'Room thirteen, second floor. And I'm going to need your ID. For the record.'

Sasza produced the document. As soon as the nurse had written down her ID number she snatched the card back and hurried towards the stairs. Before she'd even reached the top, she could hear the engine of the cleaning machine starting up. The caretaker was erasing her traces again. What a bizarre place.

You wouldn't call Magdalena Prus a classic beauty, but she most certainly took a great deal of time to look good. She was dressed up to the nines and wore immaculate make-up. She had taken care of all the details and looked like a madonna from one of Botticelli's paintings. Her intelligent, piercing eyes completed the effect. Sasza thought a woman like that had to have an intimidating effect on men, and probably inspired envy in women, too. Compared to her, Sasza felt like a grubby, scruffy ragbag. The doctor wore her dark blond hair parted in the middle and kept it neat and tidy with a silver clasp. Instead of a white doctor's gown, she wore a tight-fitting silk dress with a blue butterfly print, wrapped around her perfectly toned body like a second skin. Sasza noticed a tiny bulge at the woman's belly, only visible if you looked closely; the dress stretched over it, sticking to the skin. The doctor had a pierced belly button. Sasza would bet it sported a rather large diamond. The woman's shoes were high-heeled. Too high, considering her job, but she moved gracefully, lithe on her feet. Sasza had caught her in the act of examining a patient – an adolescent girl suffering from anorexia, as it turned out. The woman politely asked her to leave the room, and then wordlessly showed her the door to her own office.

Sasza was getting ready for a difficult conversation, setting up the tricks that would allow her to convince the psychiatrist to answer her questions. She was prepared to open up if necessary, rehearsing her story about being held hostage, battling addiction, working at the CBŚ and failing in her undercover mission. Maybe it would soften the woman up. In the end, it proved unnecessary. Prus already knew who Sasza was and what she wanted.

'He's not with us any more,' she said without preamble.

Sasza froze. She was not ready to hear that. It was the worst possible scenario. She hadn't even considered it before.

'So I came here for nothing?'

'You're here for Łukasz Polak, aren't you?' the psychiatrist asked and tapped at a thin file with the patient's name on the cover. She had been keeping her perfectly manicured hand on it from the beginning of the conversation.

Sasza regretted not thinking of snooping around the office before. The file had to have been there all along. She nodded, unable to squeeze out a word.

'He took the painting with him,' the doctor added.

Sasza couldn't breathe. How much did this woman know?

'He had it with him all along?'

The police had been looking for the painting since the start of the investigation. It would have been the main piece of evidence. They had told Sasza that Polak died in the fire, which had turned out to be a big fat lie. Now she was hearing that the painting was intact too. Did the police know? Sasza was guessing that nobody had even considered having a forensics specialist take a look at it, much less analysing it to try to form a psychological profile. It might not mean anything to anyone after all that time – just a silly painting by a crazy guy in a mental hospital – but for Sasza, it was everything. If she could see it, she'd know if the author was the Red Spider. She could open the investigation again. The original painting was the serial killer's calling card. The killer murdered to complete his magnum opus. The painting would match the photos Sasza had already memorised. And the details? She would dig them up from the archive. They'd still be up for grabs for the next thirty years – unless of course the file had been destroyed. She doubted that, however. The Red Spider had been sending Polaroids of the bodies of his victims to the police to keep them posted about his killings. The photos were in the same style as the one posted on Lidia Wrona's social media profile. The killer was leading the investigators by their noses, pointing them in the right direction. He was taking pleasure in it. He was presumably feeling unstoppable. He would recreate some of the details from the photos in the painting. Sasza had seen the painting once before, when Łukasz had kidnapped her and kept her against her will. It was supposed to resemble Hieronymus Bosch's paintings, though it seemed to her that it was about shock value more than art. Nobody aside from the killer knew the details of the murders. So, if the painting turned out to be inspired solely by the killings, it would prove Łukasz innocent. Sasza could have wiped his slate clean; though only in her head, her private archive. The authorities had already closed the formal case. But for her, it was a matter of life and death. Literally.

'He had it with him all that time?' she repeated, still failing to wrap her head around it.

Prus gave her a piercing stare and stretched her lips in a mischievous smirk.

'Three years. He would change the details over and over again. I can see a resemblance in one of the characters. A key character, to be precise.'

'What's in the painting?' Sasza swallowed loudly. 'Besides myself, naked.'

The doctor patted the file again.

'We have a photocopy right here. But, of course, I can't let you see it,' she continued, keeping her hand firmly on the documents. 'Data protection regulations, you understand. I'd have to get authorisation.'

'From whom?'

'The prosecutor's office. The minister of justice. That should do it. I couldn't show the papers even to the patient's family without his consent. But, it's the director who makes the final decision.' She cleared her throat and corrected herself: 'Gives consent, potentially.'

'He'll allow it.' Sasza stuck out a hand to grab the papers but the psychiatrist nimbly slid the file farther away.

'Go on. Call him. I'll tackle the minister next,' Sasza said.

The smile vanished from the doctor's face. Her cheeks flushed and for a while she looked older than she was. She quickly hid the documents in a drawer. *The local prom queen doesn't get humour, it seems,* thought Sasza with a hint of satisfaction.

'Where was he transferred?' she asked, not really expecting a straight answer. She was thinking frantically about her next move. This time she'd have to ask Ghost for help. There were 132 private psychiatric hospitals in Poland. They all had poetic names and an irksome rule about not granting anyone any information about their patients. Finding Polak would be like looking for a needle in a haystack.

'We treated him, he got better and left.'

'What do you mean left? Like, for good?'

The doctor nodded. She added, triumphantly: 'Nobody kept him here. He stayed voluntarily. All payments came on time and he passed all tests. Three teams examined him and they all arrived at the same conclusion: the illness had been dealt with.'

The psychiatrist wasn't going to hide the fact that she had the upper hand here. Sasza was sure that she'd strike the killing blow any time now. She couldn't count on any help or support from the woman. It was more likely she'd only make things more difficult. If she knew where Polak was at the moment, she wouldn't spill. This bitch was making Sasza's blood boil. Besides, it was never particularly hard to set Sasza on edge. Ambition had always been her Achilles heel.

'So you don't know where he is?'

'The patient wasn't sectioned, so we have no right to keep him under surveillance. He's a free man.'

'He's a murderer!' Sasza cried. She rapidly lost all semblance of control. 'I investigated him. We nearly got him. He nearly got me, too. I'm afraid he might get me yet. Don't you understand? I need to know where he is!' Her voice broke.

'He's our patient. Not a convicted felon.' The psychiatrist pinned Sasza with a steely glare. 'What do you really want with him?'

'I need to talk to him.'

'You're Milena, aren't you?'

'Excuse me?'

'His lover. You're the reason he got sick.'

Sasza didn't reply. She could feel herself blushing, and it was making her angry.

'He was my patient,' the doctor continued, 'and I know all about you two.'

'Us two?' Sasza hissed. 'There was nothing between us. He kept me locked up in a basement!'

'Please lower your voice,' Prus said, waving a hand disdainfully. Sasza immediately regretted her words. The fight had gone out of her. Not only had she come here for nothing, she had also been humiliated. And now, she knew even less than before. Prus went on, frustratingly composed and polite: 'I treated him for a couple of years. From the beginning, to be precise. And I can assure you that aside from severe depression and PTSD, he was perfectly well.'

'So everyone else was wrong? You know better, is that it?'

'That man has never been mentally ill,' the psychiatrist insisted. 'I'm certain of that. He didn't even have a mild disorder. He's just a nice guy, in need of support – not harassment.'

Sasza was close to tears. Vodka, wine, any cheap booze would do now. She was panicking. Should she go back home? Wait for her daughter? Or maybe fly to Crete for her and take her straight back to Sheffield? She was sure that if Łukasz was free, he'd want to see his child. He already knew she existed and nothing would stop him. Maybe he was already waiting at the door of their apartment in Sopot? Sasza was devastated.

'That's even worse,' she said. She was doing her best to remain calm, but it was an uphill battle. She saw red. There was an off-licence on the way here, she recalled. Only a few minutes' drive. She ignored the nagging thought like you ignore a yapping dog. She talked. That was the only way to chase away the craving – convert it into a deluge of words. Shout out the anger. Anything not to get drunk. She raised her voice again. 'You know why? Because that means that all the things he did were premeditated and he's a psychopath! The case needs to be reopened, and he has to stand trial.'

'That would mean you'd have to own up to what you've done, too,' said Prus absently. 'You've overstepped your bounds. Endangered the lives of three women. They all died, didn't they? And the killer has never been caught. Łukasz told me all about it. How are we supposed to be sure that you haven't worked with the killer? Even unwittingly.'

Sasza clenched her jaw to keep herself from saying something she'd really regret. She was shaken to the core by the psychiatrist's

gall, but she was even more shocked by the extent of her knowledge. All of that was supposed to be top secret. Not even Professor
Abrams or Sasza's family knew that much about Operation Thumbelina. Her being one of the suspects had been a secret known
only to herself, Gramps and Polak. And she had only confessed to
Łukasz in bed. They had intended to get her out of the way too.
She learned about that by chance and that's why she had allied
with Polak. They had been in the same predicament. Paradox-
ically, the fire had cleaned her slate. The authorities swept the whole
thing under the rug, failing to find anything incriminating the Red
Spider. They weren't even sure if Thumbelina had been unknow-
ingly feeding him intel. And now, years later, it might be about
to become a horrifying urban legend known to everyone in this
backwater town. It would only need the doctor to let it slip during
dinner with friends. Sasza definitely didn't want to give the psychiatrist the satisfaction. The only thing she could do was to conceal
her shock, not letting Prus know the impact her words were having.

She burst out laughing, as if she had just heard an excellent joke.
It worked. Prus was struck dumb for an instant. Suddenly, she was
in a hurry, tossing various pieces of junk from the desk into her
handbag. She clearly didn't want to extend the conversation any
more. Quite the opposite, in fact.

'As far as I know, there have been no proceedings or trials against
Łukasz,' she said, trying to close the subject.

Sasza narrowed her eyes. She was positive that Prus saw through
her charade and saw her fear. The woman was a pro. Hardly a surprise – analysing people's reactions was her job. The ball was in her
court now and the doctor suddenly decided to play a while longer.
She took Polak's file back out of its drawer and opened it, leafing
through the pages with mock interest.

'What you're saying is new to me,' she said, phlegmatically and
smugly at the same time. That was clearly supposed to piss Sasza
off even more. Prus must have realised that her armour of indifference was getting on the other woman's nerves. 'You don't have
to worry. I know who you are, and I most certainly know all about
your short but intense relationship, but it's doctor–patient privilege
and it will remain so. But you must know by now why I decided to
devote so much time to you, and on a day off, no less. Compassion.

I pity you. I would recommend that you meet with Łukasz. Talk to him. Clarify all the misunderstandings. He's not the devil, you know. I can arbitrate, if you wish. I have some experience with divorce mediation.' She grinned stupidly, as if she were on some kind of morning TV show.

'That's all I want,' Sasza lied. Then she laughed bitterly: 'You know, his address or telephone number would help me out a great deal.'

The doctor didn't react. She feigned disinterest, but she wasn't that good – she only grew tenser, biting her lip. She was getting nervous too. Very nervous. Sasza smiled inwardly.

'Don't you think so?'

'Can't help with that, I'm afraid.'

'Great.' Sasza snorted. 'I follow him to the middle of nowhere, and as soon as I start getting somewhere you tell me you've let him go and here I am, off on a wild goose chase all over again. If I had known he was getting out, I wouldn't have come here at all, just fucked off to the Arctic.'

Prus frowned with distaste at the swear word but didn't comment.

'If he'd given us his address you'd have it by now anyway.'

'What do you mean?'

'You got the letter, didn't you?'

'What letter?'

'Łukasz wrote a letter to you before leaving. It would have been sent to the police station in Gdańsk. That's where you work, isn't it? Or maybe it went to your home address?' The woman pretended she couldn't remember.

Sasza was speechless. If such a letter had come, Duchnowski would have told her.

'You seem to know an awful lot about me.' Sasza changed her strategy, counterattacking. 'Really quite a great deal. How does it feel to meddle in someone else's affairs? Where do you get the time?'

'That's my job.'

'I doubt that,' Sasza retorted. 'This doesn't sound like professional interest. And believe me, I know a thing or two about that.'

Prus blanched.

'How dare you!'

'I just happen to be an expert on these things. Sometimes I grow too interested in the cases I'm profiling on. Drives you crazy. Wouldn't you agree?'

'This meeting is over,' said Prus, but Sasza only sat back in her chair. This was starting to be fun. She wondered how the doctor would try to boot her out. Would she call security or start to scream? The former, she decided. She was the type of person who uses others to do their dirty work. Classic psychopath. In a year she'd be the boss here, or else get a transfer to another, more prestigious facility.

'You waited for me,' Sasza said suddenly. 'Admit it.'

The doctor didn't even look at her, evidently deciding that indifference was still the greatest insult she could deal. It was answer enough for Sasza. That was a confirmation and they both knew it.

'So? Am I how you imagined me?'

'Not exactly. I thought you'd look younger.'

'So sorry to disappoint.'

'Don't worry, we all get older. Not everyone knows how to conceal it.'

'So that's what's keeping you up at night. A bit shallow for a person of your stature, don't you think?' Sasza couldn't keep the smugness from her voice. 'Not what I expected either. A disappointing culmination to this talk.'

'Was there anything else? It's getting late.' The doctor swallowed the insult easily.

Polak's file was still on the desk. Prus clearly intended to leave it as it was, in plain view. Sasza couldn't believe it. Anyone could just stroll in and take a look. Anyone, but not her.

'My name isn't on any police website. I made sure of that,' she said with emphasis. 'Who helped him track me down?'

Prus stared at her with an amused expression.

'Maybe it was me. Maybe not. What does it matter now? You're overreacting. Does rejection hurt?' The psychiatrist paused, as if biting her tongue. She put on her professional mask again. 'You haven't dealt with your trauma. You're afraid of meeting him. Why else mix in legal matters and come up with this nonsense about killers and villains? That's my personal opinion. I'm being sincere – woman to woman. What do you really want? Do you still love him?'

'*I'm* overreacting?'

Sasza recalled the images of the bodies of all the murdered women. Their eviscerated wombs. Their obscene poses, arranged post-mortem by the monstrous killer. Their washed and scented skin, brushed hair, the pretty clothes he put on their bodies. The broken bones. He photographed the bodies from a height. From that perspective, splayed on grass or sand, wearing colourful dresses or wrapped in yellow tape, they resembled abstract paintings. Or that youngest one, fished out of the water, tangled in bright pink fishing net. Up close his cruelty was terrifying, but you couldn't help feeling at least a little captivated by his aesthetic sense. The Red Spider wanted fame and splendour. He was vain. Vanity had made him send those Polaroids to the police. He wanted people to talk about him. Well, tough luck. The investigators had managed to hide most of the details from the public. Such as the detail that the victims had all been prostitutes, from the kind of backgrounds that meant no one had looked for them, missed them, or demanded results. Some of their personal details hadn't been confirmed even now.

'Theoretically it's possible I might be overreacting,' she admitted finally. 'I might be nuts. Yeah, I just forgot to tell you before.'

She tucked her hands into her pockets, squeezing the pack of smokes she had there. The corner of her mouth turned up in a small smile. No, she wouldn't give Prus the satisfaction. She wouldn't break the hospital regulations by smoking. But she already knew what she'd do as soon as she left. She'd buy a bottle of booze and chug it all at once. She needed a fix. That thought immediately made her feel better. Her head would always remember how it felt to be drunk. The relaxation came with the thought itself. She could see everything clearly now. The psychiatrist had been hostile from the beginning and nothing would have changed that, but now it was obvious she was covering for her handsome patient. Sasza could understand her. She had fallen for Polak's bullshit stories herself once. Psychos can be charming. They woo you, manipulate you. Put on a mask of innocence if they need to. Oh, she knew all about it. The doctor was already one of his victims, she just didn't know it yet. He had used her as an alibi for now and as long as she stayed useful, she'd stay alive. Besides, she was too old for him anyway.

'I'm glad we're in agreement.' Prus stood up. The meeting was over for her.

Sasza didn't react but remained in her chair, immobile. She was beginning to enjoy this whole situation.

'Maybe talking to Łukasz would really help me get rid of my doubts.' She slipped into the role of the old Sasza, soused with gin and out of control. In this state she'd be able to skip between being utterly docile and pouncing on her adversary like a wild animal. That was how she had built her cover back in the day. She was a kind of a psycho herself. The psychological test back when she joined the force had confirmed that. According to the test results, she had ten out of the seventeen characteristics of a psychopath. That had made her the perfect fit for undercover work. She understood the bad guys. 'Soon as I get his address, I'll ask him how many times he thought of strangling you. Raping you and slicing up that flat belly of yours, ripping out that diamond tummy ring and cutting you up all the way from crotch to chest.'

Prus shivered.

'Maybe he'd also use you once you were dead,' Sasza continued, pretending to take pleasure in the gruesome details. 'You'd still be warm. A body doesn't get cold for a while, you know. Then he'd wash you, change your clothes and arrange your body in whatever position he wished. So you fitted into his puzzle. He'd paint you as the naked pageboy, right next to the queen.'

The psychiatrist walked over to Sasza. With a glare, she indicated that she should stand up. She was Sasza's height, but in her high heels she gave the impression of being at least a few inches taller.

'You're sick,' she said firmly. She was flushed. Sasza wondered how much plastic surgery Prus had had to look this good. Had she had a facelift? Botox injections into her brow? Were there scars behind her ears? Maybe that was the reason she didn't really show emotions. It was all botulin, not mental strength.

Prus raised her voice and said: 'There's no reason to panic before anything happens. The director has made sure that the patient will report for check-up once a month. And I will perform the check-up personally. So,' she hesitated, seeing Sasza's sneer, 'everything is under control.'

'And yet, you're afraid.' Sasza became serious again. Remembering the feeling of drunkenness brought back her composure. She could feel the taste of gin in her mouth, the aroma of juniper in her nostrils. That should be impossible. But she could really feel the burning alcohol flowing down her throat. Reluctantly, she shook the sensation off. She lowered her voice to a whisper: 'That's because you can't be sure. I mean, one hundred per cent sure that I'm wrong. You know his version, you're a good doctor, but I am a criminologist. And I can assure you that the next time I'm here, I'll have a warrant with me. I won't ask you nicely for the papers then.'

'Get the warrant and I'll show you the documents.' Prus offered a hand. Begrudgingly, Sasza shook it. But, as soon as the woman began pulling out of her grasp, Sasza squeezed it like a vice.

'Where is he?'

Prus blinked, startled.

'Where?'

'I don't know,' the doctor lied.

'Of course you do, gorgeous.' Sasza smiled.

She was sure that as soon as she left, the psychiatrist would call her favourite patient. She suspected that their relationship was somewhat closer than professional ethics allowed. But if anyone as much as implied that, she'd deny it. The papers were clean, after all. Clean like her desk, her handbag and her car – the one she had the habit of driving to the car wash at least once a week. Yes, Sasza had been subconsciously profiling the woman since she had got there. Prus had no pets. A single kid at most, preschool. Cared for by the mother-in-law or a nanny. But more likely she had no kids. Her husband would be someone important in town. A city councilman or a lawyer. They didn't have sex. If she'd had a good sex life, she would have been more relaxed. But her needs were pretty significant. She probably had a lover, maybe more than one. She surpassed them intellectually and probably liked to call herself *polyamorous*. Her fuckbuddies were most likely blue collar workers. Only a randy redneck would be able to dominate her in bed. As soon as their relationship started to feel too familiar, she'd let them go. She was afraid of closeness and having to stop pretending. Professionally – perfect. Seen as kind-hearted and ready for self-sacrifice. The missionary type. That was her weak spot. Sasza should have played this meeting out differently. She'd gain nothing here now. She had played the wrong cards. Sympathy would have been better. Sympathy and humbleness. Sasza should have allowed the doctor to feel needed, compassionate, the indispensable Mother Teresa, protector of the oppressed. *Shit*, Sasza swore silently. She'd ballsed up another operation. And the losses were impossible to rectify now.

'I'm not asking you for a specific address.' She loosened her grip. 'Just point me in the right direction. What area should I go to?'

The woman tore her hand from Sasza's and brushed it off on her dress with disgust. Sasza couldn't remember ever feeling this determined. She changed her strategy again.

'Please!' She made the most pitiable face she could imagine. 'You're the only one who can help me!'

'He's here,' came the reply.

'In Hajnówka?'

'That's the address he gave me,' Prus said and turned her back on Sasza. The dress with the butterfly print exposed most of her back. She had a cobra with its tongue sticking out tattooed on her left shoulder blade. 'Good day.'

Inspector Przemysław 'Jah-Jah' Frankowski entered the commissioner's office without knocking. Krystyna Romanowska was sitting behind her desk with her uniform unbuttoned, and was almost finished painting her nails. Jah-Jah carefully placed an uncovered carton on the tabletop. Inside was a plastic bag with the logo of a popular supermarket.

'The boys on night watch found it at the door.'

Krystyna splayed her fingers. The black 'Cairo Night' polish was still too wet to risk opening the package.

'Help me out, I don't want to ruin my nails,' she said.

She could have retired a long time ago, but she still looked great. Jah-Jah knew she ran a dozen kilometres across the forest twice a day. She also had a black belt in karate. Each year she would take a short vacation to attend the Dojo Japanese martial arts centre training camp in Stara Wieś. The crow's feet at the corners of her eyes only added to her classiness. She kept her hair short and wore no jewellery, aside from a waterproof watch with a leather and nylon strap, kitted out with a pulse meter and torch. Jah-Jah had given it to her back in the days of their marriage.

He groaned, disgruntled, but opened the bag. The commissioner leaned forward and took a peek inside. The bag contained a human skull and some bone fragments, as well as a few twigs, a clump of moss and a couple of leaves. All spattered with dirt.

'Freshly dug up,' Jah-Jah said, anticipating Krystyna's comment. 'I got people to ask around at the forestry office and the hunting clubs. Nothing yet. The forest watch is combing through the entire area a metre at a time.'

Romanowska nodded approvingly. She was finding it difficult to remain calm. Her face grew pale and she bit on her lip.

'Get this checked. You know what to do.'

'Behemoth already took pictures of the bag and the contents. He took DNA and prints from the handle but the results aren't in yet. We'd have to send it by courier to the forensic pathologist. Maybe they'll find something in the lab. We can't do much else.'

'Have you called the prosecutor?'

'That's why I'm here.'

'Good.' She stuck out a hand, waiting for him to pass her the bag. 'We'll do it on Monday. Until then, there's work to do.'

After a pause, Jah-Jah gave her the bag, glancing to the door before he did, making sure it was closed. He wore civilian clothes. A black T-shirt exhibited his muscular body and numerous tattoos. His bald pate shone with sweat. He adjusted the horn-rimmed glasses on his nose, cleared his throat and fidgeted impatiently.

'Is there something else?' Krystyna smiled politely. She started to apply another layer of 'Cairo Night'.

He shook his head.

'I can see there's something on your mind.'

'We have to do something this time.'

'With what?' She screwed the cap of the polish on. 'We have a report and the investigation's ongoing. We'll find the man.'

Jah-Jah made a vague gesture. They both knew he didn't mean the routine operations.

'If I were to decide . . .' he started and trailed off.

They stared at each other in silence. The commissioner sensed what the man wanted to say. It wasn't anything new.

'Here we go again,' she groaned. 'This has something to do with the wedding, right? You think I'm an idiot?'

'Well, tell me I'm wrong!' The officer grew agitated. 'As soon as Bondaruk announced it, the kids found the first head. In the morning, in the fireplace at Harcerska Górka, remember? No idea who planted it there. You don't know what the word in town was, 'cause you were at the dojo.'

'Oh, but I know, believe me. You'll spread panic again. We'd have people from Central breathing down our necks. This is not the time. You know we're spread thin with that damned wedding around the corner!'

Jah-Jah didn't relent.

'I went there personally, unlike you. We searched through the forest. We had our sticks and our dogs, and we even took a chopper with us. We found an old mass grave from the war. People are still hot and bothered. They want another exhumation. They're pretty upset that victims of the pogrom have been buried in a Catholic cemetery.'

'Sure, to hell with daily chores! Let's go straight to the IPN, kick up a fuss about the Orthodox community,' the commissioner replied mockingly. This was the Institute of National Remembrance, the institute in charge of national education and archives. She rolled her eyes. 'There's a meeting of bigwigs at the Carska restaurant in a minute. All the councilmen, the mayor, and the rest of the big shots will be there. I've got to go, keep things in order, so give it a rest with the history lesson. The wedding is our priority. Look,' she went on, 'there are important things and there are things that need to be done. You've always failed to distinguish between them. And besides, that's a mass event for us to secure and that takes precedence. Not to mention we don't even know if this head is new,' she finished, pointing to the package.

'We don't,' admitted Jah-Jah. 'But if that first one might have been a coincidence, which I doubt, that one has been planted at our door *today*, of all days.' He paused for effect before concluding: 'People are talking. Łarysa Szafran's case is making the rounds again. Hardly a surprise. The guy was never held liable.'

'I wasn't the commissioner at the time. Go complain to the Old Man. You won't have to go far.'

'I will,' Jah-Jah replied. 'But he can't do jack shit these days.'

'Same old.'

'We both know how it is. You're in charge. You can do things. I'm sick of doing what Four-Eyes tells us to do.'

'Find Larysa's body and I'll call the guys at Central.'

'Maybe it's her?' The officer pointed to the bag but then, seeing Krystyna's expression, instantly changed the subject: 'Błażej had the night shift. He nearly shat a brick. He's young. Too young for that post.'

'Young, my arse. He's thirty-seven!' the commissioner snapped. 'There's no position lower than duty officer. When you were his age you were already working juvies, and not long after you got the whoring division.'

Frankowski scoffed.

'Watch your language.'

'Why? I've worked vice too.'

'I always thought it weird for the entire family to work in the same place.'

'So that's what's bothering you. Want me to move?' She raised her voice. 'Move yourself if you don't like it. The way's clear.'

'Not what I meant, Krysia.'

'So what did you mean?' she asked, properly irked now. 'Get off my back. If it's Larysa, you'll know first. We'll decide then. Stop jumping to conclusions.'

'Bondaruk's wedding is tomorrow. Someone has to keep an eye on him. This is connected, I tell you. Everybody knows that. Let's stand up for ourselves for once.'

She gave in, exhausted by the constant need to prove her competence. They had been through this already. The problem was that while the others had accepted Romanowska's promotion, her ex still wanted to treat her as his little Krysia. And he had the infuriating habit of explaining the obvious.

'I know.' She adopted the strategy of pretending to be the adept reporting to him – her mentor. That always worked. 'Soon, trust me. But for now we'll do the opposite. I have orders from town hall. I already appointed four people. They'll go undercover and armed.

And a uniformed patrol too. We'll step up the safety measures. He can't get hurt.'

'Seriously?' Jah-Jah asked incredulously. 'I'm supposed to protect that cunt? With public money, too?'

'I'll give the order at the briefing today. If you have any comments, voice them then. I'll back you up as far as I can. Deal?'

Frankowski felt appreciated at last.

'But you're staying here,' she added quickly. 'The headquarters needs leadership.'

'What?' Jah-Jah couldn't hide his disappointment. He felt eliminated from the best part. 'Why do I have to stay?'

Krystyna rose and walked up to him, stopping centimetres from the man.

'Jah-Jah,' she began gently, as if talking to a child. 'Everyone's going to be in Białowieża for the night. I have to go too. Believe me, it'll be better this way. I have no one else who I trust more. This might go awry.'

He frowned, but she could see it was just for show. She felt she was getting close to appeasing him.

'You'll be the boss here tomorrow,' she assured him.

There was a silence for a while.

'Great!' he said finally, still glaring at her and pretending to be angry. 'I'll be boss, duty officer, one-man patrol and maybe a nanny for the kid, too?'

'How did you know I wanted to leave Błażej with you?'

'Krysia!'

She grinned. 'I'm kidding. You'll take Supryczyński. He's dependable.'

That clinched it. Jah-Jah liked the man, and the man liked him back. He looked up to Jah-Jah, idolising his older colleague. If there was nothing to do at the station, they could always talk about music. Supryczyński, a senior officer, played in a reggae band, and Frankowski had had his own group back in the day. The next evening in Hajnówka, with everyone due to be in Białowieża, was shaping up to be relatively quiet. Jah-Jah was just happy he wouldn't have to spend his night chasing pissheads through the forest. Bondaruk had invited the whole town and more besides. Free food and an open bar were a tempting proposition. Pig carcasses were being brought in for the grill, the Małanka choir was rehearsing wedding songs, and the local Yellow Dog brewery had already parked a tank lorry on the camping field. The crowd would be as large as it got here, as large as on Grabarka*. The word around town was that the famous Russian singer Alla Pugacheva herself would perform for the guests. Bondaruk had supposedly brought her in at the request of his mother-in-law, a long-time fan. Alla would sing her best-known songs in the local amphitheatre, the only fully natural concert venue in Central Europe.

'And besides, you won't have to guard that, as you put it, cunt. The bridegroom, I mean.'

'What about this?' Jah-Jah pointed a finger at the bag.

'Any notes attached? Anything I should know about?' Romanowska asked.

'Nope. Nothing. Just like last time.'

'Not exactly surprising. Half of the skull was burned. But this bag is new.' The commissioner studied the plastic with an exaggeratedly clueless expression. 'Maybe whoever planted this works in that shop?'

'Very funny,' the officer snapped, and added: 'I'd make this known to the public. This city has ears. We have to use it.'

'Don't!' she exclaimed. 'We'd have more work with false reports than the case itself.'

'Let them talk. They'd work for us. Whatever the truth is, it'll surface sooner or later. Let's get this out.'

'Not now!' she snapped. 'Who are you going to plant by the phone? Me? Or you? Who would sift through the emails from all kinds of lunatics? We don't have the money to employ a telephone operator.'

'It won't remain a secret for long. The city's abuzz already. Just go to the Ruble Mart and see for yourself.'

'People will always talk. For now, I refuse to comment on the case,' she said. 'He's waiting for it. First, we have to find the man. The one who planted the heads.'

'Man? Why not a woman?'

---

* The Grabarka hill is the most important place for Eastern Orthodox worship in Poland. On 19 August, during the Feast of the Transfiguration, worshippers from all around the country flock there to pray.

The commissioner nodded, agreeing. 'You think it was a single person?'

'Maybe,' he hesitated, 'they want to tell us something.'

'You'd fit right in to a cop movie,' she muttered. 'Any hypotheses? What do they want to tell us?'

'If only I knew that.' He shrugged. 'Something.'

They both looked to a corkboard hanging on the wall. It was cluttered with various ads, an army-made map of the town, pictures of wanted criminals and missing people, and an expert's receipt for examining the previous skull. One of the photos depicted an expressionless woman wearing an outmoded wig. Very doubtful someone would recognise anyone alive based on it. Next to that, there was a low-quality photo of the singed skull, based on which they had assessed the age of the deceased and prepared the composite. An expert from the Medical Academy in Poznań had cost them an arm and a leg, but he didn't put too much effort into his work – or else he was as untalented as it got. He had performed an examination faster than the Central Forensic Lab in Warsaw though. If they had decided to send the skull there, they'd have to wait for at least a year. They had sent the photos of the woman to the people in charge of Itaka's database, hoping for a miracle. It hadn't come. Neither had even a single reliable lead.

'All right, if you're so bent on it, send an email to Central,' Krystyna ordered. 'We'll need a cover story. Let's leave the rest until Monday. They won't be sending a team for some old skull, will they? Especially seeing as we've already been through this once.'

'Amazing strategy, boss.' Jah-Jah snorted. 'What you had to do yesterday, do tomorrow. Maybe the case will solve itself, or maybe people will just forget.'

'Don't be snarky,' Romanowska replied, keeping her cool. 'What if it turns out the skull belongs to a victim of the forest bands? They'll only charge us for wasting their time and won't stop yapping about how we always bother them with shit from the war. Let's get Bondaruk's wedding out of the way first. Then we'll deal with the head.'

'But the wedding will probably last for, like, a week. You know how it is. A proper Belarusian fiesta. Fake as fuck folk bullshit. Tons of people selling junk. You really want to wait that long?'

'Jah-Jah, Monday is in two days. Not in the next Five-Year Plan.'

'You're the boss.'

'I am and I take full responsibility,' she said. 'I'm sending the whole team to the party. I've spoken to the station in Białowieża and they'll cooperate. You're staying. What else do you want me to do? Put it on Facebook?'

'Wouldn't hurt,' he replied with a lopsided grin. 'Or maybe, you know, put a squeeze on Bondaruk. I'd like to put the old groom through the wringer.'

'I'll keep that in mind.'

'He knows who wants to take him down.'

Romanowska smirked at him. 'A bit surprising he didn't tell you that fifteen years ago when someone offed his girl. You interrogated him at the hospital, didn't you? I'm pretty sure it was you.'

'He wanted to save face. Nobody would look for the Belarusian girl. And he adopted her kid. A truly caring master, wouldn't you say?'

'You really must have listened closely to what the housewives on Ruble Mart had to say.' She waved him away. 'Go already. I need to change. I can't go to the party in my uniform now, can I?'

'You look good in it.'

She glowered at him until he headed for the door.

'That skull isn't from the war. Just saying.' He grabbed the handle and opened the door. 'You'll see.'

'You're the expert. Sorry, I forgot.'

'If I was chief here, I'd do things differently,' Jah-Jah declared, pointing to the bag containing the head. 'The man was suspected of killing his wife.'

'He was one of the suspects in a missing-persons case,' the commissioner retorted.

'An audacious kidnapping.'

'He didn't shoot himself and you know that. The ballistics experts have ruled it out. There was only the sound of a gunshot. Four-Eyes disappeared with Łarysa. Without a trace. If not for the gunshot wound we wouldn't have any proof anything even happened.'

'Maybe someone has just given us the proof.'

'Right, only you said the same things when we found the first head,' Romanowska said, losing her patience. She pointed to the composite image of the woman on the corkboard. 'And where did that get us? Nowhere. No connections to Bondaruk. We don't even know who it is. Jane Doe.'

'Not my fault the anthropologist screwed up.' Jah-Jah shrugged. 'Nobody would be able to recognise a face like that. Looks like a bloody alien.'

He shook the cardboard box. Its contents rattled loudly.

'*This* is a body. Old or new, it doesn't matter. It's human remains. We have a homicide here and there's only one procedure for that. And you're telling me to cover for the killer and you get angry when I talk back!'

'Jah-Jah!'

He didn't stop.

'I'm fed up with everyone tiptoeing around it! Why is everyone so bloody afraid of the man getting hurt? He's not the victim here! You tell me to lay off and drive around town, get our numbers in order. You don't care about the truth. The man's a killer but we can't touch him. Everyone's so fucking in love with him. Our very own Rockefeller. Bullshit! He's a local. A simple yokel from Hajnówka. Anyone from outside would recognise all this for what it is. A crock of shit!'

'Give. Me. Proof.'

'You only care about the procedures. Go figure. Like commander, like the team. You don't give a rat's arse about the truth.'

'Truth? The Ruble Mart truth, you mean? That's what I'm supposed to base investigative hypotheses on? Gossip?'

Romanowska stood up. Her nail polish had dried. She started rearranging the papers on her desk, closing fat files with loud thuds. She was crumpling bits of paper irritably, throwing them in the bin. Jah-Jah could see she had finally lost her nerve and was now trying to occupy her hands with something in an attempt to keep herself from throwing a fit. So, he poked the hornets' nest.

'If we get an inspection from Central, you'll have to explain yourself. You're only acting commissioner. They can give you the boot any moment. I wouldn't grow too attached to the position if I were you.'

He turned away then, ready to leave, but Romanowska snapped, unable to let him get away with an insult as stinging as that.

'I never asked for this.' She started off hissing, but with every word she got louder. Jah-Jah slammed the door shut and leaned against it to muffle the noise. He was sure the commissioner's shouting would be heard through the entire station. 'They only promoted me to save the face of this unit. I was the only one not abusing my rights. I'm also the only high-ranking female officer here. So yes, that was what tipped the scales. It was a sensible move after what *you've* done.'

'Me?' He made an innocent face.

She aimed a finger at him.

'You were there at that drinking spree. You might have died yourself, or shot someone too. That wasn't the first time you'd been drinking on duty either. And it wasn't the first time Romek and Andrzej played with their guns at the station. Good thing you didn't invite your friend, the priest. You'd have taken the cars too, if you did. I have some pretty big shoes to fill, I know. But listen, they couldn't promote you, Jah-Jah. Not now. I know you'd be better suited to this post than I am. I'm only sorry you don't have the balls to accept that your ex is higher up the ladder than you are.'

'Krysia, that's not what I meant,' Frankowski began, but trailed off.

He didn't really want to apologise now. It was hard enough on him as it was. She had humiliated him once by requesting divorce and now this: she'd got the promotion and he'd been passed over. He was supposed to become commissioner. He had even refused a transfer to Central, counting on being chosen as the new chief as soon as the position opened up. He had been in the force a lot longer than Romanowska. And he was local. She was an outsider. Besides, he had got her a post at the station in the first place. The Old Man had been preparing to retire for a while and after they had transferred Doman to Białystok, Jah-Jah had had no real competition. He had never even considered Krysia. She was a woman. His being deputy commissioner changed nothing, because it was her, his little Krysia, pulling the strings in the unit now. They both knew she was right – he envied her.

'You've got a problem, deal with it.' She cut any further discussion short. 'The briefing will begin on time.'

When Jah-Jah left, she changed her clothes, found the key and, for the first time in her life, opened the Old Man's armoured cabinet. She hadn't touched it for the whole month after she had moved into the old commissioner's office. She hadn't believed she'd keep this position for more than a few days. The cabinet door creaked. She'd have to lube the hinges. There weren't many files inside. The inside of the cabinet smelled of absinthe. She opened the door wider. Two empty bottles rolled out. Rummaging through the documents uncovered another one. Full, this time. No excise tax band. The liquor was golden-yellow. Romanowska cursed under her breath and swore to herself that she'd clean up the mess this unit was. She intended to show everyone she was worthy of her high rank. She'd do everything to keep her position, even if it meant all-out war with Jah-Jah. She flung the empty bottles into the bin, where they landed with a loud clatter. The one still filled with the home-made moonshine or whatever that was she put on the windowsill, exhibited like material evidence in a case. She wasn't going to check the contents.

Then, she picked up the box containing the human head. The plastic bag was leaky and the bottom of the box was soaked through. Romanowska fully expected her whole office to smell like a corpse when she got back. She took the bag out and hung it on the sill, outside the window, making sure the knot was strong, double-checking it to be certain. The box she put outside her room, leaving it in the corridor, next to a bin, so that the cleaning lady would take it away at first opportunity. Then she collected the files scattered across the desk and stacked them on the bottom shelf of the armoured cabinet. Finally, everything looked like it should. Romanowska turned the key, closing the cabinet. She didn't know the combination, but none of the officers would dare open it anyway. Quickly, she took out her Glock from a drawer and placed it into her elegant handbag, intending to take it to the VIP wedding dinner at the Carska restaurant. She was ready to leave.

'Oi, boss!' Błażej, her son, poked his head in through the door. He liked to tease her like that at work. Krystyna found herself thinking how similar he was to his father. A couple years more and he'd turn into a scoundrel just like Jah-Jah.

'They called from Bielsk. There's a search warrant for the Bisons' apartment. Someone's painted over the Belarusian names on the road signs in Orla. Supposedly, the youngest Bejnar had been there a week ago. He bought a shovel and took a couple of blue spray cans from Kuryluk. Maybe he dug up that skull?'

'Okay, take someone with you and go.' She assumed her formal, bossy stance and used an accordingly officious voice. 'And check if they have any black paint, tar, brushes or anything such. There's a swastika on Lipowa Street again.'

'Then we seize it?'

'If you find anything. I'll take care of the formalities. We have to get it right this time. Otherwise the prosecutor will put it down to "youthful rebelliousness" again. I don't need those wannabe patriots in my hair now. I've got a lot on my plate as it is. But yeah, go and search them. And check out if Krajnów has an alibi for this morning. Maybe he reactivated his unit?'

'Done that already. He was teaching at school. Even organised a religion test for the kids. He's covered.'

Romanowska nodded. She was proud of her son. He was a quicker thinker than his old man. Maybe he'd grow to become a half-decent cop after all.

'I'm sick of that fascist,' she grumbled. 'Keep an eye on our over-enthusiastic sermoniser. They might show up at the wedding and kick up a fuss. It would be good if we could avoid making a show of strength. Call me if you find the spray paint. The mayor will be grateful.'

'Poor Belarusians, oppressed by the evil Poles.' Her son snorted. 'Fear not, we'll protect you!'

'Stop that. Protecting them is what they pay us for. You'll see at the next payday. Dismissed.'

The door closed. Romanowska sat down behind her desk. She remained there for a moment, thinking, and then leapt to her feet.

'Błażej!' she called, rushing out of her office. She caught her son at the last moment. He had just reached the dispatch room. 'Ask him about that shovel. What he needed it for, what he did with it. Seize it if necessary. Also, look around for balaclavas and dark clothes.'

'Dark clothes?'

'Like those worn by the guy who planted the head.'

'But that's not our case. It's Bielsk's. We don't have the authority here.'

'Call them and arrange it, then. Let them know we have a new skull. Old, I mean. Another one. They'll know. We could use some support. Just be discreet. Can you do it?'

'I'll get it done in no time.'

'What happened to you?' The voice was soft, childlike.

Sasza raised her head but there was no one around. She must have imagined it.

She had been sitting on a bench in the park by the hospital for some time now, listening to the rustling of birch leaves and analysing the hopelessness of her situation. She had left the doctor's room fuming. At first, she had intended to steal the files. Łukasz's current address had to be in the hospital documents. How could they think *he* was the victim here? All it would take was a little diversion. She could have told them she had left some files behind. The nurse from reception would have let her into the doctor's office and allowed her to search the room. To take the thin file would only take a moment. To hide it in her bag among all the clutter would pose no difficulty either. They wouldn't have realised anything was wrong until Monday. And by that time she'd have been able to send the papers back. By courier, perhaps. That would have been the most effective option. But was it worth the risk?

What would she do if Łukasz decided one day to appear in her life again? What would she tell her daughter? Sasza felt for a moment that she couldn't breathe, choking on her fear.

Disembowelled bodies of women, splayed in theatrical poses. Photos mailed to the police. The macabre painting, the only evidence, supposedly perished in the fire. All of that flashed before Sasza's eyes like a grotesque movie. She could feel the noose tightening around her neck. She only wanted to finally stop being afraid, but it was hopeless. There was no telling if Łukasz had really killed those women. But she knew how to find out for sure, and it required her to meet Polak face to face. There was only one question she wanted to ask him. And even if he refused to answer,

she'd know if was him or not. She wanted to believe in his innocence so badly.

'Have you been crying?' This time the voice was accompanied
by a long shadow. Sasza turned her head toward the sound. Behind
her, next to a tree, stood a petite, blue-eyed girl. She didn't look
like an adult; more like an adolescent. Her heart-shaped lips made
Sasza think about raspberry candy. She stared at the girl, captivated. In response, the girl sent her a radiant smile. Sasza shook her
head. 'No. I'm just resting.'

The girl's flowery skirt spun and she flew graciously towards
the bench. Sasza gave her some space to sit. For a while, they were
silent. A group of patients were still occupied with their painting.
A fat man was posing now. Sasza's attention wandered to his bare
feet, swollen and red.

'Mirek never wears shoes,' the girl explained. Then, she added:
'His right leg got frostbitten this winter. He was scared they'd cut
it off. He says if you go barefoot for a long time, you stop feeling
anything in your feet. You think that's true?'

Sasza mumbled something in response. She was in no mood to
talk, and definitely wasn't going to listen to the blathering of some
mental teen. The only lunatic she was interested in was Łukasz
Polak. Only she wouldn't be able to interrogate him now. She
pushed herself up.

'I've got to go.'

The girl didn't hide her disappointment. 'Who did you come to
see?'

'A friend. See you around.' Sasza got up to leave.

'Nobody comes to see me,' the girl complained. She rolled up a
sleeve and scratched her arm. Sasza noticed the cuts on her skin.
Nothing too serious, it seemed. It looked like someone had pricked
her arm with hundreds of little needles. Most of the damage was
healed over. Only the spot the girl had scratched had some fresh
blood seeping from it. The girl rolled her sleeve down again and
continued, as if nothing had happened: 'I really miss my mum.
Dad's abroad all the time. I don't have anyone else. Besides my
brother, but he doesn't talk to anyone,' she said, pointing over to
the group of patients.

Sasza suddenly had an idea. Maybe there was still a chance to salvage this situation. No bravado though. She would act cautiously and deliberately. She looked around, scanning her surroundings for any hospital staff, before asking: 'You been here long?'

'Two years. My brother Jacek came a few months ago. The court directed him for some examinations for his trial, and then they moved him to Ciszynia. They tell me it's better for me to have him around. We were inseparable once.'

'This is a small facility. You know everyone here?'

The girl nodded vigorously.

'Do you know Łukasz Polak?' Sasza tried to hide the hope in her voice.

The girl didn't respond. She looked confused. She didn't seem to know the name.

'Blond, pretty handsome, not counting the top of his head. Thick lips, bright eyes. The quiet type. Likes to wear hoodies.'

No reaction.

'He has a scar on his arm. A little one, bluish. He fell from a swing when he was a child. Still has some paint under his skin, in the shape of a bird in flight. Everyone thinks it's a tattoo,' Sasza said, losing hope.

'Martin!' the girl exclaimed, giggling. 'He taught Jacek how to paint. Is he your friend?'

'I used to know him,' Sasza replied and sat down again. 'I need to see him.'

'He left.'

'Did he leave a telephone number or an address?'

'He doesn't have a mobile. But he came back a week ago. Took me on a trip,' the girl said, happily.

Sasza blanched. The Red Spider's victims had all been aged eighteen to twenty-five. Pretty, petite and lonely. This girl matched the killer's profile perfectly.

'Does he visit you often?'

'I only went out with him once. He lived in town until the quarantine was over. They're running a research project or something and he participated. They wanted to see how well he got on outside. They even found him a job!'

'What is it?'

'No idea. But he was happy. He told me he liked the city, that it's so quiet and green. And that the people are nice. That's what he said. He doesn't want to go back to his city. He can't go back to his parents. I think he did something bad. But, we all do.' She paused. 'Anyhow, I like his parents. They used to visit once a month. Very classy. His mum's pretty like Princess Di. If she'd lived, of course. They really worried for him.' Another pause. 'But Martin's still on his meds so he has to see the director now and again.'

'Ms Prus?'

'Mr Saczko. He's the big boss here.'

'He wasn't here today.'

'He went to the wedding. There's a big party in Białowieża today. Some rich guy is getting married. I heard the bride is only a bit older than me. And he's, like, a hundred.'

Sasza didn't care about that.

'Could you take me to him?'

'I don't know where the party is. Besides, I don't have any pretty clothes.'

'I meant Martin. Let's go see him together. What do you say?'

The girl hesitated, but it was evident she wanted to go. For a while longer, she fought with herself, finally giving a reluctant answer: 'I can't leave without permission.'

'And Łukasz got a permission for you?'

'We called him Martin.'

'Did he get you leave?'

The girl nodded.

Sasza swept the park with her eyes. 'And would it be that bad if we left now and returned in an hour? Nobody would know. When do they serve dinner?'

'I can't,' the girl whispered fearfully. 'I really can't.'

'All right, I was kidding anyway.' Sasza laughed awkwardly, trying to mask her nervousness. 'But they allowed Łukasz to take you out? Without an adult with you?'

'I'm eighteen. My birthday was three months ago. I can go on leave on my own. The doctor said okay and asked the director. I even went to Martin's apartment,' she said, beaming. 'He took some photos of me. Want to see? I look super pretty. He told me I was very photo . . . genous . . . photo-something.'

'Photos?' Sasza swallowed loudly. She couldn't believe the hospital management had allowed the girl to take such a risk. 'Can I see them? The ones he took.'

The girl nodded and immediately headed towards the building. Sasza was left alone. She fought with herself. A few minutes ago she had been ready to leave. She had felt her fervour diminishing and the whole situation had looked rather absurd. But meeting this girl had changed everything. Was the Red Spider planning another attack? Wasn't it the reason he had befriended the girl?

Sasza wanted to run to the police immediately and tell them who Polak really was. Tell them what she had seen when she had still worked for the CBŚ. It might not be too late this time. But she couldn't. Operation Thumbelina was top secret and besides, there was no proof. Only hypotheses. And there was that thing called presumption of innocence. According to the law, Polak was cured and had a right to anonymity. He could live however he wanted. Prus had been right. On the one hand, Sasza had to protect the girl against attack, but on the other, the teen knew where he lived and could take her there. She wouldn't need any files or support from the hospital staff. But if she used the girl as bait to achieve her own, private goal, she'd endanger her life. What was she supposed to do?

'Look!' The girl returned with a wad of large-format photos and a box of chocolates. She opened it. 'Martin gave it to me. Eggnog flavoured.'

Sasza was ravenous, but she refused a chocolate and instead snatched the photos. The workmanship was unmistakable. It was the same photographer. Grainy images, minimalist frames, high contrast. These photos were black and white, shot with gusto. Like a Michelin calendar. Probably made with an old-school, analogue camera. Sasza had to admit that Polak hadn't lost his touch. The young patient was indeed photogenic. She didn't simper. Didn't overdo the posing. The photographer had managed to understate her natural cuteness. The model's stare hid a dark secret, Sasza thought. For a while she reflected on why the girl might have been hospitalised at only sixteen, but she didn't dare ask yet.

Sasza had dreaded the photos being erotic in nature, but they weren't. There was no perversion in them, either, and that had been the characteristic feature of all the photos the Red Spider had sent to the police. Nothing here pointed to any bad intentions on the part of the photographer. The pictures were simply two portraits, taken in an empty apartment typical of a small town. A little fern, patterned curtains, and a gloss wall unit in the background. Sasza tried imagining the apartment Polak was renting, furniture included, probably from an elderly person. An Eastern Orthodox icon adorned one of the walls, just beneath a woven wall rug. It didn't look like a reproduction. Sasza felt that she was so close now. She'd find him even if it meant failing the shooting range exam. She could always try again in autumn and sell Ghost some excuse in the meantime.

'Was that taken at his place?'

The girl nodded and plucked two smaller photos from a file she was holding. These had been taken outdoors. One in the middle of a linden-lined street, the other in a courtyard with brick bin shelters painted over with graffiti in Cyrillic. Sasza read those: 'Wipe Out the Lakhs!'

'I look best in this one,' the girl said, pointing to the photo with the linden trees. 'I wouldn't have believed someone could take a picture like that on a normal street, just by a housing block.'

Sasza took a closer look at the photograph. The girl really did look great in it, but what the profiler was interested in was the details of the background. She focused on them, trying to commit all the little pieces to memory, just in case, so that she could recall them all later. Compared to the picture taken in the flat, it contained tons of data. Sasza was sure she'd be able to find the place, if the photo had been taken in Hajnówka. A squat apartment block from the sixties, its front facade decorated with red-and-white lines. A piece of a grocery store, it looked like, with a few letters of its name visible. Behind the girl, a signboard. Again, only the last letters were legible – 'bowski and son'.

'He took this photo right in front of his house. You can't even imagine the show we made doing that on the street. People were stopping to look at us. He has this old-school camera, you know.'

'A Sinar?' Sasza swallowed. 'With a tripod with one of the legs made of wood?'

The girl laughed.

'You do know him! What a coincidence.'

'Do you remember the address?' Sasza fought to contain her excitement.

'It's somewhere in the centre of town. I can take you there if you ask the director.'

Sasza already knew the extent of the staff's helpfulness, but she smiled at the girl.

'What's your name?'

'Danka. Well, Danuta, but no one calls me that.'

'I thought this was a private clinic and you were allowed to come and go as you please?'

'Some of us are here voluntarily, yes. Me too, but Dad is paying for my stay and he told the staff to tell him who I talk to. I escaped once already. Because of my brother. They caught us in Kłobuck. Cuffed us and hit us.' She grew silent.

'Hit you?' Sasza asked with disbelief. That was doubtful.

'The police,' Danka explained quickly. 'They've been watching me ever since.'

Sasza took a closer look at the girl. 'Why are you here?'

Danka hesitated.

'My mum died. Dad was in Afghanistan so my brother had to take care of me.'

'He's the one painting over there? The one Łukasz taught how to paint?'

The girl nodded.

'How did your mum die?'

'Jacek cut her head off.'

Sasza gaped at her, expecting a continuation, but Danka clammed up again. Sasza could see in her eyes that the girl wanted to tell her story, but was afraid of her reaction. She prodded: 'Why did he do it?'

'She didn't pay the second instalment for my skiing trip. I didn't go. I was the only one in the school who didn't. Mum said we couldn't afford it. She used to sell vitamins over the phone, but I think no one wanted to buy them. Sometimes we had to go hungry, because she spent everything on the cats. The whole house smelled of cat poo. She used to take cats from the street. Make them better. They were everywhere. Mum and Dad argued a lot about those cats. Dad shouted at her. He said we were living in a slum. But then he had to leave again. He's a soldier, you know. He has medals. He was never around, and even when he was, the only thing he did was lie and stare at the ceiling. He didn't care much. About us or the cats. So we hid Mum in the closet. She didn't fit with her head on.'

'You helped your brother?'

She hung her head.

'Dad had a saw in the basement, so I took it. Jacek put on *Sam and Cat*. I like that show. It's funny. I had headphones on so I didn't hear him. And then he came over, blood-spattered, and told me to go and buy rubbish bags. He gave me a thousand złoty in twenty-złoty bills. It was the money for my skiing trip. Mum had it all the time, but she didn't want to spend it on the trip, because one of the cats had babesiosis and the medicine for that is expensive . . .'

Danka trailed off and froze, motionless. She clutched the photos to her chest. 'Then we left,' she went on. 'We lived with Jacek's friends in the mountains until the police came.'

'How old were you?'

'Thirteen.'

Sasza glanced at Danka's fidgeting feet, and then at her angelic face. This time she seemed to have retreated for good.

'Next time I'm here, I'll ask the director to let you go with me. You won't run away, will you?'

Danka smiled. 'Will you buy me a Smurf ice-cream? They're my favourite.'

'Sure.' Sasza took her iPhone out and pointed to the pictures. 'Can I take a photo?'

'No problem,' Danka replied. 'Will you really take me with you?'

'If you behave well. Promise?'

'Promise. Hey, what's your name, by the way?'

'Me?' Sasza considered her answer for a while, setting the focus on the phone and snapping photos of all the details of Danka's pictures. 'Martin used to call me Milena. You might have heard about me in therapy.'

'Not really.' The girl shook her head. 'But he liked to talk about a Karolina.'

Sasza drove around town looking for the place where Polak had taken the photos of Danka. With no success. The authorities had ordered the refurbishment of all the buildings downtown and most of the streets were lined with scaffolding. Here and there, workers were painting facades in gaudy colours. Most of the business signage had been taken off. The city architect, either crazy or else unhealthily fascinated with confectionery, ordered all structures repainted in raspberry, willow-green or salmony colours. Soon, the entire town would look like some kind of monstrous birthday cake. Adding to the cacophony of colours, someone had decided it would be a good idea to break up the already gaudy walls with irregular indigo stripes. Most of the facades were now covered with long paper sheets to protect the windows against paint spatters, and the walls were criss-crossed with chaotic lines of contrasting colour.

Around the town market on Trzeciego Maja Street, the renovations ended. Or maybe the workers had run out of paint. The skyline was dominated by the dull, brownish colossus of the Museum of Belarusian Culture, constructed in the nineties but clearly harking back to the monumental structures erected years before for the glory of the communist regimes in Moscow or Minsk. The ground floor of the building was occupied by a restaurant, its sign reading Forest Palace. Someone trying to be funny had spray-painted below: 'Sorest Phallus'. Sasza decided to stop by. Suddenly, she felt exhausted, her frustration and hunger finally catching up with her. Professor Abrams used to say that if you were full, you wouldn't take unnecessary risks. Sasza decided to focus for the time being on the dilemma of choosing her food. The advertising display listed all the local dishes served inside: *pelmeni, solyanka,* potato *babka.* Sasza hadn't tried any of those before, and the prices were surprisingly low. She went in.

Despite the early hour, the restaurant was busy. Its decor was rustic. Embroidered tablecloths, candles in ornamental stands, decorative lacquered tree roots. Garlands of flowers hung over the high backrests of the wooden chairs. Most of the tables were taken. It seemed that contrary to popular opinion, the residents of Hajnówka liked to eat out. Sasza sat at the only unoccupied table – tucked against the back wall, right next to a window through which she could observe the outdoor section of the place, deserted save for three identical-looking thugs. They occupied a long wooden bench. Each held a thick wad of money. All three were completely absorbed in counting the bills, which they did like professionals, licking their fingers once in a while. When they were served beer, the men tossed the cash into a plastic bag from a local discount store – Sasza recognised it by its distinctive ladybird logo – and turned their attention to their drinks. Sasza's eyes were drawn to the frosted glasses, but she immediately made herself look away, instead focusing on the menu. A while later, a waitress walked over carrying a tray with a stoneware plate of lard topped with pork scratchings and a small basket of dark bread.

'This seat is taken,' she announced. She was pale like Snow White herself, and her black hair was arranged into flowing curls.

Sasza looked around. There was nothing that marked the table as reserved. She got up anyway, taking a last look around the room, but all the other seats were taken too.

'All right, today is an exception. You can stay,' the waitress said with a smile. 'To be honest, I don't think Mr Bondaruk will show up today.'

The woman placed the appetiser on the table and asked if Sasza was ready to order. Sasza chose Ukrainian borscht, garlic *ushka* dumplings and a white cabbage salad. She spread a thick layer of lard over a piece of bread and devoured the appetiser in an instant. It only made her more hungry. Bored, she glanced through the window, but the three men had taken their money and left, leaving behind only three empty beer glasses and an ashtray filled with cigarette butts. The food was delicious. Not even halfway through, Sasza ordered another portion of dumplings. They even had white tea, and not the cheap variety. Sasza decided she would stay in Hajnówka for another night and return to Sopot on Sunday evening. She wanted to confront Łukasz, wherever it would take her. She could feel her goal was nearly within reach. To look for the man like a civilian would do would take too much time, though, and time wasn't something she had in abundance.

On her way to the restaurant she had passed the local police station. She had thought about dropping in, explaining that she was a profiler and asking for help. The idea wasn't bad per se, but it wasn't exactly legal either. She knew from experience that people working in those small, local station usually didn't take experts like her too seriously. She could theoretically call some colleagues and ask if they knew anyone from Hajnówka, but she could already imagine their reaction to that. When she had driven east last time, back when she was working on the Staroń case, nobody from Tricity could even point her in the right direction.

There was only one thing left to do. It all depended on who she met down at the station and whether they would like to help her, disregarding protocol, but she could simply put her cards on the table. What would she be able to offer them? A smile and an IOU at best. Even if the impossible happened and they needed her expertise right away, they wouldn't be able to use it anyway; she had no recommendation and she'd only officially be joining the force on Monday. That meant working with the local police on the record was out of the question. Besides, what were the odds of them needing a profiler for their investigations? What they were probably dealing with were a couple of thieves, some drug dealers at the local nightclub and a throng of drunk drivers – the bread and butter of any small-town police department. When it came to murders, Hajnówka probably had close to a hundred per cent detection rate. Sasza doubted such a place was plagued by killings other than those resulting from family spats, one or two each couple of years at the most.

'Good afternoon.' Sasza was torn from her reverie by a booming basso.

She looked up. Standing at her table was an old-looking man with a bristly moustache. He was tall and lanky, with sunken cheeks, and wore a striped shirt, a scarf and a light trench coat. He had a slim, sun-weathered face, a strong jawline, and bright, piercing eyes. His hair was nearly white, thick and a bit dishevelled, brushed back David Lynch style. If not for the bushy moustache, he might have been mistaken for a gigolo a bit past his prime. He commanded respect, exuding an aura of authority. Dumbfounded, Sasza felt at a loss as to how to react. She was clearly occupying his seat. His table. For an instant she thought she had seen him before. Or maybe he just looked strikingly like someone she had known.

'I'm sorry, I've taken your seat, haven't I?' She jumped to her feet. 'I'm finished, so I'll just go.'

'No, please, stay,' he said and gestured for her to sit back down. He was composed, charming. 'I apologise for interrupting your meal. I'd be honoured if you'd sit with me.'

His lips stretched in a little smile. The wrinkles around his eyes, lips and nose – reflecting the story of one's life, if you believed in such things – testified to the man having been through quite a lot. He wasn't the ex-sportsman type or a frail intellectual. More like an ex-army man, someone used to wearing a uniform – a man in total control of his body. Not one to order appetisers. All muscle and bone, he was taut like a coiled spring. Practically no fat on him at all. Sasza had difficulty pinpointing his age. But despite his flawless posture, he had to be well past sixty.

'Everyone thinks I prefer to spend time alone,' he said, placing an empty plastic bag on the bench.

It was the same kind as the one the three thugs had had, sporting the ladybird logo of the popular discount store – probably the only one in town. It must provide equally for every social class, she thought; the man was clearly well-off, going by his self-assurance and relaxed manner.

'But they're wrong.' Sasza smiled.

'You're a wise woman,' he replied, then paused. 'For one your age, of course. How old are you, exactly?'

'Thirty-eight.'

He laughed.

'It's all downhill from there.'

He'd managed to make her laugh. She relaxed. The man seemed charming enough.

The waitress, looking spooked, approaching with Sasza's dumplings and broke up their conversation by starting to explain herself nervously, but the man sent her away with a flick of a wrist. Though he hadn't ordered anything, a short while later the waitress brought him three shots of vodka, salted pork fat with onion rings and brine-pickled cucumbers. He nodded at Sasza, inviting her to drink with him, but she refused, not even regretting it. His company had made her settle down. She didn't need booze.

'I should be somewhere else now,' he said and gulped down the first shot. Then, not waiting for her reply, he proceeded to drink the second and the third. He sighed, smacking his lips. '*Woś żyćcio kastrapataje. Choczam, kab nas kachali. Ale czamu? Hetaha nichto nie wiedaje.*'*

Sasza finished her food and decided it was time for her to leave. The vodka they served here looked freezing-cold and oily. Just as it should.

'Stay a while longer?' he asked her. There was a tone to his voice that Sasza would recognise anywhere; it was something she knew intimately. The man was an alcoholic. In the past, she would have stayed and got drunk with the guy, talking about life until morning. She had to go. Right now. She would feel the irresistible pull towards the shot glass any time now. To taste the booze again. Just the tip of her tongue. He noticed the panic in her eyes and grew sombre.

'I'm in a bit of a hurry.' She gave him an apologetic look and asked for the bill.

The waitress clearly heard her and even printed out the slip of paper, but didn't walk over, instead disappearing behind the counter. Sasza thought she would never stop filling beer glasses. Her gaze hovered somewhere between the tap and the glasses, fixed on the amber liquid and the white foam, as if hypnotised. Sasza could practically feel the bubbles fizzing on her tongue. It wasn't even two in the afternoon. She had to run, and quick.

'*Kali człowiek śpiaszaje, czort wiesialicsa,*'† the man said. He was more talkative and laid-back after the three shots. He looked like he was in the mood to talk. Suddenly, he took interest in who Sasza was and what had brought her to town. Sasza couldn't understand what he'd said, so he quickly translated the old proverb and added in a slightly patronising manner: 'You're young. Live as you like. Free. Take joy in each and every breath you take.'

Then, he grabbed her by the arm. She didn't pull away. She pitied him. Five minutes and not a second more, she thought. He'd start giving her unsolicited advice now – what to do, how to live, how to stay afloat, what's important in life. Not that long ago, Sasza used to speak to random people in bars like that too. She hadn't been

---

* Roughly: 'That is our rough life. We want to be loved. But why? Nobody knows.'
† 'When you're in a hurry, the devil's happy.' Belarusian (and Polish) proverb.

able to cure herself, but always had an idea for how to fix the lives of others.

'Life isn't that short,' he continued, 'but nobody knows how to make something of it. When you're young, you only make mistakes. Everything happens too fast, but your errors stay with you for ever. If only I could take everything back. If only I'd known then what I know now. Life isn't important. What's important is the *search*. You have to experience everything, draw the right conclusions, and never leave anything unfinished. Honesty is the only thing you have. For others and for yourself. Not money, love, or your job. All that is worthless. You have to be an egoist. It's only you and the world. My God, that sounded good!' He grinned, clearly proud of his speech. He wanted to talk more.

'I can't stay here,' Sasza said abruptly, pointing to the empty glasses. 'I try to keep away from places with alcohol.'

She couldn't believe she'd said that. It had come out on its own. She realised only after it had what it was she actually wanted. She wanted him to stop her, to call her out on her bullshit, to force her down into a chair. So she could have a drink with a clean conscience and then blame it all on him. A guy at a bar whom she didn't even know, who'd made her do it. Another classic move to duck responsibility.

But he did nothing of the sort. He frowned, grew serious, and immediately withdrew his hand from her arm. He understood.

'That means you won't come to my wedding.' He sighed, sadly. 'Everyone will be there. The old and the young. The rich and the poor. Just like in a fairy tale. I'm the king around here.' He laughed bitterly and then blew his nose into a monogrammed handkerchief. 'They'll tell their grandchildren, years from now, that they were there, at the greatest ball this town has ever seen. I've ordered a tanker of booze. And I'm certain there will be nothing left at the end.'

So this was the old man Danka had spoken about. And it was his wedding that the director of the hospital, Saczko, had been in such a hurry to attend. This was the rich bigwig marrying a girl the age of his granddaughter. He wasn't looking too happy about it. Quite the opposite, in fact. Why was he even getting married? Why was he hiding in this restaurant, drinking himself into a stupor in the company of a stranger? You don't avoid people on your wedding day. Unless you're seeking redemption. Just like Sasza had. For what did he want redemption, though? That, she didn't want to know.

'If there's vodka, I doubt I'll come.' She paid for the food and refused the change. The waitress curtsied and left without a word, but a moment later she was back with another set of shots for the man. 'But best wishes to you,' Sasza said, getting up to leave. 'All the best to you and your wife.'

He looked at her, and for a while it seemed he sobered up a little. She noticed what she thought was anxiety in his eyes. Maybe even fear. The dread of what was to come. But that only lasted an instant; then his stare grew foggy and absent again, and he downed one of the shots.

'Only you and the world,' he mumbled, gesticulating widely. 'The rest doesn't count. Listen to the words of an old man. I know how it'll end. I know the date of my own death! There's no doubt who'll do me in.'

He was still raving when Sasza left. He was in the grip of alcohol disease. Close to rock bottom. But even if she'd told him that, it would only have encouraged him to blabber on, argue. There was no sense in talking more. She wasn't on a mission. Let someone else treat him. Save him. It was probable that tomorrow, when the man woke up with a terrible hangover, he wouldn't even remember meeting her. But she wouldn't forget. His last words especially, as he'd explained why he was marrying such a young girl. A girl who didn't love him and whom he in turn didn't love. Truth be told, he'd confided, he didn't even know her too well. His words reverberated in her head until she started the engine and drove away from the restaurant. Afterwards, they seemed pitiful, idiotic, like anything out of an alcoholic's mouth did. In the end, Sasza didn't really know why they had moved her the way they had.

'For my whole life I have been hurting people,' he'd said. 'And I've done nothing to stop it. I was afraid to put up a wall. I only cared about my money, my position, my place on Earth. I only wanted power. If I'm about to make even one child happy now, I can die without regret. Because when I do die and the time of reckoning comes, I'll take nothing with me. I'll go alone, barefoot and naked, with nothing but my pride. Just the way I lived my life. What was I thinking? All I have is worthless. I fought for things that only weighed me down, like an anchor. I should have done the opposite. I know what's coming. I know what's going to happen when the monster is unleashed. I know I was the only person holding its chains. Right here.' He lifted the empty bag. Sasza was nearly sure it was the same one the three thugs had taken the money out of. 'But I'm setting it free today, and I'm going to drown my sorrows. Let the show go on, without me. Without me. I want to fly above the Earth one more time. We're all going to end up in the dirt. All of us. The Earth, our mother – it soaks up blood, cleans our conscience and only leaves a trace in our memories. Even if people keep quiet, the Earth knows. It keeps all our secrets.'

There was a traffic jam at the exit from the marketplace. Sasza stopped her car, amazed. She had been sure the inhabitants of this town, of whom there were no more than thirty thousand, didn't even know what a traffic jam was. There were only a couple of streets criss-crossing Hajnówka. She could have driven around the city twice in an hour. It was simply bizarre that she wasn't able to find Polak's house in a shithole like this.

When her car crawled closer to the market square, Sasza saw the cause of the blockage. A man pushing a wheelbarrow loaded with an enormous head of a statue of Lenin was strolling calmly in front of the line of cars. Despite the stuffy weather, the man was clothed in a wool greatcoat with golden buttons and an army hat with a red star at the front. A few porters followed him, carrying packages that looked like museum pieces: flags, a mannequin dressed in a Bolshevik revolutionary uniform, rifles, and a box filled with smaller Lenins, which might have served as paperweights in some communist functionary's office. All of these things were scrutinised and recorded by a short man wearing a corduroy suit and thick-heeled shoes that were probably meant to make him look taller. The man was then showing the porters where to place the packages in the boot of a white van.

A line of onlookers observed the show in silence. No banners, no shouting. One woman approached the man with the wheelbarrow and asked if she could take a selfie with him to post on Facebook. The man, seeming very happy, agreed. He even took off his Red

Army hat and placed it on the woman's head. Then for a short while they both grinned while her iPhone snapped the photo. Sasza noticed two cameramen at the back, recording the whole spectacle. The procession with Lenin's head had to be repeated several more times for them, so that there were two full versions – with the great-coat, and without it.

It all lasted for some time, until the drivers lost patience and the cars started to honk. From a policeman who'd appeared out of nowhere, Sasza learned that the show was down to a certain Wojciech Rynarzewski, the owner of a local bar called Volodia, losing all his possessions to the court bailiff. Until the enforcement proced-ure ended, the road was officially closed to all traffic, so all the cars in the jam had unwittingly broken a host of traffic regulations. The officer was there to fine each and every one of them. He was deaf to all protestations that the sign had been obscured by the white van. All the drivers received a fine of two hundred złoty. All except Sasza. Her car was impounded and taken to the police car park. Sasza her-self was taken to the station. It turned out she didn't have the car's registration and her driving licence, or any of her credit cards, on her, although she only realised it during the police inspection.

'CBŚ collaborator,' muttered the officer interrogating Sasza at the station.

He had been holding the white plastic card, the only document Sasza could find in her purse to confirm her identity, for such a long time that his coffee had grown completely cold and the dregs had all fallen to the bottom of the cup.

The card was a worthless little thing Ghost had given Sasza the day before. She didn't inform the officer that cards like that could be given to anyone, including a lover of a civilian police informant. She suspected the policeman knew that but didn't want to let her know he knew.

She looked around. The police station was newly renovated and smelled fresh. Larger stations all around Poland could envy Hajnówka the modern equipment the building was crammed with. The sluggish officer had mentioned it being installed not even a month earlier. The control room looked like a *Star Wars* com-mand centre. Sasza could only think about that old Chinese curse, though: 'May all your dreams come true.' She had found herself in the place she had wanted to get to from the beginning, but this wasn't how she had envisioned her visit. But it wasn't all bad. Sasza believed it wouldn't be too hard to extricate herself from her predicament and in the process get to know the local officers. She had already blown into a breathalyser, filled in an application for a police to search for the thief who'd stolen her stuff, and called her mother. Unfortunately, on a Saturday evening there was nobody at the Gdańsk headquarters who could confirm Sasza's identity. And Laura Załuska, her mother, had the irksome habit of never having her mobile with her. She treated it like her home phone and would leave it on her nightstand whenever she went out, only using it twice a day: at seven in the morning and seven in the evening.

Sasza glanced at the antique cuckoo clock hanging on the wall above the officer's head. It was nearly three. No point in calling again. Laura would call her back as soon as the metal bird chirped seven times. Sasza hoped she'd be able to think of something before then. She was in no mood to stay here for the whole day. Maybe her brother would be able to fax them a scan of her passport? He had the keys to her apartment. Unfortunately, he was not contactable; he'd be sleeping after last night's party, riding his bike in search of girls to pick up, or already trying to seduce someone on a date. It was Saturday, after all – Karol's favourite day. Sasza feared that if he picked up a new girl now, he'd call no sooner than next week. She had nobody else. Maybe she should call Ghost? No, she was too embarrassed for that. He'd only have a laugh at her expense and keep busting her balls for the next year or so. She left that option as a last resort. She wasn't worried, but tired. This wasn't the worst state she had been in, not by a long shot. She hoped they wouldn't want to search her. They'd find Ghost's Beretta and she didn't have a permit yet. That would do nothing to improve her situation.

Suddenly, a muscular, tattooed man entered the room and bellowed at the officer: 'Where's the shovel, Błażej?'

'Secured,' the policeman replied immediately. 'Behemoth is working on the prints. I'll let you know when we find something. The middle Bison supposedly bought the shovel to dig through his yard. I checked. The tomato saplings seem fresh. But then he kicked up a big fuss, because I had to check there weren't any skulls under those bushes. But no, everything was clear. Their mum nearly blew a gasket when we were leaving. I had to fine her just to shut her up.'

'What about the paint?'

'Nothing.' The officer shrugged. 'No paint, no tar and no graffiti equipment anywhere. They must have got rid of it.'

'So how did you take the shovel without a warrant? Did they guys from Bielsk issue one?'

'The boss told me to, no? I didn't screw up, did I?'

'You fucked the procedure up,' the tattooed man said and drank the younger man's coffee in two great gulps. Then he took a seat next to Sasza. 'You work for the police. Gdańsk, right?'

'I can work for you too, if you'd like,' Sasza replied. She had realised that the muscular man was in charge here. 'But I live in Tricity. That's where I get most of my commissions.'

The tattooed man introduced himself as Jah-Jah Frankowski and they shook hands. This was clearly enough for Frankowski; he lost all interest in Sasza, snatched a newspaper and began reading. Neither Sasza nor, apparently, the young officer really knew how to behave now.

'Please, continue.' Jah-Jah looked over his paper and nodded to the young policeman. 'I'm not here. There are plumbers in my office, fixing the heater. Julian accidentally broke through a wall. The whole floor is covered with pieces of brick. Let me tell you, I've never heard swearing like that. Forgive me for not repeating it word for word, but I wouldn't dare do it in the presence of a woman,' he finished.

The paper was still up in front of his face, but now he stopped pretending his arrival had been a coincidence. He froze in anticipation, listening.

Błażej, probably wanting to impress his older colleague, quickly released the CBŚ contractor card and started to ask Sasza the same questions all over again. Trying her best not to let her annoyance show, she repeated the same answers she had given earlier, glossing over some facts from her personal life. She had already given her statement on the suspected theft of her documents by one of the patients at the mental hospital. She had also said three times already that she didn't know the identity of the girl beyond her name, Danka, and that she had met her for the first time in her life today. For the time being, except filling a form, the young officer didn't seem too keen on doing his job.

'I came to meet the director of the private mental institution, a Mr Saczko. Sadly, I didn't get to speak with him. I only met with the vice-director. That's easy to confirm. The hospital treated a patient I'm interested in, for investigative purposes. An ex-criminal. He managed .to avoid trial when experts said he was mentally ill. His name is Łukasz Polak. I was hoping to question him. But he had left the hospital. The director had gone to a wedding party, so I talked to Ms Prus. My name was recorded in the reception ledger and the receptionist should remember me. I arranged the appointment officially. I've also sent a letter that should have been filed. Can you possibly send someone to Ciszynia to find this Danka and get my documents and money back? Also, I'd hurry if I were you.'

The officers exchanged glances. Jah-Jah raised his chin a bit, but changed his mind and returned to his newspaper. Błażej tensed, as if he'd farted, and took the half-finished report and picked it up, trying to look professional. Sasza noticed Jah-Jah was struggling to stifle a burst of laughter. Unexpectedly, she felt like laughing too. The whole situation was absurd. The older officer was clearly testing the youngster. She had to play their game.

'You're a policewoman,' said Błażej.

'A profiler,' Sasza cut in quickly, but the officer just took a deep breath, puffed out his chest and continued, as if pronouncing a judgement: 'In that case, the procedure is different. We need to notify your unit.'

Jah-Jah crumpled his paper and threw it on the tabletop.

'She's not in the force, son.'

'I'm an independent contractor. An expert,' Sasza said. 'I help the police in interrogations and analyse behavioural patterns. I prepare reports, draw up interrogation strategies, confront suspects and make geographical profiles.'

She paused, afraid they would be sceptical about what a profiling expert was. She had met with that attitude multiple times. Not this time, though. She suspected that Frankowski hadn't spoken to a profiler before, and that his entire knowledge came from Hollywood movies. Nevertheless, Jah-Jah clearly knew what a forensic psychologist was and simply couldn't hide his interest.

'Call Saczko, Błażej,' he ordered. 'And send someone to bring this Danka in. How long are you going to beat around the bush?'

'But the report's not ready.'

'Give her a break, man. If we catch bad guys that slow, they'll steal the stools from beneath our arses. You'll have time to fill this out later. The lady's not going to run away. Or are you?'

'I'll wait.' Sasza thanked him with a smile. 'There was eight hundred złoty in the wallet. In hundred-złoty bills. I've already blocked the cards, but I'd really like the car documents back. I need to be able to get home.'

'Do your job, son,' the inspector said. 'I'll keep the lady occupied with conversation in the meantime.'

The younger officer grabbed a large, archaic Nokia from the table and left. As soon as they were alone, Frankowski turned to Sasza. He seemed intrigued. She knew the type. At first a bit of disbelief, then a credibility test, and then questions about her professional achievements. Then, they'd start talking business. In the end, he'd make her an offer and would try to find an opportunity to barter down her rates.

'So, you work all over the country? Not region-bound?'

'There aren't that many of us,' she explained. 'And I'm not in any union. It's been more convenient thus far. Nearly every province-level HQ needs an expert like me sometimes. Each homicide or organised crime division should have someone like me on payroll. If the conditions are good, I can work for you too.' She smiled shyly.

'Any professional achievements?'

'Some.' She shrugged and pointed to her laptop case. 'May I?'

She removed from her pocket a bilingual University of Huddersfield booklet that she normally offered to her business clients. It was an abstract of one of her theses from her first year at the university, but it usually sufficed for potential clients as a brief summary of forensic psychology and her work methods. It outlined the options and told readers what to expect. On the back, there was a price list for specific services. Most were four-digit numbers. That caught Jah-Jah's eye for a long while. He let out a long whistle.

'This ain't cheap.'

'It's money well spent when you have several crimes on your hands,' she said. 'Better than a medium or cobbling up a search party of local patrolmen, believe me. Unless, of course, you want all the traces wiped out and the perp spooked.'

He laughed. 'You're very confident.'

Błażej returned. He put his immense mobile phone down and sent Sasza a strange look. Jah-Jah sat back in his chair.

'Director Saczko didn't confirm knowing you,' the officer said, turned to his superior and asked: 'What do we do now? She has no ID. The car isn't hers. Detention or fine?'

'It's my mother's,' Sasza cut in, exhaling irritably. 'I still have my English address in my documents. Can't change the owner-ship of the car yet. This is ridiculous. You should send someone to the hospital. The girl has my stuff!'

'We seem to be in a pickle,' said Jah-Jah. He slapped his thighs and pushed himself to his feet.

Sasza shrugged. She didn't care any more.

'You stay here, Błażej,' said Frankowski and threw on a jacket. 'I'll be back in an hour and a half. Call me on the walkie-talkie – there's no mobile signal in the forest.'

'What about her?' asked the young officer.

'Write a report. Do your job. We have to confirm her identity.'

Jah-Jah returned the booklet to Sasza.

'Keep it,' she offered. She wasn't sure what was happening.

Frankowski rolled the booklet up and slipped it into his back pocket. Then, without another word, her left the room.

Błażej took a seat and sat back comfortably, mimicking Frankow-ski's mannerisms. He looked like a smaller Jah-Jah, albeit less muscly, thinner, and without glasses. The shape of his lips was different too. Prettier. But that might have only been an effect of his clean shave. Sasza could bet he was related to the inspector. Similar facial expres-sions, gestures, and that macho posture to boot. The young and old officers also differed in that Błażej, as opposed to his father, had been annoying her from the moment he had opened his mouth.

'Okay, let's start over,' Błażej began officiously. 'Can anyone con-firm your identity?'

He took a new sheet of paper from the printer and wrote down the date. Sasza hesitated for a while, but finally shrugged and replied, 'Apparently not at the moment. Did you find Danka?'

'It's an ongoing investigation. We have nothing but your accusation.'

'I spoke to Ms Magdalena Prus. I told you already the director was away.' She sent a hopeful glance at the door. It remained closed. 'I believe I have made myself clear. As soon as you find the girl, you'll get my ID.'

The officer didn't seem to hear her.

'We can apply for copies of the documents on Monday at the earliest. You'll stay here until then. You'll save cash on booking a hotel.'

Sasza couldn't believe what she was hearing. 'No way,' she retorted curtly. 'The car isn't stolen or anything, so you don't have any grounds to detain me. I know my rights. You can fine me at most.'

'You're impersonating an employee of the ministry of internal affairs,' said Błażej. 'I checked the records. You're not a court-certified expert or a member of the Polish Criminology Association, or even a scientist at any Polish university.'

'That is because I'm writing my doctoral thesis in Huddersfield. My name isn't supposed to come up anywhere. And profiling is a strictly investigative operation. I don't have to have my photo posted on the police website to work there.'

'Your loss,' he said. 'Especially seeing as Ms Prus doesn't know you either.'

'What?'

'I spoke to her a minute ago. She told me she didn't have any visitors from the police today.'

Sasza wanted to tell the young officer he was a stupid prick who just liked to pick on others because he was so insecure about himself, but somehow suppressed the urge. Instead, she said: 'You've been testing me this whole time. You haven't even asked if the girl was at the clinic, have you?'

'She's not,' he replied. 'She went out today on special leave. You couldn't have met her in the park. Nothing of what you've said adds up. You've been lying from the get-go. We can't be sure you're not a grifter. You might have deceived my father, but I'm not that stupid. I won't fall for some stupid English printout.'

He opened the door and shouted:

'Oi, Supryczyński! Find me a cleanish blanket and prep the cell for our guest.'

Sasza sighed heavily.

'There's an officer in Tricity. The head of the criminal division will vouch for me. You'd have to let me call him, though.'

A slim, brown-haired man wearing a police uniform appeared in the door. Judging by his epaulettes, he was a regular constable. Błażej immediately assumed the role of the ranking officer and repeated, sporting a wily grin: 'We need a blanket. Find me something not too soiled. We don't want the lady to get lice or anything, do we?'

'The head of the Criminal Investigations Division, Chief Inspector Robert Duchnowski, can send you the official papers confirming that I'm an expert working for the Gdańsk HQ.' Sasza echoed her earlier statement with emphasis, repressing her desire to curse the arrogant youngster. The boy had a lot to learn. 'Will that be enough?'

Błażej didn't react, apart from tapping his pen on the table. 'We get the papers, you go free.'

What an idiot, thought Sasza, but kept the comment to herself. She reached into her pocket to find her phone. Pulling it out, she noticed that her ID was stuck to its back plate. She must have forgotten to put it back into her wallet earlier and it had been here in her pocket all the time. Sasza placed the plastic card on the table and smiled smugly, seeing the man stiffen.

'Is that some kind of a joke?'

'I noticed you had a rather peculiar sense of humour. I'd recommend you send someone to the hospital right away. The girl took my things and my money, as I have told you. If you do nothing I'll be sure to report this to your superiors. And I'm not talking local.'

Błażej stared at the ID, reading Sasza's name and address several times. Finally, he copied the information down on the report and slid it over to her. Hearing Frankowski's voice from the corridor, he sprang to his feet and stormed out of the interrogation room.

The door remained open. Sasza could hear them conferring. Frankowski gave the young officer a dressing-down, calling him a dumb twat and few other, even less savoury names. Sasza took out her cigarettes and lit one, not caring about asking for permission. She was tired of playing games.

Jah-Jah returned. He had her booklet tucked under his arm and unfolded it as he walked.

'Beat it, son,' he called to Błażej, dismissing him with a gesture. 'You can make us some coffee. Sugar's in the can on the lockbox. The one saying cocoa. Kick Julian in the bollocks for me while you're at it, will you? For ruining my office. And call Mum to say that I won't be coming for her. And you're on mail duty for the next month. Maybe I won't tell your mum what an arse you've made of yourself in front of the profiler.'

He sat down, putting a crystal ashtray on the table.

'If the psycho girl took your stuff, we'll find it,' he said, winking at Sasza. Finally, she was talking to the right man.

'I'm counting on it. Otherwise, I'm broke.'

'Do you have a gun?'

Sasza paled. She hesitated for an instant.

'I don't,' she lied. 'In my line of work I only need my intellect. I hypothesise and deduce, acting as support for the investigators. They catch the bad guys.'

Jah-Jah leaned back in the chair. He looked smug.

'Can you find a body?'

'First or one of many?'

'Does it matter?' he asked.

'Everything matters,' she replied. 'How much time has passed since the disappearance, victimological data, location. Also, the strategy used to interrogate the victim's friends and relatives. It all depends on the data you give me and the information I collect myself. Are you looking for someone?'

The can of blue paint ran out before Asia Pietruczuk finished the graffiti. She shook it in case she could squeeze out even a few drops more, but all she got were two small splodges. She rummaged through a satchel she had affixed to her belt. Her mobile slipped from her pocket, bounced off the thin scaffolding board and plummeted down quicker than Asia could follow. The girl imagined it crashing to the ground with a dull thwack.

Sourly, she accepted the loss, comforting herself that at least it hadn't been *her* falling to her demise. Twenty-eight metres of free fall with an abrupt end on the pavement would mean certain death. She would have to be more careful. She bit on her glove and freed one hand, zipping the satchel shut so nothing else could slip out and once again checking on her most important equipment. Just as she'd suspected, there was no paint left. Bad luck, or rather bad judgement. Climbing the water tower here on Skarpowa Street and sliding down a line, all the while risking her life (as the two old snap hooks probably wouldn't have supported her fifty kilos of weight) had taken the best part of an hour. The painting at least as long. Everything had gone according to plan, but she couldn't finish the main tag, because she had one spray can too few. She would have to return later, but wasn't sure she'd be able to in this darkness. Leaning back over the top railing and making that first step down was the scariest part. And the keys would have to be back in their place by morning. On Monday, Dad would be back from his business trip and he was in charge of the tower renovations.

Asia knew the workers would take down the scaffolding before Monday, revealing her work for all to see. The club with the scenic overlook was supposed to open on Tuesday. Nobody had seen the effects of the renovation yet. It was supposed to be a surprise for the townsfolk. The mayor would cut the ribbon and hundreds of people would be there. Polish Belarusians would gain another landmark for their cause, but Asia had had her fill of the authorities' policy. Poles were being discriminated against in Hajnówka. Anyone daring to speak out on that matter, to say that all the money went to Belarusian folk events, was immediately blacklisted as a Polish fascist. A couple of Asia's friends had been labelled as such already, and were now on trial for offences against public decency or hate speech. And they hadn't done anything bad! Can displaying a banner during Independence Day be considered indecent? Or vocally criticising the actions of town authorities during public ceremonies? The police would penalise people for as little as shouting 'Down with the commies' or 'Hail to the heroes'.

Asia hadn't been branded a fascist herself. Nobody would dare classify her as a skinhead, though she wore black cargo pants and had her head shaved like most of them. She was the daughter of an ex lumber mill worker who had become the main building contractor in town, and an exemplary student in the third grade of the local high school. The Polish one, of course. Each year, she passed her exams with honours, but it meant next to nothing; she didn't want to transfer to the second, more prestigious school, where classes were held in Belarusian, and which enjoyed all the comforts of being the town hall's favourite educational facility – scholarships, grants, extracurricular classes, a student movie club and even its own newspaper. Not to mention a volleyball team playing in the major league and funded with public money. The Belarusian high school, as the one promoting the culture of an ethnic minority, could count on grants from the EU and all kinds of ministries too. The school authorities had the full support of all the right people, including those from across the eastern border. Graduates would get scholarships to Moscow, Minsk or other universities in the erstwhile communist bloc. Students at the Polish school were given no opportunities at all compared to the Belarusians.

Asia had to listen to her dad's constant bitching and grumbling about all this. 'The Soviets have the power here,' he would tell her over and over again. 'Hajnówka has always been red. Nothing has changed since the thirties. It's a worker town, an enclave of the descendants of the proletariat! We might have democracy in Poland but here – time has stopped! And nothing will change as long as the ex-*ubeks* and commies have the power, whatever banner they fly now.'

He would give her various publications, articles from the right-wing press, and send her links via email. He never had the balls to voice his concerns in public, though. Asia agreed with her father, but had him pinned as a coward. They would argue viciously any time she accused him of conformism. Her father had never explained himself to her, sometimes only spreading his arms helplessly, saying that, as opposed to her, he had no choice any more. He had lived in Hajnówka since he was a child. The system allowed him to leave his village and graduate from university. He hadn't left town when he got the chance though, and now he had to care for his family, give them the life they deserved. He wanted his daughter to escape town as soon as possible so she didn't have to live a lie like he and his mother had.

'You'll understand when you grow up,' he would say to her.

'I'm nearly an adult already!' she would snap.

He only laughed at that. 'When in Rome, do as the Romans do.'

And her mother would add that the meek shall inherit the earth.

'Or die of starvation,' Asia would grumble in response and hide in her room to read about her heroes. They were people who didn't want to pretend, even during the war, and they had had a lot more to lose than her parents. They hadn't risked losing their jobs, their friends, or their social standing, but their very lives.

Asia was under their spell. She admired their bravery. She wanted to live like they had. Without compromise. To boldly say what she thought and to fight for her values. Bury, Inka, Łupaszka, Żelazny and Rekin – those were the people close to her heart. Her adoptive family. It was their images that she had decided to paint on the wall of the water tower. After the colossal sheets obscuring the building were removed, her graffiti depicting the 'Cursed Soldiers' would be visible from as far as the roundabout next to the church.

It was a tribute to her heroes, as well as her own coming out. Asia had enough of being the dutiful daughter, the nice girl. She agreed with her father, but that was the entire reason why she had decided to join the underground and destroy the system from the inside. She had come up with the provocation a few days before, when the Brotherhood of Orthodox Youth had invited students from local schools to a screening of documentary films. A discussion titled 'Bury – not our hero' was to take place during the event. To the local Belarusians Romuald 'Bury' Rajs was just a cruel murderer. A war criminal, a psychopath, who revelled in torturing people of any nation save the Poles. The fact that he had been posthumously rehabilitated and awarded medals, and that children had to learn about him in schools, was an issue of contention in Hajnówka.

Asia was sure that if it came to it, the Polish nationalists would support her. She was scared. Of course she was. On the one hand, she hoped that her being the author of the graffiti would remain a secret for as long as possible, or that maybe the police would never figure it out, but secretly she couldn't wait until her friends from the Danuta Siedzikówna Historical Association learned the truth. She believed she was doing something good, even if it would result in her being expelled from school. If it came to light that she had done it, she'd take the blame, just like her greatest idol, Inka, would do.

Suddenly, her foot slipped and she wobbled on the scaffolding. At the last moment she grabbed the line and the snap hook creaked, the fastening grated ominously, but held. Asia managed to keep her balance. For an instant, she looked down. She used to suffer from a fear of heights. Her mother had never let her even hang the curtains at home, after she nearly fell from the ladder once. The entire family was incredulous when Asia won a place on a language course on the training sailing ship *Pogoria* and, despite her acrophobia, announced that she was going to go.

On the trip, during which Asia had to climb the masts and hoist the sails unless she wanted to lose face and be shunned by the group, she discovered that she could overcome her fear of heights. She just had to confront it face to face. And what better place to do that than a dozen metres above the ground?

She never told her parents that she had bested her weakness. Leaving for the trip, she had promised her mother that she would never climb the mast. She was an only child and her parents had her later than they had intended to. She was their miracle, and after all the miscarriages her mother had suffered and being born as a frail preemie, she had to bear their overprotectiveness. So Asia lied for their own good. She still pretended to this day that she feared heights.

She leaned over the scaffolding, straddled the railing and detached one of the snap hooks. She cut her hand on the sill as she lifted her leg over the ledge to move inside. When she landed safely on stable ground, the second snap hook cracked and broke in two, falling and disappearing into the darkness just like her mobile had. Asia exhaled with relief.

Quickly, she ran down the stairs and turned the key in the lock. Downstairs, she craned her neck to look up at the building, and smiled with satisfaction. The scaffolding concealed most of her work, including the inscription saying WE ARE THE MIGHT OF GREAT POLAND!, which meant that nobody would discover it too early. The faces of the soldiers didn't really resemble the originals, as Asia wasn't much of an artist, but what counted was the intention. She was sure that, as soon as they uncovered it, the town would erupt in chaos.

Asia unclipped the satchel from her belt, tossed it into her military backpack, and went round the tower in search of her phone. She had just found the broken snap hook and a piece of the mobile's case when she heard hurried steps. The hairs on the back of her neck stood on end. She jumped to her feet and sprinted to hide behind the scaffolding. That white sheet wrapped around the tower was a blessing now. Nobody would be able to see her behind it.

'Asia?'

She froze, clenching her jaw, trying to make as little noise as possible.

'I know you're in there. I saw you leaving the tower.'

Asia closed her eyes. She had to think quickly. She stuffed the gloves into her pocket, unzipped her hoodie and hid the snap hooks and lines under it. She thought about Inka. What would she do?

She didn't have time to decide; someone walked rapidly up to her and pulled the white sheet away. It was the catechist.* The most handsome teacher at school.

'What are you doing here?' she whispered, then immediately regretted it. Idiot.

Asia knew through gossip that Leszek Krajnów's personal situation had changed not long ago; he was divorced now, and not really coping with living alone. He had also given his child over to its mother, his ex-wife. Everyone in town knew that under the cover of his work, he tried to be a father to all the kids from troubled local families. He helped them financially, organised 'secret complines', as he used to call his private history lessons, and led pilgrimages to the Jasna Góra Monastery. Krajnów's house was always open to the lost and the needy among the local youth. Especially those honouring the traditional values of God, Honour and the Fatherland. People said that he was secretly the leader of an armed unit of guerrillas that he taught how to shoot, hide in the forest and perform acts of sabotage, so if it came to another war, a new generation of heroes could save the region from the *russkies*.

* A religious studies teacher in the Catholic context.

Asia didn't believe that. Krajnów was deeply religious, highly intelligent, and gentle, like the Apostles. He was the only man in town who had been granted an audience by Pope John Paul II himself. But the *katsaps* would say anything to depreciate the Poles. In their devious way, they would massage even modern history to prove that they were the oppressed minority. And just look at them! They had never even organised an uprising. They just bowed their backs to Moscow and licked Putin's arse.

Asia couldn't know that Krajnów hated the *russkies* with a passion. So much, in fact, that he had changed his name by adding the Polish dash over the 'o' in his last name so nobody would know that he had Belarusian roots.

'I'm talking a stroll,' he said with a charming smile.

He reached out to her, holding an army haversack, and showed her its contents. Asia took a look inside. It was filled with miniature posters depicting Romuald 'Bury' Rajs, and cans of blue and black paint.

She produced the key to the tower and they climbed the stairs to the main hall where the grand opening was to take place. Once there, she grabbed one of his brushes and dipped it in the black paint. Together, they painted the symbol of the Jagged Sword over the Belarusian emblem. Below that, Asia wrote three letters: ŚWO. She used exactly the font that the anti-communist freedom fighters after World War Two had adorned their uniforms with. She felt like one of them.

'Death to the enemies of the Fatherland,' she said solemnly, as they walked upstairs to throw their leaflets from the top of the tower.

'Our very own Inka,' said Krajnów affectionately, patting her on the back.

Even on the sailing ship *Pogoria*, in the middle of the Atlantic Ocean, Asia hadn't felt happier.

Mariusz Korcz killed the engine of his parents' van. He glanced at Jauhien Paszka, sitting shotgun, and then turned around to the back and grabbed a film camera from the rear seat. He switched it on and centred the lens on a group of skinheads occupying the entrance to Hajnówka's Górnik cultural centre. They were standing

underneath a black-and-white poster depicting a child staring horrified at a soldier bearing a machine gun. A red inscription read:
'Bury – not our hero'.

'Should I call Błażej?' Korcz asked in Belarusian.

'Yeah, buzz him,' Jauhien replied. 'Actually, text him. If things
get rough you won't have time to talk on the phone. Leave it to him
to decide if we need backup.'

He looked through the window. 'They must have brought in all
the Jagiellonia fans from Białystok.'

'More like Wisła, man,' muttered Mariusz. He took a look around.
'They must have come in rented buses. These are not local plates.'

He quickly texted his superior and then snapped a discreet
photo of the crowd of right-wingers and sent it as confirmation of
his report. The answer came practically at once.

'He's sending a patrol car.' Mariusz smiled broadly and popped
a strawberry bubble gum into his mouth.

'Just one?'

'He's asking if they're armed and telling you to leave the camera
in the car. They'll keep an eye on it.'

'No way,' replied Jauhien, shaking his head, and left the vehicle.

They set off, like sheriffs out to get Billy the Kid himself. Only
they looked more like Laurel and Hardy. Mariusz Korcz, thin and
extremely tall, was too handsome for Laurel though. Even when
furious, he had that benign puppy-eyed look that made people
want to hug him. He wore his long hair braided, which enhanced
his effeminate air and peculiar charm and riled up the right-wing
activists like a red rag pisses off a bull. A *fag*, they would call him.
Jauhien, on the other hand, was a bald, beefy tank of a man who
could have swapped places with one of the protesting muscle-
heads and nobody would have noticed. Today – as opposed to
Korcz – he wasn't wearing a suit. He didn't have one, apart from
the old prom suit that he had grown out of years ago. He also
wasn't wearing the black T-shirt that usually served as formal
attire. Instead, he had on a Fred Perry polo shirt and a hat with
the Piła Police School logo. The right-wingers grew visibly agitated at the sight of the pair, but then, spotting their cult laurel
wreath on Jauhien's breast, they piped down and stepped aside,
obviously confused.

Inside, in front of the door to the cinema, Korcz and Jauhien met Marysia Sofińska from the Orthodox Brotherhood, who was in charge of the event. The cinema screen displayed the same poster that adorned the main entrance. Its message was clear. A psychopath with a machine gun, wearing a Polish army uniform, intending to kill an innocent child.

The auditorium was full, though none of the football hooligans were present. Jauhien carefully filmed the scene and then sat down, lighting up an e-cigarette. Korcz took his place next to him, straightening his scarf. Marysia walked over, handing microphones out.

'Thank you so much for attending,' she began, and introduced them to the audience as respectively a documentary film director and an esteemed sociologist. Jauhien and Mariusz rose and bowed. 'But before we begin this controversial discussion, I would like you to watch a short film about the crimes perpetrated in our region by a unit of resistance fighters under the command of Romuald "Bury" Rajs.'

Suddenly, the door swung open and Leszek Krajnów marched in, accompanied by a group of shaven-headed youngsters. There were a few women and girls among the mostly male protesters. They must have raided the same stall at the Ruble Mart, as they were all wearing matching red-and-white tracksuits, along with red-and-white-laced army boots and black flying jackets. They headed down the aisle towards the stage.

'I'm just a simple camera operator. I didn't think we'd have such a turnout,' Jauhien joked, but nobody laughed, so he added: 'The movie's director, Jerzy Kalina, apologises for not showing up but he's sick. We hope we can serve as his representatives here.'

A round of applause followed. Jauhien went to grab his camera, but Korcz stopped him with a gesture.

'Błażej can only get us a single patrol car, remember,' he muttered. 'Don't provoke them.'

An Orthodox priest sprang to his feet, bounded down the aisle and stood in front of the stage, guarding it like Cerberus. Krajnów and his hooligans halted, held back by the aura of authority exuding from the church official. There was a short exchange, culminating with the preacher taking the last resort.

'That man is drunk!' he declared and began to argue with one of the protesters standing near him, a stocky, bearded, troll-like man.

Krajnów signalled to his charges like a military commander and they all froze. Then he walked over to the troll, looming over him and sniffing like a dog. Without warning, his hand shot out and hit the hooligan across the ear.

'Wait outside, Konrad,' he ordered. 'We'll have a word after the screening.'

As the scolded man left, several audience members jeered him along from the back rows.

'Chop-chop, you sot!'

'They're taking collections to build a statue for Bury!'

'Go back to church, Polish pigs!'

'Tell him there's vodka shots waiting outside – he'll pick up the pace!'

Krajnów swept the room with a steely gaze, then spoke. 'We are Poles and we have every right to be here. This is a free country.'

He turned to the Orthodox priest. 'This is an open meeting. You can't throw us out, Father.' He used an ironic tone on the word 'Father'.

The priest flushed. 'Just stay civil, please.' He stepped aside.

'We're all very civil, aren't we?' Krajnów smirked and added: 'Except for the audience, it seems.'

A murmur spread among the hooligans.

'You're responsible for them,' the Orthodox priest replied, smiling. 'Do we understand each other, Lech?'

'Just who do you think I am?' Krajnów marched to the front row and took a central seat, right in front of the two main guests. Satisfied, he signalled to the back of the auditorium and Mariusz and Jauhien observed as more nationalists streamed into the room, lining up along the walls, standing to attention like riot squads at a football match. None of them sat down, but at least they had no visible weapons with them. Only their grim expressions reminded everyone that they were ready and willing to start a fight at any moment. The room grew deathly quiet. Silent, the nationalists seemed even more menacing. No one in the audience dared say anything. The lights went out, the opening credits rolled, and the first chords of a wartime song issued from the speakers. Suddenly, the film tape snapped and the silence returned. The lights went on again.

Mariusz logged in to Facebook and posted a photo of the line of skinheads on his wall. He watched, satisfied, as the likes started popping up. Jauhien put his camera down on his knees, but not before discreetly pushing the recording button. He wasn't sure what to think of this whole situation. He was worried about the number of right-wingers and the fact that the true patriots from Hajnówka numbered only a couple of teenagers and a few boys from vocational school who mainly wanted to blow off some steam and didn't really care about the motherland. Jauhien knew them all and could see their faces among the audience.

He was concerned about something else, too. Among the skinheads Krajnów had brought with him, he recognised hooligans from Białystok, Bielsk Podlaski, and even Kraków. Some real record-breakers among neo-Nazis, who just liked to fight. Jauhien knew this better than anyone – a year ago he had worked as an undercover cameraman, filming a documentary about radical nationalism. He had spent six months among those people and he knew their methods. Looking at the tight line of bald-headed goons surrounding the audience, he knew there was going to be trouble. Even if the day didn't end in bloodshed, a storm was definitely brewing in town. A big one. It was only a matter of time. He promised himself to talk to Mariusz about it when they returned to Bielsk. All of Poland would hear about the small town of Hajnówka very soon. And it wouldn't be because of the Orthodox choral music festival broadcast on Polonia TV. It would be primetime news. Each and every one of the shows would talk about it and the tickers would read 'Polish–Belarusian War' or some such. That was a given.

Korcz waved his phone in Jauhien's eyes, his face white as a sheet.

'What's up?' Jauhien whispered.

'The patrol car was here but it's left. They're looking for some girl,' the sociologist explained. 'I hope nobody scratches the van now. I took it without asking.'

'I'll have it on tape if push comes to shove,' Jauhien replied and sat back in his seat, pretending to want to pick up his camera.

Immediately, several of the skinheads protested loudly. Marysia gestured to him to set the camera down, clasping her hands as if in prayer and making a pleading face.

'Just kidding,' Jauhien called out, shrugging, and leaned over to Korcz. 'I don't think they're going to do anything today. This is a show of force. The pogrom's coming next Tuesday. Unless they get a better opportunity. But they're itching for a fight, don't you think? So watch what you say.'

'There's a back exit behind the scene. Just so you know,' Korcz whispered back. 'I don't need my teeth kicked in before the elections. I'll park the car next to the church. Wait for me there.'

Jauhien waved a hand at his friend. 'I'll manage. Just don't leave me here, you spineless coward,' he muttered. Then he pointed at something.

Korcz turned in the direction Jauhien's finger was pointing, and saw Asia Pietruczuk. That was unexpected. She was his friend's daughter. In return for getting him a construction deal in the Bielsk city hall, the man was supporting his campaign. Now, one of the bald guys, attempting courtesy, moved over so the girl had a better view. It looked like Asia felt at ease among those men. They patted her on the back, treating her as one of their own. The girl blushed when 'Snowy' – a right-winger with multiple convictions for public disturbance during the starost's* speeches – handed her his houndstooth Fred Perry shirt. She took him up on his offer and assumed her position in his place, gaining an unobstructed view of the stage. Jauhien read Korcz's thoughts, leaning close to his ear and whispering: 'She's young. Everyone's a fighter at her age.'

'I'd prefer if she fought in the ranks of the Podlasie Autonomy Movement. We need activists like her. Andriej promised me she'd join, so that comes as a total surprise. We won't be getting Little Belarus if things go to shit like that.'

Jauhien laughed.

'That not even a thing, is it? You denied wanting to move the border in that last interview, remember?'

---

* The head of the district administration (*starostwo*). Equivalent to the leader of a town or rural council.

'Little Belarus is not a thing *yet*. But give me five years and it will become a thing. And *I* am the Podlasie Autonomy Movement. But for now, I feel like we have a better chance if we go with Korwin. We agree on many issues.'

'You Belarusian fascist.'

Korcz's beautiful face lit up with a grin. 'An effective one at that.'

The lights dimmed and the screening finally started. The opening credits rolled, then the title of the film flashed up brightly: *As we forgive*.

The car park next to the Carska restaurant was full, and Acting Commissioner Krystyna Romanowska had to park on the verge and walk the remaining hundred metres. The restaurant had been converted from the town's old train station, and its tower, where the newlyweds were to spend their wedding night, was adorned with red-and-white flowers arranged in the shapes of traditional Belarusian embroidery. Romanowska passed them by without stopping. The tower didn't fascinate and delight her like it did the tourists, who stopped and gaped at the decorations. Some of them stepped out of their cars and snapped selfies on the red-and-white background. For her, the gaudy building only brought to mind a dark and foreboding Bluebeard's Castle.

There were newly renovated locomotives on the tracks, fully adapted to fulfil all the needs of the guests of the restaurant, hotel and banquet hall filling the surrounding buildings. Romanowska didn't have her invitation with her; she didn't think anyone would have the balls to even ask her for it. By the kinds of cars parked outside, she guessed that the entire elite of Hajnówka was present. A twenty-person choir and an accordion player stood at the entrance to the old waiting hall, clearly waiting for the word to start their performance. Krystyna could already feel her head pounding in anticipation.

A waitress with hair in a Russian-style bun, looking like a descendant of one of Chekhov's three sisters, curtsied to the commissioner as she crossed the threshold. She asked to take her coat, but Romanowska only stared her down. She hadn't been able to bring herself to wear an evening dress like those the wives of the local bigwigs would undoubtedly be sporting; although she wasn't in uniform, she was still an employee of the uniformed services, and in her black cigarette trousers, snow-white shirt with the top three buttons undone and a dinner jacket, she looked the part. She still had her sports watch on. The only truly feminine elements of her attire were high heels and the nail polish she had put on just for the occasion.

The interior of the restaurant was tastefully designed – you could feel the atmosphere of old Russia and each element of the décor could very well serve as a museum exhibit. There were crocheted napkins and old, rattling samovars on the tables. Walls were bedecked with icons, pictures of Russian families and genuine antique paintings. No kitsch to be seen. Romanowska had been here only once before, for work. She could remember having tea with raspberry preserve, porcini soup, blini with caviar and a piece of cheesecake. It had cost her more than a week's worth of groceries at the local market. She had to admit that the cake, while not quite worth the money, had been one of the best she ever had. Nevertheless, she had wanted to leave as soon as possible, afraid she'd stain the starched tablecloth and be made to pay for it. The room she had sat in then was empty now, the chairs arranged along the walls, revealing the old wooden-block flooring. Romanowska guessed it would serve as the dance floor tomorrow. Sounds of feasting could be heard from one of the adjoining rooms, which was adapted to more low-key parties.

'*Budte zdorovi*, Genek!' Krystyna heard the toast as soon as the waitress opened the door for her.

She nodded her head at the guests sitting at what was clearly the main table and a couple of men instantly jumped to their feet to greet her. She stuck her official smile on her lips and shook hands with everyone. It was this informal council of elders, not the figureheads from town hall or even the mayor himself, who held the real power in the town. This was no secret. Even the schoolkids knew.

Krystyna recognised Adam Gaweł, chief community elder or starost, at once; then, Tomasz Terlikowski, the previous police commissioner, referred to as the Old Man, whose office she currently occupied; Mundek Sulima, the owner of the local cable TV company, called Uncle Shortie, no taller than five foot two, barely visible over the tabletop; Krzysztof Saczko, director of the Ciszynia psychiatric hospital; and Anatol Pires, founder and ex-headteacher of the Belarusian high school, with his sphinx-still dog at his feet (being fed various morsels from the table by the rest of this 'council of the righteous'). The sixth man, looking like a tramp, wearing an old, hole-ridden suit and a spotty bow tie, she knew all too well. They hadn't talked for at least a dozen years. His head was overgrown with bristly white hair, but he was the only man at the table not sporting any kind of facial hair. None of the men were younger than in their prime and some were definitely old, but this man looked eighty or even more. There was a seventh place at the table, but it was empty and the table setting looked untouched. Romanowska assumed it was being kept for the groom, Piotr Bondaruk. Apparently, the party had started without its host.

Those who were allowed the honour of dining here with the high-ups occupied the smaller tables, arranged around the main one like planets in the solar system. Romanowska observed first that most of the officials who had ever done anything good for the city had been invited, and then that they were largely already drunk or well on their way there. She had been given a place at a table right next to the main one. Her seat neighboured the seat of that man she knew, the vagabond lookalike, and their backs nearly touched when she sat.

She looked around to see who else was there. The mayor, for starters. He was laughing hysterically at the jokes of five Belarusian councilmen. Further back, Romanowska noticed Bondaruk's three sons. They were all sitting in silence, pouting. There was the chaplain; four Orthodox priests, the constantly grumpy manager of the Belarusian radio station Ratsiya Radio, his eyes shooting nervously about; the owner of the Ruble Mart – harmless as a Labrador retriever – whose wife rented half of the Belarusian museum from the city and managed the Forest Palace restaurant; and finally the ailing director of Ciszynia hospital. Sidelined at tables further away were five entrepreneurs, mostly Bondaruk's competitors, stealing glances at the empty host's seat and exchanging comments. Most of the guests had been here for a long time, it seemed; their faces were already flushed, suggesting they had consumed a lot of vodka.

Suddenly, one of the boot-licking councilmen wobbled on his chair and spilled a glass of red wine all over Romanowska. She managed to duck away, sparing her white shirt, but the contents of the glass soaked into her chair and her suit and poured into her handbag.

'Nice reflexes,' the mayor remarked. 'A dynamite of a woman.'

'I would have already been totally drenched,' another councilman said eagerly, and began to apologise to Krystyna on behalf of his colleague. 'He's always been like an elephant in a china shop. That's why he's responsible for the construction deals!'

'Keep your trap shut, boy,' the mayor called, with a laugh. He was having a great time. 'If you ruined the commissioner's blouse, I'll have you fired!'

Romanowska pretended to be amused. She got up and took her jacket off, hanging it on the chair's backrest. She wanted to go to the ladies' to get herself in order – and check up on the Glock in her handbag – but the guest sitting behind her must have had a similar idea; he pushed his chair back at the same moment, blocking her passage.

'Grandpa Mikołaj. I'm the butcher,' he introduced himself and bowed respectfully.

'Nesteruk and Company,' someone shouted from the back of the room. 'Best damn sausage in town! And the brawn, oh my! There's still some left, if you want. Garlicky!'

People laughed at that.

'We have been acquainted,' she replied and offered him a hand. 'Krystyna Romanowska. Police. I might have changed a bit.'

The butcher was old, and his generation never shook hands with women. Instead, he held her by the tips of the fingers and gave her palm a wet kiss, to everyone's merriment.

The waitress set up a new plate for Romanowska and poured her a shot of vodka. Still standing in the middle of the banquet room, she had the opportunity to take another look around. Apart from the staff she was the only woman present.

At this point, a waiter ran up to Tomik, the blond, youngest, shortest, and handsomest of Bondaruk's sons. The man proffered a sealed envelope on a silver platter, leaned close to his ear and whispered.

Tomik clinked his crystal glass three times with a fork. He was only twenty, but Romanowska knew that he was already party to all the secrets and plans of his father's company, and was widely regarded as the old businessman's right hand. That was also the main reason why his brothers – Wasyl and Fionik – hated him with a passion. The two would always join forces against their younger sibling, although when it came to fighting for their inheritance, their alliance would quickly dissolve and they would be at each other's throats in no time.

'Everybody's here now. We can begin,' Tomik said. His hands were shaking. Romanowska wondered if that was a result of having too much to drink, or of nervousness. 'Father has been detained by some business issues but he has asked me to read this out for you. The content of this message is as much a surprise to me as it is to you – I have never seen this letter before.'

He held the envelope out towards his audience, presenting the unbroken seal. The guests stopped eating and for a while nobody even reached for their glass. The groom's absence could only mean trouble. Suddenly, a mobile rang. It belonged to Seryozha Mikołajuk, the editor-in-chief of local newspaper the *Gościniec*, who left the room rapidly, holding the phone to his ear with one hand and covering its speaker with the other.

Tomik tore the envelope open so everyone could see, slid out a piece of paper and scanned it briefly. Then he lifted it above his head. Romanowska could see that the message was short, handwritten. Old Bondaruk never used electronic devices, preferring to cut his deals face to face or by telephone. Only a select few people in town had his mobile number. Even foreign partners had to contact his assistants first.

Tomik started to read. Somewhat to Romanowska's surprise, he did so in Belarusian. She knew the language, of course, out of necessity and living here for a long time. Nevertheless, she was a bit worried she wouldn't understand the nuances of the message. And nobody was offering to act as a Polish interpreter. All eyes were on Tomik Bondaruk – everyone was waiting for the bomb to go off.

'*I, Piotr Bondaruk, son of Stanisław and Aniela, born in Zaleszany in 1948, will tomorrow enter into matrimony with Iwona Bejnar, aged twenty-five. It will be the first and last marriage in my life. If God deigns to bless me with any more offspring, which I highly doubt, I will be much pleased and hereby endeavour to secure their future, as well as that of their mother and her family.*

I would like this letter to be read to the very end in the presence of all my invited guests. Irrespective of its content or any personal objections, I would like my will to become public, and that may only come to pass when it has been read before the elite of our city.

Keeping in mind that I may die in the near future, I hereby declare that tomorrow, as the legal husband of Iwona Bejnar, I will retire. I intend to spend my time fishing, drinking moonshine and eating all the rich dishes my cardiologist tells me to refrain from. I will also hand over my company to someone younger, so that its development is not held back, and its funds are not stolen or squandered.

Each of my three sons will receive a notarised document listing all the funds and goods that they are to inherit. The factory, being the property of not only myself, but of the entire local community, as it has been established and cared for by us all, with me being simply its steward, must be managed by a highly competent individual. None of my sons satisfies this requirement. Tomik may be well-educated, but he is a coward . . .'

Tomik paused for a moment, clearing his throat. The room fell completely silent.

'I' don't know what Father wanted to achieve by this,' he said in Polish.

'Father told you to read, so read, brother,' Wasyl called out with a chuckle.

'It's your funeral, mate,' Tomik replied and straightened out the letter again.

'*Fionik would only spend the money on hookers, and Wasyl has never taken an interest in the company, so I'll save him the trouble. Therefore, let it be known to all that I hereby pass my estate down to my fourth son. You may know him already. I'm of course referring to the* Gościniec's *editor-in-chief, Mikołajuk. Seryozha, forgive me. I wanted to tell you but this was your mother's will.'*

The room erupted into pandemonium. Romanowska observed the guests and simultaneously fought to keep herself from laughing. It was like being in a play. Bondaruk's sons were already balling their fists. They'd probably boycott the wedding, not to mention sue their father, before long. She liked Mikołajuk. He was a smallish, crafty, but ultimately harmless fellow. He often provided informal

intel to the police. Back in the day people would have called it nark-
ing. Times change, though, and now it was called 'doing favours'.
Romanowska pitied the man. After this mess he would be utterly
screwed. Nobody would have the guts to officially criticise Bondaruk's decision, but people would talk. And that meant trouble. For
the commissioner, it only meant that security at the wedding would
have to be doubled. She took out her mobile and texted Jah-Jah to
send a patrol car to the restaurant right away. Just in case. You can
never be too careful. Anything might happen when the guests got
really drunk. Her deputy responded after a few seconds that the
car was already there, but he wouldn't be able to come himself, as
something important had come up. Then he sent another message:
'Some troll looted the national emblem from the culture centre.
The director's nagging me.'

She didn't reply. He had enough to do; she would leave him
alone.

'Read the rest. There's booze to drink yet,' the mayor called
impatiently. He, along with everybody, wanted to know what else
the eccentric Bondaruk had written. Romanowska wondered if this
was just only a silly joke on Bondaruk's part – a father's way of testing his sons, his allies, and his various business partners. It wasn't
entirely improbable; Bondaruk was known as a man who did whatever and whenever he wanted. He had never cared for what people
might say. This detached attitude, and his ruthless drive to achieve
his own goals without looking back, had been the reasons he was
able to accumulate such an impressive fortune in such hard times.
But he had outdone himself now. This was his best prank ever.
The man had balls, it had to be said. 'Your father told you to read
on whatever happened. So read on – or give the letter to me,' the
mayor boomed at the young man.

Tomik glared at him for a while, but then lifted the letter and
continued:

'*If Seryozha wants to work with my other sons, I'll allow them to
retain their positions. If he refuses to take up my offer, I shall declare
a competition in which anyone can participate, irrespective of sex. The
only conditions are that participants be Belarusian, less than fifty years
old, and competent in the field of managing a timber industry company.
If any one of you, dear guests, feel themselves worthy, you may enter the*

competition, and good luck. In the event of my unexpected and violent death, or else my death from natural causes – or a demise having all the hallmarks of natural expiration – Grandpa Mikołaj Nesteruk shall appoint the manager of the company. Being of sound mind and memory, I hereby declare my will to be final and binding. Moreover, I have made my decision while sober, though I doubt I will still be so by the time you read this. Nor you, for that matter.

Piotr Bondaruk'

Tomik put the paper down. He poured himself a shot of vodka and gulped it down. Then he inhaled, as if to say something, but instead only slowly collapsed into his seat. 'Dad's gone mad,' he whispered.

'Calm down,' the mayor called out laughingly' 'He's just stressed out before the wedding. The girl is so young, high-maintenance, and his cock's all flabby by now. He has a right to be a bit jittery. Everything is going to go back to normal after the wedding. Besides, without notarised papers, nothing is binding, so don't worry. Drink up!'

'Gentlemen,' said Anatol Pires, the high-school founder. He mumbled it quietly, but Romanowska was close enough to hear. He was known mainly for being utterly and irreversibly broke. Several years before, he had been Bondaruk's competitor in the timber industry, but he had made some mistakes and lost everything. 'It seems that I satisfy all the criteria, barring age,' he went on. 'But the papers shouldn't be too hard to tweak, so who knows – maybe in a few months you'll be ordering your stairs and floors from me. I'll knock New Forest Hajnówka out in no time, or my name's not Pires!'

That got him a few muffled laughs. Some guests resumed eating, still chuckling, and others whispered among themselves, outraged:

'What do you mean he's not going to show up? The audacity!'

Wasyl and Fionik, Bondaruk's two oldest sons, got up and left ostentatiously, with Tomik hot on their heels. As far as anyone knew, this was the first time ever that the three had presented such a united front. A couple more guests left too, clearly upset by Bondaruk's letter.

As soon as the restaurant was clear of naysayers, the mood grew more cheerful. Romanowska suspected that some of those present had known about Bondaruk's letter before the dinner. He had probably at least discussed his decision with the elders. They had definitely known, yes, she thought, looking at them. Their expressions were triumphant rather than astonished or shocked. She took a deep breath and smiled at the butcher, Grandpa Mikołaj, who had been sitting still, utterly impassive, since the beginning of the confusion. He winked in response, though it could have been a nervous tic. Encouraged nonetheless, Romanowska grabbed a fork and helped herself to some delicious-looking potato sausage and a hefty serving of bison stew. She might as well treat herself to some luxury while she was here.

Just as she started to eat, the door opened and Seryozha returned. He had a black eye and a bloody nose. Seeing that, the mayor jumped to his feet, led the man to his seat and started to wipe his face clean with a napkin, calling for someone to get some ice.

'Sit down, son, and calm down. Don't you worry. That's a leader's life for you, right there. You lose a bunch of friends and get a dozen enemies in return. It seems you're the man of the minute,' he chortled. 'The king is dead! Long live the king.'

'I'm not Bondaruk's son,' Seryozha was weeping, his voice breaking. 'I'll do the tests. I'll prove it. This has to be some kind of misunderstanding.'

'Oh, but you might well be. Why not? Besides, who cares about the truth?' Grandpa Mikołaj said, unexpectedly. All eyes turned to the butcher. It was a rare sight, him taking the stand. Very rare. 'What's important,' he went on, 'is that Piotr doesn't need anything more than a rumour to begin the slaughter.'

Polish Radio's morning show was drowned out by the roar of a motorbike. Bożena Bejnar, dressed up in a peach-coloured taffeta frock with lots of frills and lacing, walked to the window. Frowning, she stared out at the handsome young blond man leaning nonchalantly against a bright-yellow motorbike. As soon as her daughter stepped out of the shower, she drew the curtains. 'Don't you dare go out,' she hissed, untangling curling pins from her hair.

Iwona didn't react apart from a faint smile of satisfaction that flickered across her face. She didn't have to go to the window to know who was waiting in the courtyard. She knew the sound of that engine. She hadn't thought that Quack would show up at the wedding. Not because he was a coward. On the contrary – the man had rivalry in his blood. He did know who not to mess with, though, and Bondaruk was top of that list. It had to be said, Iwona found her ex-fiancé's behaviour very flattering, but the fact that he had decided to show up could only mean trouble. For both of them, though mainly for him. Iwona had to talk to him right away.

Quickly, she donned the outfit that had been delivered from the seamstress early that morning. Both the skirt and the blouse when she put them on were perfect. They smelled of lavender. Iwona tied a sash around her waist, completing the costume. The person she saw in the mirror wasn't her, but some overdone doll straight out of local folklore. She untied the pinny and threw it over the backrest of a nearby chair , and started to brush her hair. Meanwhile, her mother dialled a number on her mobile. Whoever she was calling wasn't picking up. Iwona was still standing looking in the mirror when Bożena strode to the kitchen to use the landline. Some mascara and then vivid red lipstick. Quack liked her in heavy make-up.

'He's here,' Bożena whispered into the receiver. 'I know, I thought he wouldn't, but here he is, in front of my house, with that idiotic bike of his.'

Then she was silent for a long while, before plucking the last cigarette from the pack and digging through the things strewn across the table in search of a lighter. In the end, she bent over the stove and lit it that way, turning the stove off just in time to avoid a fiery disaster as one of her curling pins unrolled and her hair cascaded over the gas jet.

'I'll watch her,' she promised into the phone. 'Don't you worry, son. You'll get your land. We all want that, and Iwona will do her part.'

She heard a slam. She let the receiver go and sprinted to the living room. The curtains were rippling as the air gusted in through the open window. There was no trace of Iwona apart from the embroidered pinny on the chair and the rhythmically swinging plywood door. The motorbike revved and a few moments later the only sound was the radio. The news presenter was announcing another hot Sunday. June was going to be beautiful and sunny. In three weeks' time there was going to be an Orthodox choral music festival in Hajnówka, and a similar event in Białystok, but that one hadn't received the blessing of Archbishop Sawa. Furious, Bożena switched the radio off.

'I've changed my mind,' Quack declared when they stopped in front of a shed in the middle of an unploughed field.

The motorbike had got stuck in the dry sand and Quack had thought they would have to go on foot, but he had managed to drive across the wasteland onto a narrow road. The land hadn't been worked for years. Quack's mother, Dunia Orzechowska née Załuska, used to plant potatoes there, but that had been a long time ago. In the eighties, she had given most of her land over to the state and they'd had to live off her meagre pension ever since. She only kept this rough patch of earth. Before the war, this was where the richest village in the region had stood. It had been called Załuskie. His mother's ancestral home had been the biggest structure in the village, and successive men of her family had held the position of headman since time immemorial. During the war the settlement had been burned to the ground and its inhabitants shot or burned alive. Those few who remained had moved to neighbouring villages or to workhouses in the city. Quack's mother had done the same, buying an old forester's lodge near Hajnówka and putting down roots there. The house still didn't have running water or a bathroom, but she had never needed much. Most of the time she prayed, went to church and helped those in need. People called her a folk healer, a witch doctor, a *szeptunka,** though she always said she was no different from any old recluse. God had only started supposedly speaking to her in her twilight years, but people said she had had strange powers since she was a child. When the needy visited her, she always said it wasn't her doing the healing, but the patient's faith. If you didn't believe, she couldn't help you.

Many refugees from Załuskie had returned to their faith only decades after the war. The Eastern Orthodox creed wasn't looked upon with favour in the new communist reality. And besides, animosity between Poles and Belarusians remained alive. Belarusians couldn't forgive the Poles for turning them over to the roaming

---

* Literally 'whisperer'; a term for traditional Polish healing women practising predominantly in Podlasie.

bands of militant radicals. When democracy finally came, the towns-folk started to buy land en masse. You could get a few hectares of low-grade land for peanuts. Dunia used to dream that her only son would settle down and build a house on their ancestral land. Quack, however, thought little of farming and had always been ashamed of his background. To be called a peasant was to him the greatest affront. Dunia tried convincing him that most city folk had their roots in peasantry – the majority of the old aristocratic and burgher families had been killed during the war. Landowners had had their land and the records of their rights to it brutally seized and the poorer farmhands had gone to work in factories. The contemporary plutocrats were descendants of those downtrodden wretches.

Quack and his mother had missed the moment to cash in on their piece of land. But the potential buyers quickly found other sellers, and people from the neighbouring villages who might have been interested in expanding their fields had too little money to convince Dunia to sell her ancestral domain. And later, when money started coming in from the European Union, those same people preferred to buy cars, plasma TVs or brand new combine-harvesters that could be tax-deducted. Quack hadn't even applied to the young farmers' support programme, though he could have received substantial financing. He could have bought more land of his own and lived as God intended. But no. He didn't even want to hear about it. He rented a room in town, too embarrassed to even be seen with his mother. When she asked him if he had been approved by the programme, he replied that he had filled in the wrong form. There were no more opportunities. The locals knew Dunia's land was of the worst grade, good for nothing except planting potatoes. So the Załuski family land turned into a wasteground and their old house grew ever more dilapidated. Nothing suggested that was about to change any time soon.

Quack, with a charming smile, offered Iwona a hand and she got off the motorbike. During their ride, she'd had to lift her skirt, revealing her thighs. Now, she straightened and lowered it, noticing Quack's greedy glances. They hadn't seen each other since winter, when she had visited him in prison.

'Have you sunbathed yet?' he asked, feigning indifference. He noticed that she still wore his ring, but said nothing.

'A bit, behind the house,' she muttered, pointing to the shed. 'Let's hide before someone sees us and tells my brothers. You shouldn't have come.'

When he'd wheeled the bike inside and closed the door, she backed away until her back touched the wall. She thought he might pounce and try to have his way with her, taking advantage of their isolation. But strangely, he didn't even try to hug her.

'What's going on?' She tilted her head. 'Are you mad at me?'

'I've changed my mind,' he said fiercely, finally walking over to her, and lifted her chin. The gesture wasn't tender, it was a show of dominance. She didn't fight back. Interpreting her submissiveness as consent, he caressed her face, delicately now. She snuggled against his hand, grabbing it and holding it tight in her own. He leaned closer and kissed her hair. There was real affection in the gesture. When she looked at him, there was lust in his eyes. Despite that, he kept his voice cold and composed, saying: 'I won't agree to that arrangement we had. I won't wait for you.'

That startled her.

'But we had a deal.'

'That was your idea,' he replied. 'Your plan.'

'But you agreed.'

She walked over to the only window, barely transparent with all the bird shit spattering it. Dead flies were scattered across the windowsill like a crusty blanket. The shed was stuffy and she wanted to open the window, let some air in. But she knew she couldn't do that. Someone might notice and report an intruder. It should look abandoned if they were to remain unseen.

Iwona headed to the other room, used as storage for farming equipment. She opened the door to a small space that had long ago housed animals. There weren't any windows here and it was completely dark. Her eyes adjusted quickly, and she soon discerned the silhouettes of wooden vessels filled with blackish slop. Those had to be old pig feeding troughs. She didn't want to know what they contained now.

In the corner of the room, behind a bale of hay, lay a small triangular shape. When she got closer, she realised it was travel bags – three bundles containing what looked like sleeping bags, a canister of fuel, a little stove and a military backpack. Quack had packed some buckwheat, noodles, preserves and a water bag. If they rationed it, the food should last them about two weeks. They'd change their hiding place then. Maybe a few days sooner, if Quack managed to find them a car. He would bring them water from the nearby creek under cover of night. When they had had their holiday here three years ago, the creek had flowed with the votive tissues the Orthodox faithful used to wipe their hands with so that the 'holy water' might ease their pains. The Krynoczka, as the creek was called, was said to release its power once a year, bringing in throngs of devotees from all over the country. Iwona didn't believe in all that religious stuff. Quack did, though, being from an Orthodox family. So, when she had found a silk scarf in the water, she'd washed it and ironed it and worn it until it frayed. Quack's mother had said it was bad luck, because the thing was supposedly soaked through with someone's worries and concerns and now they would be transferred to Iwona. She had brushed it off as nonsense.

Iwona produced a torch from the backpack and aimed the beam at Quack's face.

'Stop it!' He covered his eyes. 'Are you mad?'

She laughed and pointed the light towards the ground. The floor was black and damp. She swept the tip of her coral-red lacquered shoe in an arc across it, revealing wooden splinters, sand and clumps of grass. It was bare ground they were standing on. And now it really dawned on her that they might spend the next month in this place. Where would they sleep? There was no inflatable mattress or even a camping mat. Was she crazy? Doubt swept over her, but just as she was about to protest, she noticed a table. New, metal, shiny. As if someone had scrubbed it clean. It was the only element of the furniture that reminded her that it was indeed the twenty-first century. There was a metal suitcase under the table. She didn't know what Quack kept in there, but it suddenly didn't matter. Iwona grabbed one of the sleeping bags, unfurled it and spread it over the table. Quack shook his head, though, so she moved it onto the hay and lay down.

'Come,' she said, beckoning him. He didn't move, still hesitant.

'My beautiful, lovely Quacky.' She got up again and approached him, whispering into his ear: 'I'm all yours. Only yours. You know that, don't you?'

She pulled him towards her, placing his hand on her breast, and kissed him on the lips. He didn't remain passive for long. With some difficulty, he started to untie the straps of her wedding blouse, and finally managed to get the job done with her help. He watched her take off her skirt and the rest of her clothes, hanging them on a rusty meat hook affixed to the wall.

Iwona stood naked, waiting. In the twilight, Quack could only see the outlines of her body.

'What about your hairdresser today? You'll be late,' he said, voicing his last doubt, but only perfunctorily. His hands moved of their own accord and soon he could empirically confirm that Iwona's skin was as soft as the satin sleeping shirt he had stolen for her.

'They'll notice,' he added, unconvincingly.

'Keep talking and I'll really be late,' she laughed and undid his belt.

They kissed greedily.

'It'll be all right,' she whispered in his ear when she could breathe again. They lay on the damp, earthy-smelling hay, face to face. Not even animals would stoop so low as to sleep there. But she didn't care. She was drowning in his eyes.

'Have you slept with him?' he asked softly.

She smiled and shook her head. 'Don't be jealous. He's on our side,' she said. 'He'll protect us while he can.'

'Why?' Quack asked, and added: 'Why is he doing this?'

'I don't know.' She shrugged. 'It's his business. But while it serves, we should use it. Just . . . don't fuck this up, Quack. Do you trust me?'

'No.' He looked into her eyes. 'But I do love you.'

She grinned. He was beautiful, and disarming. Like a little boy. She liked him, she really did. Maybe she could even love him again?

'That's why I need to marry him.'

'I can't allow that,' he whispered, then moaned as Iwona slid her hand down his belly.

The church was filled to bursting, but nearly everyone was standing with their backs to the altar.

'Where? I can't see,' a child called.

'God sees all,' a woman standing behind a counter, selling candles and devotional items, reprimanded the boy.

She wore a golden-braided headscarf and glared at the deep cleavages and revealing clothes of younger women with disgust. They wouldn't come to church dressed like that if she had any say in it.

The priest, wearing a golden mitre and a golden cassock and holding a golden censer, the full regalia of an Orthodox cleric, stood in the corner, having a lively conversation with the groom. Bondaruk nodded his head meekly. Finally, he bowed and touched the ground with a finger. The priest stuck out his ringed hand for the man to kiss. Piotr smooched the shiny ruby the size of a mirabelle plum encased in red Russian gold.

'The groom's pissed,' Jah-Jah muttered to Romanowska, glancing at his watch. They were standing in the vestibule, observing the situation.

'A bit old for a groom, ain't he?' a woman standing next to them chuckled. 'Slipping on your old *rubashka** doesn't make you any younger. Neither does marrying a young *dzyaushka*.† Assuming she shows up at all. Shame.' She hid her face in her hands and shook her head, feigning concern.

Meanwhile, Bożena Bejnar was striding from the small rug the couple were supposed to stand on during the ceremony, all the way to the exit and then back again. She had never had an occasion to show off her only evening dress to so many people at once. After some time, the less informed guests started pointing at her, thinking her the bride. After each nervous tour up and down the church, Bożena walked over to Bondaruk and whispered something in his ear. His only response was to pat her on the back and give her a brief hug, trying to help her rein her fury in.

'She's just trying to be fashionably late, is all,' he assured her. 'She probably lost track of time at the hair salon. You know how five minutes can turn into half an hour. Keep calm, Mother dear.'

Bożena knew better. She could still hear the roar of the yellow motorbike, but she couldn't just tell Bondaruk that. Her sons were

---

* A type of flaxen shirt worn in the region in the 19th century. Nowadays only worn in traditional costume contexts.
† Lit. 'young woman/girl'.

still out, searching for their sister. They had orders to bring her in by force if necessary. But as yet there was no trace of either them or Iwona.

Piotr had shaved off his moustache and didn't look his age now. Come to think of it, he didn't behave his age either. People knew he must have been over fifty, but nobody would have guessed that he was nearing seventy. Tall, reedy, thin, he stood with his back straight, like a soldier at attention. His hair, snow-white, contrasted starkly with his black eyebrows and together with the aquiline nose made him resemble a bird of prey. There was no nervousness in him. But it didn't mean he was calm. Those who knew him suspected that inside, he was quivering with concern.

The witnesses stood one to each side of him, wearing suits paired with Belarusian *rubashkas*, their hands sheathed in white gloves. The young couple's crowns were waiting on special silk pillows. After yesterday's sensational news, which had spread like wildfire around the whole town, they were worried Bondaruk's sons would wreck the wedding. People said that trouble was brewing and tragedy could strike at any time. Police cars had spent the entire night parked at the houses of both the editor-in-chief and his alleged father. The commissioner had also gathered a unit of volunteers to intervene if it came to rioting. With the large numbers of hooligans staying in the city overnight, anything might happen.

Suddenly, the church door swung open and a person wearing a long, flowing robe entered. The sun was shining from behind her, so nobody could see who it was at first. Only when the person passed the vestibule did the crowd let out a collective sigh of relief. People turned back to the iconostasis.

The bride was wearing full, traditional Belarusian garb, flower crown and embroidered belt included. Her striped grass-green skirt reached the ground, and as she walked, the tips of her lacquered coral-coloured pumps could just be glimpsed. She had on a white shirt with colourful hand-embroidered flowers, edged with traditional Belarusian trim. The bride's face was covered by a thick veil that hung from an enormous wreath of red-and-white flowers. Her hair was tied back and up so that not even a single strand could be seen. Instead, dozens of silk bands cascaded down her back like a coat made of rainbows. In her hand, she held a braid thick as an arm.

The priest gestured to the young couple and together they walked to the altar. Even those sceptics who favoured the classic white wedding dress over the folk attire had to admit the girl looked gorgeous.

'Is that a Belarusian coif?' The gossipers took an immediate interest. 'Why is the braid not attached?'

Though Bondaruk's sons hadn't graced the ceremony with their presence, everything seemed to be going perfectly smoothly. The guests, relaxed again, were looking forward to the week-long party that would follow the church ceremony. The sawmill workers had been given time off until Wednesday; Bondaruk had announced that the company would be closed until then. Even the glue lab, usually open 24/7, would be shut down.

'I'm only going to have one wedding,' he'd explained to local TV. 'I'd like my employees to celebrate with me.'

Bondaruk's competitors were rubbing their hands in anticipation of the gains they'd make. Especially as there was going to be an interregnum after the party; the fight for the throne would take some time. Nobody really believed that the newspaper editor would be able to keep his new position for longer than it took to file a lawsuit. None of Bondaruk's sons would allow the outsider to snatch the multimillion capital of the company from under their noses, the competitors were sure. Seryozha at this moment was standing with his back against the wall, clearly frightened to death by the responsibility Bondaruk had thrown at him. Two bodyguards in baggy suits stood either side of him.

The choir began to sing. The witnesses lifted golden crowns over the couple's heads. They would keep them raised like that for the entire two-and-a-half-hour mass. Bondaruk had warned them there would be no excuses if they failed. When the couple accepted communion – wine from a decorative chalice and pieces of prosphora* – Jah-Jah leaned over to Romanowska and said he was going for a smoke.

'I'll keep watch here,' she replied with a smile.

---

* A small loaf of leavened bread used in Orthodox Christian services.

There were horse-drawn carriages standing in front of the entrance, ready for the celebrants. The horses wore decorative bridles and the coachmen were in full livery. They were smoking Russian cigarettes and turning their moustached faces to the sun. They had a lot of driving ahead of them. The more impatient guests could also take the buses. Only a few had arrived by car; everybody had known there would be no parking spaces at the restaurant today. The police had already announced they would be checking the sobriety of everyone leaving the neighbourhood by car.

Citizens of Białowieża were gathering on the courtyard. The crowd was growing larger by the minute. Everyone wanted to see the bride of the famous magnate. People were bunching up around the church door, holding little bags of spare change. Florists had had to get in extra supplies. Business hadn't been this good in living memory.

Jah-Jah smoked three cigarettes and tried to return to the church, but the crowd made it impossible. He darted a glance at Senior Officer Karol Supryczyński, who just spread his arms, resigned. The only thing they could do now was pray nobody started a fire. There were no emergency exits in the church and people would trample each other to death in no time. Jah-Jah headed to the side door, but still he had to elbow through the mob. All of a sudden, he spotted Bożena Bejnar, the bride's mother. She was trying to push herself through the crowd too to leave the church. The flow of people carried him in the opposite direction. The ceremony must have been over; people had started thronging around the couple. Everyone wanted to touch the bride's dress for luck, give the newlyweds their best wishes and pluck one of the silky ribbons from the bride's wreath. Jah-Jah noticed Bożena had black streaks down her cheeks. Had she been crying? Must be motherly emotion. He pushed his way back to Krystyna. There was a lot of space around her now; everybody was moving towards the exit, keen to grab the best seats in the carriages.

'Strange,' Romanowska said, as soon as Jah-Jah reached her.

She spoke in a whisper, nodding to passing guests with a smile stuck to her lips, and Jah-Jah followed her lead. Many people knew them, so they had keep nodding, over and over again. Jah-Jah thought they must look like those styrofoam dogs with bobbing heads that truck drivers liked to stick on their dashboard.

'What's strange?' A nod to the mayor.

'She hasn't revealed her face,' Krystyna replied. 'She was veiled for the whole ceremony. I'm not sure, but I think that's not really in line with protocol.'

'Protocol is for people like us, Madam Commissioner,' Jah-Jah teased. 'This is a traditional ceremony. Did you show your face during our wedding?'

'I didn't wear a veil, as you might recall if you tried.'

A nod to the owner of the TV station.

'Maybe someone gave her a black eye for being late.'

'All the more reason to check it out up close,' the commissioner replied and sent a brilliant smile to Alina Gryc, the head of the town library in Hajnówka.

'Want me to strip-search her?'

'I'll deal with that.'

A cold and shallow bow to the owner of the funeral parlour, reciprocated with only a scrutinising look. Then, the butcher, and a few doctors. Scout troop leader. Kindergarten nurse.

'We've got a profiler in town.' Jah-Jah suddenly changed the subject. 'I've already talked to her.'

'Who?' The commissioner momentarily taken aback, didn't return their son's teacher's nod.

'Karol detained a woman yesterday. Name's Załuska. An investigative psychologist and a criminologist.'

'The name sounds familiar.'

'She's not a local though. Came from the seaside. Red like a squirrel but with a temper.'

Romanowska stared at Jah-Jah for a while.

'Red-headed,' she said. 'That's only a colour. Doesn't mean she's mean.'

'I wouldn't discount it,' Jah-Jah said and snorted.

'What has she done?'

'I'll tell you later,' he said firmly. 'But it's been pretty amusing, I can tell you that. She's looking for Doctor Death.'

'Shut up. Don't let Saczko hear you,' Romanowska hissed and took a look around. 'Okay, I think he's not here. Interesting.

He and Bondaruk are generally inseparable. Wasn't he the one who confirmed Bondaruk's innocence after Łarysa disappeared? And what's going on with the criminologist, really?'

'I kinda promised I'd help her. And then – wait for it . . .' He paused, preparing his surprise.

'Well?'

'You know she can find bodies.'

'And?'

'We don't have to mix up the guys from Central in our shit. Let them come, do whatever they want. But they didn't want to give us their profiler – no problem. We'll have our own. And for free!'

'Jah-Jah!' she scoffed. 'That's unacceptable. I cannot let you recruit people without my knowledge.'

'Well, you know *now*.'

'You should have told me earlier.'

'Why would I do that? I know what you would have said. *Nyet.*'

He leaned over to Krystyna, bringing his face close to hers. She could smell his stale breath. He grabbed her by the shoulders.

'Listen. That woman has an agenda. She wants to act. She's a lone wolf. All we need to do is keep out of her way. We'll throw her some clues, give her an address or two and point her towards the witness. And the doc is here, no?'

'I haven't seen him.'

'I have. He came with that posh genius lad. I can't believe they're not sleeping together. Have you seen her dress?'

'I think you're wrong. Saczko's not here.'

'Yeah, whatever. What does it matter anyway? Załuska will find him herself. And then, as repayment, she'll take care of our skulls. She'll find the bodies and we'll let her go, take over the case and get the bonus from Central.' He smiled triumphantly. 'Besides, she doesn't know anything yet. I haven't told her a thing without telling you first. Don't worry. I checked her out. We're not risking a thing.'

'You have it all figured out, don't you?'

'I have dirt on her, just in case.'

'What dirt?'

'Driving without a licence and registration. And no gun licence.'

'Gun?'

'She's carrying a piece. That's potentially dangerous and we can make a case out of it. I searched her car discreetly while Błażej was playing the retard. I've made a report. It's waiting for you on your desk. But I haven't filed it yet, just to be sure. We can attach it to the files later if we need it.'

'You want to frame her?'

'Not if she helps us. But you know, better safe than sorry.'

Romanowska mulled it over, regarding her ex with half-closed eyes.

'So you took her to my office and pretended to be the boss.' She chuckled. 'Come on, let's talk outside. I still don't get some of this.'

'What don't you understand? A guy would have got it. You women,' Jah-Jah scoffed, but a wide grin lit up his face as the priest, having changed into a less dazzling cassock, walked past them.

'*Slava hospodu, batyushka!* Great wedding. See you later?' he asked, tapping the side of his nose tellingly.

'Franek, Franek, Franek.' The priest clicked his tongue and wagged a finger at the officer. The town had been abuzz not that long ago with news that the cleric had lost his driving licence. The preacher had been utterly hammered when the police pulled him over. But now he made an innocent face. 'Grow up.'

'Right back at you, *batyushka*.'

The priest retreated.

'Boy, am I glad we're not married any more,' Romanowska muttered. 'You'd be the end of me.'

'Who? Me?' Jah-Jah looked genuinely surprised. 'It's you who turns down all my ideas.'

'I undo their consequences.'

The church was nearly empty. A while longer and their voices would start reverberating across the building. Krystyna glanced at the door and gestured for them to leave. This whole conversation had made her lose track of the newlyweds, who were now standing in the courtyard, receiving congratulations. The bride was still veiled. 'Maybe she's not showing her face because she's not the person everyone thinks she is?' Jah-Jah joked and burst out laughing, waiting for Krystyna's acerbic retort. Instead, his ex just looked at him with something approaching admiration.

'Go and check it out,' she ordered, poking a finger into his solar plexus.

'Don't be stupid. I was joking.'

'I'll let that Załuska of yours take care of our skulls.' Her voice was determined.

'Firstly, not *my* Załuska,' he said. 'I don't know her. Secondly, I'm not even sure she'll go for it. And *número tres,* this is just bonkers. I was only having a laugh.'

Romanowska grabbed him by the arm and squeezed.

'I want to know who's behind the veil. Maybe it's Dunia! Maybe she finally caught him. How often do I ask you for a favour? Be a man!'

'Idiot,' Jah-Jah snapped, and waved her away. But he shoved himself through the crowd and took up position at the end of the long line of guests.

Suddenly, the crowd parted. An ancient woman wrapped in rags was shambling towards the couple, supporting herself with one hand on a cane. It was Alla, the seamstress. A gorgeous Belarusian girl wearing military boots was holding her by the other arm. The stench the elderly woman exuded was overbearing. People discreetly covered their noses, turning round. Alla approached the newlyweds, lifted the bride's veil and stuck her head underneath.

'She kissed her on the forehead,' people were saying. 'What does it mean?'

'A traitor kisses on the cheek, a lover on the lips, and a parent on the forehead,' someone said, citing a fragment of the Belarusian national epic. 'She blessed her.'

Alla left the church. She was holding the bride's black braid in her gnarly hand, but in the crowds nobody noticed. Soon after, the couple stepped into one of the horse-drawn carriages and drove off towards the restaurant. The train of guests followed in their wake.

Romanowska walked over to Jah-Jah.

'So?'

'I couldn't see.'

'It wasn't her,' said Tomik, passing his gold iPhone around.
His older brothers squinted in turn at the blurry photo Tomik had received from a paid-off security guard.

'It's some old lady,' Marta, Tomik's fiancée, said. 'Look at her hands. See? Where the glove ends. Look at the veins.'

Everyone leaned in to see the phone, staring at the photo.

'She was veiled like that for the whole ceremony,' Fionik said. 'People are talking.'

'So' maybe she's a stand-in?' Marta asked in a theatrical whisper. She drew out the syllables for dramatic effect.

'Stand-in?' Wasyl scoffed. 'Who can tell? This picture is blurry as hell.'

'Well, you should have gone and seen for yourself then. The guard only had an old Nokia. He did the best he could,' Marta snapped. She had been the one to bribe the man. 'Now it's too little, too late.' She couldn't forgive her fiancé for forbidding her to attend the ceremony. Now nobody would see her new dress with its raccoon-fur ruff. Another opportunity to wear the outfit wouldn't come any time soon. Unless Tomik took her to the Żubrówka Hotel for New Year's Eve. She'd forgive him then. Maybe. She wasn't sure yet.

'Whatever happened back at that party, we should go to the wedding and keep a unified front. Maybe your father can be swayed?' she'd tried to persuade him earlier in the morning.

But Tomik had only said, 'I won't make myself a laughing stock,' and that was that.

Marta had been sulking ever since.

Now they were all sitting in the Starówka, Wasyl's bar. Apart from them it was completely empty. First they had argued, then they had eaten. Finally, the men had decided to contest their father's will on the grounds of mental disturbance. There was precedent; they only had to unearth the papers from Bondaruk's stay at Ciszynia years ago. And embellish a thing or two. Their father's diagnosis of Othello syndrome had been his defence in Łarysa's murder. There would have been a trial otherwise, though circumstantial, as the body hadn't been found. But thanks to Saczko, Bondaruk hadn't even been charged. Now his sons were puzzling over how to defeat their father with his own weapon. Bondaruk would have to go back to the hospital. They had a justification for this too: Fionik's and Wasyl's mothers were both missing. The only issue was the facility's director. Bondaruk had been friends with Saczko for ever and the doctor would never certify their father as mentally incompetent. He owed him too much. Finding a psychiatrist from another city wasn't an option either; it might suggest that Bondaruk's sons had bad intentions. The whole family now knew that the plan was a lost cause – unless someone changed Saczko's mind. Scared him badly enough or handed him a cheque. The only thing was the brothers didn't know how much they should offer the man for such a service. Or who to send to actually do the thing and not botch it.

'It would be easier to hire a killer,' Marta grumbled, then gave a nervous laugh.

'What are you saying?' Fionik asked, shocked. These were his first words since dinner had been served.

'What? You threatened your brother with that very thing not that long ago,' Marta replied. 'Don't you remember? Don't worry, Wala can't hear us.'

Walentyna, Fionik's wife, sat apart from the group. She never joined in family discussions. *God's will,* she'd said when the news of Bondaruk's decision became known. She didn't care about the money. What counted was that her family was well and had a roof over their heads. She was a spokesperson for the town hall and had a cooking blog. Fionik ran a network of grocery stores. God doesn't like the greedy, Walentyna would say. She had only come to the family meeting as that was what any good wife would have done, but she was mainly occupied with looking after their son. Five-year-old Leo was a very lively child. Currently, he was trying his best to pull a gigantic flower pot from a counter straight down on his head.

Fionik knew how this was going to pan out. If their father got his wish, they'd lose everything. Wala would change her tune as soon as creditors came knocking and threatened to take their house away. Fionik had had to take another mortgage a year ago. Keeping his grocery stores afloat was a losing battle, and he was only able to keep things together because of his father's financial support. And besides, his wife would probably lose her job the day Bondaruk went out of business.

'He's not even your real dad,' Marta said, shrugging. She'd got her confidence back. 'You have to face the truth. Yeah, okay, he adopted you, paid for your education. But he isn't your blood.

Not to mention the other things. I only don't say what we all know because of the kid. We don't want him to repeat things at school.'

Tomik flushed. 'Shut up, woman!' he cried.

Wasyl silenced him with a gesture. 'Hard truth, but the truth,' he said. 'Let Marta finish. If it weren't for our common enemy, we wouldn't even be sitting at a table together.'

'Hear, hear,' Walentyna called from the other side of the room.

That surprised them. Nobody had thought she was listening to the conversation. Marta leaned back in her chair, took a deep breath and thanked Wasyl and Wala with a smile.

'Old Petya doesn't have too long to live. He knows that. The will only proves it. Maybe he's ill? I read people do all kinds of weird things when they're sick. Nobody gets it until the autopsy. A brain tumour pressing down on the nerves or some such.'

'I don't think that's what's happening.'

'Whatever.' Marta waved away the comment. 'But if he died abruptly, you'd all benefit. I'm not talking about anything spectacular. An accident. Something quiet. You know, he dies in his sleep. Happens all the time with old people. You'd share the money three ways. We could pay off the Żubrówka and forget the whole thing ever happened.'

Tomik grabbed the mobile and displayed the photo of the bride again. 'But what is *this* all about?'

Nobody wanted to revisit the subject of the veil. They sat in silence, digesting what Marta had said. Leo pulled at the tablecloth, toppling over a candle holder and sliding a full set of porcelain crockery off the table. Fortunately, the candles went out before hitting the boy's head.

'I know a guy,' Wasyl croaked. 'Has a business in Białowieża. Girls, protection, et cetera. Everything from the East, of course – no papers. They'd take up any job. I asked him once and he promised he'd help. Remember?' He fixed his eyes on Tomik. 'Said he'd send someone. I can call him again.'

Nobody responded, because at that moment, despite the 'Closed' sign hanging outside, the doorbell rang. Without waiting, an old man in a crumpled hat entered the bar. He had long, wild, knotted, white hair and a beard like Santa Claus. An old yellow-brown

AmStaff dog trudged unsteadily alongside him. The man nodded at the group but kept his distance.

He headed straight to the bar, ordered two lagers and sat down in the corner of the room with his two mugs. Bondaruk's sons shot him furtive glances.

'Go talk to him,' said Marta, pulling at her husband's sleeve. 'He won't stay for ever. Tell him to talk to Saczko. Just don't forget to negotiate the price.'

'But I don't really know the man,' Tomik said, trying to worm his way out of talking to the older man.

'He used to teach you German,' Wasyl said in a low voice. 'Remind him who you are. He'll be happy. Maybe give you a discount.'

'You called him, not me,' Tomik retorted.

'But I only ever got Cs in his lessons,' Wasyl riposted. 'You go. You were always the nerd.'

That did it. Tomik pushed himself to his feet. He looked at the old dog sitting like a sphinx at Pires's feet, never letting the child crawling across the floor out of its sight. Bondaruk's youngest son brushed invisible crumbs off his sweater, straightened his collar and reluctantly headed towards the man's table. The rest of the family followed him with their eyes.

'Good day, Professor.'

He couldn't even bring himself to sit down; he had re-assumed the role of the timid student, shaking at the sight of the strict Professor Pires, as if the man was still the principal of the Belarusian high school. In his time, he had been charismatic, confident, and radical in his views.

During the reign of the communist regime, he had been one of the very few people in town who never had any problems getting a passport. He used this to his advantage and travelled around the world. He used to have all kinds of customs stamps in his papers, including all the countries of the Soviet bloc. He knew seven languages, not counting German. The secret police had never detained him, even though people had said he was a bad apple and probably a spy.

After his wife died he had sold everything, bought a yacht and founded the floorboard company that he hoped would rival

Bondaruk's own business. It went bankrupt within the year. He turned to drinking, lost his yacht in a game of cards, and became the local weirdo. He now lived like a beggar, sleeping in a little shack next to the town landfill, where he had worked as the keeper since losing his fortune. Aside from that, he wandered around the city with the dog, which he had taken from an animal shelter. He had been the target of several attacks by skinheads and other hooligans. Once some still unidentified individuals had tried to bury him alive in the old gravel pit. He had seen their faces but had kept his mouth shut. But, that same day, the parents of three local right-wing activists lost their jobs at the sawmill and nobody would ever employ them again. Since then, not even the most radical nationalists had attempted another attack on him.

Anatol Pires never lost his standing among the older generation. He knew people and had dirt on everyone. Some thought he was the real power behind the throne, a member of the informal council of elders, though he rarely showed up to their meetings. If he wanted, he could have led a completely different life, but he had chosen to live like a tramp. He liked to say that he was *indie* – the last independent, free man in the city. That only made people laugh.

'You call this a good day? The world's going to shit,' Pires muttered, taking off his hat.

Tomik dropped his eyes.

'We called you about some business, Professor. Everything has gone wrong. Father's out of his mind.'

'Well, he lasted a damn long time,' the old man said. He spat into his hand and flattened his hair. Tomik shot his family a glance.

'My brothers. They'd like to talk to you, too,' he began. 'Listen to your plan.'

'I ain't got no plan.' Pires took an enormous swig of his lager. When he put the glass down, it was half-empty. 'But you can buy me another beer.'

Tomik nodded at the waitress. Pires slapped him on the back with such force that the young man bent over the table.

'We thought you'd pass our idea to the director of Ciszynia,' Tomik said. 'This is pretty important. We have the money.'

'If you have the cash, I'll make the arrangement with Doctor Death. No problem,' Pires replied. 'Half the city is on your side. But if I'm to talk to Saczko, you'll have to pay me too.'

'I'm willing to pay double.'

Tomik immediately regretted his words. He could already see Marta's expression.

'What do I need money for?' Pires laughed loudly. 'I want something more valuable than gold. That which binds people for ever. Focus, boy, and understand once and for all that your father got where he is now only because he knows that one golden rule. I'm talking about a favour!'

Tomik was finding it difficult to remain calm. He knew this was only a prelude. Pires was lighting a fire under his arse. And he really didn't have an idea what the old beggar wanted.

'You'll find papers in your old man's house.'

'What papers?'

'A file of old documents. Identification papers for a group of carters murdered during the pogroms of Orthodox villages after the war. Forty-nine documents. I want them all. Originals. No copies. You understand, fancypants?'

'Those documents didn't survive,' Tomik said, collecting himself. 'The second exhumation was a year ago. There were thirteen bodies. They've been buried at the army cemetery in Bielsk.'

'Listen to me, boy,' Pires growled, bristling. 'I don't care about the official story and I'm certainly not going to try to educate you now, since you've managed to get where you are without basic knowledge of your own family. Your father has those documents. All forty-fucking-nine. Trust me. Only one file was burned. I won't tell you which one. Actually I don't know.'

'How am I supposed to get them?' Tomik whispered.

'If I knew I would have taken them myself, wouldn't I?'

At that moment, Leo ran up to the table and gave Pires' dog a great hug. The animal allowed the boy to pet it, remaining calm and still. When Leo touched its tail though, it snapped at him without warning or any sound. The child immediately burst into tears. Walentyna bounded to the rescue.

'You keep your beast on a leash,' Pires snarled and, giving no heed to the woman's protests, turned back to Tomik, saying: 'There were fifty carters. Only those thirteen bodies were found. The rest are still rotting somewhere, wild dogs gnawing at their bones. Forgotten. Or maybe not. Not entirely, at least. People remember. But only someone with those damned documents would ever be able to find them. Whoever knows where they are might be keeping quiet out of fear. But curiosity beats fear nine times out of ten. Someone will come clean.'

Tomik turned his head to look at his brothers. They were pretending not to listen, seemingly engrossed in whatever prattle Marta had for them. She was showing them a gift Tomik had bought her – a pair of antique carnelian earrings.

'I think it won't be as easy as that,' Tomik said after a long pause. 'I'm rather pessimistic on that matter. Father never told me about it.'

'And has he told you how your mother died?' Pires smiled slyly, revealing his blackened gums.

Tomik straightened up and froze, suddenly unsettled. 'I was adopted.'

'Just like those two other bastards whose mothers Four-Eyes offed.'

'You're telling me Bondaruk knew my mother? And they were secretly in love?'

Pires looked at Tomik with something approaching respect.

'Do what I tell you and I'll lead you to your grandmother. She lives in a village near Ciechanowiec. She's been looking for her daughter for a long time. And if she's dead, I'll give you the case number and you can read about your family at least. It won't be pretty though. Why do you think he adopted you? Ask your dad about Jowita. That was her stage name. She was a pretty one. I fell for her too. Come to think about it, you look just like her.'

Tomik sat immobile, as if someone had pulled his plug.

'Are you sure about that?' he asked finally.

'You've got your story and I have mine,' Pires replied. 'As I said, I don't need your money. Well, maybe a little bit, for the expenses. My father was among the carters. They murdered him. I need to find his grave before I bite the dust myself.'

An awkward silence descended. Tomik was lost for words. He wanted to ask the old man why his father would want to keep those documents. What did he have to do with that old tragedy? And most importantly, what did the old codger know about the death of his mother? Was it possible she was still alive? Everybody had always told him she'd left him and vanished. Tomik wasn't sure he wanted to know the real answer. But he didn't ask any of those questions.

'I'll look for the papers,' he promised instead.

'I'm glad to hear that.' Pires sighed. 'Because, my dear boy, I never lose hope. And besides, if I know Four-Eyes, he's got all kinds of dirt on each and every one of us on the council of elders in that little notebook of his. Find it. That's when you'll enter the real labyrinth, young Theseus.' He got up, finished his second beer in one enormous gulp and tucked both glasses into the pockets of his coat. 'Oh, by the way, the last will is a lost cause. Iwona gets it all. The bride was never swapped.'

With that, he snapped the leash onto the silent dog's collar and left, the glasses in his pockets clinking like a minibar on a plane.

Before Jah-Jah had released Sasza from the police station, he had shown her a picture of the director of the psychiatric hospital, but there were so many people outside the church that her chances of spotting the man were slim. Instead she looked for Jah-Jah, finally catching him when he stepped out of the building to have a smoke.

'Even if I wanted to, I can't make the doctor talk to you,' he said and, like Pontius Pilate, seemed to wash his hands of the case.

'You can't or won't introduce me?'

He adjusted his glasses and lowered his head to hers.

'I didn't say that.' He grinned. 'Listen. Doctor Death really likes the local tanning salon. And his favourite colour is green.'

She looked around. She couldn't see anyone sufficiently tanned and wearing a green suit, and such an outmoded outfit would have stuck out like a sore thumb in this crowd. She suspected the two men didn't feel much affection for each other. That they were acquainted was obvious. Everybody knows everyone in a small town like this. At least by sight.

'You have to be clearer,' she said. 'I'm not that good at charades.'

'That's a pity. I hoped you would be.'

Jah-Jah definitely didn't intend to make her work any easier. He just turned round and left, and became occupied with flirting with some woman with close-cropped hair. They looked like a couple, at least from a distance. She tried catching his eye, but he ignored her.

Nearly all the guests had already left, in the horse-drawn carriages or the colourfully decorated buses. The commotion was accompanied by folk music and singing. Sasza hated weddings. Modern and traditional alike. And she definitely didn't want to go to a public binge. She still didn't feel strong enough to participate in events where vodka, wine and beer were the main attractions. It seemed she didn't have any choice though, so she reluctantly joined the long procession of guests.

She got into her car and drove towards Białowieża. On the way, she briefly stopped at the hospital, but no one had found her documents. The police had been there already and had apparently sent a couple of patrols in search of Danka. They had all the ways out of the city under surveillance, which wasn't hard to do; no trains stopped at the local station these days and the building was closed and empty. A bus came just twice a day – at five in the morning from Warsaw and at three p.m. from Białystok. It seemed Danka had simply vanished. Sasza cursed her naivety. The girl had stolen her money and run off. A couple of hundred złoty would allow her to cross the country and survive until she found another dupe to rip off. They would never find her. Sasza wasn't worried about her credit cards – she had blocked them immediately after discovering the theft. But if the girl crossed the border or committed a crime using her papers, that would be bad.

Despite the fact that the local officers had settled on fining her and impounding her car for a while, last night she had decided to tell Ghost and had sent him a text. He called her back at once.

'You messed up,' he'd said.

In the background, she could hear children playing. She felt déjà vu. Gramps, when she had talked to him in the spring. Then it struck her. She knew where Danka might have gone. Maybe she hadn't left town after all. That's why they couldn't find her. She was here, but lying low, like Łukasz. Maybe *with* Łukasz. Okay. She could kill two birds with one stone. If she found the apartment from the photo, she'd also find her stuff, and from there she'd be able to safely return to Sopot.

'Can you talk?' she asked.

'Sure. My ex is just cooking dinner,' Ghost had replied. 'We're sitting with her current husband, having a beer.'

Sasza couldn't wrap her mind around that weird set-up, but she wasn't in the mood to listen to Ghost's personal stories.

'Can you move the date of my exam? I've filled in the forms. I've passed the tests. It's only the shooting range left.'

He said nothing as she told him what happened, except that once in a while he would snort or laugh at her clumsiness. In the end, he told her the next date would be in the autumn, but he wasn't sure if Sasza could join his team that late.

'Sweetheart, people dream about joining my team. And my old office is a luxury not many can afford,' he said.

'I know, I know,' Sasza laughed. 'Genuine chipboard, no paid overtime, and hardcore grind twenty-four-seven. So exclusive. But I'm not one for luxury, Ghost. You know I do my best. I'm not having a holiday here. This is serious. Just don't say I didn't warn you. I'll take the risk.'

'Want me to come and get you?' he asked. 'If you can't drive on your own.'

''I'm not drunk, Ghost. They haven't taken my licence,' Sasza retorted. 'If they find my stuff by Sunday, I'll get back on time.'

She had kept to herself why she had even gone to Hajnówka in the first place. Łukasz Polak was her private affair. She also didn't tell him about her search for Saczko. Or the details of how she'd got mugged. To him, the story was simple – she couldn't drive and couldn't afford a ticket home. She needed help. His strong arm to lean on. She calls, so he has to play the macho man. That was where his offer came from. Sasza sighed, thinking about the simple-mindedness of the man.

'You there?'

'Yeah,' she muttered. 'If they don't find my stuff, I'll come back by bus or train, or I'll hitchhike. I'll get duplicates of my papers and come back for the car later.'

'That'll take you at least three days. You told me no trains stop at that shithole.'

'I'll manage somehow,' she said with finality.

'Send me the address of the hotel. I'll eat, grab a few hours of sleep and come and get you.' He wasn't relenting.

He really wanted her to pass that exam. It was obviously a matter of honour for him. After all, he had vouched for her; if she missed her appointment, he'd lose face.

'How many beers have you had?' she said.

'Three,' he replied. 'And a half. But I won't finish the last one.'

'All right, don't bother. You can't drive like that,' she said. 'If something goes awry, you can collect me from Białystok tomorrow. It'll be faster that way. I'll check the train schedule and call you back.'

'Okay,' he grunted and took a sip of his beer.

'So, everything good besides the obvious?' he asked.

She hesitated. She wanted to tell him more. Ask him to check Łukasz Polak's files. But she thought better of it. She could still do it on her own.

'Yeah. Have a good one.'

'Catch you later.' He hung up.

She started the car again and drove on to the party. Jah-Jah had turned a blind eye on her not having a licence and had issued a special permit that would allow her to drive her car on his turf. Outside the jurisdiction of the local police station, though, she'd have to fend for herself.

Bożena Bejnar was full of misgivings, even though everything was going according to plan. Iwona had come to the wedding and everyone was talking about how good she had looked. Her father was probably lying somewhere drunk – anyway, he hadn't made it to the church in time to make good on his earlier threats. He had done as Bożena wanted, for once, and hadn't ruined their daughter's wedding. After the ceremony, Bondaruk had signed the perpetual land lease contract for her oldest son, against a symbolic fee of one złoty. Władysław would soon be able to build a house there. Maybe he'd even get a legal job. A company. They'd finally move out of the slums of Chemiczna Street.

Bożena had a sinking feeling, though, that Quack hadn't turned up at the apartment for no reason. Iwona's assurances of 'Don't worry, Mum, I don't love him any more' did nothing to placate her. She knew better. Her experience told her that it wasn't that easy to just stop loving someone. And why else vanish with your ex for hours on the day of your wedding? What can a couple of young people, madly in love with each other just months before, do for such a long time alone? Bożena wasn't deluding herself. Something was amiss. And she hadn't been in on the plan. Things happening behind her back wasn't something Bożena was used to and she couldn't let it go. She sat at the dinner table, brooding, stealing glances at Iwona and watching for suspicious behaviour. Finally Irek told her she was overreacting.

'She's married now. She won't be screwing around any more,' he said with a laugh. 'You sold her well, so chill out. Eat something.'

'I'm gonna eat till I puke,' her younger son cut in. His comment went down well with the guests sitting next to the family.

The tables were laden with food, but Bożena didn't feel like eating. The guests started chanting, 'Gorzko, gorzko!'* The couple smooched under the bride's veil. People started jeering and whistling. That wasn't what they had been waiting for. Bondaruk raised a hand, though, and that simple gesture was enough to silence the shouting. Bożena admired the man. She caught herself thinking about what kind of man he had been years before. If Iwona hadn't come along, she'd probably have suggested he married her instead. She would have married him happily, truth be told, but she also knew he wouldn't have wanted her – she was too old for his liking. His loss.

The VIP dinner had been served in a restaurant located in a historic carriage house neighbouring the concert shell. The other guests had their party outside. The festivities were just starting, but there were already no places left at the tables outdoors. Waiters kept bringing in whole roast pigs. People ate and drank like it was their last day on Earth. They nearly trampled each other to get to the free food. There were plastic cups for the drinks, but broken remains of vodka bottles were littering the ground. Parties of this size didn't happen too often around town. The sun was setting, but

---

* Literally 'bitter, bitter'. Traditionally chanted at a wedding party, until the couple kisses. Refers to the 'bitter' taste of the wedding vodka that their kiss is supposed to sweeten.

more people were still arriving. There would be dancing, a concert by Alla Pugacheva, traditional wedding games and fireworks.

The choristers ate their due and left the VIP table, bowing to the groom and signalling their readiness to work. Bondaruk gestured that they could leave. In fifteen minutes there was going to be a choir competition. Church and folk choirs were attending and the event was to be transmitted by Białystok TV. The main concert would start right after they finished their performance. The Russian singer, Alla Pugacheva, had a contract stating that she'd stay in her hotel until the last moment. But that didn't prevent crowds of her fans occupying the entrance to the restaurant.

Bożena discreetly left her table and headed to the door. There was enough space in the amphitheatre, but there were only a few benches to sit on, all reserved for the couple's families. She intended to find a place in the front row and forget about her worries.

'Miss Bożena, beautiful as always.' Somebody pulled at her scarf lightly. She froze. It was Quack. He wore a leather overall and had a biker's helmet tucked under his arm. He flashed his perfectly white teeth in a wide grin. 'I just wanted to say goodbye. And to thank you. For everything. You know, anything happens, it's not my fault.'

Bożena kept her eyes on the man for a few moments. It was no wonder at all that Iwona had picked him. Her husband had been handsome like that too. Both mother and daughter had a soft spot for bad boys. And hopeless paupers, it seemed. But Bożena had gone through a lot and knew that marriage was first and foremost a legal contract. You marry out of good sense and keep your feelings out of it. If there's love, great. If there isn't, even better. All those emotions just pile up and make a mess, and it's best to have your life in perfect order.

'What are you up to, you snake?' she hissed.

'I'm leaving,' he replied. He sounded sincere.

She felt relieved. She put out her hands and embraced him like a wayward son. If someone happened to be keeping an eye on them, they would see two people very close to each other, even though nothing could be further from the truth.

'Don't ever come back,' she warned him quietly and squeezed him to her so hard, he could smell her sweat. What she could feel was vodka. Something wasn't right. She let him go and added: 'I'll kill you myself if you do. Do you understand?'

'Or, you know, maybe the old gaffer croaks and I'm free to show up again.' Quack laughed.

She laughed too, but her smile didn't reach her eyes. She could see that his eyes reflected her own feelings. He was a worthy opponent, despite being a good-for-nothing layabout.

'Iwona's husband hasn't felt or looked this good in years,' she said, eyeing him up and down. 'I'll let you know if anything changes. Until that time comes, stay out of the way. We're not friends.'

They parted. Bożena took a seat on one of the benches and observed Quack getting on his bike and driving away. She wiped away a single tear. She liked the scoundrel and she couldn't help it. But now, she felt like an old queen. She was the one calling the shots and she liked it. It showed, too. People were looking at her while pretending they weren't. It was her daughter's wedding party and the first day of Bożena's grand triumph. Iwona had changed her life for the better and, as her mother, she, Bożena, had made it possible. She couldn't allow anyone to ruin it now. She had to keep vigilant.

'Scram,' she barked at a photographer who had sprung up from nowhere.

As soon as the TV cameraman arrived, though, she instantly straightened up and started posing. Bondaruk took a seat next to his new mother-in-law and they both smiled for the camera, looking like a couple. Tomorrow they'd be on TV and in the meantime all over the Internet. Bożena hoped she looked good.

Someone shouted that Alla Pugacheva was on her way from the hotel. The make-up people were already waiting for her in her flower-filled dressing room. A bottle of champagne and a platter of strawberries, along with a piece of the wedding cake from a local pastry shop, had been left on the table for her too. Nobody had dared comment on the absence of the traditional home-made *korovai*.

Bożena couldn't wait for the private audience with the singer that Bondaruk had promised her. She had all of Pugacheva's albums with her and had wanted an autograph on every single one. She had even fantasised about spending a nice, friendly evening with the star. That's what money can get you, she'd thought, regretting that she had never had enough to buy things like that. Happiness *could* be purchased. It was only a matter of price. She might have learned that late in her life, but it was better than not having learned it at all. Bożena wouldn't let her daughter be stupid like that. Common sense trumps love. Always.

'Where's Iwona?' she asked Bondaruk.

'She went to the toilet,' said Bondaruk.

He stood up to greet Saczko, giving the man a bear hug. That wasn't easy, as the doctor was horribly obese and his mahogany-tinted fake tan did nothing to improve things. He looked like a greasy pork scratching. There was a beautiful woman at his side, with a perfect body and the self-assurance to show it off. She wore a long, revealing, pistachio-coloured dress that showed her back down to the very bottom. A muslin scarf more or less obscured a tattoo on her shoulder blade. Picturesque, thought Bożena. And she had boobs many a younger woman would die for.

'Magdalena Prus,' she introduced herself and apologised for not attending the wedding ceremony. Something had come up at work.

'One of our patients decided to head out and visit town,' she said with a smile.

Bondaruk kissed her outstretched hand. He kept it at his lips for a while longer than necessary, and the woman blushed. They know each other, thought Bożena. They're *closely* acquainted. She felt a twinge of envy. Saczko didn't seem to notice.

Bożena turned on her heel, offended that she hadn't been treated the same way. That was when she noticed the bride's green skirt, right at the top of the stairs that led out of the amphitheatre, between two pine trees. It flickered briefly and then merged into the forest. A second later Bożena thought she heard the familiar roar of a motorbike. She leapt to her feet and ran towards the sound.

Sasza had never spent as much time in traffic jams as here, in Podlasie. Of all places . . . This time the line of cars reached from the entrance to the national park to the Jagiellońskie resort. Going by car had turned out to be the worst possible idea. There were patrol cars everywhere, blocking the road. All drivers were checked and their details committed to police notebooks. It was obvious that the traffic wouldn't dissipate for at least another hour, when Pugacheva had finished her show and returned to her hotel.

Sasza had the slip of paper Jah-Jah had given her but she didn't want to explain herself to overzealous officers again. She turned her car around and drove down a side street. She intended to take the quiet route around the village of Teremiski and then the forest road, which was used only by local rangers. The last time she had been here, people had told her the best car to drive through the forest was a Fiat 126p, which years before had been the most popular car in Poland. Sasza was, however, in her Uno. It was similarly small and could fit anywhere. And it had good suspension, so she should be able to drive through the forest without any problems. If the road was clear of tree branches, she'd arrive in fifteen minutes or so. She would avoid her documents being checked and she'd arrive in Białowieża before everyone else. At least, that was the plan.

She googled a detour on her mobile, and spread a paper map over her knees just in case. It had all the forest paths as well as the national park borders marked. There was a small road leading through the forest straight to the amphitheatre. Finding this short-cut made her day, provided she didn't run into any forest rangers on her way. But even if she did, she already knew what he'd say. She'd tell them Jah-Jah sent her and show them his permit. She was counting on the man being as important as he had made himself sound.

At first, everything went according to plan. The evening twilight disguised her escape perfectly. She drove away quickly. The forest was quiet; she could hear nothing aside from the singing and music far off. Sasza slowed down and drove carefully, around ten kilometres per hour. But then the road suddenly ended. She glanced at the map. It wasn't marked as a dead end. The road was too narrow to turn the car around, so she had to reverse.

Suddenly, in her rear-view mirror, between the trees Sasza noticed a girl. She was running, hard, as if fleeing from something. She wore a folk outfit. One of the choristers, Sasza thought. But when the girl came closer, she recognised her as the bride. A black Mercedes was driving down the forest road, chasing her. It was a distinctive model, with four headlights. Four-Eyes, people called that kind. It was covered in dents, the black paint chipped and scratched in multiple spots. Smoke was spewing from beneath its bonnet. It forced its way through the forest at breakneck speed. Sasza stopped at the last moment to avoid a crash. The other car didn't even try to brake. The girl sprinted to the passenger door of Sasza's Uno, grabbed the handle and jumped in.

'Go!' she cried, panicked.

For an instant, Sasza was dumbfounded. She looked around. They were trapped. She couldn't drive either way. There was a wall of trees in front of them, and the black car behind. It stopped now, blocking the only way out. Suddenly, Sasza heard the slam of a door. In her rear-view mirror, she saw someone, a man, walking towards them. He wore a folk outfit, too, traditional Belarusian wedding attire. And a balaclava covered his face.

'Who's that?' Sasza asked. 'You know him?'

Instead of responding, the girl lost it. 'Call for help! Oh, God, no! He's going to kill me!'

Sasza hit the central lock button and heard the click of the doors locking. She fished her mobile out of her handbag and pressed it into the young woman's hand.

'One-one-two,' she commanded. 'And stop crying! Give them the coordinates.'

She tossed her the map.

The man leaned down to the passenger window. With the mask, Sasza could only see his eyes. They were green, with bright lashes. Blond. The girl jerked away from the door. She was scared witless.

'Go away,' Sasza called to the assailant. At the same time, she rummaged through her bag in search of her Beretta. 'She doesn't want to talk to you.'

The man didn't seem to hear. Out of nowhere, he produced an enormous axe and smashed it into the car's window. The glass held, but thousands of long cracks spread radially around the point of impact. Now they couldn't see him any more. Sasza blew a fuse. The goddamned punk had ruined her car! She had no idea what was going on between these two, but this was too much. She finally found the gun. In her side pocket, where she had tossed the bullets, she could only feel two. No time to search for more. Barely keeping her composure, Sasza loaded the Beretta. The guy outside was going crazy. She opened the door on her side and stepped out, propped her arms on the roof and aimed the gun at the man. If she wanted, from that distance she could shoot him right between the eyes. He froze, taken aback.

'It's loaded,' she warned. 'Move over slowly, or I'll shoot. Step away from the car.'

He did as he was told.

'Lie on the ground, face-down. Hands on your head.'

He didn't move. Sasza felt a trickle of sweat running down her back.

'Hands on your head,' she repeated. 'And lie on the ground, douchebag.'

They locked stares. She could see his bright, emotionless pupils, perfectly still. They made her think of a snake. He began to lift his hands, slowly. Suddenly, he blinked. His eyes shot to his left. She spun in that direction. Too late. Someone struck her on the back of her head but the hit missed and only managed to stun her. She fell. The attacker twisted her arm, trying to wrest the gun from her hand. Accidentally, she pulled the trigger. She didn't know where exactly, but she knew she had scored a hit; the person behind her wailed in pain. Briefly, she registered the high pitch and thought it sounded like a woman. For an instant, Sasza was afraid she had shot the young bride. The person stamped on her arm with all their weight. The pain was unbearable, as if someone was drilling a nail into her hand. The Beretta fell to the ground. She heard the crack of breaking bone. Her hand started swelling immediately. She tried to get up, but that only won her another knock on the head. This time with something hard. And this time, it didn't miss. Before she collapsed to the ground and lost consciousness, she heard another gunshot.

STASZEK

(1946)

Katarzyna Załuska, twenty-five years old, climbed the hayloft ladder with difficulty. Her hands couldn't feel anything. She had given her woollen mittens to her eight-year-old daughter Dunia so that the child could make snowballs. When she reached the top, she was wheezing. With each exhalation, little clouds of steam puffed out of her mouth. The weather was better than the day before, but it was still around twenty degrees Celsius below zero. Katarzyna wore an old padded jacket or *fufaika*, her husband's long johns and all three of her skirts. She had taken her thick patched-leather coat off before she started climbing, unable to fasten it over her bulging belly. She'd been afraid one of its tails would catch on a rung and she'd fall. Now, shaking with cold, she regretted that decision.

Suddenly, she felt a cramp. Clamping her mouth shut so as not to alarm Olga, her younger sister, waiting above her, she balled a fist and looked at her nails to ward off bad luck. It wasn't time yet. It was only the end of the seventh month. When she had been pregnant with Dunia, she had to work the potato fields until the day she delivered the child. Back in those times nobody had believed there was a war brewing. People had been more interested in digging up potatoes than bombings in Warsaw. She had her daughter in the evening, stayed in bed the next day, and then it was back to work with the toddler wrapped up tightly and sleeping in the grass just next to the forest. Katarzyna had to finish her chores before the Red Army or the Germans rolled through the borderland. That's how she was: brave, proud and hard-working. At least that's what people said to Bazyli, the owner of the Załuskie manor house, when he had come to ask for her hand. They weren't wrong. Her cottage was always immaculately clean. There was always dinner on the table, even if there wasn't much in the way of food to make it with. Her numerous siblings were taken care of and the animals were well-tended.

Bazyli Załuski, her husband, was the richest *kulak*, or landed peasant, in the region, as his father and his father's father had been. The entirety of the land between the village of Załuskie and the forest was his. And not a single patch of it was unworked. That meant he didn't really have the time to stay at home. Katarzyna had to take care of the farm by herself. But she didn't complain. She was organised and cheerful, and she often even found the time to sew something for herself or other village women. Even during the last bombings, when everyone was huddled in their root cellars, she would remain at her sewing machine. She just didn't like leaving work unfinished.

It was much like that now too. Another expectant mother might use her pregnancy as an excuse to refuse to help her neighbours. Not Katarzyna, though. She had promised the Mackiewicz family to help them clear the loft of pumpkins, which were to be taken by cart to the root cellar in the forest. In return, her family would get twenty big, healthy gourds. Katarzyna knew it would take them the best part of the day and that, when they returned, they would be hungry. They'd enjoy a real feast: a pumpkin pie and some milk soup with *zacierki*.*

She stood on the ladder's highest rung for a while longer, resting. Her legs were shaking like aspen leaves. For a while she worried about her ability to descend the ladder – but she couldn't think about that now. There was a more pressing matter to attend to first: how to climb all the way up without hurting the baby she was carrying. It was getting agitated and kicking. Katarzyna was certain it would be a boy this time. Her belly was round and hard like the gourds taking up the loft and the baby's little feet sometimes protruded through her thin skin. Dunia, like the good girl she was, had never kicked her like that. Olga held out a helping hand and, with her help and the last of her own strength, Katarzyna hauled herself up and rolled over the edge to the hayloft's floor. She stayed on her back for a long while, stroking her

---

* Small dumplings made of coarsely grated wheat dough.

belly and trying to catch her breath. Her head spun and her heart was pounding.

'I won't let anyone hurt you,' she whispered in Belarusian.

She finally raised her head and appraised the neighbours' riches. She was shocked at just how much work it represented. Suddenly, the price the Mackiewicz family was paying didn't seem that generous. How were they supposed to get all this down? What cart would hold that many pumpkins? Katarzyna straightened her headscarf, which she had knitted herself from sheep's wool, and sat up. Olga was already rolling the pumpkins towards the hole in the middle of the floor. One of them plummeted down and smashed into pieces on the ground. Katarzyna stared at her.

'How are we supposed to get them down with just the two of us?' Olga asked defensively. 'Only you could have promised to do something this stupid!'

Unlike her sister, Olga didn't like to exert herself. She was short and bony. A weakling, their father used to say, laughing. Katarzyna had always been his favourite and Olga had never forgiven her for that. She was clever, though, and quickly learned how to avoid work. She was a real expert at procrastination. Today, she had no excuses – Katarzyna had promised to make her a new shirt. Nevertheless, Olga couldn't help herself. She'd started moaning as soon as the work began.

'It'll take a week if we're to do it one by one. I can't waste that much time.'

'We won't drop them down,' Katarzyna said decisively. She straightened her skirt over her belly. The child seemed to have gone to sleep. She grabbed a roof beam to pull herself up and accidentally pulled down a saddlecloth, revealing a cubby-hole beneath the thatching. Katarzyna peeked inside. The morning light illuminated a cache of machine guns and ammunition belts. Katarzyna froze, unable to even breathe. Who were her neighbours keeping all that for? To their neighbours, they would always declare that they had no interest in politics. For generations they had been living on the farm neighbouring Załuskie. It didn't matter that her family went to an Orthodox church and the Mackiewiczes to a Catholic one. Nobody cared. There was only one God, as far as they were all concerned. They had never had a conspirator in the village before. At least not officially. Katarzyna knew she'd have to talk with her husband about this. The commandos were on the lookout for new weapons all the time. They took bloody revenge on the peasants who helped the new authorities. All guns were seized and their owners killed. For an arsenal like this, their whole village could be burned to the ground. Unless the stash was being kept here for the Polish guerrillas. Katarzyna quickly but carefully covered the weapons as if tucking in a child in bed. As Olga approached, she withdrew to a safe distance, trying to keep a neutral expression. She could breathe again.

Olga went deeper into the loft. She just wanted to get this over with and return to her warm stove. Meanwhile, her sister meandered between the pumpkins. At the other end of the room, propped against the wall, was a trough for feeding cows. It was broken on one side. Katarzyna bent over it and rolled a pumpkin down its length. It was a perfect fit. She gestured to Olga and called for the children, still throwing snowballs outside. They skipped inside and deftly climbed the ladder.

'Slowly, slowly, one at a time,' she laughed. And then she added, in Belarusian: 'Some of you have to stay down there. We're playing marbles, but the marbles are gigantic!'

'Olga, you go down,' she said. 'I'll hand you the trough when you're halfway down. The children will hold it.'

'Why?' Olga asked. She didn't get the plan. 'Why don't we do it normally? Throw them all down one by one? Our boys will be back later and they can help us out.'

'We can manage ourselves,' Katarzyna replied.

'The more a woman does alone, the more her man lazes about,' Olga muttered.

Katarzyna refrained from commenting, though it had to be said, her sister wasn't wrong. Without a word, she passed Olga the trough and told her to move it towards the hole in the floor. She spread her skirt and sat down, cross-legged, then gestured to Olga to stand on the ladder and told the children to roll the pumpkins her way.

'Now prop the trough at an angle. Let's go!' Katarzyna called. She was suddenly excited.

The kids could feel it too. They rolled the pumpkins down in the trough, giggling. The ones on the ground caught the vegetables and placed them along the fence. It was snowing again, so Katarzyna told them to cover the pumpkins with some juniper sprigs. It was all going fabulously. When there were enough yellow and orange pumpkins on the ground to form a giant golden heap under the juniper, she spotted a man behind the fence. He was watching them curiously, but not moving to help. Katarzyna recognised him as Staszek Gałczyński. He had used to help out with the easier jobs on the Załuskis' farm for a bit of money. He was a scrawny man with a squint and none of the girls in the village took him seriously. It wasn't all about that eye of his either. His family had never had any land of their own. Staszek lived with his mother in a hovel by the forest, in the neighbouring village of Zaleszany. People said his father had left his wife before she'd given birth, joined the commandos and never come back. His mother had had a hard time raising him; if not for a merciful Orthodox priest from the nearby town of Kleszczele, they'd have both died of starvation. The man had taken Staszek's mother on as a maid. She didn't care that she had to work for an Orthodox priest and he, in turn, respected her faith. So Staszek grew up and did his *scharwerk** in the Orthodox parsonage. Sometimes he would also repair the roof, sweep the building and even help out with the mass.

But the priest didn't survive the war and neither did the church. The Russians blew it up while retreating, and Staszek and his mother were left without any means of support. Bazyli Załuski took pity on the boy and employed him on the farm, though Staszek hadn't been too keen on hard work in the fields; he only really came to see Olga. But Olga never even noticed him. No farmer, even the richest, impressed her. She dreamed of someone who would take her to the city. When soldiers visited at night, demanding food, she would give them additional portions of meat. If they said the word Warsaw. Later, people said that it was because of Olga that Staszek started collaborating with the Polish guerrillas.

---

* Compulsory physical labour undertaken by local residents for the state. Mainly assisting with public works, building roads, bridges, dykes, etc.

'Call him to help us,' Katarzyna called out to her sister in Belarusian.

Olga looked at her and hissed: 'He's a runt.'

'A man's stronger than a woman even if he's a runt,' Katarzyna replied and gestured to Staszek. Somewhat reluctantly, he started walking in their direction.

'Need a hand?' he asked in Polish.

'*Nye treba*,' Olga scoffed, replying in Belarusian. He could understand her; he had been living in a Belarusian village since he was a child. If you looked into the family trees of Polish families around here, you'd find Belarusian ancestry. Poles and Belarusians had always lived hand in hand here. 'You're a bit late,' she carried on. 'I'm not on the ladder any more, so you won't get a good view of my arse.'

'Olga!' Katarzyna cried and turned to Staszek. 'Please, can you help me? I don't know if I can get down with this fat belly of mine.'

Staszek rolled up his sleeves and bowed gallantly.

'I shall carry you down, madam,' he announced. 'On my own back, if necessary.'

'I'm not a madam! Call me Katyusha,' she called back. 'And wait just a minute more. We still have a few of these pumpkins to roll down.'

Before the sun set, the Mackiewicz family gold was stacked under the juniper. People from neighbouring houses came to see the results of their work. Katarzyna let some of them take a pumpkin for themselves. People were hungry. It wouldn't be right to keep all that food and not share. The children, flushed from their hard work, were throwing snowballs at each other again. Katarzyna couldn't wait to sit down by a hot stove and cook some delicious milk soup. They still had four cows in their shed, and would hide them behind the farm machinery when the guerrillas came. The animals had learned to keep quiet, which had allowed them to survive the last years of the war. Now, the country was free again and the family would bounce back. Katarzyna raised her head to the heavens and made the sign of the cross with three fingers, the Orthodox way.

Staszek had sat down with Olga on a tree stump and they were talking in hushed tones. Katarzyna watched discreetly, not wanting to interrupt them. From the corner of her eye she saw Olga slapping the man. That could only mean he had insulted her in some way. The whole village had always laughed at his clumsy advances. Suddenly, Katarzyna's daughter Dunia ran up to her. She put her ear to Katarzyna's belly and pretended she was knocking.

'Tonia? It's me, Dunia,' she whispered. 'We'll play together very soon. Mummy will get you out and I'll take you to the pear tree to see Grandma Alla. I'll put you in a carriage like a doll. And I'll feed you milk. And if you're a boy, I'll show you the tree house. You'll love it!'

Katarzyna fixed the *ushanka* hat on her daughter's head and leaned over her, rubbing noses with the girl. Dunia's was cold, like a dog's.

'Let me see your hands, little pumpkin,' she said, alarmed. 'Aren't you cold?'

The girl stuck out her hands, still in her mother's too-large mittens.

'I was running the whole time, like you told me. Aren't *you* cold?'

Katarzyna hid her hands deeper into her sleeves. She didn't want her daughter to see the frostbite. The skin on her fingers had grown even more red and cracked than normal and she felt ashamed of it.

She heard the sound of a horse's hooves on the ground and rushed to the road to look. Someone was approaching, riding bareback and pulling two empty carts. Katarzyna recognised them as her brothers'.

'Hide the children, Katyusha!' called her cousin. Mikołaj Nesteruk. He wasn't yet fifteen and still had the facial features of a child; but he was built like a bull and was just as strong. The war had turned him into a man too early. 'Mackiewicz won't be coming for the pumpkins. The pack took him. They took your cart, too.'

'What about Bazyli?' she asked, fearing the worst.

'He went with the rest of the carters,' the boy replied. 'He had a good horse. They sent me away because my mare is limping. I'm riding to warn the people in the village that they need to hide.'

'Who's coming? The Russians?'

He looked at her, hesitating. Then he slowly shook his head.

'One of them had a Soviet uniform on. But I don't think he was Russian. They spoke in Polish. They'll come and ask whose side we're on.'

She sighed with relief. The Russians didn't care who and how they were robbing. They sometimes killed people just for looking at them the wrong way. They raped the women and burned them alive in their homes. The straw roofing caught fire easily and the conflagration soon spread across whole villages. That's what people said. The village of Załuskie was lucky – it was nestled beside the forest, off the beaten track, and had survived the war practically unscathed. The villagers might know what starvation and poverty were, but at least they were alive.

'Their leader had on a hat with a crowned eagle and a skull-and-bones gorget, and he had a picture of the Virgin Mary in his lapel.'

'Bury! God save us!' Katarzyna cried.

The soldiers of the National Military Union were hostile towards the locals and treated them as collaborators of the new communist authorities. Romuald Rajs, known as 'Bury', nursed a particularly burning hatred for the villagers.

'Hide the children,' Mikołaj repeated. 'Get the Catholic painting out and light a votive candle. And may God have mercy on you.'

Katarzyna immediately gathered the children. She herded them to the road and put one of the younger boys on the cart, telling Dunia to do what her uncle said. Then, she ran as fast as she could over to the other cottages and warned the neighbours. The men grew pale, their eyes wide with terror. The women wailed in fear.

Halfway back to her house, Katarzyna looked round. She hadn't taken her payment in pumpkins for the day's work. Maybe Olga and Staszek would at least grab a few. The sun was setting, but it wasn't dark yet. She realised she couldn't see her sister and her suitor.

'Kola!' She pulled at her cousin's sleeve. 'Where's Olga?'

He looked around.

'She wasn't with you?'

'She was,' Katarzyna replied. 'She was sitting over by the wood-pile with Staszek.'

'Olga?' he asked. 'With that Pole?'

'He may be a Catholic, but he's a good boy. Help me look!'

They searched everywhere on the Mackiewicz family farm. Dunia didn't want to stay with her uncle any more, so Katarzyna hoisted her up in her arms and carried her. It grew dark. If not for the snow, she'd have asked the neighbours for an oil lamp, but they had barricaded themselves into their cottages, and wouldn't want to open up. Katarzyna was exhausted. She popped her head into the barn again, just to be sure she hadn't missed anything.

'Olga!' she called. 'Staszek!'

Suddenly, she heard a muffled voice from the haystack. 'Sister, help!' Olga stumbled out, clothes dishevelled, and ran towards Katarzyna. Her breasts were bare and her hair was a mess. Katarzyna covered her daughter's eyes. Staszek appeared behind Olga. He was putting on his jacket and buttoning up his trousers.

'I didn't hurt her!' he rasped.

'He would have if you hadn't turned up! Bastard!' Olga cried and hid behind her sister. 'I'm cursed now! Dishonoured.'

Olga tried to pull her towards the door, but Katarzyna stepped forward instead, closer to Staszek. Without a word, she spat in his face. Dunia stared at her mother, gripping her hand tightly. At that moment, the door opened and Mikołaj barged in. When Olga started crying again, he gave her his coat and, without warning, swung his whip at Staszek, crying, 'I'll kill you, you dog!'

Staszek cowered. When he lifted his head again, his face had two cuts across it. Blood was streaming into his eyes.

'Leave him alone,' Katarzyna said.

Mikołaj would do no such thing.

'Good boy, the Pole,' he jeered, shooting daggers at Katarzyna, as if she had been to blame for this. 'I'll fuck up the little *lakh** here and now!'

He kept swearing and striking the boy with the whip. He didn't even stop when Dunia grabbed his arm, and she nearly got hit with the tip of the thick lash for her efforts. Katarzyna took the hit instead. She bent over in pain.

---

* A term historically used by Eastern European people to refer to Poles. Depending on context, it can be derogatory (as it is here).

'God will punish him,' she told her daughter, hiding her hand in the pocket of her coat so that Dunia couldn't see the blood. The cold helped a bit with the pain, but it still stung.

She withdrew farther away. Dunia sobbed silently, too scared even to cry aloud. Olga, on the other hand, was hysterical and Katarzyna had to haul her away by force. She could still hear the whistle and crack of the whip as they left the barn.

Her legs shook. She was exhausted and worried out of her mind. The child in her belly kicked. She hoped that Mikołaj wouldn't hurt Staszek too much. Staszek might as well just pack up his things and leave now; people wouldn't forgive one of their own such a transgression. He would be lynched. Katarzyna didn't care about that, though. With the utmost difficulty, she scrambled up onto the cart and urged the horse on. There were more pressing matters to attend to now. She wasn't sure if they would survive the coming night, or whether she'd see her husband again. There were just three words buzzing in her head, repeating over and over again: 'Bury is coming.'

The sentry heard a crack from the forest. He reloaded his gun and squinted into the darkness. A shadow flitted between the trees. A moment later, a scared hare skipped across the road. The forest was deathly quiet, but the sentry was certain someone was watching his hideout from the thicket. He whistled twice, like a bird. One of the commanders popped his head out from the hut. He was wearing a *fufaika,* obviously taken from a Belarusian peasant, and a *ushanka* hat in an effort to look inconspicuous. But his steely gaze and worn officer's trousers gave him away as the soldier he was. He was the head of the Extraordinary Special Operations Unit, a legend: Romuald Rajs, better known as Bury. He had grown a bushy moustache in the Belarusian style to try to further blend in.

'Someone's coming,' the sentry reported and pointed with his chin. 'Somewhere over there.'

Bury signalled to his men. Three soldiers in Polish uniforms approached. Their black epaulettes had cloth triangle badges sewn into them. 'Death to the Enemies of the Fatherland' they said. In their lapels, they wore pictures of the Holy Virgin and small medallions bearing a skull-and-bones motif. The commander handed out a single light machine gun and a couple of grenades. 'Take him out.'

The soldiers rushed to fulfil the order. An owl hooted in the distance.

Bury returned to his hut. There was a makeshift table in the centre, cobbled together from some mossy boards. The commanders of the other brigades stood around it, listening to Zygmunt Szendzielarz, *nom de guerre* Łupaszka. They were: Wladyslaw 'Młot' Łukasiuk, Marian 'Mścisław' Pluciński and Kazimierz 'Rekin' Chmielowski – Bury's second-in-command. They were studying a hand-drawn map pinned to the table by a compass and a German-made torch. Łupaszka was holding a pair of callipers, measuring the distance along a railway line. A red dot, resembling a drop of blood, marked a nearby town – Hajnówka. Tomorrow, the last Red Army unit was supposed to head back to the Soviet Union from there. Accompanying the troops, there would be tanks, weapons and food. The guerrillas planned to hijack the train and seize the supplies, killing the soldiers in the process. Hanging anyone who helped them by the neck. It was going to be a massacre. The operation was intended as a show of force of the Polish counter-communist underground. For the guerrillas, the war was far from over. They had weapons, anti-tank cannons and ammunition in droves. Those few Poles living in the local villages cooperated with the commandos, keeping their equipment in barns and pigsties and waiting for a sign to hand over the valuable weapons. The guerrillas predicted that the Russian soldiers would get drunk to celebrate striking out for home. They planned to attack before dawn, with the enemies still asleep and inebriated. Informers had brought news an hour ago – the town had been thrown into disarray by the Soviets' celebrations.

'You won't find an available whore in the whole city,' they had reported.

'We've got a snooper,' Bury said.

Łupaszka's eyes didn't leave the map. Only when he was finished with counting and had noted down the number twenty-seven (too far for a safe retreat on foot if the operation went awry) did he reply: 'I want him alive. Even if it's a *katsap*.'

Bury remained in his place, keeping his mouth shut. Everybody knew how much he hated the Belarusians. Some years before, Bury's brother had been taken to a nearby town, Zanie, to recuperate after sustaining a wound. On 17 September 1939 a group of Belarusian nationalists from the international Soviet army had barged into the field hospital where he lay and murdered each and every Polish patient.

The lands the guerrillas were currently operating in were widely recognised as the least hospitable to Polish armed forces. The workers from Hajnówka, similarly to the local populace, were strong supporters of the communists and openly hostile towards an independent Poland. Since the very first days after the liberation they had fought tooth and nail to strengthen the communist regime. They would openly voice their support for the authorities, proud of their efforts to rebuild the industry in the local towns. They would declare that, having had enough of the unending war, the only things they wanted were bread and work.

The local peasants were officially disinterested in politics, but they did supply the communists with firewood and food. There had been a few incidents, too, that additionally stoked the fire of Bury's hatred. When units of Polish guerrillas had arrived in some villages, the peasants hadn't only refused to hand over their belongings; they had also informed the UB* and the militia of the location of the Poles' hideout. Bury had barely managed to lead his people out in time. For months after that they had hunkered down in various self-constructed hovels, starving and seething with hate. They didn't want to die like dogs, preferring to meet their ends in glorious battle. Bury had sent out a couple of patrols to gather food. Two of them brought in only a measly haul, along with news: *they are calling us 'bands' and are openly hostile. Peasant brats spat at us!* The third patrol hadn't come back at all, and some Poles living nearby told the guerrillas that their colleagues had been attacked by a bunch of peasant communist collaborators, who ran them through with pitchforks. Their weapons were taken. The Polish

---

* *Urząd Bezpieczeństwa* or Department of Security: the secret police, the internal and foreign intelligence agency responsible for monitoring anti-state activities. Played a large part in the Stalinist reign of terror in Poland during the early communist era.

villagers had warned Bury's men about aggressive locals before. People they had to live cheek-by-jowl with.

People said there were secret weapon caches in Belarusian homes, under hay bales or piles of firewood. The villages were supposedly full of communist sympathisers who kept official, secret documents, and worked as informants for the secret police.

The Poles kept telling the guerrillas that they feared the Belarusians. They asked for help, said they weren't feeling safe in their own country. Bury had promised them vengeance for all the wrongs they had suffered. Soon the tables would turn.

'They're well armed, if my patrols keep disappearing,' Bury would try convincing Łupaszka. But the commander had other things on his plate. He had no time to deal with the locals. His order for Bury was for the officer to remain alert. Nobody had been caught red-handed before, so they couldn't exactly do anything. But Bury didn't need proof. The testimony of the local Poles was enough for him. Why would his compatriots lie to him?

'It's enemy territory,' Łupaszka had said then, adding: 'This war isn't over for us yet. One day, there will be a reckoning.'

All members of the unit knew they couldn't count on any support from the Belarusians. This was the birthplace of the Polish Workers' Party and the best recruiting grounds for the Białystok Security Service and militia, as well as other cogs in the state machinery. All the more reason to treat the attack on Hajnówka as a show of strength by the Polish armed underground forces. The soldiers of the 'bands' all considered Orthodox Belarusians to be traitors.

'Change the orders,' Łupaszka said, turning to Bury. 'We'll have a talk first. If he's a *katsap*, he won't leave alive. You have my word.'

Bury clicked his heels and left the hut. He rolled a cigarette, waiting for his men to return, but hadn't finished it when they appeared, leading a man dressed like a peasant. The wretch couldn't be any older than his patrolmen. Barely out of adolescence.

'He says he's Polish.'

Bury gave a little laugh. He flicked the cigarette away.

'There are no *russkies* here. When you strip them naked and chain them to a forge furnace, they're suddenly all Polish. Say a prayer,' he ordered.

'Our Father, who art in heaven, hallowed be thy name, thy king-dom come, Thy will be done,' Staszek Gałczyński started to whisper frantically. 'Hail Mary, Full of Grace, The Lord is with thee.'

'Cross yourself.'

The man, scared witless, made the sign of the cross with a shak-ing hand. Full hand. The Orthodox always did it with only three fingers. That wasn't proof enough, though. Bury had seen a lot. The locals were smart and they had quickly learned that the guer-rillas would treat them better if they pretended to be Catholics. By now, most of them knew a few Polish prayers. With a single rapid pull, Bury ripped the man's shirt from his chest. He had a necklace with a Catholic cross round his neck.

'Father fought in Rekin's brigade. He died in battle back in forty-four. For the Fatherland,' whimpered the prisoner, saluting awkwardly.

Bury looked him up and down.

'I thought you were a *katsap*,' he said, grabbing Staszek by the chin. 'We nearly blasted your brains out.'

'Captain, sir, I bring news. You keep guns and bullets at my neighbour's house. She told me where to find you. I looked for you for hours.'

Łupaszka emerged from his shack. His personal guard trailed after him, a few steps behind. He aimed a loaded rifle at the vil-lager. Recognising the commander, Staszek blanched and fell to his knees, as if seeing God Almighty himself.

'Please, don't kill me, Major!'

Bury looked down at the man with disgust. He lifted him by the collar. 'What news do you have? Talk. We don't have all night.'

Staszek straightened up, but he wasn't able to keep his head from lolling. Bury loosened his grip a little and Staszek fell back to the ground. One of the soldiers poked him with his bayonet and the prisoner jumped back to his feet at once. He stiffened, standing to attention, raised his head with a grimace, and said: 'You're looking for Belarusian saboteurs, sir. There is a village called Załuskie, next to my own, Zaleszany. There are three saboteurs there. They keep weapons in the pigsty. They've been supporting the communists for years. They killed your patrol.' Staszek turned his head to look at Bury. 'The ones you sent for food. I know who did that.'

'Have you seen these weapons?'

Staszek shook his head vigorously. 'People at the Orthodox church were talking about it, before it burned down. I used to fix the roof there,' he said and immediately added: 'But I'm not a *russkie*! You'll find their uniforms, too. They didn't have time to ditch them. They're in a house next to a cottage where there are a lot of pumpkins in the yard.'

Bury grabbed him by the lapels of his coat again. 'Names.'

Staszek's eyes bulged, staring at the hands that held him a few centimetres above the ground.

'I'm on your side,' he said, gathering his courage. He seemed to feel a bit bolder now that his words appeared to have fallen on fertile ground. 'Those three should be punished. And there's only one punishment for traitors. Death.'

Bury let the boy go.

'The men are two brothers,' Staszek went on. 'Stepan and Leonid Pires from Zaleszany, my neighbours, and the oldest of the Nesteruk boys from Załuskie. Mikołaj Nesteruk is especially dangerous.' He touched his bruised face. 'He did this to me. He's stirring up the locals against you. People like him want to give this land up to the Soviets. They say he's the one who killed your soldiers. He's young but everyone's scared of him. I'll show you where he lives. Just let the Catholics live, please. There aren't many of us back there, only five families. We all pray for you and you'll always be welcome at our houses.'

'What do you want for this information?' Bury narrowed his eyes distrustfully, looking at Staszek. This seemed too easy for his liking. They had been looking for the killers for months now. Nobody had known or suspected anything and now, out of the blue, comes this whistle-blower. And today, of all days. One of the most important days for the Fatherland. That had to be a ruse. 'We have no money,' Bury added.

'We may pay you with a bullet to the head, though,' Rekin cut in.

The boy shrugged. 'Everything I'm telling you is true. Would I risk my life coming here if I didn't hate those *russkies*? I want justice. I want to live here in peace. We only have a little hovel, my mother and I. I also want the church to be rebuilt. Poland should be for Poles.'

Bury patted the boy on the cheek. 'Since you're such a little fighter, you'll come with us. Boys, get Steffie a bit of training,' he said, shoving the new arrival towards the soldiers. 'You like your new name?'

The men all laughed. Staszek hadn't expected that.

'But I have to go back,' he tried. 'I left Mother all alone.'

Bury walked over to him and said coldly: 'It just so happens we need a local guide.'

'Congratulations,' Łupaszka chimed in. 'You've just joined the unit.'

He mounted his horse and turned to Bury. 'This is an important day for Poland. You're in charge. No bravado.'

The scout moved out first and the rest of the unit followed.

'Well, Steffie.' Bury smiled. He took out a flask and allowed Staszek to have a swig of pure spirit. 'You'll show us the whoresons. If they're the ones we're looking for, I'll let you go. You'll live. I believe we have a common interest in punishing those *russkie* pigs.'

He turned to his men and ordered:

'Tie him up.'

Bazyli was chilled to the marrow. When the order came that they were to do *scharwerk,* he had dressed himself in a rush and gone out to get this over with. He took the shorter of his two coats because it was easier to work in, but now he'd give everything for a warm *fufaika.* With a group of other carters, they had spent the night huddled on a pile of lumber that should have already been hauled to and unloaded at the school in Orle. There were thirty of them. Twenty were from his own village and seven from neighbouring settlements. He used to see those from his village in church. The rest, he only knew by sight.

There had been twenty Catholics with them, too, but they had been taken off by Bury's unit. They were the unlucky ones – most of them wouldn't return. Bazyli didn't intend to be a hero. He had his land, his wife and his daughter. Another child on the way, too. He had people to live for.

When he saw a pair of shiny military boots stopping at his feet, he didn't even raise his head. The soldier wore full uniform and carried a rifle. Bazyli kept still until he heard the gun being cocked and saw the muzzle aimed at his face. He jumped to his feet immediately. The soldier didn't have to say a thing. New orders had come – that much was apparent from the man's expression. Bazyli smiled inwardly. Maybe they'll finally be let go.

Bury and his unit had headed out to Hajnówka before dawn. Though there were still some shots to be heard, from the fragments of conversations Bazyli had overheard he guessed that the Poles had been defeated. The Red Army had a train full of ammunition and overwhelming numerical superiority. A wounded soldier had arrived at the camp about half an hour ago and with his dying breath had passed on some dark news, which spread like wildfire. The Security Service had known about the attack before it happened. Civilians from Hajnówka, units of the militia as well as agents of the Service had been conscripted to fight off the assailants. When Bury had arrived, they easily repelled the assault, massacring the Polish forces. Nearly half of Bury's men were dead. The rest were wounded. Only a couple of officers had retreated into the forest, waiting for support, which had come too late.

Bury had ordered immediate retreat. The carters were to head through the forest out to Hajnówka to pick up the wounded. Other carters were secretly happy that the Poles had been defeated. They thought the Soviets would free them soon. But Bazyli had eavesdropped on a conversation between a guard and the wounded soldier and he knew Bury's unit was not being chased. It looked like nobody cared any more. For now, he refrained from sharing the news with the other men, instead waiting for a moment of distraction so he could flee. The situation wasn't getting any better, though. Bury and his unit were marching from village to village, burning everything in their wake, free to do as they pleased. No trace of any militia or the army. For them, the civilians, that only meant one thing – death.

'You know this forest?' the uniformed man asked Bazyli.

The farmer stared at the face of the child dressed up as a soldier, wondering how long the boy would last on the frontlines. He should be at school, chasing girls, dancing at parties. He was too young for soldiering. Too delicate. And now, also too scared of being caught by the enemy. That the unit would be caught eventually was a certainty. As soon as the Security

Service operatives found their 'band', they'd hang them for all to see, from trees if need be. Even if the Poles managed to escape from the forest, they'd soon be court-martialled. He felt pity for the boy. He nodded.

'You'll go first,' the soldier barked. 'They'll be at the weeping willow in a few minutes. On the crossroads. Know that place?'

Bazyli kept staring at the soldier from under the brim of his frosty hat. He didn't react.

'Don't you understand Polish, filthy *katsap*?' The boy's face creased in fury, and he smashed the butt of his rifle into Bazyli's face.

The man didn't even register surprise and didn't dodge the hit. He was hungry and sleepy. And now, he could also feel blood in his mouth. He spat out a couple of teeth and rolled onto his back. That only made the soldier more eager. He kicked Bazyli with his heavy army boots, desperately trying to mask his own fear. Bazyli managed to get up, and took the next hit without losing his balance. The other carters observed this apathetically. None came to his rescue. None of them wanted to share Bazyli's fate.

'I know where it is,' said Staszek, stepping to the front of the group. Bazyli glanced at the Pole with gratitude, wiping away the blood trickling down his chin. 'May I?'

'We're moving out in three minutes.'

The soldier cut Staszek's bonds, pointed him to the seat next to the driver's, and left in a hurry. When the creaking of the snow under his boots had died away, Bazyli spat out another tooth in a wad of bloody phlegm. He eyed the other carters. They seemed resigned to dying. None of them even tried to incite the others to rise up against their oppressors. Someone handed Bazyli a piece of chewing tobacco. Everyone was hungry. None of them had expected to have to spend another day doing *scharwerk*. One man, Janek Korcz, pulled out a bottle of moonshine and passed it around. When it reached Bazyli, he took a long swig, feeling the alcohol burn his mouth, and swallowed. He patted his trusty old horse tenderly, straightened her wool saddlecloth and grabbed the reins. Staszek was already sitting on the bench, head nestled in the collar of his worn jacket.

They drove down a narrow forest road. The rest followed them. Fifty carts in all. Most were empty, saving space for Bury's retreating soldiers. The last one bore the dead messenger. The young guards-man had wanted to bury him in the forest at first, but then changed his mind, fearing court martial. Bury enforced strict discipline among his men. His unit was famous for instituting draconian pun-ishment for any kind of insubordination. The commander would lash his soldiers or make them go through exhausting training.

'Boy!' Bazyli patted Staszek on the back, but the young man only waved him away. The carter leaned over and asked in a whisper: 'Why did they take you? You don't have a cart or a horse. You're not a *russkie* either.'

Staszek muttered something by way of response but Bazyli didn't catch it. For a while, they drove in silence; then, suddenly, Staszek turned to Bazyli, pulling a silver cross from under his shirt. 'If they ask you, tell them you're Catholic.'

''I'm a Pole. You know that. Only Orthodox,' Bazyli replied. 'When they wanted to move us to Belarus, I refused. This is my home. My land. How could I ever reject that?'

'You'll die, then,' Staszek sighed and turned away. 'Heed my words.'

Aleksander Krajnow, the secretary of the Polish Workers' Party in Bielsk Podlaski, got off the train at Zaleszany and headed to the station building with a sprightly gait. Usually, when he visited town to attend secret meetings of Belarusian conspirators, the railway workers would lend him a bicycle. If he caught a tractor passing by, he'd hitch a ride to see Marek Frankowski, the head of Zanie village, who also worked as the *poviat** chief. Krajnow had been a tailor before the war, and despite not having sewn even a single shirt since the liberation, he always kept a package of unfinished trousers for his cover story. When the authorities stopped him for inspections, he would show them the clothes, presenting the tack-ing with pride and grumbling about the prices these days, the lack of proper labour with all the people moving in to Hajnówka to the lumber mill, and having to import thread all the way from Warsaw. This worked like a charm. Always. It never took him more than a couple of minutes to get rid of nosy officers.

---

* Regional government unit, equivalent to a county or district.

His wife always told him that his trick was as plain as a pikestaff and he'd get arrested eventually, but Aleksander stuck to his story.

His cause was righteous, but he knew he should keep acting carefully. Especially taking into account that beneath the package of unfinished trousers he was smuggling propaganda leaflets for the Free Belarus movement. In the beginning, the local villagers wanted nothing to do with any kind of politics. They would tell him the only thing that mattered was their land and the fruits it bore. The land fed them, whereas politics only brought war. And idle talk had never fed anyone. That, Krajnow thought, was a lie. He participated in party meetings, both local and general, made speeches on various events in the region and various rallies. And since he had left his trade and taken up politics, his pantry was brimming with meat. He was better off even than in the days when he used to spend whole nights sewing, neglecting his family.

He sighed heavily, remembering how much work they'd had to do with Frankowski to talk the local community into attending their events at the town club. They had finally come round, sensing profit and growing more eager, only when the local farmers' wives' associations kicked off and the Peasants' Self-Help Cooperative started giving out loans. There were more women than men at the meetings, as there was singing, colour magazines and recipe exchanges. A week previously, Krajnow had even brought them a washing machine. It didn't work, but that wasn't an issue, or the point; the simple act of bringing in something as technically advanced as that had brought round everyone to his cause. He knew the women would now do everything in their power to make their husbands join the party and electrify their villages.

Krajnow kept striding. He had some serious business to talk about with Frankowski.

The lumber mill in Hajnówka needed more people. The last strike had been pacified, but only just, and the workers were growing more bold by the day. They needed peasants, who would consider a move to the city social advancement and would do anything to achieve it. Krajnow knew this from his own experience. Even more so when they came from large families and couldn't count on inheriting any land. Usually, only the eldest children would take over the estate; the rest were destined to be farmhands in their own homes, often turning to alcohol (usually distilled in the backyard barn) and chasing around after women. The party, on the other hand, provided a place to stay and a stable wage.

Krajnow intended to convince young villagers to leave their homes and support their families by earning proper money in the city. He really believed everything would change for the better with the coming of the People's Republic of Poland. He had driven a Chaika with a dignitary from Hajnówka once, and had been promised that if he kept up the good work, he'd soon earn his own chrome-wheeled limousine. His only problem was the unions. The labourers from Hajnówka had recently established one, inviting other dissatisfied workers to join, and as many as eighty per cent of the local workmen had signed up already. Krajnow's order from his superiors was to swap the bunch of entitled ingrates with landless peasants, who wouldn't even think of rebelling against their benevolent communist comrades.

The bike was rusty and squeaked with each rotation of its wheels. Its narrow tyres slid on the icy road. Krajnow reached the outskirts of the village of Zanie sweaty and exhausted. He got off the bike and started walking, pushing the clunky contraption along. The houses around him looked abandoned, as if the village had been decimated by plague.

All the blinds were shut. Some farmers had also clearly hidden their animals. The silence, broken only by the odd bark from a solitary dog, was unsettling. Reaching the centre of the village, Krajnow saw a woman and a child in a window in one of the houses. She seemed to be gesticulating to him, but he couldn't make out the meaning of her frantic movements. He walked closer, but the woman retreated and drew the curtains. He left his bike propped against a fence and continued walking.

He was getting hungry. Maybe Frankowski's wife would cook him hot soup, as she usually did. He was still thinking about the coming meal when he spotted a group of people in the distance. A few steps further and he stopped abruptly. He had lost his appetite.

There was a unit of armed soldiers on the other side of the road. Carts were standing in a line alongside the village buildings. Wary drivers turned their heads, eyeing the newcomer impassively. One of them, his face bruised and battered all over, warned him away with a gesture. Krajnow spun on his heel, jumped behind a pile of firewood and hunkered down. It turned out to be a great vantage point.

It seemed that there was some kind of secret meeting taking place in the culture and education club building. Surprising. And worrisome. He hadn't been informed of anything of the sort. A while later, the group of villagers entered the building, which had been cordoned off by the soldiers. Only a couple of uniformed men remained outside. A few steps away, a group of children were throwing snowballs. One of them hit a soldier on the back and the man turned, aiming his rifle at the youngster, and said something that instantly made the children rush away screaming. Krajnow hadn't heard what had been said, but he knew this was serious. Something really bad was going to happen here. Still hunched over, he crept behind a shack, heading towards the carters. They looked chilled to the marrow, standing apathetically beside their vehicles. None of them wanted to talk to him.

'What's happening here?' Krajnow tugged at a burly man, the one with the bruised face. He thought he recognised the man and, when the other spoke, Krajnow knew for sure; it was Bazyli Załuski, the chief of the neighbouring village of Załuskie. Bazyli had chased Krajnow away some time ago for spreading communist propaganda, saying his people wanted nothing to do with politics and would rather live and raise their children in peace than die as communist heroes.

'They're looking for Frankowski, comrade Krajnow.' Bazyli recognised the secretary at once. 'They say someone from this village told the Security Service that Bury was planning to attack Hajnówka. They say a member of the Communist Party lives somewhere around here.'

'Someone local?' Krajnów swallowed loudly, glancing around. 'Have they found him?'

Bazyli shook his head' 'People say it's a lie and nobody has any interest in politics here. But the soldiers keep repeating that there's some kind of central party bureau here. And that there's an informer among us. Bury wants the people to deliver him the conspirators. Otherwise, he'll punish the whole village. Help us, comrade. You're an important man, aren't you?'

'Don't tell them you saw me,' Krajnow hissed, and went on in a hushed voice, moving away at the same time: 'I'll notify the authorities.'

While he could be seen, he tried walking in a confident manner, back straight, but as soon as he passed the last carter, he dropped his package and ran.

'Hey! You lost something!' one of the carters called out. He picked up the package, spilling hundreds of propaganda leaflets. A few drifted down the road with the wind. One of the soldiers noticed and started walking towards the carter.

Krajnow didn't listen or turn back. He grabbed his bike and rode off as fast as he could.

When he reached the train station an hour later, the sky was already ablaze with fire. The village was burning. It didn't take much imagination to deduce what had happened.

Reclining in his seat on the train, Krajnow turned his head away from the view and leafed through a party bulletin. But he wasn't reading; he was composing a report in his mind. Later that day, the station manager telegraphed it to the Security Service office in Hajnówka. The orders came immediately. Do not take action. The authorities know about everything. The situation is under control.

Back at home, Krajnow sighed with relief. 'I had a lot of luck today,' he said to his wife. The room was pleasantly warm. The stove was on. 'I'm hungry as a hog.'

A while later, a bowl of steaming-hot mushroom *borscht* was standing on the table. The soup owed its slightly sour taste to a few drops of apple vinegar, home-made by his wife. That was a strictly local delicacy. You wouldn't get this kind of soup anywhere else.

'Any news on Marek?' his wife asked. 'Are the kids well?'

'Yes, yes.' He nodded, slurping his soup. 'Same old, same old.'

The fire was consuming the roof of Załuski's house. The wind stoked the flames and soon the neighbouring cottages were ablaze too. Within three hours, the richest village in the region was lost to the fiery conflagration. The sky looked like an enormous orange wall. This year's Candlemas would go down in history as one of the most tragic events ever experienced by the local populace.

Soldiers bearing rifles aimed at the entrances stood guard in front of each and every house inhabited by the Orthodox villagers. Their orders were to shoot on sight anyone trying to escape the fire. Earlier, they had been given matches and had used flares and flamethrowers to set fire to the houses. The flames didn't touch the cottages of the Poles, though. Bury had ordered his men to keep away from those. The Poles were to live. The Belarusians would die and be left to rot.

Katarzyna had told Olga and Dunia to stay under the bed. She wrapped herself in her thickest blanket and observed the fire consuming the shutters. If she had crawled under the bed with her family, she would have never got out. Her belly was too big. Half of her face was buried, but she didn't feel any pain. Only fear.

It was unbearably hot inside. Smoke filled the whole room. Out of breath, Katarzyna headed to the pantry and broke the small window just below the ceiling. She climbed up on the milk churn and pulled all the slivers of glass out of the frame, preparing an escape route. She pulled her half-conscious sister and daughter from under the bed and ordered them to jump through the window.

Olga rushed towards it first but, after several attempts at squeezing herself through, she had to withdraw.

'I don't want to die like that,' she wailed.

'Pray,' Katarzyna ordered. 'Aloud.'

'That won't help!' Olga collapsed to the floor, resigned, and howled like an animal. 'They're killing us!'

'God will have mercy, if you believe. *Otche nash. Vyeruyu. Izhe hyeruvimy,**' she intoned in Belarusian.

'I don't believe,' Olga moaned. She grew silent, falling into a stupor.

Katarzyna didn't have the time or the strength to try to motivate her sister any more. Instead she picked up her daughter and lifted her up to the window. Dunia slipped through easily, but then she stopped halfway through and turned to her mother, a silent question in her eyes.

---

* This is the 'Cherubic Hymn', part of Eastern Orthodox liturgy.

'Jump!' Katarzyna barked harshly, but immediately added in a softer voice: 'It isn't that high. You can do it.'

The girl landed softly in the snow. Katarzyna clambered up and stuck her head through the small hole.

'You did well, dear.' She smiled. Then she pointed to the forest. 'Now run, Dunia. Run as fast as you can.'

'What about you?' The girl's lower lip started to tremble. 'I'm scared to go alone.'

'I'll catch you at the weeping willow,' Katarzyna replied. She did her best to keep herself from crying. She couldn't show weakness now, in front of her daughter. 'Hide in the shack. If you meet anyone, speak Polish. *Not* Belarusian. Do you understand?'

'Mummy!' the girl cried and threw herself at the wall, trying to climb back inside. Her small hands pawed at the wooden planks, her booted legs slipping with each attempt to find a foothold. 'I want to stay with you!'

'Dunia!' Katarzyna shouted and wagged a finger at her daughter. 'Daddy will be angry if you don't do as I say. Now run and hide in the forest. Now! Go!'

The girl was still hesitating. She wiped the snot from under her nose with her coat sleeve. Weeping, she picked up her hat from the ground. 'But . . . I want to stay with you.'

Katarzyna felt tears rolling down her cheeks. She couldn't stop herself from crying any more. When she spoke, her voice broke.

'I'm here, Dunia, my dear,' she said. 'I'll always be with you. Remember. I'll always be your guardian angel. I won't let anyone hurt you. Now go, little pumpkin, run.' She let out a sad little laugh, masking her despair, then added, not believing a word she was saying: 'We'll meet at the shack in a while. I'll come and find you and I won't leave you ever again. I promise.'

The girl seemed to believe her. She started to run, stumbling over snowdrifts, getting up and running again. Then, a gunshot. Katarzyna froze. She leaned out of the window. Just around the corner of the house, she could see a young soldier. He stood with his legs apart, a cigarette in his mouth, aiming at her daughter like a huntsman eyeing a doe. A few other uniformed men were standing right behind him, cheering him on.

'Run, Dunia!' Katarzyna called at the top of her lungs in Belarusian and immediately doubled up in a fit of coughing. The pantry was filling with smoke. Her voice caught in her throat. 'I love you,' she croaked, silently. She crossed herself and started to pray, not taking her eyes from her daughter for even a moment. Please, God, don't let them hurt her. Saint Anne, mother of the Virgin Mary. Have mercy on our souls.

Another shot. Katarzyna closed her eyes. They were streaming with tears now. Her face contorted in a grimace of anguish. 'Take me instead,' she pleaded. 'Save her.'

She opened her eyes again. The soldier was thrashing in the snow, on fire, like a living torch. The other men were trying to put the flames out, but couldn't. The rifle lay at the soldier's feet, its magazine cracked open like a flower in full bloom. It must have happened at the second shot. Wailing with pain, the soldier drew his last breath. Dunia, safe and sound, disappeared in the thicket.

'*Slava Hospodu*,'* Katarzyna whispered. 'For ever and ever. Amen.'

Once she was certain that none of the soldiers were going after her daughter, she turned to look at her sister. Olga huddled on the floor, half-conscious and dazed by the smoke.

'Get up!' Katarzyna shook her and stuck a large votive candle in her hand. She picked up a Catholic painting, depicting the Holy Virgin, covered in cobwebs and dust. It had been left behind by one of the Polish milkmaids her family had employed before the war, when they still had an entire herd of cattle. They had kept it just in case. 'Speak Polish only,' she told her sister. 'When we get out, turn left and head to the Mackiewicz house. They'll hide you. I'll keep the soldiers occupied. They won't shoot a pregnant woman, will they?'

The two women left through the front door, bumping straight into Bury's men. Olga made herself scarce, just like her sister had told her. The soldier standing guard at the door was too confused to react. He focused on the pregnant woman lugging a Catholic painting.

'Belarusian?' He ripped the Holy Virgin from Katarzyna's hands, and started studying it.

'I'm Polish, sir,' Katarzyna said, blushing. She had never been any good at lying. 'Ask Mrs Mackiewicz. She's Catholic too.'

---

* 'Praise the Lord.'

She started reciting the traditional Candlemas prayer. The soldier, visibly unsettled, gazed at her bulging belly. Finally, he let her go. She quickly joined the other survivors, clustered at the fence. She dropped her head, eyeing the line of bodies splayed on the ground in unnatural poses, most of them lying face-down. The backs of their heads were universally shattered. By bullets, stones, or wooden staves, she didn't know. One of them was lying face-up and she recognised him. Janek Karpiuk, a man her age. Once, they had attended the same school. They used to dance at village festivals until the break of dawn. They would have made a pretty couple, people used to say. She had nearly married him. His head must have been caved in only moments ago; his eyes were still open. There was also a gaping wound in his stomach and thick blood was still flowing from it. It bubbled, making a gurgling noise, and quickly soaked into the snow. Katarzyna stifled a scream. He was still alive and conscious. His hands were twitching, his eyes trailing after her, but he couldn't speak. And she couldn't help. Couldn't even walk the few steps dividing them to hold his hand in those last moments of his life.

'God save us,' she whispered to herself, raising her eyes to the sky. 'And save Dunia. Don't let her get hurt. *Spasi i sokhrani*,'* she whimpered.

Bury's men were looking for gun stashes. They interrogated the captives one by one. Katarzyna felt nauseous. The lives of her people were in her hands. It was as simple as turning in her neighbours. But when her turn came, she couldn't rat on them. She just shook her head. Stealing a glance back, she noticed the Mackiewicz house, a Catholic house, was still untouched by the fire. The pumpkins she had taken from the loft earlier were still piled up under the juniper branches. They weren't even chipped.

A while later a soldier holding a woman in a vice-like grip stumbled into Katarzyna. His face twisted in a furious grimace.

'Let me go, you oaf!' the woman cried.

It was Beata Szymańska, the daughter of old man Mackiewicz, the owner of all those pumpkins. Her son had played with Dunia at their house as recently as two days ago. They had known each

---

* 'Save us and protect us.'

other for years. Katarzyna was the older of the two, and theoretically part of a more affluent social group. At least before the war. She remembered sewing a wedding dress for Beata and not taking any payment for it. In return, Beata had often helped her with Dunia, having been unable to have children herself for a long time. On one occasion the Mackiewicz family had been without meat and Katarzyna had asked her husband to give them some of their pork ribs left over from the winter. She had never asked for a favour in return. Now, she smiled at Beata hopefully.

'Is she Polish?' the soldier barked at Beata, pointing at Katarzyna.

'That's what she told you?' The woman let out a croaking laugh.

'You're a *katsap!*' The soldier stepped towards Katarzyna, raising a hand to hit her, but then stopped, unsure. He squinted, bringing his bayonet up to her chin.

Katarzyna raised her head haughtily. 'This is my land. This is Poland and I was born here.'

He sized her up. 'Your land, filthy *russkie* pig? *This* land, you say?' he asked, pointing a finger at the ground. 'You'll be buried in it, in that case. Right now.'

A couple more soldiers approached them. One of them stepped out of the line, pulling a crumpled piece of paper from his pocket. *This has to be the leader,* thought Katarzyna. Maybe it's Romuald Rajs himself. He had epaulettes and officer's markings on the lapel of his uniform. Deep-set eyes and a pronounced jawline made him seem even more imposing. Suddenly, at the back of the group of men, she spotted Staszek Gałczyński. Dressed as a civilian, but he had to be part of the unit; they seemed friendly towards him. Katarzyna felt renewed hope. She fixed Staszek with her gaze, trying to catch his eye, but he pretended not to see and didn't speak even a word in her favour.

'Rekin,' she heard another soldier say. He was taller, with a goat-like beard. 'Leave her alone. She's expecting.'

The unit was herding a group of men. Captives. They all wore *ushankas*. One of them had on only his underwear. His hands were tied. So were his legs. He could walk, but only barely, his steps short and uneven. The soldier escorting the man hit him between the shoulder blades with the butt of his rifle. The prisoner's face was a bloody mess. From that distance, Katarzyna couldn't identify him, but she knew it wasn't her husband. He was hunched over and submissive. Her Bazyli would have walked proudly.

In a solemn voice, the man the others called Rekin read out a sentence from the crumpled piece of paper, then shot the man in the back of the head. He repeated this six more times with the other captives. Katarzyna prayed silently and stared at the forest, where her daughter had run. Some of the men who fell to the ground at her feet died with an expression of disbelief on their faces. The ones still moving were struck in the heads with staves or stones by the lower-ranking soldiers. Some were shot a second time, in the stomach, but those were a minority. The Poles didn't want to waste bullets on Orthodox peasants.

'She's a *katsap*,' said the soldier that had been guarding Katarzyna's house. 'She lied.'

'She's a *russkie*,' Beata chimed in. 'And her sister's hiding under the juniper in my yard. Over there!' She pointed to the neighbouring house. Olga emerged from the pumpkin pile and started running. Katarzyna couldn't believe it. What was Beata doing? She looked her in the eyes, feeling nothing but hate. The child inside her was strangely calm. It had probably died from all that smoke, she thought. God had already taken it. Suddenly, the only thing she could feel was calmness. She was ready to die herself.

'Let her go,' Bury said. 'We have work to do. Let's go.'

Suddenly, a snowball flew through the night, hitting the second-in-command in the back. Someone giggled. A child. Everyone froze. Katarzyna noticed two boys, hiding behind the fence of Beata's house.

'Stop it right away!' the woman shouted. Bury sent her a glare. 'Forgive them, sirs. They're only children. We're Catholic!'

'Mum!' A call from back down the road.

A child was running their way. Another snowball. Another giggle. A soldier raised his rifle. Katarzyna noticed it first. She lunged towards the child. After a few steps she knew it wasn't Dunia, but Beata's son. But it was too late. She was in the line of fire.

The shot came without warning. Katarzyna clutched at her belly and sank to the ground. She rolled onto her back before she hit it. Wisps of smoke in the sky. It wasn't cold any more. The snow was only pleasantly cool on the burnt skin of her face and hands. Soft and comfortable.

The boy didn't manage to reach her. He collapsed, hit with another bullet. Out of the corner of her eye, Katarzyna glimpsed the gun in Staszek's hand. He seemed surprised. One of the soldiers immediately took the weapon from him. The rest burst out laughing and patted Staszek on the back.

Dunia, Katarzyna thought before she died, *I'll be your guardian angel. Remember.*

Shots from a machine gun broke the lull. The people lined up at the fence fell one by one. Having killed a pregnant woman and a child, the soldiers had to eliminate all witnesses.

Dunia could hear the shots but they were muffled, as if coming from behind a window. She was huddled in a shack in a pine copse, terrified. She wanted to go to her mother, but she couldn't move. Instead, she waited for Katarzyna to come to her, tell her everything would be all right, give her a motherly hug. She wept quietly, afraid to make too much noise, until finally she fell asleep. When dawn broke Dunia woke, chilled to the marrow, and walked back home.

Their yard was strewn with bodies. People were tossing them into carts, and then arranging them in a line along the fence. Dunia found her mother. Katarzyna's body was lying some distance from the others. Her face was turned towards the sky, her lips slightly parted in something approaching a smile. The girl lay down next to her mother, snuggling against the cold corpse.

Golden-orange pumpkins, neatly stacked under the juniper in the yard, reflected the rays of the sun.

Staszek stood with the others at the weeping willow, waiting for his turn. The carters were being shot, one at a time. The procedure was simple and efficient. Bury read out the judgment and the soldiers did the dirty work, bashing in the villagers' heads with stones, staves, or rifle butts. They didn't squander ammunition on civilians. When it was Bazyli's turn, Bury had to intervene. The man fought like a lion, getting up after each hit, lunging at his oppressors and nearly poking a soldier's eye out. Eventually, he was shot in the gut, then finished off with a blow to the head.

Staszek didn't believe he was going to be saved. Not even God Almighty could help him now, he thought. The village of Puchały Stare could be seen in the distance. Its inhabitants must have heard the shots and the cries of the dying. They could possibly even see the unit at work. None of them even thought of coming to the rescue. Nobody left their homes to watch. An hour ago, Staszek had been one of those tasked with excavating root cellars, where the locals normally kept food through the cold winters, and where the murdered carters would find their final resting place. Now, propped against his shovel, he was standing to the side of the main group and observing the line of men waiting for their death. He wasn't even able to pray for them.

His hands were calloused, seeping pus that instantly froze in disgusting patterns on his skin. He didn't feel any pain. It all felt like a dream. He spread his fingers, turning his palms this way and that. They were no different to the hands he used during Holy Mass to pass the chalice to the priest, who would hand out the sacramental host to the dozens of the faithful. Those hands had the blood of the innocents on them now. The blood of the child he had shot accidentally, out of his mind with fear. He had held a gun for the first time in his life then. He had just pulled the trigger. The boy had doubled over and fallen to the ground. The blood of those Belarusian conspirators Staszek had pointed out to Bury's men, though he had no idea if they actually had ever been informers to the communists. The blood of all those hundreds of people who had died during the unit's terrible rampage across Belarusian villages. It wasn't supposed to play out like that. Staszek had only wanted a bit of vengeance. For the humiliation he had suffered at the hands of Mikołaj Nesteruk. For being disgraced in front of Olga.

Now, Staszek only wanted someone to end this. He knew he wouldn't have the strength to tie his own noose and hang himself. He didn't believe in God any more, much less the Fatherland or 'honour'. What he had seen wasn't heroism in the name of universal values, but instead cruel, atrocious, senseless slaughter of the innocent. That's how he saw it.

There were Catholics, Orthodox and even two Jews in Bury's unit. All of these men had fought for Poland's independence during the war. Then they had fought the communists. They were lucky – they genuinely believed in what they were doing. Death to the enemies of the Fatherland. Poland for Poles. Their sadism found justification in empty slogans such as these. They thought Staszek a coward.

After the execution, the bodies were kicked down into the root cellars like sacks of potatoes. Staszek couldn't watch any more. He squatted down and occupied himself by digging little holes in the ground. One of the carters had dropped a small knife earlier. It was lying on the frozen ground and, looking at it, Staszek felt a pang of remorse. The man hadn't had the time to use the knife. It was still clean, its blade gleaming in the sun. Staszek picked it up and read the Cyrillic letters engraved on the wooden handle: *Hleb nash nasushnyi.** The knife was made to cut bread, not human flesh. Staszek clamped his hand over the handle and carved an Orthodox cross on one of the trees with it. That was when Bury found him. Staszek spun abruptly, standing in front of the carving, and aimed the blade at the commander. It only made the man laugh.

'Here,' he said, handing Staszek a dirty package. 'You'll burn it.'

Staszek lowered the knife and stared at Bury, fully aware that he wouldn't be able to do any harm to him. Surprisingly, he realised he wanted to live. At any cost. Bury's uniform was spattered with tiny droplets of blood. In places, pieces of brain matter and hair were stuck to the fabric. Bury brushed them off like breadcrumbs after a breakfast and straightened his hat, moving the eagle emblem to its correct central position. Someone handed him a wool coat and lit his cigarette for him. Bury puffed out a cloud of smoke and continued: 'You'll never tell anyone what happened here.'

'Yes, sir,' Staszek stammered out automatically, looking around, genuinely surprised that he wouldn't be sharing the carters' fate after all. He wanted to ask why, but didn't get the chance. Bury was talking again. 'This blood was spilled for the Fatherland. You will be forgiven.'

'I will keep silent,' Staszek said.

---

* 'Our daily bread.'

'As you should,' Bury replied. 'We all saw you shoot that child. That wasn't necessary. But each of us has sacrifices like that on our conscience. This is war.'

Some time later, Staszek pointed the unit in the right direction through the forest and looked on as they left. As soon as they'd vanished over the horizon, Staszek lit a fire and unwrapped the large, embroidered handkerchief from around the package. Inside were the personal documents of the murdered carters, which he tossed into the flames. Only one burned away completely. Bazyli Załuski's. The rest, Staszek pulled out at the last minute. They were only seared at the edges. He wrapped them up in the handkerchief again, adding in the Belarusian's knife. Then he set off for home. He felt the bundle burning the skin of his chest, but he didn't stop.

It took him two days to reach his village. He slept in the forest, eating everything short of snow. When he finally got back, he saw that the village had been burned to the ground. He walked to the next one, where people surrounded him and told him what had happened. He recognised Mikołaj Nesteruk in the crowd. The boy averted his eyes.

Staszek told his mother that Bury had released him before capturing the carters. He lied that the commander of the 3rd Vilnian Brigade had remembered his father from the war. She cried, recalling her late husband's heroic actions, but forbade Staszek to repeat the story to anyone.

'It's not something to be proud of nowadays,' she explained.

A week later, Staszek went to a secret Mass for both the Catholic and Orthodox faithful, in remembrance of the civilians killed around Hajnówka. The authorities had organised support for the victims of the fires. As one of the few men who'd managed to survive the pogrom, Staszek earned some pats on the back. The women and children who had also survived, and were in line to inherit the land in the burned-down village, were moved instead to neighbouring settlements. People helped them rebuild. Some, like Staszek, left for the city and found employment in the lumber mill in Hajnówka. Nobody looked for the murdered carters. Nobody talked about them. Staszek, too, tried to forget about the executions.

That same summer, the hovel he had lived in with his mother collapsed and disappeared under a blanket of grass. It was ankle high when Aniela Bondaruk, daughter of the principal of the school in Hajnówka, approached Staszek during a party meeting and whispered that they could go for ice cream together, if he wanted. Staszek said yes. People said the next Sunday was going to be hot. It was. Staszek's short stature and his rheumy eye didn't seem to bother Aniela.

At the end of March a detachment of militia moved out to apprehend Bury's unit. The commander himself, as well as some of his most loyal companions, including his second-in-command, were caught in southern Poland some two years later, in November. By that time, Staszek was already the director of the greenwood processing plant in the lumber mill. He had seventy subordinates. Workers from local villages he had employed personally. They were all grateful and brought him bottles of vodka each year for his name-day. He would drink alone, after his shift. A few months later, Staszek and Aniela moved to a state-owned flat in one of the worker blocks in Hajnówka. He managed to renovate the apartment before his son was born. The proud parents named the child Piotr. Staszek's father-in-law suggested that the boy take his last name. It was Belarusian, and that was an advantage. Staszek had no objections. A year later, they swapped their hearth for a large tiled stove – a real luxury in those days.

When Piotr went to school, the village of Załuskie was no longer marked on the maps in geography textbooks. The remains of the burned-down houses had been dismantled and used as firewood by the locals, while the surviving inhabitants of the village moved to neighbouring settlements. Of the village of Załuskie, nothing was left but beaten ground.

Hajnówka, 2014

The search party advanced through the forest in a loose line, maintaining a three-metre distance between people. Making their way across the thicket, they combed through the underbrush. Most had high-power torches. Some had brought portable power generators. The woodland clearings were bright as day. Animals, alarmed by the sudden illumination, flitted beneath their feet. A group of drunken wedding guests had only barely made it out alive; they had been nearly trampled by a herd of elk fleeing from the light.

The police had managed to scatter the crowd without causing widespread panic. An emergency response squad had been called from the central station as support for the local force. Additional units had also been mobilised from the neighbouring *poviat*. The search had been joined by firefighters, Scout troops, and all able-bodied wedding guests. The people responsible for the fireworks show lit flares to further illuminate the thick forest. But the girl was nowhere to be found.

People started going home and by dawn, the wedding venue was deserted.

A patrol returning to base found an abandoned blue Fiat Uno on one of the forest roads. The front right window was broken and the passenger seat was speckled with blood. The bride's wedding dress lay crumpled on the floor.

Jah-Jah recognised the car immediately. It was the profiler's. He had let the woman out of the station yesterday with a document allowing her to drive back to her hotel. He kept his mouth shut. A moment later, his walkie-talkie chimed. A woman had been found tied to a tree a few kilometres away. She was badly bruised, gagged, and had on nothing but her underwear. But she was alive. The police assumed she might have been a witness to the kidnapping.

Jah-Jah ordered the search to continue and rushed to the hospital. Romanowska called as he was nearing the building.

'We have Four-Eyes.'

'You brought him in?'

'Remember the car that disappeared in ninety-nine with Łarysa Szafran?'

'That Belarusian? Bondaruk's first girl?'

'Well, the car's black now. The plates are missing. But the technicians discovered old gunshot holes under the floor mats. The calibre matches.'

'Call Central.'

'I already have. They're sending us a special team.'

Piotr was standing at the window, observing the rising sun, when the housekeeper announced that his mother-in-law had arrived. The freshly married man hadn't slept a wink last night. Fifteen minutes previously, he'd changed into trousers and a yellow sweater. His eyes were ringed with dark circles. This one night made had him look ten years older.

'She'll be back,' Bożena said by way of greeting.

He pointed her to an armchair and she collapsed into it, resigned. Her dress was dirty and crumpled. She had been searching through the forest with the rest of the party and hadn't had time to change. He threw her a zipped canvas jumper emblazoned with the logo of the company, a buzz-saw and a young spruce, of the kind that Piotr's employees wore to work. She put it on and pulled the zipper all the way up to her chin. Though grateful, she couldn't entirely stop shaking. He offered her a thick, chequered blanket, which she wrapped around herself.

'Tea?'

She shook her head. 'She'll come back or I'll make her. My boys'll find her,' she assured him.

He sat down and nodded at the housekeeper. She brought a steaming kettle and a plate of jam. Piotr added a couple of spoonfuls of the preserve to a cup of tea and stirred. 'That wasn't the arrangement.'

She dropped her head.

'I know it's not your fault.' He pushed the cup across the table towards her. 'You must be freezing. Drink. It'll help.'

She sent him a grateful look, but he averted his eyes, staring out of the window.

'You can keep your land,' he said. 'And the money. But everything else in our agreement is void.'

Bożena took a sip of the tea. It burned her lips.

'I'll find her. People will forget.'

'*I* won't,' he growled. 'She doesn't have to live with me if that is her wish. She could have told me. I didn't make her marry me.'

He spoke calmly but surely, his words uttered with absolute authority. Bożena didn't dare reply.

'Announce that I am offering a reward,' he went on. 'Fifty thousand if she's brought to me alive. You'll pay it out of the money I gave you. If she's back by tomorrow morning, we'll have a talk. She will be able to save face. You'll keep the rest of the money.' He paused and poured himself a cup of tea. She noticed his hands were shaking. He didn't sweeten his tea, just took a swig immediately and continued: 'She's not worth a thing to me dead.'

Bożena shot him a wary glance.

'Dead?'

'I only asked for loyalty. I didn't need her faithfulness. She could eat the cake and have the cake. But she has made her choice. Now, I'm a laughing stock for the whole town and we cannot remain married.'

Bożena put her cup down. Her lip was trembling, and her eyes brimmed with tears. 'What did you do to her?'

'You can go now,' he said, drily. 'We have a long day ahead of us.'

When she had left, he stretched out on the sofa and pulled the chequered blanket over himself, head included. Only his bare feet stuck out. He wasn't about to go to sleep. He was thinking. For another hour, he remained perfectly still, eyes wide open. Then he got up and went to the garage. His three brand new cars were all parked in their spaces. The fourth space, further down the spacious garage, with its own gate, was empty. Right in the middle of it, there was a sticky splatter. He crouched down, rubbed the substance between his fingers and sniffed. Motor oil or maybe brake fluid. He swept the drive with his eyes. The driver must have taken off fast. There were clear tyre marks on the ground. Bondaruk walked to the door. The padlock had been sawn through. He took it and hid it in his pocket, replacing it with a new one. Then, he went back to the house, fired the housekeeper – paying her a hefty severance fee – and drove to the sawmill. There would be no one around at this hour, but he needed to work. On his way, he made a few calls, one being to a notary.

'I'd like to change my last will,' he said when the notary called him back. 'I'll need a few hours of your time. Come alone. No witnesses. Bring all your seals.'

Then he went into the woodshed and chopped wood until, completely drained, he sank down.

The cast was done, but the doctors told her to remain in bed. They had X-rayed her and tended to the bruises on her head. It wasn't as bad as she had feared. Somebody had brought her belongings. The suitcase was open, but the laptop was in one piece. Nobody had turned it on. She was changing into her own clothes when a nurse knocked on the door of her room.

'I need to check your blood pressure.'

'I'm good,' Sasza snarled, trying to pull on her jeans. She couldn't button them up with one hand. The woman walked over and helped her.

'There should be a comb in my suitcase. Could you get it for me?'

The nurse rummaged through Sasza's belongings.

'Maybe in the washbag,' Sasza suggested.

'You can't leave the hospital yet,' the nurse said. 'You have a concussion. We have to keep you for a few days.'

Sasza ignored her, running her good hand through her tangled hair. Finally the nurse found the comb. It was wrapped in a colourful hairband with a little, crystal unicorn figurine attached to it. Sasza felt her throat constrict. She had to call her daughter right away.

'The police want to question you. They'll be here any minute,' the nurse said as she combed Sasza's hair.

'Can you tie it in a ponytail?' Sasza asked.

The nurse did so, but then suddenly Sasza felt faint. She flopped to the bed. The nurse put a hand to her brow. 'You're burning up. I'll get you something to help with that.'

She folded back the duvet and straightened the sheet.

'Lie back down, please,' she ordered.

Sasza was too exhausted to take her clothes off again, so she collapsed on the bed fully dressed and closed her eyes. It felt like just a moment, but when she opened them again it was getting dark. A short-haired woman was standing in the doorway. Sasza recognised her as the policeman's companion from the wedding. A uniformed officer was standing a step behind her. The same one Frankowski's son had sent for a blanket back at the station.

'Commissioner Krystyna Romanowska,' the woman introduced herself. 'How are you feeling?'

'I've felt better,' Sasza groaned. She didn't have the strength to play the badass any more.

'I can only imagine. Unfortunately, we're short on time. We need to talk.'

Sasza nodded. She understood the gravity of the situation. She propped herself on her good arm, ready for the questions.

'I couldn't see his face,' she said. 'And I've already told the policeman in the ambulance what happened. Hope I've been helpful.'

'He told me everything,' Romanowska replied and pointed to the young officer next to her. 'This is senior officer Karol Supryczyński, who's also our sketch artist. Orders from Central. You know the drill. I know you won't recognise the man, but we need something on paper.'

Sasza placed her good hand to her forehead, covering her eyes too. She had been asking for trouble from the beginning. And trouble never turns down an invitation. She should have been at the shooting range in Gdańsk now, instead, she'd slept through the whole day. She hadn't had a chance to tell Ghost she wasn't coming. He'd think she'd backed out like a coward. She was furious with herself.

'Slim, five foot nine, give or take. Black balaclava. Folk outfit. Biker gloves.' She was repeating her earlier statement.

The sketch artist showed her various composite images, one after another. She couldn't decide. It could have been anyone under that balaclava. She described the man's eyes in great detail, though she knew it wouldn't be of much use to the investigators.

'Bright eyes, green I think, if he wasn't wearing contacts,' she said. 'White-blond eyelashes. I don't think they were dyed. I didn't see the other attacker,' she went on. 'I was assaulted from the back. He must have been a lot weaker and shorter than me, though – he missed with the first blow and only smacked me in the temple when I bent over. Actually, I think it might have been a woman. Wearing high heels.'

'A woman?' Romanowska jotted it down in her notebook. 'Anything more specific?'

'Rather petite.' Sasza tapped at her cast. 'Something stuck into my hand. Could have been a high heel. And the person wasn't too heavy. That's what I thought at the time.'

'How about the car?'

'Black Mercedes. An old model, but in good condition.'

'"The four-eyed kind,"' the officer read from the report. 'You're sure?'

Sasza nodded.

'It had pretty distinctive headlights. He had them on while he was chasing after the girl. I didn't get the licence-plate number though.'

'We've secured the vehicle,' Romanowska said. 'It had a broken oil sump. That's why it died.'

Romanowska dismissed the sketch artist but didn't leave the room herself. Sasza kept her eyes fixed on the commissioner, who asked her, 'What brings you to our town?'

Sasza hesitated. 'Private matters,' she said, finally. 'I was supposed to be back in Gdańsk by now, celebrating my return to the force. But it looks like I'm knee-deep in shit. Again.'

Romanowska kept a poker face. She shut the notebook and glanced at her watch. 'Do you think the assailant might be older? As in, past sixty at least.'

'I doubt it.' Sasza shook her head. 'He was strong, large. I felt his biceps through his shirt. Muscular. I don't think he was more than thirty, forty at the most. But I can't be sure, I suppose. He did have a balaclava on.' She lay back on the bed again. She was still exhausted. 'I don't think it was a jealous husband, if that's what you're thinking. I saw Bondaruk, or whatever that guy's called, up close. We sat at the same table for an hour at the Forest Palace.'

Romanowska knitted her brows.

'A chance meeting,' Sasza explained. 'Saturday, around three in the afternoon. I was finishing my meal when he came in for a drink. We spoke for a while. I thought he seemed depressed. Didn't look the happy groom, anyway. More like he was getting ready for a funeral. But he did invite me to the wedding. I turned him down. I had no idea I'd end up here then. I didn't even know who he was.'

'And it couldn't have been him?' The commissioner was doing a poor job of masking her excitement.

'I didn't say that,' Sasza replied quickly. 'I might pick him out in an identity parade. Or if he agrees to a visit to the crime scene. You know, my head is spinning. I might not remember everything now. I'll let you know if I come up with something.'

'We'll have to question you again, I'm afraid.'

'I know.' Sasza grew sullen.

'We're waiting for a team from Central precinct. Until then, we're all alone in this. Now tell me about the girl.'

'I'm not completely sure it was a woman,' Sasza said. 'It could have been a smallish man. Shorter than me. When that thing stuck into my palm, I thought it was a high heel. But I'm not that sure. Maybe I assumed that because I'm a woman. I'll think about it some more.'

'I mean Iwona Bejnar. Bondaruk's wife. Was she cooperating with the kidnapper? Was she only pretending?'

'Absolutely not,' Sasza replied immediately. 'She was horrified. Hysterical.'

'Do you have a gun licence?'

'Not with me.' Sasza dropped her eyes. 'I don't have any papers with me. But you should know that by now. Have you found Danka from the psychiatric hospital'?'

'We're working on it,' the commissioner said. She wasn't easily distracted. 'Your gun hasn't been registered as yours. Do you know that?'

'Have you found it?'

Romanowska nodded. 'The fingerprints have been wiped off. Someone was very thorough. They left it in your glove compartment.'

Sasza let her head hang and came clean: 'I got the Beretta from a colleague before I left Tricity. It was all above board. I'll call him right away. I know this looks weird, but please believe me, I'll get you the papers for everything.'

'Make sure you do that. When people from Central show up, we'll have to have all the formalities sorted out. Until that time, I'm giving you the benefit of the doubt. I don't know how long that'll last though.' She smiled.

Sasza could feel the executioner's blade hanging over her neck. If it came out that she had been using an unregistered gun, her dream of getting back into the force was as good as dead. Then Romanowska stubbed out the measly ray of hope she still had.

'We've also found ammunition in your bag. Fits the Beretta. Pretty little thing, by the way. There are fingerprints on the bullets.'

Sasza said nothing. She was already in trouble and she knew that, but it seemed that was just the tip of the iceberg.

'They're mine,' she confirmed. 'You don't have to have them tested.'

She waited for more. She no longer cared. But Romanowska stood up, ready to leave. Surprising. A pretty rushed questioning, as far as they went. The commissioner must have just been sounding her out.

'That'll be all for now. Thank you.'

'I can go home?'

'They won't want you to leave the hospital tonight. But if you do, we have your personal details. Chief inspector Duchnowski has confirmed all documents today. I believe you. He assured us he'll be here tomorrow morning at the latest to take you home.'

'You called him? He knows everything?'

Romanowska confirmed with a nod, then smiled softly. 'Well, not everything. Only the gun and the documents. He asked me for this as a favour.'

She checked outside to make sure the corridor was empty, then placed a grey envelope on the table. When it landed on the metal, they both heard the quiet clinking sound of the bullets.

'It would be best if you kept them hidden for a while. I haven't destroyed the papers. For now.'

Romanowska was an ally, Sasza realised.'

'I've also swept it under the carpet that you were driving without a licence,' the commissioner said. 'And, of course, I didn't start an investigation into the Beretta, though I really should have, considering it was fired three times.'

'Three?' Sasza echoed. 'I only loaded two bullets. I couldn't find any more in my bag.'

'Are you sure?'

'Positive.'

The commissioner mulled over this new information. Sasza broke the silence.

'Why did they leave the gun?'

'I've been thinking the same thing,' Romanowska admitted. 'We'll see what the inspection of the car tells us. Your vehicle has to stay with us for now. The technicians are working on it as we speak. If the guys from Central have any doubts, I'll try to deal with them.'

'What about the gun? Three shots. How will that look in the report?'

'The ballistics expert checked it out. We already have a preliminary report,' the commissioner said. 'We've written that the crime weapon hasn't yet been found. I have to trust that your intentions are good.'

'I'm in your debt.'

Romanowska nodded and glanced at her watch. 'I guess so. But if the investigation takes a different turn, I have dirt on you.' She said it with a playful laugh, but Sasza sensed a darker undertone to the joke. She let it pass without comment. She felt immense relief, but also a little anxiety.

Romanowska continued: 'I'm sorry you had to go through this, but at the same time, I'm really glad you're our witness.'

'Can't say I share your optimism,' Sasza muttered. She shot Romanowska an enquiring look. The woman had gone back to her formal demeanour. 'Why are you helping me?'

The commissioner looked taken aback Clearly she hadn't been ready for that question. She wanted to say they needed Sasza's professional help with a profile, but then she thought better of it. Coming clean this early wouldn't help.

'Everything will become clear in time,' she replied. 'I'm sorry your visit here ended like this.'

So, she was weaseling out of having to answer. Sasza attempted a smile. Her lip stung.

'I'm sorry too. I'm at your disposal though,' she said. 'Free of charge.'

Romanowska took a long look at Supryczyński's drawing and clicked her tongue with dissatisfaction. Nobody would recognise the perpetrator from this. They had another phantom kidnapper on their hands. Just like years before, when she had been a newbie on the force.

'I'll keep that in mind,' she said nonchalantly. 'Take care of yourself. I can see trouble follows you.'

'You can say that again.'

The commissioner jotted something down in her notebook, tore out a page and placed it on Sasza's bedside table before leaving.

'Łukasz Polak, Saczko's patient you were looking for, lives at this address.' She stopped in the doorway. 'And the telephone number is my private mobile. Next time you find yourself in a pickle, call me.'

'Pickle?'

'If you're in trouble, better you have another woman at your back. It'll spare us the paperwork. The shredder at our office can only work so fast.'

Sasza glanced at the piece of paper. 18/4 Trzeciego Maja Street. She had passed that street a couple times. She felt the stress dissipating, grabbed her phone and dialled her mum.

'Granny can't talk right now, but you can call later,' came Karolina's voice on the voicemail.

She fell back onto her pillow, crumpling the priceless piece of paper in her hand and tossing it into the drawer. A few minutes later, she was asleep.

The ground was freshly trampled. Islands of black soil poked out from the lush grass every couple of feet. Vandals had dug up the symbolic grave again, although at least this time they hadn't stolen the cross. Instead it had been tossed into the bushes. It was missing its Orthodox cross-beam. Dunia Orzechowska grabbed a large pebble and, supporting herself on the stave she had made for herself, hammered it back into place until it stopped wobbling. Then she knelt, panting heavily. She prayed for the victims of the war buried under the mound. She recited an *akathist* and bowed, touching her forehead to the ground three times. Having pushed herself up to her feet with some difficulty, she brushed off her ragged clothes. Her bones ached, but it wasn't because of the weather. They ached every day lately.

Her house was a few kilometres away. Going through the forest would be quicker, and she wasn't afraid she'd get lost. She had been raised here and knew every inch of this land like the back of her hand. The problem was, it hadn't rained for the last month, and she'd probably get stuck crossing the sandy forest dunes. She settled on the longer walk along the main road. Hopefully someone would give her a lift; if nobody stopped, she'd reach home well after sunset.

As soon as she reached the road, a brand new lorry with the logo of the meat processing plant pulled up. She withdrew to the side and covered her face with her headscarf. A man stepped out of the car. Mikołaj Nesteruk. She knew he was around ten years her senior, but he didn't look it; lately, Dunia had lost a lot of weight and it had aged her, while he in turn seemed to have got plumper and more youthful. He walked over and took her by the hand.

'Come, Dunia. Ride with me,' he said and opened the passenger door. There was a woman in the driver's seat. Dunia recognised her at once. It was Bożena Bejnar. She nodded to the elderly lady, saying nothing.

'I have to feed the chickens,' Dunia said. ''I've left the dogs alone, too.'

'We'll give you a lift.'

'I wouldn't want to get your seats all dirty,' she replied and continued along the road.

Mikołaj followed her, silently, staying a step behind. Bożena swung the car door shut, leaving the engine running, and walked towards them. From a distance, they must have looked like the smallest imaginable funeral procession. Suddenly, Dunia stopped and turned round, facing Nesteruk.

'What does she want?'

He produced a silk ribbon. Bożena stayed at a safe distance, but could clearly hear every word.

'Her daughter has disappeared. Your boy kidnapped her,' Nesteruk said.

That piqued Dunia's interest at last.

'Her daughter?' She pointed a crooked finger at Bożena. 'She was her daughter?'

Mikołaj nodded.

'I promised I'd ask you.' He paused. 'Where did Jurek hide her?'

'I haven't seen my son since winter. He came home and stayed for a week when they let him out of jail. Sometimes he would come in the night and leave his bike in the woodshed. I'd hear the sound of its engine. But he never entered the house. When I woke up, he would already be gone. I think he's ashamed of having been to jail. As if I don't know how life can be.' She spoke in Belarusian.

Nesteruk fixed his eyes on her, waiting. She didn't continue.

'Maybe you could pray for her?'

'She's not a believer,' Dunia spat, but took the ribbon from his hand and begun muttering an Old Church Slavonic prayer. It sounded like a magical spell. She broke off after a while, shaking her head.

'What does it mean?' Nesteruk asked.

'I didn't feel anything. It's been like that recently. I'm losing my touch.' She seemed to be joking, but her face remained utterly impassive.

Nesteruk touched her arm and gently pulled her to him. She resisted the hug but stood still, and they stood there for a while, backs bent and heads bowed – an elderly couple knowing their time could come at any point.

'How did you find me, Uncle?'

'Today is the anniversary of their death, Dunia, my dear.' He shrugged. 'I didn't need to look far. You come here every year.'

'Someone tore out the cross again,' she complained.

'Bah! The dead don't care!' He waved his hand dismissively. Seeing her expression, he added: 'I'll take care of it.'

'No need now. God will judge them.'

'Can't you help us?' he asked. 'The girl's mother just wants to know if she's all right.'

He passed Dunia a photo of Iwona and a green comb with a broken tooth. There were a few black hairs stuck in it.

'It's all we have left. And the ribbons.'

Dunia eyed the photo for a while. It was from an ID card of Iwona at about, she thought, eighteen. Her hair was long, with a fringe. She stared at the camera intently.

'*Krasavitsa*,'* Dunia complimented the girl's appearance. But then she frowned. She asked: 'What does my son want with her?'

'Don't you know?' Nesteruk seemed perplexed. 'They're saying she ran away from her wedding party with him. People saw them together. Your boy beat up some outsider before he escaped. They must be hiding somewhere.'

Dunia walked a few steps towards the forest and closed her eyes. Nesteruk stayed where he was and gestured for Bożena to return to the car and kill the engine. Dunia started to whisper under her breath. More Orthodox prayers. She didn't stop even when a speeding car zoomed past them, its horn wailing frantically. Suddenly, she fell silent and struck out down the road at a brisk pace. Bożena got out of the car and ran up to Nesteruk.

'What did she say?'

'Not a thing,' he replied sadly. He took off his hat, clutched it to his chest and crossed himself.

Bożena grabbed him by the lapel of his jacket. 'What does that mean!'

She launched herself after the old lady. 'Please! Is she dead?' she called, desperately. Catching up with Dunia, she grabbed her by the shoulder and yanked, nearly toppling the other woman. 'Tell me. Please. Tell me it's not true.'

Nesteruk reached out for Bożena and managed to get her back into the car before going after Dunia again.

'Don't let her return here, Kola,' she said, before he'd had a chance to ask anything. 'She should hide or leave for ever. Tell her if you see her.'

Nesteruk bowed his head, took Dunia's hand in his and placed a tender kiss on it. When he looked at her again his eyes were watery.

Bożena couldn't hear the woman's words, but she understood instantly. A great sob burst out of her throat and she started crying.

'She's lying!' She wailed. 'It can't be true. She can't know that!'

---

* 'A beauty.'

Nesteruk didn't say anything else. Dunia turned round, though, and spoke to Bożena in a cold, steely voice.

'It's your fault,' she hissed. 'You sacrificed her. Let him devour her.'

Her words were like a curse. Bożena stopped crying at once, shocked.

'I . . . I didn't know,' she moaned. 'I only wanted her to never be poor like me.'

Dunia opened one hand. Her skin was surprisingly clean and delicate. In the middle of her palm were the few black hairs from the green comb.

'You don't have faith,' she said. 'You believe in nothing. But your daughter is calm now. Happy. Away from you, at last. But you'll never be calm or happy. I curse you for all the times that child had to suffer because of you. You'll have to bear this burden for the rest of your life.'

She spat on the ground, spun on her heel and walked away. A few dozen metres down the road, she found a birch stake. It was the cross-beam from the mass grave. The vandals had thrown it out of the window of their car. She picked it up and slid it into the canvas bag she wore on her back. She'd burn it with the kidnapped girl's hair and her photo.

'Doman!' Romanowska sprang up from her chair and fell into the arms of a tall, dark-haired man wearing a leather jacket. He was the centre of attention in a group of other officers from the local station.

The commissioner hadn't expected her old friend to be among the group sent from Central. This was a pleasant surprise. 'Chief Inspector Tomasz 'Doman' Domański, a Hajnówka local, had been transferred to Białystok only a couple of years ago. Romanowska had seen him on TV when, working with a profiler from Katowice, he had solved a case involving child murders in Białystok.

He grinned widely and lifted her in a bear hug. For a while, Romanowska thought she could see Jah-Jah stealing a jealous glance at them. That was wildly satisfying. Doman and Jah-Jah had been partners and Jah-Jah owed the other man a debt of gratitude. Doman had caught Jah-Jah taking a bribe but, instead of selling his colleague out to the boss, had kept the news to himself. He had also helped him weasel out of the predicament and massaged the paperwork. He had done it for the sake of Krystyna and Błażej.

'How's Liliana?' Romanowska asked, feeling the ground beneath her feet again.

'She's due in August,' Domański replied, unable to keep the thrill from his voice. 'I've turned into her personal herring and pastry delivery service lately. We've already been through the pickle stage.'

'You must be proud?' Still smiling, she led her friend to her office. Jah-Jah didn't follow them. 'I hope your days of foolish bravado are behind you.'

'I'm a new man. I guess I've grown up. How about you?' he said, winking playfully and pointing to the commissioner's desk. 'That chair's had never had a woman sitting in it before. Congrats!'

Romanowska blushed.

'If you hadn't left, you'd be in charge here now.'

She put the kettle on and poured a couple of spoonfuls of instant coffee into a mug with a logo of the Police Academy in Piła. They were both graduates. She added two generous scoops of sugar to each mug.

'Even if they chose me, I wouldn't have accepted. You know that.' Doman grimaced, then chuckled. 'How's Jah-Jah? Or rather, how's he coping with your new posting?'

'Barely.' Krystyna didn't want to go into the details, but he could read her meaning in her eyes. He knew Jah-Jah too well not to realise that the man was squirming with envy. She added: 'He brought it on himself. They tell you about the Old Man's fuck-up? Jah-Jah was with them. Sober as a nun, thank God. He was supposed to drive the whole bunch home.'

They had known each other since for ever. She couldn't remember how many parties and barbecues they had been to together when Chief Inspector Domański had still been living in town. He was the husband of Romanowska's best friend. For years, he had worked at the local station in Hajnówka; he had never cared for climbing the corporate ladder and the only thing he had ever wanted was to be transferred to a homicide division. Central HQ in Białystok didn't have one, but he got the next best thing – the criminal division. Having your dreams fulfilled is the worst thing that can happen to you, he used to complain, but Romanowska knew he wouldn't change a thing.

Now, Doman went silent, his expression growing serious.

'Tell me about the missing girl.'

Romanowska passed him his coffee and a couple of biscuits on a saucer. She sat down.

'You're the only one they sent?'

'You kidding me?' He frowned, pulling out his mobile and glancing at the screen. 'I have a whole entourage. Fantômas and his lackey will be here soon. Luckily, the prosecutor is okay. Reasonable. We're supposed to use your team. I think they're counting on us getting this mess sorted out quickly. Just like last time.'

'You really are a sight for sore eyes.' The commissioner smiled and went to the cabinet to take out the case files, which she placed on the table in front of the chief inspector. 'I'll be brief, then. The case may look simple, but it's anything but.'

Doman turned his head to look at the door. It was closed. Romanowska walked across the room and slid the latch, just in case.

'We have another head.'

'I've heard,' Doman said, lowering his voice. 'You don't even know how many strings I had to pull so they'd send me.'

'You must have been really keen to see me,' she joked, but deep down she was glad he cared.

'All of them, Krysia. All my contacts. But that's not important now. I'm here. Jah-Jah told me he had a theory about that skull.'

Romanowska let that go without comment. Jah-Jah hadn't told her anything of the sort. She decided to continue. There wasn't much time. She had to brief Doman before the other officers and the prosecutor arrived and, together, they would decide on how much to tell them. When they had found the first skull, Doman was already working at Central. They had given him the case because he was local. Even though the skull had been moved, they still had to treat Harcerska Górka, near Hajnówka, where it had originally been found, as the crime scene. Doman knew the place and, most importantly, the people here, and they knew him. He had ordered the entire forest to be scoured, but the rest of the body had never been found. Nobody had reported anyone missing. The police hadn't managed to reconstruct the pre-mortem appearance of the deceased, either. Based on the bone structure, they concluded that the deceased was a woman nearing thirty, and that the cause of death had been blunt trauma. Neither the police database nor the Itaka foundation's files had been any help. The Jane Doe file had been put with other unsolved cases. They had known a thing or two more, but had kept it out of the report.

'We suspect Bondaruk is the key.'

Doman didn't seem the least bit surprised. Romanowska suspected that Jah-Jah had already brought him up to speed. Jah-Jah was supposed to be having today off – he hadn't slept for nearly two days and his face was swollen and his eyes bloodshot – but he'd been afraid he'd get left out. He wouldn't; Romanowska had intended to give him the case anyway. Under Doman's supervision, Jah-Jah would play nice.

'He's dodged the bullet how many times now? I don't see how we can get him,' Doman muttered.

'I'm not saying he's our suspect, but I'm sure he's at the centre of this mess. We have to pressure him into talking. Jah-Jah's all fired up about it. The first skull was planted on the day he announced his engagement to the missing girl. The second one came the day before the wedding ceremony. Iwona Bejnar went missing a day later. We have a witness to the kidnapping. A woman. The kidnapper spared her. We found her, nearly naked, tied to a tree. He escaped in her car and left it in the forest. He must have found another one, and had help, because the trail ends there. He's just vanished. Just like Łarysa back in the day. What's interesting is a day before all this, Jah-Jah had brought in the woman, the witness, for questioning. She didn't have a driving licence or registration, or any other ID aside from a CBŚ contractor badge. She said her name was Sasza Załuska. A profiler from Gdańsk. I have no idea what she was looking for in our forest and Saczko, the director, couldn't or wouldn't tell us either. If you ask me, something's off about all that.'

Doman looked up. 'You think someone planted her to put us off the scent?'

'The head of the criminal division in Gdańsk verified her identity and vouched for her,' the commissioner replied. 'I don't know the guy, but he's on his way here to get her. He didn't seem too pleased about it, though. The woman has a broken arm and can't drive. And her car is still being analysed. Anyway, she seems clean. She's told us she always works incognito. There's nothing on her in the police database or the experts list. Long story short, she doesn't exist. But she did give Jah-Jah some booklet about profiling. It has the seals from some English university on it and we've verified she works there. As a scientist in the Forensic Psychology Institute under some guy called Abrams. We found publications by her in psychology periodicals. I've checked myself. I think she's some kind of genius criminologist, though she's definitely a bit crazy.'

'I only know one forensic psychologist and I can tell you the guy's also pretty nuts. But he *is* effective,' Doman said, taking out his notebook and jotting things down. He underlined the profiler's name twice and added a question mark after it.

'I'll ask Meyer,' he added. 'If she's good, he'll know her. There are only about a dozen experts in that field in Poland. So if she's a fraud, we'll know.'

'I saw her this morning. She seems all right.' Romanowska pointed to a thin case file. 'You can read her statement. Aside from the broken bone, some bruises and mild hypothermia, she's okay. I told her we might need her.' The commissioner was businesslike now. 'I haven't given recruiting her much thought, but since she's a key witness, I don't think letting her in on the details makes much sense. I've said she can go home as soon as the hospital lets her out – but I also asked the hospital staff to keep her for a bit longer than strictly necessary and the nurses to keep an eye on her and let us know if she looks like she might leave. I want to try to stop her getting into another mess.'

'What do you mean?' Doman asked.

'She's looking for some nutjob from Ciszynia psych hospital. Says it's personal, but the guy killed a couple of people and got away with it. Spent some time on a nice vacation there.'

'No shit.'

'You got that right.' Romanowska nodded. 'Prus caught him in her snare. She used to talk to him every day. Three years! She knows him inside out. So anyway, this profiler has some business with the man, but she won't tell me what exactly.'

Romanowska changed tack. 'Anyway, the girl's family suspects the kidnapping is a cover-up and that Iwona Bejnar simply ran off with her ex-boyfriend. Even the girl's mother defends Bondaruk. She's one of the rednecks from Chemiczna Street.'

'That explains a thing or two.' Doman nodded. 'People down there aren't exactly well off. She sold her daughter. And Bondaruk must have been around a hundred back when I left. Who's the Romeo? I'm starting to understand, I think.'

'Jurek Orzechowski, a petty thief. Nickname Quack. Thirty-six. Fond of drug-dealing and drunk-driving. His mother used to work at the sawmill. Now she lives in the village. People say she's some kind of healer. You know, praying away illnesses, stuff like that. A ghost whisperer. Name's Eudokia Orzechowska, but people call her Dunia. Don't know if you heard about her.'

'I'm not exactly a witcher, if that's what you're asking.'

'Her son was convicted for attempted burglary and theft as well as dealing in stolen property. Unemployed.'

'Must have got into the business after I left,' Doman said. 'But not as good a catch as the old man, eh? The grandad does have a slight advantage in the form of a couple of million quid. The kid has what? A big dick and a shiny smile.'

'The thing is, we can't locate the man,' Romanowska continued. 'He's gone into hiding. The missing girl's mum sent out her sons to try to find him. The three Bison boys from Chemiczna. You know *them*, don't you?'

'Sure I do.' Doman nodded. 'If those guys can't find her, I don't know who can. Definitely not us.' He laughed. 'Unless she's dead and buried.'

'Besides, half the town is looking for her, because Bondaruk is offering a reward.'

'How much is he willing to pay for his beloved wife?'

'Fifty thousand.'

'Not too much. But, he probably bought her for less in the first place.'

'This morning,' Romanowska was saying, 'we found this in Quack's mother's shack.'

She showed him pictures of the shed. There were suitcases in the corner, a stockpile of food and two sleeping bags. Also, fragments of the wedding dress.

'These are their things?'

Romanowska nodded. 'We haven't released this info yet. The shed is secured. I planted a man there just in case Quack wanted to return. He left his motorbike there. It's in working order. We found the helmet next to the building too. The technician is already back. We have fingerprints, hair, even some semen.' She paused. 'If we find the girl, we'll have the whole set. I think the kidnapping really might only be a hoax. The perp was in a balaclava and he had a helper. Pretty audacious. And a whole lot like in the movies. Things like that don't happen around here. The woman from Gdańsk must have thrown a spanner in the works. So, what do you think happened?'

'Fuck knows.' Doman sighed. 'I'd like to talk to her.' He pointed to the picture of Dunia Orzechowska's shed. 'The helmet was found outside, yes?' He tossed one of the pictures onto the desk. 'So maybe the loon from Ciszynia is somehow connected to Bondaruk's girl?'

'I doubt it.' Romanowska shook her head. 'But I gave the profiler the Ciszynia guy's address. We'll keep an eye on her. Discreetly. And about Quack, I have no idea. Looks like they left their stuff in haste, don't you think? Maybe someone spooked him?'

'Or the Bison boys took him and now they're only pretending to be looking for her. Maybe they're counting on Bondaruk raising the reward money.'

'We've left them alone for now, anyway,' the commissioner admitted. 'We only discovered the shed today. It seems probable the two escaped and used the kidnapping as a cover story.'

'So what does the skull have to do with it? How does that connect to the groom?'

Romanowska walked over to the corkboard on the wall and took down the facial reconstruction image prepared by the Medical Academy in Poznań. She flicked it onto the table. Doman nodded. He knew that case. He didn't need an explanation.

'I'm pretty sure it's the same case,' Romanowska said.

'Look, we won't be able to connect the two skulls at this stage. It's too early.' Doman moved the pictures of the heads to a separate pile.

'Oh yes we can,' Romanowska insisted. 'Guess what car the kidnapper drove.'

There was a silence. Finally, Doman's face brightened in a smile. 'No,' he said. 'I don't believe it.'

'You better,' Romanowska said. She placed photos of the car found in the forest in front of him. A black Mercedes E-class, W210, the four-eyed type. 'It's the same that was used to kidnap Łarysa Szafran. The paint job is new, but we found bullet holes on the inside. All things considered, the car is in pretty good condition. Someone must have kept it in a garage all these years.'

'That car was white.'

'Correct.' She nodded. 'As I said, the paint job is new. But the numbers are the same.'

'Repainting that old rust-bucket must have cost more than the car's worth. Doesn't make any sense.'

'It has brand new tyres and a tank full of petrol. A year ago someone fitted it for gas too. We found the papers.'

'Get me the address of the garage. What about the licence plates?'

'The originals. I asked the traffic division to check any fines, tickets, speed camera photos, drivers, all that stuff.'

'Good job.'

'I gave it to Behemoth yesterday. But we could use some help from the main lab. Can you get us someone? They could also check for any old traces. Maybe they'll find something connected to the old case. Łarysa's blood, anything.'

'I doubt that. After all these years?'

'Won't do us any harm.'

'You've got someone willing to double-check old data? Must be a pretty patient guy.'

'He's my son.' She smiled. 'Poor boy doesn't really have a choice. What can you do if you've spent most of your childhood at the station? Besides, he was never good at interrogations. As soon as he's told to question someone, he starts acting like his dad. Only a lot clumsier.'

Doman gave a short laugh. He took the picture of the woman found at Harcerska Górka, then put it back down. He took out a pack of cigarettes. Romanowska reluctantly passed him a lighter.

'So, if I understand correctly,' he puffed out a cloud of smoke, 'Iwona Bejnar is the third wife of Piotr Bondaruk's who's gone missing.'

'First *wife*,' the commissioner corrected him. 'But she's the third woman in an intimate relationship with him to go missing.'

Doman continued, unfazed.

'We have the car that Łarysa, the mother of one of his sons, died in. But we don't have her body.'

'And that's the same car in which Mariola was seen last, before she left for work and vanished,' Romanowska added. 'No body here either.'

'And we have two skulls that need to be identified,' Doman concluded. 'Because our Jane Doe is definitely not Łarysa or Mariola. Is that right?'

Krystyna stood up and tried to open the window, but it was stuck. She returned to her desk and waved the documents around, trying to fan away the smoke.

'You still do that karate thing?'

She shook her head. 'Don't have the time nowadays. But I run twice a day.'

He sized her up. 'It shows.'

'Thanks. I know it sounds crazy,' she started with renewed vigour. 'But maybe someone's trying to help us out here? Everything seems to lead to Four-Eyes.'

'Who's questioned him? I can't find the report.'

Romanowska kept her stare fixed on Doman. She said nothing for a while, then finally answered, lowering her voice.

'I was thinking you'd do it,' she said. 'Or at least someone from your team. An outsider. I have to keep the mayor satisfied. My hands are tied. I haven't told anyone anything yet. The search lasted until morning.'

'You're scared.'

'Not at all,' she said, too quickly. They both knew she wanted to keep her job. 'But I'd prefer it if you took it on yourselves. He'd have more respect. You know how it is.'

She pointed to the picture of the girl, then walked back to the window and tried again to prise it open.

'I think we need to send the skull for another analysis,' she said. 'I called Warsaw, but the man's so snowed under, the fastest he can get to it is three years from now. Maybe you could do something to get it done faster? We have new info. It's looking a lot more serious now.'

Doman pushed himself up.

'I'll spin him some yarn.' He put out his cigarette and walked over to the window, opening it without any difficulty. 'Let me see that skull.'

Since her husband's death, Eugenia Rączka had started to take care of herself again.

For years she had been focusing on one thing only – his illness. Nursing him, calling the doctors, attending to his needs at night, checking if he hadn't choked to death. Over time, Kazimierz stopped recognising her. He lost the ability to discern fantasy from reality and sometimes accused her of cheating, murder, or stealing his things. He would call the police or chatlines without her knowledge, and she'd only find out when the exorbitant bills arrived.

She knew her husband's tiring behaviour was an effect of the unimaginable pain he had been in since the beginning of his battle with cancer. But there were moments when it was just too much and Eugenia quietly prayed for him to finally die. In fact she would beg God to take them both, for she simply didn't have the strength to endure.

Finally, a few years ago, when Justyna, their only daughter, was visiting for the holidays, Eugenia's prayers were heard. Kazimierz kicked his wife out of his room, greeted his daughter with unexpected tenderness, ate a portion of pierogi that Eugenia had blended to a pulp, and died quietly in his sleep that same night. Eugenia felt sad and empty, of course, but above all she was immensely relieved. Before Kazik's funeral, she confessed to everything to a priest, who didn't chastise her as she had thought he would. Instead, he asked her when had been the last time she'd thought about herself. Eugenia realised she hadn't really thought about herself since Justyna was born.

Becoming a mother had flipped her priorities. Tending to her family took up the whole day. Those rare moments when she could have done something for herself, Eugenia usually spent tending to other people's kids – those who would come to the youth centre for music lessons, or to her house for private tutoring, or the ones for whom she had set up an amateur theatre and ran accordion classes. Eugenia also arranged concerts for schoolchildren. Her students later tended to find work as accompanists in local bands and folk choirs.

Eugenia had realised now that while she had always been there for everyone, nobody had ever cared for her in return. And the only time that could really be called 'hers' were the moments when she took a couple of minutes to smoke a cigarette in the bathroom. Two or three times a day, in total secrecy, so that her husband, who hated smoking, didn't get a whiff of it.

After the funeral, the first thing she did was go to the local kiosk and buy herself two packs of Marlboro reds. She smoked a couple on her way home, and didn't care that her students might see her.

Eugenia was well known in town. She was one of Hajnówka's honorary citizens, though she hadn't been born or raised here. She had been born in Vilnius into the old Jakubowski family, who sat out the war in a small worker block in the Kolejki district of Hajnówka. After the Red Army liberated the region and life became something like normal, Eugenia graduated from music school in Białystok and then the Higher State School of Music in Warsaw, where she met Kazimierz Rączka. For a few years, Kazik and Eugenia played in the orchestra together. Then they married. When Eugenia became pregnant, Kazik decided they'd move to Hajnówka, where life was slower, and where it was easier to make a living than in the bombed-out ruin of Warsaw.

Justyna was born a frail and anaemic child and was frequently ill. No doctor knew how to treat her. Once when she was unwell, a neighbour told Eugenia that she knew a *szeptunka*, or whisperer. The woman cast a charm and sent Eugenia a package of odd items – bitter herbs and poppy seeds – with instructions for how to deploy them. Eugenia was baffled, but complied. Two weeks later, Justyna recovered, and Eugenia was never again sceptical about local beliefs or about the whisperer. She didn't tell Kazimierz about the healer; Eugenia knew he wouldn't have been pleased about his daughter being tended to by this woman, whom he thought of as a local witch. For many years, though, she visited the woman with various, more or less serious issues, and recommended her to her students' families.

When she had first seen Dunia, Eugenia was taken aback. The whisperer was a polite and pretty girl, at least a decade younger than Eugenia herself. The two quickly grew to like each other. Some people were afraid of her, crossing themselves when they saw her and doing everything in their power to avoid her stare for fear of accidentally getting cursed. Dunia would laugh at this, though she did remember each and every affront. She had never been vengeful, but she always refused to help non-believers. And sometimes people without faith did come to her, asking for a prayer when all the usual methods had failed. Eugenia would stubbornly defend her friend, telling people that she wasn't a witch, but rather a good-natured healer and guide. Dunia was highly educated. She had graduated from the School of Rural Economy in wood technology, but she hadn't gone to work at the lumber mill, instead choosing a career as a midwife at the local hospital. After hours she would prepare herbal mixtures and recite healing prayers. Tradition dictated that she help the ill for free, but people believed that being indebted to someone like Dunia could end badly and would pay for her services with what they had: milk, meat, colourful beads. So Dunia's lifestyle and finances were always comfortable.

Over time, Dunia lost all interest in matters material, refusing even those forms of payment for her services and growing more and more destitute, slowly turning into the folk-tale witch some people had always imagined her to be. She wore rags and walked with a staff, inspiring fear and dread among younger people. Eugenia, though, knew that life hadn't been kind to Dunia and she always defended her friend.

Justyna left for France as soon as she graduated from university, and didn't visit her parents for some time, but sent them a photo after three years away. The photo showed Justyna and a thin German girl, who Justyna told them was called Ines. It was apparent that the two women were more than friends. Justyna, snuggling against Ines's reedy arms, stared at the camera, silently challenging the world. The eyes of both expressed the elation and contentedness of lovers.

Kazimierz had never accepted that his only daughter was a lesbian, though he liked to say that it could have been worse – Justyna might have fallen in love with a 'Negro'. As well as being a racist, he was an anti-Semite, and had never treated homosexuality as anything other than a mental disorder. He also sent monthly payments to Polish nationalist organisations and subscribed to the extreme right-wing magazine *Szczerbiec*. Eugenia didn't understand her daughter's attraction to women and, for a very long time, chided herself for raising Justyna the wrong way, but finally she accepted it. Once a week, never telling her husband, she went to the post office and ordered an international telephone call. She listened to her daughter talk about her life, and felt happy that Justyna had found love. She would always end the conversation with a blessing, saying that she hadn't lost Justyna, instead gaining another daughter.

Ines came to Hajnówka to Kazimierz's funeral. She and Justyna looked like sisters. They came with a little boy they had adopted, Sambor. He had dark brown eyes and skin the colour of walnut. The boy spent the holiday with Eugenia while Justyna and her wife travelled across Poland. The boy would come to visit his grandmother twice a year from then on. The fact that people would talk about his skin colour for the rest of the year amused Eugenia.

Now, she picked up a fly-swatter and smacked a bug with one quick motion. She looked out of the window. The neighbours were keeping rubbish on the balcony again instead of throwing it out in the public bin.

She lived in a block in a residential development dubbed the 'Millennium', one of the oldest multi-storey complexes in town, which had been built right after the war. The authorities had been planning the demolition of the old buildings, but the cost of moving the residents was at the moment too high. Finally, the town hall settled on renovating the blocks instead and, for a time, they had been the city's calling card. All pipes and roofing had been replaced and central heating had been installed as a substitute for the old stoves that had been standard as recently as the 1980s. Public utility buildings were separated from residential flats, and shops and other outlets now lined the streets. Years ago, that had been truly revolutionary; before the renovation, the only commercial district in town had been on Buczka Street, whose name was later changed to Priest Wierobiej Street. But despite the authorities' good intentions, the area didn't become prestigious. Quite the opposite. The residential blocks now housed the lowest classes, the worst rabble, as Kazik liked to call their unemployed neighbours. They left their rubbish to rot in the corridors and stored their discarded household appliances and various bits and bobs in the stairwells. They didn't shut their doors, brewed illegal moonshine, and had the extra-annoying habit of slaughtering pigs in the basement in the spring. As if they still lived in a village.

Hajnówka had been established as a small settlement next to the lumber yard and had developed in stages as people arrived from around the country in search of a good job. It was the global centre of absolutely nothing. Even its name meant 'new forest' (from the Belarusian *haj,* which meant forest, and *nowka,* meaning new), and was bestowed only in order to mark the godforsaken place on the maps so the railway companies knew where to go to pick up wood and strip the natural forest of its riches.

There had never been a town architect involved, so no cohesive urban structure. And though Hajnówka was nearly a hundred years old now, and had proudly borne its status as a city for nearly fifty, it looked as if nothing would ever change when it came to aesthetics. Since the eighties, and the great boom in the town's development accompanied by the unchecked destruction of the surrounding woodland, the place had stagnated. Today, the forest was a mere shadow of its former glory, and strict laws limited logging. After the border of the national park was moved to the outskirts of Hajnówka, most locals started importing lumber from Ukraine. You had to bribe the regional forestry officials if you wanted to win a bid for even a single square metre of woodland.

In 1939, the town had numbered close to 18,000 inhabitants; today, though official documents listed 27,000, everybody knew that the actual number was closer to half of that. The citizens of Hajnówka were mostly elderly people whose children and grandchildren had gone to work somewhere else. It was a town of old people nostalgic about the 'good old times' of the communist regime when Hajnówka had been – just like them – in its prime. These people were utterly resistant to the efforts of the more socialist parties, various businessmen and cultural figures. The authorities did whatever they could to keep the citizens happy, including indulging the smaller political parties who were completely outnumbered and disregarded in other regions of the country. Candidates from the two main political groups, PIS and PO, stood no chances here; since the war, this had been the bastion of post-communist and peasant parties. Hajnówka still had a cemetery for the unknown soldiers of the Red Army and hardly any of the names of streets and squares had been changed since the sixties, which was a point of contention between the few representatives of the opposition and the local authorities. The city was called Red Hajnówka for a reason.

Around a year ago, Eugenia's block had been repainted pink, blue and willow-green. The new look had been designed by a well known local artist – Ryszard Wróblewski. In return, he received from the city one of the old lumber mill buildings, where he set up his workshop. Sometimes the artist would hold exhibitions there, but Eugenia had only been once. The sculptures depicting victims of the war were too much for her. They reminded her of her own experiences.

Besides, the sculptor was a Belarusian activist. He vocally protested against a plaque in memory of the local soldiers who had served in the armed anti-communist underground under the command of Zygmunt Szendzielarz, alias 'Łupaszka'. Two days after the artist's outburst the city was awash with the news that his photo and address had been uploaded to the website of the Blood and Honour far-right group. Nationalists blacklisted him as someone to be 'pacified'. That same night, the police were called to the sculptor's studio, where they foiled an attempted break-in. But the case was quickly closed. To have something to show the media, the police arrested the headteacher of the local Belarusian high school, who had taken bribes and defrauded large sums of money. Belarusian activists immediately latched on to the arrest and used it as a pretext to organise a large-scale protest, complaining to the Ministry of Internal Affairs that the Belarusian minority was being oppressed.

Eugenia sat in the window of her flat, framed by the pink walls of the building, and observed the street.

The fifty-metre flat she was left with after her husband's death was simply too large for her needs; and she was abroad for the best part of the year. So she rented out the spare room. A long hall allowed both her and her tenant some privacy. She preferred renting the apartment to men. She had 'raised' three such wards to date. Her tenants were invariably people in difficult situations. Eugenia took pride in helping those men get back on their own two feet. A helping hand, some motivational speeches, and some rudimentary material support was all it took. But now the additional room had stood empty for nearly a year. People didn't come to Hajnówka for work like they used to. In fact, even those already living there had difficulty finding employment. So, when a young lad recommended by a doctor from the Ciszynia private psychiatric hospital had arrived looking for a place to stay, Eugenia had been surprised.

Łukasz had come with close to nothing. He only had a single travel bag, half empty. A washbag, a couple of old black hoodies. On his head he wore a thick beanie, though the day was hot, and under his arm he held an empty stretcher for a painting and a tripod for a camera. Later, she also saw he had a metal suitcase containing a professional camera and some painting supplies. He was clean, polite and handsome. Taking a thick wad of money out of a crumpled envelope, he paid for six months up front. In his first weeks he didn't leave the apartment often. His room smelled of turpentine. One time, he went out in a hurry, leaving his door open, and Eugenia saw his painting. It was a bit strange, but the man had undeniable talent. She went to her bookcase and started to leaf through her various photo albums, trying to find some reference to her tenant's art. At first, she thought it resembled Bosch. Maybe that had been his inspiration, or maybe he was copying one of the master's works. Eugenia knew that the local painters often worked like that, though they were reluctant to admit it. She had a copy of a painting of Saint Catherine that she had bought for a lot of money years before. Its artist preferred to remain anonymous.

When Łukasz had finished his painting, he propped it against the wall, facing in so that its front couldn't be seen, and thoroughly cleaned his room. Eugenia never again smelled turpentine in there. He took up photography instead. Each day at different times he would watch the old lumber mill. Though he had his equipment set up the whole time, he only took a picture on the last day. During one of his sessions, he was noticed by old man Schabowski, the first photographer in town. There had been a time when Schabowski had run a successful studio, and most locals aged sixty or over had his photos in their albums – family meetings, baptisms, first communions, weddings and funerals. Nowadays, people had cameras in their phones and largely only came for pictures for ID cards and driving licences.

With time, though, photography became popular again and Schabowski (although he had officially retired long ago he was still working) found himself with more commissions. He'd tried talking his son into taking over the family business, but to his father's regret, the man had no talent and even less patience for the business or the art. When the old photographer noticed Łukasz setting up his antique Sinar for the umpteenth time, he felt emotional and, believing the young man would revitalise his old studio, offered the outsider a job. He also lent him his digital Canon camera and a couple of basic lenses.

So, for the last month, Łukasz had been employed snapping photos at weddings and first communions, and old man Schabowski displayed all his works in the window of the studio. They were a sight to behold. Eugenia knew next to nothing about photography, but she was as proud of her tenant as if he was one of her students at the music centre.

Since he'd moved in, she didn't feel as lonely. They would talk over dinner. Łukasz listened to her stories and asked her questions, seemingly fascinated by her life. It flattered her. A couple of times he brought a girl. She seemed rather young to be his lover, and when Eugenia carefully asked about her, he told her the girl's name was Danka and she was a friend from the hospital. There was nothing between them besides a shared passion for photography. The next day he showed Eugenia the photos he had taken of Danka. She was left speechless at first, and then asked if he would take a photo of her too.

Now, she sat on the windowsill and looked for Łukasz. She hadn't seen him for a while. People nodded to her from the street and she nodded back. She knew all of them, at least by sight. Eugenia didn't try to engage anyone in small talk, as she knew they were all racing home for lunch. The traffic would get lighter around three in the afternoon. Then, around six, the younger generations would come out. Dating couples, throngs of schoolchildren. And later, around nine, adolescents would start congregating at the bus stops, drinking beers and smoking pot. Hajnówka had been living at its own, steady pace for years. As she was thinking about the passage of time, Eugenia noticed a red-haired woman with a cast on her arm walking along the street. An outsider.

The woman wore a chequered shirt with one sleeve cut off to accommodate the cast, blue jeans, and shoes that would look better on a man. She walked around the housing block for what must have been at least twenty minutes. Eugenia guessed she was looking for the entrance. The staircases were located on the other side of the building, but an outsider wouldn't know, or spot them through all the scaffolding. Eventually, the woman stopped another passer-by and was pointed in the right direction. For a while, she disappeared from Eugenia's view and the street was deserted. Bored, Eugenia went to the kitchen to have a smoke and prepare dinner.

She put out her cigarette in a porcelain ashtray, peeled two potatoes, defrosted a couple of meat patties, grated some apple and a few carrots and sat at the table. A big fat fly landed on one of her beautiful, round patties. That was strange. There wasn't any over-ripe fruit lying around to attract them. She shooed the fly out of the window and drew the blinds. The doorbell rang and Eugenia went to the peephole. It was the redheaded woman with the cast.

'What's this about?' she asked.

'I'm looking for Mr Polak. I was told he rented a room here.'

Eugenia opened the door. She could hear buzzing. She took a quick look around but couldn't see a single fly in the room.

'I'm sorry to bother you,' the woman said.

She was pretty in that modern way – thin as a skeleton. Aside from the broken arm she seemed okay, though she had several fresh bruises on her face. Eugenia examined her, uneasy.

'My name is Sasza Załuska,' she said.

'Załuska?'

Eugenia opened the door wider. She knew that name. She was searching her memory, trying to match it to the face of one of her students, but there were no hits. The open door and windows were creating a draught.

'Please, come in,' she said. 'It's blowing like the devil in here.'

Sasza entered the apartment and looked around. *This might be the flat from the picture*, she thought.

'I'm sorry, but the nice gentleman isn't home,' Eugenia said, and added: 'I don't know where he went. I've only just returned from a trip.' She pointed to the unpacked suitcase.

Sasza frowned, worried. 'Do you have his number?'

Eugenia shook her head. 'As far as I know, Łukasz doesn't own a mobile phone. We only have a landline here. Old people don't need those modern inventions,' she said, smiling, and headed to the kitchen, Sasza following her.

Sasza hoisted up her bag. With her good hand, she tried fishing something out of it, but couldn't. She hissed in pain; Eugenia realised the edge of the bag had caught at a cut on her healthy arm.

'Shouldn't you go to a doctor?' Eugenia asked, concerned.

'Officially, I'm at the hospital right now,' Sasza tried to smile, but instead she grimaced in pain. She had a cut at one corner of her mouth. Seeing the other woman's stare, she added, seriously this time: 'I've only left temporarily. I have urgent business with Mr Polak. Could you write down my number for him?'

Eugenia dutifully went to the cupboard and took out an old music notebook and a sharp pencil, and wrote down the number Sasza dictated. Then the younger woman stood in the doorway, seeming unsure of what to do next. Eugenia looked at her with sympathy, but it was time to say goodbye.

'May I help you with anything else?'

Sasza nodded. 'I know this might seem strange,' she began. 'I hadn't seen him for years. I'm not even sure he's really the one renting your room. You know, if I'm looking for the right man.'

'I don't know either, dear,' Eugenia replied with an amused smile.

'The name matches, but I'd like to make sure.'

'Do you have his photo? If you do, let me see it. Even if it's old,' the older woman suggested. 'Once you're my age you get good at recognising faces.'

Sasza took out her mobile and showed Eugenia the photo of Danka.

'Was this taken here?' she asked. 'It's the only photo I have.'

Eugenia took a careful look and grinned. 'I remember that girl. She's visited a couple of times. But I thought you were looking for my tenant?'

'Was this picture taken in this apartment?' Sasza asked again.

A nod. 'As soon as he's back, I'll give him your number,' Eugenia promised. Sasza didn't move.

'My dinner's getting cold,' the older woman grunted.

'Did he tell you when he'll be back?'

'Sorry, love. No.'

Sasza hesitated.

'Could I . . .' She paused. 'I'd like to see his room. I'll only take a moment.'

Eugenia studied her warily and was about to refuse, but relented. 'All right. If you two know each other, Łukasz shouldn't have a problem with that. He's a polite young man and you look nice too. I'd wager he's your sweetheart.'

Sasza gave a nervous laugh.

Eugenia took a key from a hanger and led Sasza down the hallway. The closer they got, the stronger the smell of turpentine became.

'Please, don't hold the mess against me,' Eugenia said. 'He's just my tenant, not my grandson. I allow my tenants their privacy.'

'That's a rare quality these days.'

A turn of the key, and the door opened. Sasza stuck her head inside. The room was dark and the curtains drawn. Everything was just like the photo. A wall unit, flowers in pots. Various knick-knacks on the shelves. A sofa bed along one wall. A painting stretcher facing the wall.

And someone sleeping on the bed. Eugenia had also realised. She closed the door immediately.

'Mr Polak!' she called through the door. She was visibly alarmed. 'I thought you were out. I'm sorry.'

Nothing but silence in response.

'The room could do with some fresh air,' she said apologetically. 'Łukasz is a painter. A great artist. He must have worked on a painting overnight. I'll wake him up.'

Sasza nodded and took a few steps back. The room hadn't only smelled of turpentine. There was another odour there too. She knew it well from her time on the force. As promised though, she stayed back. But she pulled out her phone and dialled the commissioner. Her heart was pounding.

Eugenia knocked a few more times, but there was no answer. Another fly landed on the door handle.

'Maybe something happened to him?' she said, turning back to Sasza. 'Why isn't he responding?'

She read the silent confirmation in Sasza's eyes and pushed the door open again, then walked over to the bed and tried to shake the sleeping person awake. After a minute or two Sasza followed the older woman in and, with a single, firm motion, pulled she sheets off. And instinctively covered her mouth with a hand. It wasn't Łukasz. It was a thin girl, curled up like an embryo. Wearing the same flowery skirt she'd had on two days ago in the park. Her hair was spread around her head on the pillow. Her hands and legs were tied with industrial grade tie-wraps. She was beautiful. She was dead.

'Holy mother of God,' Eugenia whispered.

This was the same bed that her Kazik had died in. Black butterflies flickered before the elderly woman's eyes and she collapsed to the floor. Sasza instantly launched herself forward to help, but midstride, she noticed something on the bedside table. Her documents folder. Her driving licence was on top of it, showing her address in Sopot. Beneath it, a fragment of a photograph. Sasza recognised it at once. It had been taken a year ago at the seaside and she had carried it in her wallet since then. Someone had ripped the photo in half, leaving only part of Sasza, and taking the rest. Of her daughter Karolina, only a hand remained.

'Something is rotten in the state of Denmark,' said Doman.

They were sitting in the main conference hall of the *poviat* police station. Chief inspector Domański, his team of technicians from Central HQ, Romanowska, Jah-Jah and Anita Krawczyk, the prosecutor from Białystok.

Anita had arrived in a short, black skirt, with her hair tied in a bun, and wearing high heels. She was visibly embarrassed. She had apologised for her appearance a couple of times, explaining that she had been on her way to the concert hall, where an Orthodox liturgical music concert was taking place. First impressions of the woman were misleading. She wasn't only a glamour-puss, she knew her stuff. Krawczyk immediately realised that the technicians were commencing a visual inspection before getting to the photographic documentation proper. As soon as she heard they'd have to wait at least half an hour for the video equipment, she produced a hand-held camera and told them to record a video on the spot. She didn't try to interject again. Some prosecutors like to take their frustration out on investigators. Not her. She liked to act as if she wasn't even there, simply supervising the collection of evidence, like a benevolent protector. When a young technician, clearly out of his mind with stress, started trying to pick up each and every hair and piece of thread from the sheet the body had been covered with, she approached him and whispered in his ear so that Domański couldn't overhear:

'Just cut out a fragment.'

Behemoth grew red. After he'd finished the job, Krawczyk pulled the technician to the side, offered him a cigarette and smiled at him. 'Now, describe it in detail. I don't want to look bad in court, all right?'

The officer assured her that he'd do everything in his power to please her.

'I'm pretty pleased with myself as it is. So just make sure you don't screw it up,' she said and left, heading to the local clothes store to buy a pair of sneakers.

She came back in a pair of green sports shoes and sat de-husking sunflower seeds.

'We don't think your outfit is out of place, Anita. On the contrary,' Doman teased. 'You're always welcome to our briefings. And we're not going anywhere for a while yet, it seems.'

'Well, it sure as hell feels out of place to me,' she replied coldly, fingering her pearl necklace, as she had no more seeds to de-husk. 'Because it seems I won't be going to the concert after all. My husband spent months trying to get those tickets. We only got them from the mayor's office in the end. So get a move on, Doman, 'cause I need to get there, even if I only catch the last part.'

She pulled a plastic bag from under her chair and studied her evening shoes. The heels were worn.

'Anybody got any nubuck spray?'

'I have mosquito spray,' Jah-Jah offered, grinning. 'Be my guest.'

Romanowska shot him an icy stare and turned to Anita: 'My son will bring you some from home. I've texted him.'

'The things people do for their career . . .' Doman said. 'I'm a pretty good singer too. Under the shower. And you wouldn't have to wait months for a ticket.'

'Your recitals suffer from lack of attendance,' the prosecutor riposted. She was losing patience.

'You'd be surprised.' The inspector laughed. 'But you can't bring your husband.'

Anita tossed her shoes under the table.

'Her husband is a lawyer,' Doman said loudly, so everybody heard. Nobody knew how to respond to that.

Only Romanowska smiled, with one corner of her mouth. Doman had treated his ex-lovers like his property since she had been at high school with him. His break-up with Anita was probably still a sore spot. Romanowska doubted his qualities as a faithful husband and thought that Liliana's pregnancies probably did nothing to curb Doman's nature. People like that didn't just change. Even on his deathbed, she thought, the man would try his pick-up lines on the nurses.

Doman was just getting started. Evidently, he was taking his revenge on Anita and didn't intend to stop. He continued: 'The worst douchebag in town. His only redeeming quality is his pay cheque. Everybody knows diamonds are a woman's best friend.'

'Oh, so that's what's bothering you, sweetheart?' The prosecutor sighed heavily. She pushed the remains of the sunflower seeds away. 'Let's talk about the murder, shall we?'

There was an empty coffee pot on the table. The centre of the wall was dominated by a corkboard covered in photos from the inspection of the site where the body of Danuta Pietrasik had been found, as well as a few images of the suspect, Łukasz Polak, drawn from the psychiatric hospital's files. The criminology technician had delivered a video from the preliminary post-mortem just a few minutes ago. Doman slid the CD towards the prosecutor.

'Have a gander. It'll take the wind out of your sails.'

Anita retained her cool demeanour. She took the CD and asked Romanowska to summarise the findings.

'The deceased is a woman. Eighteen years of age. Cause of death: strangulation. Murder weapon: telephone charger cable. She was tied. Numerous abrasions and petechial haemorrhages. The court pathologist will be able to tell us more after the autopsy. The victim was in situ for forty-eight hours tops. She was found in the apartment of one Eugenia Rączka, a retired music teacher who rented a room to one Łukasz Polak. Rączka has just returned from abroad and hadn't left the flat since. We're assuming that the crime was committed on Sunday, most probably in the afternoon.'

'The day of Bondaruk's wedding,' Jah-Jah cut in.

'Yes, the same day as the bride went missing,' Romanowska confirmed, sending her ex-husband a sharp look. 'Let's hold back on any hypotheses for now.'

'Did I just hypothesise?'

Doman chuckled.

Romanowska approached a whiteboard and began writing down the information.

'Personal identity number, tax number and personal information of the suspect have been added to the file. We've established that the man left the city a week ago on Saturday for an open-air painting workshop in a place called Dubicze Cerkiewne. He didn't attend the workshop, though he had gone to the school where it was held and paid an advance in the amount of one hundred and forty złoty. The school secretary was the last person to see him.'

The commissioner attached a receipt to the board with a magnet.

'Polak left his personal belongings, photographic equipment and paintings in Eugenia Rączka's apartment. He must have been in a hurry. We have secured a half-packed bag in his room. Some of his things have been tossed inside seemingly without care. Randomly. A nurse at Ciszynia recognised the bag and its contents as Polak's property. He did not have a mobile phone or a bank account. On Friday, before he left, Polak asked his employer for an advance. Mr Schabowski paid him a thousand five hundred złoty plus his expenses and outstanding amounts. Thirty-five hundred in total.'

'That's a lot of cash around here,' Jah-Jah chimed in again, but this time Doman sent him a glare, shutting the man up.

Romanowska continued:

'Sunday morning, Polak was supposed to work at Bondaruk's wedding. He didn't show up at the meeting in the Carska restaurant, where they were going to discuss the details of a private session. As I said, the man doesn't own a phone, and he didn't return home. Schabowski had to bring in his son as a substitute photographer for the wedding and the subsequent party. Both the victim and the suspect were patients at the psychiatric hospital, Ciszynia. They had known each other for three years. Danuta Pietrasik was transferred to Ciszynia before him. Her brother is still a patient there. He has an alibi and hasn't left the facility since being hospitalised. To be clear, he has not left the premises even once. He refused to visit his father, his last remaining relative. His sister, however, left the premises several times. Not counting her escapes, that is. She visited Polak at least a couple of times in his apartment, as confirmed by Mrs Rączka. The hospital authorities agreed on that. Polak was made officially responsible for Danuta during her stay outside the facility and signed off on all her official leaves.'

'Isn't the man . . . ?' Jah-Jah trailed off.

'That's right, but two months ago he was deemed cured. Here's the psychologist's assessment.'

Romanowska pulled a single page from the file and passed it to Jah-Jah. He scanned the assessment and passed it down the line. The prosecutor took a while longer to look through it, reading it thoroughly, before putting it down.

'Polak participated in a research programme supervised by a Norwegian foundation collaborating with Ciszynia,' Romanowska went on. 'If I remember correctly, the foundation financed the renovation of the park and the fence at the hospital. Anyway, before the incident, the patient had always returned from leave on time and had taken his pills without complaint. Nobody ever had anything bad to say about him. He missed his last psychiatric consultation, but that was because he was at work. His employer verified that. He was due to have another in two weeks' time.'

'I bet he won't be attending this time,' Jah-Jah muttered, but nobody laughed. He added, louder this time: 'From a PR perspective, that's pretty bad for the hospital, right? Just wait until the media catch the scent. We have an arrest warrant being printed as we speak.'

'Polak wasn't referred for treatment by a court of law. He had no obligation to remain at Ciszynia,' Romanowska was saying. 'I sent a man to question the personnel. I have the official reports here.'

A thick report was passed to Doman, who only briefly glanced at it before pushing it towards the prosecutor. She didn't open the report either. Romanowska shrugged and took it back.

'Mr Saczko, the director, appointed the doctor responsible for Polak's case. Doctor Prus will be at our disposal twenty-four-seven. She has already been called and will join us within the hour.'

'Oh! I know her!' Jah-Jah exclaimed and whistled loudly. He turned to Doman and grinned. 'You'll like her.'

'What about the girl?' Anita asked. 'Did nobody report her missing? Didn't anyone look for her?'

'No. We sent two patrols out to find her on Saturday. We had reason to believe she had appropriated the documents and money of a resident of Tricity by the name of Sasza Załuska, a profiler, I went to Ciszynia to meet with . . .' Romanowska paused for effect and pointed to the suspect's picture on the board.

'That guy,' finished Doman.

Romanowska nodded.

'Załuska is also the only witness in the case of Iwona Bondaruk's kidnapping. We called you about it on Sunday. She was beaten up by the assailants and tied to a tree. She's still in hospital. Załuska was first at the crime scene in Eugenia Rączka's apartment, too. She discovered Danuta Pietrasik's body. We received an anonymous call from her number. She was seen at the bus station after that, and we caught her an hour ago on the road to Białystok. She was trying to hitch a ride.'

'Is that some kind of a joke?' Doman asked, turning to Jah-Jah.

'Not at all.' Romanowska sat down. 'Jah-Jah will get you up to speed on the rest of the story. I think Doman should know the details of your acquaintance with this profiler.'

Doman raised his head. He looked intrigued. 'I'm all ears.'

Jah-Jah briefly summarised his meeting with Załuska, and then produced the rolled-up booklet she had given him on Saturday during the questioning. He tossed the document on the table.

'I believe there's no such thing as coincidence,' he said. 'I'm not naive. I think we should treat this Załuska as a suspect in both cases. I don't know how she's connected to them, but life in our town was simpler before she arrived.'

'Poetic as fuck.' Doman snorted. 'Care to give us some hard data on that?'

Jah-Jah presented the profiler's zip-up bag, packed into an evidence bag, and placed it on the table. Next to that he placed a scan of Sasza's fingerprints taken from the police database.

'Years ago, Załuska was the subject of a disciplinary procedure. She filed for discharge from service. Either they made her do it or she came up with the idea herself. Either way, she got away with whatever she really did. However, I kept digging and a source that wishes to remain anonymous told me the CBŚ is still keeping tabs on her. She could have been an undercover operative. We'll know more when her superior arrives from Gdańsk. He was the one to verify her personal info. He's the head of the local criminal division. Vouched for her.'

'If he turns up,' Romanowska cut in.

'And to think this used to be such a peaceful town,' Doman sighed. He got up and kissed Anita on the cheek, making her blush. 'I'm off to Hades. Go team.'

Sasza compulsively scratched her arm under the cast. She had dark half-circles under her eyes. Her freckled face was pale, with reddish blotches on nose and cheeks. But, though she was exhausted, her brain was in overdrive. They were going to frame her for murder. She had seen through their scheme. Was this Gramps's doing? Or were her paranoid fears finally coming true and the Red Spider was finally exacting his long-planned vengeance on her? If you wait long enough, you'll get what's coming to you, as her mother used to say. Your thoughts determine your energy. If this somehow panned out in her favour, she'd be an incurable optimist from now on. She'd never give in to her doubts and suspicions ever again. Her fear threatened to overwhelm her but she did her best to hide it.

'Your proposition was meant as a test, wasn't it?' she asked.

Romanowska and Jah-Jah, watching Sasza's interrogation from behind a one-way mirror, exchanged glances.

'I didn't make you any offers,' Doman replied. 'It's in your best interest to find the suspect as soon as possible. Long and the short of it, either you're with us or against us. If I haven't made myself clear already – you don't really have a choice.'

'There's always a choice,' Sasza protested. 'But as it happens, I had nothing to do with that murder. If you'd like me to work for you, you'd better stop insulting me.'

Doman fidgeted in his chair. 'You're hard to trust and you made things even harder for us.'

'You made them hard yourselves,' she grunted and extended her hand, palm up. 'My phone please. I need to contact my daughter.'

Doman just slid the mobile closer to his side of the table.

'You turn up in town and suddenly people start dying or disappearing. Coincidence?'

'That's too far-fetched, and you know it. It's too early to charge anyone.'

'Who's talking about charges?' Doman scoffed. 'I'm only saying that you were at both crime scenes. And you own an unlicensed firearm. We've kept it out of the reports, but that could still change. Try putting yourself in our shoes. I can't let you go.'

Sasza stood firm. She wanted to say something about absolute necessity or special social interest, but she had had about enough of being someone's lab rat. She had enough troubles of her own and didn't need someone else's shit. Her daughter would return from her holidays in a week. Everything was supposed to be clear by now, but instead her trip to Hajnówka had only made things worse.

And Ghost was staying silent. He wouldn't answer her calls or texts. She knew he wasn't coming, even though the commissioner had told her that they had issued an official call. If he had been coming, he would have told her first. Personally. He was at work, poring over some case file, most likely. Or maybe he'd just finally got pissed off by her absence of the exam, or been dragged over the coals by Chief Waligóra. One thing you could say about Ghost was that if he had something in his head, there was no reasoning with him. Sasza could imagine him right now. He'd seen her actions as belittling him and thrown a tantrum. Besides, why would he sacrifice his own time to come to her rescue? Who was she to him? A colleague, an acquaintance. Nothing more. What had she been hoping for? Even worse, she realised she had feelings for him, and he wasn't exactly boyfriend material. Whatever. Have it his way. She'd never ask for anything again. And she definitely wouldn't apologise. She had more serious problems to deal with. Time to prove she was innocent. As always, she only had herself to count on.

'Stop playing games,' she said coldly. 'I made my statement. We're on the same side. You know I'm not a criminal.'

Doman's face remained serious. 'I do hope so.'

Sasza was getting angry. If you want to beat someone up, it's never hard to find a sufficiently heavy stick.

'You have nothing on me.'

'For now.'

'So why are we even talking? You lock me up, I call a lawyer. You do your thing, I wait in a cell. You get the investigation going, I sit on my ass and try to be patient. But let's wait for the evidence analysis and then we'll see who was right all along.'

'Sounds like a plan.' He gave her a challenging look.

Sasza believed him. What would happen to Karolina if they threw her in prison? She glared at Doman but pulled in her horns.

'All right. What do you want from me?'

Doman smiled. 'I want you to be frank with me.'

'Well, right back at you,' she muttered.

In short, simple words, Doman explained just how the situation looked from his perspective. He didn't beat around the bush.

'You need a scapegoat,' Sasza said. She was ready to cooperate. Her only weapon was her knowledge of Łukasz Polak. That might be of some use to them. They wouldn't find a thing on him by themselves. Everything was buried too deep. And they knew as much. That was the only reason they were even talking to her. Sasza didn't quite grasp the extent of her predicament. What was Doman's trump card? Had she missed something?

'As I said before, I came here to meet Polak,' she said. 'I suspected that he was a dangerous criminal, though officially no charges were ever filed against him. When I worked for the CBŚ, he was a suspect in several murder cases. I went to the forest and the apartment on Trzeciego Maja Street for the same reason. Him. The commissioner gave me the address herself. She knows my story. Me and Polak were . . . close.' She hesitated, then inhaled and let out her breath heavily. 'We had an affair. A short one. I don't want to get into any details. It's private stuff.'

'Not any more.'

Sasza ignored the riposte.

'Until very recently, I thought Łukasz was dead. I'd been told so by my superiors. When I learned that he was alive and had been released from hospital, I knew there were going to be more victims. And that's not doom-mongering, is it? There's a body. I know his MO. I know how he works. His weak spots. I could help you find him,' she said. Without waiting for a reply, she added, pointing to her profiling booklet sticking out of Doman's breast pocket: 'I believe you're more interested in what I can offer you than putting me in jail. That would be short-sighted. I'd file for damages for being unlawfully held as soon as you let me go. And you *will* let me go. Trying to frame me for a murder is absurd. Sooner or later you're going to have to accept that. When you find more bodies.'

Instead of replying, Doman tapped his pen on the table. He switched the recorder off and chucked it into a drawer. Then he took out an ashtray and placed it on the table, offering Sasza a cigarette, a roll-up. She hesitated but then took it.

'Did a letter come to the station? A photo maybe?' she asked.

'Not that I know of.'

'It will.' Sasza grimaced. The cigarette was awful. She breathed out a puff of smoke and flicked the ash from the tip, then stubbed out the roll-up in the ashtray. 'If the Red Spider killed Danka, he'll send a photo. He used to send us photos of his victims, stylised, like paintings.'

'I hope you know how this sounds.' Doman got up, went to the door and took a peek outside. 'We're in Poland, in a happy little town where nothing ever happens.'

'Psychopaths are everywhere.' Sasza wasn't going to allow him to rattle her. 'They're not only in large cities. And he's not just some ordinary criminal. He's got experience. He knows how to erase his traces. He's had a lot of time to practise. Maybe someone went missing before? Inspector Frankowski asked me some time ago if I knew how to find a body.'

'Ask and ye shall receive.' Doman smirked.

'Łukasz Polak could leave Ciszynia any time he wanted. All he had to do was return from leave the same day. And he did. Always on time. He could have killed up to about a hundred kilometres outside Hajnówka. Look for young women who've gone missing in the region. I can prepare a profile of the typical victim.'

Doman nodded. 'Thanks for the offer, but we're talking about you now. And the case at hand.'

Sasza dropped her eyes. 'I'm telling you it was just a case of wrong time, wrong place.'

'I don't believe in coincidence.'

'Me neither.' Sasza pursed her lips. 'I don't get it. Maybe he's hunting me? Maybe my arrival somehow activated his urges?'

A silence fell over the room. Sasza suddenly realised that was it. They needed her as bait. That's what this was about. Someone knocked at the door. Doman pushed himself up and opened it, letting Romanowska in.

'Can I see you for a second?' she asked him.

Doman left the room. Sasza immediately darted to grab her mobile and called her mother. Hearing the recording of her daughter's voice again made her eyes tear up. She couldn't help it. When Romanowska, Frankowski and Doman returned, they found her crying. Their expressions were apologetic. The atmosphere grew visibly less strained. Sasza wiped her tears away with a sleeve, trying to hide her emotions.

'We have confirmation that the fingerprints from the crime scene are not yours,' the commissioner started.

Sasza kept her eyes on her telephone screen. It took her a while to understand what was being said and focus on the words.

'It's too early to form a hypothesis. We're still waiting for the expert opinion, but the local newspaper received this.'

Romanowska showed Sasza a printout in a plastic bag. It was a black-and-white photo snapped from above. Danka was lying on her side, like an embryo. The picture made Sasza think of an ultrasound image of an unborn child. In the photo the bruises and lividity she had seen on the victim's face were practically indiscernible. What was immediately visible were the plastic tie-wraps on her hands and feet. Sasza took a long good look at the image and finally nodded.

'Who was it addressed to?'

'Sergiusz Mikołajuk, the editor-in-chief of the local newspaper. We call him Seryozha. He's waiting in the corridor. He's told us he hasn't shown the evidence to anybody, but the photo is already on the Internet. If it's been leaked, we can do nothing to stop it from spreading. TV stations are already calling. We need to make an official statement.'

'Before, he only played his game with the police. Now he's involving the media,' Sasza said. 'He wants fame.'

Jah-Jah pulled out a few photos from his breast pocket. He hovered them in front of Sasza. The images were a composite that made up a face.

'You said you can find a hidden body,' he said. 'We have a few disappearances that have never been solved. Maybe that was your friend's doing too.'

At first, Sasza shot the photos only a reluctant glance, but then she looked more carefully. The composite was lousy, but the similarity was undeniable. Sasza took the photos from Jah-Jah's hand and laid them on the table, then rummaged in her bag for the photo of the two women and the handsome middle-aged man that Marzena Koźmińska, the Wasp, had given her. She compared them, then shook her head.

'Her name is Monika Zakrzewska. She also went by the name Jowita. A prostitute from Warsaw's Bródno district. Her body was never found. I don't think her disappearance was connected to the Red Spider though. She went missing in the year 2000 and he didn't start killing until much later.'

Sasza put her photo on the table next to the police images and pointed to the image of Koźmińska.

'This woman was charged with kidnapping, but she denies it. She thinks that guy kidnapped Jowita.' Sasza pointed a finger at the man in the photo. 'Four-Eyes. That's what people called him.'

Romanowska looked at Jah-Jah, who turned to Doman. He nodded. 'That is Piotr Bondaruk,' the commissioner said and added, stating the obvious: 'The new husband of the girl who went missing in the forest.'

Sasza looked up at her sharply. 'Are you sure?'

'I've been living here for years,' Romanowska flared up. She glanced at Jah-Jah.

'Yeah, I think so too,' he growled. 'Can't be a mix-up.'

Doman ruffled his hair in a nervous gesture.

'All right, but how is that connected to the murder of the Ciszynia patient?'

'I can look for him.' Sasza reached out for the case file.

Doman hesitated but finally slid it towards her. 'Call Anita. Tell her we have a change of plan,' he said to Romanowska.

'I work alone,' Sasza said and shot Doman a cold stare. 'You don't get to poke your nose into my process.'

'Can't promise you that.' He shook his head.

'I'll keep you posted,' Sasza said. 'And I believe you're forgetting something.'

Doman raised his eyebrows.

'Apologise to the lady!' Jah-Jah poked Doman in the gut, smirking with satisfaction.

'That's not what I meant,' Sasza hissed. 'If I was in your place, I would have been suspicious too. Comes with the profession. But you need to straighten things out with HQ in Tricity. I want you to promise you'll keep your report to yourself. You know how it is with gossip. Hard to debunk. I was given the gun by Duchnowski. Ask him yourself.'

Doman didn't respond.

'And I want it back,' Sasza continued determinedly. She pointed to the photo of Łukasz on the board. 'That man kept me imprisoned once. If you want me to be the bait, I need a gun.'

Silence. Romanowska shook her head. Jah-Jah grinned ironically.

'It's either that or I'm out,' Sasza added.

'Then you're out.' Doman shrugged.

Sasza put the documents back on the table and crossed her arms.

'I won't say anything more without my lawyer. And I'm not going anywhere. I'm safest here.'

'All right, have it your way,' Doman capitulated. 'I was bluffing anyway. Your friend, the cop who gave you the gun, doesn't know anything yet.'

Sasza smiled with one corner of her mouth.

'Fucker,' she said.

Doman laughed at that, as if she had complimented him. Romanowska sent Jah-Jah for the Beretta and a set of bullets.

'My aunt's moved to a farm close to the Belarusian border,' she said, turning to Sasza. 'Her flat is empty. It's located on Piłsudskiego Street. Only a couple of hundred metres from the station. Błażej will give you the keys. You'll be able to work undisturbed there. We can't really keep you here . . .' She paused.

Sasza looked at her gratefully. She tapped her cast.

'I need a driver too.'

'It would be my pleasure!' Jah-Jah exclaimed, flexing his impressive biceps.

'I said a driver, not a bodyguard.'

'You're wrong.' Romanowska cut her short. 'If someone's hunting you, better to have one of ours watching your back.'

'How tall are you?' Sasza sized Doman up.

He froze, dumbfounded, but answered: 'Hundred and ninety-nine centimetres.'

Sasza shook her head.

'Too tall. How about your son?' She turned to Jah-Jah. 'No more than a hundred and seventy-five, right?'

'Eight,' Romanowska said. 'What's this about?'

'I want my car,' Sasza replied. 'As soon as the technicians are done with it. If I'm to act as bait, I should look natural. A Fiat Uno won't fit a basketball player like one of you two. I need someone shorter. I'd blow a fuse if I had to listen to your constant complaining about how cramped it was. For now, a patrol car will do.'

Romanowska called Błażej, who was standing outside, holding a can of shoe spray. He had gone home for nothing. The prosecutor had already driven back to Białystok. When they were done with Sasza, they were supposed to call her and bring her up to date.

'I need a few hours,' Sasza said. 'And if you find out anything new, I'd like you to call me asap. We can't afford to work with out-of-date intel.'

She snatched her bag and tried throwing it over her shoulder, but failed. Błażej bent over and started collecting all the things that had fallen out. Sasza's head spun. She collapsed back into the chair, breathing heavily. Romanowska studied her, alarmed. 'Is everything all right?'

'No.' Sasza got up with difficulty. 'I need to lie down for a while.'

'Maybe you'll learn a thing or two from a CBŚ agent,' said Jah-Jah, smiling at his son.

'I wouldn't count on it,' Sasza replied before Błażej could open his mouth. 'Unless it's getting mixed up in someone else's affairs. For no pay.' She handed the files to the officer and headed towards the exit. 'Oh, about my car.' She turned to Błażej. 'Third gear doesn't work. You have to really step on the clutch.'

'I'll keep an eye on you,' Doman said quietly, certain that Sasza would be too engaged with talking to Błażej to hear him.

She turned round and smiled.

'If I let you.'

The well was deep and dry. Iwona bent over the rim and threw a pebble down, listening for the splash.

'Echo!' she called.

In response, she only heard her own echoing voice, not the stone hitting the bottom.

Suddenly, someone wrapped their arms around her waist. She stumbled and nearly fell down the shaft, but her fear turned to glee as soon as she turned round and saw Quack. He embraced her and placed a kiss on her lips.

'My lovely, divine Quack,' Iwona purred. She pushed herself against him, breathing in his scent – smoke, sweat and leather.

'How long do we have to stay here?'

Instead of replying, he pulled out a crumpled bouquet from under the lapel of his leather jacket. She squealed happily.

'So I'm going to get us some groceries.' A woman's voice ruined the moment.

Iwona waved at Kinga Kosiek, the nice Belarusian girl she had met during the *korovai* baking ritual, and whom she had immediately taken a liking to. Since they had gone into hiding here, the two of them must have talked about all their relationships, told each other about their dreams, complained about boys and various family members. Kinga had become a Belarusian activist only recently. Previously, at school, she had been against political activism. Her parents were ashamed of their peasant origins and Kinga went to the Belarusian high school only because she had wanted to learn foreign languages, and the school's language study classes were better equipped than at the other – Polish – school. She had had to learn Belarusian, as most classes were taught in that language and, unlike her friends from around Hajnówka, her family had never spoken it.

Returning to Hajnówka after university, Kinga had found work teaching English at her old school. When her teaching hours were cut down, to make ends meet she had taken over the classes of a retired Belarusian history teacher. From feeling a hundred per cent Polish just a couple of years previously, Kinga was now promoting Belarusian culture and tradition, teaching the local kids to love their Eastern European homeland.

However, most of her money came from her side job at Pizzeria Siciliana.

'Just don't come back too soon!' Quack called after her now and pulled Iwona towards the house.

It was a typical semi-detached local house made out of wooden beams painted black, with white window shutters and a richly engraved veranda. It stood right in the middle of an old orchard. The house was ringed by a fence that had been ordered by the church in Mikołowo as an enclosure for the local cemetery but had never been collected; Kinga's father had bought it for peanuts and simply painted it in a white and pink pattern to make it less dour. When the Mazury residential project was constructed in the eighties, Kinga's dad didn't sell his land, and now the parcel was surrounded by apartment blocks. The fence did nothing to improve the privacy of the residents of the little house, so he'd planted a line of junipers along the border of the plot. They had grown to resemble a dense copse. This rural farm in the very heart of the city was now Kinga's. It was the perfect spot to lie low. Everyone in the area assumed after Kinga's father died that the house was empty.

Iwona heated up some soup for Quack. She placed a freshly baked cake on the table, sat in his lap and stroked his hair affectionately.

'Does it hurt?' Quack asked, looking at her bandaged arm.

She nodded. 'You could have shot me,' she whispered.

He placed a tender kiss on the spot.

'All right, you.' She laughed. 'It's all good.'

He snuggled against her breasts and breathed: 'I don't know what I'd do if something happened to you.'

She thought she could hear him sobbing gently, so she wrapped her arms around him, asking: 'How long do I have to stay here?'

'It's not so bad, is it?' He glanced at the bruises on her face. 'Treat it like a surprise holiday. How's that sound?'

Iwona softened. She allowed him to touch her, caress her skin. But as soon as he tried unbuttoning her shirt, she stiffened again. 'There's no TV or Internet. I don't even have my phone.'

'They'd just track it down.'

'So let's get a new one. Prepaid.'

'I'll think about it,' he said abruptly.

Maybe Quack simply didn't have the money, she thought. She studied him for a while, trying to hide her resentment.

'Does Piotr know?'

He nodded.

'He's offering a reward.'

'Fifty or a hundred?'

'Fifty. Everybody's looking for you.'

'Shame. A hundred would sound better.' She sighed. 'What an old penny-pincher.'

'Do you trust her?' Quack pointed to a photo of Kinga and her parents that stood on the cupboard.

'Do I have a choice? I'm one of you now. A Belarusian.'

Quack pushed his plate away. Iwona asked if he wanted some more soup. He shook his head. 'I've got bad news. The car was a set-up.'

'You mean it was stolen?'

'Worse. People say it was used to murder someone way back when. Should have taken it with us or dumped it in the bog. It's probably full of our prints. And that woman driving the blue Uno, the one that jumped us? She's police. There's gonna be trouble.'

Iwona mulled this over. She got up and went to the window, took a peek outside, then drew the curtain. Its dark claret fabric robbed the room of all light.

'Do you regret it?' Quack walked over and put his arms around her waist. She rested her head on his chest, staying quiet for a long while. 'It didn't pan out like we planned,' he added.

'Not if I don't have to spend the rest of my life here,' she replied finally, nimbly sliding his phone out of his pocket. He tried snatching it from her hand, but she danced away, laughing out loud. 'Or if you stay here with me.'

Quack managed to get the mobile back. He stuffed it back into his pocket and zipped it shut.

'I don't trust her,' he said, nodding at the photo on the cupboard again.

'You don't trust anyone.'

'Even you, you mean?' he asked. 'Don't start with that again. It just came out. I was mad. I didn't understand the situation.'

'You know, you really should start trusting me. I'm the only thing keeping us both alive.'

'All the more reason to panic that he'll do it again.'

'Take that back!' She stiffened.

'All right. Forget it.'

Quack grabbed his rucksack and started to unpack sets of men's clothing. He also pulled out another motorbike suit and an old blond wig.

'Want me to role-play a glam-rock star for you?' Iwona asked.

'We're leaving.'

'When?'

'Now.' He smiled.

Iwona felt her stomach knotting with excitement. She was falling in love with Quack all over again. He was such a rogue! And she might be stupid, but she just couldn't help but feel great when she was with him. She wouldn't fight her feelings any more. No other man made her feel like this.

'Does Mum know?'

He shook his head.

'How about Piotr?'

'You'll tell him yourself. He's waiting for us at your mum's flat. He has the cash,' Quack said.

With a single motion, Iwona pulled her skirt off and grabbed the motorbike suit. Quack approached her as she was trying to untangle herself from her underskirt. He clasped his hands around her waist and started to kiss her breasts above her bra. She laughed, still struggling with her clothes, but didn't stop him.

'We can be a couple of minutes late, can't we?' he whispered.

The suit dropped to the ground. Iwona swept the plates from the table. Quack picked her up and sat her down on the tabletop. She reclined, feeling him pull her knickers down with his teeth and nestle his face between her legs. She closed her eyes.

Neither of them heard the car driving up to the house. The driver slammed on the brakes and stepped out. Leaving the engine running, he marched towards the well and took a look inside. Empty. No water. He took a little package wrapped in rags out of a plastic bag. Then he folded the bag, hid it in his pocket and tossed the parcel into the dark shaft of the well. It was heavy and he heard a dull thump when it reached the bottom. Then, with a can of blue spray paint, he drew the symbol of Pahonia* on the wall of the well. Beneath the emblem he wrote: 'Wipe Out the Lakhs!' As soon as the deed was done, he jumped back in his car and drove off, leaving only faint traces of the tyres on the grass.

'You'll tell them everything.'

'Everything?'

'Everything they want to know.' Krzysztof Saczko took a pair of new blue Crocs from the wardrobe, peeled off the label and placed them carefully on the floor, next to the desk. He took off his suit jacket, loosened his tie, and bent down to untie his shoes, huffing and moaning, trying to reach his feet over his enormous paunch. With his head under the desk, he grunted: 'Get me that white coat, please.'

Magdalena Prus arched an eyebrow – she had never seen him wear one before – but got up and picked up the coat, which was in a plastic bag on the coffee table. When she turned back to Saczko, he'd changed into the Crocs and was spreading files over the desktop, arranging them in a way that was clearly supposed to lead any visitors to think he had been hard at work.

'Expecting someone?'

---

*The national emblem of both Belarus and Lithuania, as well as being a symbol used by nationalist groups sympathising with one of those states.

'Guests are rather inevitable at this stage. Don't let the cleaning lady touch anything.'

'She wouldn't dare.'

'*You* don't touch anything either.'

'Unlike you, I actually know what you keep here.'

'That's why I chose you.' He smiled brightly.

'I'm honoured,' Prus said, and smirked. She had never seen Saczko in a white coat because it was years since he had worked night shifts at Ciszynia. As its frontman, he was often away at symposiums, always travelling business class. Prus had to do all the dirty work for him. She spent most of her free time here, keeping the staff in line. She liked to think of herself as Ciszynia's Cardinal Richelieu – when the time came, all she'd have to do was to reach out and the crown would be hers. For the time being, though, she needed Saczko. Manipulating the man couldn't be easier. He did as he was told. Besides, he liked being the centre of attention. Today, though, Saczko didn't want to go to the police station for attention. Was he afraid they'd figure out that he was a mere pawn? Surely it was just a matter of time.

'Who do you want to fool?' she asked.

'Me?' He feigned surprise. 'That's not how I'd frame it, sweetheart. Who do *we* want to fool would be better, don't you think? We're in it together.'

She hated it when he called her sweetheart. He knew that and only ever did it to annoy her.

'Should I know anything specific?' She picked a tangerine from a wicker basket and started to peel it.

'They'll ask you about everything.'

'Do I give them papers?'

He loosened his tie some more. Finally, he ripped it of, and undid the top button of his green shirt.

'Of course.'

'What about patient–doctor privilege?'

'You are to be helpful and supportive. Be a friend and an ally, but don't let them dominate you.'

'That's my speciality.'

'Thank God they didn't find that body here. That would have been catastrophic.'

Prus ate her tangerine. A thin trickle of juice dripped down her chin and she wiped it with a napkin. Saczko didn't even notice.

'We're safe,' she mumbled, still chewing. She took a few more tangerines. 'The girl escaped. We've reported it. They looked for her. And Polak has been certified as healthy by three separate experts. We can't be responsible for what our patients do outside these walls. We're going to be okay.'

'This is just the beginning,' Saczko said, staring at her. 'It's not about the Pietrasik girl or even about Polak. They're going to ask us about Bondaruk. Maybe not today, but who knows what they'll dig up? Then they'll shake us down. Why was he hospitalised? Why didn't we keep him? Who parked his Mercedes in front of the clinic? Who drove it? And who found it? If they figure out our whole west wing was funded by his New Forest, they'll stick to our arses like leeches.'

She shrugged.

'The Warsaw city guard found it. Based on an unpaid ticket. They towed it away and impounded it. The prosecutor kept the car until the case was closed. Then they gave it back, and he could legally drive it again. As far as I know he locked it up in his garage. He had the right to do that. Though in his place, I would have got rid of it. Too many bad memories. Especially if those memories lead straight to proof of guilt.'

Saczko shook his head. 'I picked it up. I signed the papers. Personally.'

'Seriously?' Prus laughed out loud. 'And you're afraid they're going to discover that?'

'Yes.' He nodded. 'What's worse, I can't just tell them. He's my friend.'

'That's a bit of an overstatement.'

'Perhaps. But it's my signature on the papers. If they get them, I'll be done.'

Before she could reply, a clattering from outside the room distracted her. A woman was shouting: 'He broke all the Christmas trees! And he keeps threatening me! And now he's hung his stinking undies in the maintenance room. And he's stirring up the crew against me!'

The door flew open and the woman barged in. She was from the cleaning company to whom the hospital outsourced its cleaning and maintenance work, young and attractive. The moment she saw Prus, she clamped her mouth shut and curtsied meekly. She had her regulation cap clenched in her hand and she must have sprayed herself with an inordinate amount of perfume before entering, as the smell quickly spread across the entire room. And it wasn't the cheap kind. How does a cleaning lady get the cash for Dior Addict and then waste it wearing it to work?

Saczko trotted over to the woman with a cat-like softness that clashed starkly with his girth. Prus backed away. She took the last two tangerines, sat down at the desk and occupied herself with peeling them.

'Director, sir, I'm going to have to fire that lout!' the woman went on, then, seeing Prus's expression, finished more quietly: 'I just can't work with him any more.'

'Not now, Halina dearest!' Saczko pushed the cleaning lady out of the door and added in a patronising tone: 'I'll come to see you in a minute. I'm having an important meeting.'

He shut the door and reached for an empty file, which he used as a fan.

'What a hyena,' he mumbled. He turned to Prus. 'You need to talk to him. Tell him to pipe down a bit.'

'Poor, dumb Halina,' Magdalena said. 'Why do you feel you need to run after her? You fucked her a couple of times but that doesn't mean you owe her anything.'

Saczko pinned her with a hateful gaze.

'All right, all right.' Prus lifted her hands in a placating gesture. She laughed. 'We all make mistakes. But at least you got her that perfume as a goodbye, eh?'

Saczko blushed. 'Kuba won't listen to anyone else,' he said, 'and I can't let her get rid of him.'

Prus knew that the hospital had never been as clean as it was since Kuba had started working there. He scrubbed the floors, lifts and showers, and more, all for a pitiful two hundred złoty a month. He could dry his pants wherever he wanted for all she cared. But more to the point, Saczko had told him practically everything.

'We can't let her get rid of him,' Saczko said now, obviously thinking the same as her. He wiped the sweat from his brow. 'But she said it – technically he's her employee. She's the one who can fire him if she wants.'

'*We* run this place,' Prus said with emphasis. '*We* signed his contract. That's why he accepted the job. Your fuck-buddy must have forgotten to check his paperwork.' She threw the tangerine peel in the bin and rose from her chair. 'I have to go now. They're waiting for me at the station. I'm telling them everything, yes? Sure?'

He nodded. 'Only the truth can save us.'

'There's no such thing as the objective truth,' she said. 'Which one should I give them? Mine, yours or your idiot of a girl's?'

'I told you already. The half-truth. Tell them everything about the new case. When they start asking about Bondaruk, go with Othello syndrome, unproven guilt and Łarysa Szafran's lover. Give them some snippets from our evaluations, but only the stuff that's already in the papers. Add nothing from yourself. There's nothing worse than over-explaining. Let them feel like you've let them in on the deepest secrets. You're good at that.'

'Just don't let them know about the west wing, right?' She smiled. 'I should start with that, you know. Keep a step ahead of them. That way they'd stick to the official audit, sniff around a bit, looking for corruption and stuff— Oh, right, you and Four-Eyes are best buds!' she exclaimed, as if she had just remembered. 'You signed the car pick-up papers. A year after his treatment. They'll connect the dots soon enough and put you through the wringer.'

Startled and trying to hide it, he stomped across the room, stopping very close to her and clasping his hands on her bony shoulders. He couldn't help but notice she looked younger today. He didn't comment on it. It wasn't the time for compliments. There was a crisis to avert.

'Have you seen the car lately?' he said.

She shook her head, standing rigid. His touch wasn't making her comfortable.

'Piotr has about seven cars,' she replied. 'I was never interested in that one. It's an old wreck. And it's got a bad reputation.'

'You know nothing,' Saczko sighed. 'You didn't see inside it.'

He cocked his head, spreading his lips in a wry smile. 'Don't tell me you've never driven with him. Even when the two of you—'

'Nothing but hearsay,' she cut in coldly and shook his hands off. He walked back to his desk and reclined in his chair. His eyes never left her. He was waiting for a response. 'If you keep what you know about me and Piotr to yourself, I won't tell them about the west wing,' she promised finally. 'We're in this together.'

Saczko leaned towards her. 'We both know nothing ever happened between the two of you, right?'

'That's not what people think, unfortunately.'

'All right. Go now.'

She grabbed her Jane Shilton handbag, buttoned up her jacket and left.

'Look closely,' said Inspector Paweł Leśniewski, the chief technician from the Białystok station, who had arrived in Hajnówka along with Tomasz Domański. For the last twelve hours, the man had been working on collecting evidence from the two cars impounded in the forest after Iwona Bejnar's disappearance.

He and Doman were now standing in front of an old Mercedes that had seen better days. There were numerous scratches on its bodywork, and twigs and other debris from the forest. In some places the paint was chipped, and white smudges of base coat showed through. The bottom of the bumper was corroded right through. One of the rear quarter panels was missing.

'Tell me what you see.'

'An old clunker, but no worse than my own. What am I supposed to see?' asked Doman, helping himself to a cigarette.

'No smoking.' The technician stopped the chief inspector with a gesture. 'As tempting as it would be to have one with you.'

Doman reluctantly slid the pack back in his pocket and got out his chewing gum instead, offering one to Leśniewski, who refused.

'My dentist tells me it's bad for the teeth. Periodontitis.' He took out a pack of nicotine pills, tossed one into his mouth and smacked his lips. 'I got my candy. They don't really work. I still grind my teeth at night.'

'Right. I should have known why you were so lively,' Doman grunted. 'How many times have you tried quitting this month?'

'Oh, fuck off. This time I promised my wife I'll stick to it. She quit two years ago and I'm still trying. Can't lose to a woman, can I?'

'Okay, how about we talk business. I have an interrogation coming up in a minute. Do the numbers match? Has the mileage been tampered with? And: blood, hair, fingerprints. You got all that?'

Leśniewski didn't even pretend to listen. He waved his hand dismissively and walked to the other side of the car.

'Boring,' he said. 'The report is already on your desk. I have something better.' He opened the car door. 'Clunker, you said?'

He pulled a lever by the steering wheel and the car instantly rose a few centimetres. The technician looked out, seeing the effect that little show had on Doman's face. The chief inspector had the expression of a little boy who'd just got a toy fire engine.

'Out-fucking-standing! That would have saved the oil sump on my own hunk of junk so many times,' he said. Seeing Leśniewski's scornful stare, he added: 'I mean, pretty useful mechanism, Chief.'

'Give it a few seconds and the old four-eyes turns into an SUV. Not the same as a real off-roader, mind. It won't go up a sand dune but a forest? Like around Białowieża? No problemo.'

Doman whistled.

'That's why the guy drove through the woods and was able to catch up with the girl.'

'That's right.' The technician nodded and pointed to a set of plastic strips on the car's undercarriage. 'They may look cheap and they're pretty banged up, but they're practically indestructible. Titanium reinforcements. Like a tank, or at least close enough. The scratches are just in the Teflon layering – strictly cosmetic. What may be useful to know is that this wasn't that car's first foray into the local woods. I'd say it was mainly used to drive round that way. At least since last winter. We've found traces of moss, leaves, earth and fragments of animal faeces on the undercarriage and the tyres and they're old. More recently, the car must have driven over a bird's nest too. We found traces of protein.'

'What? It drives up trees too?' Doman smirked.

'I'm only telling you what we found. May come in handy when you look for the body. We can figure out what kind of bird it was. Maybe it lives on the forest floor?'

Doman grew serious. 'You think he used it to transport bodies?'

'Too early to say. We've sent the samples for analysis. I'll let you know as soon as we get something. There was a lot of hair and numerous fingerprints. There's blood, too. I'm getting there.'

Doman glanced at his watch. 'If I'm late to the questioning, Baldie's going to start without me. And he might cock up the whole case if I don't keep an eye on him. So please, just keep this quick.'

'Patience is a virtue, my friend.' Leśniewski smiled. 'I promise, you'll love it when I'm finished.'

Doman sighed. 'If you think I'm going to hug you, you've got another think coming.'

Leśniewski grimaced, but continued: 'He didn't visit the car wash too often. And the traces I'm about to show you aren't the same as those from the last trip. I've secured those in a separate batch.'

'Uh-huh,' Doman grunted. 'Any specifics? What about the reinforced undercarriage?'

'I'm not a mechanic, only a simple technician. Give it to Lech if you want more data. He'll be happy to help,' Leśniewski replied. 'But look at this. This is the real shit.'

He opened the door on the passenger side. The soft lining had been ripped off and there were four large holes in the metal sheet.

'These are bullet holes. Remember Łarysa Szafran's disappearance? I analysed this car personally back in 2000. I'd like to remind you that it was a different colour then. Ambulance white. It had been missing for more than a year, then it was miraculously found, and then got lost again.'

Doman nodded.

'The bodywork was repaired,' Leśniewski went on. 'New paint job. High-gloss T4W Tiefschwarz. Original Mercedes colour. One hundred forty złoty per can. It's only sold by Mercedes, you can't buy it outside an official retailer.'

'I bet you can get it on the Internet though.'

'I don't know. I'm only telling you what I see.'

'So? What's the big deal? I like shiny cars too.'

'Really? Last time I checked you were driving your wife's ride,' Leśniewski retorted.

Doman puffed up.

'Anyway, someone must have really wanted to keep those bullet holes as a souvenir.' The technician pointed to the holes. 'Look, even the ridges have been coated with anti-corrosion paint. The holes themselves have been polished from the inside. They look bigger than they should.'

'A new paint job is one thing, but replacing the whole door gets expensive,' Doman mused. 'Maybe the man just didn't want to overspend?'

Leśniewski wagged a finger at his friend. 'That's where you're wrong. This car has been renovated thoroughly, without skimping on expenses. And those holes, in my humble opinion, are a totem. Look!'

He pulled out the passenger seat. It was covered with faux-leather and had a factory label on the underside. Year of production: 2010. Leśniewski nodded to his assistant, who approached, bearing the car's lining.

'Everything in this car has been replaced. The seats, the lining, the steering wheel. Even the speedometer. Some of those things aren't even a year old. But most importantly, this old clunker runs on a brand new Mercedes S350 computer. BlueTEC. You don't get any more modern than that. That thing is smarter than most drivers. It sees in 3D and recognises road bumps to select the best damping profile. Three-sixty field of view. It even sees in the dark, way farther than the lights can reach. It reads you your texts and emails. It can heat up the window washer and it manages over five hundred LEDs. You know why the kidnapper took the profiler's little Uno? Because Four-Eyes here suddenly died.'

'Anti-theft system?'

'Better. The car recognises your fingerprint. It won't go more than five kilometres before turning off and engaging something called the "really dead" system. It plays dead. Literally. In order to start it again, you need the owner's finger – or you can call an expert from Mercedes to reboot the system. That thing only gets put in government limos and cars belonging to the very richest people in the country, like King Zygmunt.'

Doman arched an eyebrow.

'Like that guy who took out the biggest loan in Polish history. Remember? A hundred billion to buy a mobile phone company.

Has his own bank, an insurance company and radio that only plays classical, 'cause the king loves Rachmaninov.'

'How do you know that?'

'I keep an eye out. Read the papers. Usually the red-tops. They write about King Zygmunt all the time. Probably some old dispute. Anyway, you can buy yourself one of those for as little as fifty grand.' Leśniewski hesitated. 'Well, maybe a hundred.'

'So you're telling me this is our own Knight Rider?'

'Looks like it.'

Doman scratched his head. 'How much did it cost? The whole modification. Including the computer.'

'A fuckload.'

'Who sticks that kind of equipment into an old rust-bucket like that?'

'This is a small town,' Leśniewski said. 'As they say: what the eye doesn't see, the heart doesn't grieve. That's how I see it, and I'm a redneck myself. If Mr Four-Eyes bought himself a flashy paint job and sprinkled some chrome on his ride, people would say he was showing off.'

'You're right. This is not about money,' Doman admitted. 'What else? Because that's not everything, is it? I know you too well.'

Leśniewski walked over to the driver's seat with a wily smile. 'The car has an unlicensed liquid petroleum gas system. Homemade, you might say. What's interesting, the tank has been removed. The only things left are the switch and the fuel fill. Over here.' He jabbed a finger at the missing piece of bodywork. 'See? Ripped off.'

'Not your work?'

'It was missing from the get-go. The hooks are broken. Whoever did it, they didn't care for proper procedure. Besides, he'd have had to report the removal. So he just drove on petrol instead. Didn't use LPG at all. The papers probably say that the system is still functional. All you need is someone to sign the documents once a year.'

'We'll find the piece of shit. I have a few addresses already,' Doman said, disappointed. 'LPG system. Nothing out of the ordinary. And here I was, thinking you'd regale me with stories of infrared parking sensors or . . . I don't know, a cache of anti-tank missiles.'

'Sorry to disappoint, but I'd recommend taking a look at the car's history in the motor vehicle department. They might have a few interesting snippets. This machine has been through a lot.'

'As has its owner. We'll check everything. Tickets, speed cameras, insurances. Don't sweat it.'

'That's what I like to hear.' Leśniewski grinned. 'Remember – the car drove five kilometres from its parking space. Not a metre more.'

'So Bondaruk wasn't the driver.'

'He didn't participate in the kidnapping,' the technician said, nodding. 'Didn't lay a hand on it. In the literal sense, of course. He could still be our driver. We have a fuck-ton of prints. Check in tomorrow for the results.'

'You're suggesting we should look for garages within five kilometres of the crime scene?'

'Bingo!' Leśniewski puffed out his chest, arms akimbo.

'But the forest extends for more than thirty kilometres. There's nothing there. The car would have to have been kept in the woods, maybe in some kind of a shack?'

'That's what's been bugging me from the beginning, mate.'

They stood for a while, saying nothing. Doman lit a cigarette before Leśniewski could stop him.

'So, he installed a computer that cost a hundred grand but got a cheap-ass fuel system?' Doman mused. 'What for? To feel more eccentric?'

'Everything in this car has been thought through.'

'You've left the best for last, haven't you?' Doman guessed. He straightened up and waited.

Leśniewski took off his hat and ran his fingers through his hair. He stepped towards the boot. Doman followed.

'This is where the spare wheel should be.' Leśniewski lifted a felt cover. 'But instead, we have this.'

There was a parcel wrapped in a chequered blanket.

Doman couldn't resist. He pulled on a glove and swept the blanket aside. Beneath it lay a whole set of tools and weapons ordered by size. There were hand saws, cleavers, iron bars, and an old British Bull Dog revolver with the barrel sawn off right below the cylinder. Doman made to pick it up to take a closer look, but Leśniewski stopped him.

'It's not functional,' he explained. 'Besides, this is only half of the arsenal. We're sending all that to check for fingerprints. I've left this stuff here just for you.'

'Just to see the smile on my face, you mean?' The chief inspector cocked his head.

'Just so.' Leśniewski's face brightened in a wide grin. 'Of course, we're going to check if the six-shooter over there fits the holes in the door.'

'That would make things so simple,' Doman sighed, a dreamy expression on his face. 'God's will, I guess.'

'What we found in this old rattletrap is the real treasure, though.' The technician walked over to the wall, turning towards the second car – Sasza Załuska's blue Fiat Uno. He lifted a plastic camping fridge by its single, broken handle and opened it. Beneath a layer of frozen meat, finely chopped vegetables and boxes of vanilla ice cream was a cluster of long plastic containers with elastic tubes attached to one end. The tubes in turn terminated in IV cannulas. They were all labelled in detail and contained a brownish red fluid.

'Human blood,' Leśniewski said before Doman could ask. 'One was broken, so I satisfied my curiosity. We'll use agarose gel. There's no older or simpler method, but it's also the best. The boys at the lab will do a PCR test, and you'll know before sundown if it's a man's or a woman's.'

'How much is there?'

'Nearly six litres. More or less the amount you or I carry in us.'

'This has been taken from a single person?' Doman asked, faltering.

'Yes. Or, at least, the labels say so,' Leśniewski said. 'We'll have the blood tested anyway, obviously. And this is generally how you label blood for transplants. The bags are professional too. If I were you, I'd poke around the hospital, maybe look into the employees. Assuming they know we have both cars, they've probably already started wiping out traces.'

'If this is one guy, he bled out, is that right?' Doman asked hesitantly.

Instead of looking for the killer of the Ciszynia patient, he should order a helicopter, a ground radar, and an army detachment to look for Knight Rider's bride's body. He could already picture the expression on his superiors' faces when he told them about the extra expenses.

'Not necessarily.' The technician shrugged. 'He might still be alive and kicking.'

'Bullshit.' Doman spun on his heel.

The cover of the fridge slammed shut. 'Our bloodless friend may be okay if he got a full transfusion,' said Leśniewski. 'The lab will let us know tomorrow just who we have living in the fridge here. Julka can't do it any sooner, I've already asked.'

DUNIA

(1957)

The flimsy canary-yellow cloth sandals were hideous, but Dunia couldn't take her eyes off them. When she went to sleep she sat them on the windowsill, so they were the first thing she saw when she woke up. Mikhail Gaweł, her aunt's husband, who had taken Dunia in after her parents' death, had bought them on the market with the cash left over after selling last year's harvest, and had given them to his adopted daughter with an apology that he couldn't afford anything more fancy. His own children had received more valuable presents that day, but Dunia was happy nonetheless. Usually, Mikhail only gave her small handfuls of sweets or bundles of trimmings from the tailor. He knew that Dunia loved to sew, like her mother before her.

The sandals were a perfect fit, but for weeks, Dunia didn't even dare wear them at home, much less go out in them. But today was going to be a special occasion. A perfect excuse to finally show them off.

She and her uncle were to go to the town hall this morning so Dunia could pick up her identity document. This was a momentous occasion for the whole family. Dunia Załuska was the sole inheritor of her parents' property and land. With the identity documents, she could go to a notary to transfer the ownership of the Załuski estate to her benefactors – Mikhail and her Aunt Olga.

Everyone in the village wondered why Dunia wasn't engaged to any of the local boys, unlike most of her friends. She was an attractive young woman. People said she'd grow old and miss out on marriage. Would she live at her aunt's house for ever? She had a good dowry and should marry before it was too late. But the girl didn't want to hear about it.

She envied Adam, her stepbrother, seven years her junior; he was allowed to take private lessons in the city. The boy had already been writing applications to the authorities on behalf of the villagers for years and could count better than the shop-keeper at the Self-Help Cooperative, where the Gaweł family bought their farming equipment and feedstock. Mikhail had been collecting funds for his son's education since the boy was born. Adam was to graduate from a good high school and go to university. Move to the city and become a building surveyor. His future job was as good as guaranteed; Mikhail had arranged it with an erstwhile neighbour, Aleksander Krajnow, who was now a borough secretary in Bielsk Podlaski. The Gaweł family sent him half-carcasses after each pig slaughter. Adam's role was simply to survive until he came of age, then satisfy his father's ambitions.

As a girl, Dunia, though equally intelligent, had no right to a formal education. She could sing beautifully, and danced at other people's wedding parties. She should learn how to be a good house-wife and find herself a good husband. Since she had been living here she had had to get up at dawn, work around the farm, and tend to the seven children Olga had given birth to.

Mikhail had married Olga not even three months after the Załuski family were murdered. Her house had been burned down like every other Orthodox dwelling in the area and she had had nowhere to go. Nobody saw anything wrong with her getting mar-ried so soon after her family's tragedy. It would be worse if she had lived with Mikhail without the priest's blessing.

She'd only hesitated a moment. Poverty had a way of making people forget about their dreams. Olga didn't want to wait for Prince Charming from the city any more. And Mikhail wasn't too old, didn't drink too much, and worked hard on his small farm. He took Olga as his wife because the Załuski family land neigh-boured his own. It was convenient. He had numerous siblings, including an older brother, which meant he wouldn't get a scrap of land when the time came to divide the family inheritance. The only thing he could expect was to become a farmhand for his brother. Meanwhile, Dunia had a dozen hectares of land, not to mention the forest and the pastures. The Gawełs planned to take over the land officially. They deserved it, didn't they? They did take Dunia in after the war, after all.

Everyone seemed satisfied with this solution. Dunia had a roof over her head, and Olga had someone to do all the hardest house-work for free. And when they married Dunia off – perhaps to one of Mikhail's cousins – the estate would remain in the family. Załuskie, the village where they had lived, was no more, and only a fragment of their old house was left, nothing more than a patched-up shed they used for tool storage. After working his own small piece of land, Mikhail helped out with tending to the land of the more afflu-ent peasants. He would curse and complain; they didn't even let him speak his own language. All the landed peasants were Polish. But for now, until all the formalities were taken care off, he had no choice. This was all supposed to change when he took over the Załuski estate.

Olga was an obedient wife, though not nearly as resourceful as her dearly departed sister. And Mikhail always took her side. She was of slight build, sickly, and should be cared for, he said, and ordered Dunia to do all the hard work. The girl was tall for her age and had been lugging sacks of potatoes and crates of straw with the men since she was eleven. She had only com-plained once; it got her twenty lashes doled out with a heavy, wettened belt. Olga had administered the punishment herself and, afterwards, was completely drained and had to go to bed for the rest of the day.

Since that day, Dunia had never complained or said a single bad thing about her aunt. She knew her uncle wouldn't believe her. When Mikhail was around, Olga would swear that she loved her niece like her own children, though the truth always surfaced at mealtimes; Dunia was allowed to sit at the table only when her chores were done, and she was only given a spoon for her food when the rest of the family had had their share. Often, there was nothing left for her. Dunia was hungry all the time. Sometimes, when they had guests, Olga would send her to the pantry to get sausages or various preserves, and Dunia would stick a finger into the butter churn and at least have a taste of the cream gathering on the surface. She wasn't allowed anything more. If she stole any-thing, Olga would have immediately notice and told her husband.

Mikhail kept out of Olga's affairs at home. The kitchen and the household were her domain. He was an honest man and would not tolerate lying or thieving. Once when Dunia and the younger children took a little piece of sausage, Olga told him about it and Mikhail beat each and every one of them black and blue with a horse bridle. Dunia was the oldest, so she got the worst of it. For a month, she had to sleep sitting upright. She was afraid the bruises would never go away. But she was ashamed of her behaviour and promised herself that she would never again give her aunt or uncle any excuse to beat her. She kept that promise. From that time onward, each autumn Dunia would collect wild pears for herself. She dried them and nibbled on them for the rest of the year.

Olga always had more chores for Dunia. As she herself was always either pregnant or bedridden, she couldn't really work in the fields or keep the house. And Dunia was more of a mother to the other children than was Olga. Maybe this was why she didn't want her own family; acting like a mother since she was seven, when Olga and Mikhail had their first son, had knocked any notion of having her own children out of her. After Adam, the firstborn, her aunt gave birth to Andrzej, Stefan, Vera, Luba, Tosia and Alla – the last one was just the sweetest child. She was always happy and didn't cry at all. Dunia loved the girl as if she was her own unborn sister, who had died in the pogrom along with her mother.

Dunia didn't remember her mother, Katarzyna. She knew her face only from her parents' wedding photo, which Olga had ordered to be locked up in a chest. When Dunia was young, she had wanted to look like her mother. She hadn't inherited her regular features, only her slim, aquiline nose and high cheekbones. For years, people had told her she looked just like her father and that it would bring her luck. Bazyl might have been handsome, but nobody would have referred to him as 'pretty'. Dunia had his thick lips, large brown eyes and drooping eyelids, which made her look permanently sad. And even if she fasted for weeks, her cheeks were always slightly chubby. Whenever she smiled, a little dimple formed in the right one. Her body was stick thin, bony even, and her breasts were small, but because it was the trend at the time to wear multiple layers of clothes – even during the summer – Olga managed to talk everyone into thinking that Dunia was secretly overeating.

Sometimes, Dunia dreamed about her mother. The dreams were never vivid but more like flashbacks, snippets of the past: her mother standing up to defend her; the timbre of her voice, the playful sparks in her grey eyes, the carmine lips, or the touch of her delicate hands. Dunia wasn't sure if that was a real memory or just her imagination. She did remember the lingering feeling after each such dream, though. Strength, courage and mental fortitude. When people asked her what Katarzyna had been like, Dunia only shrugged and replied: 'Strong and wise. If she had been weak and stupid, she would have survived.'

She tried not to think about her mother too much. Nobody at home spoke of her at all. The subject of how she had died was a complete taboo. Aunt Olga always cut discussions short, saying that Katarzyna's only living daughter didn't deserve to hear about those horrible times. In time, Dunia's mother grew less clear in her memory, darkened by morbid images of murder and ruin. The girl did remember the last words Katarzyna had said to her though. 'I'll be your guardian angel. I won't let anyone hurt you.' When Dunia was still a child, sometimes she had thought she could feel her mother's presence. She would hear Katarzyna calling out to her. In such moments, Dunia would race to the river and call back, crying for her mother. And when life felt too difficult, she would imagine jumping in and floating away, never to return. But she never gathered the courage to do that; instead she would go back home and endure her aunt's disciplinary lectures. Olga would be angry that Dunia had been wandering around instead of doing chores or taking care of the children.

As she grew older, Dunia stopped believing in her mother's protective presence. She went to church, as it was the only occasion to dress up, but she had stopped believing in God years before. How does God allow murderers to be hailed as heroes? If God was making her suffer in Olga's house, she didn't want anything to do with Him. Dunia dreamed of studying medicine. She wanted to treat people, help the needy. She wanted to be God; only better, because unlike the real one, she would actually help. Miracles? There were no such things.

When she was thirteen, she delivered a baby for the first time, Olga's. After that, she was often called to assist the old midwife from the neighbouring village. A year previously, she had started visiting pregnant women on her own. She kept the money in a metal can. Just in case. Nobody else would pay for her studies, after all. She had no right to study. She wasn't even supposed to dream about it. One day, she would have to run away. This was her reason for not keeping anything she could call her own; she wouldn't be able to take anything with her. Anything she received as payment in kind from the women she helped, she exchanged for cash. Once, she'd told her aunt and uncle about her dreams. They laughed, but watched her closely for weeks.

There was one single time when Dunia had decided to go to the city without telling them, to buy books. As soon as she got back, Olga had beaten her bloody with a pole. The books that Dunia had spent all her savings on, she tossed into the fireplace. All the time she yelled at the top of her voice that she had had to carry the water from the well herself, feed the animals and milk the cows, and she hadn't raised Dunia so she could spend her time on idiocies like reading instead of doing her work around the farm.

It took all of Dunia's strength to get back on her feet after that beating. Finally, she understood her role. She had been grateful for the roof over her head and the opportunity to have something resembling a real family. Not any more. Now she was sure that, if it was up to her aunt and uncle, she would never be able to escape Wólka Wygonowska. Dunia would be able to leave only if she was moving to her new husband's place. But in their eyes she was already too old, and marrying her off would mean they'd have to pay a dowry. So, even if someone showed up at the doorstep asking for Dunia's hand, he'd have to pay them off. But that wouldn't change a thing in her life, would it? No farmer would allow his wife to go to the city and get an education. Her new husband would make her work her fingers to the bone, get her pregnant each year, and beat her up when he felt like it. She'd be his property. After Olga burned her books, Dunia was left with nothing. She would have to deliver dozens of babies to be able to buy a ticket and run off. The prospect of that was the only thing keeping her alive.

'Get us something to eat,' Mikhail said now.

He was sitting at the table with their wealthy neighbour, Artem Prokopiuk, for whom he worked tending to pigs, shearing sheep and digging up potatoes. Dunia shot a glance at the bottle of moonshine they were drinking and went to the pantry for some food. When she got back, the men were guffawing loudly and drunkenly.

'I can see, Mikhail, we're going to make a deal!' Artem raised a glass of spirit, ogling Dunia's backside lasciviously.

She cut some sausage into bite-size chunks, took a couple of sour gherkins from a stoneware jar and broke up some bread. Alla started to cry in the other room and she placed the food on the table and then went to her.

'Come over here, daughter!' she heard Mikhail calling .

When he was drunk, his face always grew less stern. Sometimes he even cracked a joke or two. He couldn't hold his liquor and only drank rarely. Only on special occasions. This had to be very special. He and Artem had already downed half the bottle.

Dunia returned with the child in her arms, cradling her and humming a lullaby.

'Grandfather Prokopiuk wants you to be his wife,' Mikhail said matter-of-factly. He didn't wait for a response. 'I've already agreed. He will help us get your land back. Your small dowry isn't a problem.'

Dunia nodded her thanks, as was the tradition, but kept silent. She knew her dowry boiled down to what she was wearing. They wouldn't even give her the wall-hangings or bed linens her mother had sewn and which had been saved from the fire. The only thing they'd maybe allow her to take was the old holy icon. And that was only because they had bought themselves a new one a month ago and the old one, burnt at the edges, had been put in the attic.

'I won't bend the knee, girl. I'm too old for that,' the old widower laughed.

He was older than Dunia's uncle and had been married twice already. Both his wives had died in childbirth. Dunia had assisted during his second wife's labour. She knew the woman had died because her husband had made her work the fields until the day she was due, and he didn't want to pay the doctor when she became ill. He also didn't call the midwife until the last moment and when she and Dunia had arrived, it was already too late. They only managed to save the child. Artem didn't seem too worried. He had gained another heir, after all. Now, he was just looking for someone to look after his children.

'I see she has some experience with tending to children,' Artem said, turning back to Mikhail. For him, the deal was already done.

'She's very good with children. Very good,' Dunia's uncle enthused.

Dunia felt she was jumping out of the frying pan into the fire. She stood rooted to the spot, saying nothing. They didn't expect her to. They didn't even look her way as they talked, joked and drank. They discussed business, the political situation. Artem knew someone in town. He promised he'd get Mikhail some farming equipment. Their plans were ambitious. They wanted to develop the farmland together. They laughed, patting each other's backs.

'Mum hasn't returned,' Dunia said. 'She should be home by now. The cows haven't been brought in.'

Mikhail shook his head like a wet dog. He took a look outside the window. It was growing dark.

'Well, go fetch her.' He waved a hand, as if shooing away an irritating fly.

'The children are alone. Alla has a fever.'

Mikhail extended his arms. Dunia handed him his daughter.

'Hurry up,' he said. 'We have to wake up at dawn tomorrow.'

Dunia headed for the door. Artem rose and staggered after her, stopping her just before she reached for the handle.

'We have an accord, then,' he said. He was sporting an obscene smile. He licked his lips. On his moustache, Dunia could see droplets of grease from the cold cuts he had eaten. She felt sick. 'We will announce our betrothal on Sunday, and we'll marry after the holiday,' he went on. 'I see no reason to put this off. You're not that young, after all.'

'Well said!' Mikhail burst out laughing.

Dunia excused herself, but Artem didn't budge. He shot out his arm, wrapping it around her waist, and pulled her to him. She pushed him away and slapped him with all the strength she could muster. That only made him laugh.

'Hot-blooded gal!' He grinned, massaging his reddening cheek. The hit had sobered him up a bit.

Mikhail said nothing. He put his knife down and tried pushing himself up, arms propped on the table, but slumped back down. 'Apologise to our guest,' he mumbled.

Dunia stood in the door, petrified, blushing.

'Apologise, girl! You have to respect your husband.'

'He's not my husband yet!' she replied, raising her chin defiantly.

Artem waved a hand dismissively, amused. 'Let it go, Mikhail. I got carried away. The girl's handy, I have to give her that. And she's only defending her honour.' He chortled. 'I like it. That's why I chose her.'

Mikhail finally managed to clamber to his feet. He headed to the wall, grabbing a thin rawhide lash hanging on a hook there. Then he walked over to a bucket of water by the stove and dipped the strap, shaking the excess water off.

'Apologise. Now.'

Dunia recalled the time when he had smacked little Andrzej's head on the stove. He had never recovered; now he was slow and could still not read. She didn't want to share the boy's fate.

'Please forgive me, sir.' She was looking down.

'Raise your head,' Mikhail ordered.

She looked up.

'Forgive me,' she hissed through clenched teeth. 'I was out of line.'

Artem brightened up. 'You have raised her well, friend. She will be a good wife.'

Dunia stifled a sob. She felt helpless. Her hand balled into a fist, but she kept it in her pocket. She could feel the nails biting into the flesh of her palm.

'May I go now?'

'Come back soon,' Mikhail replied as if nothing had happened. 'And don't drive the cows too hard or the milk will go sour.'

'Yes, Father.' She left.

Instead of going to get Olga at once, Dunia huddled in the pigsty and cried, trying to make as little noise as possible. She was adept at keeping quiet by now. She wept silently every day, and the short moments of tearful solitude were as much a part of her day as morning ablutions. She couldn't remember a time when she had no reason to hide in the pigsty. When she felt calm again, it was already dark. Olga might have already driven the cattle back. If she had told her husband that Dunia hadn't gone out looking for her, the girl would be in even more trouble.

Dunia rushed to the road. Olga was just turning away from what looked like a friendly conversation with their Catholic neighbour. Her face was flushed. She had probably had too much to drink at the neighbour's house. She also looked unusually happy. But what really drew Dunia's attention was the new, flowery shawl her aunt had wrapped around her head. Olga was also holding a paper bag carrying the name of a city confectioner's. She must have been to the city.

'What happened to you?' Dunia asked. 'Father is worried.'

'I had the most wonderful day,' Olga explained with a self-satisfied smirk. 'I found a can full of money behind the barn, next to the stanchions. It wasn't much, but it was enough to buy sweets for the children. Just look how much I got.'

She pulled the bag open. Inside was a heap of colourful sweets. Dunia felt the blood draining from her face. Suddenly, she couldn't breathe. Olga snatched the bag away.

'Not for you. When I divide it between the children, you might get one,' she barked.

'That was my money! Mine!' Dunia shrieked. 'You knew that!'

'Yours?' Olga asked. 'Since when do children earn money? Even I don't get anything. And I work way harder than you, you leech.'

Dunia pointed a finger at her aunt.

'I was saving that. It took me a year. I was supposed to pay for school. Take the sweets back to the shop.'

'Shush, stupid!' Olga spat. 'Or I'll tell your father you've been stealing. I'll tell him everything and I'll show him that cubbyhole of yours. School!' She snorted. 'You're bad in the head, you ingrate. You won't go to any school. I'll teach you a lesson! And Mikhail will beat all the knowledge you need into you. You won't sit down for a week!'

'I earned it. I earned it myself.' Dunia started to cry.

But Olga wasn't listening. She continued her tirade. 'You must have stolen from your own father. Taken his spare change.'

Dunia collapsed to her knees and grabbed the hem of Olga's dress. 'No, you know people paid me for helping out with delivering babies,' she whispered pleadingly. 'You can take the money. Give the sweets to the children. Just don't tell Father, and please give me back whatever's left.'

'Nothing's left!' Olga laughed loudly. She smoothed her new scarf. 'You like it?'

Dunia stood back up. She fixed Olga with a glare. Tears streamed down her cheeks. She remained perfectly quiet, though. The only thing she could feel now was pure hate. For the first time in years, she could feel the presence of her mother. *Run away*, she said. *Go. Go wherever your legs take you.* Dunia could hear the words clearly in her head. *God will help you. I will be there for you. Always.* The spectral voice vanished. Her aunt stepped closer and wiped the tears away from Dunia's face with the corner of her scarf. She had to raise her arms above her head. She was shorter than her niece, reaching no higher than her chest. Dunia could feel the smell of fruit liqueur on her breath.

'Stop snivelling.' Olga's expression grew less severe. She hugged Dunia, snuggling against her chest like a cat. 'We'll buy you a scarf just like that when you marry. I won't tell your father anything.'

The girl stared coldly into the distance, frozen rigid.

'For a moment there, you looked just like Katarzyna, you know?' Olga went on. 'You grew all pretty. I was scared it was her inside you. As if her ghost was telling me something, you know?'

Dunia closed her eyes. She started to pray. That made her feel calmer. The world started to spin around her. She could die right now. There was nothing in her head besides an image that appeared and then became the centre of her universe. It was Katarzyna. She stepped down from heaven and pulled Dunia into her arms. She cradled her, just like Dunia had with little Alla. For the first time, she could see her mother's face so clearly. Each detail: the shape of her eyes, nose, jaw; the pores in her skin. Katarzyna smiled warmly. *So you do remember me.* And then Dunia felt something tugging at her and her mother vanished. She opened her eyes again. There was a drunken old hag standing in front of her. It took her a while to realise it was Olga, trying to shake her out of her stupor. Dunia didn't want to go back to reality. She floated away again. But her mother didn't reappear; this time, Dunia could only see Olga's face. Decades older. And then, flashes: she chased away her oldest son, and cried on the grave of her husband, and then sat alone, surrounded by empty bottles and rubbish, and then clutched at her chest, and then she was lying dead in a coffin. All this flew past Dunia's eyes in one, lightning-fast sequence. It must have lasted for only moments, but it felt as if she had been witness to her aunt's whole life.

'You'll die in your bed,' she said in an empty voice. 'Your heart will burst. You will live long, but you will bury three of your children. You will bury your husband too. A horse will kick him to death. Then, you will die too. In winter. In pain.'

Olga blinked. Her mouth hung open slackly. She looked shaken. 'What are you saying?'

'They'll find your body during harvest season, months after you die. You'll be dry as a husk by then,' Dunia finished.

They looked at each other, both knowing something out of the ordinary had just happened. Dunia clutched at her head. It was throbbing. 'What is happening to me?'

Olga was out of her mind with fear. 'People were right,' she whispered and backed away. 'You have power.'

'What? What did they say?'

Olga waved it away. Her demeanour changed. She leaned over and spoke in Dunia's ear.

'I won't tell anyone. Nobody should know. They'll say you're a whisperer. Or a witch. They'll chase us away,' she hissed. She meant to scare Dunia, and it was working. The girl nodded meekly. 'But you won't tell anyone about the money. It will be our secret. Here. Take a few,' she said, fishing out a couple of sweets from the bag.

Dunia shook her head and disentangled herself from her aunt's embrace. She walked home, not looking back. She went to bed early and didn't even get up when she heard little Alla crying. She felt like a monster for leaving her little sister like that. But something had broken in her on that road. She had regained her mother and there was nothing to keep her here any more. She had had enough of being the housekeeper, labourer and servant to her adoptive parents. She wouldn't let them sell her for a strip of land, like a cow or a sow.

When Olga woke the next morning to Alla crying, she called out to Dunia to deal with it. But her niece didn't reply. Her bed was empty.

Olga went to the window and looked outside. The horse was already harnessed. Of course – Mikhail and Dunia were going to the city today. Olga looked around the room. The yellow sandals had gone, as had several sets of sheets and Katarzyna's photograph from the chest. She realised she'd never see her new scarf again as well. She cursed her niece silently.

Dunia had been wandering around the forest for at least an hour now. She had left home before dawn but had lost her way in the darkness. A storm was brewing. The air was thick and hot like winter stew. It would start raining any time now. She thought she could already feel solitary raindrops on her face. She wouldn't be able to go home again. She wouldn't get her land back, probably. But she'd rather die than return anyway. Only humiliation lay that way. Dunia needed a good hiding place. She had stolen a loaf of bread and a ring of sausage from the pantry. If things took a turn for the worse, at least she'd die with her stomach full. She'd jump into the river. They wouldn't catch her. They wouldn't marry her off against her will. She wouldn't live the life they had planned for her. Her ancestral land didn't matter to her. The only thing that mattered was freedom. For now, her only idea was to hide in the old shed by her real parents' ruined house. She didn't know the way through the dense forest, but she marched at a brisk pace, feeling the raindrops pattering on her head faster now. If she got too wet and cold, she'd have no chance of survival.

Dunia reached a clearing that forked out into three paths. She stood there for a long while, unable to make a decision. She closed her eyes, letting fate decide for her. Her legs took her across the glade. After a few dozen steps, her foot caught on a protruding root and she nearly fell. She opened her eyes. It was now raining heavily. She wrapped herself tightly in her new scarf, and then she noticed an outline of a shack between the trees. There was a light in one of the windows. Dunia brightened up. She had no idea who lived there, but she didn't hesitate, running over to the building and knocking on the door. It creaked ominously. She saw that only one hinge kept it in its place. No one responded, so she pushed it open. Inside, at the hearth, sat an old woman wrapped in rags. She was stirring something in a large pot. The house was dirty. It smelled of old things and poverty. In the centre of the room stood a table holding a couple of Orthodox icons. The *rushnyk** around the painting of the Holy Virgin was clean and starched. Dunia was sure nothing bad would befall her in this place.

'*Slava Hospodu Isusu Christu,*' she said by way of greeting.

'*Vo vyeky vyekov,*' the old woman replied.

Only now did she look up, revealing her face. She tried standing up but reached back to rub at her lower back, moaned softly, and sat back down. Dunia dropped the small bundle containing her things at the door and rushed to the woman to help her. The poor woman was so thin, she seemed as if she would break in two.

'Please, Grandmother, lie down!' Dunia helped her host to a metal-framed bed strewn with dirty linens.

'I was about to have some herbal tea,' the ancient woman croaked in Belarusian and grew silent, gasping for air. 'I didn't finish making it. I don't have the strength any more.'

Dunia finished brewing the tea, strained the herbs and gave the infusion to the woman, who took a sip.

'I cannot help myself any more, so I doubt I'll be able to help you,' she sighed. 'It's nearly my time. My cow gave birth, but the first calf is dead. The old girl is too exhausted to push out the other one. She should be destroyed, so she doesn't suffer. I wish God would take me too. I'm not good for anything any more.'

Dunia placed a hand on the old lady's brow. She was burning up. She must have had a nosebleed recently; there were fresh scabs around her nose. Dunia went back to her bundle and took out a slice of bread and some sausage. She fed the dying woman piece by piece, like a little child. Then she covered her with the old blanket and recited a quick prayer. Her whispering seemed to calm the woman down. She closed her eyes and her face relaxed in an expression of bliss.

---

* A ritual cloth embroidered with symbols; used in sacred Eastern Slavic rituals, religious services and ceremonial events.

'May God bless you,' she breathed. 'When I die, write "Nina" on my gravestone. That will be enough.'

Dunia nodded, and then huddled against the woman. She didn't know why she did it but for a time, they stayed like this, embracing. Dunia felt her mother again. Katarzyna's ghost was standing right behind her. Her mother was still young, pregnant, and dressed in her winter clothes. Just as Dunia remembered her from her childhood. She imagined Katarzyna smiling at her, placing a hot hand on her forehead and saying, 'Shhh, quiet, it's okay.' But when she turned her head, there was nobody there. Only a brown cat skipped across the empty pots by the stove. The old woman was asleep. She was breathing steadily. Dunia got up and took a step back, saying more to herself than her host, 'I'll go see the cow. You stay here, Grandmother.'

She went to the door and opened it. There was a man standing outside. He wore a padded coat. His chin was covered with stubble. He had a crumpled *ushanka* on his head and an unfiltered cigarette between his lips. He was soaking wet. Water dripped from the peak of his hat.

'There you are,' said Artem, Dunia's would-be husband.

He reached out but didn't catch her, as she took a quick step back. The sky was suddenly lit by a thunderbolt. In the brightness, Dunia thought she glimpsed an angelic host. Her mother was among them. Her face was white, covered with a shawl, only her eyes visible. They were perfectly still, like the eyes of saints in paintings. Dunia blinked, but the vision would not go away. She wasn't afraid of them any more. She was getting used to them. Then the thunder rolled, deafening. She smelled something burning.

Artem was lying at her feet. She crouched down and turned his head. His face was blackened. He wasn't moving. The lightning bolt must have hit him right on the top of his head. His hat had a giant hole in it. There was a burnt spot on his head, and the hair around the wound was charred to the skin. But all of a sudden, his eyes snapped open. Seeing Dunia looming over him, he came to his senses immediately. He jumped to his feet and raced away, as if chased by the devil himself.

Dunia got up and her lips spread in a smile. Artem would never try to touch her again. Another realisation dawned on her.

The rumour would spread like wildfire. People would fear her. She knew by now that on the wintry morning in 1946 when her mother was killed, a rifle had exploded in the hands of a soldier who was going to shoot Dunia, and that people said it was *because* of Dunia. And now, a lightning bolt had nearly killed Artem. People in this region still believed in the old folk nonsense. Dunia clenched her teeth, but couldn't stop herself from crying. She begged God to take the power away. She didn't want to be a witch.

Mikołaj Nesteruk decided to finish his chores earlier than usual. His mare pulled the wagon with difficulty. It was loaded to the top. He had more scrap metal than he needed. The blacksmith for whom Mikołaj collected metal junk wouldn't be able to smelt it until Christmas. He stopped in a clearing and allowed his horse to nibble on the fresh grass. Grandmother Nina lived not far from here. Mikołaj's father used to come to the old whisperer for help. Mikołaj strapped down the wagon and travelled the rest of the way on foot. Like every year, he wanted to ask the ancient woman for a prayer for the people who had gone missing or were murdered during the war. He still had hope that his old friend, Bazyli Załuski, had hidden away during the turmoil, and that he'd return someday. Just like he himself had.

Instead of the old hermit, he saw a young woman by the well. She was pulling buckets of water from the shaft and pouring water into a large tub. It looked like she was washing linen; white sheets were strung between the trees. Mikołaj took his hat off and greeted the girl respectfully, but stopped dumbfounded when she turned to look at him. He saw the ghost of his long-dead sister-in-law. Or rather, her new incarnation. The girl must have noticed his confusion, as she didn't say a thing, just stood there with her sleeves rolled up, her trusting eyes locked on Mikołaj.

'Is Nina home?' he asked dumbly, unable to think of anything else to say.

The girl nodded. A strand of hair slipped down from beneath the braid wrapped around her head like a crown. She brushed it away. He remembered Katarzyna making that exact same gesture. His knees felt weak.

'She's by the stove,' the young woman said and returned to work.

Mikołaj sighed with relief. The unnatural similarity had vanished as soon as she spoke. He'd had no idea Nina had an adult daughter. She'd never been married and the whole time he had been visiting her, he hadn't seen any man apart from those who came here for the woman's help. He didn't want to offend the girl. Maybe the whisperer would dispel his doubts.

He was shocked again when he stepped inside the old house. The place had never been this clean before. Old Nina had always been focused solely on her mission. God had given her the power to heal and exorcise the devil, and she never refused to help. Way back when, people used to queue to get an audience with her. Nina had stopped caring about the material world years ago, and when her own health started to deteriorate, she had just accepted the fact that her house looked more like a cave than a proper cottage. She lived like an animal, sleeping, eating and preparing and performing rituals in the same room. Now, even the bad smell of a room divided from the cowshed only by a thin, hole-riddled wall was gone.

'*Slava Hospodu,*' he said.

'For ever and ever,' he heard Nina reply from somewhere beneath a stack of feather blankets by the stove. Mikołaj headed that way. The old woman attempted to get up, but he stopped her with a gesture.

'Don't get up on my account, Mother. I was just passing by. Everything is all right.'

'How long is it since you stopped drinking, Kola?'

'Eight years, give or take. I do as you told me, to the letter. Each year. I still have the poppy seeds and the herbs. Thank you.'

'Don't thank me. It's not my doing. It's faith. *Hospodi miluyet.*'

'But my cow has got sluggish. It's probably the evil eye. A curse. And maybe you could also pray for Kasia and Bazyli.' He placed a few bills on the table.

Nina shook her head and pushed the money away.

'Too much.'

'Take it,' Mikołaj insisted. 'You're a good woman. You can buy something for your daughter in town.'

Nina didn't have a chance to protest; Dunia entered, nodded to the guest and went into the other room.

'Do you recognise her?' Nina pointed at the closed door.

Mikołaj muttered something vague.

'She's your niece. Kasia's and Bazyli's daughter.' Nina bobbed her head and for a while sat in silence, taking in Mikołaj's stunned expression. 'God brought her to me. Olga threw her away. She's afraid to go back.'

Mikołaj balled his fists.

'Don't lose your temper, dear boy,' the old whisperer said placatingly, and handed him a small greasy piece of wood. It had probably had a painted image of a saint on it years before. Now, because of all the rubbing and touching, all that remained was its golden frame. 'Do you feel the warmth?'

Mikołaj squinted and nodded.

'I do.'

'Your faith is still strong.' Nina nodded approvingly. 'You'll take the girl with you and drive her to the city. As far away from this place as possible. The ground here is soaked with her ancestors' blood. She cannot stay here. She cannot return here, or she'll waste away. And, most importantly, she cannot make any decisions here. She needs to travel the world. It is her fate.'

Mikołaj's eyes snapped open.

'It burns!' He tried pulling his hand away from the painting.

Nina gave a sinister laugh. 'It's her,' she whispered, lowering her voice and pointing to the door to the other room. 'She has the power. She's young. Good. Like her mother. She'll serve the people. I taught her everything. God has never given me a daughter, but he has brought her to me. Praise be.'

'Does she . . .' Mikołaj hesitated. 'Does she know who I am?'

'She'll know soon enough,' Nina replied calmly, as if it were nothing important. 'You can take your hand away. God gives everything you need. And lets you forget everything you don't. Remember.'

Mikołaj pulled his hand away. He stared at the old woman expectantly, but she didn't burn any linen like usual. She didn't sprinkle his head with ash, and she didn't pray thirteen times, bowing deeply. Instead, she went to the wardrobe, took out a set of her best linens, wool scarves, her best coat, lacquered shoes with a stubby heel – probably from the time of her own wedding – and a white shirt with an enormous embroidered collar. Finally, she put a bundle wrapped in paper on top of the pile. She lifted one corner of the paper to show Mikołaj its contents. It was money. Mikołaj protested, insisting that she keep at least some of it for herself, but the woman only slapped him gently with an open hand, as if swatting a fly.

'Go now,' she said. The effort had clearly exhausted her and she crawled back into her blankets.

'Piotr! Come here!' Aniela Bondaruk called to a black-haired boy who had just climbed onto the windowsill and was now jumping up and down like a bouncing ball, trying to reach a dragonfly that had flown into the apartment. Glistening with rainbow-like colours, it buzzed loudly as it tried to escape through the window, bouncing off the glass now and again.

Aniela, already in her fur coat, was collecting up her son's things. School bag, lunch, scarf. She cleared plates from the table and then, seeing her son was wobbling on the sill, she rushed to the window and caught him just before he hit the floor. The boy, tall for his age, ten, nearly squashed her as he fell. But at least this time he didn't break a tooth, as he had done when he climbed onto the roof of the toilet block at school.

'You'll be the end of me,' she said, panting.

She sat down on the sofa, red stains blooming over her cheeks, and stared at her son. Piotr giggled, amused by his mother's panic. He extended a hand and opened his palm. In the middle lay the dragonfly. Dead. Its wings seemed deep purple now. Aniela had never seen such an exotic insect before. She pushed Piotr's hand away with disgust. She hated bugs. Too many of them in the hospital in Hajnówka, where she worked as an ambulance dispatcher.

'Staszek, you take him.' Aniela called, looking over at the other room, where her husband was sitting at his desk. Most of the desktop was strewn with papers and his abacus. He didn't so much as raise his eyes, just carried on muttering calculations. The metal wood-drying chamber he had designed was supposed to be made ready later today. A delegation all the way from Warsaw had arrived in Hajnówka the previous evening and they would be at the lumber mill later. Staszek was supposed to show them how the prototype worked. If the central office decided to buy a few sets, he'd be promoted to manager.

'Are you listening to me? I won't put up with him any more,' Aniela repeated.

Staszek pushed a stack of documents away and put his pen down. 'Piotr is not a newborn. He can find his way to school on his own,' he said and winked at his son, who was just filching a box of matches behind his mother's back. He poured them into his pocket and stuffed the dead dragonfly into the box.

'Sure, I'll find my way,' he called. 'Dad's right.'

'Just make sure it doesn't end like the last time,' Aniela grumbled. 'Go to school, not the swings at the park.'

'He's embarrassed that you still walk him to school, like he's a baby.'

'That's right!' Piotr was now drilling a hole in his glove with a finger. 'Don't worry, Mum.'

'All right. Then I'm off.' Aniela left, slamming the door shut behind her.

Her shift began in twenty minutes. If she hurried, she'd still have time for a coffee with her colleagues.

Staszek and Piotr exchanged glances.

'Right. Off you go too, Bondaruk.' Staszek got up. 'We're leaving. But if you disappoint your mother, you little shit, I'll beat your arse black and blue.' He wagged a finger at his son.

The threat didn't seem to frighten the boy at all. Nobody had ever hit him at home. He got his coat and bag together with surprising alacrity and was out of the door before his father had realised. Instead of school, he went straight to the Soviet Army cemetery, where he was supposed to meet his buddies. It was usually empty, apart from on public holidays. His pockets were stuffed with the matches, a number of cigarettes he had been stealing one by one from his father for the last week, and the dead dragonfly in the matchbox, which he intended to publicly deprive of its wings. Maybe he'd also be able to scare some girls at school with it. If he ended up there, that is.

There was a wagon filled with junk in front of the cemetery gate. A peasant in a *ushanka* hat sat on its bench. He was talking to a girl wearing felt boots, too large for her feet. It was obvious she came from the villages too. Piotr hid behind a tree. He waited until the peasant drove away. They'd only ask why he wasn't at school.

As soon as the wagon had rolled off, Piotr climbed the cemetery wall and jumped on the girl from behind, but she moved away at the last instant. The scarf slipped from her head. She was young and pretty. And the worst part was that instead of fleeing, she laughed.

The boy fell awkwardly to the cobblestone pavement and howled in pain, then burst into tears. The girl's expression grew sour. She helped him up, but he couldn't stand on his own. He pushed her away, so she placed the bundle she was carrying in the grass. Intoning some old Belarusian song, she managed to untie his shoe, but he jerked away again, kicking her in the nose in the process. She withdrew and sent him an angry look. He grew meek all of a sudden and mumbled something akin to a proper apology.

'Calm down. You're not dying,' she scolded him. 'Let me see. Or do you want me to leave you here?'

His ankle had swollen up and was getting more swollen by the moment. It had to hurt like hell. Tears were flowing freely down his face. The girl felt for the kid, but she didn't intend to get all mushy. His hands were shaky. His face reminded her of the children in the reproductions of famous paintings by Wyspiański that she used to look at through the library window. He didn't resemble the little devil he probably wanted people to see him as.

'It's broken.' She crouched down next to him and added: 'Don't kick me again.'

Piotr gave her an unexpected hug. She didn't know how to react at first. Nobody had ever hugged her before. Finally, she wrapped her arms around him, and realised that her eyes were tearing up too.

'We're going to the hospital,' she said gently. Her voice held affection, concern and fear. He felt them all.

Piotr grew visibly frightened at first. He shook his head desperately, crying and moaning. Dunia kept her stare fixed on him. She got it. He was a little tough guy. He'd only respect someone strong.

'Be a man,' she barked. She couldn't help herself though, and wiped the snot from under his nose. 'I'm Dunia,' she said. 'You'll be all right. Do you know what it means to die?'

'Mummy!' he screamed.

The kid was spoilt, apparently. A boy from a good house. He wouldn't have made it at Mikhail and Olga's house. She felt a sudden wave of irritation.

'Quit screaming,' she scolded him. 'At least you have a mother. Some people aren't as lucky as you.'

She placed a hand on his brow and started to whisper something that Piotr couldn't understand. He grew calmer though, and finally fell asleep. Dunia stood by the cemetery wall and watched the street, hoping someone would appear. There was nobody. No one ventured this far from the town centre at this time of day. She thought about going to the church to ask for help, but decided against it. She didn't want to leave the boy alone. Suddenly, in the distance she spotted a black Volga and rushed to the road. The car raced straight at her and she jumped aside just in time, then turned back, panting. The car stopped a hundred metres or so down the road. She ran towards it and knocked at the window. Behind the wheel was a man wearing a uniform cap. In the back seat were two more men. One of them wore a sweater and a sheepskin coat, and the other a grey suit. He held a file of documents on his knees. He looked extremely irritated that someone had dared to interrupt his journey.

Dunia blushed. She saw that the other man in the back, the one in the sweater, had rolled the window down a bit. He kept his eyes fixed on her. He was a large man. Ugly like a gargoyle. Despite his casual outfit, he had to be important. Dunia had never seen such a beautiful car before. Chrome handles, polished bodywork. She felt intimidated. She managed to stammer an apology in Polish, and then pointed back to the boy lying by the cemetery wall.

A few minutes later she was in the back seat of the Volga. The boy's head rested on her knees, and his dirty legs were leaving dark smudges on the dignitary's sheepskin coat. 'What's your name?' the dignitary asked her from the front passenger seat. He and the other man had moved so they could lie the boy across the back seat. He could have been no more than twenty-five, but he seemed too mature for her to call him by his name, even though he had said she should. He'd introduced himself as Anatol Pires.

'Dunia Załuska.' She inclined her head gracefully. They were speaking Belarusian now, and Anatol spoke it like she had never before heard anyone speaking it. It was beautiful; a natural lilt and melody.

'And this guy is Stepan Orzechowski,' Anatol said. The man in the front turned and extended a hand to her. It was bony and well-manicured. Not the hand of a manual worker. Blushing, Dunia shook his hand, though she was embarrassed that the skin of her palm would be too coarse to the touch. He clearly noticed both the roughness of her skin and the adorable way in which she blushed; he smiled, revealing a set of perfectly white teeth, and placed a kiss on her palm. She immediately pulled her hand free and stuck it into her pocket.

'Which high school do you go to?'

Dunia raised her head haughtily and replied: 'I will apply to the medical school in Bielsk next year. I'm looking for work for now.'

Stepan Orzechowski measured her up with his eyes. 'Where do you live?'

'I'm renting a room,' she lied and pointed to the sleeping boy. 'And this is my nephew.'

Anatol Pires smiled. 'As it happens, I could help you out. I'm the headmaster of the local high school. But you'd have to pass an exam. Are you from the countryside?'

She nodded.

'Larysa Hienijuš,' Anatol went on. 'Our first revolutionary. She never accepted Soviet citizenship. She emigrated to Bohemia. It was the only country that helped the Belarusian people. That's where she lived and wrote. After she was released from labour camp, she decided to return to her ancestral land. She died in Zelva. A true freedom fighter. Do you know her?'

Dunia shook her head. She felt so bland, ugly, and useless.

'You should read some of her work. Maybe you'll learn something. Knowledge – that's the only freedom worth fighting for,' Anatol said.

'Stop confusing her, Anatol,' Orzechowski chimed in, also in Belarusian. Dunia was surprised. She'd thought he was Polish. 'Come to the mill tomorrow. Tell the man at the gate I sent you. The plant needs strong young women to lay floorboards in the drying room. It's hard work, mind you, and I don't really think you'll last – but it's worth a try.'

'I've worked since I was a child,' she said defiantly. 'I want to learn *and* work.'

The men exchanged glances and laughed.

'Women like you are nothing but trouble,' Orzechowski said without turning round. 'You should curb your pride. At least pretend to be humble. You know what they say: only cowards survive wars. The heroes are the first to die. It's just how the world works.'

Dunia stared at the dignitary's back.

'The war is over.'

'Sometimes it's about what you can't see.' He sighed and returned to his papers.

Meanwhile, Anatol was unable to stop shooting lustful glances at Dunia. 'Have you got your ID yet?' he asked.

Dunia dropped her eyes shyly but didn't respond. Instead, she just thanked the 'kind sirs' for their helpfulness.

'There are no "kind sirs" here,' Orzechowski bristled. 'Only comrades. Belarusian brothers in arms, girl.'

The car stopped at the hospital gate. Anatol offered to help Dunia carry Piotr, but she threw her sack over her shoulder, took the boy in her arms as if he weighed no more than a bundle of sticks for the fire, and carried him all the way to reception. A nurse jumped up from behind the desk. Another nurse appeared with a stretcher. Anatol followed Dunia with his eyes until she'd disappeared through the door, and then turned to Stepan. 'Strong and feisty, eh?'

'She's not Belarusian. Can't be. A German or a Pole. Some kind of fascist half-breed. Have you seen her face?'

Anatol laughed out loud and patted his friend on the cheek. 'You really don't like women, do you?'

'Unlike you. Always playing the field. While your Jagoda waits at home.'

'She's waiting, all right. And besides, she does my job for me. She's translating my articles into German for *Allgemeine Zeitung*.'

'Let me tell you: if I met someone like her, maybe I'd consider marrying too.' Stepan sighed.

'Oh, sure, if she has a pair of balls you would.' Anatol snorted. Stepan stared him down, then shot a glance at the driver, who must have overheard the conversation. He'd have to fire the poor man now.

By that evening, when he was on his way to meet the priest, his lover, he had already forgotten about the incident with the peasant girl.

Anatol, however, had jotted down Dunia's last name and now went to the town hall, where he asked for the pictures she had submitted with her ID application. Now he was staring at the feisty girl's intelligent face. There weren't many people with the courage to stop an intimidating black Volga clearly belonging to a regime official just to help a child. He would remember her. He remembered everything and everyone. That was why he was good at his job.

When he arrived at work, he didn't even pop into the common room to say hello. Instead he went straight to his office, from where he called his friends at the secret police, asking them to dig up everything they could about the girl's family down to the third generation. Anatol ordered the agents to find the girl and keep an eye on her. He wanted to know everything about her. He sat back in his chair and smiled.

He already had a wife and was quite happy with her. His life was good, and he wouldn't want to turn it upside down all of a sudden. More trouble wasn't what he needed right now. After all, he had lovers of all kinds, eager to please him. But the fact remained that he hadn't been this excited for a long time. He couldn't help it – he had to have that girl. She might have been poorly dressed, bad at holding a conversation, straight-up uncivilised, but she was proud, bold and most probably totally innocent. An idealistic and audacious woman who wouldn't give her most precious possession to just anyone. She'd rather become an old spinster than marry someone she didn't love. Anatol knew it would take an effort to soften her up. No simple sweet talk would be enough here. She'd resist. But, deep down inside, he was counting on just that. For the rest of the day he remained in good spirits. He even finally agreed on a trip to Germany to spy on an enemy of the state – a mission he had been refusing for months now. All in all, it was a good day.

Hajnówka, 2014

Twenty-three square metres, not counting the cluttered balcony, had become Sasza Załuska's temporary base of operations.

When she entered the stuffy apartment on Piłsudskiego Street, she decided that Romanowska's aunt must be part of the town's intellectual elite. There were no gaudy pieces of furniture, soft armchairs, copies of paintings by Matejko, pastel landscapes on the walls or any of that stuff. No purely decorative bric-à-brac, no fake-gold Russian cuckoo clocks. There was simply no room for any of that here. The entire flat was filled to the roof with books.

The material standing of the 'intellectual elite' was evident. The bookshelves were cobbled together from chipboard and weren't even lacquered. They were simple, screwed together with cheap steel bolts and supported on hooks and frames made out of old railway tracks. Decor like this was the wet dream of every hipster in Warsaw. The resident of this place must have had serious mental fortitude to keep this stuff while every other inhabitant of the small town instead spent their hard-earned cash on high-gloss furniture and wall units filled with faux-crystal tableware. Romanowska's aunt was apparently only interested in knowledge. Sasza felt a sudden need to learn all she could about her.

The living room had a space where you could sleep or entertain guests, though probably no more than two at a time. There was also a small kitchen annexe. The majority of the flat, however, fulfilled the role of reading room and office. The living part of the living room was cramped; Sasza had to edge along the wall to fit between the bed and the kitchen. The office part was like a breath of fresh air. Each wall was lined with shelves stacked with numbered books, now gathering dust. There were hundreds of them. In the midst of all this was a small space where nestled an old TV. It had been turned around so the screen faced the wall. The tiny amount of space around it was filled with books too. To Sasza it felt like being in Professor Abrams's office at the Huddersfield International Forensic Psychology Research Centre. She felt safe and hidden away.

'My aunt has a log cabin by the river,' Romanowska said, placing a cardboard box stuffed with case files on the table. 'Her son bought it for her. To ease his conscience. He lives in New York and practically never visits. Auntie won't be back before winter, and if it's mild she might stay away until spring.'

Sasza brushed off the dust from a bentwood chair standing by an old-fashioned desk covered in green felt and took a while to gather her thoughts. There was a basket of walnuts on the windowsill. She didn't dare help herself to any. They were probably older than her.

Meanwhile, Romanowska, prattling about the light illuminating the room from morning until at least six in the afternoon, was opening and closing kitchen cabinets and turning the fridge on, putting away the basic groceries they had bought on their way. Finally, she took up a knife and occupied herself with slicing bread.

'I'm not hungry,' Sasza said.

She glanced at a chequered foldable sofa bed. It took up most of the passage between the living zone and the library. She wondered how she'd be able to fold it out with one hand.

Romanowska sat down, lacing her fingers together.

'You're right, Ms Załuska.'

'Call me Sasza.' The profiler offered her healthy hand. 'It's probably a faux pas on my part, but being on first-name terms would make it easier to work together.'

'Krysia.'

The two women smiled at each other.

'I haven't brought you here myself for nothing. I wanted to talk about some things off the record.'

'Case-related or private?'

Romanowska nodded vaguely, not really answering the question.

'With how things stand at the moment, you're not in a good spot. We both know it's only—'

'A hypothesis,' Sasza finished the sentence for the commissioner, trying to fish out a cigarette from her pocket. 'I'm not mad or anything. The only thing I have a problem with is the way you people run a case. Though that's not really your fault.'

Romanowska tensed. 'My aunt doesn't like it when people smoke here.'

'That's her right.' Sasza finally managed to pluck a smoke from the pack and got up to open the balcony door. It was easier than she thought. She was getting used to working with one hand. 'Now, talk to me. My eyes aren't what they used to be, but I'm still a good listener.'

'Have it your way, but we'll have to air the room.'

'I won't stay until winter.' Sasza smiled. 'I'll be gone like the smoke before you know it. Without a trace.'

Romanowska didn't protest. Sasza felt her confidence returning. She kept her eyes locked on the tip of her cigarette.

'I don't understand everything right now. If I am to be of any use, you can't hide things from me.'

'I won't,' Romanowska replied, but didn't continue.

'So maybe this is a good time to spill? Or would you rather wait until someone else dies?' Sasza paused. 'Why did you give me Polak's address?'

Romanowska shrugged. 'I felt bad for you.'

'That's it?'

'Isn't that enough?'

The commissioner walked over to one of the shelves and pulled a book out, looking at the title. '*Wood is my hobby*'. Then she took out another. '*Chipboard Production Technology*'. She blew away the dust, opened the book and yawned.

'Do you know why I'm here?' She turned to look at Sasza and continued without waiting for an answer: 'My first cousin once removed was a wood technology specialist at the local lumber mill. He was an inventor, too. He constructed the first bandsaw in town. You can see his photo in a golden frame at the town hall. Standing by his machine, proud as a peacock. Back then, Bond-aruk was already the manager of the drying department, despite being a decade younger than most of the workers. My aunt used to run the library at the culture centre. The senior citizens' club too, later. She used to organise winter holidays for the local kids. They both used to work fourteen hours a day, six days a week.

What you see around you is all they had. They were never party members. Most of the books here were second-hand. The stuff libraries disposed of. Nobody else wanted them. My aunt bought them for peanuts. It was before the devaluation.'

Sasza listened patiently, without interrupting. Romanowska continued:

'One year – I was still at school – Mum couldn't send me anywhere for the winter holiday, so she brought me here. I met Jah-Jah during that holiday. I was eleven. He was four years older. When you're that young, that seems like a lot. At first, I hated him. He hated me right back. Everything that pisses me off in that man today was equally irritating back then. The showing off, the shallowness, his inability to read human motivations. He always preferred playing the smart-arse over having serious conversations. He didn't like to read. Still doesn't. Watching a game, working out, throwing around misogynist jokes. That's Jah-Jah for you.

'Anyway, later on I would come here every year. I was impressed by this boy who always knew what he wanted. He would become a lawyer, he said. But then, when he failed all his exams, he changed his plans without a second thought. That impressed me too. He decided he wanted to be a policeman or a soldier. He dreamed of joining the special forces, or maybe the ZOMO. Though he was too smart to join that bunch.

'I didn't know what I wanted. I was afraid most of the time. I think I was just looking for a father figure. I wanted someone to take responsibility for my life. When I was eighteen, I got pregnant. We married a year after Błażej was born. I didn't want to be pregnant during our wedding. I didn't even want a wedding – I didn't like the thought that I'd spend the rest of my life peeling potatoes and hoovering rugs – but my family was embarrassed that I had an illegitimate child. So they planned it all, and now I've lived here for years. But to the locals I'll always be a city girl from Wałbrzych pretending to be a local. What you have to understand about this place is that it doesn't mean a thing if you're Catholic, Orthodox, Jewish or even Muslim. There are only the locals and the outsiders. I am and will always be an outsider. The ashes of my ancestors weren't buried here.'

'Fascinating,' Sasza muttered. 'But what does all this have to do with our case?'

'Bondaruk has always been an important man here. I've been keeping an eye on him for more than forty years. That's a long time.'

'Hard to disagree.'

'I remember everything about him. All the stories that surfaced over the years. Most of them are just gossip and hearsay. Nobody has ever charged him with anything. Nobody cared enough. Or else, nobody had the balls to take on the local monster. There's someone like him in every small town. Everyone protects and supports him, simply because the man feeds the whole community. My ex-boss said that when I wanted to kick up a fuss about Łarysa and Mariola. Everyone knows Bondaruk killed his two wives.'

'Excuse me?' Sasza was lost for words.

'Well, he didn't exactly marry them,' Romanowska said. She smiled. 'But you heard me. Two of his lovers died. First, Łarysa – an unknown perpetrator took shots at her on the road to Białystok. Then, Mariola – one day she went off on a business trip and never returned. Now, Iwona – kidnapped in the forest. No bodies in any of those cases. None ended up in court. In fact he was never charged for any of them, even though evidence was collected. For example, in Łarysa's case, Bondaruk ended up in the Ciszynia hospital, so there are his treatment files. And, of course, we had the car.'

'The black Mercedes?'

'That car has turned up in every one of the three cases.'

Sasza needed a moment to think. She closed the balcony door, wrapped herself in a blanket, and went to the kitchen to put the kettle on. It was ancient.

'Tea or coffee?' she asked, placing two plastic-handled mugs on the counter.

Romanowska walked over to the desk and started taking files out of the cardboard box.

'That's why I brought you the files for our case – but also everything I've collected on Bondaruk through the years. I know the man. I used to know him even better way back when. Jah-Jah still can't forgive me for our little fling, even if nothing really happened. Or not much, at any case.'

'What do you mean?' Sasza asked, knitting her brows. 'Either it happened or it didn't.'

Romanowska grew serious. 'Not really. He has a certain problem . . .' She paused and waved the thought away. 'Anyway, it never really changed anything. He always loved women and they reciprocated. Some probably still have a thing for him. He has a peculiar . . . how to put it into words? A certain sadness about him. But also charm and surprising tenderness. That can be intriguing. At least, I was intrigued. There was a time when I really needed to feel . . . worshipped, I guess. You know how Jah-Jah can be. You've seen it yourself. Before the divorce he rarely noticed me. *Now* he's trying. But what's done is done. My point is, there's not a single woman aged forty plus who hasn't been the target of Bondaruk's advances. He might be old now and I know it's difficult to believe, but just ask anyone.'

'I had lunch with him that one time. I do believe it,' Sasza replied. 'What's your point?'

'Six months ago, we discovered the first skull. A bunch of Boy Scouts found it in a campfire at Harcerska Górka. The day before, Bondaruk had announced his engagement to the girl who's missing. The Bison boys' sister. The city erupted in chatter. The old *katsap* had chosen the young Bejnar girl – a rowdy lass who liked hanging out with football hooligans and skinheads. If the outrage of all the women Piotr had spurned over the years could be converted into energy, we'd have a tornado on our hands. You wouldn't notice at first glance that something was wrong, though. Nobody says anything openly here. Whispers and gossip. Small talk. Conversations you have in the safety of your home. Like us now.'

Romanowska showed Sasza the picture of the woman they were looking for, placing the photo of the half-burned skull next to it.

'Is this the woman I recognised?'

'Yes, the prostitute. Though we're still waiting for official confirmation. Then, on the day before Bondaruk's wedding, someone planted another skull. I don't know who it belongs to yet, but it can't be a coincidence. We're looking for the person who delivered it on CCTV footage. We have an idea. Jah-Jah is doing the field work.'

'Wait. You've lost me.'

'The first skull was thrown into a fire on purpose. So that the Boy Scouts could find it. We ran some tests and discovered there were traces of dirt on it. It must have been buried for years. We can't be sure exactly how long, but the soft tissue was thoroughly decomposed. Nothing but bone left. At first, we suspected it was from the war. The forests were the old stomping grounds of bands of freedom fighters. All kinds. The Ukrainian UPA, Polish anti-communist guerrillas, the Red Army, the Germans, you name it. This was a borderland and a lot of people were murdered here. Back in forty-six the last contingent of the victorious Red Army left for home. People still find bones in the forest sometimes. Take a stroll yourself and you might trip over some remains, too. Anyway, we sent the bones for identification.' Romanowska fished out another photo from the box. 'The second skull was in a plastic bag. I haven't said this until now because it sounds like some kind of conspiracy theory, but I think Danuta Pietrasik's murder might be connected to Bondaruk.'

Sasza cleared her throat, trying to keep a serious expression.

'Are you suggesting that we're dealing with our very own Bluebeard who is seducing women, immediately offing them and then hiding their bodies in the forest so people thought they've just gone missing? And he does all that with a ghost car. An old Mercedes that shows up and disappears without a trace.'

'Pretty much.' Romanowska was serious. 'But it's not only women.'

The kettle was boiling and spurting puffs of steam, but both women sat still.

'So, there were more disappearances? How many? Who else went missing?'

Romanowska got up and went to the kitchen. She took the kettle off the stove and shut off the gas valve on the small propane cylinder standing on the counter, dousing the flame on the stove.

'Make sure to shut the valve every time you finish cooking,' she called. 'It's safer that way.'

'I don't intend to cook,' Sasza barked and repeated herself: 'Who else went missing?'

Romanowska was still ignoring her. She carried the two mugs across the room and went to put them down on the small table.

She misjudged the distance and bumped the table with her knee. It sounded painful and her face creased.

'Damn it, this place is like a doll's house,' she hissed.

Sasza smirked but helped the commissioner by taking the mugs from her so she could sit down.

'Your hands are cold,' Romanowska said.

'They always are,' Sasza replied. 'The only times they warm up are when I have a fever or after sex.'

'I hope you don't have a fever right now,' Romanowska said. 'Otherwise, I'd have to take you back to the hospital.'

Sasza took a sip of her tea. 'And that second situation doesn't apply any more. For the last seven years, as far as I recall.'

'Eleven for me,' Romanowska replied, doing a quick count in her mind.

Sasza laughed. 'Now I understand why you helped me. It wasn't pity. You're just pissed off with the patriarchy. You think I'm a victim, but also a fellow unwilling sexual abstinent.'

'Think what you want. The fact remains that helping you felt good,' Romanowska admitted. 'I had no idea it would turn out to be such a clusterfuck.'

'What do you mean?'

'Well, it's a bit meatier than my celibacy and a backwater power struggle, wouldn't you say?'

'Backwater or not,' Sasza raised her mug in a toast, 'down with feminism!'

Romanowska grimaced.

'What? I'm a traditionalist,' Sasza explained and laughed out loud. 'A man should carry your bags and keep you entertained. Always on his toes. That doesn't mean I'd let myself be humiliated for love. I'd rather be single. Like you.'

A silence fell over the room. Romanowska sipped her tea.

'When I started working in the force, I just had to do all the paperwork,' she began. 'I was responsible for disappearances. Only nobody ever disappeared without the involvement of the Security Service. When they wanted someone gone, they knew how to get it done. Their main office was in the building by the roundabout. I remember it rained cats and dogs that day. A pretty woman dressed in a nylon coat and homespun trousers barged into the station, soaked through. As soon as she took off her headscarf, I saw that her hair was tied in the most elaborate bun I've ever seen. It looked like a crown of snakes. I have no idea how long her hair had to be, but that detail really stuck in my mind. And the colour – pitch black. Same as Iwona's. The woman was called Dunia Orzechowska. She was the wife of the director of the lumber mill, Stepan Orzechowski. He was Gaweł's man – the head of the Security Service – and everyone knew that. A commie through and through. Bondaruk was a young engineer at the mill back then, in charge of modernisation. And he was the party bigwigs' favourite pet. An ex-head of the local Socialist Youth Union and an activist respected both by the old guard and the new generation. He was the centre of attention as early as then. But people never really trusted him. When you graduate with top marks in Warsaw and then go straight back to Hajnówka instead of kick-starting your career in the capital or pretty much wherever you want, you either have powerful friends in the party HQ or you've been sent to this backwater on a mission.'

'A spy, then?'

'Who knows. But he was supposed to take Orzechowski's place as the head of the mill. Not that he wouldn't be a better pick. Bondaruk has always been a smart guy. His father invented a machine for drying planks that was supposed to increase production volumes, but the company never bought the patent. It was too expensive to roll out on a large scale. Bondaruk changed two things in his old man's design – he increased the load capacity and increased the motor's power a bit. Today, most lumber mills in Poland use machines based on his improvements.' Romanowska sipped more tea. 'Anyway, Dunia reported her husband missing. Supposedly, he went away on business and never returned. We did our jobs. It was a priority case. We had all our men on it. But, no more than a week later, it was closed. First, the old commissioner got a call from Gaweł. He ordered it swept under the carpet. Then Dunia withdrew her statement. It was a pretty big thing in the media. Then, two days later, Dunia brought in a letter. Unfortunately, it's since been lost. The whole town had a big old laugh at her expense. People poked fun at her for at least a year. That's when she turned into a recluse.'

'What was in the letter?'

'A coming-out. Stepan wrote that he was gay and was leaving his wife for a Catholic priest. It contained a longish confession that he never loved Dunia, and that he married her out of pity and to have someone at his back when he grew old. So, he left her his property and the money he had in his bank account so she could raise their son properly. Dunia was pregnant at the time.'

'The son is Jurek Orzechowski, Iwona's ex-boyfriend?'

'Just so.' Romanowska nodded. 'It looked legit. The priest had been beaten up and chased off by an angry mob some time earlier. The Church authorities had nothing against it. They probably knew more than they let on and wanted to keep the story quiet. Stuff like that used to be taboo. People just said the priest was indecent, drank too much, and stole collection money. Before he left, he did just that. Took all the cash from the collection box and the entire fund for the construction of a new chapel at the town cemetery. Two days later, Stepan went missing too. Years later, when the force upgraded to a central computer database, I tried to get a fix on him but couldn't find anything. There were no traces. No data. The man didn't exist any more. Same thing with the priest. The last record dated back to seventy-seven. I know shit happens, but to two guys at the same time?'

Sasza blinked twice.

'Let me guess,' she said. 'Dunia had an affair with Bondaruk.'

'Clever girl.' Romanowska smiled. 'It was a big thing. Dunia had been Bondaruk's first and greatest love. People say that Iwona Bejnar was supposed to wear her dress to her wedding. It had originally been made for Dunia. For a while I even thought it was her at the altar.'

Sasza shook her head. 'Dunia went missing too?'

'No,' the commissioner replied. 'But she went mad. You might have met her. She looks like a witch now. She's our local whisperer. Apparently, she has powers.'

'Local folklore . . .'

'I'm serious,' Romanowska said with emphasis. 'She's weird. You'll see. Some people are afraid of her.'

Sasza's mobile vibrated. She sprang to her feet and dug around in her handbag, finally fishing out the phone. The screen showed

Sasza's daughter, wearing a black leather jacket and a pink sequinned shirt.

'Hey! Everything fine?' Sasza said sweetly, her voice totally different from the professional coldness of her conversation with the commissioner.

Romanowska smiled. She saw the glimmer in Sasza's eyes and heard the joy and sadness in her laugh at something her daughter was saying. This was a mother missing her child.

Romanowska headed to the kitchen, wanting to give Sasza at least some semblance of privacy. The conversation lasted for a quarter of an hour. When Sasza put the phone down, she looked calmer. With a deep sigh of relief, she took a bite of the sandwich Romanowska had placed on the table for her. The commissioner took a seat and bit into her own sandwich. For a while they ate without speaking.

'I don't think I've ever tasted anything that good in my entire life,' Sasza said finally.

'It's local sausage. A guy by the name of Nesteruk looks after the production process. He's eighty years old but he still likes to personally slaughter pigs at the processing plant. Likes teaching the youngsters how to kill without causing them to suffer,' Romanowska explained.

Sasza swallowed and pushed the plate away.

'He actually got rich by collecting scrap metal. A close friend of Bondaruk's, too,' Romanowska was saying between bites. She also finished Sasza's sandwich. Finally, she returned to her story as if the interruption had never happened. 'So, as you know, Jurek Orzechowski is Dunia's son. He's a petty thief. Goes by the alias Quack. He's our main suspect. I have reasons to believe he was planning to abscond with Iwona.'

'That's why you asked if she knew the assailant. It's beginning to come together now. A family squabble. Even if they're not officially family.'

Romanowska shrugged. Sasza started to count on her fingers. A smile bloomed on her face.

'If you ask me, we have a solid case here. One body, two heads, and five disappearances. And all that because of our sixty-year-old Don Juan.'

'Four-Eyes.'

'Yeah.' Sasza produced the photo she had received from Marzena Koźmińska. 'People used to call him that everywhere. He must have been pretty happy with that nickname if he boasted about it at party HQ.'

Romanowska looked up enquiringly. She didn't get it.

'Fancy a trip to Gdańsk?' Sasza said.

'What, now?'

'No. I need to get the data in order first. But tomorrow? We can leave town together, can't we? I can even play the part of the suspect for a while longer if you need me to. I'm actually starting to like it.'

Sasza walked over to the bookshelf and picked one tome at random. *The Man-Eating Myth* by William Arens. The book was new, not from a second-hand shop. She opened it to a random page and read aloud:

'"To eat another man is to possess him fully, experience oral ecstasy."' She closed the book, smirked, and said: 'Maybe he eats them? That's why there are no bodies. He only leaves heads and bones.'

Romanowska sent her a weird look, choosing not to react to her taunts this time.

Gdańsk, 2014

A strong pain radiating all the way around her hip threw Marzena off her chair. She quickly stretched out her leg to fight the cramp. It only made things worse, as usual. A moment later and she couldn't feel her feet. She allowed herself to collapse and lay on the floor, perfectly still. Her eyes teared up. She clenched her teeth, suffering in silence. It would pass. She waited. Everything passes. That's what you learn in prison. When the pain was bearable, she released the sewing hoop and needle threaded with red that she was clutching. John Paul II smiled his unsettling smile from the unfinished tablecloth. He was still missing the upper part of his face. At this stage it could still be Batman and not the Pope. Three years ago she would have done just that, just for kicks. Today, she didn't even have the strength to refuse soup, despite knowing the guard had stuck her dirty middle finger in it when she passed it through the hole in the door. She ate whatever they gave her. At least that way she had something to throw up. She did that a few times a day lately. Her sciatica wouldn't let go those last couple of days, tormenting her non-stop. It was because of her back. A spinal defect. Maybe something even more serious. Her lumbar region had hurt ever since she could remember. She got used to it – the constant, buzzing, dull pain. Ever present, like a feeling of guilt. She didn't really want to know what it was. During the day, when the pain died down a bit, she raged, hating the way they were treating her. At night, she rolled around her bed, sleepless. Inmates like her didn't get physiotherapy, or even potassium pills. So, she just dealt with it. Smoked a lot and drank tea. She had nothing else left. If not for the kids, she'd have hanged herself already. She would still do it as soon as her family were safe and financially secure.

The Pope was supposed to be finished before tomorrow afternoon. That was still doable if she worked double-speed. The convoy would take the tablecloth to the Castle. They'd pull it over a frame and hang it from the main wall of the prison chapel. It was supposed to be her gift for the seventieth anniversary of the prison maternity ward. As strange as it sounded, she wanted back in. Each scratch on the wall of that hateful fortress, each dirty wainscot – she knew them like the back of her hand. She had never spent this much time in one place and, ironically, that's where she felt the safest.

The door creaked. Someone pulled on the latch. That someone must have taken a peek inside, though Marzena couldn't see. With the utmost difficulty, she lifted her head a bit, but that was as far as she could move. The door opened wide. Marzena stared at the snow-white stockings and cappuccino-coloured brogues of the person who entered. The ward head. They hated each other, but always spoke to one another with sickening sweetness.

'The chaplain is waiting and you're lying around,' the guard purred.

Marzena turned her head. She could barely breathe. With the rest of her strength she propped herself up on her elbows. She met the guard's eyes. Was it concern she saw in them? No, impossible. She must have gone mad from all that pain and helplessness. Nobody cared about her.

'How are you feeling?'

The guard offered her a hand. Marzena groaned. She shook her head. Pulling herself back up into the chair was too much.

'I'm done until morning. When can I go home?'

'Home is where the heart is, love. I read that once. A crime novel or some such,' the woman said with a snort of laughter. She patted down her uniform. The baton at her belt dangled limply, and the handcuffs played a clinking tune. So no, after all. The concern had been fake and Marzena had fallen for it. The guard was sure Marzena was faking her sickness because of the upcoming court hearing. She dropped her amicable manner. 'The doctor's out. There was a birth, and a bucket handle to extract from an inmate's throat. A petty dealer. All she got is three years and she wanted to off herself.' She snorted. 'So, you're too late. You can stop the show now.'

Marzena did not reply.

'You have a guest, but if you're not well enough, I'll get rid of them.'

'Who?'

'Maybe I could even arrange for some "special conditions" for your meeting. If you stop acting the fool. But don't count on getting an empty cell for the two of you.'

'A man?' Marzena sat up instantly. She massaged her back. 'Gromek?' She shook her head. 'I don't talk to snitches.'

'Get your shit in order.' The guard laughed. 'You'll have fifteen minutes. Piotr doesn't have much time.'

Marzena took a while to think. Impossible. The psychologist couldn't have found him this fast. But she didn't know any other Piotr. Besides, nobody had visited her for years. Nobody she'd wanted to see, at least. She got up slowly, then collapsed into the chair, gasping for air. When her breathing had calmed down, Marzena noticed a long run in the guard's left stocking. It went all the way up from the heel to the hem of her dress. Nobody's perfect.

At first, she didn't recognise him. His hair had gone white, he had grown thinner. He looked like an old goat. Too much drinking. She recognised the symptoms at once. The swollen cheeks, the goitre on his neck, the bloodshot eyes. Compared to him, she looked great, even in her orange prison onesie. But apparently he didn't use mirrors too often, as he started mocking her own appearance as soon as she entered.

'You always knew how to take care of yourself, sweetheart. Nice tracksuit. You on a diet? I can see you still have your boobs, at least. Haven't they got saggy on prison chow?'

Suddenly, the penny dropped. The memories clicked into place. It really was Four-Eyes. His visit had to be connected to the psychologist's. It couldn't be coincidence. Marzena had to give it to Sasza – she was good. She had underestimated her.

'How did you do it?'

He pretended he didn't understand the question. She didn't intend to offer him any help.

'Chickenshit? The princess ain't protected enough?'

'Fuck off.'

'Give me the name and I'll get you a lawyer. A good one. You know I can do it.'

'What name?'

'The guy who offed Jowita.'

She aimed a finger at him. He shook his head.

'Wrong.'

'I'll tell them it was you when they ask. I know it was you.'

He cleared his throat with an offended expression.

'Marzena, sweetheart, I know I hurt you. But to turn against me like that? We were supposed to conquer the world together. "Fuck everyone and everything, they won't get us alive." Remember?'

She laughed sharply. 'Oh, please. I'm too old for this shit.'

'That, at least, is true. It's downhill from here,' he muttered. 'I'll ask you again. It's for our own common good. We're in it together. I can't believe you're not afraid for yourself.'

'For years you didn't care and now, out of the blue . . .' She paused. 'What's your angle? Why now, when even I've stopped caring?'

'You should start caring again,' he replied. 'I need the name of the man who stole my car and smashed it near Ciechanów after Jowita ran away. Someone reported dangerous driving to the police. I'll find him, dig him up if needed, and hang him from a tree.'

'Look at you. Bloody knight in shining armour,' she snorted. 'Why now?'

'My arse is on fire, so to speak,' he said. 'I need to hold off an attack. That's the only thing on my mind now.'

She shrugged.

'You have my word: it wasn't me,' he repeated, his voice growing gentle.

'Wasn't you what?'

'Me and Jowita were close. I took care of her. I didn't want anything in return.'

'She would have ended up better if she fucked a battalion of soldiers. Maybe then her mother would at least have a place to go on All Souls Day.'

'I wasn't there. But sometimes I think to myself that maybe you could have helped her. You vanished so fast with that man of yours.'

'Right,' Marzena scoffed. 'I'm in here for murder anyway, so you might as well pile some more shit on me. I don't care. And besides, Jowita was younger and prettier than me, wasn't she?'

She paused, wanting him to think she was envious.

'Are you jealous?' He looked genuinely puzzled. 'Of something like that? A gang-rape?'

'Doesn't matter now, does it? Men always have a reason to do anything but what a woman wants. It took me some time, but finally I got it. At least I don't have hope any more.'

Once again, he couldn't help but feel surprised at the fact that Marzena had only ever graduated from high school. He recalled reading somewhere that she had passed her final exams in jail. Her vocabulary was more refined than before. Maybe she read a lot? And she didn't look *that* ugly. That was a fact.

'We wouldn't have made it,' he said. 'We were just fooling around.'

'I trusted you,' she hissed.

She knew it sounded like a scene from a soap opera. She didn't care.

'I appreciate that.'

'So, who was I for you?' Marzena whispered, and immediately regretted her words when he replied without a moment's thought: 'Nobody.'

She bit her lip. She must have cancer. It couldn't be anything else. That's why she kept getting thinner and couldn't sleep. That's why the radiating pain never subsided. She felt angry. That was good. Anger poured down her throat, cascaded down her eyes, and made her forget the tingling in her foot. She even stopped feeling the pain in her back for a while.

'Nobody?' she asked. 'After all the risks I took?'

'Not for me, though,' he replied with a smile. 'Only for yourself. We both did it for ourselves. You used her, I used you. I'm sorry.'

'You won't find him.' Marzena folded her arms. She was shaking inside but couldn't let him see that. 'He won't confess. Maybe he's dead already.'

'It would be better for him,' Piotr said matter-of-factly. 'He fucked up bad. Like your other boyfriends. How you miss from that short a distance, I don't even know. But I must admit, I am curious about why he hasn't ratted you out yet. Or maybe that's part of the plan?'

His face brightened with a knowing smile. Marzena felt queasy all of a sudden.

'It wasn't supposed to end like that,' she assured him. 'I was young and stupid. I cared for you.'

'For my money, you mean.'

'Sure, that too.'

'So, it seems we both have a reason to find the man. If you don't help me, I'll tell them about you. You'll join Jowita and Łarysa. It'll be the end of you. For me, it's downhill now.'

'How do you know I'm not planning to do the same? And it might not be that hard for me.'

'I'm perfectly sure you're not planning anything of the sort, sweetheart. More than sure.'

She sent him a look of grudging admiration. They could have been such a pretty couple. Like Bonnie and Clyde. They could have been better versions of them. They would never have been caught. If he hadn't cheated on her with Jowita – her stupid, pretty friend. Men who say they're after a woman's character or her internal beauty lie. A pretty package and some sweet talk is what they want. If Marzena had had the money and the smarts then that she had now, she wouldn't have ended up in jail. She felt a surge of strength. She could fight again. There was hope. An ATM had just marched into her cell. All she had to do was figure out the PIN code and stick a credit card in.

'I also know it isn't true that your life is as bad as it gets,' Piotr was saying. That didn't surprise her. It was her only weakness. 'You have children. Patryk, Agnieszka, and Robert, if I recall correctly.'

She let the information flow in one ear and spill out straight out the other. It was worth it – she was already in. Now, the only thing she had to do was negotiate the rate. Maybe she'd get a physio. Potassium, morphine, and a small flat somewhere quiet, when they let her out in some thirty years. She'd never accepted the thought that she'd have to spend the rest of her life locked up. There's no such thing as 'for ever'. What she needed now was a beachhead. If she could only put her foot down firmly on the ground. That would be all she needed.

Meanwhile, Piotr took out a piece of paper and wrote something on it. She noticed the liver spots on the back of his hand, and the thickened, rheumatic joints of his fingers. His physical appeal was all but gone. He still had the same voice and those snake eyes. Always alert. He wouldn't leave without the thing he had come here for.

'A lawyer and a payout. Want to negotiate the rate?'

She shook her head.

'Let's say thirty.' She knew it would only be the first instalment. They both knew it. She needed the show to go on for a while longer, but she couldn't overdo it. She whetted his appetite. 'Half for me, half for my kids.'

'All right,' he sighed.

She paused to gather her thoughts.

'It's not even a secret,' she said. 'You know the name already. You just need to think a bit harder. The flatmate of that archivist from the IPN.'

'Shaggy from Wiolinowa Street?'

'Yeah, the hairy guy.'

They both burst out laughing. Piotr grew serious first.

'The guy who hadn't slept with anyone for seven years?'

'The guy who never slept with anyone. He was so desperate he fucked me. Imagine that,' Marzena said, still smirking. 'We went here and there together. Scanning materials and partying after the job was done. He wasn't even that ugly. If not for you, I might have become Mrs Shaggy from Wiolinowa Street. He got you the papers on your war stories.'

'Have you read them?'

She shook her head. 'Nah, there was too much. Besides, I wouldn't remember a thing by now anyway.'

He knew she was lying but decided to let it slide.

'Fifty if you have the copies of the carters' documents.'

She made a Mona Lisa face.

'And if I had the originals?'

He stared at her in anticipation. She was tired of stringing him along. It was satisfying to be able to fool him. He cared. At least as much as she cared for getting leave to see her kids.

'I only had the copies of your denouncements. And a file on your old man. A tragic story. The Security Service rarely offed their own like that.'

She got up and stretched.

'But I won't give them to you. My daughter burned them along with my stuff.'

'Nobody throws money into the fire,' he hissed and headed to the door. He stopped at the threshold, waiting for Marzena to take it back, to say that she'd cooperate. Nothing of the sort happened. She kept silent, bit her lip, and shrugged.

'If you're stupid enough and don't know cash from loo roll, it can happen,' he said eventually. 'But that doesn't get you anywhere. You always stay a pauper.'

'You know best,' she replied, and when he turned round and disappeared, she felt more gratified than she could remember feeling for a long time.

Later that evening, she bought a SIM card and called her son. She told him to hide the document file in a secure locker at the train station, and then wait for the postman. He would have to give the money to his sister. She would repay their debts, send her mum a proper parcel and buy her son a present from Grandma.

That night, Marzena didn't throw up, and she slept like a baby.

After leaving the prison, Bondaruk stopped at the gate for a brief moment. It was drizzling lightly. He turned up the collar of his coat, pulled his frayed straw hat lower over his brow and started walking. Someone yanked him to a halt. Bondaruk jerked away on a reflex. His hat fell off, landing in a puddle. Black butterflies swirled before his eyes.

'Chief Inspector Robert Duchnowski, police,' the aggressor introduced himself and apologised for his abruptness. He shot a brief glance at his watch. An old Nokia phone chirped, signalling a text received. Both men reached for their pockets. 'I nearly missed you. If you'll come with me, I'll take you to the station in Hajnówka. The whole unit is looking for you. You haven't been returning calls.'

'I had some business to attend to here,' Bondaruk growled. 'What do you want from me?'

Ghost put a soggy cigarette between his lips. 'We'll talk on the way. We have a few things to discuss. One of them is Sasza. To be honest, I don't really care about the rest at the moment.'

Bondaruk studied the officer for a while.

'I don't believe we've been introduced,' he said finally, in his most polite manner. Ghost stifled a laugh. 'I assure you, I had nothing to do with your lady love. You can rest easy.'

Hajnówka, 2014

'Alcoholic paranoia. Considered a subtype of delusional disorder. Also called Othello syndrome. Chronic, persistent, obsessive jealousy. And resulting issues with anger management. That was Bondaruk's initial diagnosis.' Magdalena Prus paused and slowly crossed her legs. She hadn't chosen her minidress on purpose, but it had to be part of her subconscious coping mechanism. As soon as she and Saczko had decided she'd only tell half the truth during today's questioning, she had gone home to change. The snug white skirt felt like the natural choice. It was brand new. A visit to the station would be the perfect debut for it. Besides, if they discovered she was lying to the police, she'd at least look good enough to try to work her charm. She'd put on red knickers, just to be sure she made the appropriate impression.

The older officer, who had come from central headquarters and was now standing propped against the wall, had presumably seen the film with the Sharon Stone scene that Magdalena was trying to imitate; he straightened up instantly, desperately trying to keep his eyes from wandering lower than Magdalena's breasts. The muscle-head from the local station on the other hand, the one who was just there to write down her statement, seemed to have missed the movie altogether. He was impassive.

'He locked a woman in a gilded cage and followed all her movements,' Prus continued. 'Obsessive checking of her bedlinens, rummaging through her underwear drawer. Every attempted delivery note left by the postman was a potential love letter. She had to pee with the door open. He would look for her lovers in the wardrobe, under the bed. Everywhere. He was absolutely paranoid that Łarysa was two-timing him. Classic symptoms.'

'Was he aggressive?'

Prus nodded.

'The police files were sparse, but Łarysa Szafran behaved like a classic victim of domestic abuse. She reported some incidents, but mainly emotional abuse. No forensic medical examinations were made, but she had no bruises or anything of the sort. Later, she withdrew the motions for prosecution, but I can tell you she had been our patient for a while too. Both of them used to drink. Rather a lot, too. They met through Belarusian minority meetings. He started identifying as Belarusian because of her. She used to say that love of rock music and local moonshine brought them together. I have a list of some events from his medical history. I also have her confessions recorded. I can make them available to you. I haven't listened to those cassettes yet, but I admit that I wanted to study their case more closely. I always thought their relationship bordered on the pathological. I even mentioned it in one of my articles for the *Journal of Clinical Psychiatry*. It wasn't met with too much enthusiasm, though – there are literally millions of other Othellos around. So I quickly lost professional interest in Bondaruk's behaviour.'

'How about personal interest?'

'Personal?' she repeated and frowned, clearly taking the question as an insult. Doman looked embarrassed but didn't withdraw the question. She continued. 'At first it was strictly professional for me.'

'How did their relationship deviate from the norm?'

'She suffered from the same disorder. We just hadn't diagnosed her in time.'

'Guess he met his match then.' Doman smiled.

'You could say that.' Prus shrugged. 'Though it would be an oversimplification. Disorders like that are rare in women. Have a read through our files if you find the time.'

'I doubt I will. That old story is more of a curiosity. Supportive evidence at best.'

'I thought as much.'

The officer gestured to his colleague, who got up, sending Prus an indifferent look. The psychiatrist's eyes wandered from one officer to the other. They had said nothing worrying yet, but she couldn't help feeling unsettled. She felt her left eyelid twitch. She couldn't control it. Fortunately, she had her glasses on and they didn't seem to notice the tic. She didn't know how long they'd keep her here.

'Milk, sugar, or black?' Doman broke the silence.

'Black,' she replied. He nodded to his younger colleague, who left the room. Prus sighed with relief and pointed to the documents spread on the table. A mugshot of Bondaruk taken after his arrest was on the top of the pile. Despite his age at the time, he could still be considered attractive. His hair was already turning grey, but the square jaw, worthy of a Roman sculpture, and his piercing, stern eyes still gave him charisma. Magdalena remembered the electrifying effect they'd had on her when she first saw the man. She used to joke that he had the petrifying gaze of a salamander, or an alligator breaking the surface of the water. Bondaruk's stare had nothing romantic or melancholy in it; it just made people's skin crawl. She had once said that to him, counting on making him laugh, or at least relax a bit, but his eyes hadn't even twitched. He had clearly known he couldn't afford to loosen up yet; the psychiatrist would have registered even the smallest grimace. That hadn't exactly been the truth. She had fallen for him on their first meeting, though if anyone asked, she would have denied it strenuously. Today, she was ready to admit it for the first time. That was part of her plan to distract the officers. She was just waiting for the right moment.

'He always knew what his greatest weakness was,' she continued. 'That wasn't normal. It's like with an addict, you know. He should be telling us he's got it under control, refusing to acknowledge his problem. An Othello should try to assure us that he wasn't jealous at all. That we were making things up. He should have tried to mask his issues, perfecting his denial mechanism. Instead, he knew he wasn't well and had no qualms with talking about it. He even called himself a psychopath, an antisocial bastard. He said he knew he should be treated. He told me his pathologic jealousy felt like cancer, consumed him. He asked for help.'

The coffee arrived in brown mugs. The officer had got himself hot chocolate from the vending machine. He took a loud, slurping sip. The sound visibly irked Doman, and after a short while he asked his colleague to step out for a moment. The psychiatrist was spewing nonsense, Doman thought, trying to lead them off track.

None of what she said sounded like information that could lead to a breakthrough in the case.

The young officer left and the investigator returned to his questioning. 'So, you treated him.'

'And with good results,' Prus confirmed. 'We used antipsychotics to stabilise his mood. The paranoid projections disappeared after a month. I'm willing to risk saying that he felt better at the hospital than at home. Everyone took to him from the beginning, including the other patients. Not without reason, of course. He bought everyone presents. That wasn't really allowed, but nobody ever caught him red-handed. I know for certain that none of the staff accepted any pay-offs, though Bondaruk offered them "gifts" several times. The treatment progressed according to plan and he got better extremely fast. That doesn't happen very often. You have to understand – we only try to help people. We don't judge them. For us, he was a patient, not a potential criminal.'

'The best kind of patient, right? A generous one.'

She smiled and corrected him: 'A paying one, like any other. Each day of therapy has a cost. That's just how it is. But in this case the order to treat him came from the prosecutor's office, so the payments came from the state. And those are significantly lower than private donations. Anyway, I was the first to say that he wasn't ill.'

'You're saying he was faking it?'

'We weren't sure at first. All his symptoms, including physical, were in order. That particular disorder makes people act erratically. A patient accuses their partner of cheating, insults them, calls them names, only to grow tender and loving the next moment, professing their love, and then crying and complaining again about having their heart broken. You know, like in the movies.'

'I hate comedies.'

'Well, I don't.' Prus took a sip of the thin coffee and grimaced as she swallowed.

'Delicious, isn't it?' The officer smirked. He hadn't touched his mug.

'There were times when you could get proper coffee here.' Prus sighed.

'Were there?' He looked interested. 'Have you been here before?'

She smiled widely, showing her immaculate teeth, but not wide enough for him to see her gums. Just like she'd learned in her French etiquette guides.

'Yes, and for the same reason. That's when I first had one of those sandwiches from the little place on Trzeciego Maja Street. I'm still a fan. You should try them.'

He didn't react to that, so she decided to continue, reverting to her professional manner.

'In time, I started to suspect that the delusions were just a cover story. At least for him. I know, that's a bold hypothesis. It could effectively ruin his line of defence. You understand, if he wasn't mentally disturbed, he could be prosecuted for kidnapping his wife. He was, after all, the main suspect. His attorney came to me to try and convince me to drop my idea. I couldn't agree to that. In my report, I wrote that Bondaruk wasn't suffering from Othello syndrome.'

Doman raised his head. 'What are you saying?'

'It's a small town,' she said. 'We were told that the missing woman wasn't entirely blameless. Well, I was told at least. We were friends back in school, before Łarysa turned into a Belarusian activist. She went to Minsk to fight against President Lukashenko; meanwhile I graduated from university in Warsaw and worked for a while at a hospital there. Then, I returned here, as the vice-director of our clinic. I didn't look for her at first. It was she who called me and told me she had a new boyfriend. It was simple, really. Bondaruk was jealous of her, but he had reasons. We noticed that he had a very low anxiety threshold. She used it to stoke his psychosis. I think she just didn't want to leave him with nothing. She wanted to get something out of that relationship. They'd been together for five years and he'd never proposed. For some women that is a very important thing. Love isn't everything, you know. For women, anyway.'

Doman had a hard time listening to her fruitless monologue, or 'fucking around' as he liked to refer to long tales spun by witnesses, riddled with unnecessary digressions. He liked his data concise. If she weren't an expert, but an ordinary witness, he would have cut her bullshit short long ago.

'So, you're telling me he was afraid?' he asked. 'Who was he afraid of?'

She nodded but instantly changed her mind and shook her head.

'No. He's one of the most self-confident men I know. I'm talking about past trauma. Something that threw a shadow over his sense of security, generally speaking. She had to know the details. She was blackmailing him.'

Doman leaned closer, intrigued. 'I'd like the specifics, please.'

'What I mean is he wasn't consciously afraid of anything. His anxiety surfaced when he was asleep, when he lost control, and when his "Not-Me" took over.'

'All right, that's enough,' Doman exclaimed. 'Was it his "Not-Me" or whatever that killed her? Or did the other guy do it? What's his name . . .' He glanced at the old report. 'Wiesław Zegadło, the PE teacher.'

Prus placed her empty coffee mug on the table. It splashed and spilled a few drops onto her white dress. She hissed. 'Your data isn't exhaustive,' she said. 'After the first incident, we let him go. In fact, my boss practically threw him out. When Łarysa went missing, he came to us for the second time and his Othello syndrome was nowhere to be seen. He was healthy and stable. We gave him Noveril and that was enough.'

Doman considered this. 'But he was spared a trial because he claimed Othello syndrome.'

'Yes, his lawyer did a good job. He used that to clear Bondaruk of all charges. The case didn't even go to court,' Prus replied. 'But this was a year or two after Piotr left our clinic. When Łarysa and Piotr had already stopped dating and she'd moved to her new apartment, which he bought for her. The son decided to stay with his father.'

'Her son, you mean?'

'Fionik Szafran. Bondaruk officially adopted him when she went missing, and gave him his last name. Otherwise the boy would have had to go to live with his grandmother, whom he didn't know, and his real father, who left him when the kid was barely able to walk.'

They sat still for some time. Doman slowly arranged the data in his head.

'So, Bondaruk had two spells at the clinic. Why didn't anyone inform us?'

'Not two,' Prus said, shaking her head and smiling. 'Three times is the charm. The first one he paid for himself. He was admitted at Łarysa's request. The second time we treated him as ordered by the expert working for the prosecution, and the state paid. We are certified to conduct psychiatric observation for the purposes of criminal investigations. That was the time he got shot and nearly died. He would have bled to death if he hadn't received immediate help. And then there was the third time. He admitted himself and paid with his own funds. That was when Mariola went missing. As you probably remember, she went on a business trip and never returned. They just found Bondaruk's car. That damned Mercedes made people think that he killed her too. You know, to get her son. But there was nothing to corroborate that story. There was something about Mariola living in Bytom, then being seen in Dublin. Her father, Mikołaj Nesteruk, supposedly received a postcard from her, though it wasn't signed. I really don't know. You should have all that in your files.'

'And if you're wrong?' the officer asked. 'What if he really did suffer from Othello syndrome? How often does a man with a disorder like that kill his wife?'

'Contrary to what the novels say, it is a rare occurrence. Not entirely impossible, though.'

'With the knowledge you have of Piotr Bondaruk's mental state, do you think he would be capable of committing a crime out of emotional distress? I mean, currently.'

Prus shrugged. 'I haven't examined him for some time. Things change.' She kept her eyes fixed on the coffee stains on her dress. She was thinking about the cost of having it dry-cleaned. Maybe putting it on hadn't been such a good idea after all. She looked up. 'Strictly speaking, every murder of someone close to the perpetrator stems from emotional distress. Even if the prosecutor decides the motive is, say, robbery. But since we're talking about Bondaruk, if you're asking if he kidnapped those two women and then killed them, I highly doubt that.'

'How can you be so sure?'

Prus hesitated. 'If it wasn't such a serious accusation, a convoluted case, and all those things happening in the meantime, like Miss Bejnar going missing, I wouldn't disclose my information. But, as it is, I think I have to.'

Doman kept quiet, smirking to himself.

'After Łarysa was killed, I spoke to Bondaruk.' She dropped her head again. 'It was off the record, on my own initiative. I was fascinated by his case, I admit. I wanted to write an article about it. He was such a great research subject.'

'You said your interest was strictly professional.'

'As I said, at first. I wanted to get an article in a prestigious journal,' she said. 'He told me I didn't know him at all. That I thought he was better than he really was. And that I was wrong, though he had nothing but respect for my professional knowledge. I didn't believe him. I thought that he was claiming responsibility because of the post-traumatic shock. That was when he told me he had done something horrifying.'

'What? Fired a hundred workers from the lumber mill?' Doman snorted. He was certain Bondaruk would never confess to committing any crime.

Prus remained deadly serious.

'He told me his whole career had been built on crime. He killed a man and used to be an informant for the Security Service. They protected him. He was untouchable for years after the regime fell. He always wanted to help people as much as he could, but only because he used to do really bad things. But he wouldn't have succeeded like he did if he had nobody to help. You know how it is. You lived here. This works both ways. You have dirt on someone, and that someone has dirt on you.'

'Names. What "someone" are you talking about?'

'He didn't know who had decided that his time was up. Or why. But what made things worse, instead of attacking him directly, they were targeting his loved ones. His women. Long story short, he thought someone was – how would you put it – ah, framing him for those murders.'

'And here we have it.' Doman burst out laughing. 'And you believed him, took pity on him and didn't go to the police? Isn't this how any conversation between a patient and a psychiatrist looks? He can confess anything he wants, but unless it gets into a report and is then confirmed at court, it counts for jack shit.'

'We weren't talking at the hospital,' Magdalena replied, bristling. 'And I did report it to the commissioner. Twice. First to the old one, then to Romanowska. Though she wasn't so senior then.'

'There isn't anything about that in the files,' he retorted. 'Besides, I would have known. I worked here.'

'I remember,' she said. 'There isn't anything in the files because my ex-husband, a lawyer at town hall, made sure that no detail of that conversation saw light of day. And that's because Piotr told me all that after we had sex. At my place. When my husband was away. He was afraid of the outrage. What would people say? And now he hates me so much, he'll surely stick to his version. He doesn't work at town hall any more. They gave him the boot. He runs an office at the roundhouse near Hajnówka. Right by the business incubator and the chainsaw store.'

'You had an affair with a patient?' Doman asked, still unable to stop chuckling. 'You and that old fart?'

'Seven months,' the psychiatrist confirmed, haughtily. She was losing her composure. 'And I'd like to remind you that, unlike Łarysa and Mariola, I'm still alive!'

'So, you're saying they're not?' Doman asked immediately.

Magdalena Prus clammed up. She'd messed up big time, and she knew it.

PIOTR

(1977)

'You asleep?' Piotr put his hand on her small breast. Her nipple was still hard.

'Yeah,' Dunia muttered and turned her back on him. The bed creaked. He felt her backside brush against his belly.

'Leave with me,' he whispered, wrapping his arm around her waist. Her belly was rounded, but he could feel her ribs under his fingers. She was so lithe and nimble. Like a cat. He hadn't thought a woman that thin could ever have such an effect on him. Her leanness made her look a lot younger than thirty-seven.

She said nothing, but he would bet her eyes were open now, and that her expression was astonished. It was getting dark outside. They both stared at the walnut tree, stripped of its leaves, its naked branches whipping to the rhythm of the wind. They were that tree, he and she. Unified into one, strong trunk, but having to submit to the blowing gale. They could just wait until it passed, but Piotr had had enough of hiding. He felt his strength leaving him. His parents had taught him one very important thing – he could achieve anything he wanted, but only if he acted purposefully and was always prepared for the consequences of his actions. It was because of Dunia that he was still living in this sad, grey place. It was a workers' town. *You don't work, you don't eat.* And 'work' only ever meant gruelling physical labour. There was nothing here for intellectuals. The humble labourer was king here and it would always stay that way. His mother had said that, as she gave him her last money so he could take private French lessons.

Piotr had left for a while. He had gone to the University of Life Sciences in Warsaw, where, as far as he could tell, students learned the theory behind shoving piles of shit from place to place. But

Piotr had wanted more. When he graduated he'd stayed in Warsaw, applied to the Socialist Youth Association, started working, as an intern at first, at a party newspaper. Its motto was the classic communist adage 'Workers of the world, unite!' He stayed there, did well. He only went back to Hajnówka in the holidays. This time, though, something had changed.

Dunia, after meeting the ten-year-old Piotr and helping him get to the hospital to have his broken ankle treated, had come to live in Piotr's family home with him and his grateful parents, her life with her adoptive parents being unbearable. When Piotr was younger and she a teenager she'd taken care of him. She'd become the sister he had never had. And when he'd left for Warsaw they had become less close. But while he was home for this holiday, he'd started to see her differently, and she him. They both liked to say they had finally fallen in love at first sight. Now, it was the beginning of November, and he was still in Hajnówka. He had lied to his boss that he was collecting intelligence on the lumber mill and then, when that excuse had run its course, that his mother had fallen ill. Finally, someone else took his place at the newspaper and he had nothing to go back to Warsaw for. He did have other options. A job at the ministry, for one; but he simply couldn't countenance the idea of living without his beloved. So, he stayed in Hajnówka, even though Dunia had asked him to think about his career. He paid her no mind. He knew she loved him. He felt they had been created for each other. Physically, mentally. He could read her mind. It always made her uncomfortable; she had never allowed anyone this close before. When he'd gambled his whole career for her, letting his love win, she'd broken down in tears. Never before had he seen her in such pain. It was proof enough of her love for him.

'This place eats anyone who's not just a worker. They aren't welcome. Don't be stupid!' She'd thrown herself at him, hitting him in desperation. Later, they'd made love. Passionately, angrily, as if she wanted to be punished for his lost chances.

He looked for employment for six months. But there were no newspapers here, just the brochures handed out at the lumber mill. And there was already a tight-knit group of loyal bootlickers who tended to the official party bulletin. Piotr had no connections. He was blacklisted. Everybody knew his father, Staszek Gałczyński.

A traitor. It didn't help that his parents had adopted his mother's name, Bondaruk. People remembered. If his father were still alive, he would have driven Piotr away from here by force. He hadn't given him all that education only for the boy to have to fritter it away, living through the same hell he himself had experienced. *A dishonour like mine cannot be forgotten or forgiven,* he said on his deathbed. He'd died in excruciating pain.

Piotr's mother wouldn't even talk to him, so he moved to a workers' boarding house. He had little money and quickly got used to being hungry, the high point of his day being when Dunia brought him his dinner in a basket. She couldn't visit him every day though – there were appearances to keep up. They met two, sometimes three times a week, when she was working the night shift on the hospital maternity ward. It wasn't any way to live and he knew it, but leaving Dunia was not an option. Piotr was twenty-eight and still afraid to grow up. He didn't want to fight. There was nothing of the warrior in him, but he couldn't settle for becoming a journalist either, on the leash of important communist comrades, dancing to their tune.

Dunia, though considerate and supportive, didn't intend to risk her hard-earned life for him. She had been forced to run away too many times to forget the taste of not having a place to call her own.

'Love isn't enough to start over,' she would say.

Now, she extended a hand and he slid his own into it, interlocking his fingers with hers. They stayed like that, motionless, until she stirred. Piotr knew her well enough to know that in a moment she'd spring up and start dressing. Her shift was starting at nine that night. It was only seven; they still had time. But she squirmed out of his embrace, just offering a cheek for a goodbye smooch. She pulled her knees up and allowed herself to rest her face on his chest for a moment. She swept her nose across his skin, taking in his scent.

'I like this place,' she breathed. 'I'll remember it for ever.'

'Leave with me,' he repeated. 'We'll start over. Just you and me.'

'I'm too old for you.'

'It's only eight years. It doesn't matter to me.'

'It matters to others. To me.' She pushed herself away, pretending to be amused. In truth, she was unbearably sad. She was right.

'I can already picture your mother. Not only am I a married woman and way older than you, I'm a *russkie* to boot. Belarusians killed your father. You're Judas's son. You won't be able to make people forget. Even if you stood up to your mother, she'd blame me for ever for ruining your life.'

'We don't need anyone. We only need ourselves.' He stroked her salt-and-pepper hair. The first strands of grey had started appearing in it before Dunia turned thirty, but she never wanted to dye it. Instead, she wore flashy headscarves. She was never seen without one. 'We'll go somewhere new where no one knows us.'

'He won't give me a divorce. You can't divorce when you're Orthodox. What God has joined together—'

'You don't love him!'

'I don't.' She agreed, shaking her head. 'But he's my husband. And I can't leave Irma. I'm the only thing she's got.'

'I can get rid of him, if you want,' he offered. 'I'll do it for you. Because I love you.'

'Shut up, stupid!' She clamped a hand over his mouth. 'But it would be best if he had never existed.'

She pushed herself up and bent over to pick up her bra from the floor. Then, looking for her knickers, she paused for a moment, stroking her belly. *Had she gained weight?* Piotr asked himself. Her breasts seemed larger too. Not that that was a problem. He adored her body and she had told him that she adored his. They matched in bed, she liked to say, always blushing. To find pleasure in bed was a sin, after all. *We'll be damned*, she cried sometimes.

She finally found her knickers, on the coffee table and pulled them on. Then, fumbling a bit, she pulled on her suspender belt. 'It must have shrunk when I washed it,' she said, seeing him look as she wrestled with the fabric. Finally, she put on a slip and then the rest of her clothes, which were folded in a neat heap on the chair. Dunia always folded her clothes. The bed creaked when she sat down to pull her shoes on.

'Stay a while longer. We have time.' He touched her back, trailing his fingers from the back of her neck down her spine. She arched in bliss, froze for an instant as he gently touched her ear, but shook him off and pushed herself up.

She straightened up and stood tall, legs apart and arms on her hips. She looked strong, brave, and haughty. It might have fooled someone else, but Piotr knew it was just a mask and that inside, she was soft and yielding. Like the beeswax the locals used to use as caulking, which hardened with every minute after application, Dunia hardened with each layer of clothes she put on, losing the softness she only allowed him to see. He was proud to be able to watch her when she was naked – both physically and emotionally.

'My love, why fritter your life away at my side?' she cried. 'You're young, beautiful. Go out, conquer the world! I have to stay here. I don't have a choice. I work here. I live here. This is my place. This is where I die. Irma goes to school here. How can I leave her?'

'Let's take her with us.'

'She wouldn't want to go.'

'We don't have to marry,' he pleaded. 'I don't need that. You don't either.'

'But what can you offer me?' She turned to him, challenging. 'You'd like me to leave all I have. What will you give me in return?'

Piotr sat up, slapped his pillow back into shape, and helped himself to a cigarette. He offered it to Dunia, knowing she sometimes liked a drag or two, but this time she refused.

'I'll find a job.'

'What job?' she scoffed. 'You're no good at physical labour.'

He flexed his bicep. He was thin, and his delicate hands had scratches on them. He had been chopping wood. He had tried working at the lumber mill, but had only lasted six days.

'Something is going to happen,' she said ominously. She started to comb her hair with quick, jerky movements. The ends had tangled into a knot and she lifted it, studying the twisted strands, seeing something only she understood. 'Something bad. It might have started happening already.'

'Come on!' He waved his hand dismissively. Sometimes, she told him about the visions she had. She saw things before they happened. Piotr knew people came to her, asking for help. She prayed for them. Piotr was sceptical. He'd never believed in folk tales. Or in *whisperers*, as people referred to Dunia. He preferred the real, blood and bones Dunia. His beautiful Dunia. His Dunia was no witch.

'I'll go first, if you like. I'll find us a home. There are all kinds of opportunities in big cities. I'll send for you and Irma.'

'She won't want to leave her daddy.'

'You haven't asked her.'

'She doesn't like you.' Dunia grabbed a pair of scissors and cut off the knotted strand of hair. Then she took a box of matches and burned the strand, muttering something under her breath. The room quickly filled with the stench.

'How do you know that?'

'She knows about us. Everybody knows. He knows too.'

That took Piotr by surprise. Dunia laughed. 'Don't worry,' she said. 'He doesn't care. He hasn't touched me since I can remember. And I doubt he ever will again. At least he's open about it with me.'

'I don't understand that. How can he resist your charms?' He pulled her closer and kissed her on the lips.

She pulled away and laughed again.

'He's got a daughter, remember. He only married me so I could raise her.'

Piotr knitted his brows. He didn't understand.

'But *he* likes you.'

'Is he some kind of pervert?' he asked, his face screwing up in contempt.

'You should be happy. It's the only reason he tolerates what we do.'

'Tolerates?'

'He finds it amusing. He asked about you yesterday. What kind of person you are. I didn't say anything, but I know he finds you attractive. Don't tell me you haven't noticed.'

'Somehow, I've missed it.'

'Look closer, then. I wouldn't turn your back on Stepan if I were you.'

He threw the pillow at her.

'You're beautiful,' she said. She touched his chest, slipping her fingers into his chest hair, and slowly slid her hand down. He immediately got an erection. She pulled the bedsheet away and smiled. 'I've never felt so good with anyone. Not that I've done it with a lot of men. Why can't we just keep living like this?'

'I want you to be mine. Only mine.'

'You can't buy me, you know,' she said, frowning. 'I'll never be only yours. It's not about you. I'll never be anyone's property. I want to be free. Are things so bad as they are?'

'I don't want to see you just once a week. I want to be able to hold hands with you. Out on the street.'

'You mean walk side by side. We're in Hajnówka.'

'You know what I mean. I want to be able to live with you, go to sleep next to you. Wake up and see your face.'

'Stop it, please.'

'I don't want to pretend we don't know each other when you talk to people I know.'

'You're the last romantic in the world,' she sighed. 'All the others have died out.'

'I'll be able to provide for you.'

'We'll see.' She hesitated. 'We'll have to discuss this seriously some time.'

'So, you're thinking about it? There's a chance you'll run away with me?'

'I'll bring you breakfast after my shift,' she replied, not looking at him. 'We'll get back to it then. But for now, you should know something important.'

'Nothing's important,' he cried, passionately. 'Irma can't stop you. You deserve to be happy!'

'It's not that simple,' she replied, but then brightened up. 'Maybe we really would make a good family.'

There was a noise from the corridor. Footsteps. Dunia shot Piotr a worried look. He just shrugged.

'Probably the guy from one-oh-seven. He likes to snoop around. And you're not exactly quiet in bed, sweetheart.'

She stifled a laugh and put a finger to her lips. Piotr piped down. The footsteps were growing louder.

'No,' she whispered. 'He's coming here. Is the door closed?'

He nodded.

'I'm off then, my love.'

He liked it when she called him that. She planted a kiss on his forehead and then spread some Vaseline over her lips. She threw on her coat and tied her satin scarf around her neck. Suddenly, the door lock clicked. Whoever it was had a key. The door swung open just as Dunia was picking up her wicker basket. A middle-aged man was standing in the doorway.

'*Dobry vyetchar,*' Stepan greeted them in Belarusian. His mouth spread in a sly smile. 'Have you lost your way, wife?'

Dunia shot him a brief glance and rushed out without replying. He grabbed her by the arm and she hissed in pain.

'They called from the hospital. They need you. Breech delivery or something.'

'I'm on my way there now,' she replied without a hint of concern. 'I just need to get Irma ready for school tomorrow.'

'Irma is a big girl. She'll do it herself,' he said. 'There's no time. Jagoda Pires is about to have a baby, so you'd better hurry up. I promised Anatol you'd help.'

'I'm not a doctor.'

'Just go and be there,' he barked. 'My driver will take you.'

She said nothing more, just stepped out and closed the door behind her. The men remained silent until her steps died away, and then Stepan took a chair, setting it down by Piotr's bed. He stared at the younger man's ruffled hair and his sweaty chest. Piotr threw the bedcovers off and got up. Stepan licked his lips and put a pipe in his mouth. He didn't turn his head away. On the contrary – his eyes trailed the naked man. When Piotr approached Stepan's chair to pick up his trousers, Dunia's husband blatantly and keenly observed the younger man's genitals. Piotr caught his look. He recalled Dunia jokingly warning him about Stepan, but he didn't want to give him the satisfaction of reacting. He calmly pulled on his underpants and trousers. They locked stares. When Piotr, still naked from the waist up, took out a pack of cigarettes from his pocket, Stepan sat upright and offered him a light.

Piotr breathed smoke into his rival's face. He saw how Stepan was looking at him. 'I'll fight for her. She doesn't want to be with you any more,' he said in a cocksure manner.

Stepan burst out laughing. 'Don't make a scene, boy.' He pulled out a car catalogue from his breast pocket. He pointed to a Chaika with chrome handles and then to a classic Volga with roll-down windows – the newest model. 'Come look at the car I've just ordered. The first such automobile in Hajnówka. They've just promoted me.

I'm the new director of the lumber mill. Stick with me and you'll go a long way.'

Piotr frowned.

'What are you saying?'

Stepan got to his feet, walked over to the radio and switched it on. It screeched at first, and then they heard music and singing.

'I need you to do something,' Stepan said coolly. 'You can write, yes? You'll write something for the newspaper. I'll get them to publish it. You'll be sorted for life. But the kid is mine.'

'What kid?'

'Your kid.' Stepan's face remained impassive. Only his eyes narrowed. 'Didn't she tell you?'

Piotr waited. He felt the blood draining from his face. He swayed on the chair. He thought he might faint.

'Dunia is four months pregnant. You can fuck her all you like. Or rather, all she likes. But the child comes to me. You in?'

Stepan looked out of the window. It was way past shift start time, but there was a throng of male labourers outside the lumber mill building. There were women and children too, the women with meals for their husbands. The men sat on cardboard boxes around glowing portable braziers and talked, warming their hands. All the locomotives and gondola cars had been linked together and were now blocking the track to the tool warehouse. One of the largest engines had a skull-and-bones flag attached to it. There were banners saying: 'Sit-in protest – day 2'.

One of his men, Wacław Mariański, went out to address the crowd.

'What is the meaning of this foolishness? We have lumber to process. Get back to work. The director will fire everyone who does not comply.'

The protesters responded with loud jeers and whistling. They crowded tighter together, standing in a large half-circle. A few moments later, eggs and flares started flying out of the group. Mariański retreated into the building.

Stepan drew the office blinds as one of the eggs splattered on the window. He puffed out smoke from his pipe, picked the black telephone on his desk and ordered an intercity call. Warsaw picked up after a few rings.

'They want a thirty per cent raise for piecework. They also want firewood allowance. Two metres of wood per month. Also, they want us to stick to safety regulations and comply with their future requests,' he reported.

Then he listened, nodding and cutting in once in a while:

'Yes, of course. I fully agree with you, comrade. Yes, I have the means. No, if we arm the militia, it will only make things worse. When will they publish? Understood.'

He put the receiver down. A moment later, the phone rang again.

'Front desk here, comrade director. Engineer Bondaruk asks to see you.'

'Let him in. Have him talk to the workers. Tell him to come to see me at home afterwards. I'll wait.'

Stepan ended the call and looked out of the window again. He saw Bondaruk enter the square, climb a pile of wooden crates and start to address the crowd of workers. They clearly didn't want to listen, but when he passed them a microphone, they started to shout their requests and complaints.

'We want work and bread!'

'He's a snoop! One of them,' someone shouted from the crowd.

'Shut up, let him speak. The country has to know about our situation!'

A patrol car drove up and uniformed officers stepped out and secured the back exit. Stepan left in the car, unnoticed by the workers, and was driven home to safety. Dunia was just finishing doing Irma's homework with her. He planted a kiss on his daughter's forehead and said to his wife: 'I have to go to Warsaw.'

She nodded.

'If I'm not back soon, don't do anything. I'll be safe. We have to wait until the storm blows over. The protests have to end by tomorrow, or else they're going to transfer us to the other border. If they don't . . .' He paused.

'What am I supposed to say if you don't come back?'

'You know nothing,' he replied. 'Best it remains that way.'

That night, when Stepan was having his evening cocktail and his wife and daughter were already asleep, someone knocked at the door. The director put on a suit jacket over his crumpled shirt. It was Bondaruk. He passed his superior a few pages. Stepan took them and scanned the text. He smiled approvingly and invited the younger man inside, but Piotr only shook his head. Stepan took his coat from the hanger and left, shutting the door behind him. There was a brand new limousine parked by the entrance to the building. The driver opened the door for his boss. Stepan and Piotr stepped into the car. They drove to the post office and woke the manager. The man, still in his pyjamas, telefaxed the editor's office of the *Gazeta Współczesna* newspaper. When he was finished, Stepan placed a voucher for free firewood on his desk. The post office manager bowed deeply.

'Good job, boy!' The director patted Bondaruk on the back. 'Can you drive?'

'Only a motorbike,' Piotr said. 'I've never driven one of these limos.'

'It's a lot easier than fucking a woman, I can tell you that,' Stepan said, snorting with laughter. 'All you have to do is keep to the road. Never waver. Come on, *molodets*! The world is your oyster from now on.'

The driver took his hat and left on foot. Piotr got into the driver's seat.

'We're going to Warsaw, boy. But first, we have a meeting to attend.'

They drove down a forest road.

'Switch the high beam on,' Stepan said. 'Nice feature, eh? A gift from the party.'

A black building loomed in the darkness, illuminated by the car's headlights. Piotr drove over to it slowly. The structure, a holiday house, was made of wood. Black with soot. Run-down. Back in the house's glory days, the window frames had clearly been white – probably freshly painted before every holiday. Now, they were grey and scratched, crumbling. Some of the windows had chipboard in them instead of glass. The roofing was in desperate need of repair, cascades of thatch dangling from it.

'Kill the engine,' Stepan ordered.

He hauled himself out of the car and wrapped himself tighter in his coat. It was blowing a gale. Piotr remained in the driver's seat. He was wondering where they were. They were well away from the city and had nearly got lost on the winding, narrow roads. Stepan had missed the turn several times, and Piotr had had to keep reversing the enormous limo. He wasn't sure if he'd be able to find his way back in the moonlight – and at the moment he had no idea if he'd ever even return.

Piotr turned the key and shut off the engine. For a while, the only sound was the whistling of the wind and the throaty snorting of pigs, who presumably shared the building with humans, as there wasn't a pigsty in sight. Piotr pulled on the handbrake and rummaged in his pocket for his cigarettes. The pack was empty. He crumpled it into a ball and tossed it into a compartment in the car's door. A moment later, he changed his mind, reaching for the pack and putting it back in his pocket. His instinct told him he shouldn't leave any traces in the limousine.

'There is a fisherman's box in the boot. Take it out,' Stepan said through the window. 'And a bag with some food.'

As Piotr was leaning into the boot to take out the bag and the box full of vodka bottles, he heard a whistling whisper. He looked up. There was another man standing by the house. Short, fat and, as was revealed when he took his hat off, balding. He was talking to Stepan in a low voice. He took him by the arm. They obviously knew each other. Piotr slammed the boot shut, turned the key in the lock and headed towards the house door.

'What's he doing here?' the priest asked when he spotted Bondaruk. He stared at Stepan's handsome face, and then back at the younger man. He was clearly doing his best to hide his jealousy.

Piotr knew this priest. Jerzy Świerczewski. A few days ago, the townspeople had chased him out of his own house. Stepan must have been hiding him here so they wouldn't lynch him.

'I'll wait in the car,' he offered, but Stepan took him by the shoulder and pulled Piotr towards.

The gesture felt intimate. Too intimate. Piotr shook off Stepan's hand, bristling.

'He's coming with us,' Stepan told the priest and added: 'Be nice to him. Remember, you're prettier when you smile.'

Piotr regretted not having his knife with him.

'I knew your father,' the priest, told him. His eyes, lacking eyelashes, narrowed into two fat-rimmed slits. 'I used to take his confessions.'

'Keys!' Stepan shot out a hand. 'And stop boring the kid with your stories.'

Piotr gestured that neither of his hands were free. The fresh cold cuts in the bag he held smelled delicious and he suddenly felt very hungry. Despite having promised himself he'd never accept anything from Stepan, he was close to breaking that pledge. His mouth watered. He hadn't had a proper meal in ages.

Stepan gestured to the priest, who reached into Bondaruk's pocket for the car keys. There was another, older key hanging from the chain and he opened the creaking door with it. A fat rat zoomed out, passing between Piotr's legs. He jumped and nearly fell over a low chopping block with an axe firmly lodged in it.

'What a pansy.' The priest laughed. 'You can tell he's a city boy.'

Stepan lit an oil lamp, which gave out a faint light, just enough to illuminate a table with several chairs upside down on it. They were identical to those in Stepan's office back at the lumber mill. Brand new. Two equally unused sofas stood on either side of the room. Bedding hung from hooks, wrapped in plastic foil, like monstrous cocoons.

'What are we doing here?' Piotr asked. And then added: 'What am *I* doing here?'

Stepan raised his head. He slapped the bottom of a vodka bottle, unscrewed the cap and took a big swig.

'We have a deal, don't we? Do your part, and you can go free.'

'I've already done my part. What about my payment?'

'Have you?'

Stepan placed a piece of paper on the table. Half of it was printed. He called to the priest. 'You write, Świerczewski. Informant recruitment report. Security Service, Hajnówka division. I, the undersigned, Piotr Bondaruk, son of Stanisław Bondaruk and Alina, née Bondaruk.'

The priest put on a pair of glasses and licked the tip of a pencil. He wrote down what Stepan had said, then paused and took a look at Piotr.

'What codename should we give him? Such a pretty face!' He reached out to stroke Bondaruk's face. Stepan slapped the hand away.

'No touching. First we work, then we play.'

Piotr retreated a couple of steps. 'I won't be a snitch!'

Stepan took a bite of sausage and motioned to the priest, who took his glasses off and pushed the papers away. He took out a loaf of bread and cut a slice for himself and another for the director. He put the knife down. The ivory handle was sturdy, held together with thick bolts. The blade itself was paper-thin and sickle-shaped.

'Suit yourself,' Stepan said with his mouth full. He took a chicken leg and bit into it. Then he unwrapped a fat ring of brawn and helped himself to a large chunk.

They ate in silence. Bondaruk observed, hypnotised. He couldn't believe they had let him off so easily.

'Have something to eat before you go,' Stepan said pleasantly. 'You have a long way to travel. It's dark. You might get lost. In fact, maybe you'd better wait until morning. You can sleep here.' He pointed at the two sofas.

Piotr sat down at the table. He allowed a glass to be filled for him and gulped down the drink. He realised it was pure spirit. It burned his throat and he knew would quickly go to his head. He took a few bites of sausage, which he followed with a slice of bread. He drank a couple more glasses of alcohol and felt his head start to swim. He could hear the other two men laughing at him, but he didn't care any more. Consciousness left him as suddenly as if someone had switched off the lights.

He woke up to loud squeals and a horrid stench. Then he felt a tearing pain in his rectum. His hands were tied to a fence, and his face had been pushed into pig shit. The pigs, crazed with fear, were squealing, huddled against the wall. His nose, eyes and mouth were plastered with their excrement. It was hard to breathe. Suddenly, someone jerked him up by the hair. Piotr opened his eyes, lifting his head. What he saw were male genitalia. The priest was touching himself, looking on with a hideous grin as Stepan raped Piotr. The young man could do nothing to defend himself. Finally, Stepan finished. Piotr kept still. He was bent over the railing, his trousers around his ankles. He wasn't able to speak, much less to fight.

'Shush.' The priest stroked his shit-spattered face. 'Your first time, pretty boy?'

Piotr managed to pull his head away. He wanted to spit in the man's face, but he felt something unbearably hot, burningly painful, slipping between his buttocks. He screamed and fainted.

'Now try to fuck her,' Stepan growled, buttoning his trousers. 'She's all yours.'

Then he wrapped his arm around the priest, and they both left and went back to the house. The priest gently washed the dirt off his lover and they lay down on one of the sofas. Jerzy tried to cuddle up to him but Stepan shooed him away, exhausted.

'I'm jealous,' complained the vicar.

'You should be,' Stepan said. 'I've never had such a lovely lay in my life. I think I'll go at him again tomorrow. And the day after tomorrow, and so on until I break him. I think I'm in love.'

Jerzy looked at his lover with reproach. Stepan shrugged.

'At least, it feels like love.'

The sun was rising when Piotr woke up. He was lying in a pool of his own blood. His testicles were horribly swollen. His cut-off penis lay next to him. He reached out for it and cradled it in his hand. It didn't feel like a part of himself. After some time, he wrapped it in some cheesecloth he'd found. There must have been a cow here before, he thought absentmindedly. He shambled towards the house, dragging his feet. In the entryway, he found the axe lodged in the chopping block and pulled it out, then moved on, into the room where his tormentors were still sleeping.

He chopped without warning. Chopped, and chopped again. He felt he'd be drained of all his strength soon, so he kept chopping. Stepan died after the second hit. He had sharpened the axe well. When Stepan's head was already cleaved in two, the priest scrambled up and started running. Piotr caught up with him on the porch. The man was still alive. He was making gurgling noises. His eyes, frenzied with terror, darted back and forth. Piotr didn't put him out of his misery. He had no strength left in him. Instead, he crawled back inside, curled up on one of the sofas and, still gripping the axe, fell into an uneasy slumber. Disjointed fragments of thoughts flashed through his mind. At one point he thought he could hear the rumble of a car. Had someone come to help him? Or to help *them*? As much as he wanted to get up, take the brand new black Chaika and drive away, he couldn't as much as twitch. He was sure he wouldn't wake up again. His only regret was that when they found him, they'd think he was a sodomite like the other two. Mother would be devastated. She would never forgive him. Dunia would know, but she would tell no one.

The pigs were awake but they didn't make any noise. They were trotting around their enclosure, waiting patiently for someone to feed them.

Hajnówka, 2014

The old wall-hanging depicting rutting stags had never enjoyed so much attention as when Sasza stabbed it with dozens of pins, putting up photos of young women. All of them were either missing or murdered.

From the left, they were: Łarysa, Mariola, Iwona and Danka. They looked good with the backdrop of the idealised forest. It suited them. They had all disappeared in the woods.

Beneath them, Sasza pinned the photos of Bondaruk and his white car, and slips of paper with the names of his sons. She had to consider them suspects too; they had been the ones to lose the most after Bondaruk's wedding. Below these she pinned the names of people connected to the case, but who she couldn't yet categorise as either suspects or witnesses.

When she had finished the 'occupational therapy', as she always thought of this stage of visualisation essential for the preliminary phase of a profiler's job, Sasza transferred all the data she could to large sheets of paper Romanowska had sent her. It looked like a family tree. Individuals were connected by a range of relatives, some closer than others. Sasza marked them with vectors and continuous (friends) or dotted (enemies) lines. Just as she had suspected, there was no one who would count as a complete outsider. Everybody knew everyone. Theoretically, this might make her job easier, as a web like this could be helpful in unearthing perpetrators' motivations, but at the same time it meant she'd have to plough through dozens of lies, half-truths and manipulations. People who know each other tend to make investigations harder by being obstructive, out of either not wanting to upset people or the fear that their neighbours, acquaintances or relatives might hold their statements against them. You have to read between the lines in such cases. That was a job for later, though.

Now, Sasza took a detailed map of the city and its surroundings and marked key locations: the place of disappearance of the women and where the skulls were discovered, as well as the residential and work addresses of every person involved. She traced the routes of power lines, overpasses, railways and the local river, the Leśna, which the locals called the Stink Stream because the chemical plant used to dump waste into it. There still wasn't a single soul in town who would risk swimming in it.

It quickly became apparent that Danka's case was different from the others. Aside from the employees and patients of the psychiatric hospital, there were no connections with any locals. Sasza thought of taking Danka's picture down, but something stopped her. Instead, she just moved it a bit farther away from the rest, next to the arrest warrant for Łukasz Polak, which had been released to the media earlier that morning.

She divided the case files according to victims, and then stacked them into neat piles on the desk. She read each report and started making notes. At first she did this on her laptop, in the professional profiling software she favoured, but after a while she decided there was just too much information. Lacking Post-its, Sasza instead cut up some printer paper. A victim is a book and you have to know how to read it. And though at first glance the missing women were as different as it got, some similarities did start to appear as Sasza worked. They were all under thirty when they had gone missing. Each case involved the same car. They had all been emotionally connected to Piotr Bondaruk and all had the same blood type – 0Rh–. Sasza had realised this earlier in the day and had verified it with the commissioner. It had to be important; the investigators had found a portable refrigerator filled with blood plasma in the boot of the car that the perpetrator had chased Iwona Bejnar in and that was the same blood type too.

No body, no crime. Disappearances are the hardest and least rewarding type of case. They always require you to question dozens of witnesses multiple times. Even worse, most of them were cold; you never knew if you'd be able to dig up anything new. And Sasza already had a jumble of data on her desk. She decided to start the analysis with the case that seemed the least connected to Four-Eyes, but which at least had a body to start from. It would be the easiest to create a profile for. Sasza decided to ignore what she already knew, instead creating new hypotheses.

Danka Pietrasik had been lying on the bed, covered. The sheet had been smoothed down, giving the appearance of tidiness. In Sasza's opinion, the murderer had obsessively and meticulously arranged the crime scene, ritualising the killing. The sheet was supposed to look like a shroud. Removing it had revealed a macabre scene. The woman had been bound with tie-wraps and a telephone charger cable had been wrapped round her neck. A thin charger socket for a simple old Nokia, the most popular mobile phone around, sold for one złoty if you signed up to a contract. Sasza found that interesting. Eugenia Rączka, Polak's landlady, had told her that neither she nor Polak had owned a mobile phone. That didn't necessarily mean anything, of course; the murderer might have stolen a charger, or bought it just to commit the crime. There were no fingerprint matches with the database.

The woman's body had been arranged in a foetal position, but she hadn't been naked. The perpetrator had made sure that despite the first impression, which was undoubtedly grotesque, Danka's dignity was intact. Her dress had been buttoned up and her knickers untouched. Although she was under the covers, her dress had revealed only the lower half of her thighs. The murderer must have gone to some trouble to keep her clothes this way. *As if he was parting with a loved one*, thought Sasza. As if he had known her or been emotionally attached to her. The same went for Danka's hair. It had been braided. Maybe even combed. Her lips had been slicked with protective lip balm, the pot of which the investigators later found under the nightstand. They hoped to find matching fingerprints on it.

At first, Sasza had thought that all of this was intended as a gruesome exhibit. Like those the Red Spider used to present years before. But if that were the case, why cover the body with the bedsheet? Why lock the bedroom door and the apartment? Why didn't the murderer take away his things? There was something inconsistent about this. Finally, why did the killer murder Danka in Eugenia Rączka's flat? He didn't leave the body there to be seen, like with the previous victims. Normally, the answer would be obvious: he did not want the victim to be found before he had managed to find a new and safe hiding spot. But is there a place in Hajnówka where you can lie low and feel safe? The forests and villages, the abandoned huts in the woods would be good guesses. But they don't have the Internet, and a killer such as this, prone to showing off, always keeps tabs on what the police are doing. He has to keep on top of things to be able to control his actions. He wouldn't have changed his MO so drastically just because he had moved to a small town. Sasza had to seriously consider the hypothesis that this killer was a Red Spider copycat.

Eugenia Rączka had opened Polak's room with her own key. There had been no signs of a break-in. She had only noticed the first fly the day after the murder. The victim's body had been in the apartment for no longer than twenty-four hours, so the murder had been committed without Eugenia around. If the murderer was her tenant (and that seemed likely), he had had a lot of time to pack up his things and leave. However, he had left personal belongings that made identifying him all too easy; his the photographic equipment – and the painting. Under the pretence of making a private call, Sasza had asked Eugenia to leave the room, and had hidden the painting under her jacket. It was her, and she couldn't bear the thought of the police finding it at the crime scene.

Now, she spread out the small canvas and studied it. It was an idealised version of herself, but it offered answers to the questions Sasza had been wanting to ask for a long time. It felt like a crushing weight had finally lifted from her shoulders. Her phone rang. Romanowska.

'The woman was bound post-mortem,' the commissioner said as soon as Sasza picked up. 'Cause of death is strangulation. Probably with a pillow. There are multiple petechiae that suggest the killer straddled the victim. The physician said it was a quick, humane death. The cable was wrapped round the neck at a later time. The victim was also arranged in her pose post-mortem. It was not ligature strangulation, as we first assumed. There are only minor abrasions on the neck. Nothing serious. The tie-wraps were also put on after death. Remember the lividity on the face? It's only on the left side. The pathologist says the killer rolled the girl onto her side and that's why blood pooled there. Tell me, why all the theatrics?'

'Go to Ciszynia,' replied Sasza. She was breathing heavily, picturing the man she had seen in the clinic's grounds, painting, in a blue hoodie. She glanced at the painting again and then away, shuddering with disgust. 'Check if she had any over-eager admirers. Maybe someone had a crush on her? I know one thing – the killer had to be someone close to the victim. Maybe her brother? I need to be present during his questioning.'

'I'd rather keep you out of it for now. We'll manage on our own.'

'Suit yourself,' Sasza sighed, though staying on the sidelines wasn't to her liking. Before Romanowska hung up, Sasza added: 'Can you go to Jacek Pietrasik's room? That's the victim's brother. Secure any paints, painting equipment and clothes he might have worn while painting recently. Can you get a warrant for that? Oh, and check the make of his mobile. And if he borrowed someone's charger and cable. Maybe he lost his? Or, if someone else lost one or had one stolen. You know.'

'It's a pretty popular phone,' Romanowska said. 'Besides, been there, done that. He's got an alibi. We still have his psychiatrist at the station.'

'Prus?' Sasza switched the mobile to speaker mode and bent down to pull on her biker boots. 'Don't ask her anything and, more importantly, don't tell her anything. I'll be there in a minute.'

'As I said, I'd like you to stay under the radar for now. No official questioning,' the commissioner said, but Sasza wasn't listening. She was already on her way to the door. Before she left, she snatched the painting and quickly slid it under her jacket. She stopped by the mirror to check if it was bulging out. But no. Nobody would know.

Gdańsk, 2014

Jarosław Sokołowski, aka Shaggy, was writing an advert for a job in the Białystok IPN Document Access and Archiving Department when his colleague Ariel called from outside his door, 'There's a letter for you. There was a mix-up with the address. Marian opened it, but he didn't look inside. It was supposed to come to you direct.'

Jarosław muttered a response and carried on typing. The job advert was nearly done. He just had to insert the usual formalities.

'Other duties as needed.'

He looked up. The corner of a blue envelope, printed with childish designs, jutted beneath his door. He couldn't imagine anyone over the age of seven choosing that type of envelope. Jarosław didn't have children or a wife and he was quite happy about that. Not having to support anyone was a luxury. His last lover, of the paid sort of course, he had dumped over ten years ago. His mother didn't write to him either, so that was another option he could discount – he visited her in Siedlce every week, returning with a bag full of jars of fried fish, pork chops or dumplings. That left his father. But he never wrote letters of any kind, not counting official correspondence with town hall and other authorities. And he would never, ever use stationery depicting characters from kids' movies. Drab, grey, cheap envelopes and paper were his thing. The cheaper the better. Right from when Jarosław was a child, his father had taught him to save money.

Jarosław's father's teachings were the main reason Jarosław himself now had no loans or mortgages. Not a single one. What he did have were numerous savings accounts. Some amounts he had frozen for as long as fifty years. The rate of return on them amounted to as much as twenty-two per cent, so it was a no-brainer. Jarosław didn't think about the things his deposited cash would someday buy him, or about the people who would potentially inherit his savings. He liked to have them just in case. Once a day he would call his stockbroker and ask about his investments. He paid them more attention than any of his friends and relatives.

Presently, he stood up from his chair. It creaked. He walked over and picked up the envelope and opened it. Inside was a Polaroid photo. It showed himself, naked, years younger. His body was covered in a thick blanket of hair. Back then he hadn't been able to afford full-body laser hair removal. Next to him, on a bed, lay an unattractive woman, spreadeagled and also naked. Her most striking features were her large breasts. He recognised Marzena 'the Wasp' Koźmińska immediately. You don't forget women like that. Especially when they vanish into thin air, taking your work laptop with them, and the next time you see them is on the TV, being led by two policemen to court, charged with murder. But Shaggy had no hard feelings. Marzena had sent the computer back. No files had been missing. She had only put a couple of porn films on the hard drive for a laugh.

There was no sender's name or address on the envelope, but Jarosław recognised the Wasp's handwriting. There was a case file number on the back, in the same hand. He instantly knew it referred to the case of Romuald 'Bury' Rajs and his massacre of Orthodox villages in Podlasie. The case had been closed a year back. Forty or so thick tomes were still stacked somewhere in the archive but, aside from the occasional local journalist from Białystok, nobody took any interest in them.

Jarosław returned to his desk shakily and sat down, his thoughts racing. When would Marzena contact him and which files would she ask for this time? She wouldn't explain her reasons. She never did. He wasn't afraid. In fact, he was mildly happy that she had been released and he'd have the chance to see her again. But what if Marian or Ariel – or whoever was in the postroom that day – had opened the envelope or been tempted to peek inside it? It wasn't that he was ashamed of his hairiness. Not any more. He even laughed at his own nickname, which had stuck even though he could now afford laser hair removal. However, if one of his colleagues recognised the woman, that was another thing altogether.

The case was notorious. They would immediately connect him to Marzena's trial and her friend Jowita's disappearance. He couldn't allow that. Not when his career was finally on the right track.

Jarosław quickly checked who had been working in the postroom earlier that day, wrote a job advert for that position, and wrote adverts for Marian's and Ariel's positions too. He'd have no problems finding a couple of young, idealistic historians who'd like to work in the archive for the slave wages the IPN offered. After all, he had started out that way. And he sure as hell intended to keep his position.

Hajnówka, 2014

Damian peeked out from behind his cover of spruce branches cut from the trees. There was a clearing before him. Crossing it would be the hardest part; the glade offered no trees to hide behind. He thought quickly. Was he supposed to risk entering the bog? He wouldn't be noticed there. Or maybe he should continue on his way and risk getting shot. He didn't have his wellies on. He reloaded his rifle. There was a handful of plastic rounds in his pocket still. He had used the gun only for training since winter. And he had never had to shoot a living enemy before.

He heard a rustle. He shot a glance behind him, but there was no one there. Must have been an animal. A hare or a doe, flitting through the underbrush and vanishing in the darkness. His two companions had been lagging behind. They couldn't have got here as fast as him; he was always the best at 'hare and hounds'.

Damian was a natural at boxing, which his father had been expert in until he had an accident at the lumber mill, for which his parents hadn't got a broken penny as it had happened before the fall of the communist regime. Paralysed from the waist down in the accident, he had hanged himself on a ceiling beam when Damian was six months old. All Damian got from the man was his name and an old communist medal he had received for being one of the thirty most productive workers on the thirtieth anniversary of the Hajnówka Lumber Industry Plant, or, as it was now known, Piotr Bondaruk's New Forest Hajnówka. Damian hated the communists with a passion. They'd killed his father.

Damian had perfected his strength and boxing technique with a sack full of sand and had been invited to join the guerrilla unit he was now training with – not to mention the brawls between football hooligans after each Jagiellonia game. The other hooligans often invited Damian to join in, which he did only reluctantly, knowing that the whole affair had nothing to do with real patriotism.

He heard footsteps, then the sound of someone dropping to the ground and crawling along the left-hand side of the clearing. Damian corrected his aim. It wasn't easy to make a decision, but the longer he stayed there thinking, the more afraid he would get of screwing up. It must have been at least twenty degrees Celsius and sweat was trickling down his spine, but Damian pulled his balaclava over his face and turned up his collar so that none of his skin was visible. He ran across the clearing. The shots came from ahead of him. He managed to dodge the first and second one but, before he could take aim and start returning fire, he was dead. The plastic bullets hitting his body hurt like hell. And they ruined his jacket, which had been his father's, with their fluorescent splotches.

'If you act, don't be afraid. If you're afraid, don't act,' Leszek Krajnów, the commander of the opposing team, said, appearing from behind Damian. And then he took him as a prisoner.

They didn't talk on their way back. The catechist kept quiet out of pity. Damian kept his mouth shut because he was ashamed. There'd be time for a debriefing at the campfire. He was ready to be reprimanded by the unit commander.

When they reached the base, Damian watched Krajnów's men leading the other prisoners in. His two companions, Tadek and Arek. He found some comfort in the fact that he had only got shot twice, while these two sported brand new camo splotched all over with fluorescent splatters. They didn't seem worried that they'd lost, though. They had their sandwiches out, their Thermoses too, and were sitting on a fallen tree, tucking in. At this point, Damian's own commander emerged from the thicket. Artur Mackiewicz took the tree branch camouflage off his head and patted the boy on the back.

'You nearly reached their base, boy.'

'Nearly isn't good enough, Captain.'

Krajnów and Mackiewicz exchanged looks.

'He really is fierce.' Krajnów nodded at Damian. 'You were right. He's going to be your best fighter.'

'Soldier,' Damian corrected the man.

He wasn't satisfied with the praise. What did he mean by using the future tense? He was already the best. But he kept that thought to himself.

'You're right – soldier.' Mackiewicz nodded at the marks on Damian's jacket. 'But you acted alone. You didn't cooperate with the rest of the unit. That is why you lost. You didn't use your companions as recon or decoy. You wanted to be the hero. But this isn't a movie.'

Damian gaped at the commander. It was the worst thing he could imagine hearing. Guerrillas are blood brothers. Like musketeers. One for all and all for one. Mackiewicz threw Damian a box of matches. Firewood lay in a neat stack, prepared by the prisoners, who had been waiting for the rest of their team for an hour now. Damian easily lit the fire, using only one match. The commanders sat down, took swigs from their flasks, offering the alcohol to the adults among the unit, and began their assessment. For some, Damian knew, this was the boring part. He liked it the best though. All around them silence, darkness. The world was theirs and it ended where their light ended. What counted was this moment. Just men talking about honour, the Fatherland, and war. Damian was too young to feel annoyed by the solemn and bombastic tone of the meetings. On the contrary – he felt proud of being a member of such an elite unit, known to so few. Currently there were seven of them, plus the two commanders.

Two members of the unit, one of them Konrad Lewandowski, hadn't been allowed to participate today because they had arrived at the meet-up spot one hungover and one drunk. The commander was strict. He also liked to dress up like Romuald Rajs and often used his alias, 'Bury'. Today, as punishment, he had ordered the two drunkards to gather firewood, which was usually the girls' job. Today, though, Damian couldn't see any of the girls. That was fine by him. He had never felt comfortable in their presence. They always stared at him. He didn't want to know what they were thinking about him. They were probably laughing at him because he was so thin and really too young to be part of the unit. What they were doing was serious, after all. They trained and fought like real soldiers. Artur 'Bury' Mackiewicz had told them there was a real war coming. They had to be prepared.

'Real victors do what the others can't,' he'd said. 'Your Fatherland needs you. You never know when the call to arms will come.'

He handed the vodka to Damian. The boy looked at it, shook his head and handed it down the line. The commander smiled with satisfaction. He believed in Damian. He had been the same, years before. Or, at least, that was how he liked to remember himself.

'In the current situation, Poland has to be ready for a guerrilla war,' 'Bury' Mackiewicz began. They were all ready for one of his stories. Unfortunately, they were out of food. There weren't even sausages to roast over the fire. No potatoes to bake in the hot ash, either. 'Every time I speak about it, people smirk, laugh. Think it an anachronism. This is partly because of the stereotype about guerrillas. All those war movies about armoured units and old agents are wrong! We have to topple those stereotypes. Grind them to ash. Soldiers! Do not think about underground resistance units as groups of a couple of dozen men, marching through forests with smiles on their faces, singing war songs and parading across towns and villages. Modern guerrillas are formed into small groups. Units of no more than five men. Moving quickly, well hidden, always knowing their arena of operations like the backs of their own hands. Sometimes such small units merge into larger groups only to disperse again and disappear in their expertly masked bases or among the local populace. A real guerrilla fighter can easily replace his gun with a plough and the other way round. Without being exposed.'

Suddenly, laughter rang out. Two young women appeared at the campfire. They planted a large pot on the ground and lifted the lid, revealing thick, savoury split-pea soup smelling of smoked pork. Krajnów beamed, greeting Asia, who wore all black. Damian knew her. She was the best student at school and the daughter of one of the town's dignitaries and the richest real estate developer around.

'Artur, you forgot about the most important thing,' Krajnów said. 'Guerrillas always enjoy the support of the locals. It's the local populace that supply the soldiers with information and warm clothes. And it's their patriotic wives who bring in the food.'

A package of Nesteruk barbecue sausages landed next to the pot of soup. Mackiewicz sent one of the 'casualties' for some sticks to spike the sausages on.

'Only a unit with such support has a chance of winning the war!' Mackiewicz slapped his thighs and took out his canteen to fill with soup. 'You've showed real spirit during our mission today, boys, and I know you're tough, but what I'm most impressed with is the base you've built.' He gestured around. 'Because the most import-ant thing in our fight is staying alive. It's not about going blindly into battle and getting killed. Remember about always staying in cover and, if needed, about the possibility to withdraw. Tactic-al withdrawal is no dishonour. You fight to win. It doesn't matter who you're fighting: communists, fags, or atheists. It's all the same. War doesn't change. The aims justify the means. History knows many kinds of patriotism. There are always victims. But remember, Damian – a tree offers scant cover,' he said, turning to the boy sit-ting next to him. Damian blushed, though thankfully nobody would realise; all their cheeks were flushed with the heat of the campfire.

'A tree won't do,' Mackiewicz went on. 'Do I need to remind you that we're not preparing for all-out war? We're guerrillas, fighting from hiding. We attack where the enemy doesn't expect us. Our main asset is the element of surprise. Our greatest strength is the ability to strike surgically. Defeat the enemy piece by piece. We're like a virus – small and unseen, but able to defeat the strongest tiger. We eat away at the enemy slowly. We destroy the body organ by organ, shutting the monster's eyes, clogging its ears, and then, finally, killing it. That is our role. We would stand no chance in open warfare.'

One of the girls laughed. A few of the boys chuckled too. Mackiewicz stared them down. He didn't like it when his soldiers played and flirted when he was speaking. Only Asia remained silent. She sat rigid, back straight, listening intently. They'd never accepted a girl before, but Krajnów had told Mackiewicz that she wanted to join the unit and was a good markswoman. Krajnów had also told him, without giving any further details, that she was good at sabotage. Mysterious; but he had promised to consider enrolling the girl. Krajnów had invited Asia to the meeting tonight so he could take a better look at her. When she caught Mackiewicz's stare, she averted her eyes. She was cau-tious and sensible. A big advantage, especially for someone as young as her. He hoped she wouldn't blow their cover gossiping with her girlfriends.

'Your knowledge will come in handy any day now,' Mackiewicz continued. 'The communists could strike at any moment. You have to be ready – if you really love your country. Do you? Well?'

The girl who had laughed earlier was trying to keep a straight face now. She covered her face with her jacket, pretending to be cold. Asia jabbed her with an elbow. Then she gestured to Krajnów and he nodded. Asia got up and left without saying goodbye. The other girl, who had been trying to catch the attention of the young guerrillas, seemed to realise she was wasting her time; she followed. Mackiewicz reflected on Asia. She was composed, serious and had none of that irritating sweetness characteristic of most girls her age. She could come in handy in a fight, if they trained her. Inka herself had also started out cooking for the soldiers and tending their wounds, and she had turned out to be a better shot than most of her unit. And she didn't give anyone away when they arrested her. She would die for her unit. If not for her, Bury wouldn't have escaped the eastern hinterland where the Polish military was considered the enemy.

Damian didn't turn his attention back to his comrades immediately. He was listening to be sure that the girls had really gone. What did they really want? Were the commanders testing them? Or maybe they were spies? He also thought about who would have to take the soup pot back.

'Poland is not a girl you can dump and then come back to when you feel like it,' Mackiewicz was saying. 'When it demands the enemy's blood, will you defend it or cower? Are you ready to die for your country? Will you be proud to do so?'

Everyone, Damian included, nodded eagerly. Those questions didn't require answers. To even contemplate refusing would mean being booted out of the group. The army is not a debate club, the commander had told Damian, when he had once asked a philosophical question about the need to inflict death on civilians in the name of the greater good.

'But, if your country lays you to eternal sleep in its hallowed ground, its embrace is sweeter than any lover's.' The commander pointed to the ground. 'You'll remain with her for ever. Like everyone who has ever given his life in its defence. Your country is your land. The Fatherland. You should rise up against all the foul enemies who treat the very name of our country as a challenge.'

Everyone grew silent. Tadek gestured at Damian.

'He's a *katsap*,' he said. 'Who do you love?'

'Poland,' Damian replied without a moment's hesitation. 'Just like you.'

'Your forefathers were Belarusians. They sold us out to the *russkies*. They even collaborated with the Germans. They wanted to get their land back. They got shit and good riddance. They got nothing from the Germans, nothing from the Soviets, so now they pretend to be Polish. *Katsaps* rule this town. Go to them, where you belong. What are you even doing here?'

Mackiewicz raised a hand. Tadek piped down immediately.

'Ancestry isn't everything,' the commander said. 'Religion neither. My mother is Orthodox, for instance. So, as you would put it, a *katsap*.'

An awkward silence fell over the camp. Tadek dropped his eyes.

'Leszek here is a Catholic,' Mackiewicz continued. 'Like his father and his father's father before that. A true Pole with an aristocratic pedigree. And still we're friends. Because the measure of our friendship is our enemies.'

'His enemy is my enemy,' Krajnów added. 'Amen.'

'His friend is my ally. We are one unit. In Bury's, Łupaszka's and Młot's units there were Catholics, Orthodox and even Jews. What counts is what you feel. Or rather, who you feel you are. Communists, atheists and homosexuals – we're fighting them today and we will fight them tomorrow. All those who have succumbed to media manipulation and are the victims of the decline of the education system do not deserve to be called Poles. And women should be true ladies and we should treat them as such, according to the code of chivalry. And a lady shouldn't meddle in a man's affairs. A woman should not wear the trousers. Even the Bible says that. It was Job who said that a man's life is war. He said nothing about women—'

Krajnów raised a hand to interrupt his friend.

'I need to pick up my daughter from her mother's.' He stood up and rested his hand on Mackiewicz's shoulder. He pointed his chin at the soup pot. 'Will you take it back to the girls?'

'Damian and Tadek will do it,' the commander said. 'Godspeed.'

The guerrillas followed Krajnów with their eyes until he was gone.

'A man brought down,' the commander sighed. 'Such a fine man. A historian with a doctorate. Deeply religious, and yet, he had to suffer through a divorce. And he was made to live here, in this damned country, so utterly demoralised, where young people only focus on material things. He can't move out, because he has a daughter here. If he at least had a son, he'd raise him to become a warrior. A good man like himself.'

Nobody said anything.

'At least he isn't gay,' Tadek chortled.

Mackiewicz took the bait. 'Faggotry is a serious disease. It eats at thousands of young Poles, like a maggot. What's even worse though, they have the audacity to still go to church, showing off their vile deviancy!' He stopped abruptly.

Where the lecture would go from here was anyone's guess. One of the gathered didn't manage to stifle a yawn. Others followed suit, covering their mouths.

'But you're different,' the commander continued. He must have realised he had gone too far. 'You are the first generation free from any insecurities, the phobias of communism, the burden of war. Your motivation is strong and you're ambitious.'

He patted Damian on the back. The boy poured himself another portion of soup before it went totally cold.

'It's for you that Leszek makes his sacrifices. He can still believe in you. Boys, you can still change everything. You are the new Columbus generation. You respect and celebrate national dignity, the greatness of your country, the sacrifice and bravery of the generations before you, honour and pride. Those are the things that shape you. Military service will only help you in your endeavours. I don't believe in militarised scouting formations and their tradition any more. Paramilitary units such as ours are the future. Never let yourselves be told otherwise, because soon *we* will be the ones to defend our country against the enemy. Never let yourselves be told that you're fascists. Poland for Poles – those are beautiful words. Poles are warriors. And if you fight, you win. Because warriors can be beaten, but they never surrender.'

'Commander, sir. Does that mean there's going to be a war?' Tadek asked, his voice shaky.

'It never ended, son.' Mackiewicz smiled warmly. 'Our people were resigned to communist occupation and the current dictate of the post-communists. Then, we were manipulated by the imperialist European Union – the flood of goods, the genetically modified foods and the dreams of riches. You can see how that turned out.'

They nodded.

'My parents have been unemployed for more than two years now. If not for Grandmum's pension and some part-time jobs felling trees, we'd have starved to death,' one of the boys muttered.

'So you see,' Mackiewicz said, 'if you're a true Pole, you'll fight for what should be yours. I'll signal the commencement of Operation Poland. You'll know before the civilians do. The first local defence militias have already started popping up all around the country. They don't act within the remit of the local administration and the Church, though some wanted them to. Here in the east, that wouldn't work. Catholic and Orthodox parishes are at each other's throats. If I deem you ready, you'll join those units. We have the upper hand over the authorities. Unlike the police, army and border patrol, we really know the land, the local people. We have true local intelligence – and that's something no state official can ever aspire to. A modern freedom fighter should have the ability to get secret intelligence from civilians. And in turn, those civilians should be certain that they may count on the freedom fighters to defend them.'

'So why didn't we help out with searching for Iwona Bejnar?' Damian dared to ask.

'Who told you we should have?'

Damian and the rest of the boys looked surprised. The commander continued:

'Our people saved her from the Belarusian corrupt elite. We hid her and ordered our local units to fake a kidnapping. Now we're waiting for the blame to land to the old man on top of their vile pyramid. We'll kill two birds with one stone, boys. Smart, isn't it? Sure it is. But we're not only active there. Commander Krajnów is receiving new intelligence as we speak. For now, I can only tell you that to kidnap a pure-blooded Polish girl is one of the elements of the ongoing Polish–Belarusian war. You know how the First World War started, don't you? What happened in Sarajevo. We have to be on high alert. Anything could happen.'

'How much time do we have?'

'A month. Maybe as little as two weeks. Or even less.'

'What about weapons?' Tadek was growing agitated. 'Will we get real guns?'

Mackiewicz was silent for a long time before he spoke:

'Blood may be spilled. You will be trained. This is not a good time, though. The police are everywhere, snooping around the forest. For now, we have to keep scouting. We need to be alert. Remember, ninety-nine per cent of the time it's better to disengage. Tactical withdrawal. You should cover each other. Don't play tough guys and don't put yourselves in danger without good cause. You need to be brave, but most of all, you need to be smart. And do not use traditional camouflage on your missions. You cannot be exposed.'

The fire was dying down. The young freedom fighters gathered their things. The commander picked two men to smother the embers, and set off back towards the car he had parked at the Orthodox cemetery, near the Hajnówka–Białowieża road. It took him half an hour to reach it.

He wiped the camo paint from his face with half a bottle of mineral water, packed up his equipment and military outfit in a leather bag, put on his work suit and started the engine. As he was driving towards town, he spotted Damian walking along the road, alone. As they passed, they simply exchanged looks. But Mackiewicz couldn't help himself and, after he'd driven by, he looked in the rear-view mirror and hailed the boy with a raised hand. Damian raised his own in response. To a bystander it might have looked like the Nazi salute, but they both knew it meant something else entirely.

When Mackiewicz got to work at the law firm, his secretary met him at the door and whispered theatrically that he had a visitor and that she had tried calling him. The visitor, Inspector Jah-Jah Frankowski, had refused to leave. The best the secretary could do was to make him wait outside the lawyer's office.

'You should have let him in,' Artur Mackiewicz told her.

He greeted Jah-Jah like an old friend. They had been friends, once.

'Any news?' Jah-Jah asked.

'As you know, I have been representing the sons of Piotr Bondaruk for a couple of days now. From what I can tell, the letter read the day before the wedding, and the last will, bear all the hallmarks of a forgery,' Mackiewicz replied, reclining in his chair.

Behind his back stood a plinth with an enormous parrot perched on top of it – a gift from the last mayor, which he had received when he still worked for town hall. Jah-Jah walked over to the bird as the secretary brought in coffee.

'Who issued that opinion so quickly?'

'A graphologist from Białystok. A buddy of mine. It's all legit.'

Jah-Jah pressed a button hidden beneath the colourful bird's wing. 'Don't bring a knife to a gunfight,' the parrot croaked.

Jah-Jah chuckled. He sat down and pushed his espresso away.

'So that was just for show? Bondaruk played us?'

'It certainly seems so,' Mackiewicz replied, composed. 'Anyway, what's up? What do you have for me?'

'Two questions. About the same thing, you could say. I'd like you to answer them truthfully before we start with the official part. Off the record for now.'

'I'm at your disposal,' Mackiewicz said. 'We're friends, aren't we?'

'Did your wife have an affair with Bondaruk?'

'Not that I know of,' Mackiewicz said. 'But best ask her yourself.'

'I already did.' Jah-Jah smirked. 'On to question number two.'

'Let's hope it'll be one I can answer.'

'Did the oldest groom in the world personally eliminate anyone back in the seventies and have the secret police cover it up?'

'How the hell would I know *that*, man?' Mackiewicz snorted. 'That should be your area.'

'You know everything.'

'Only God knows everything.'

'You're the commander of the Local Territorial Defence Militia. An *illegal* paramilitary organisation. I can charge you with employing Nazi symbolism, inciting unrest, criminal possession of weapons and unlawful threats. I can arrest your men and ban you from ever practising your profession again.'

'You can try.' Mackiewicz clammed up.

'But you don't deny it? Huh. And here I was, thinking this was just some bullshit Krajnów likes to tell kids during religion classes.'

Jah-Jah produced a search warrant for Mackiewicz's firm and his apartment, It was blank apart from the signature. Mackiewicz blanched.

'I need a name,' Jah-Jah said. 'Call me if you remember anything.'

Jah-Jah walked out. As he left the office, passing the secretary, he said with a wink, 'Watch out. The espresso machine might be an imperialist listening device.'

Psychological profile of an unidentified offender

Author: Sasza Załuska

Evidence: under investigation

Codename: 'Four-Eyes'

Pertains to case file no.: Ds. 560/14, Ds. 2478/00, VIIIK 54/00, IIIK 345/01,

supportive – Ds. 1342/77

This document is to be further revised. It is not a typical profile as it does not concern a single offence, but instead a number of seemingly unrelated cases. It does not contain the typical psychological characteristics of an unidentified offender, instead covering exclusively select data isolated from cases of disappearances of women connected only by the owner of an impounded Mercedes (E-class, model W210) car, licence plate number BHA 3456 (black or white colour). What is more, on account of the identity of the suspect as well as certain circumstances constituting valuable sources of information, this analysis is supplemented with case no. Ds. 1342/77, not connected to the vehicle referred to above. The cases in question have been selected with regard to the close relationships between the missing persons and the suspect (excluding Ds. 1342/77). The vehicle is currently being held at the police impound yard in Białystok. It has been subjected to criminological analysis (data in the case file).

Circumstances of the offence

Ds. 560/14

The victim, **Iwona Bondaruk**, née Bejnar, daughter of Bożena and Dawid, resident of Poland, Polish nationality, was audaciously kidnapped on 13 May 2014 around 10:20 P.M. from Teremiski near Białowieża (last seen alive in the Jagiellońskie amphitheatre). There were two kidnappers. One of them, male, was masked (balaclava + traditional wedding outfit – regional attire) and armed. The second kidnapper, sex and appearance unknown (possibly a woman). The kidnappers used a car: Mercedes E-class, model W210, licence plate BHA 3456, colour black. The victim had probably been followed from the vicinity of the Jagiellońskie amphitheatre, from where she travelled on foot, reaching a forest road in Teremiski, where the kidnappers attacked her and gave chase. Their pursuit was thwarted by Sasza Załuska, driving a Fiat Uno car, licence plate GDA 5439, registered to Laura Załuska. Despite undertaking actions to resist the attackers, attempting persuasion and resorting to hand-to-hand combat, as well as firing a warning shot from a Beretta 950 handgun, the victim was not rescued from the perpetrators. Sasza Załuska was injured, tied to a tree, stripped of her clothes, and left in the forest. Despite searching the forest and its vicinity, the victim has not been found. No body was secured either. Iwona Bondaruk does not have children. Status of the case in the Public Prosecutor's Office – ongoing.

Ds 2478/00

The victim, **Łarysa Szafran**, daughter of Ludmiła and Aleksy Kozłowski, resident of Belarus, Belarusian nationality, was kidnapped in the year 2000 during a work trip she had left for in a Mercedes E-class, model W210 car, licence plate BHA 3456, colour white. According to the statement of the victim's partner, Piotr Bondaruk, she was shot with an unidentified firearm. The body has not been found. Piotr Bondaruk, son of Alina and Stanisław Bondaruk (father's family name Gałczyński) was injured during the gunfight. The man was resuscitated. He was considered one of the suspects and hospitalised for psychiatric observation in the specialist psychiatric ward of the public hospital from 1999 to 2001 (the hospital is now the Ciszynia private clinic). The missing vehicle was found in the course of a routine road-side check. The driver, using a driving licence identifying him as one Jarosław Sokołowski, was not able to explain how he came into possession of the vehicle. He was accompanied by a woman by the name of Marzena Koźmińska, who presented the patrol officers with car lease documents issued in the name of Piotr Bondaruk. The vehicle was impounded and subsequently returned to the owner after a period of two years (all expenses covered by the state). At a later date, Piotr Bondaruk legally adopted Łarysa Szafran's son (Fiodor Bondaruk). Status of the case in the Public Prosecutor's Office – closed.

VIIIK 54/00

On 3 March 2000, the victim, **Monika Zakrzewska, alias Jowita,** was lured out of her family home in Ciechanowiec by Marzena Koźmińska, who had arrived on scene in a Mercedes E-class, model W210 car, licence plate BHA 3456, colour white. The mother of the victim reported her daughter's disappearance a week later. The body of the victim has not been found to date. Marzena Koźmińska, currently incarcerated as punishment for crimes referred to in another case (murder of a student in Warsaw), was also convicted for the kidnapping and assault on Monika Zakrzewska. With regard to the nature of the case (both women were prostitutes), the family did not publicise the case. At a later date, Piotr Bondaruk legally adopted Monika Zakrzewska's son (Tomasz Bondaruk). Status of the case – final decision issued by the District Court in Pułtusk, offender Marzena Koźmińska.

IIIK 345/01

On 4 April 2001, a police patrol in Brok (road from Hajnówka to Białystok) stopped a Mercedes E-class, model W210 car, licence plate BHA 3456, colour <u>black</u>, for a roadside check. The driver, **Mariola Nesteruk,** was intoxicated with alcohol. A blood test showed 1.2 per mil alcohol in her system. The driver did not possess any registration documents for the vehicle. She had been driving recklessly, causing danger to other drivers. Her erratic behaviour had been reported by another driver through a CB-radio. The vehicle referred to above, with the driver's wing mirror broken, was towed to a police impound yard. The owner, Piotr Bondaruk, was notified and collected the vehicle after two days. Mariola Nesteruk was held for a single night in the local police detention facility. She did not appear at any court hearings afterwards. The sentencing judgment for drunk driving was issued in default. Mariola Nesteruk paid the fine via postal order. Mariola Nesteruk, remained in a close relationship with Piotr Bondaruk. Her son, Jan Nesteruk, called Wasyl, was legally adopted by Piotr Bondaruk a month before she 'left'. Currently, Mariola Nesteruk cannot be found in any PESEL or NIP-based register. She has also not been entered into any missing person database kept by the Itaka Foundation or the police.

Ds. 1342/77

On 26 August 1977

Sasza stopped writing, read through the text, crumpled the page into a ball, and threw it into the bin. She stayed at her desk for a couple more hours, but the only thing she wrote was Bondaruk's car's licence plate number. She gave up and went out to the balcony for a smoke. Her mobile beeped. The message, from an unknown number, said 'the MMS could not be delivered'. She frowned. Who was trying to send her an image? She pressed 'delete', but just as she did so it occurred to her that maybe it was from Gramps. She tried to return the call, but got an automated voice telling her that the number she was calling 'had not been recognised'. Sasza couldn't think of anyone she could ask to check the number for her right away. She returned to her cigarette.

When her mobile beeped again she snatched it up immediately. A text: 'Call me'. No sign-off. Was it the same number? She couldn't remember. She wrote back: 'What do you want? M.' The reply came after a moment. 'To talk to you.' She felt her legs buckling beneath her. Her hands were shaking. She fumbled with the phone as it beeped again with another text. 'I need to see her. Ł.'

Warsaw, 2014

The gypsum bust of King Bolesław's head stood on the cupboard, flanked by the likenesses of other, lesser-known people. Junior Inspector Dariusz Zajdel poured scalding hot water into a cup of instant coffee, helped himself to two doughnuts and sat down at his PC.

He had already taken photos of the skull he had received earlier that morning. Now, he uploaded the images into a program he had written himself, marked the distance between the eye sockets with red arrows, measured the length of the jawbone and the width of the frontal bone. He kept working on it for a few more hours until all the measurements were in place, and the images of the skull were covered with a neat network of vectors and markers. Then he started the time-consuming work of applying fragments of images he had made over the years to various areas of the skull. He had in his database thousands of human noses, eyes, bits and pieces of cheeks, brows, earlobes and lips. The anthropologist Zajdel had been working with for years had told him the skull belonged to a male. Slavic type, with a tendency towards obesity. Green, grey or blue eyes. The probable cause of death was a blow to the head with a sharp object. An axe or a cleaving knife. The skull was cracked in two places. Before the sun set, Zajdel had completed an almost full image of a man from his puzzle pieces. It just lacked hair, which was always the last thing he applied. It was too misleading to choose any earlier.

Zajdel took a break. He went to the police canteen, called his wife and told her he'd be home soon. Then he went back to his office.

He uploaded the image he had constructed to Itaka's missing persons database. Thousands of similar faces immediately popped up.

He checked the face's details – the man had gone missing sometime in the seventies or eighties. The anthropological analysis noted a propensity for balding. The skull had arrived from the eastern border. Podlasie region. He applied hair, giving the missing man a comb-over, and then added a bushy moustache. It was the staple look of any self-respecting Polish worker back then. But he wasn't happy with the effect. The guy looked like a freak. Using Photoshop, he shaved the moustache again, applied a straw-blond hairpiece to the bald spot and swapped the man's old-school sweater for an equally outdated wedding suit with wide shoulder pads. Way better. But something was still missing.

Zajdel's job was forensic knowledge and artistic talent, fifty-fifty. And he had both in abundance. Some people called his talent a 'sixth sense', as nobody else was able to reflect a person's 'soul' in a reconstruction like the old specialist did. But Zajdel himself liked to call it simply imagination.

It was not enough to perfectly apply forensic techniques if you didn't feel, know, or like people. Each time Zajdel created one of his reconstructions, he felt the enormity of his responsibility. He couldn't stop thinking about who the people he recreated had been in life. What did they do for a living? What had their dreams been? Passions? Flaws? Most of the time, those questions remained unanswered; the police stations who commissioned him always asked him to treat their cases as a priority, but somehow never remembered to let him know the results of their investigations. That was why Zajdel had created his own database, so he could keep tabs on his cases. This time, they had promised him that if the case was ever solved they'd send him the files. He was counting on Sasza Załuska, who had asked him for a big favour, to keep her word. Usually investigators had to wait months for him to find a free couple of hours. Sometimes over a year. Zajdel had never been quick, but he was thorough. And he never left his work unfinished.

He had been about to leave when Załuska had called.

'Call me in a week,' he'd grunted.

'I'll bring you *Alice in Wonderland* in Korean if you hurry it up,' she offered.

She knew about his wife's collection. She had only a few translations left to find.

'She already has that one,' he laughed.

'How?'

'A profiler from Katowice. Met him during training.'

'How about Belarusian?'

'Worth a try. I didn't know there was a Belarusian version.'

'If there isn't, I'll go there myself and make them write one. Just for Amelia. Anyway, got anything yet?'

'A bit.'

'Show, don't tell.'

He glanced at the sleazy guy he had created. 'Need to sleep on it.'

'My arse is on the line here,' she said. 'And I have a lead. It just popped up. The suspect has been avoiding punishment for years. Everything here is a fucking conspiracy. Nobody talks. Like in the fifties, you know? The case of the wedding guests from the bus. Nobody spills anything. If we at least had a single body, even an old one, we could bust our guy. It's easy to lie over a cup of tea, but you rarely keep your shit together locked up in a cage.'

'I was just about to leave,' he grumbled. 'I promised Amelia she'd be able to go out with her friends today.'

'Tell her she'll get a copy of *Alice* in Belarusian. That should do it.'

'I doubt that,' he muttered, but clicked the 'send' button. 'Just don't show it to anyone yet, okay?'

'Sure thing.'

He smiled and shook his head as he finally closed the door to leave. It was plain as day that the whole station would see the sleazy guy first thing tomorrow. He decided to work some more on the image over the week and charge them extra.

He was surprised to say the least when, having finally got through Warsaw's rush-hour traffic, he reached home and his wife told him there had been a call for him. Someone from the Church authorities.

'He's a priest?' Zajdel couldn't believe it.

'He's been living the life in the Dominican Republic since the eighties. He was one of the suspects in a paedophile scandal there too, if you believe it, and was the only one whose contract hasn't been terminated. Apparently, they're afraid of another shitstorm.'

'Well, that may be the first modern case of miraculous resurrection, honey,' Zajdel laughed. 'Because his skull is safely tucked into a cardboard box by my desk.'

'You must be exhausted. I'll make you dinner.' Amelia shrugged.

That was why he had married that woman. Since school, he had seen her as the sweetest girl. Living together for twenty years had changed nothing – he was still completely in love with her. And their daughter was an exact copy of her mother. Zajdel didn't know how he'd feel when she started bringing boyfriends home.

'What was the surprise you had for me?' Amelia asked.

Zajdel frowned and fished in his briefcase for his phone. He tried to call Sasza. Busy. He took his shoes off and hung up his coat. The landline rang. Amelia answered, listened, and held out the receiver.

'It's your boss,' she said. 'The Church would prefer if your guy was alive. You're to send in a report asap. They want the news amended.'

Zajdel shook his head and motioned for her to make an excuse for him. He needed to speak to Załuska first.

'I haven't showed it to anyone,' she said when he finally reached her. 'I haven't looked at it myself yet.'

'I have priests calling me,' he said.

'I don't go to church.'

'The guys at the top are calling me too,' he added.

She grew serious instantly. 'I'll take a look,' she said. 'Hang on.'

He sat down. His wife was setting the table.

'All right, I'm opening it,' Sasza said. 'I don't think I know the guy.' Pause, then: 'Holy fuck,' she breathed.

There was a bowl of tomato soup in front of Zajdel now. He started to eat.

'What's wrong? Did you get it or not?'

'My PC's just gone down,' Sasza said. 'It looks like it's been wiped. Everything I have has just evaporated.' She sounded panicked.

'Just take it to our technicians. They'll get it back for you,' he replied calmly. 'But they won't take a book as a thank-you. Those bums know nothing about real art. You've got me into a pretty big mess, I have to tell you.'

Zajdel looked at his mobile, his wife's and the landline. They were all ringing.

'You know what? Get your shit together and let me finish my dinner,' he told Sasza. 'Then call me – if they don't block your mobile.'

He hung up. Amelia was holding out the landline to him again.

'The local priest,' she whispered. 'Maybe I'll stay in tonight. What's happening, honey?'

'Why won't everybody just fuck the hell off!' Zajdel shouted, and immediately felt ashamed. He never used such language in front of his wife. He apologised, thought for a while, and decided he had to go back to the station, though he hated eating his food cold and, more importantly, disappointing Amelia. He hadn't even had time to take a look at his sleeping daughter. For the first time since she was born.

Back at work, Zajdel logged into the National Police Information System, the Central Vehicle and Driver Database, the central convict register, the missing persons database, the register of wanted criminals, the register of paedophiles and sexual offenders, and then he even manually searched through the list of people pardoned by the president. Nothing. Not a single hit. He thought for a moment, then, like a mere civilian, googled 'priest, Polish Peoples' Republic, Dominican Republic, Hajnówka, Security Service, disappearance'. After several hours, close to exhaustion, he found a feature by one Iza Michalewicz. Published in 2005 in the *Duży Format*, it described the case of the strangely speedy promotion of a priest who had collaborated with the communist Security Service. Jerzy Bołtromiuk from Hajnówka, alias 'Świerk', had gone missing in 1977 after being chased away by his parishioners for immoral conduct towards young boys. He had been allocated his 'pink file' in that decade, long before comrade Kiszczak had ordered the Citizens' Militia to commence Operation Hyacinth. Zajdel knew what that was: a secret operation to create a national database of all Polish homosexuals, along with anyone who was in contact with persons known to be homosexual.

At the time the Białystok Church washed their hands of the Bołtromiuk affair, so the locals took matters into their own hands. But in the end the priest outsmarted everyone. He vanished with the money he had collected for the construction of a chapel in the local cemetery. The case was swept under the rug, and the man's name didn't surface again until the nineties. This time he didn't steal or abuse boys, and he was a lot more discreet in selecting his lovers. He also got promoted rather quickly. Maybe the Church authorities had just wanted him out of the country; he seemed mainly to work on missions abroad.

As Zajdel read the piece he became less sure of anything with every minute. There was just one photo in the article. A thirty-year-old Bołtromiuk was standing on a pedestal in front of a town hall, with a backdrop of an old Soviet tank – the erstwhile symbol of the town, most likely. In his outfit, a padded jacket and wellies, it wasn't obvious he was a priest. Zajdel enlarged the image. He was absolutely certain that the reconstruction he had finished earlier was this man's face. He knew now what it was that hadn't worked – he should have given the sleazy guy a pair of glasses. 'Świerk' was wearing in the photo an old-fashioned round-rimmed pair. Zajdel quickly copied the text of the article and sent it to Załuska in a private message. He had no idea who had borrowed Bołtromiuk's identity to convert heathens in Africa, but it was clear that nobody had looked for him for years. For everyone, the Church authorities and other national administration units included, it was more convenient that 'Świerk' be alive.

Hajnówka, 2014

'What do you mean you didn't have a firewall?' Jah-Jah, clearly disoriented, was shaking his head, turning Sasza's Mac laptop round in his hands.

She only shrugged. 'I didn't pay three thousand for that thing to have to instal anti-spyware programs on it,' she scoffed. She sat down on a tiny chair she had found in the bathroom. Jah-Jah was pretending to tinker with the laptop, clicking and opening various files, but Sasza quickly realised he was probably using a Mac for the first time. She sighed with resignation and scanned the room with her eyes. 'At least I've practically made no notes on it regarding the case,' she said, taking out her notebook and pointing vaguely at the various papers taking up the majority of the free space in the apartment. 'It's just that my whole archive was in there. The work of years of my professional career. Not to mention my doctoral thesis . . .' She hid her face in her hands.

'Yeah,' Jah-Jah grunted. 'Pretty simple interface. User-friendly. Where's the external drive?'

Sasza raised her head and nodded at the black plastic box with a cable sticking out from its side.

'Gone too. See for yourself. As soon as I connected it to the laptop it died. I realised something was wrong only when it got wiped too. Someone snuck some spyware in and deleted everything that was there. Only state intelligence does that. I'm not going to let that slide. I'll report it and I'll find the bastard,' she growled.

'I know a guy—' Jah-Jah said but was cut off by a knock at the door.

Sasza opened it. It was Romanowska and Doman.

'I don't think there's enough space here for the both of you,' Sasza took a shot at brightening up the atmosphere. 'Unless someone sits in the sink.'

She could see Błażej, Jah-Jah's son, behind the others, but as soon as he saw how cramped the flat was he turned round and headed back to the car.

'Seeing as I'm the lightest, I'll take the sink,' Doman replied. He had to bow his head to keep it from hitting the doorframe on his way in.

'That seat is already taken!' Jah-Jah called.

'Sweet Lord!' Doman whistled as his eyes trailed along the book-lined walls.

'Not too shabby for a home collection, right?' Sasza smiled.

'Never mind the collection. This looks like Hannibal Lecter's lair.'

'Guilty as charged,' Sasza replied, taking a look around.

The pastoral wall-hanging was nearly completely covered with case-related photos and brightly coloured scraps of paper. A large map pinned to the curtains obscured the window. Towering stacks of case files were arranged in long lines, open on specific pages and organised chronologically. Sasza had also been to the town library, where she had copied more articles and documents. She'd glued the copies together into long scrolls, which were furled into rolls, waiting for their moment.

'That's just your everyday profiler's work,' she laughed. She grabbed a printout of the reconstruction prepared by Zajdel. 'Does the DNA match?'

Romanowska shook her head. 'Still too early to tell. Is the profile ready?'

'Which one?'

The officers exchanged worried looks.

'Those cases should be separated,' Sasza explained, and pointed at the photo of young Danka. 'I think this one isn't part of the Four-Eyes case after all. It looks like a family affair. The murderer wanted to set her free. There's no need for a profile. What you need is a proper interrogation.'

'Her brother won't say a thing,' Romanowska said. 'He's slipped into some kind of stupor. He doesn't answer questions. There's no way we can interrogate him. Maybe he's just acting. Or maybe he really is crazy. We know the prints on the lipstick match, however. He knew Polak and his story. Turns out everyone at the clinic knew it. What do you think, Doman?'

'But he's still under arrest?' Sasza asked. 'Better not to have to look for two guys at the same time.'

Doman silenced her with a gesture.

'Not your business any more. I've already asked Meyer to help. He promised to come and take a look as soon as he can. He's going to make a profile.' The chief inspector emphasised the last word. 'He thinks we need one. Says the cases should be connected at this stage. Let Danka's brother try and escape Ciszynia. Good luck with that. Prus will find him and drag him back by the balls.'

Jah-Jah chortled.

Sasza walked over to the wall rug. She pointed at the line of photos of Bondaruk's women.

'The first one who went missing was attacked in the suspect's presence. He was wounded badly. He was lucky there was a witness who helped him, or else he would have died. It's possible that he and the woman were both meant to die in the shooting.'

'Or the police were supposed to think that afterwards,' Jah-Jah cut in.

Sasza nodded, agreeing, but quickly added: 'Or the killer was a beginner. He hesitated, got spooked, lost his cool and cocked up.'

Then Sasza moved her finger to the next photo – Mariola Nesteruk.

'The second victim was driving the suspect's car. Bondaruk is the last person who saw the woman alive. At least, that was the assumption of the investigators. However, there is no real proof for that. It's only a hypothesis.'

'Corroborated by the girl's father.'

'Who hasn't been interrogated.'

'I personally received his statement,' Jah-Jah said.

'There isn't anything that would confirm it in the files,' Sasza replied. 'Mikołaj Nesteruk should have been a suspect. Today, that doesn't mean anything any more.'

'His record is as clean as it gets,' Romanowska protested. 'The director's friend.'

'And he was the one to come to his rescue in the first case. Isn't it a bit too convenient that he was at the crime scene? In the middle of nowhere?' Sasza asked.

'The disappearance was reported as usual. Forty-eight hours after the girl went missing. Nesteruk has an alibi for the entire period,' Jah-Jah said.

'Just like Bondaruk. Everyone's covered. Who's covering for whom? You scratch my back, I'll scratch yours. Quid pro quo, et cetera. Maybe someone just made it look like a kidnapping?' Sasza added: 'I don't want to sound too nosy, but you were here at the time. Who headed the investigation? Did the lead investigator have any reason to cover Four-Eyes' arse?'

'The old commissioner,' Romanowska replied. 'And I doubt that. He had been the chief here for years.'

'So he knew the girl's father and her boyfriend. If I wanted to kill off another woman, I'd do just that – make sure I had an alibi. That way nobody would even suspect it was me,' Sasza said.

A silence fell over the room.

'Are you suggesting Mariola's father had something to do with her disappearance?' Romanowska asked sharply.

'I'm not suggesting anything. I'm stating the facts. The only name other than Bondaruk's that shows up in the papers is Nesteruk's. And didn't he found a prosperous meat processing company right after the shooting?'

They all went silent. Sasza continued:

'The third victim left the amphitheatre and disappeared in the forest. Bondaruk was seen by at least a hundred people at that very moment. When unidentified assailants were chasing the girl across the forest, he was searching for her with the police and other volunteers. You can't write off the possibility that he ordered the kidnapping, but he didn't commit any of those murders – if they even were murders. If he gave the order, the killers did their job in a pretty splashy manner. A bit too showy, if you ask me. Only Mariola – Bondaruk's second woman – was killed quietly. That case makes sense. If you're a bad husband, that's how you get rid of your cheating wife. And that is another thing that connects the victims. They were all unfaithful.'

Another moment of silence.

'What are you suggesting?' Doman asked finally.

'Bondaruk knows who's hunting him.'

'Ha! Didn't I tell you?' Jah-Jah chimed in. 'We need to have a proper talk with that guy. And I didn't even have to turn my flat into a creepy nerd cave to realise that.'

'Another person who knows is the one who planted the skulls,' Sasza continued, unfazed. 'He's the one we should be looking for now, if we want to save Iwona Bejnar. I believe she's still alive.'

'Outstanding,' Doman muttered, then added: 'Unfortunately, we haven't been able to identify our mysterious delivery guy yet. This balcony opens? I could do with a smoke.'

He opened the balcony door. Sasza joined him outside.

'I think it's pretty obvious,' she said. 'Bondaruk planted them himself. He wants you to catch him. That's his only chance of wriggling out of it without losing face.'

She turned to Jah-Jah. 'Your turn.'

Jah-Jah recounted his visit to Mackiewicz's office. Nobody seemed surprised that the lawyer was secretly the commander of a paramilitary organisation. It did surprise them, however, to hear that he had given Jah-Jah the name of the man Bondaruk had killed years before.

'Stepan Orzechowski, the missing husband of Dunia Orzechowska,' Jah-Jah announced. 'The chief homosexual in town and one of the first managers of the lumber mill. He kept the job only for a short while. Our man Four-Eyes took his position and still has it now. Everyone knows Stepan ran off with a priest, but it seems their destination was the afterlife, not the Caymans. Orzechowski's wife had to know about it, though I'm not saying she had anything to do with it. Both of them were secret collaborators with the authorities. Bondaruk was, too. It could have been an internal bureau affair.'

Sasza glanced at her watch.

'I think what we're working with is a tight-knit group holding the real power in the city, not an individual. Iwona's kidnapping was a slap in the face for the insubordinate ex-secret agent. They wanted to remind him that you don't just leave that line of business other than in a body bag. I think Bondaruk forgot his place. Times might have changed but the people have not. It's a free country now, but it's the same people in the same places. I did my research.'

She threw a bundle of old newspapers on the table.

'Old news,' Romanowska said. 'We won't prove anything to anyone now. But since you seem to be such a great detective, why don't you tell us why you think those particular three kidnappings are linked in the first place? There have been more than three women kidnapped over the years.'

Sasza had to admit the chief inspector was right.

'Good point. This is the pièce de résistance of our case. They could just be unlucky – easy targets at the point when Bondaruk was attempting to wriggle himself out of the deal. You know, the secret pact. The Council of the Righteous, let's call them. But no. I don't think it was like that. This was something more personal. Something that sparked off the whole silent conspiracy and is still keeping it together. Their plan from the beginning was to get Bondaruk into a pickle and then cover for him.'

'You're starting to talk like a local.' Jah-Jah smirked.

Sasza kept talking. 'Who runs this town? Who's the head man?' she asked, but was only met with doubting looks. 'Who had been at the helm during the regime and got promoted when it fell? He might not even be a leftist any more. Maybe a Polish nationalist? People like that tend to know which way the wind is blowing. They never have their own opinions. What counts is what gets them to power.'

'Wait a second. I think you've lost me.' Doman stubbed his cigarette out in a planter and stuffed the butt into his pocket.

'We need to look at the older generations. They might not even want to talk, though.' Sasza turned to the commissioner. 'You said that the bride came to her wedding in a heavy veil and that there was an older woman who approached her and lifted it and kissed her on the forehead, as if giving her her blessing. Accepting her. Who was that? You might laugh at this, but I really think we're witnessing some kind of ritual. Or rather, fragments of it. We can't wrap our heads around it yet, but it has to be important to the locals. Their history. Legacy.'

'Pathetic.' Doman shut the balcony door with a bang. He cast a glance around the room. Sasza followed his gaze. It did look a bit like a psychiatric patient's cell. 'You've let your imagination get the better of you. If that's all you have for us, you can pack your bags.

I'm not going to stop you if you decide to leave first thing in the morning. Go read the Tarot somewhere else.'

'Wait.' Romanowska cut him off with a gesture. 'I remember Bondaruk once told me that he knew how this is going to end.'

Sasza nodded. 'He told me the same thing,' she whispered. 'Twice. I asked: How? He said: Like fighting dogs end up. He didn't mean by dying in a fight – that would be too easy. He meant that to make a dog utterly dependent on you, you punish it often and reward it occasionally, and over time the lack of punishment becomes a reward in itself. But the dog eventually attacks you and runs away, so you stalk it until you catch it, and you kill it. If the dog has been trained to fight well, it will wound you before it dies. And if it's really lucky, you'll both die. The dog is happy to die side by side with you, because a dog always loves its owner.'

'What the fuck is that supposed to prove?' Jah-Jah had clearly had enough.

'That we have to question Bondaruk's friends from the VIP table at the Carska restaurant.' Romanowska smiled at Sasza. 'They're our Council of the Righteous.'

'What about my computer?' Sasza asked Jah-Jah.

He nodded and called his son. 'Błażej, send me the number of that computer guy, will you? Let him know it's off the record. We have a little something for him. And tell him to call his sister.'

A while later, Błażej texted the number and Jah-Jah gave it to Sasza. 'He's a hacker. I don't know if he'll be able to help,' he warned her. 'He's pretty weird.'

'IT people always live in their own world.'

Jah-Jah took another, pointed look around the room.

'Not just IT people.'

The men left Romanowska and Sasza alone.

'I'm scared for Piotr,' Romanowska said. 'I don't pity him, but I think what you said might be true. It does make sense and those two bloody numbskulls know it.' She nodded at the door. 'That's why they don't want to get in too deep without good reason. Everyone who was sitting at that table in the Carska is an old communist. The current starost was the chief of the local Security Service branch until it was dissolved. Nothing has changed here since then. The only difference is now there's money.'

'Money is power.'

'And power is even more money. And the cycle goes on.'

They both knew they were on treacherous ground. This had stopped being a simple murder case.

'Let's go see him right now,' Sasza suggested. 'Bondaruk. Let's have a chat.'

Krystyna dropped her gaze.

'I can't,' she breathed. 'I have to protect him. I can't bother him. I'm not allowed to take him in without good reason.'

'On whose orders?'

'The powers that be.'

'Power is money.' Sasza sighed. 'Who?'

'I really can't tell you.'

Sasza propped her fists on her hips.

'How do you mean?'

'You can leave. I have to stay here. I have a husband here. A son.'

'Ex-husband.'

'When you marry someone in an Orthodox church, it's for life. Even if I don't accept it, for the locals I'll always be Jah-Jah's wife.'

Sasza capitulated. 'Have it your way.'

'But I can ask around discreetly.'

'Won't do us any harm.'

'I need a reason though. An excuse to start digging. We need to find the bodies of the priest and the other guy. Stepan Orzechowski. They won't be able to keep us away then.'

'Can you get a geographical profile request?'

'Possibly. If there's good reason,' the commissioner repeated. For a moment, Sasza thought the woman was avoiding her eyes. 'Find a body. No body, no case.'

'Can't you help me at all?' Sasza pinned the town map over the curtains again. 'I bloody hate geographical profiling, but I don't see another way. It's just that I don't know the region.'

Romanowska took a reluctant look at the map criss-crossed by various markings.

'Maybe let's get your laptop in order first? I'll take you to the hacker and then come and help you when you're back.'

Sasza agreed and called the number Błażej had sent her. She had barely introduced herself when the person at the other end gave her an address and then hung up. Sasza repeated it to the commissioner.

'That's the address of the army cemetery in Bielsk Podlaski.' Romanowska frowned. 'About thirty kilometres' drive.'

'Well, the IT magician is there right now.'

'The city looks dead,' Sasza said, looking out of the car window. There was no one in the street, in the park, or even outside what had been the cinema, now a supermarket.

'It'll come to life in the morning.' Romanowska smiled, keeping her eyes on the road. 'Enjoy the silence while you can. Where you come from it's probably partygoers, traffic and constant hubbub, right?'

'When you're here for a few days the quiet seems so relaxing,' Sasza replied. 'But after a while you realise it's only a facade. On the surface, everybody's so nice and polite. People know each other. But that's an illusion too. It hides a need to spy on others, a morbid fascination with what's happening in other people's houses. People put up all kinds of walls here. As a way to isolate themselves. I think I prefer the anonymity you get in Tricity.'

'You're not a fan of good neighbourly relations then?'

'I tried questioning Bondaruk's neighbours and talking to that Dunia woman. Asking around about her son. Everyone pretended they didn't even know the name of his street. When I mentioned the name "Quack" they all clammed up. The only thing I learned about the missing girl's brothers is that they're "good lads". Here, let me play you a recording.'

They listened.

'Do you know the girl that's gone missing?'

'A nice girl. Decent.'

'How about her brothers? Father? How did they treat her?'

'Good lads, all. And she was a decent, polite girl. They treated her good.'

'Maybe they didn't like that she married a Belarusian? Much older than her, too.'

'Don't know that, miss. But I can tell you Bondaruk is a decent man, too. He gives people work. I worked at the mill when I was younger myself.'

'You're still young. You don't look more than forty. Am I close?'

'Seriously, miss? I'm thirty-three. But I'm pensioned off. For my back, you see. The doctor didn't want to sign the papers, but one of the Bison brothers had a talk with him and he changed his mind.'

'Decent lad?' Sasza said.

'As I said, miss. As I said.'

Sasza pressed 'stop'. She knitted her brows and put on an ugly grimace to mimic the 33-year-old with a Bison-prescribed medical pension.

'You're a decent lass yourself, Krysia. Very decent.'

She went back to her own voice.

'So that's that. A successful victimological analysis. The rest were more or less the same.'

Romanowska shot the profiler a glance.

'What did you expect? We're in the east. It may be Poland, but it's the hinterland. The border. For generations this land has been a bone of contention for politicians, and the ones who really suffer are the locals. Some people call this region Little Belarus. We have always been closer to Russia than the West and you can still see the Russian influence. Mentality, culture, religious customs, even the way people dress and what they eat. The centuries of conflict taught people to be silent aloud. Talk, but not tell you anything of value. They seem open. They invite you to their houses, feed you, let you sleep in their beds. Maybe they even open up a bit for real, if they think you're a *dobry chelovek*. A "decent person". But even if they do, you won't get much out of them. Outsiders have always come here to patrol the borders, to strip the land of its precious wood. To take land away from the locals. Sometimes they stayed, married local women and had children. Became locals and were buried here.'

They passed the city limits and then a few villages. The buildings were growing sparser the farther they went, until there were none. The road was bordered on both sides by endless expanses of lush, winter crops. To the right, a beautiful, old, leafless tree caught Sasza's eye. Cypress trees in Tuscany were nothing compared to this, she thought, though Tuscany undoubtedly had better PR.

'Winter crops,' Romanowska said, pointing her chin at the field of succulent grass spreading as far as the eye could see. Its colour even at this time of year was the vivid green of hope.

Now she indicated something else.

'There was a village there once, by that old tree. It was wiped out after the war. Burned down. The Załuski brothers used to have their farm there. That was also the name of the whole place. Załuskie.'

'So that's why you asked me back at the hospital if I had family here.'

'I don't know anyone around here by that name. Nobody alive, at least. Practically everyone in Załuskie and the neighbouring settlements was murdered. I wouldn't be surprised if the survivors changed their names to something more . . . proletarian. Those were the times.'

'Why was the village burned down?'

'Polish soldiers. It was an Orthodox settlement. Back then, that meant Belarusian. Bury, the commander of the unit that did this, is a national hero now. One of the Cursed Soldiers. He hated all *katsaps*, as Belarusians were referred to. When he retreated with his unit after a botched attack on a Red Army convoy in Hajnówka, he burned down every Belarusian village on his way. He blamed the locals for selling the Poles out to the Soviets. There's an execution ground by that copse over there. There was this old dugout by a village called Puchały. The bones of a couple dozen carters were found there. They'd been taken by the soldiers, ordered to transport the men in their carts, and then brutally murdered. The bones stayed there for fifty years. The locals still go there to pray. There was a priest who used to go and consecrate the ground twice every year for decades. People say the carters didn't have their documents with them. Only thirteen victims have been identified even now. They were exhumed a couple of years back and taken to the army cemetery in Bielsk. The one we're going to now.'

Sasza fell into a pensive mood.

'I don't think my family come from here,' she said after a while. 'My father was from Tricity, my mother from a place near Lublin.'

'You'd be surprised if you knew where the locals here come from. Some came from the east, some from Vilnius, or Ukraine. There are people from France and Germany, most of them Jews. They mixed with the locals and today they're all considered to be the same as them.'

'Because their fathers were buried here?'

'Exactly.'

'What about Bondaruk? Who were his ancestors? Not Belarusians? Belarus didn't exist then.'

Romanowska took a moment to think, then said, 'People say his father was Polish. He went to church, just like his mother, though her grandmother was Orthodox. I'm not sure, but I think the father, Staszek, was one of the survivors of the pogrom. Just like Dunia Orzechowska and old man Nesteruk. They're Orthodox as far as I can tell. I've definitely seen them in the Orthodox church. The rest, I don't know. Hard to tell, really. People changed their names, you know. Most chose the lesser evil and joined the communist party. They accepted what they were given to get a job and an apartment. To survive.'

'So how did Bondaruk become a Belarusian and what do people care if everyone here lives in one big melting pot?'

'Oh, they *do* care. You couldn't even start to imagine all the antagonisms we have here. Take for instance our local Polish nationalists. We've got a real problem with skinheads. They fight for what they think is theirs, like there's a Polish–Belarusian war about to start.'

'I've seen both swastikas and Belarusian slogans on the walls.'

They reached a roundabout. The road signs were in two languages. Some of them had spray-paint splotches on them.

'Orla was the first place to introduce Belarusian signage. Polish nationalists keep destroying road signs here. Each year on the anniversary of the pogroms of the Orthodox populace all kinds of journos come here, stirring up old stories. This year, bands of football hooligans arrived first. They patrolled the village and came to the doorsteps of old people, with baseball bats. Nothing more, but it was enough. When the journos arrived the next day, nobody wanted to talk to them.'

'A warning?'

'A signal for them to keep their mouths shut. A young sociologist found the diary of a daughter of one of the pogrom victims. Not an educated woman, so there was nothing really eye-opening in it. It was sent to the IPN during the ongoing investigation into the murders. But it contained the names of her neighbours, who were still alive at the time. They had collaborated with the Polish freedom fighters and then the Citizens Militia and the Security Service. There was a hypothesis that the pogrom took place with the consent of the authorities. Belarusians didn't want to leave their land, so the communists found a way to use the nationalists to eliminate them.'

'Why?'

'To take over their houses and land. Why else wage a war? But that's not the worst thing,' Romanowska continued. 'Bury wouldn't have been able to burn down a dozen villages and murder civilians for a week on end without the support of the local populace. Nearly five hundred people died in this area. Two hundred survived, but they were so afraid for themselves and their families that they didn't tell anyone about the place where the murdered carters have been buried until nineteen ninety-five. The woman who gave the diary to the sociologist had to move to the other end of the country. Someone nailed a dead rooster to her door. It's our local shameful secret. Like Jedwabne.' This, Sasza knew, was a massacre of Polish Jews in that town in 1941, during the early stages of the Holocaust. Men, women and children locked in a barn that was then set on fire. It was later confirmed that non-Jewish locals were the main perpetrators of the massacre.

'Nobody likes those old wounds reopened,' Romanowska went on.

They had reached the cemetery gate. Sasza picked up her laptop bag.

'Want me to come with you?' Romanowska asked.

'I don't even know where I'm supposed to go.'

The commissioner pointed to the sexton's booth.

'There's a light on in there. I'll keep the engine on.' She zipped up her jacket. 'It's getting cold.'

Sasza headed towards the booth at a brisk pace. She knocked on the door, which opened with a creak. Inside was a thin man wearing a tight-fitting cycling outfit. He had a lean face topped with a chequered flat cap with a Fred Perry pin at the front. He took this off and extended a hand. Sasza noticed that his ring and little fingers were disfigured and limp, and the skin on them scarred as if burnt.

'I'll see what I can recover, and I'll call you,' he said simply. Anticipating Sasza's question about what on earth he was doing in a cemetery, he added: 'I just work here part-time. I'm supposed to keep watch over the graves. The *belarusskies* come here to venerate their murdered ancestors or some such. The skinheads will show up any time now.'

'How much will it cost me?' Sasza asked.

'Seeing as Błażej asked me for the favour, I'll discuss the payment with him.' The man waved a hand dismissively and smiled boyishly. He seemed laid-back and composed, and behaved with a studied nonchalance that didn't leave Sasza any room to argue. This wasn't really a conversation, more of a monologue. He made statements with utter conviction and took compliance for granted. Sasza immediately felt at ease. The hacker clearly knew his job.

'I can't guarantee I'll get your data back,' he said. 'Any passwords or other security measures?'

She shook her head.

'I'll call you. This might take a while.'

'Seems like I don't have a choice.' She sighed. 'I really need a folder named "doct" back. And my kid's photos. That one should be called "Karo". And maybe another called "profile". I have some work documents in it that I haven't copied yet. The rest I've backed up.'

'Does it hurt?' He pointed at her arm.

'It just itches,' she replied dismissively. He had it worse. His hand wouldn't mend. Hers would, sooner or later. 'It's not too easy, though, living one-handed. Besides, people keep asking me about it.'

'Believe me, I know.' He waved his mangled hand.

She wanted to ask him how it had happened, but the man had already moved to close the door.

'I heard there's a mass grave here where Bury's victims have been buried,' she blurted out.

He studied her warily. 'I can take you there.'

'No, don't bother.'

'It's not a problem. I could do with a walk, actually.'

They set off. Sasza saw a group of people in the distance. They were sitting around the mass grave, cheerful and carefree. Some of them had bouquets and funeral wreaths. There were a couple of candles burning on the marble gravestone. As soon as Sasza and the man approached the group, someone passed her a bottle. It was gin. She could smell the juniper in the air.

Kinga Kosiek served a customer a steaming hot pizza, then checked the time. Two hours until the end of her shift. Today was dragging, mainly because the place was almost empty, as it had been for a few days now. The pizzeria was close to Ciszynia psychiatric hospital and close to nothing else except the forest. And ever since Iwona Bejnar had gone missing and the murder of Danuta Pietrasik had been made known, the thought of a killer stalking the city streets at night had effectively shut down any nightlife there was in this town.

Kinga wasn't afraid, though. She knew that Iwona was perfectly safe and that she and Quack would be leaving the country soon.

On the day Kinga was supposed to admit to faking Iwona's kidnapping, the commissioner hadn't showed up at the karate dojo where they both trained. Kinga had called the station but the officer on call sounded hostile and her courage failed her. She had just hung up.

Now Kinga tried calling Quack from the pizzeria's landline. He didn't pick up. Kinga's anxiety was slowly turning into fear. Normally when she called him, he always picked up. Had he and Iwona been captured?

She dropped the receiver and ran out of the pizzeria.

She walked down the embankment running along the old train track, then crossed the dilapidated footbridge over the Stink Stream. The bridge hadn't been used for its intended purpose for years. It was only frequented by 'the derailed', as her mother liked to say. The local youth liked to loiter here, skipping over the broken spans and crumbling arches, sometimes lighting fires in the middle of the structure, bingeing on booze and drugs. It was also the perfect vantage point. You could see people approaching from pretty far away, and if the coppers decided to bust your party, you could always dump your drugs in the river.

This time in the evening there were only two people on the footbridge, men, sitting by a little campfire that was so small and dim that Kinga only spotted them when she was halfway across the bridge and almost upon them.

One of the men looked up at her. 'What's a pretty piece of ass like you doing here, eh?' he said, then turned to his companion. 'Oi, Tadek, grab the lass and invite her to the party.'

The other man jumped to his feet. Kinga watched, wondering what to do. The bridge was narrow. They could easily block her way if she tried to walk past. She didn't feel that scared, though. The boy who had called out to her was just looking for a diversion. Something fun to do. Anything, really. She knew the type. Dressed like a guerrilla soldier, his jacket spattered with fluorescent paintball splotches. Some wannabe from one of the local vocational schools. Probably preparing for war, like most of the local losers looking for thrills in one of the numerous paramilitary groups in the region. It was hard to tell if he was Polish or Belarusian; he had spoken in Polish, but that didn't count for much. She decided to keep quiet. If the man caught her Belarusian accent she might be in trouble. She bowed her head.

'Hey, it's Kinga from Siciliana,' the man in the paint-spattered jacket said now. That took Kinga by surprise. She didn't know this man. He called out to the other guy, Tadek. 'Leave her alone, mate.'

Tadek hesitated. 'Let the lady get by,' the other man said, more aggressively now. 'Can't you see she's in a hurry?'

Tadek reluctantly stepped to the side, leaning over the railing to make way. The other guy did the same. Kinga breathed out with relief and resumed walking, picking up the pace.

'Thanks,' she muttered as she passed them.

As she crossed the footbridge, her feet started getting stuck in the soggy ground and she lost one of her flip-flops. She kicked off the other and continued barefoot. The ground was cold, wet and disgusting.

Kinga could see the gate leading to her garden now. Lights were on in most of the flats, and she could see cars speeding along the narrow street. The familiar sight instantly calmed her down.

She could still hear the two men behind her, arguing about something.

Then something else. A different voice: 'I'm going for a leak, baby-doll.' It was a man, somewhere behind her. There was a splash, then another. Someone wading through the water of the Stink Stream. It grew louder. Kinga turned round. In the distance, she could see a dark silhouette. The man was stepping out of the water. He started running towards her. Kinga spun on her heel and ran for home, but the man gained on her effortlessly and grabbed her by the arm. She could do nothing to resist, her years of karate training instantly forgotten. She felt numb, limp. She managed to let out a short yelp before her assailant put a hand to her mouth and pinned her to the ground with a knee. She could smell turpentine. Kinga howled as the man bit into her arm, clamped his jaw shut, ripping through the skin and muscle, and tore out a chunk of her flesh in a welter of blood. She squirmed and thrashed, but his knee just pressed into her back harder and she felt his hand covering her mouth and nose, cutting off her air. Kinga's head spun. Dark patches encroached on her vision. She couldn't breathe. She couldn't scream again. The fear was paralysing. The only sound that escaped her throat was a quiet mewling. As he pulled at her hair, yanking her head up so she couldn't see his face, she spotted the two men in paramilitary outfits running away from her. There was nobody else around. Geographically, this was the dead centre of the city, though you wouldn't have thought so, bordered as it was by the river on one side, and grassland and an orchard on the other. It was the best hiding spot in town and that was why she had brought Iwona here. Nobody would hear or see anything that happened here. Nobody would come and help. She was all on her own.

That was when instinct kicked in and she fought back.

Sasza woke up parched and with a revolting, sour taste in her mouth. Her eyes were gritty, like she had sand under her eyelids. And her head was throbbing with pain. Sitting up wasn't an option. The midday sun shining through the window did nothing to help. She pulled the duvet over her head and hid in the darkness. Was that the reek of metabolised alcohol seeping through her pores with the sweat? What had happened at the cemetery? And how had she got back from Bielsk and to the apartment on Piłsudskiego Street? She didn't remember. She must have got drunk and blacked out. She had known these feelings and thoughts intimately, before, but she had hoped she wouldn't find herself going through them ever again. Despite the feelings of humiliation, shame and fury at herself for getting plastered again, the only thing she could think of right now was having some more. A small beer or, better yet, a drop of gin with a squeeze of lemon juice would work wonders. If she got up now, got dressed and left the flat, she would go straight to the off-licence. The closest one was just across the street from the station.

Trying to distract herself, she looked down at her body under the duvet. Her chest, thighs and belly were all marred by countless tiny bruises, as if she'd been bitten by lice. There had been similar marks on Danka's arms. The murdered girl. They itched. A lot. She scratched a spot just below her collarbone, immediately drawing blood. A trickle of it ran down her skin, right along her scar. It looked horrible.

She peeked out from under the duvet. Then she sat up. She felt not too bad. She got out of bed slowly, swayed a bit, then stood for a moment. Still not too bad. She headed towards the shower, following a trail of yesterday's discarded clothes. She picked her shirt up. It was torn. She must have had quite a struggle to rip it off with the cast still on her arm. She passed the mirror in the hallway, trying not to look at herself. But she couldn't completely avoid glimpsing herself in the large bathroom mirror. Her eyes weren't as bloodshot as they usually were when she was hungover. Her face wasn't swollen, either. She was standing straight. Her head wasn't spinning any more. She breathed into her palm, trying to smell the alcohol. There was none. What the hell? She was sober as a judge. How?

She turned on the bath taps, then brushed her teeth and combed her hair. Her messy curls were even more unruly than usual. In an attempt at some semblance of order, she pinned them back with a cotton hairband. She stepped into the bathtub, trying her best not to think about the blanks in her memory and musing on how her hangover must have been strictly psychosomatic. She laughed. It wasn't all bad. The only job now was to recall what had happened.

After her bath, she put on a dressing gown and went back into the main room. She intended to vacate the place later that day. She needed to pack and tidy up.

But as she looked around, she saw what she hadn't seen before in her psychosomatic hungover and self-loathing state. All of her working documents were absent. Only her home-made Post-its remained, scattered everywhere. The cartons Romanowska had brought her the files in were still lined up under the table. Empty. The day was hot, but Sasza suddenly shivered. Someone – the police? Romanowska herself? – must have taken them while she was getting hammered with random people in a cemetery. She sank to the floor. Still on the wagon or not, she was at rock bottom again.

From where she sat slumped on the floor, she could see under the sofa bed. She realised, with a sick feeling, that her painting was gone too.

As she sat there her mobile chimed with a text. She'd forgotten about the phone. She followed its sound and found it half-under the bed. The text was from the IT guy. 'You can pick up your computer today at eight P.M. I've only recovered the data you asked for. The rest would take a month at least. I'll be at my workplace. Ciszynia hospital, employees' entrance at the back. Don't use the main one!'

The icon for missed calls was showing seventeen. She also had six texts. Karo, her mother, Ghost, Romanowska, and two from unknown numbers. She went through the texts first. Karolina was returning from her holiday the day after tomorrow, landing at midnight. Laura, the girl's grandmother, was asking Sasza to pick them up from the airport. Laura said she'd promised Karolina that they'd visit a dog shelter and adopt a puppy as soon as they returned. 'It might come in handy in the garden. Hunt for moles. A small one. Not too fuzzy,' she wrote. She also asked Sasza to call back. Her daughter was missing her. Sasza felt like crying.

Ghost's long and rambling text said he was in Gdańsk. He couldn't come for her as his car was at the garage and his daughter was having an exam. He had to keep an eye on her so she would focus on her revision. 'There's a lot of bus lines from Warsaw to Hajnówka. Redbus for example. 67 złoty direct line, would you believe it,' the text went on. He added that he was already in touch with the local police. 'Romanowska will take care of you. She promised.' His conscience obviously wasn't clear though; the message ended with him writing that he'd check that Redbus line for her.

Sasza felt like someone had slapped her. She felt abandoned, alone, angry. How she hated men at this moment. She had pinned too much on her and Ghost. What had she believed would happen? Men could never be counted on. Nobody would help her. She was all alone again. Like always. All he had said were empty words. 'Eat a dick,' she muttered and deleted his text. Then, she deleted his number too. *Fuck you!* Doing that felt good. The unjustified fury, the viciousness, the thoughtless, reckless action. A fleeting moment of relief, and then the inevitable feeling of guilt. Shame. The need to hide. Always in that order. Now, on to damage limitation. She scrolled through all her old texts, looking in vain for Ghost's number. Nothing. She had removed Ghost's details for good. Great . . .

She sighed, tried to put it out of her mind, and called Karolina. The girl squealed with joy as Sasza promised that they'd really go to the dog shelter, and that she could choose a puppy.

Another text arrived as she and her daughter were saying goodbye. It was Romanowska. 'Where are you? Briefing in an hour. Good job yesterday.'

Good job? What had she done, exactly? She could remember nothing.

The text string showed that Romanowska had sent her a message two hours ago as well: 'Pack up the files. I'll send Błażej your way. He'll help you bring them over.'

She panicked. She stared around as if the files might suddenly reappear. She looked in the most unlikely places; she opened and slammed shut kitchen cupboards, flicked through books and peered behind them and underneath the shelves. But the files were definitively gone. Sasza collapsed to the floor and cried. She could think of only one thing to do now. Run. Disappear and go as far from this bloody place as possible. Go home.

Calming down slightly now she had some kind of plan, she packed her suitcase and even tidied up a little.

She picked up her suitcase and left the apartment. On the street she stopped a passer-by to ask how to get hold of a taxi and he directed her to the rank, by the church.

It was quite a walk. On her way, Sasza called the IT guy. He made a few excuses, but finally agreed that she could come for her laptop right away. She finally reached the taxi rank, got into one and asked for Ciszynia.

The IT guy let her in through the back entrance. He looked different in what looked like a caretaker's uniform. He allowed her to tuck her suitcase into a corner of a large maintenance room. The space was filled with various cleaning agents, dozens of mops, and some spare uniforms. There were also, propped up against or hung on the walls, shovels, saws and spiked metal bars. Pretty typical for these kinds of rooms in these kinds of institutions. What wasn't as typical were the two fridges. They were the same kind, she realised, as the one that was found in Bondaruk's car.

'My sister can't see you,' the man whispered.

Sasza looked up at him. And suddenly she remembered. She had seen him on the first day she came here, when she had tried to meet the director. He had been driving a huge industrial floor cleaning machine and wearing – she remembered this now too – that uniform.

She tried to play dumb, keeping her face blank, but she was sure he had noticed the flash of recognition in her eyes. He was too smart not to have.

'Come and join me in my kingdom,' he said. He guided her over to another part of the room. All the windows, Sasza noted, were barred and the entirety of the walls and ceiling covered with metal sheets. Like a submarine. Or a can of sardines. She could see another door, half-open to a room fully lined with white tiles like an operating theatre.

Her laptop was sitting in the middle of a desk. Next to it, his own equipment, as well as screens monitoring the entire place. The camera feeds skipped rhythmically, showing various rooms as well as the park. People were working, strolling. A car was entering the garage. Sasza saw Magdalena Prus walking down a corridor and then bending over a patient's bed. She wore her signature high heels and a tight-fitting mini.

'Would she have a problem with me coming back here?'

'You know how it is.' The man smiled and scrolled through some surveillance feeds, then stopped. The image was of a resident's room and a man sat in there, perfectly still. 'This was the Red Spider's room,' he said. 'Well, if the man really was the Red Spider, anyway.'

'There never was a Red Spider,' Sasza replied. 'It's an urban legend. It was whipped up to distract the media from other unsolved cases. A bank robbery, Bohdan Piasecki's case, the "Night Psycho". Not to mention that it served pretty well as a cover-up for political shenanigans. There were no murders back in the communist days. Or, rather, the authorities had a one hundred per cent clearance rate,' she amended.

'Right. But I know Lucian Staniak's* case made it into the files of the FBI. He's still the only Polish serial killer even mentioned by them. Even the Zagłębie Vampire didn't earn that honour.'

'I can see you've done your homework,' she said. 'Zdzisław Marchwicki hasn't been listed, because he wasn't our biggest case. He was charged with a lot of things he didn't do. Staniak's case was another thing entirely. It had been doctored expertly. And the media took the bait. The files were supposed to be lost at a later date.'

'Were those things top secret?' The man opened her laptop and logged in.

'Well, not any more. You know.'

He relaxed. 'It's very careless to leave such things unprotected. Very unlike an ex-CBŚ agent.'

Sasza pursed her lips. 'You seem to know an awful lot about me.'

He didn't reply. A light on his CB radio blinked. The device sputtered and then a voice came over it: 'One-thirteen-eight-one.'

The IT guy got up and picked up a swipe-card, then went over to the door. As he did so he turned round and put a finger to his lips. She nodded.

'Don't touch anything. I'll be back in a minute,' he said and closed the door. She heard him on the other side keying in the code. Locking her in.

The lock clicked, and then there was silence.

Sasza got up and walked to the white-tiled room. She pushed the door fully open and went in. In the middle of the room was

---

* One of Poland's most notorious real-life serial killers.

a metal slab and on it an IV cannula and a bag of 0Rh– blood plasma. Sasza touched it. The blood seemed warm. She retreated to the other room and the CCTV screens. She could see the IT guy on one of them, driving his cleaning machine. He stopped in the middle of a corridor, nodded to a doctor, and then pointed at the camera. Sasza jumped away. For a while longer, she waited in case someone came and opened the door, but nobody did. She decided to take a look into things. The man's computer was password protected. She tried entering the sequence of numbers the voice on the CB radio had said earlier. Access denied. She looked around. There was a corkboard on the wall, boasting a cleaning inspection sheet and also an old photo of a young girl. It had clearly been taken years before, during the previous regime. The girl wore a navy blue school uniform and wore her hair in two braids. It was Magdalena Prus. Aged seventeen, the girl hadn't looked anything like the elegant woman she was now. Sasza took the photo down and hid it in her pocket, then continued her reconnaissance.

She dug through the work clothes on the hangers. Something caught her eye. She lifted a baggy work apron to reveal a traditional Belarusian man's outfit. A wedding outfit. The trousers were spattered with blood, and a worn balaclava was sticking out from one of the pockets.

ŁARYSA

(1995)

'I'm not going back,' Łarysa Szafran said plainly, rifling through the music cassettes in the glove compartment and settling on a recording of last year's Belarusian music festival. After a dozen songs or so, a Polish song came on. Łarysa rewound the recording to the beginning and pressed play. She only ever listened to Belarusian rock. A few minutes later, the tape got tangled in the cassette player and the music stopped with a warbling noise. Łarysa swore and pulled the cassette out, sitting back to wind the tape back in. That recording was seriously rare. She wasn't prepared to part with it.

'Now it's going to stutter like Fionik's dad at the maintenance hearing.' She laughed in her hoarse alto; but, seeing Piotr's expression, she added in Belarusian: 'All right! You have to give him that he at least has the balls to stand up to that Lukashenko guy. As far as I know, his only aim in life now is to blow his fucking brains out. Come to think about it, I could make a living as a revolutionary's wife. Why don't you buy me a gun for my next birthday?'

She was younger than Bondaruk by some twenty years. They had met seven months earlier, but her swearing was still something that he had trouble getting used to.

'By the way, I still can't wrap my head around how they could give that guy the presidency,' she mused, pursing her lips. Her innocent appearance had always clashed with her vulgarity. '*Hospodi pomilui!*'

'You didn't vote,' Piotr pointed out stoically. 'You've contributed to him becoming president too.'

'There's no such thing as free elections in Belarus,' she scoffed, indignant. She had studied English at the State Linguistic University in Minsk before she got expelled for subversive political activity after three years. 'There's no such thing as *freedom*. And *independence*? It's not even listed in dictionaries. It's been swapped for *indoctrination*. The worst thing is I'm not even exaggerating. I can show you. I have the damn thing in my collection. Published Minsk 1994. Fresh from the press. I'm going to take it west with me – if I ever leave this place. Nothing demonstrates the current situation in the homeland better. The only winner there is the great white bear. Moscow. Lukashenko is a puppet. And ordinary people are just scared. The tanks, the soldiers, the secret agents. The poverty, you know? But they'll come around. Sooner or later. That they didn't vote for the opposition doesn't change anything. Shit, the people even stopped talking in their own language. *Our* language.' She paused. 'Anyway, I feel like this is going to be my home from now on. I can do something good here. Besides, my dad's dad lived here. I would have been born here if not for the war. And I think I want my kids to live here too. By the way, want to make kids with me? Like, right now?'

She looked at him sweetly. When she didn't swear, drink copious amounts of alcohol, or smoke her stinky Parliaments, she really looked like an angel. Piotr knew her too well to see her that way, though. He grimaced.

'You're as much a Pole as I'm a Belarusian.'

She leaned over him and planted a kiss on his cheek, gently placing a hand on his thigh.

'Maybe we're mongrels, but we're not outsiders. We're local and that has to count for something.' She pointed to a birch cross by the road. 'Over there, by the weeping willow. That's where Jan, my grandad, lies. I've never visited the place. Even when my family still lived here. Or if I did, I was too young to remember. When we left, I wasn't even Fionik's age.'

'Ran away out of patriotism.'

'Fuck you,' she barked. 'Mum didn't want to go. She pretended to be Polish. Dad wanted to go back, but it was really about the job he got at the university. He had next to no chance of having a career in academia here. Who the fuck needs a Belarusian literature teacher around those parts? But I'm gonna change that. I'll find the place where the ashes of my ancestors lie, and that's where I'll stay.'

'Let's hope it doesn't come to that too fast.' He looked at her.

He wanted to add that he'd like to feel the same fire, purity and faith she had inside her. He found it fascinating. It was out of this fascination that he'd decided to protect her. Even from herself. But at the same time, he envied her. He didn't intend to strip her of her pure, childish enthusiasm and naivety, even though he knew it was foolish. Let her keep her childhood as long as she could. Oh, to be naive, but pure and full of bright ideas, again. He smiled with affection. She took it as encouragement and slid her hand up his thigh. He could feel her nails gently trailing a line towards his crotch.

'If you don't want to have sex before we're married, we can marry right away,' she offered.

Piotr tensed. He shrugged her off his leg and changed gears.

'Aren't you a goody two-shoes,' she said with a smirk.

'Can't you act like a lady for once?' he retorted, knowing she wouldn't. Łarysa turned away and stared out of the window.

'The Poles killed my grandad because he was Belarusian. Orthodox. That was enough back then. That's war for you.'

She rummaged through the glove compartment again and fished out another cassette. Her favourite singer, he realised, glancing at the cover. She squealed like a little girl in a sweetshop and put the cassette into the recorder. When the song started, Łarysa started to sway to the rhythm. Her asymmetrical fringe of bright, but clearly natural-coloured hair swung to the right side of her face, partially obscuring it.

'*Vaina!*' shouted the singer through the speakers. *War.*

Łarysa put on a red beret and tied a scarf round her neck. In these, with her mother's green duster coat and worn low-heeled pumps, she looked like someone from a French movie about the resistance fighters during World War Two.

She was bobbing her head to the music, once in a while calling out with the singer. *Vaina!* Piotr studied her earrings, sporting Pahonia emblems. She had made them out of beer bottle caps, spray-painting them gold. He knew the locals saw her as an eccentric, but that was what he liked the most about her. Also, the fact she didn't really care about the little details. Details such as the fact that she was unemployed, poor, and practically homeless. She didn't care about domestic life like any self-respecting local woman would. She didn't hoard clothes, shoes, or handbags. Books, maybe. But even those she gave away as soon as she'd read them. She needed to pass on her passion for fighting for what was right and her obsessive pursuit of Truth.

She also didn't really bother much with motherhood. A lucky coincidence, as Fionik was a good, self-sufficient child. He was practically raising himself. Since she'd started working at the Dialog foundation for supporting refugees from the Eastern bloc and had managed to get her son Polish citizenship, Larysa didn't pay the kid much heed. And the kid didn't seem to hold it against her. He loved her just as she was. Little Fionik didn't find it hard to assimilate in his new country, even though he was still too young to even grasp the concept of nationality. Other kids liked him. And he could already speak Polish way better than his mother. Larysa, filled with revolutionary spirit, seemed to live exclusively for her lofty ideals. Her only goal in life was to wake the Belarusian people from their deep winter slumber, as she liked to say. And you had to give her that – she was pretty convincing in that role. A lot more convincing than all the opposition politicians back in Minsk.

'Turn here,' she ordered.

Piotr didn't comply at once, though he wasn't surprised. Earlier in the morning Larysa had told him she had to catch a train. That night, she was supposed to go to Minsk; they were supposed to arrive at the train station before five in the afternoon. But instead of packing her things, Larysa had dawdled. She had read some documents, taken a thorough inventory of her old clothes, changed a dozen times, torn up some photos, and looked at arbitrary newspaper cuttings. She hadn't seemed to be in a hurry at all. She had finally packed her suitcase, but the thing was so light Piotr wondered if what she was taking back to her homeland was Polish air and a handful of dirt. The bottle of booze and some sweets for Larysa's parents – which Piotr had had to tell her to take – rattled around as if the bag was empty apart from them.

Larysa had left Piotr a couple of power-of-attorney papers for the foundation and copies of her and her son's IDs. She did this every time she travelled out of the country, even for a few days. Just in case she got abducted by secret agents. Her obsession had only grown stronger with time. In the beginning, Piotr was worried, but he grew used to her paranoia soon enough. Most citizens of ex-Soviet states were afflicted by the same more or less rational suspicion.

In the morning, sipping her coffee, Łarysa had cuddled Fionik as if she were never going to see him again. Piotr had never thought her capable of such affection. It had to be a ruse. But he decided to go with it, and took the empty-feeling suitcase, throwing it into the car boot. Later, at the city limits, Piotr's old Polonez had broken down. The radiator had spewed smoke. Piotr had had to get his hands dirty repairing the damage. As they waited for the radiator to cool down, Łarysa had grumbled that a man of his stature – the high-and-mighty-father-director, as she used to call him mockingly – should drive a Mercedes instead of that old clunker. Piotr had refused to comment, only smiling slightly. He had been waiting for just such a car for the last month. A brand-new Mercedes E-class. 'Four-Eyes'. As soon as the car dealer had shown him photos of it, he knew he had to have one. He was already looking forward to seeing Łarysa's expression as he showed her his new toy.

'You turning or not?' she asked nonchalantly, but something in her voice made him hit the brakes at once. 'Cause if not, I'm jumping out right now.'

'What are you saying?' he asked, stopping the car abruptly. They were both yanked forward. The tyres screeched.

She hummed along with the music, then shouted out the chorus at ear-splitting volume.

Piotr jabbed at a button and ejected the cassette. 'You're not going back to Belarus?'

'I don't hear people begging me to come back.' She took out a pack of her Parliaments.

Piotr persisted. 'What about Fionik? Where will he go to school? Won't your husband look for you? What about the country? Do you think it won't go looking for its runaway citizen?'

'I highly doubt that.' Łarysa lit her cigarette and took a drag. She tossed the matches into the glove compartment, then stepped out of the car and slammed the door shut behind her. Piotr stayed in his seat, trailing Łarysa with his eyes. She had her old handbag in her hand, and was swinging it like a pendulum to the rhythm of her steps. He sat still a moment longer, hoping she would stop. Then he drove the car closer to the line of trees and killed the engine.

Checking all the doors and windows were closed, he headed Łarysa's way. She waited for him. She knew he would come. He always did.

'What exactly are we looking for here?'

'A butcher. Do you know that this was the birthplace of Ivan the Terrible?'

Piotr hadn't. He was astonished. Ivan Marchenko, Treblinka prison guard, who was eventually charged with and tried for genocide during the Holocaust. He was nicknamed Ivan the Terrible in reference to the infamously bloodthirsty Tsar of Russia of the same name.

Łarysa took out another cigarette and started rifling through her handbag. Piotr had foreseen that. He took out of his pocket the matches she had thrown in the glove compartment earlier. She lit her cigarette, then straightened her beret and strode down the path, her heels sinking into the sandy ground. It had to be something important, then. She wasn't the type of woman who'd spend any time in field conditions if it wasn't absolutely necessary. She much preferred long discussions at the table, particularly those accompanied by vodka shots. Wandering through forests was something she'd elect to do only if it paid out in knowledge. She was always hungry for more of that. Truth be told, Piotr was getting curious himself as to what they were looking for, and especially what knowledge exactly was so important to Łarysa.

'His original name was Jan Marczuk,' Łarysa went on. 'After the war, back here, he would always glorify Germany. He greeted his friends with the old *Heil Hitler*! He took beatings for that from the police, but he never changed. Of course, he also hated Jews. I heard that a guy who used to drink with him liked to say that Marczuk confided in him. Apparently, the old fat-ass dreamed of being able to feel human blood on his hands again. That's when people started saying that he used to be a guard at one of the concentration camps.'

'Nonsense.' Piotr wasn't sure why he should trust the hearsay of these 'people' Łarysa seemed to have been talking to.

'Hear me out,' she insisted. 'Some local amateur historian, Krzysztof Wieremiuk – he's a German teacher in his day job – looked into it and learned that Ivan Marchenko has never been found. And Marczuk used to tell people he worked in a Nazi camp.

Wieremiuk also told me that auxiliary units of the SS tasked with pacifying the Warsaw Ghetto, and some concentration camp guards, were recruited from the Ukrainian community. Is it so hard to believe one of them was in fact a Belarusian from around here? Or a Russian? The historian tried researching Marczuk's family history and looking for people who used to know him and could tell him something about his life during the war.'

'Even if what you're saying is true, this Wieremiuk shouldn't have expected to unearth anything of value,' Piotr said. 'Time goes by and people forget. Evidence gets lost or destroyed.'

'But he did find a marriage certificate for one Olga Wołosiuk. He also found a priest from Dubicze Cerkiewne. That priest performed her marriage ceremony and baptised their daughter. But there's more. Bielsk Podlaski has a large Ukrainian community. They speak a different dialect, and their culture and traditions are different from Belarusian ones. Not the same as in the villages around Hajnówka.'

'So what? What do we care about some Ukrainian guy? Even if he is the Butcher of Treblinka. There were so many evil men during the war.'

Łarysa waved him away. They had reached a small house surrounded by a dilapidated wooden fence. It was old. Probably dated from well before the war. The windows were broken and the roof had partially collapsed. There was a stork's nest on the chimney.

'Krzysztof Wieremiuk found Olga and his daughter. The latter told him Marczuk was a drunk. He was only with her mother for a little while before she threw him out and married someone else.'

'So what about Treblinka?' Piotr said. 'Could she confirm that he used to be a guard there?'

'She doesn't remember. She barely remembers him. He disappeared in nineteen forty-three, when she was little. Then he reappeared after the war. Lived right here' – she pointed at the ruined house – 'and in nineteen eighty-six he tried to see Olga. Turned up at her house. She didn't let him in. He was drunk again.'

'And we've come here so you could tell me this?' Piotr asked. 'That's why we're not going to the train station?'

'You want me to leave already?' Łarysa turned away. 'You won't get rid of me that easily.'

She opened the gate and went into the garden. It was overgrown with blackberry bushes. Piotr thought he should stop her so she didn't rip her duster coat on the thorns, but after a few metres, he realised the bushes had been cleared and there was a narrow path.

'Marczuk died a month ago in a hospital near Białystok,' Łarysa called back to him.

'Thank God,' Piotr said. 'He won't murder another Jew or Pole, then.'

'He never officially claimed responsibility. He never answered any questions about Treblinka or the SS. He kept quiet until the very end. But he did say a thing or two to Wieremiuk. And he left him something too. Something that I think you'll find interesting. It concerns your ancestry. Your family and your very nature. Your *genes*. I think you should know about what I'm about to show you, oh high-and-mighty-father-director.'

Piotr grabbed her by the arm and jerked her towards himself.

'Are you out of your mind?' he hissed.

'Wait. He's coming. Don't make a scene now.'

'You could have told me! You spent all that time singing your stupid songs when you could have—'

He shut up mid-sentence. A man was coming out of the house. He had the thin, sly face of a rat. Skinny, wearing a collarless three-buttoned shirt, peasant-style, untucked. He had a military sweater tied around his hips and wore glasses. A canvas bag hung from his hand. It had a bottle of milk sticking out from the top.

'Piotr Bondaruk?' the man asked, brushing wood shavings and ants from his trousers. He must have been sitting on a rotten tree trunk. He could have been lurking anywhere. He had probably heard their conversation. Or at least some of it. The man extended a hand. It was soft. 'Or maybe I should call you Piotr Stanislavovitch Gałczyński? Have you never thought about why your mother, Aniela, and your father Staszek, and you yourself kept the name of your distant aunt from the eastern hinterland? Anastazja Bonda? None of you even knew her. Bondaruk is a Ukrainian variation on that name. Nothing more than a pseudonym. A nickname. The suffix nothing but an ethnic identifier.'

The ratty man must have already smelled the money he was about to get showered with. He looked flushed with self-satisfaction. Piotr did a quick calculation in his mind. How much would the man want from him, what currency, and how long would he keep blackmailing him. Until he died? Then he looked at Łarysa. The stupid woman was probably still thinking this was all about her bloody ideals.

'Are you alone?' Piotr asked in the most calm and polite manner he could manage in the circumstances.

'Lonely and alone. Solo.' Wieremiuk nodded eagerly. 'But if I don't return, my friend, the commissioner in Bielsk will know where to look. He also knows who I've come to meet.'

From the corner of his eye, Piotr noticed the grin melt away from Łarysa's face.

'Show me the proof,' Piotr demanded.

Wieremiuk rummaged through his canvas bag and took out a brightly-coloured plastic one, from which he produced a package wrapped in a black rag that looked like a small devotional *matatka*.* There were some letters in Cyrillic script on it. The amateur historian unwrapped it, revealing a stack of old documents.

'Marczuk asked me to do something before he died. He told me to send it to the media. He hated Poles. Catholic Poles, to be precise.'

'Just like you?' Piotr smirked.

The ratty Wieremiuk was still smiling, though.

'Keep your wits about you, Bondaruk,' he said. 'I'm on your side if you're on our side. And that's how it'll stay.'

Piotr reached out for the documents. Wieremiuk stepped back instantly and wrapped them back up in the rag, then stuffed it into his rucksack. He nodded at Łarysa.

'You want to know where your grandfather's buried?'

She nodded in return.

'I'd like to show you. I really would,' the rat replied, turning to Bondaruk again. 'Now, filthy *katsap*, it's time to show us the place where the carters were murdered. Enough of silence.'

---

* A typically Polish small wall-tapestry type cloth, sometimes embroidered with religious script.

Piotr sat down on a tree stump. He shot Łarysa and Wieremiuk a wary glance and sighed. Then he shook his head, feeling defeated.

'People already know,' he said. 'It's not a secret.'

The rat lost his verve.

'How do you mean? Who knows?'

'Everybody knows. It's just that nobody wants the place to be officially found. What is it to you? Why stick your nose in something that's none of your business. You're an outsider, aren't you?'

Wieremiuk didn't respond. It was enough confirmation for Bondaruk.

'It's your bloody damned obligation,' Wieremiuk grew agitated again. 'Your responsibility. You've been playing the wolf dressed in sheep's clothing for years. You've been paying your father's debt your whole life, even if you don't know it.'

'He's right, you know,' Łarysa chimed in. 'They'll listen to you. The community, the authorities. Someone has to start talking.'

Piotr didn't pay her any attention. 'You're either a Don Quixote or simply a fool,' he said. 'The country doesn't want to know. Neither the Poles nor the Belarusians.'

Wieremiuk didn't back down. 'That's what you think,' he hissed. 'People want to know. A special institute for those kinds of things is in the works. The IPN. All the materials, the entire archive of all the crimes against the Polish nation will be there. Our entire national memory! The glories and the moments of shame. All the future generations will know, and anyone will be able to learn about it.'

'Complete and utter nonsense.' Piotr waved a hand dismissively. 'What's done is done. Look around. People care about money. They don't need proof of the crimes against their ancestors. Nobody wants old wounds reopened. Just ask around the local villages. The last living witnesses keep quiet, and their children simply don't know. That keeps them safe. And the authorities will defend me. I put all of those bigwigs in their positions in the first place.'

'Who?' Wieremiuk frowned in incomprehension.

'The starost, the mayor, the police commissioner, the director of the Belarusian high school. Even the director of the culture centre. Countless businessmen. They received denationalised assets. I lent them money. They're still repaying their debts. None of them has any interest in biting the hand that feeds.'

'Until they have repaid their debts,' Wieremiuk growled. 'Everything ends.'

'The officials will rip you apart, man. You're too small to swim with the big fish.'

Piotr reached out for the documents again. This time Wieremiuk handed him the package. Piotr unwrapped it and read the names. Seven of them.

'That's not everyone,' he said. 'There were fifty carters. Didn't the people in Puchały tell you? That's only the Council's bargaining chip.'

'What Council?' Łarysa asked. Wieremiuk was silent. He looked confused. Out of his depth. 'Does this mean all the people in charge of the city are descendants of the murdered carters?' Łarysa went on.

'Those who stayed and kept their mouths shut. Those who cut themselves off, who didn't like how the situation panned out, have either left or are dead.'

'Dead?'

'Some of them, yes,' Piotr admitted. He returned the documents to Wieremiuk. He was disappointed. 'Money, as I've already told you. People are fed up with being poor. Capitalism gave them the opportunity to get rich. New cars, houses with central heating and stable jobs make up for the moral decline. Nobody cares for nationalism any more. The differences between nations are the least of everyone's concerns. Ecumenism. Tolerance. Go read some election slogans.'

'There's no such thing as a Council!' Wieremiuk said, in a last attempt at staving off the new information. 'We're not living in a movie.'

Piotr smiled at him.

'Is that right? Tell me, who runs things around here? Who's the starost? The mayor? Who put them in their place? Are you sure the Bielsk commissioner hasn't already ordered his men to bring you in? What you're holding is a bomb, and you know next to nothing about pyrotechnics. You have a wife, kids, friends. Aren't you afraid for them? Bury wasn't a murderer, either. He was just following orders.'

'That is simply not true.'

Piotr raised his hands, surrendering the case.

'That's debatable, at least. But it isn't pertinent to our discussion.'

'How is it not pertinent?' Wieremiuk exclaimed. 'It's fundamental!'

He hesitated for a while, seemingly unsure if he should continue the dialogue. Finally, he just slid the package back into its bag. 'I don't want money. I want the truth.' He bowed to both Łarysa and Piotr. 'I will do all I can to uncover it. The location of that grave must be discovered. We will meet again.'

'I don't think so,' Piotr muttered. More loudly, he said: 'Take care of yourself. Take my advice.'

Piotr and Łarysa were left alone. Bondaruk looked at her. 'Well, you got what you came here for. Happy?'

A week later, Łarysa barged into Piotr Bondaruk's office at the lumber mill, tears streaming down her flushed face. Piotr was sitting behind his desk, surrounded by the various trophies, medals and diplomas he had received during the previous regime as well as in the current, nascent capitalist era. The statues and framed certificates did not elicit as much respect as the enormous bison head hanging on the wall, which was now the object of the full attention of a fat, bald man. The man sat in a wobbly chair facing the lumber mill director. His huge, fat buttocks spilled over the seat on both sides. He looked like a grown man sitting in a kiddie chair.

'I need a word,' Łarysa barked sourly. Her colourful skirt whirled around her as she turned to slam the door behind her, showing her thighs and garters. She instinctively smoothed it down with a hand. 'It can't wait.'

'Włodzimierz here was just bringing me up to speed on the intricacies of creative accounting, dear,' Piotr replied without taking his eyes off the obese man. A polite smile, normally reserved for visits to schools and town hall, where he played patron of the arts and philanthropist, was plastered across his face. It didn't reach his eyes. 'Thanks to his ideas, we'll earn heaps of money. *That* is what can't wait. Give me thirty minutes. We'll be finished by then, won't we?' He nodded at the accountant, who eagerly nodded back before turning his head and eyeing Łarysa lasciviously.

'I need to speak with you right *now!*' Łarysa shouted.

Her outburst just made Piotr's smile widen. He imagined she would start stomping her feet like a spoilt child any time now.

'Unless you want me to say what I'm about to say with that hog present,' she added.

The accountant reddened in outrage.

'Would you give me a minute?' Piotr addressed the man before he could respond to Łarysa's insult. 'Please, use our canteen, help yourself to a meal on the house. My secretary will call you back. And please, forgive my fiancée. She's a foreigner. Hot-blooded, eastern girl. Quick to anger. I think it's best if you don't have to hear it any more.'

The fat accountant started to collect his papers, but they kept spilling from his hands, which were shaking with suppressed anger.

'Please, forgive us,' Piotr asked once more and gestured for the man to leave the documents.

As the door slammed shut behind the accountant, Piotr pointed Łarysa to a leather armchair at the wall, but she took the accountant's warm seat instead. She needed Bondaruk close for this.

'He's dead,' she hissed. 'What did you do to him?'

'Who?' Piotr seemed lost.

'Wieremiuk, of course. The kids at school were informed they'd have a new German teacher. For now, Anatol Pires has taken over. I heard he just sent the kids home.'

'*Ausgezeichnet*,' muttered Piotr. *Just great.* 'Well, at least the brats are happy now.'

'The funeral is in two days. They're going to do a post-mortem first, but people are already talking. Apparently, it was suicide. I heard he got fired and a week before that they gave his wife the boot from her job too. They were left with nothing. Nobody's wanted to employ the poor man for the last month. Not even as a nightwatchman. I'm wondering, did you have something to do with it?'

Piotr took a sip of his cold tea.

'What are you talking about?'

'He killed himself!' Łarysa pointed an accusatory finger at Bondaruk. 'And you're behind it.'

He turned away from her and stared out of the window. 'Don't be stupid.'

'I *was* stupid. I was stupid to trust you.' She got up. 'I'm going back to Belarus.'

Piotr knitted his brows and rubbed at his reddened eyelids. 'As you wish.'

Łarysa stiffened, squinted, hunched over and froze. She looked ready to pounce. She looked lovely.

'Won't you stop me?'

'I've never promised you anything.'

'That's what I'm talking about. You only needed me for your pleasure! I was a pet!'

'You never complained,' he retorted, but she wasn't listening any more.

'But now, I don't have anywhere to go,' she continued her tirade. He hated it when she tried making him pity her. As she lost composure, her Eastern lilt became more clearly audible. 'I can't go back really. You know that.'

She was clearly about to cry, holding on to some semblance of self-control only by the thinnest thread.

'Nobody wants you back home, my love,' Piotr cooed. He walked over and wrapped his arms around her. She tried pushing him away, but his grip was vice-like. His fingers clamped around her frail shoulders. She'd have bruises later. She bruised easily, with that thin, alabaster-white skin of hers. He spoke to her, his tone affectionate, his words anything but. 'Nobody will look for you, dear. Nobody needs you there. Nobody needs you anywhere. Neither in Belarus nor here. You sow the wind, you have to reap the whirlwind. Don't be surprised when the storm starts. But here, now – that's only a single lightning bolt. And it's still far, far away. I told you already – don't meddle in my business. Let others do their work. Your foundation is nothing. It has no power across the border. If you leave, you die. And you have a son to take care of. He's such a good boy, our Fionik.'

She stopped resisting. As soon as he felt her softening, he loosened his grip.

'Who are you?'

'I'm the son of a traitor. A spy for war criminals,' he said plainly. 'I'm a murderer, if that's what you want to call me. A multiple murderer. Is that what you wanted to hear?'

Tears rolled down Łarysa's cheeks. 'I don't believe you,' she said defiantly. That took him by surprise.

'I fell in love with your courage,' she went on. 'I risked my life, my honour, and my good name. And now you reject me. You haven't even fucked me! Am I that ugly to you?'

He turned his face away. 'Don't confuse sexuality with love. Those are two separate things.'

'What are you saying?'

'Most people I've loved I haven't had sex with. Sex isn't the same as love. They rarely go together. Very rarely.'

'So you do love me?'

He hesitated.

'I like you,' he replied. 'I trust you. I care for you. As for a wife. Isn't that enough?'

She started squirming again, trying to break free. That wasn't the answer she'd wanted to hear.

'I'll discover that grave. I'll tell everyone,' she hissed angrily.

'Wieremiuk said the same thing. Now he's dead.'

'I'll succeed where he failed,' Łarysa dug in. 'Why won't you help me? Just a bit. One of the villagers from Zaleszany kept secret notes. She wrote down her father's and uncle's conversations. They've probably been destroyed, but I'll find that woman and make her talk.'

'Stop.' He put a finger to her lips. She managed to break free.

'I won't. You can't stop me!'

He waved his hand at her dismissively.

'You're just a bored city girl. Do some work for a change. Real work. You'll lose your fighting spirit. Maybe you'd like to work in the export division here? Nobody really knows English around these parts. You could come in handy. What do you say, my beautiful, young and highly educated sweetheart?'

She slapped him, leaving her hand on his jaw for an instant. He pushed it away and rubbed at the spot. Łarysa's eyes bulged. What had she done?

'I take it you accept my offer?' he said.

'Only if you help me reveal the truth. For the homeland. It's a national memorial.'

'You're doing it only for yourself,' he snarled. 'You just need pay-back, don't you? For your failures. For the youth you lost. Just out of spite. You can't get back at your husband – that bloody paparazzo disappeared as soon as it turned out you were pregnant. He doesn't care about you and you can't deal with that. So you're looking to retaliate, substituting your personal hurts with those lofty ideals. But it's your own *vaina*. Your own war. You need a victory, don't you?'

'I'm leaving,' she cut in. She needed him to shut up. She burst out: 'You don't want to live with me, so you won't! I won't beg for your love.'

'This works both ways. I'd advise you to think about it.'

'Take me there right now,' she ordered. 'I want to honour the dead.'

He smirked and shook his head. 'You don't get it, do you? Better not to know. You can listen to rumours, suspect where it is, investigate all you want, but you *can't* see the place. Just like Bigfoot or Nessie. What the eye doesn't see, the heart doesn't grieve. This knowledge has a terrible cost. You don't want to play with fire, Łarysa. The sly rat paid with his life for doing just that.'

'You told me you had nothing to do with it.'

'And I stand by my words. The little man picked a fight with a beast and he didn't even have a knife to defend himself. I don't even go into that labyrinth. Let the Minotaur stay in his lair. As long as he does, everyone is safe.'

'Everyone?'

'Our fathers' generation wants to forget. Live out their days in peace. *We* are scared. Our children don't give a damn. Our grand-children will be the ones to feel the need to revive their national identity. I'll be old by then and I won't care. That will be the time to reveal all there is to reveal. To take revenge and to ask forgiveness. It will be a time of clear divides. Of protests and demonstrations. When the killers die out and the innocent have their bloodless revenge, your dream will come true. The world will be pure once again. But not yet. That's just the way it is.'

'What do you mean?'

'I'm saying that if you start digging now, you'll have to face the beast. Alone. Weak. Without any allies. Nobody will have your back. I won't be strong enough to protect you. Not that I don't want to.

I'll do my best. You can count on me. I will show you the place. But only if you really want to see it. Your choice. You don't have to ask around those villages, opening old wounds. Don't put those people in danger.'

Łarysa stared into Piotr's eyes, full of love and devotion. She threw herself into his arms. 'If something happens to me, you'll take care of Fionik, okay?'

'Until I die.' He stroked her hair. 'He will be safe and he'll never want for anything. You have my word. He won't know war. He won't want to remember.'

'But I want to,' she burst out at last. 'I want to bury my grandfather.'

'The old man doesn't care any more.' He took her by the hand. 'Work for me.'

She nodded. He smiled. She'd fight for him. They'd win a battle or two together, fighting for the only cause that never grows old: wealth.

'Do you have those documents?' she asked shyly. 'I want to see if he's there. If he lies in that mass grave by Puchały Stare.'

Piotr tensed. So he wouldn't be able to save her after all. This woman would always keep looking for trouble. She'd always choose the wrong option. If she could walk any one of a dozen roads, she'd choose the most winding. He wanted to say to her: 'Run. Find someone who'll love you. Forget about me.' But he said something else.

'I'm sorry, but I don't have them. This is the only riddle that I still haven't solved. Whoever has the treasure of Little Belarus holds all the cards. I'd give half my wealth for the knowledge and power – to be able to show who the murdered carters were and all those who collaborated with the secret police. But the truth will surface sooner or later. We'll know just who has it when the blood starts flowing.'

Hajnówka, 2014

When she bent over to pick up the last of the cardboard boxes from the apartment Sasza Załuska had been working in, blood flowed from Romanowska's nose. It was exhaustion. She had always seemed to need more sleep than everybody else. Nine, even ten hours. It was part of her life motto – the 'three S' rule, or 'sleep, sex and serenity'. Those things were better for keeping your beauty and youth than even the most expensive cosmetic surgery. But since all the chaos had broken out in town, she'd had to make do with about four hours of shut-eye a night. And it didn't look like things would change any time soon. The night was turning out to be rather busy. Doman had had to go to the rescue of Hubert Meyer, his pet forensic psychologist from Katowice, who was supposed to be driving to the station but who had got lost on the local roads.

At the station Romanowska had noticed that a rolled-up painting had got mixed up with the case documents. She'd picked it up and, tired and fumbling, had dropped it, and it had partially unrolled itself. The commissioner had stiffened, startled, then, with shaky hands, spread the small painting out on the floor.

It depicted Sasza Załuska. She was five, maybe ten years younger in it than she was now, but there was no doubt that it was her. In the lower corner was the author's signature, 'Łu', and a dedication: 'For Milena's 29th. Romanowska had wondered if defending the profiler all that time had been such a good idea. Since she'd arrived in town, all she'd seemed to do was bring trouble. The other investigators had a hypothesis that her real goal here was not to solve the case, but rather to bog it down. Sasza had a broad knowledge of criminology. That was a fact. And they had shown her the majority of the files. She really had done a good job – but more,

Romanowska reflected now, in the sense of successfully making things Byzantine and convoluted than clearing them up.

Until yesterday, Sasza Załuska had had a single ally – the commissioner. Romanowska had tried convincing the other investigators during the last briefing that the woman was simply chaotic by nature. But now she felt a pang of unease that was slowly but surely turning into full-blown panic. Maybe Sasza hadn't showed up by chance after all? All the things she had said about hating Łukasz Polak might have been a smokescreen. She might still be in love with the man. She hadn't made any attempt to find him, despite knowing the man a lot better than anyone else around here. But if Sasza had come here only to free Polak and help him escape, they were all going to take the fall for that. The entire station. What was even worse, Romanowska had been the one to order the files delivered to Sasza. And the guy who had vouched for her, Robert Duchnowski, still hadn't arrived.

The director of the New Forest Hajnówka lumber plant was keeping quiet. He had turned himself in earlier that morning, but refused to make a statement or answer any questions, only admitting that it had been he who planted both skulls. But why had he done it? He clammed up about that. How had Sasza Załuska known? Had they talked? He hadn't denied it. But it had been she who'd come up with that hypothesis in the first place, hadn't it? Bondaruk had told them nothing more. He had only called his lawyer and asked the officers to cuff him. His position in town was too prominent, though. The starost, Adam Gaweł, had called and bailed the man out. Bondaruk had promised he'd be at the detectives' disposal and left. Apparently he hadn't turned up at work today, instead staying at home and not returning any calls. His housekeeper had told them that he was drinking himself into a stupor. Only Jah-Jah had any contact with the man. What the hell was happening?

Romanowska decided she couldn't protect Sasza any more, and called the forensic technician team in to examine the apartment. The commissioner told herself she had to watch her every step from now on. She must take the profiler off the case immediately, before it was too late and she had to pay for her mistakes with her job. She intended to show the painting to Doman and advance a new plan: if push came to shove, she had enough evidence to arrest Sasza and keep her in detention indefinitely, blaming her for all the mistakes in the investigation. She could start with illegal possession of a firearm.

She finished loading the boxes into her car and got behind the steering wheel. When she turned the radio on, Radio Zet was broadcasting a news story about the search for Łukasz Polak, or 'the Red Spider copycat' as they were referring to him. Then, a short feature from Hajnówka about Kinga Kosiek, the Belarusian Pizzeria Siciliana waitress, who was still unconscious in hospital. 'The new killing grounds of the Cannibal,' the reporter said. That was what the media had dubbed the murderer, who had literally bitten off a chunk of Kosiek's arm. The investigators now had his DNA, his teeth imprint, and more evidence, all of which should help police to catch him soon. For the time being, though, the man was still at large, and all police, military and voluntary units had been put on high alert. The local detention centre was full of suspects being questioned, the report said.

Romanowska was afraid this chaos would only help the real perpetrator escape. What was absolutely certain, however, was that the 'Cannibal' wasn't Łukasz Polak. They had eliminated him straight away. This had been kept from the media, though; it would show up the fact that the force had a whole bunch of unsolved cases on their hands instead of one. Rumours were flying, nonetheless; the talk around town was that the Cannibal had intended to eat the Belarusian girl alive. There were speculations about conflicts between nationalists. People talked about the swastikas daubed on walls around town, the arguments between Poles and Belarusians about Romuald 'Bury' Rajs and his band of freedom fighters – or murderers, depending on who you listened to. While Romanowska knew that all this was just a way for people to cope with their fear, she was sure too that the situation would only keep escalating until they finally caught the Cannibal. What she wasn't sure of was how many criminals they were chasing. Was it just one deviant or an organised group?

Kinga Kosiek was liked in town. She had no enemies. Ideological motives seemed likely. She was part of the Orthodox Brotherhood, after all. She had participated in the quasi-religious traditional ceremony leading up to Piotr Bondaruk's wedding. She was also part of the Union of Belarusians in Poland and as a student had actively worked for the Belarusian nationalist cause. People had also seen her with the missing girl, Iwona Bejnar, before she was abducted. It had looked like they were friends. The investigators couldn't rule out the possibility that she knew something about the bride's abduction and had been attacked because of it. The police had already checked the Polish nationalist groups, but they all gave each other alibis. There was no point in continuing to dig there.

The report went on. Facebook users were sending out chain posts asking for support for the Red Spider, whose whole bio had been miraculously unearthed as soon as the story hit the papers. Łukasz Polak's paintings were fetching exorbitant prices in galleries.

Romanowska switched the radio off with a grimace and parked her car by the station.

Sasza was waiting for her on the steps. She was holding her sticker-covered laptop and a file of papers, which she offered to the commissioner by way of a greeting. Romanowska tried to find a speck of enthusiasm for the profiler's newest revelations.

'You missed the briefing. It was eight hours ago,' she grumbled and took a glance back, making sure she hadn't left anything Sasza could take an interest in on the back seat of the car. She hoped the psychologist didn't know they had already taken her off the case.

'I had to get my data back,' Sasza said, pointing her chin at the laptop. 'Your man did a good job. Read these.'

Romanowska didn't feel like indulging the profiler any more. She did take the papers, though, and stuck them under her arm, then headed to the watch-room, Sasza hot on her heels. The commissioner nodded to the officer on guard, hovered her card over the scanner and went inside. The security gate clamped shut before Sasza could get through and she sent the officer an irritated look. Romanowska didn't have the courage to look her in the eye; neither, it seemed, did the guard.

'I'm only asking you to take a look at it,' Sasza said. 'I've spent the whole day preparing it.'

'I will, when I find the time,' Romanowska promised unconvincingly and quickly disappeared behind the glass door leading to the 'employees only' zone.

Deflated, Sasza turned away and left the building. Outside again, she lit a cigarette, narrowed her eyes and lifted her face to the sky, taking a moment to bask in the sun. Anything to stop thinking about the case, even for a moment. She heard tyres screeching, and saw an older man wearing glasses getting out of a large SUV. He walked briskly around the vehicle, leaned into the boot, and took out a leather briefcase and a thick paper roll secured with a rubber band, then headed up the steps into the building. For a minute Sasza wondered if this was the famous Hubert Meyer, psychologist. The man didn't look like a police officer. And Doman, who was supposedly friendly with him, was nowhere to be seen. He was also not a journalist – his eyes were too intelligent for that. Besides, he lacked that irritating self-confidence common to all people of the media.

She finished her cigarette and watched the man trying to convince the officer on duty to let him in. He failed. A while later, he came back out and stopped next to Sasza. His expression was sour. He looked disappointed. At least she hadn't been wrong about him. Not entirely, at least. They would have let him in if he was the other profiler. He ignored her completely. So he wasn't a reporter either. And he wasn't a local; she wasn't sure how, but she could tell that without having to look at the licence plate of his SUV.

She looked anyway, out of curiosity. 'You came from Warsaw?' she asked.

'That's my wife's car,' he replied, briefly eyeing her cast. 'Have you been at the demonstration?'

'I'm not sure which one you mean. A lot has been happening here lately. But if you intend to drive back to Warsaw, could I hitch a ride? My car's broken.'

She pointed at the blue Uno in the police car park, still sealed shut. At that moment, a small unit of officers wearing combat uniforms jogged out of the station in formation and hopped into a police van. Its siren blared and the vehicle drove off. A moment later, a couple more officers came out, these in civilian clothes. They seemed in a hurry. Romanowska's son, Błażej, was among them. He passed Sasza without acknowledging her and jumped into an unmarked police car. He was the only high-ranking officer among them. The rest were probably still at the briefing. Maybe Meyer was already inside?

Meanwhile, the man with the glasses had obviously realised that Sasza wasn't police, and visibly lost interest in her. He had an absent look on his face. Suddenly, it became clear to her. He was a scientist. For an instant, she wondered if she should call Professor Abrams.

'I have a few more things to take care of here,' he said, nodded goodbye and headed back to his car. Before he stepped into it, he took off his jacket, folded it inside out and carefully hung it from the backrest of his seat, then placed the paper roll on the back seat. Then he hesitated, looking around, squinting. Eventually he wound down the window and called, 'Can you tell me where the local water tower is?' to Sasza.

'I'll show you,' she replied, and, moving fast, opened the passenger door and sat down in the car before he could protest. Sasza sat back comfortably and smiled. 'So, what do you do for a living?' she asked.

The man still looked shocked. Maybe he was afraid the crazy woman would hijack his car or abduct him. Sasza introduced herself and offered the man a hand. He sighed with visible relief when he heard that she was a police expert. Okay, she might have lied just a little about that. He produced a calling card and passed it to her. His name was Professor Anton Czubajs. It told her exactly nothing. The professor looked offended at her blank face.

'I am a psychotherapist in Belarus,' he explained. 'The best in the region.'

'Oh.' Sasza tried to sound appropriately awed. It didn't work. She tried changing the subject: 'So when are you going home?'

'Maybe this evening,' he said, clearly wanting to sound as non-committal as possible. 'Or maybe I'll stay a while.'

'What brings you here?'

'I'm the best psychotherapist in Podlasie. That's because I'm the *only* psychotherapist in Podlasie. I'm also the only proponent of Lacan's psychoanalysis around.' He laughed hoarsely. Sasza was beginning to regret getting into his car. She wasn't sure which one of the two of them was the weirder: she or Mr Freud here. The regret grew stronger when he added: 'I've developed my own method of graphic representation of intergenerational transfer in families. I call it the genogram. It's a bit like a genealogical tree, you know? It allows me to illustrate the connections and relations between relatives, but focusing on the image of the familial inter-relations that a person inherits from their forebears. This in turn makes it possible to pinpoint the most likely reasons for a given person's standing, their general situation in life. It's a very useful tool in psychotherapy. Especially in my very own approach to it. My theory, you see, is that history is psychoanalysis and vice versa.'

'And who have you treated this way?'

'Forgive me, but I cannot disclose the names of my patients.' But he winked playfully as he said it. Or maybe it was just a nervous tic. 'But most of them are public personas.'

'Everything is public here.' Sasza nodded gravely, which finally elicited a laugh from the professor. Emboldened, she said the first name that came into her head. 'Piotr Bondaruk?'

Czubajs stopped laughing instantly. 'No, but close. His partner. She came to me after they broke up.'

'All Bondaruk's partners except one are dead,' Sasza said. 'So you're talking about Dunia Orzechowska.'

She saw something like respect in the professor's eyes then. He lowered his voice to a whisper. His eyes were wide and wild. Only geniuses or diagnosed psychopaths, in Sasza's experience, got that unhinged look in their eyes.

'I need to speak with someone from the police right now. I have information that can help solve the case in which Mr Bondaruk is a suspect.'

'Bondaruk is *one* of the suspects. He has not been charged with anything.'

'Are you in charge of the investigation?'

'Not any more. I finished my work on it today.'

'Your work can't be finished. Or, if it is, your conclusion is erroneous. You didn't have all the information.'

'Oh, really?'

'Did you know that Bondaruk has only one biological son? His name is Jurek Orzechowski; the ex-fiancé of Iwona Bejnar. She married Bondaruk at his behest.'

This certainly was new information. It completely changed the context of Iwona's kidnapping, as well as giving Dunia Orzechowska a motive.

'I'll take your silence as a "no",' Czubajs said. 'You really should have known that, though. It's no secret.'

'The locals aren't exactly forthcoming.'

'Tell me about it.' The man bobbed his head. 'But I'd advise you to speak with Mr Bondaruk. He won't let me in, but he does like women. But!' he went on. 'I have to clear one thing up. It wasn't Mrs Orzechowska who ordered the genogram. It was Ms Prus. The local psychiatrist and a colleague of mine. I've been her academic supervisor for years.'

'Had she been in a relationship with Bondaruk too?'

'Not at all,' Czubajs replied. 'I have reason to believe that she lied in that matter. Actually, I'm actively working to have her permit taken away.'

'Why?' Sasza asked. She couldn't hide the satisfaction in her voice.

'She is suffering from a severe disorder. She should be treated.'

'What's wrong with her?'

'Forgive me. Doctor–patient confidentiality.'

They drove up to the water tower. The scaffolding had been taken down and the enormous graffiti depicting the Cursed Soldiers was now uncovered, there for all the town to see. There was a group of city officials trying to gain access to the building. They were being cut off by a large group of young men carrying banners reading 'Poland for Poles'.

Marianna Mackiewicz stood in the library doorway surveying the room, which was filling up with a heap of shoes and never-worn suits and coats; books, records and old VHS cassettes. Packed into cardboard boxes lined up against the wall were old porcelain tableware sets and various other bits and bobs including, she saw, a collection of Czechoslovakian crystal saucers, so valued during the communist regime.

In the library, wearing slippers, pyjama bottoms and an old, faded fleece, was Piotr Bondaruk. An hour previously, he had told Marianna she could take anything she wanted for herself. The rest would be thrown out or given to charity. Bondaruk had told her that he didn't want any of his sons to be able to enjoy his things. The housekeeper had been suffering the man's manias and depressions for years; she just promised him solemnly, 'None of it will go to waste,' while thinking that the local hospice would probably take the clothes and shoes at least.

Piotr took a sip of herbal tea and helped himself to another cigarette, breaking off the filter first. The apple pie she had brought in was still on the table, not one piece eaten. He hadn't had a proper meal since his visit to the police station. Despite this, Marianna still laid the table every mealtime, taking the untouched food back to the kitchen later. She didn't have the courage to caution her employer about the dangers of fasting. He wouldn't have listened anyway.

The doorbell rang. Bondaruk had told her not to let anyone in apart from the police officer who checked up on him three times a day. She didn't know the reason for those visits; she wasn't sure if they were about keeping an eye on Mr Bondaruk's activities or keeping him from committing suicide. Marianna thought the whole situation peculiar, to say the least.

Officer Frankowski never even tried to hold a conversation with Marianna. When he arrived, he would sit at the kitchen table and silently eat whatever she gave him. Come to think about it, it wasn't so bad having him around. He ate everything, and for Marianna there wasn't anything worse than having to throw out food.

She still remembered Przemysław Frankowski as a plump and pimply adolescent. Nobody would have suspected the boy would end up in the police. He had been fat and was bullied for it. Other kids had often thought he was slow, as he would never give in to their taunts and fight back. His mother had often had to come to the school principal and make scenes. She had urged her son to defend himself, but Przemysław had kept his stoic demeanour and never did. Maybe he was smarter and more mature than the other children, or maybe he just hadn't known how to fight back. At times, Marianna thought he was like the Buddha. Just sitting there with that benign smile on his round face, observing the others spitting acid at one another. He had a Zen-like calmness about him. Nobody had been able to provoke him, not even Marianna's own son Artur, with whom he had had to share a school desk and who had been Jah-Jah's most vocal tormentor.

Przemek had only acquired that nickname a lot later, when he and Artur had finally buried the hatchet and had started to go to the gym together and formed a reggae band with some friends. They had both worn their hair in dreadlocks and worn colourful clothes that Marianna sewed for them herself. She had suspected they smoked weed. The boys' friendship had blossomed and they had become inseparable. Later they had applied to law school together, but only Artur had passed the exams. Frankowski's parents had had no money to bribe the university authorities like Marianna had done. She had started working for Bondaruk by then and he had lent her a large sum of money and helped Artur with his legal career. Marianna had used some of the money to pay for a thanksgiving service at the local church and had promised herself and God she'd stay loyal to her benefactor for the rest of her life. She simply had to make sure her Artur achieved more than her late husband, who had been just one of many machine technicians at the lumber mill.

Artur had never known about the bribes, though it wasn't much of a secret in town. In his misplaced confidence, he still believed he had passed his exams without any help. Jah-Jah had tried applying to law school three more times, even stooping so low as to try his luck with exams at the local branch of the University of Warsaw, which he saw as beneath him. He never passed. Finally he settled on joining the militia. He had harboured something of an envious grudge against Artur, and had largely cut ties with him; they barely saw each other nowadays. Artur still sometimes mentioned Przemek though and clearly missed their friendship. But Marianna knew the situation wouldn't change; Jah-Jah hated it when other people beat him to something. She understood that about him. She even had some admiration for it.

She could have quit her job at Bondaruk's house – Artur had suggested she do so, numerous times – but she dug in her heels and stubbornly clung to it.

'If I leave, who will take care of him?' she asked Artur, who was now a respected lawyer. Her son was still embarrassed that his mother was a simple housekeeper, but she didn't care. 'Mr Bondaruk has no one but me. On his deathbed, there will be nobody to bring him a glass of water. His evil sons are only waiting for their inheritance. They care about nothing else. They can't wait for him to pass away.'

One day, Artur told his mother that Bondaruk's sons were in fact his clients. He was currently in the process of preparing a masterful legal manoeuvre to undermine Bondaruk's credibility. It would make him, in the eyes of the locals, not much more than an impoverished lunatic. Hearing this, Marianna pleaded for her son to rethink his decision. He refused. For the next week she cooked only the best meals for her benefactor: *gołąbki,* potato *babka* and soufflé. She couldn't look him in the eye and, after a while, he asked her what was the matter. She told him the truth. His only response was to laugh bitterly and give her a few days off. She went to her son, ready for a fight.

'A man who spends his entire life building an empire must have enemies,' was all Artur said in reply. He mocked her for her 'good heart'.

It never occurred to him that his mother was simply lonely, like Bondaruk. Since his divorce from Magdalena Prus, Artur was living the high life, while Marianna had never even thought about another relationship after her husband had died. Taking care of Piotr had always given her a sense of security, as well as a use for her time. In a way, the two had grown close, though they never talked about anything personal and had never been physically close.

'If your dear employer loved a person instead of just his money, he wouldn't have spent his life alone in that enormous mansion of his,' Artur had said. 'Remember, Mum, success is the domain of people who are determined, inquisitive and ruthless. Intellectual faculties and personal charm are nothing but garnish. The road to the very top is full of obstacles and you have to be a special kind of person to overcome those. It's always easier to climb up when you have other people's backs to plant your feet on. And it's even easier when stepping on others gives you a boner. And that sly fucker definitely gets off on hurting other people. That's my take on him, anyway.'

Marianna hadn't wanted to listen any more. She had never heard a single bad word from Mr Bondaruk, not for all these years. He had always been straight with her. And the few times when she had asked him for help, support or advice, he had always come through for her. People only considered her influential in the town because of Bondaruk's support; she was just a simple woman from nowhere. Piotr, on the other hand, had always had his network of connections, most of them among the ruling elite. He never wanted anything in return from Marianna. She believed he was a good man. She had never bought into all the things people said about him. Murderer, wife-killer, drunkard and thief? No. She had tried considering those accusations, but always ended up taking Bondaruk's side. She knew him to be none of those things. And even if all the women whom he had ever invited into his life had disappeared in mysterious circumstances, in Marianna's opinion they deserved it. For her, they were always intruders, vampires sucking her benefactor dry.

She went to the front door and peered through the peephole. She frowned. It wasn't the police officer. It was Dunia Orzechowska. The whisperer hadn't visited Mr Bondaruk for years. In fact, Marianna hadn't seen 'Demented Dunia', as people called her, around town for a long time. There was another person with her, standing a step behind like a shadow. It was the mute, Alla. Her visits meant the house had to be thoroughly aired afterwards.

Marianna hesitated. The doorbell rang again and was followed by an impatient knocking. Bondaruk didn't call out to her to answer it. Well, if he wasn't reacting, Marianna would do the same. She went to the kitchen to get on with dinner and pretended she wasn't there.

The doorbell and the knocking fell silent.

'Dinner will be ready in five minutes!' she called. When Mr Bondaruk didn't deign to respond, she went to the library and added: 'It was your friends Alla and Dunia Orzechowska at the door.'

Bondaruk jumped to his feet and started to frantically stuff some papers back into a suitcase. That was surprising; he had never tried to hide anything from Marianna before, but now he looked as if he had finally found what he'd been looking for and didn't want her to see what that was. She had cleaned his library hundreds of times, and had moved that old suitcase around even more. Once or twice she had even taken a peek inside. Aside from some Russian newspapers and a collection of even older magazines, she could see nothing of value in it.

'Call them back and set the table for three,' Bondaruk ordered.

He was trying to get rid of her. Marianna nodded, withdrew and went briskly to the main door. The two women were almost off the premises, but when they heard the door opening, Alla turned round with an expectant stare. Dunia also turned and, rather than saying anything, glared at Marianna. They had never liked each other. But Marianna knew how to be diplomatic.

'Mr Bondaruk asks if you would have dinner with him,' she said coolly and went back inside, leaving the door open.

When she emerged from the kitchen sometime later, carrying the tureen, home-made bread, and cutlery for three, the two were waiting in the hallway. Bondaruk was nowhere to be seen and the door to the library was closed, but they could all hear heavy items landing on the floor and being shuffled around. She led the women to the dining room.

Dunia sat at the head of the table. Alla remained standing at the door. She was perfectly still and silent. Like a Sphinx. Marianna had a hard time breathing, with the reek the woman exuded. Why couldn't she just take a bath? And more importantly, what did Mr Bondaruk see in her? Actually, she didn't want to know. She had seen a lot in that house. Too much to be able to sleep soundly most of the time.

'We'll be quick,' Dunia said. 'And thank you for your offer, but we've already eaten.'

Marianna made no attempt to remove the three lots of cutlery.

'Maybe you'll take some tea? Coffee?'

Dunia shoved a hand into her pocket and took out a little fabric bag. She passed it to Marianna. 'Boil it and let it stand for five minutes. Then pour it though a strainer. Keep the leaves. You might need them. They're good for women our age. Calms your nerves and makes your hair stronger.'

'Thank you,' Marianna muttered, keeping her irritation in check. She looked way younger than those two witches. 'That's very kind of you.'

Dunia did not reply, just smiled weakly, laced her fingers and waited. Piotr appeared at the door. He was still in his dusty pyjamas. He hadn't combed his hair. He motioned for Dunia to come with him, and she obliged. Marianna was staring after them when:

'I'll have a coffee,' said Alla out of the blue. Her voice was coarse and shaky. 'Milk and sugar, if it's not too much.'

Marianna nearly dropped the tureen lid in shock. Since she had moved into town, she had never, ever heard Alla utter a single word. Everyone thought she was mute. In fact, some people – including Marianna – assumed that if she was mute, she was probably also deaf, and gossiped in her presence. They even mocked Alla herself. Marianna tried desperately to think whether she had ever spilled too much when the old woman was in earshot. She felt deeply embarrassed. She blushed like a schoolgirl.

'Is there a problem?' Alla asked.

'No, not at all.' Marianna quickly turned on her heel and headed for the kitchen.

On her way, she passed the open door of the library and slowed down. Dunia was standing with Mr Bondaruk, who was pointing at the suitcase. It now, Marianna saw, contained a new set of papers. Documents in grey files, the covers all featuring his handwriting.

'Why are you showing me this?' Dunia asked, watching as Piotr walked over to close the library door. They hadn't been in such a situation for years, the two of them alone together.

'They're not safe here any more,' Piotr said.

'I can't take them.' Dunia's hands were shaking. She had come all the way here on foot. Her worn boots were spattered with mud and she felt drained; she could barely keep her balance. 'It's too much of a responsibility.'

Piotr offered her a chair. 'I could have sent a car for you,' he said. Gratefully she took a seat, and said: 'It's too conspicuous. Jah-Jah would have seen it, or heard about it. I hate him. You know why.'

'Did he go to Nesteruk?'

Dunia shrugged. 'Kola won't come. We're too old to play soldiers, Petya. Find someone young. Someone with some fight still in them.'

'Has your son been found?'

She shook her head. Her lips trembled. Her face grew tense. It took all her strength to hide her distress. She still wanted to believe it would all end happily.

'How about Iwona?' Bondaruk asked, his voice shaky.

'No news is good news.'

'You know I'm doing it for us. For him.'

She kept silent for a while. Finally, she took a deep breath and said: 'I never wanted anything from you.'

'That was a mistake. Mine as well as yours. You know how much I regret everything that happened.'

She didn't respond, just shrugged.

Piotr sat down next to her. For a minute they just looked at each other – two elderly people who had lost at the game of life. There was no hope for them any more. He broke eye contact first. She had never before seen him defeated but, in this moment, he didn't resemble the daredevil she had once loved. Now, she only pitied him. She put a hand on his shoulder and he placed his own hand over it. His fingers were deathly cold. Dunia shivered and took back her hand.

It wasn't hard for him to read her thoughts. She loathed him. For the briefest instant he felt a spark of anger, but he let it go. He knew she had never forgiven him, and that she would never again learn to trust him. He'd had to let her go. He had made himself let her go. Not without a lot of sacrifices and a good fight, but he had finally done it. But he was still the only one who knew why Dunia had become a recluse and lost contact with reality, escaping into her world of strange rituals and magic.

'Take it to the police.' She pointed her chin at the suitcase, then stood up and withdrew to a safe distance. Her breath was raspy. The farther she was from Piotr, the calmer she felt.

'They will destroy it.' He shook his head. 'They'll do everything in their power to bury it. Do you know what's in there?'

He unzipped the suitcase. She turned away. 'I don't want to see it. I don't want to!'

'So, nothing has changed.'

'Burn it.'

'No!' It was his turn for an outburst. 'If this disappears, I'm the first one to die.'

'You're already dead. You don't have much time.'

He hung his head. She was right. 'It wasn't supposed to be like this.'

'It is what it is,' she said. 'Is this all? Did you only want to see me because of those old papers?'

He slowly shook his head, defeated. 'This is my life. Our life. Our son's life. And the lives of the generations to come. They have the right to know the truth.'

'Truth,' she scoffed, suddenly bristling. 'Whose truth? Yours or the politicians'? I thought you wanted to show me your testament. So he'll at least be able to regain his honour.'

'You've already buried me,' he growled.

'I buried myself. A long time ago. I'm not afraid any more. And I have one piece of advice for you too: make peace with God. You don't know when your time will come. You're not twenty any more.'

'So you don't want my treasure?' He laughed bitterly and opened the lid, ignoring her protestations. He pulled out one of the files. It was labelled 'Twig'. An alias of one of the secret collaborators from the previous regime. There were a lot more of those in the suitcase. 'This is worth a fortune.'

'It would be blood money.'

'All money is blood money.'

'Neither I nor my son would stoop so low as to deal in blackmail. Frankly, I'm astonished you're still keeping those papers. I don't think they would even interest the police – or anyone else for that matter. Better tell the truth. Show them Stepan's grave. Admit what you've done. Maybe you'd feel better about yourself.'

He stared at her in disbelief. 'Why don't you do it then?' he asked, a smile blooming on his face.

'It doesn't matter to me.'

'So I am to take this on myself?'

She stayed silent. He closed the suitcase and slid it back into hiding under a chair. There was deep disappointment on his face. He had wanted her to finally set him free. To redeem him. But it was just wishful thinking. He had been dealing with this for years and he couldn't forgive himself; why should he expect her to do it? What had he been thinking? Of course Dunia wouldn't want to do it. She had already sacrificed too much. She knew everything and had kept it to herself. If he decided to confess, she would help him, he didn't doubt that; but admitting his sins was just too difficult. That was because this trove of secrets had one more thing inside it. Another secret. One that he had never told anyone. Not even the love of his life. Neither of them had ever talked about it. Neither of them could be sure how the other would react. Or what would happen when the truth was eventually allowed to be spoken.

'Irma,' Dunia said quietly. 'She's alive.'

Piotr slowly shook his head. He was clearly not sure if he had heard correctly.

'It wasn't your fault,' she added quickly.

His face softened in profound relief. His eyes watered. She didn't get to finish. An instant later, they were both crying. 'Kola and I helped save her,' she said.

He stepped forward and embraced her. Her body was rigid, stiff. Her lips formed a thin line. She only suffered his touch for a short while, then squirmed free.

'She's using a different name now and she lives right here. I know for certain that she's all right.'

He looked at her pleadingly.

'I'll never tell you her new name.' She shook her head. 'You don't need to know. But don't blame yourself. We saved her. So, do with that what you will. Don't let the skeleton out of the closet. Nobody needs to dig up the past. We're all safe from it. The only person it can still harm is you.'

Bondaruk collapsed back in his chair and hid his face in his hands. When he raised his eyes again, he was smiling shyly.

'What would you do in my place?'

Dunia shrugged and smoothed down her long skirt. She tied her headscarf under her chin. For a moment, he could see her white hair. It was greasy and thin. Barely more than a few strands left. For a moment, he felt déjà vu. He recalled her taking just such a scarf off, and braiding her thick, long hair, wrapping it around her head.

'There're more and more cases like this being unearthed now.' She rubbed at her wrinkled eyelids. Her skin was waxen, thin and crumpled like parchment. It used to be alabaster white. 'The young will understand. National identity is a thing people need now. Read the papers, watch the TV. The young are taking to the streets, bearing banners. We couldn't do that. Just look around. The times have changed.'

'You don't have the slightest idea how wrong you are,' he replied and laughed out loud, only to suddenly grow sullen again. 'Who will believe me? Who will believe old Four-Eyes, a wife-killer and a well-known profiteer?'

'Then talk to him,' she said, passion returning. 'You know him! You have all kinds of dirt on him.'

'My supervising officer is not the issue. The real problem is the old guard still in power here. As soon as they catch on that I have dirt on them, all hell will break loose. It will be like opening Pandora's box. They'll rip me apart. And I'll drag you and Kola down to the bottom with me. I know how this will end.' He grew silent again.

They both knew what he wanted to say.

'So destroy it,' she said. 'For your own good. You'll pay off who you can, and the rest will forget. People forget.'

'Not the locals.'

'Belarusians do remember, but they never tell.' She got up and made herself approach him. She patted him on the back. Like a dog. 'Go with God, Petya.'

Romanowska unfurled the paper file. At the top was the profile of the unidentified offender. Only the first few pages had text on and the rest was blank. She looked through the file again, lifting the pages and flipping them back and forward, finally tossing them back to the desk. As she did, she spotted something on the back of one page. 'BHA 3456'. It was written in pencil, barely visible. She called Sasza Załuska.

'What the hell is wrong with you?' she hissed. 'Bondaruk's car's licence number is in the files. Is that some kind of a joke?'

'It was the only thing I knew would make you call me,' Sasza replied coolly.

Romanowska wasn't sure how to play this. If she did it by the book, this conversation would be a way for her to save face. The pro-filer was practically asking for dismissal on disciplinary grounds. All Romanowska had to do was round up everything they had on her: her illegal gun, theft of evidence from a crime scene and being the first person at each of the crime scenes, to name just a few. Plus driving without a licence. If the commissioner told her superiors, Sasza would never again work for the police. She wouldn't even get a job as a security guard at a supermarket. She would have to forget about profiling work too. Maybe some kind of second-rate detective agency would employ her one day. But only the kind whose personnel are the dregs of the police. In the short term, though, Sasza would have to leave the country. Spend some time doing research somewhere abroad and keeping her mouth shut about what had happened here. Just like in Łukasz Polak's case. She had run away and kept quiet, and the case had been swept under the rug.

'You're giving me no choice,' Romanowska said. 'I'll show this report to the prosecutor. You're fucked. I'm done playing games.' She added, 'And leave your gun at the station.'

'Not going to happen,' Sasza replied and then addressed someone else, probably standing next to her and listening in on the conversation. Romanowska could hear them talking. 'It's the local commissioner,' Sasza said to the other person. 'You've been looking for her, right, Professor? She's a bit nervous.'

Who was Sasza talking to? Romanowska wondered. For a moment she was afraid it was one of the other high-ranking officers. Or maybe the prosecutor herself? But her doubts were dispelled a moment later.

'Professor Anton Czubajs wanted to see you earlier,' Sasza began, her voice impassive. 'He's got some interesting hypotheses about your current predicament. If you're not interested, he won't press further. We have a lot of eager listeners here. Mostly journalists. They'll be more than happy to hear us out. But I wager you wouldn't be too thrilled if you learned what we've discovered from the media.'

'Who?' Romanowska asked, puzzled. 'What professor? What are you talking about?'

In response, both Sasza and the man listening in laughed. Then, a moment of companionable banter at the commissioner's expense. 'Nah, that's not anything out of the ordinary. She's just like that. But she's okay, really. Trust me. She's saved my arse a couple times.'

After a while, Sasza put the mobile to her ear again. 'History is psychoanalysis and psychoanalysis is history,' she said. 'That's what Professor Czubajs says.' She paused. 'Anyway, I did start working on the profile but it was a lost cause. I didn't have enough info. You haven't told me everything. In fact, I'm starting to believe you haven't actually given me anything of value. Even the numbers in the files were wrong. To be honest, I'm a bit disappointed in myself. I should have figured this out earlier.'

Romanowska saw red, but managed to reply. 'What on earth do you mean?'

'The files you gave me lacked even a single transcript from Bondaruk's interrogations. They were left out of all the cases. Also, you didn't tell me that Stepan, Dunia Orzechowska's husband who went missing in the seventies, was a Security Service agent tasked with recruiting union dissenters at the lumber mill as secret informers. He mainly dealt with Poles. And Bondaruk was a Pole. An educated engineer, working part-time at the newspaper as a Party mouthpiece. And he didn't come here looking for work, but out of love for a woman. And what's even more interesting is that he was fired from his journalist job and transferred out of town. But there's more. Right before Stepan went missing, Bondaruk had been employed as the chairman of the union, a so-called cultural and educational instructor, and as soon as the previous lumber mill director vanished, he came up with a design for a lumber dryer that revolutionised the industry. He began climbing the corporate ladder at an unprecedented pace. Not even a year later, he took Orzechowski's place at the top.'

Romanowska only just stopped herself from asking how Sasza knew this. The reports she had given her – as Sasza had realised – glossed over those facts. The knowledge was strictly off limits. Unless she had got it from some rumourmonger. But who? Nobody would be that stupid, surely? People knew that some things were meant to stay hidden.

'How does that tie in with our case?' she asked, trying to sound indifferent.

'On a fundamental level,' Sasza replied. 'History has a way of leaking down to younger generations. In this way, people's psychological profiles are irredeemably altered. It's a bit like if you bury radioactive waste. You can't see it, and nobody remembers, but it's still there. And the ground gets contaminated.'

'The fuck are you babbling on about?' Romanowska lost it now. Sasza didn't let her interrupt, though.

'We can say that all the cases are a consequence of the original one. The vanishing, or rather the elimination, of Stepan. You know how that went, don't you? Like any other botched job during the regime. The key to all the cases is this: a guy goes missing. He's a Security Service agent and communist dignitary, openly gay and in a relationship with a local priest. We have to get to the bottom of that first, if we want to solve the rest of the cases. We all leave imprints, so to speak, which determine our thought patterns and actions. What keeps happening in your little shithole of a town, the vanishings of Bondaruk's lovers – excluding Danka, that's an entirely separate case – stems from the man's communist activity. Professor Czubajs has done his homework, you know. Bondaruk wasn't officially an agent, but he still might have been a secret collaborator. In fact, everything points to that being the case. And it seems he was one of their best. What's more, we can't rule out the possibility that he's still under supervision by his handler from those days. Deals like that don't just disappear, even when a regime falls. They just carry on discreetly. But, as you've already told me, discretion is people's forte around here, isn't it? Nobody ever says anything. You're not an exception. You know a lot more than you've let on.'

'Hold your horses,' Romanowska cut in. 'Is there anything more to what you're saying than the wild theories of a wacky old historian?'

'There might be, if you help me,' Sasza replied, still keeping her composure. 'I'm surprised you haven't dug up Bondaruk's backyard or that private piece of forest of his in search of the bodies. Maybe that's where you'll find them. Or maybe that's where he keeps the dirt he has on everybody, using it to blackmail half of the town to keep their mouths shut—'

'You don't know what you're saying.' Romanowska didn't let Sasza finish this time. 'We have dug up his land. No bones. No documents. At least, no documents of that kind.'

'You don't need a profiler here at all,' Sasza said. 'Who you need is a single law-abiding investigator who won't shit his pants at the mention of interrogating Bondaruk. Your case is as simple as it gets. He didn't off any of those women. They were killed to keep him in line. But that would mean admitting that the Council of the Righteous you've mentioned, thinking I'd take it as a joke, is real.

Besides, if you don't get your shit together, you'll have a regular war on your hands. Polish and Belarusian skinheads are both only too eager to fuck your town up. If I were you, I'd get that GPR from Białystok right away.'

'Thanks for the advice.' Romanowska snorted. 'I'll make sure to pass on your drunken blather to my superiors. You want that?'

'I'm not sure whether I'm talking with the right person any more,' Sasza said gravely. Was she recording this conversation, Romanowska suddenly thought? She decided to watch her words very carefully from now on. Maybe she had been underestimating the profiler after all. She did let her continue though. She had to know what else the woman had dug up.

'I don't know whose side you're on,' Sasza was saying. 'But if it's mine, take me to Bondaruk and let's question him together. So you don't have any more doubts about my competence and motivation.'

'He won't talk,' Romanowska said. 'We've tried.'

'Let me try. I have my means.'

'A lot of people smarter and stronger than you have tried and failed.'

'The situation has changed,' Sasza said, still unfazed. 'He knows he's about to die. And he can't run.'

'How can you be so sure?'

'Bożena Bejnar's telephone bills. The woman talked to Quack yesterday. His mobile is in Hajnówka. Not Mexico or Arizona, where you probably wish he was. And why don't you arrest the Bison boys? Why not fill your cell block with suspects? You're doing nothing.'

'We have nothing on them. We can't take them in,' the commissioner retorted and added, just in case she was being recorded: 'We're only a local station. Call Doman. Maybe he'll believe you.'

Sasza laughed bitterly. 'He's not taking my calls. But I'm still digging. I'll do your job for you, don't worry. That data recovery guy, Kuba, used to work for one of the telecom companies. He checked some stuff for me. Didn't take him long. It was all below the counter, of course, so we won't be able to use it in court, but I still learned some really interesting things. Did you know that the hacker attack on my laptop came from the station? The IP address matches. Care to explain?'

Romanowska was temporarily lost for words. 'I need to go to the briefing now,' she managed.

'If you're on my side, postpone it,' Sasza barked. 'Or even better, take Meyer with you. If he's so good, he should know how important it is to collect victimological data. I'm a bit worried that he missed it. If he's received the same papers as me, you might as well flush his expertise down the loo. Even if he really is a genius, you can't polish a turd, as my ex-boss used to say. By the way, I've found Iwona Bejnar's kidnapper's outfit. The balaclava and wedding suit were stuffed into the sleeve of Łukasz Polak's work clothes. They're in my boot now. Professionally secured. I wanted to tell you that before, but you wouldn't let me into the station.'

'Why haven't you called in forensics? Are you out of your mind?' Romanowska exclaimed.

'Because Jah-Jah has already done it,' Sasza said. 'I heard they've finished collecting samples.'

'Nobody told me.'

'Well, then talk to your husband and agree on a single version,' Sasza replied and added: 'If you're still going to use me as a smoke-screen, I'll stir up so much shit you might as well start packing your things right away.'

'Are you threatening me?'

'I'd call it "asking for support",' Sasza purred. 'Because I'm not letting it go. You can be sure of that. You've got me into this, and I've gone too far to turn back now.'

Romanowska saw her second line light blinking. Someone else was trying to call her.

'I'll get back to you,' she said and switched the connections. It was Doman.

'The bitten girl woke up,' he announced. 'Told us where Iwona Bejnar has been hiding. I sent a team to the old Kosiek house. It's by the Mazury housing project. The old shack with an orchard, right in the middle of the place.'

'I thought that was abandoned.'

'We all did. The perfect hiding spot. No place better than right under our noses,' Doman admitted. 'Anyway, we have her.'

'Alive?'

'Never been better,' he replied. 'Not even a scratch on her. She was in the middle of pressing fresh apple juice when the SWAT team went in. Call the spokesman. We've done it. Tell Jah-Jah he can pop the champagne.'

'Good job. Get her questioned,' Romanowska ordered. 'We'll pin the mental girl on her even more mental brother and then we're out of the woods. Good job this one will actually be done by the book. The phone charger fits, we found the profiler's daughter's photo in his room, so now all we need is to get a match on the teeth imprint. Tell Saczko to get his papers in order. We might need them.'

'Already done that,' Doman said. 'And the Bejnar girl? She was already packed and ready to leave. Guess what we found in her things. Fifty grand in cash. The same amount Bondaruk offered for her head. I'm going to level with you here – this stinks. She was more scared about her apple juice spoiling than about our team barging in. And she keeps asking about Quack. The little fucker's vanished like a fart in the wind. I sent in forensics to comb through the premises. I'll let you know if they find anything.' He paused. 'But tell me, don't you want to oversee all this personally? Don't you want to know why the girl ran away from Bluebeard?'

'Believe me, I do, but first I need to address an issue with our problematic profiler.'

'Oh, give me a break. There's no body, so we might as well close the case. Let the ginger bitch run home. I don't want to see her ever again.'

'I'm afraid you'll change your mind when you hear what I have to say,' Romanowska retorted coldly, then paused for effect. It worked; Doman was quiet. 'Załuska is digging up old stuff,' Romanowska went on. 'She latched on to Orzechowski's vanishing. Found some egghead looking for attention. They're jabbering about Security Service agents and old communists. I don't know what they're on to, but it looks like they've pooled efforts with the nationalists. Maybe they got some papers from the IPN. I don't have a clue, really. But it looks serious.'

'They're small fry. Gaweł will deal with them. What the mayor can't do, the starost will handle.'

'Listen to me. I think the profiler will get us in trouble. Seems like it's her speciality,' Romanowska said. 'She's an outsider. She doesn't know or care about the rules. I underestimated her.'

'Do what you think is best.' Doman brushed her off. 'All I care about is that the papers are clean.'

'They will be,' the commissioner sighed. 'As always.'

'Okay. I'm going to handle Iwona Bejnar now. Give the boys the green light to bring in her mum and the Bison boys. I've been waiting for this day for years. I feel like I've won the lottery now.'

'Don't overdo it with the celebrations, but put on a show for the journos.'

'You can count on that. It's going to be spectacular. I'll even let them take photos inside. Let the leeches have some fun too.'

'Hey, and don't let anyone steal your glory. Don't give this over to the spokesman.'

'I'm too smart for that, love.'

Romanowska hung up, issued the orders and headed to her car. She took her Glock with her.

'Meet me in five at the lumber mill,' she said, switching the phone back to the line Sasza was waiting on.

'I'm already at Bondaruk's house,' the profiler replied. 'Get a move on. There're some groupies loitering about. Sixty plus, by the looks of it. One of them is the witch.'

'Best he can afford right now,' Romanowska managed. Instead of going to Bondaruk's house, she took a turn to Red Pig Town, the local name for the exclusive red-brick residential project where all the town officials lived, including the current and ex-mayors. Romanowska had a flat there too. She knocked on her neighbour's door. The starost's daughter opened it.

'Hi, Gosia. Is your dad home?'

She slipped into the flat without waiting for a reply. The daughter was trying to shush her, whispering that she had just managed to get her newborn to sleep. Romanowska didn't care. She raised her voice so the starost could hear her.

'I have some really important business. Four-Eyes is making a fuss.'

Adam Gaweł appeared immediately, wearing a bathrobe and slippers, and ushered her into the living room.

'I'm not in the mood, Krysia.' He let out a deep yawn. 'Keep it down unless you want to wake up my grandson. I spent an hour getting him to sleep.'

'I need a budget right away,' the commissioner said flatly. 'The profiler from Gdańsk is sniffing around Bondaruk. And the man's close to breaking.'

The starost didn't respond, so Romanowska added, 'He's going to give us away.'

'How much?'

'She won't take a bribe. It's for me. Let's say . . . thirty. Polish złoty of course. Not euros.'

'Who are you going to send after her?'

'I'll deal with it officially.' She shrugged and smiled, recalling the painting Błażej had mistakenly included among the case documents. It would be the perfect piece of evidence in their second case – the murder of Danka from Ciszynia. By the time Sasza managed to clear her name, if she did so at all, it would be too late. Nobody would take her story seriously. A witness has to be credible, and the profiler had done the best she could to look suspicious. Plus, there was the issue of the unlicensed gun. She wouldn't get away. They had her car impounded. There was a lot of dirt on the woman. It would be enough. She wouldn't be able to get back up after this.

'Good,' the starost commended her. 'So, where's the problem?'

'There isn't one,' Romanowska said. 'It's only that my job isn't entirely secure yet. Before I start the procedure and call the prosecutor, I'd like to be sure you won't swap me for Jah-Jah. And I'm talking about a long-term deal. Are we clear?'

'You're putting me in a difficult position. You know I've promised him that job.'

'A prudent businessman like you has to take difficult decisions. Make the right choices,' she offered.

'Wouldn't you rather be a part of the Council? The elections are coming. You'll sit around some boring meetings and then we'll make you mayor. You'll have my support. Plus, I can get you some Treasury bonds.'

Romanowska's jaw dropped. 'I . . . hadn't thought about it.'

'You'll cut some ribbons here and there, make some speeches and have a lot of free time,' he continued. 'And the nationalists will

be happy with their first Polish mayor. You could run with the con-
servatives. You don't have anything against throwing some shit at a
few Belarusians, do you? You know – show your teeth a bit. Like a
fighting dog.'

'Yeah, I can do that.'

'Good.' He patted her on the back. 'You'll make a great polit-
ician. We'll kill two birds with one stone. Take the wind out of the
anti-communist underground's sails.'

Romanowska's mobile rang. She excused herself and stepped
out into the hallway to take the call. It was Sasza again.

'You can start without me,' the commissioner told her. 'Something's delayed me.'

'You sure?' Sasza asked. 'A while ago those two women left and
Jah-Jah went inside. I'd prefer to talk to Bondaruk without him. You
think that's possible?'

'Sure, if you manage to get rid of Jah-Jah,' Romanowska said
sweetly. 'You can tell him you're acting on my orders. I'll confirm
it. If you get something from him, let me know at once. Meanwhile,
I'll send a team to search the lumber mill,' she lied.

'Great! That's what I was counting on.' Sasza thanked Romanowska profusely and hung up.

'What search?' The starost loomed up behind Romanowska.

'Just something to keep the profiler away for a while.' She smiled
charmingly. 'You know what? I've thought this through. The Swiss
franc went up, we have a hell of a case of inflation. The crisis is just
around the corner. This new offer of yours is more risky. In a word,
I want a hundred now. And five grand up front for ongoing operations. After all, I need to look good for the elections. And the spa
doesn't do discounts. So, what will it be, Agent Giewont?'

The starost's only response was a threatening glare.

One of the files was labelled 'Supervising Officer: <GIEWONT>'.
Sasza opened the Security Service agent's record. A moment later,
she slammed it shut. Adam Gaweł, the starost, might not be in
there under that name, but she already knew he had been the man
responsible for the operations of the Security Service in Hajnówka
for decades. He had held on to his position until the unit was finally
disbanded and its headquarters turned into a kindergarten. A short

while later, Gaweł had become the starost. Sasza couldn't wait to read the whole thing, but first she wanted to hear out the confession of Piotr Bondaruk, or Secret Collaborator Stach.

They had been talking for what must have been hours, the passage of time only showing in the number of empty coffee cups and apple pie plates on the table and the fact that the sun had set. Piotr had told Marianna to stay away from his office while he and Sasza were in there, instead ordering the housekeeper to leave them a flask of hot water, some teabags and a jar of instant coffee. About three cups ago, he had called her and told her she could have the rest of the evening off. Jah-Jah had not returned and neither Romanowska, nor any of the forensic technicians the commissioner had been supposed to send, had turned up. Sasza wasn't thinking about that at the moment, though. Bondaruk's story was so shocking, it overshadowed anything else.

'Will you have a drink with me?' Bondaruk asked. Sasza shook her head. Piotr didn't bother pouring glasses for himself, instead chugging the Żołądkowa Gorzka vodka straight from its golden bottle.

'So that's my story, Your Honour,' he concluded with an apologetic smile. 'I don't know who cleaned up my mess. I came to at the hospital, connected to an IV and a catheter and with my head wrapped in bandages. I'd lost more than three litres of blood. Nobody came to question me afterwards. I never even had to visit the police station to make a statement. But, some time later, the town exploded with the news that two pederasts had gone missing. That's what we used to call homosexuals back then, by the way. Pederasts. They were both public figures, so Hajnówka was abuzz with the news. With time, the whole thing was forgotten, though, and a year later I was in charge of the lumber mill.'

'The case has already expired, but we should make this public,' Sasza interjected. She swallowed drily and shot a glance at Bondaruk's crotch. How was it possible that he'd had three more sons later? She decided not to ask for now. 'The family needs to know where he is buried.'

'The only family Stepan had was his wife,' Piotr retorted bitterly. 'And she doesn't even want to remember his name. With that scandal the Security Service had fabricated, people started shunning her. Though that he had been a homosexual was at least true. Dunia knew that when she married him. That was the deal. They didn't have to forge any papers. Anyway, it ended up the way you saw. Dunia lives as a recluse now. If you ask me, she's coping pretty well. She is the only person who doesn't care if I make my story public. I spoke to her today.'

'I saw her leaving.'

He nodded. 'Only she didn't want to pay for keeping the thing silent, so I had to protect her. I promised to secure her son, Jurek.' He hesitated. 'My son too. He's my only rightful heir. At first, she didn't want to hear it. She wanted to keep him away from it all, and for me to change my last will. But that didn't work out. I made an attempt before my wedding with Iwona. Now I know my other three sons will do anything in their power to discredit any document that disinherits them. They were adopted, all three,' he explained. 'I had no choice. I had my orders. And it's not like they have it bad. When I die, they'll still be the richest people in town. I know they're itching to get more of my money though. I've done good by them, in memory of their mothers, even though we've never been close. It's a dog-eat-dog family, you might say. And a young dog will always prevail over an old one. That's just the way it is. I don't blame them. They know nothing. At least, I believe they don't.'

'Why didn't Dunia want to talk about it to me?'

'Would you have? Those are old, painful stories. And Dunia lived through the war, half a century of communism, and then capitalism when it was new and lawless. It's hard for her to find a place in the modern world. She doesn't understand that the past isn't only a memory.'

'The past projects on the present and the future,' Sasza agreed.

Piotr smiled. 'Have I told you you're a very wise woman?'

'Several times.'

'That's good,' he said, nodding, and added, 'Dunia only wants to be left alone. Like me.'

'But you're talking to me.'

Bondaruk pointed to the suitcase full of documents. 'Everything's in there. All the answers to all your questions. All the hopes and all the solutions.'

Sasza had already scanned through the papers that had kept Bondaruk untouchable for decades. The files only contained the aliases of ex-collaborators of the communist secret police, not their real names, but between them and Piotr explaining things, she'd easily worked out who was who in town and how they'd got to where they were. Some, like the starost, most of the older police officers from the local and central station, and a lot of business-men, like the owner of the TV station, the meat processing plant guy, Mikołaj Nesteruk, an erstwhile friend of Bondaruk's – the first one to betray him – were particularly easy to expose. They had all received large sums from the Ministry of Internal Affairs on top of their official income. They were legally employed as secret Security Service informers. Still. Decades after the body had been formally dismantled. And they all still held the power in town. Hajnówka was still ruled by ex-communists. They had just changed their bios and found new professions, and took good care that nothing of their shameful past would ever surface. Who knew, knew. The rest understood nothing, and it would stay that way. They didn't care about anything. Except money, of course.

But that was becoming a problem for the provincial oligarchs. The town had lost its lustre, no longer the promised land for the socially ambitious that it had been. Lumber was getting scarce, and so was wild game. Hajnówka was slowly but surely declining. The more of a backwater the town was becoming, the more everyone wanted to sustain the folk myth of tolerance for multiculturalism and the friendship between Catholics and Orthodox. The reality was different, though, and Sasza already knew that. Nationalist ideologies were in full bloom.

The young generation yearned for 'purity'. They based their misbegotten pride on the origins of their ancestors. Either Polish or Belarusian. Youth needed segregation. Self-determination. But they would understand nothing if they wouldn't reach deeper. And what really mattered had happened only half a century ago. Sasza knew that the elders couldn't keep such a ticking bomb under the radar for much longer. The fuse had been lit a long time ago and the time of explosion was nearing.

'And I can just take these papers?' Sasza asked.

'Well, without them, nobody would believe you.'

'I need to know where Stepan and the priest are buried too,' she said. 'I need to be able to go ahead with the exhumation and clear the case once and for all.'

Bondaruk studied the bottom of the vodka bottle for a while. It had been empty for the last fifteen minutes. Sasza hoped the man wouldn't want to open another. She wasn't sure how much longer she'd be able to stay with that temptation in front of her. She stayed silent, waiting.

Meanwhile, Piotr was thinking: *How many graves have I shown already? To how many women? And none of them survived.* But he didn't voice this. He didn't want her to back away now. He needed her. She was an outsider. His only hope. Hope for what, exactly, he wasn't sure. One thing was clear though: there would be no more lies. Sometimes he thought that this was what he was best at – tricks, lies, manipulation, hiding and running. But he had been honest with Sasza Załuska. He needed to confess before he died. Needed to heave the burden off his shoulders and die a free man. How, where and when they'd eliminate him wasn't important right now. Who'd do it was also of no consequence. Bondaruk just wanted the profiler to reveal everything he had had to live with for all these years.

'I'll take you there,' he promised, and saying that instantly made him feel better. He drank the rest of his coffee.

It was still a long time until dawn. 'What, now?' Sasza asked.

'Why not?' He pushed himself up and took his car keys from the table.

'I'm only guilty of killing the agent and the priest. I murdered them as vengeance for what they had done to me. For raping me. It wasn't political. There was no higher ideal behind it. Nobody paid me. But I don't regret it. I hated them. And I don't know where Łarysa, Jowita or Mariola were buried. I never actually saw any evidence that they were dead.'

'Jowita's skull has been identified,' Sasza pointed out.

'I never believed they'd save her, even though they promised as much. They never leave witnesses alive. That would have been a textbook mistake. The girls died so I would keep silent. And I did. As a reward, they gave me the lumber mill. But I didn't sell them out for it. I was supposed to share their fate back in ninety-nine.

I still don't know why they spared me. Sometimes I think it's history's revenge for my father. He was a traitor, you know. He ratted out the Belarusian conspirators to Bury. I chose the alias "Stach", an abbreviation of his name, for myself to remind me where I come from.'

'All this sounds rather fanciful.'

'You're too young to get it. But I'm sure you'll fill in the blanks soon enough.' He pointed to the files. 'People must know their history to be able to decide their future. It's not in line with the interests of the locals, but frankly, I don't give a shit.'

'Okay. I still don't understand one thing,' Sasza said. 'Why was Iwona kidnapped? And who did it?'

'I told you already. It was a deal everyone agreed to,' Piotr replied impatiently. 'Jurek did something stupid again and went to prison. I managed to get him a shorter sentence, but I didn't want to show my hand. I could expose the boy to a lot of unpleasantness if it was revealed that he's my blood. I've managed to keep it under the rug with Dunia. Fionik, Wasyl and Tomik would be on to any news about a new claimant to my inheritance in a flash. I needed to keep Jurek safe, but all I can do is leave him money. I've never taken any part in his upbringing. I didn't see him growing up. I was afraid they'd use it against me. And I'm ashamed to say, I only thought of myself. When the first opportunity came, I befriended his girlfriend. I know, it sounds twisted, but I needed to know my own son and I could see no other choice – Dunia never allowed me to get anywhere near him. And Iwona couldn't stop talking about Jurek. He's like me, in a way. He probably won't settle down until he's at least forty.'

'He's gone for now. Disappeared. Do you know where to find him?'

Piotr shrugged. His face expressed no anxiety at all. He must have been sure everything was going according to his plan.

'He's with Iwona,' he replied. 'I've secured their immediate future, so they could leave if they wanted. They're safe. I hope they're managing to have a good time, despite the circumstances.'

'Where are they?' Sasza pressed.

'I don't know that,' he admitted. 'Alla found someone trustworthy to hide them. She helped me with everything. She's my guardian angel, you know. She and Dunia have been friends ever since I can remember. When Dunia learned what I did to Stepan, she started to despise me. She was physically repelled by me. She still can't stand my presence, let alone my touch. We couldn't be together, though there's nothing that binds people stronger than crime. Alla knew about us. She used to help us hide. But she knows nothing about politics. Some women prefer their own worlds. Knitting, singing, keeping the house. She's like that. I trust her more than anyone else in the world.'

'So, how did that kidnapping go?' Sasza pushed him. She wouldn't let him pull her off track with his digressions. 'You weren't in the forest then. It was someone else. Someone stronger. And there was a woman with him.'

Piotr sighed. 'Everything slipped out of control when I made my first mistake. That letter the day before the wedding was unnecessary. I got drunk and felt depressed. I wanted to reveal the truth all at once,' he explained. 'At first I was afraid to bring the youngsters in on my plan, so I played Iwona's admirer. And I had some fun doing that, I confess. A young lass like her can really breathe new life into an old man's bones. Only the mothers knew the specifics: Dunia and Bożena. I knew I could trust Dunia. And I paid Bożena off. She still doesn't know all the details. Then we told Jurek. At first, Iwona didn't want to do it. She was faithful to him. She really loves that numbskull. I wanted to secure their future, as I said. I thought back to the one woman I'd had that kind of relationship with in my entire life, and I softened up.'

'You're talking about Dunia, aren't you?'

He nodded. 'She changed, you know? She used to be different – brave, bold and fearless. I could have changed, too.' He paused. Sasza was afraid he'd drift away into one of his stories, but he snapped back to reality. 'But no. I doubt that. People stay the same. I let myself be cowed. They played me well. I was too ambitious. Too vain.'

'Tell me about the kidnapping.'

'Yes. We planned to use their own weapon,' Piotr continued. 'If they killed my women, I decided to pretend to do the same to them. I knew I was playing hardball. But I was right. Everyone was struck dumb. They sent their people to thwart us. They took the only evidence that could mark me as the perpetrator. The car.'

'Who exactly are you talking about?'

He smiled and opened the file on top of the pile, then threw it over to Sasza. She read the label: 'Twig'.

'Adam Gaweł, the starost.'

He passed her another file. This time the label read: 'Nile'. 'Przemysław Frankowski,' he said.

'Jah-Jah? He must only have been in his teens back then. The Security Service didn't recruit adolescents, surely?'

'He was sixteen and had missed out on law school. He was a peasant boy with no views on social advancement. He had to join the party and collaborate with the agency. He joined the army. That's where they recruited him. He was frustrated and ambitious. His mission was to woo Romanowska. Her father was a well-regarded engineer. She used to visit her aunt in Hajnówka every year. They had known each other since they were kids. But he only made her fall in love with him when he was ordered to do so. He monitored Romanowska's uncle and the small but active community of local intellectuals. I don't know if you know, but the commissioner's uncle and father were two of the most important opposition activists in the region. They ran an illegal printing den when the Solidarity civil resistance movement became popular in Gdańsk and Warsaw. Officially, they worked for the weapons industry. In the lumber yard alone, fifteen per cent of the people were informers. No one who ever wanted to be promoted could refuse the party. So people joined, and still went to church in secret. I let it go. I recruited young mothers by getting their kids a place at the nursery. Not only Belarusians; I had some Poles, too. But you know what's the worst? They all believed they were in the right. They told themselves that those were just the times. The capital was far away. The Solidarity even farther. And all the time, Moscow loomed over the horizon to the east, just a stone's throw away. Do you know that Białystok was supposed to be split off from Poland? The communists were deeply rooted here. They had a lot of support among the populace. Stepan did his specialist training in Moscow. He was the worst type of Stalinist rat. Truly one of a kind. But at some point they started treating him like a nuisance. He stopped acting in the spirit of progress, as we used to say. I think they used me to eliminate him.'

'You said it was a crime of passion.'

He nodded. 'I thought so for years. But it's evident to me now that it was in line with their interests. Just like in forty-six. The communist authorities used the hatred brewing in the Polish freedom fighters' hearts and used Bury's unit to off some Belarusians who stood in their way. Why do you think nobody allowed a search party to go after them? Why were they allowed to burn and pillage villages for a week, killing pregnant women and innocent children? The Orthodox didn't want to leave their land. Only Poles live there now. Belarusian families have been all but forgotten. If you go to Zaleszany, Zanie, Wólka Wygonowska, they'll tell you in Polish that the previous occupants of their houses had gone to the Soviet Union and that they found the land fair and square. All of them identify as Poles now. So, the purge was a resounding success. Thirty-year-olds nowadays don't even know they have Belarusian roots. And even if they do, they're not really patriots. It's all about the lifestyle. Going to festivals, singing folk songs, not to mention being admitted to the prestigious Belarusian school. Kids have it better there. Language classes, volleyball games, all that stuff.'

'I don't agree,' Sasza protested. 'People need to know their roots. Jews, Germans, Russians, it's the same for everyone. Belarusians will get there too eventually. Their great-grandparents were scared, their grandparents wanted to forget, and their parents pretended nothing happened. It's only the fourth generation, the angry middle-school-aged kids, who want to revisit it all. Exhume the dead and dig up old graves. They need a reckoning. They need to know who was guilty and who was innocent. The names of the traitors need to be known. That's why you get the nationalists – Little Belarus and Polish Hajnówka. Two extremes, both fighting to preserve their identity. And all they really want is the truth. It's not up for debate. It's a fact.'

Piotr only laughed at that. 'You're wrong. It's a masquerade. Kids don't choose the Belarusian school out of sentimentality. They do it out of calculation. They know it's going to score them more points in the future, when they go to university. And guess where they go. Prestigious Polish universities. It's simply the better choice. I can't rule out that the two people who kidnapped Iwona were Polish nationalists. Sure, they might have been riled up by their older compatriots, the sly bastards that hold the power among such groups, using nationalistic language. It's an old trick, using nationalism for your own ends. But those at the top only care about money, mark my words. And don't let the cult of martyrdom cloud your vision; the same happened with Bury. People's property was pillaged and their old homes empty. The authorities divided up the land, settled it on the "docile" and the "loyal" and those from "good backgrounds". There is no such thing as Polish Belarusians any more. Just as nothing is left of the village of Załuskie.'

Sasza looked up. 'Romanowska showed me that place. There's nothing but a field left. No man's land.'

'Do you know that there were two Załuski brothers among the murdered carters? Bazyli and Janek. Maybe they were your family?'

'I doubt it.' Sasza scanned through the secret informer aliases on the old files. 'Twig, Nile, Shark, Hammer. Only Łupaszka is missing. Those are the aliases of the Cursed Soldiers.'

'All the files you're holding now are Belarusian freedom fighters,' Piotr said. 'They wanted to get their land back as early as the seventies.'

'You're Polish.'

'I don't know who I am.' Piotr shrugged. He was scribbling something on a piece of paper he had ripped out of a desk diary. He was one of those people who didn't find multitasking taxing at all. 'I used to be Polish, but then I became a Belarusian. Besides, who really knows their identity? There's no such thing as pure blood. Only a theory. Especially around these parts. That's why those pathetic activists are so damn funny. On both sides of the conflict.'

'So, Iwona's alive.' Sasza changed the subject. She unwrapped a new pack of cigarettes, discarding the crumpled wrapper on a used plate. 'And she's okay?'

'She's with Quack. They're waiting for forged papers so they can leave the country. I'm doing my best to help them. I might visit them when it all quietens down. I've never been to Ireland.'

'Who's forging the papers for them? Your handler?'

Piotr pointed at the documents. 'Skinny. Read the files and you'll figure out his real name. I won't waste our time here explaining it all.'

Sasza stood up.

'I'll call backup. The police need to see it.'

'If that's how you want to play it.' He nodded, then crumpled his notes into a ball and shoved them into a pocket. He also pocketed the cigarette wrapper. It looked like he was covering their tracks. He placed the flask, cups and plates on a tray and took them to the kitchen. The table now sat empty. Nobody would know they had had a long debate here.

'But I'll only show the grave to you,' Piotr said. 'You can deal with the exhumations yourself. Without me.'

Sasza tried to phone Romanowska, but the commissioner rejected her calls. Jah-Jah and Doman did the same. Finally, Romanowska texted that she couldn't talk because she was 'on a job'. Sasza replied, telling the commissioner that she was going to the crime scene and asking her to call back as soon as possible. There was no reply, but Sasza wasn't surprised. She'd expected that.

'Okay. Let's go,' she said. 'Call a car.'

'Not going to happen,' he replied. 'I can't trust anyone except you.'

Alla was stepping carefully, quietly. It hadn't rained for days. The sun was scorching, like in the middle of summer. Though the river provided some respite from the drought, the meadow had dried up and now, in the light of the moon, it resembled a stubble field. Alla had walked this particular path twice before, and she had never felt this frightened. The shrubbery obscured the entrance and she wasn't sure she'd be able to find the gate. She had a torch but kept it switched off, fearing she'd draw attention. When she came within sight of the Kosiek family house, her concerns turned out to have been groundless; even from this distance, she could see the whole place was enclosed with red-and-white police tape. She ducked under it and went to the gate. It was closed and sealed with more tape. She pushed the key into the lock and snuck inside.

She could turn the torch on now; the dense shrubbery would mask her approach. Breathing heavily with her exertion, Alla headed straight to the well. She grabbed the bucket and unspooled the heavy old chain. The sudden, deafening ruckus sent cold shivers down her spine and she picked up the pace. Finally, the bucket hit the bottom of the shaft. She heard a splash, and then the clanging of metal on metal. Alla squinted, trying to make out the bucket in the darkness. She focused on her task. Her prize was somewhere in the water. She pulled out bucket after bucket, pouring the liquid into an old tub next to the well. She was dripping with sweat. Her hands were sore. She wanted to sit down and take a moment to rest, but that wasn't an option. Wheezing and salivating uncontrollably, she continued her work. This time she found it. When she pulled the half-empty bucket out, there was a small package in it. She fished out the foil-wrapped bundle. It was smallish, but heavy. Alla started unwrapping the thing with stiffening fingers, but quickly realised it would take more than that to free the contents from their protective casing. She would need scissors or a knife. That could wait; she could already see that it really was what she had come here for. The shape was right. The half-ripped plastic wrap revealed the handle of an old Bulldog-type revolver. It was corroded. The barrel was sawn off an inch down the cylinder.

'Need a hand?' came a man's voice behind her. She jerked around. The wet package nearly fell out of her hands.

In the night, the forest was nothing but blackness. The trees sheltered them from the wind. The silence was total, aside from the hooting of owls and the quiet crack of twigs as wild animals moved around. Piotr parked the car in a clearing. They'd have to walk the rest of the way. Equipped with torches and a map on which Sasza was marking the way so she could retrace her steps, they reached a copse of trees dominated by a tall weeping willow. Even from a distance Sasza could see the birchwood cross marking the grave; its white silhouette contrasted starkly with the dark background. Piotr approached it and picked something up from the ground. A short piece of wood. He stuck his hand in his pocket, pulled out a hammer and, with a few hits, attached the Orthodox cross-beam to the woodwork.

'People think this was an execution ground. They come here to pray. Maybe they're right,' he said. 'Only the individual buried here doesn't deserve their prayers. But that's just my opinion.'

Sasza was getting cold. She was dressed too lightly for the weather. During the day the sun was scorching, but the nights were still freezing cold. Her teeth chattering, she took out her mobile and snapped a photo of the grave. She was still sceptical.

'So you're telling me this is it?'

Piotr nodded and pointed to a shack standing in the distance. 'It happened over there.'

The old farm was surrounded by a dilapidated, decomposing wooden fence. It looked deserted.

'Dunia lives there now,' he added.

'She knew from the beginning?'

'I think so,' he muttered evasively. 'But you'll have to ask her yourself.'

'I've already told you how she reacts to my questions,' Sasza reminded Piotr. 'She says nothing.'

Piotr wasn't really listening. He approached an old oak tree and scratched a layer of moss from the bark, revealing a small Orthodox cross cut into the wood.

'I don't know who did this, but there's one just like it near the carters' mass grave. Someone still visits the site and restores it when it starts getting overgrown,' he said. 'But there's also someone else who regularly comes here, rips that birch cross out of the ground and throws it into a nearby ditch. As if telling us *russkies* aren't welcome here.

'The bodies of those two bastards are buried six or more metres down,' he went on. 'If I had a choice, I would have left the country then. I'd have signed a loyalty pledge and fucked off to France, England, or maybe Australia. As far away as possible. Maybe then they would have lived, the girls. But they were unlucky. That they met me. You can't change what happened.'

Sasza shone her torch on the spot and studied it. The ground was black. No grass grew. One of the young trees was toppled, its roots sticking out. It was lying to the side, like a weed someone had uprooted.

Sasza looked up at Bondaruk, surprised. 'Someone dug this up.'

'I did that two months ago. I dug up one of the skulls and sent it to the police,' he explained. 'That's how I'm sure the rest of the bones are still there.'

Sasza grimaced. She felt sudden revulsion at the old man – and then fear. She was in the middle of nowhere, her only companion a brutal murderer. How sure could she be that he had told her the truth? If he attacked her now, she wouldn't stand a chance. Bondaruk wasn't infirm or frail. He was still wiry, limber and strong enough to overpower her, cave her skull in with that hammer and bury her with his other two victims. Who would even think to look for her in an old post-war grave known only to a select few? Her broken hand didn't do anything to improve her chances.

'Don't be afraid,' Bondaruk laughed, misreading her expression. 'There's nothing but bones there. We're all going to end up like that. I don't believe in ghosts; but sometimes, when I come here, those old memories come back to me.'

He covered his face with his hands, took a deep breath and shuddered.

'I can feel it again,' he said. 'I can't remember the details though. I can't recall everything that happened. The order of events. How it ended.'

'Physiological affect,' Sasza said and continued with her diagnosis: 'Temporary loss of consciousness and denial as a mechanism of self-defence. Allows you to go on. A perfectly normal reaction.'

He nodded slightly. 'I don't even dream about it. But I'll never forget the metallic reek of blood. And its taste on my tongue. And then the smell of the hospital. And that catheter.'

'Why did you dig up that skull?' Sasza changed the subject.

Piotr hesitated. He didn't respond at once, but spoke after a long while, his voice raspy.

'I want you to make this place known. You can say you've deduced it with one of your scientific tricks. Geographical profiling, clairvoyance, a leak from someone in the know. Whatever comes to mind. Just keep Dunia out of this. And me,' he added.

'How?' Sasza asked, raising her eyebrows.

'What? You thought I dug the grave for the two slimy fucks all by myself? In the seventies?'

Sasza stared into Piotr's eyes. 'You've just said someone cleaned up your mess. Not even half an hour has passed, and you're already changing your story.'

He squinted and grimaced, growing irritated, but then seemed to calm down. He raised a hand in a placatory gesture.

'The house was cleaned up and the bodies were hidden in a double wall in one of the garages at the hospital's isolation ward. My mother and Dunia used to work there. When the new hospital was built and the old one was sold, I needed to move the bodies so the workers didn't find them. People from one of the nearby villages helped me dig the grave. Some guys from the lumber mill. I've always done my best to keep them happy. Most of them are dead by now, but their children aren't. I've been a benevolent leader to them. They had it better than the rest. They made quite a bit of money for themselves. Maybe their fathers hadn't told them the reason for my kindness. But it's better to be safe than sorry. As to who cleaned up the mess at the shack, I don't know. Probably the Security Service or the militia sent someone. But I did dig the grave, along with the others. Everyone who helped me knew who was buried here and who killed them. They treated me like a hero who'd vanquished the beast. That's provincial thinking right there. Everyone knows, but no one talks.'

'Maybe it was the men whose files you gave me today? Maybe you want to dump the responsibility on them.'

Piotr smiled cunningly. 'Maybe they're the same people.'

'So why are you acting against them? Why do I need to know all this?'

Piotr wavered for an instant, and then pulled a thin package from inside his jacket.

'These are the documents of the murdered carters whose bones were beneath the old hovels in Puchały Stare until ninety-five. Right where Bury and his men executed them. They waited for an exhumation for fifty years. For half a century nobody felt like calling the authorities. Not even when the communist regime fell in eighty-nine. There were two men among them by the name Załuski.'

'You've told me that already.'

'Dunia's family name is Załuska.'

Sasza burst out laughing. 'Do you know how many Załuskis there are in Poland? Not to mention the world.'

'And how many of them shorten their cosmopolitan names like Aleksandra to Sasza?'

Sasza waved him off. 'Bollocks.'

'Maybe. But ask your father who his grandmother was. Where she came from. Maybe I'm wrong. But as I look at you, I think I can see some eastern genes. And that fierceness, that eastern ferocity. You have our blood in your veins.'

'Belarusians aren't exactly known for their fighting spirit. They don't have a single uprising in their history.'

'That's because their land was taken and retaken by Poles, Russians and Germans, time after time. But that is changing. I've already told you about the Belarusian nationalists, the Podlasie Autonomy Movement. Tell them you have Belarusian roots, and they'll start taking you seriously. Believe me.'

'You want me to lie?'

'If you have ancestors among the carters, you're a local. And you don't become one if you're a Jew, a Pole or a German. You only become one if the ashes of your ancestors lie in local earth. You know it yourself: there is no such thing as pure blood. You've been an outsider. Nobody wanted to talk to you. You feed outsiders with your best pork scratchings, you offer them your purest vodka, you let them sleep in your bed and tell them sob stories about the hardships your nation had to go through. But to a local, you say how it really is. Because the locals will always keep it to themselves. It's a simple trick. But it will work wonders. No investigator on the case will ever get as much from the locals.'

Lights appeared on the nearby road. A car. Piotr grabbed Sasza by the hand, clamping his other hand over her mouth and pulling her deeper into the forest. She couldn't scream. As the lights receded and Bondaruk let her go she scrambled to the road, panicked and furious, calling after the driver to stop, waving her arms. She called Romanowska desperately.

'It wasn't the police,' Piotr said.

'Who was it then?'

'You should talk to Dunia,' Bondaruk replied.

He had sobered up and now looked older than he was. Resigned, Sasza followed him to the car. He opened the door for her.

'I'll take you to the hotel,' he said. 'They should be after me by now. I'm supposed to report in every few hours. Remember – you have to keep up appearances. There's nothing as important.'

They set off.

'There's one thing still bothering me,' Sasza said after a while. 'Who did the dirty work? Who killed your fiancées? That must have kept you awake at night for years. Providing, of course, that you've told me the truth and they aren't buried somewhere remote too.'

'You still don't believe me?' Piotr asked. 'After all I've told you?'

Sasza didn't respond to that. It was too early to take a side. She was still too confused.

'Who did it?' she repeated. 'Or at least, who do you suspect?'

'People say Stepan had a daughter from his first marriage. She used to live in a boarding house and didn't visit home too often.'

'Wasn't Stepan gay?'

'There weren't gay people back then,' Bondaruk said without a hint of irony. 'It used to be a deviation, a mental disorder to be treated. When you were gay, the first thing you did was to find yourself a wife. I told you that Stepan popped up out of nowhere after being trained in Moscow. Nobody knew his story. Where he came from. People used to say that he was a local, but who really knew? Besides, he was your typical Stalinist bootlicker. Small fry. Not one of the great powers behind the throne. He wouldn't warrant an interview in the modern media like some others did. When he died, Irma was seventeen. I've never met her. Me and Dunia, we were seeing each other in secret, and she never told me anything about her stepdaughter. Their relationship wasn't anything to write home about, I think, but she played the dutiful mother.'

'Let me guess,' Sasza said, shaking her head. 'The girl vanished without a trace after you murdered Stepan and the priest?'

'Dunia tells me Irma was the one to save me,' Piotr replied. 'That I owe her my life. I can barely recall, but before I lost consciousness I think I saw a pair of black pumps with large bows, standing in a pool of blood. Her father's high standing allowed Irma to wear good clothes, you know. Though I'm not sure if I haven't made this up in delirium. Giewont once suggested that the girl was offed, but I think they simply recruited her and kept it from me. They must have taken her abroad, trained her and given her a new identity. They were good at that kind of thing. But you asked if I suspected anyone. I do. I think it was personal vengeance for killing her father and dishonouring him. She's the only one I have no dirt on. In fact, I didn't know she was alive until earlier today. Dunia told me.'

'Or maybe you're lying and she's buried with her father. Or somewhere underneath an old hovel or a ditch your loyal men dug for her,' Sasza said. 'And that is the reason for your theatrical anguish. You don't regret killing Stepan, but an innocent seventeen-year-old is a different story.'

'Maybe,' Piotr agreed. 'But if that is the case, I don't know who else could have hated me enough to kill the women I loved and collect dirt on me for years. I bribed everyone. And this is not about the money.'

'I'm having trouble believing you don't know her new name,' Sasza said. They stopped at the Bison Motel.

This was where she had started her journey and where, she remembered, she had thought that the entire case would only take her a few hours. Nearly a week had passed since that day and the end was nowhere in sight. Only two letters of the motel's neon sign were left now.

'Unfortunately, I'm telling the truth. She's too well-concealed. I really don't know who she might be today,' Piotr replied. 'She'd be fifty-four now.'

Sasza stepped out of the car, grabbed the files Bondaruk had given her and leaned down to look the man in the eye.

'You take care of yourself.'

'You too.' He smiled. 'Don't forget to make copies. There's a photocopy machine at Ciszynia. Don't let those files out of your sight.'

'Don't you worry about that. I know what to do.'

'I'm not worried about much these days.' He pulled a small case from his breast pocket, sorting through its contents and finally plucking two old documents from within. 'These are the Załuski brothers' IDs. Show them to your parents. Maybe they'll recognise them. If not, take these to the IPN.'

'What about the rest?' Sasza asked, pointing her chin at the case full of the files of the other murdered carters.

'When I die, they'll be given to their rightful owners. They'll do with them as they please. Don't forget, I'm local. I need to play by the rules. If they want to keep those old crimes buried, I don't have the right to object.' He revved the engine and drove off, tyres screeching.

JOWITA

(1999)

'I put on my best Sunday tracksuit. The one I go to church in. Nicest fuckin' outfit in town—'The beefy musclehead broke off as someone knocked on the door.

Marzena flicked a cigarette butt into an empty beer bottle and sprang up from the couch with a pirouette. She opened the door. It was Piotr. At the sight of the suited man, the meat-head rose slowly from his seat and crossed his arms, flexing his steroid-fed muscles.

'Chill, Igor. He's okay,' Marzena said soothingly, as if calming down a dog. She took a quick look out of the door before closing it.

The muscular man did as he was told, sitting back down and helping himself to a thick chunk of pâté and a slice of bread. He chewed slowly, his eyes never leaving the guest.

'Is Nikolai in?' Piotr asked. He lowered his worn tennis bag to the floor by the wall. The gesture was hesitant and delicate, as if the bag contained something made of glass. Judging by the numerous spatters of glue and wood chippings it featured, it had never been used for sports. As he let the handles drop, the top of the bag caved in. It was half empty. The bodyguard shot it a wary glance.

'Groceries,' Bondaruk explained and repeated his earlier question. 'Is the boss in?'

Marzena shook her head, and then repeated the gesture with her hips. Her blond perm à la Madonna's *Like a Virgin* look was lacquered rigid and didn't so much as wobble on her head. Image was everything when you worked in her trade, and hers was classic, though out of date by at least a few years. She hadn't been pretty to begin with, but the perm and all the gaudy accessories made things even worse. Nobody cared. Her clients' attention was usually focused solely on her enormous cleavage.

'He went to fetch some piss for the customers,' Marzena replied giddily, sending Igor a lopsided grin. The man was spreading a thick layer of lard over another slice of bread. He gobbled it and nodded.

Marzena pointed Piotr to the couch. Igor moved so that the man wouldn't sit too close to him.

'An hour ago, give or take,' the woman went on. 'Something must have kept him. Maybe they ordered it frozen? Our fridge died, the useless cunt. Jowita put hot toast inside yesterday. The fucking thermostat didn't stand a chance. Well, now she's working her arse off to buy a new one. Literally,' she said with a rough laugh. 'She charges triple now, up front.'

Piotr stared around the spacious flat. Four rooms neighboured the one they sat in on all sides. There was little furniture, just a coffee table made of old pallets, the couch and two fabric-covered armchairs. The windows were clean. The blinds were closed. There was a green-and-pink-striped rug on the floor. The door to each room was secured by sturdy locks with the warranty stickers still on. Nikolai had installed the locks because he knew the business. The customers that ended up here needed complete privacy. The clients had to be safe. Nothing could disappear. Nobody could see them. The girls were personally tested by the head of the nearest hospital each week. Healthy, clean and, at least theoretically, drug-free. Nikolai had invested a lot in his stable. That was why he kept the girls under lock and key when they weren't working.

The Manhattan residential project was supposed to be opening to the public in a few months' time, but a few residents had been allowed in already – if they had the right connections. Nikolai and his girls were some of the first people to receive keys. Previously, they had operated out of Białowieża. The top brass of the police, a local journalist, the head of the TV station and all the important town officials had attended the housewarming party. They had received their share of freebies; Nikolai had introduced them to his girls and walked them around the apartment. The hotel manager had provided the vodka, and the girls themselves had prepared the food – bowls of vegetable salad, *borscht* and *kalduny*. Piotr had been there too and had helped himself to the VIP package. Marzena had kept him company. They had watched *Dark City* in her cell.

Fully dressed, like old friends. She hadn't even asked him what was wrong with him. Maybe she had been afraid the director of the lumber mill preferred boys. Nikolai wasn't catering to those kinds of needs. Yet. Even though he didn't have to, Piotr had left her two hundred in cash, telling her to keep it from her pimp. The pair had entered into a silent alliance.

Jowita, Marzena's friend, had enjoyed the interest of most of the guests. Though enjoyed might not be the right word. Nikolai had tended to her, bringing her hot broth and Ballantine's whisky. He had also unofficially acknowledged her as his most productive employee. When she had finally recovered, he even allowed her to leave for a few days to spend some time with her kid. He had kept the keys to her room, though. Her documents and the rest of her cash had been locked inside. Otherwise she might not have returned.

There were three more girls. None of them had a visa, so they wouldn't leave. Going to the capital without an ID or any knowledge of the language was too risky. Besides, they had all they could have wanted right here – the status their jobs as luxury call girls gave them, and the comfort of understanding what was being said. Everyone in town knew Khakhlak Russian. And Nikolai was their fellow countryman. It was better than back home for them. The local girls worked part-time during the day, ten to four, when their kids were at school, while the residents slept off the nights.

Today, only one of the doors was half-open, revealing the sound-dampening lining around the frame. Piotr glanced at Marzena. Instead of answering, she took out a key and quickly shut that door too.

'Theoretically, I'm on duty right now, but no one's showed up. Maybe it because it's the middle of the week. Or maybe the weather. A stroke of luck, I say. Or not,' she said cryptically, but pointed her chin at one of the doors.

Piotr concluded that one of the big shots from town hall or someone equally important was visiting, and the apartment was deserted only because he had paid for it. Piotr didn't ask who it was. Marzena wouldn't tell the truth with the security guy around. Igor was rather nervous by nature. He rationed his energy. Now, he was in 'standby mode', but if shit hit the fan and someone decided to kick up a fuss, he would turn into a pitbull in a flash.

Marzena turned to her colleague with a sly smile.

'You were saying? Bond's one of us.' She winked at Bondaruk, or at least he thought she did. Marzena Koźmińska was cross-eyed and her eyes tended to wander at times. Her most charming characteristic was that she didn't give a damn about it.

The musclehead didn't react at once. His steroid-dazed brain needed some time to process the information. But eventually he picked up his story where he had left off. Piotr half-listened, trying to look polite. Something about having to lie low here after he had burned his bridges in Warsaw. About selling drugs, and hookers, and a man who gave him what he describes as 'bullshit' about Polish–Russian friendship.

He eventually concluded: 'So, I've been lying low doing nothing here for eleven months now. But, whatever. Let's have a drink. Pour us a shot, Wasp.'

Marzena did as Igor suggested and drank with the men. Igor kept talking. After three, or maybe five, rounds, Piotr asked again, 'The boss should be here by now, surely? Can't you call him?'

Igor took out his brick of a phone and dialled a number with his meaty finger. Leftie, thought Piotr. That's why he knocks people out so easily. Nobody suspects a hit with a left. Igor put the mobile to his ear but said nothing, just listened. Then he jumped up and headed to the door.

'The lovebirds have half an hour left,' he grunted, indicating Jowita's room. 'As soon as they're over time, they pay double. Ten per cent for you if you manage to throw the cunts out. If I know our little daisy, and I do, we'd have to send her to physio after so much work. And Nikolai wouldn't like that. Though he's in no state to say so right now. Doesn't look too good.'

Marzena stood up. 'What's wrong?'

'Nothing much. He got hammered, the bloody pisshead, and blacked out on the street. They took him to the ICU. It was some quack at the hospital who answered. I got to go. Keep an eye on things, will you?'

He didn't wait for a response. The door slammed. Piotr and Marzena sat in silence for a long while.

'Poppy-seed cake?' Marzena asked finally. 'Not home-made, but it's pretty good.'

Piotr shook his head. The silence resumed. They could hear muffled laughs and cursing from Jowita's room. A moment later, a dull thump and the sound of the door latch sliding open. A man Piotr's age peered out, nodding his flushed, fat, moustached head by way of greeting. Gaweł, the starost. Bondaruk hated the man with a passion, but nodded politely in response.

'Where's the booze, Wasp?' Gaweł called out to Marzena.

The woman passed him a bottle without a word.

'It's warm.' He grimaced, but retreated into the room.

'You have thirty minutes. Nikolai said—' Marzena broke off. The man had already shut the door.

'Who's there with him?' Piotr asked.

She shrugged and took a sip of vodka.

'How many?'

She raised four fingers. He raised his eyebrows.

'And she's with them alone?'

Marzena nodded. Piotr sprang to his feet and went to Jowita's door. He put his ear to it, but could hear nothing.

'How long have they been in there?' he asked, genuinely worried.

'I've seen worse, believe me. If you don't want to fuck, tell me what you came for.'

Piotr went back to the couch, sat down and pulled out an oil-cloth-bound notebook from his breast pocket.

'A few years ago someone topped Wieremiuk, the German teacher at the high school. I want to swap this' – he wiggled the notebook in the air – 'for the papers he had with him.'

'Not my business, love.'

'I don't care about the man or how he died. I only want the stuff taken from his body after he did.'

'Did he owe you?'

Piotr didn't reply. Instead, he went back to Jowita's door.

'We need to go in there. The man's a pig. She won't survive. I know him.'

'Since when are you such a gallant knight?'

Piotr sat back down, but he was growing nervous. 'I only need some old, yellowed papers.'

'Yellowed papers? They worth anything? More than what you have here?'

'No,' he said. 'But I'm getting old now, so I like old things.'

'Some dirt on that old commie? Political?'

Before Piotr could respond or react, Marzena grabbed his bag and opened it. She pulled out a thick wad of clean, new hundred-złoty bills, still wrapped in their excise tax bands, the way they come from the bank.

'You robbed some place lately?'

'Tell your man I'll swap this for the teacher's files and I'll throw in this notebook to sweeten the deal.'

'I'm just a simple girl, what can I do?' She shrugged, slid the bag's zipper shut and went back to her seat. She smiled at Piotr playfully. 'Besides, I couldn't care less about Nikolai. But wait, maybe you have the hots for him, eh?'

'I'm not homosexual,' Piotr replied calmly, but didn't look her in the eye.

She raised her hands in apology, looking scared. Maybe she thought she'd gone too far.

'I'll tell him,' she promised. 'But he won't be able to do a thing. He's not local.'

'The teacher was offed by a professional,' Piotr said. 'Maybe he ordered Wieremiuk killed? But he definitely kept his own hands clean. If Nikolai wants that flat at Red Pig Town he'll do it. I've promised it to him, but I can always change my mind.'

'The fuck you want me to do here?'

He didn't reply. Marzena pulled on a hoodie and zipped it up. She frowned.

'But I might have something for you. Two weeks ago there was a guy here. He was talking to Nikolai but I might have overheard a bit. He was asking for the same German teacher,' she said, lighting a cigarette. 'Maybe my dear boss hasn't just passed out in a snow-drift. I hope Igor comes back in one piece. Otherwise, I'll have to start looking for a new job.'

Piotr grabbed her by the arm, but his grip was loose and he slid his hand down to hers, briefly caressing her palm.

'Twenty grand for you,' he said, 'if this information turns out to be legit.'

She wrested her hand from his grip. 'If only I could leave here. Twenty grand means shit.'

'Are you suggesting you'll deal with this yourself?'

'Nikolai was part of it. He took money. He won't talk. And the guy I told you about wasn't from around here. He was from the capital.'

Piotr gripped her by the shoulders. He was determined.

'The files the teacher had are the IDs of carters murdered after the war. The IPN is already sniffing around for them.'

'Keep your hands off me!' she growled, and slipped away again.

'An investigation into that case could ruin a whole lot of local fat cats. I thought those papers were lost.'

She grimaced. This was boring her. 'I don't need to know what's in the files. I don't give a flying fuck about politics or history or old wives' tales. I only want the money. I'll snoop around and tell you who has the documents. You'll have to do the rest yourself. Pay someone to lift the stuff from the right house. My specialities lie elsewhere. Armed robbery and sucking cock. But I doubt you're interested in the latter.'

She shot a glance at her watch and produced a key. Then, she walked over to the cupboard and switched off the camera that had been recording everything happening in Jowita's room. She rewound the tape and took a look at the screen. Her eyes went wide and she covered her mouth. She slammed the cupboard door shut and looked over at Piotr.

'I need a hand with something,' she said, clearly trying to remain composed. 'I need to throw these deviant fucks out. It's a fucking slaughterhouse in there.'

'I'm no Igor.'

'You'll do fine.' She sent him a half-smile. 'Just follow my lead.'

She positioned him on one side of the door and herself on the other and they opened it together on the count of three. The first thing they saw was Adam Gaweł's naked arse and his skinny legs. The young editor-in-chief of the local newspaper, Vadim Trots, was asleep on the bed, fully dressed. Only the zipper of his jeans was undone. He didn't have any underwear on and his small, shrivelled balls were sticking out through the opening. There was a man trying to wake him up. Przemysław 'Jah-Jah' Frankowski. Unfortunately, he was so drunk he only managed to kick over a line of empty bottles. Trots woke, startled, and wrapped himself up in the sheets.

Jowita was lying next to him, naked, on her back. She was bruised all over. Her nose was broken and she had an enormous swollen weal under one eye. Her hands were tied. She appeared to be unconscious. The police commissioner, Tomasz Terlikowski, was standing over her, legs planted wide and a thick leather belt in his hand. His shirt was unbuttoned and covered in sweat stains. He must have been exerting himself for hours.

'What are you doing here? I'm not finished yet,' he rasped. 'We've paid. The whore's doing her job. She got another hundred for S&M.'

'Time's up.' Marzena rushed over to Jowita, who opened one eye and tried to whisper something, but her voice was so weak, Marzena couldn't understand a word. She could smell blood and other secretions. Marzena tried to lift her, but Jowita was limp in her hands.

'She's dying!' Marzena screamed. Her eyes teared up. 'You motherfuckers!'

'Look, Terlik! You've fucked her up so good she shat the bed!' Gaweł burst out laughing. He patted Terlikowski on the back. The commissioner was already getting dressed. 'All right, boys. Let's get out of here. We'll have a word with Nikolai about the lousy customer service. He can get his little whorehouse out of my town. We don't want no dirty whores here, do we?'

Piotr, standing in the doorway, was rooted to the spot. No one paid him any attention. As Terlikowski was passing, he shot out an arm, grabbed the officer by the throat and slammed him into the wall. The commissioner's face went red, then bluish. His eyes bulged as he desperately tried to inhale. Gaweł threw himself on Bondaruk in an attempt to pull him away from the officer. Piotr let the commissioner flop down to the floor and attacked the starost. He grabbed an electronic alarm clock from the bedside table and crashed it over

Gaweł's head, but the man only shook his head, as if shooing away an irritating bug. Next, Bondaruk lunged for one of the empty bottles, broke it over the table and slashed the jagged edge across the starost's neck. He misjudged and only managed a shallow cut, from which blood initially spouted like a fountain, then stopped.

'Are you out of your fucking mind?!' Gaweł roared. 'She's only a whore. And we've paid up front!'

Jah-Jah crawled out of the room. As he was passing Piotr, the man kicked him in the arse so hard the young officer rolled across the living room, leaving a trail of piss behind him. Trots managed to make it out of the room without a scratch on him, by flattening himself against the wall and then sprinting out like his arse was on fire when he saw a chance. Terlikowski, recovered, snuck up on Piotr and smashed a great stoneware jug over his head. Piotr dropped to the floor, and blackness engulfed him.

Jowita lay on the sofa with her eyes closed. She was muttering something. Dunia Orzechowska, whom had already administered the semi-conscious woman some strong painkillers, was stitching her face up and tending to her numerous bruises and cuts.

'You have to take her to the hospital.' She looked at Piotr, who was sitting in a chair, pressing a bag of frozen spinach to his throbbing head. He glanced at Marzena.

'Nikolai will find us and kill us,' she said. She was chain-smoking, flicking her cigarette butts to the floor. 'First he's going to kill me, then Jowita, and then he'll get you.'

'I'll sort this out,' Piotr said. 'Don't panic.'

Marzena hid her face in her hands. He thought she was going to burst out crying, but in fact she started laughing.

'Maybe you feel safe, but my head is already on a spike. And I only have one, you fucking dimwit.'

Dunia passed Piotr a cup of herbal tea.

'It's hot,' he hissed.

'Drink it before it gets cold,' she replied.

He sipped it slowly.

'Did you hear me?' Dunia demanded. 'The girl needs to be taken to the hospital. They've cut her up, down there.'

A silence fell over the room.

'She'll die if you don't. Call an ambulance.'

Marzena jumped to her feet and stormed off to her room, emerging a while later with a travel bag.

'I'm off,' she said and headed to the door.

'What about your friend?' Dunia asked, clearly shocked.

'In my business you don't get to have friends, lady,' the Wasp said and curtsied. 'Have fun, kids. Better they don't find you here when she dies. Else they might pin it on you.'

Dunia gritted her teeth. She turned to Piotr and fixed him with her glare. 'Won't you do anything?'

He got up with difficulty, reached into his pocket and pulled out the keys to his car. 'I parked it on Kolejki, by the grocery shop.'

Marzena stopped at the door, looking unsure. 'I don't have a driving licence.'

Piotr looked back at Dunia.

'Ask Kola to come,' she said. 'Maybe tell him to bring someone strong with him. Someone who he trusts. We won't be able to carry her out alone. And you, call Bielsk. Maybe the director will see her at his house. And keep talking to her. Don't let her sleep.'

Marzena sighed deeply, put her bag down and took the car keys.

'How much time do we have?' Bondaruk asked Dunia.

'An hour, give or take.'

'We have to hurry.'

Jowita was playing with her son when her mother came into the room with a grave expression on her face.

'Someone wants to see you,' she said. 'Says you're friends, but I'm not sure about that. She looks like a harlot.'

Jowita planted a kiss on her son's brow, tied a bandana over her head and walked to the lobby. It hadn't even been six months, but Marzena had changed. Jowita could almost smell the money on her. Her friend leaned over a white Mercedes, wearing a miniskirt shorter than Britney's in 'Baby One More Time'. The speakers in the car blared out some pop mega-hit.

'Turn it down or the neighbours will come out,' Jowita said.

She went over to Marzena and kissed her on the cheek. Before the woman could opened her mouth, Jowita added, 'Mum found me a job at the dairy. I'm staying.'

'You're milking cows now?' Marzena grimaced.

'Better than whoring around.' Jowita instinctively touched her crooked nose. 'I still haven't fully recovered.'

Marzena walked around the car and knocked at the windscreen. A young, ugly man stepped out. He wore glasses, and his face was flat like a frying pan. And he had hair everywhere. Jowita had seen gorillas more attractive than him.

'Let me introduce you. Shaggy, this is Jowita. Jowita – Shaggy.'

'It's Monika,' Jowita said.

'Jarek,' the man replied.

They shook hands and smiled at each other, then Jowita invited them inside, but the pair refused. She felt mildly offended. The house wasn't anything special, that was true. In fact, it didn't look inviting at all. It smelled of manure. The squealing of pigs could be heard.

Jowita looked back, to see her son standing in the doorway. Judging by his expression, he was scared Mummy would abandon him again, leaving him with his strict grandmother. If she so much as suggested doing so, Jowita knew the boy would break down in tears. He was delicate, skittish, like a rescue dog left too many times to trust anyone again. She walked over to him, taking him by the hand.

'This is Tomek,' she introduced the boy to the others. 'He's almost six. And this is Aunt Marzena and Uncle Jarek. Aunt Marzena has children too, Tomek. Three of them.'

The Wasp bent down and started talking to the boy, but Jarek stood rigid. He looked like he was in a hurry. It didn't look like they were a couple. He looked like an intellectual, a clerk maybe, and the Wasp had never liked that type of man. He was probably her new sponsor, Jowita thought.

'Is there a café anywhere near?' the man asked.

'We only have a bar, and I'd rather Tomek didn't go there,' Jowita replied and stroked the boy's hair. He huddled against his mother. 'I don't go there either,' she went on. 'Not any more. We'd need to go to town.'

'So, let's go,' Marzena said enthusiastically. 'We can take the kid. You like chips?' she asked the boy. 'Any real man loves them. And I know what I'm saying, right, Shaggy?'

The man frowned at hearing her call him that, but got behind the wheel meekly.

'I don't know.' Jowita lowered her voice to a whisper. 'I like it here, Marzena. It's boring, it's hard, but at least it's calm. Please don't be mad, but I won't go with you.'

She turned round and started walking back to the house. Marzena gripped her by the arm. It hurt. The boy started to cry. The Wasp instantly let her friend go and Jowita hurried on.

'I've got business. Pure gold!' Marzena called after her. 'I can't do it without you.'

Jowita bit her lip and turned round. 'No. And don't come back here any more.'

Marzena rummaged through her handbag and took out a VHS tape. Jowita furrowed her brow.

'They have to pay,' Marzena said, gently.

'Give me a break.' Jowita waved her away. 'They don't exist for me any more. Who would take the case? You know who they are. And who I was. We don't stand a chance.'

'I'm not talking about an investigation.'

Jowita shook her head. She was afraid. 'No.' She implored Marzena with her eyes. 'Please, don't do it. Don't get me into this.'

'If you don't want to get rich, I'll rip the cash from their throats myself. But you won't get a penny. You could have your nose done. Surgery is cheap as chips now. You're young. You can still be pretty. You can still meet someone new.'

'Like Shaggy?'

'A man doesn't have to be handsome. It's enough I'm a beauty.' Marzena pursed her lips, then burst into infectious laughter. Jowita joined in. She couldn't help herself. Marzena had always known how to make her laugh. 'Besides, he's really good to me,' Marzena went on. 'And he doesn't need much. Well, he needs what every man needs. But I have a manual and know what makes him tick.' She giggled.

'Good for you,' Jowita said, but she was already caving in. Marzena had found her soft spot. Nobody wants to be alone.

'You needn't be afraid,' Marzena tempted her. 'I'll take care of everything. We'll make all four of them pay. And, if all goes according to plan, they'll keep paying for ever. Piotr will give us a hand.'

'He promised?' Jowita asked hopefully.

Marzena burst out laughing. 'He doesn't know yet. But he will. I'll talk to him. I need to give him his car back. Are you getting child support?'

Jowita dropped her eyes and that was answer enough.

'He's still in Germany?'

Jowita shook her head and shot a frightened glance at her son. Finally, she replied in a whisper: 'My brother saw him with some floozie. Utterly hammered. Wanted to beat him up but the bastard hailed a cab and got away. But it seems he's got the better side of the deal. I'll never get anything from him.'

'We'll get him too,' Marzena promised. She embraced both Jowita and the boy. Then she called to Shaggy: 'Jarek, sweetheart, get a pillow or something for the car. The boy needs a kiddy seat.'

'He'll sit on my knee,' Jowita said.

In the car, she looked around at the interior. The light upholstery bore dark smudges. She touched one, realising it was her own blood. Then she looked into the wing mirror. *I'll never look pretty again,* she thought. *Nothing is going to be the same again.*

'You look good,' Marzena was prattling. 'Considering the circumstances, of course. But, I almost forgot! Nikolai and Igor send their best wishes. They don't hold anything against you. They've opened a new place in Narewka. The police are friendlier there.'

Jowita stifled a sob.

'What's Mum sad about?' the boy asked.

'She's sad because she has no money,' Marzena replied, turning round to look at him. 'But that is going to change, love. Money makes everything better. Remember that.'

She turned back to face the front and pushed a cassette into the player. The speakers reverberated with Madonna singing 'Material Girl'.

Hajnówka, 2014

Each Tuesday, Mrs Antonina 'Tosia' Rosłoń ate breakfast for dinner so she could drive to the Wednesday wholesale market in Bielsk Podlaski first thing in the morning. At three in the morning, she brought the fresh vegetables she had bought there back to her market stall in Hajnówka, which she had named TO-MI-TO for the first letters of the names of her husband Tolik, her son Mirek and herself. At six, local housewives and stock boys were already lining up to buy her produce. Her son helped her with transporting, unloading and restocking the stall. Her daughter-in-law Angelica joined in too after she'd dropped her son at nursery.

Today, as usual, they were lugging bags of potatoes, rolling barrels of sauerkraut, moving boxes full of ripe tomatoes, shining aubergines and pre-peeled onions.

Business was good. Mrs Rosłoń had worked hard – and honestly – for everything she had now. The only thing she had had to bribe someone for was her stall. But that had been years ago, when the Ruble Mart had been a real black market, and the main currency used there really was the Russian ruble. Russians used to come here from across the border on a regular basis. The Rosłoń household was full of Russian gold, Uighur hand-made knives, Belarusian thin-sheet pots, Lithuanian drugs, Azerbaijani earthenware pots and Ukrainian clocks and watches, and even wall-hangings from faraway Georgia. In those days you could also have bought a stolen car or an old machine gun.

But there hadn't been any real *russkies* around for years. Today, the stalls sold Chinese crap like everywhere else and only the name remained. But the locals, out of tradition or habit maybe, still came here every Wednesday and left with their shopping bags stuffed full.

Mrs Rosłoń opened the stall for business and her first customer asked for half a kilo of sauerkraut.

'Making *bigos*, aren't you?' Mrs Rosłoń asked.

That must have inspired the other customers; one after another they all asked for sauerkraut. Mrs Rosłoń stirred the cabbage in its barrel, all the while informing the queue of the scarcity of true, traditional sauerkraut on the market nowadays. Hers was organic and she liked to emphasise that at every opportunity.

She dug down into the barrel to mix the water in a bit more. The ladle met resistance. Something hard. She pushed it down and wiggled it a bit, then pulled the ladle out and leaned over the rim of the barrel to take a look inside. Surely her supplier hadn't tried to scam her by hiding a brick in the barrel to increase its weight? But what else could it be?

Among the top layer of the pickled cabbage was floating a human head. White hair, half-dissolved in the acidic brine, looked like Medusa's snakes, making the swollen face look even more macabre and grotesque.

Mrs Rosłoń didn't scream. She didn't faint. She just gestured to her customers that the stall was closing, turned the sign on the door to 'Closed', found her phone and dialled 112. She thought anxiously about her losses. It wasn't just that specific barrel. She might lose her life's work. If the rumour spread, as it surely would, nobody would as much as look her way any more. TO-MI-TO would become nothing more than that place where they sell sauerkraut with dismembered bodies inside.

Doman was just finishing his interview when Błażej barged into the room, panting. Seeing the attractive woman, whom he recognised as a journalist from a popular radio station, packing up her equipment, he bowed to her and blushed before asking his superior to come with him.

The journalist hung about, doing her best to listen in on their conversation, but all she caught was the phrase 'Ruble Mart'.

When Doman returned, he was suddenly in a hurry. Just a couple of minutes earlier, the handsome cop had been trying to get her to go out to lunch with him.

'Maybe another time, Marta,' he said now, with a polite smile, indicating the door.

The journalist bobbed her head and made her way out. As soon as she left, Doman called his driver.

The whole area around the local market had been cordoned off. Members of the public were clustered around, as well as a large group of reporters (including the radio journalist). A press operations centre had been thrown together at the Forest Palace restaurant. The presence of police tape suggested the Ruble Mart had become a place of tragedy. People were talking about the cannibal again. About a body found at one of the stalls. Their stories were growing in intricacy and scale by the minute. Now, the cannibal was a mass murderer. In the middle of all this stood all the market vendors, surrounded by volunteer militiamen.

Romanowska, who had arrived a moment ago and met up with Doman, had a terrible headache. She was just about to start digging through her bag for some painkillers when her walkie-talkie screeched:

'Calling all patrols. I repeat. Calling all patrols. The wanted criminal Łukasz Polak has been seen at the bus station. The suspect is moving towards the church right now. Over and out.'

Magdalena Prus switched on the light in her huge wardrobe and stared with pride at her life's work: her clothes. Mainly skirts and dresses she hadn't even worn. Balls, parties and banquets were a rarity in Hajnówka. There were weddings at least, but Magdalena hadn't been invited to any lately. She heard that people in larger cities liked to celebrate divorces like they did weddings now. Unfortunately, divorces were also a rarity in Hajnówka. The few that did occur were quiet affairs, dealt with quickly and forgotten even faster. The alternative was living together like enemies under one roof. People did that, too. Priests kept the locals on a short leash.

Magdalena's lover, Marek, had a wife by the name of Jadwiga. She had given him seven children and didn't intend to carry on the conjugal duties any further, so Marek could do as he pleased now. The two of them met once a week. In the meantime, they didn't call each other, though Marek always remembered important dates like Valentine's Day. They both liked this arrangement. Magdalena never had to look at Marek in a sweaty undershirt, slumped on a sofa watching TV. He always arrived at her place immaculately clean and perfumed. His dirty socks would never lie around her flat. She never saw him in a bad mood, and she never had to listen to him complain about his work.

From the very beginning, Marek had realised that he was fucking someone way above his station, so before he came to her place he always bought good wine, perfume he worked half the month to afford, or an item of clothing, size 36. He never chose the clothes himself, of course. Magdalena would send him a link or lead him to a shop and point out what she wanted. He had the comfort of always knowing what his lover would like. And she had the guarantee that everything would stay the way she wanted it. Marek had never ever let her down – in any way. If there was one thing about Magdalena Prus, it was that her sexual needs were nearly limitless. She enjoyed only the highest quality when it came to everything in her life.

Today was their tenth anniversary and she was standing in front of the mirror, deciding which dress to wear tonight.

She decided on her Audrey Hepburn look. She slid into a modest floral skirt with a broad waistband and tied her hair into an old-school bun, which she had practised carefully.

The door buzzed. She didn't have to look at her watch to know that it was Marek, ahead of schedule. He would never learn that classy people should always be late. She swore under her breath, ripping a long run in one of her stockings. The door buzzed twice more, but she didn't hurry. She took her time choosing her shoes. They were the frame to the painting, as she liked to say. Only after she'd found a pair of antique snakeskin pumps and slid her feet into them did she go to the door to greet her guest.

She buzzed Marek in and waited, but he didn't appear, so she decided to go out to meet him instead. She could see from the window that the night was bright. It was a full moon. They'd kiss in the moonlight. She licked her lips at the thought. Magdalena opened the door to step out, and fluttered her eyelashes flirtatiously. Her smile froze on her lips. It wasn't Marek. It was Łukasz Polak.

He looked like shit. Rugged, unshaven and stinking of machine lubricant. One of his arms was all scratched and he had a small bruise under one eye. Despite this, she still found herself attracted to him – she had done as far back as his days at Ciszynia, but he had never reciprocated her interest.

'May I come in?' he asked, stepping over the threshold without waiting for a reply.

She stood still at the door for a moment, confused. What would she do when Marek arrived? She slammed the door shut. Maybe she'd just pretend she wasn't there? But that would mean another month without seeing him. Not to mention the stockings, worn especially for him, would go to waste.

'Going out?' asked Polak. 'I've been hiding in the old isolation ward. Rats bit me as I slept,' he continued, holding out his scratched arm.

She went off to fetch the first aid kit. When she came back she asked him, 'Did anybody see you?'

She started cleaning his wounds, her movements rushed and not very delicate. He hissed with her every touch.

'I wanted to turn myself in today.'

'Good for you,' she muttered.

'I wouldn't rat on you.'

'Right. Just like you kept your mouth shut during therapy. I know everything about you, boy. Besides, that woman keeps looking for you.'

'For me?' He took a frightened look around. 'Sasza's here?'

Magdalena bandaged his arm. 'She's in town. She really wanted to see you. I tried to talk her out of it, but she dug in her heels. Her stubbornness only got her a broken arm and a lot of trouble.'

Polak jumped to his feet. 'Why didn't you tell me?'

'How was I supposed to tell you? You're not taking any calls.'

'I was afraid my phone was tapped,' he said. 'I'm in trouble.'

'The whole country knows that.' She laughed and turned the TV on. The news anchor was talking about an African summit in Paris. She muted it. 'Well, okay, you're not front-page material any more. But you were everywhere until yesterday. I'm surprised they haven't caught you yet.'

'I wasn't running,' he said. 'I didn't know.'

'Typical.'

'Do you have anything to eat?' he asked, shooting glances at the exquisite dinner waiting on the marble kitchen counter.

She rolled her eyes, but headed to the kitchen and opened the fridge. She took out some bread, butter, sausage and a carton of milk. He started eating greedily. She didn't want to ask him what it was he had been doing since his escape. She didn't need to know. She just wanted to know how much longer this would take; and she had to think of how to let him know he wasn't welcome. Finally, she packed the remaining food in a plastic bag , tossing in a bunch of grapes for good measure.

'Take it and get out,' she barked. 'Chop-chop. I'm not going to give you any money.'

He was dumbstruck.

'Where am I supposed to go?'

'Call your mother,' she offered.

'They're waiting for me there, I'm sure.'

Her was getting on her nerves. 'What do you expect me to do?'

'Tell them it wasn't me!'

'If it wasn't you, they'll realise that sooner or later. Why did you have to run like a coward?'

He added his half-eaten sandwich to the bag.

'Take me to Ciszynia and let me stay there,' he pleaded.

'Are you joking?'

'In your rejuvenation room,' he added and fixed her with a hopeful stare.

She glared at him. 'I don't know what you're talking about.'

He smiled. 'You can stop pretending. I've been there.'

'Get out!' she screamed.

He frowned, finally understanding. 'Either you take me to where you keep the blood, or I go to the police and tell them all about it,' he said coldly. After a pause he added, less sharply: 'I'll wait out the storm there and vanish later. Nobody will know.'

'I'd have to deal with you for years then,' she hissed. 'People have already tried to blackmail me.'

Polak looked up. 'Tried and failed? Does that mean you . . . dealt with them?' he asked. 'Is that what you're doing there?'

'It's none of your business. Better deal with your ginger girlfriend. She's in trouble, as I said.'

He didn't respond to that.

'Medical experiments? Organ trading?' he asked, but saw he hadn't hit the bullseye. He tried once more. 'You're dealing in blood. That's the only cure for Alzheimer's, isn't it? I've seen the printouts on your desk.'

He moved closer to her. Eyed her delicate skin. She had practically no wrinkles. Then he shot out his arm and grabbed her by the shoulder, pulling her to the mirror alongside himself.

'How old are you, oh queen?' he said. 'You think I'm an idiot? I've known for years it's all about the money. Big, big money.'

'Let me go!' She squirmed and tried to free herself.

The doorbell rang and they both started at the sound. Magdalena seized the moment and sprang away. She picked up the receiver, but Polak managed to clap a hand over her mouth. He leaned close to her ear and whispered, 'I'll kill you if you tell them.'

'Get out of this room,' she ordered, just barely keeping it together.

'I'll go and get something to eat and then I'm going to take a nap,' he said. 'I won't see or hear anything. Have a nice evening.'

She pushed him into the bedroom and turned the key in the lock before tossing it into a drawer filled with a set of sharp new kitchen knives. She took one of them out, leaving it on the counter. Just in case. She was breathing heavily. The door went again and again, announcing the arrival of her lover. She thanked God he had built her that wardrobe.

She smoothed down her dress, applied some more lipstick and calmly went back to her initial plan. The moon, a kiss, dinner, and then they'd go to the rejuvenation room. Łukasz Polak would learn all about their experiments. Only it would be the last thing he'd learn in his life.

'You look beautiful, if a bit menacing,' Marek said, offering her a gift – a large flagon of Chanel No. 5. It wasn't the cheaper *eau de toilette* or even *eau de parfum*. It was pure extract. She smiled. He was one hundred per cent right, for once. She opened the bottle and sprayed herself with the perfume, shutting her eyes in ecstasy. She had everything under control.

'I know. But you don't have to be afraid,' she purred.

'Why don't I believe you?' he breathed and kissed her.

She opened her eyes and looked at the sky. The damn moon had already vanished behind the clouds. It started to drizzle. Nonetheless, Magdalena decided that they didn't need to hurry.

'Tell me something nice for our anniversary,' she said.

'I love you,' he said, predictably. Then he offered her another gift. A pair of horrid earrings with garnets too large to be genuine. He must have chosen those by himself. 'The garnets are real,' he said, seeing her expression. 'Mum bought them at the Ruble Mart. Back in the good old days. Russian red gold.' He beamed.

'All right, that's better.' She threw herself into his arms. For some reason that had touched her. Maybe her good mood stemmed from her plans for after her date. She could already taste the coppery tang of blood. 'I kinda-sorta like you too,' she said.

He frowned. This wasn't what he had been expecting to hear.

'Just kidding,' she added quickly. 'I love you too. You built me a palace for my treasures, didn't you?'

They changed the normal order of things this time. First, they had sex, and only then dinner and wine. She took the knife with her when they went up to bed, discreetly hidden in a towel, and left it close enough to her to be able to grab the handle quickly. It had come back from the grinder yesterday along with the rest of her knife set. The blades were sharp enough to cut through skin with a single motion and bleed a still-living body. Normally, Magdalena used rabbit blood for her baths, but she wouldn't have a problem with swapping it for human. But she needed someone strong – a man – to keep the victim pinned down. Besides, she had never bled anyone at home, let alone someone fully conscious and not drugged. *Well*, she thought, *there's a first time for everything.*

This time, Sasza didn't get the Bison Motel's honeymoon suite but a regular single room. It didn't have an enormous bison head on a wall, just a window with a view of the inside of a bin shelter. She ordered the salted pork lard with onions the receptionist had recommended last time she visited. It wasn't as tasty as in the Forest Palace or the Starówka, the best restaurants in town, and it certainly bore no resemblance to the delicacies served in the Żubrówka Hotel in Białowieża, but she ate her breakfast with good appetite nonetheless, washing it down with white tea. She had requested a late checkout, so she took her time reading the files over her breakfast.

Her mobile played the theme song from *Madagascar*, which meant Karolina was calling. Sasza picked up immediately.

'Mum?' came her daughter's sweet voice. 'Remember what day it is today?'

She froze.

'Uncle Karol's birthday. Grandma says you probably forgot.'

Sasza smiled. It wouldn't make sense to call her brother before one in the afternoon. He was probably still fast asleep.

'I haven't called him yet, but I will. I remember. Did you call him?'

'Yes. We even sang "Happy Birthday" with Grandma. I miss you, Mummy.' Karo's voice broke on the last sentence.

Sasza's eyes teared up. She thanked God every day for this child. Only her little girl allowed her to keep all her problems at a healthy distance. Everything she was going through in this strange place suddenly felt less important. The only thing that counted, the only thing Sasza cared for, was her daughter. She wanted to go home.

'Will Uncle come for you by car?' she asked. 'When are you landing? Can you pass the phone to Granny, please? We'll talk later, sweetheart.'

Laura came on the phone.

'Where are you? Karol says you haven't been taking his calls.' She was starting, characteristically, with a reprimand.

Sasza sighed. Karol hadn't called her even once. But she couldn't stay angry with Laura. A strict mother is a good thing. She kept the family together. And besides, it meant she was still in good form, feeling well. Everything was okay. Nonetheless, an alarm blared in Sasza's head as she recalled something.

'Mum,' she began in an innocent tone. 'Where did my grandparents come from? Your parents and Dad's.'

'What is this about?' Laura was immediately suspicious. 'I've told you. Gołąb near Zamość. The south-east.'

'But is it possible that Grandma moved there or, I don't know, was relocated there after the war? From Białystok for example?' Sasza felt she was scrabbling for ground.

'No,' Laura replied. 'We owned land there. A manor. It had been our family's for generations. Why would you suddenly take interest in my past? You didn't even want to take a look at our family tree when I tried showing it to you.'

'How about Dad's mum?'

'Seaside. What is this all about?'

'It's a work thing,' Sasza said evasively. 'I'm working on something. Can't tell you the details. I've found two men here – Załuski brothers. Bazyli and Jan. They call him Janka here, but that's a regional thing.'

'Jan?' Laura paused. 'Dad had a cousin. The Germans killed him during the war. A tank shot at him.'

'Which year?'

'Around the end of the war. I don't know the particulars.'

'I have their documents. Would you recognise them? Or an aunt or cousin?'

Laura was quickly losing her patience. 'I have a whole album of old photos at home. Come back and I'll show you. It's not a conversation for now. Do you know how expensive roaming is here? Not to mention Karolina wants to talk to you again.'

'All right, bye,' Sasza managed before her daughter snatched the receiver back. They talked for a while longer, professing their love and longing for each other. Finally, Sasza had to end the call.

'We'll see each other tomorrow, pumpkin. Granny can't afford to pay any more for roaming.'

'Mummy, are the stars angels?' the girl asked before they hung up. 'People who died and watch over us? Because the stars here are different to our stars.'

Sasza bit her lip. 'I think you might be right,' she replied. 'You could say that.'

'I chose one and I know it's Dad.'

Sasza balled her hand into a fist, crumpling the napkin she was holding.

'If Daddy's dead, he is watching over us, isn't he? He sees everything now. And he's doing everything he can so we stay safe.'

'I'm sure he is,' Sasza stammered. 'God watches over us.'

'With Daddy and Grandpa?'

'Grandpa would be proud of you.'

'I was born on Grandpa's Day. So we swapped places. He turned into a star and I was born.'

'You're so smart. Smart and brave. I love you so much.'

'Do you think that if I talk to my star more, Daddy is going to talk to me too?'

'I don't think so, honey.' Sasza couldn't bear more of this. She couldn't keep lying to her daughter like this. 'Stars and angels don't speak. They just are. They keep watch.'

'I miss Daddy very much.'

Sasza paused, not sure how to respond to that.

'Well, I'm your mum *and* dad at the same time now,' she said in the end. 'Everything will be okay. Tell Grandma Karol is going to pick you up. My car broke down.'

'Okay! Bye! Love you!' Karolina squealed. 'I got to go. They opened the pool. And Grandma told me we don't have to go to the beach today. And I'll swim with a floaty thing. By myself. I'm the best!'

'You are, sweetheart.' Sasza breathed out with relief. She heard scratching, as if someone had dropped the phone and was scrambling to pick it up.

'What do you mean it broke down? You've just had it repaired.'

'Mum, I broke my arm. Tell Karol to pick you up. And keep Karolina at your place for another day, please. I'll try to come straight back.'

The response was silence. Sasza looked at the phone screen. Laura had hung up. Sasza wasn't sure how long she had been talking to herself. She tried to call back, but nobody picked up. She tried again. It was no use. With a shaking hand, Sasza placed the mobile back on the table and waited until the screen blacked out. A moment later, it came back on. The *Madagascar* song played again.

'Okay. I have to deal with everything as always. And what do you mean you broke your arm?' Laura asked coldly.

'You're wonderful, Mum.'

'I know,' the older woman replied, some warmth returning to her voice. 'I recall now what happened to Jan.'

Sasza understood now. Laura hadn't wanted to talk about it with Karolina there.

'He died right after the war,' her mother went on. 'He can't even have been twenty. I think it happened in the winter. I was told the bands were roaming the forests and many died. And they couldn't even be buried, because it was too cold to dig. But why the sudden interest?'

'Don't worry about it,' she said, trying to maintain a neutral voice. 'We'll talk about it when I'm back. This isn't something to discuss over the phone.'

'All right. I take it you've been to a doctor and are keeping safe? You'll have to get some physio. Do you realise that? A bone fracture at your age isn't something you can just shrug off.'

'I know, Mum. I'm taking care of myself. Have a nice flight home.'

'We'll pray for you.' Laura hung up, as was her way, without waiting for a reply.

Sasza turned to the files again and took out the Załuski brothers' papers. She looked at the photos of the two men. They didn't look like anyone from her family she could think of.

She picked up her phone again and scrolled through her texts until she found what she was looking for.

'I need to see her. Ł.'

She called the number and raised the phone to her ear. Her hand was shaking. Nobody picked up. Relieved, she dropped the connection, took a deep breath, and collected the documents into the file again. She went to the reception desk to pay for her room, but the receptionist only waved her away.

'The director already paid.'

He slid a package towards her. It was wrapped in paper printed with the hotel's logo.

'As fresh as it gets. For lunch,' he said with a roguish smile. Sasza frowned and shook her head. 'It's pork lard from Nesteruk,' the man explained. 'It's so good. On the house.'

Sasza thanked the man and headed towards the exit. Halfway to the door, she swept the lobby with a look. There was no one else there, just the two of them.

'Not many guests at the moment, eh?' she asked. 'Would you drive me to Ciszynia? The director would be grateful.'

The receptionist lost his smile, but reluctantly agreed. He took a ring of keys from under the counter and pulled off his company blazer. Underneath it, he was wearing a T-shirt with a likeness of the Cursed Soldiers and a slogan reading: 'Glory to the Heroes!' He led Sasza to an old off-road truck, a Tarpan. He made some space on the passenger seat, tossing food wrappers to the floor. It wasn't the pork lard he seemed to adore so much, but good old KFC. He snatched up as many old energy-drink cans and coffee cups as he could and threw them on the back seat. Then, with an expansive gesture, he invited Sasza in.

'It may not be a ZU-32 pick-up truck,' he laughed, 'but you can stick a machine gun on top and rip holes in houses still loyal to the government.'

'Is that what you're planning?' Sasza asked, pointing her chin at his T-shirt. 'Shoot up a bunch of villagers?'

'I was only joking.' He looked flustered. 'But, you know, if the shit hits the fan we have enough hardware to get things done.'

'Who exactly are "we"?'

'National Hajnówka, of course,' he replied with pride. 'Check out our Facebook page.'

'I thought you were on the director's side,' she said, puzzled. 'How do you manage to keep in his good graces with these nationalist ideas?'

'It's only a job. And besides, the director likes to have it both ways, haven't you noticed? He financed our last training camp. It was a blast, I tell you.' His wide grin made Sasza think of the Cheshire Cat.

'What about that?' She pointed to the receptionist's tattoo. It stuck out from under his sleeve each time he changed gears. It was a so-called 'falanga', a heavily stylised hand holding a sword, ready to strike. The symbol of Polish nationalists.

'Oh, you know.' He pulled his sleeve over the tattoo. 'I was young and stupid.'

Sasza took a better look at the young man. His head was clean-shaven. He was athletic, muscled, though rather slight of build. She noticed now that he had another tiny tattoo behind his ear. The number 88.

'And this?' She indicated it.

He didn't reply for a while. He stopped the car, though they were still a couple of hundred metres from Ciszynia.

'I think it's best if I'm not seen with you.' He opened her door.

'Thank you very much.' She managed a polite smile and got out, standing still and following the old Tarpan with her eyes as it made a U-turn and headed off down the road back to the hotel.

As soon as it had disappeared, she took out her phone and wrote down the licence plate number. She knew who she had been dealing with. The 'falanga' and the number 88 were symbols used only by fascists. 'H' is the eighth letter of the alphabet. Two eights made a double H, then. 'HH' – *Heil Hitler*.

Panic among nationalists in Hajnówka.

Some time ago we notified the Prosecutor's Office that the website National Hajnówka was publishing photos of people wearing fascist symbols banned by law. Young people wore clothes adorned with the Nazi Totenkopf *symbol while marching in the demonstration in memory of 'Bury', a war criminal who murdered so called 'enemies of the state', including innocent children. Descendants of the people murdered by Bury and his band still inhabit Hajnówka.*

During the war the soldiers of the underground resistance collected the Totenkopf *pins as a token of how many enemies they'd killed, marking them with the letters ŚWO, which meant 'death to the enemies of the fatherland'. However, nothing justifies the wearing of Nazi symbols by young, misguided people in 2014, during a time of peace. Next time you go to a demonstration, why don't you wear swastikas instead?*

The police are investigating those instigating such behaviour. And this *has been dubbed a scandal.*

I've been called a 'left-wing activist' in Parliament. Dear nationalists: I am neither an activist, nor do I associate with the left wing. I simply know that wearing Nazi symbols and using the National Hajnówka website to write things such as: 'Bury should have eradicated all Belarusians. Pity he didn't have the time' is absolute evil. What is more, I will do everything in my power to make those responsible answer for their actions.

Poles and Belarusians of Hajnówka had been living in peace for generations, until a group of Polish pseudo-patriots started meddling and inciting nationality-based conflicts. No formal inquiries will change the fact that what you are doing is pure evil. Belarusians have the same right to live on this land as Poles.

Asia folded the newspaper so as to leave the article visible so her father wouldn't miss it, and put it on the table. Just as her mother was about to serve him dinner. Pietruczuk gave his daughter an admonishing look.

'I'm going to the demo,' Asia announced and turned to leave. Pietruczuk watched her taking her leather jacket from the hanger and tying a bandana around her neck.

'You stay right here!' he called, but she didn't listen. Her mother retreated to the kitchen, taking the dinner plate with her. Asia's father pushed himself to his feet and shuffled towards the door. The girl was already running down the stairs. 'Asia!'

She didn't even pause. Only when she reached ground floor and was fiddling with the chain securing her bike to the handrail did she call back, 'People are readying for war! I'm not going to stay here and watch as the commies sweep this under the rug!'

'Who put this ridiculous notion into your head?' her father scoffed.

'Ridiculous? Read the damn article. You'll get it then. And you're asking who? You! You taught me what's important. God, Honour and the Fatherland. Those are *your* words. Pity they're just words.'

Pietruczuk capitulated. 'Let's talk.'

'The time for talking is over, Dad. There's going to be a war. You'll see.'

Suddenly it became clear to him that his daughter hadn't been trying to untie her bike but a gigantic banner. She threw it over her shoulder, like some kind of knight readying his sword for battle. A moment later, he saw two boys enter the stairwell. They wore hoodies and baggy trousers. At a distance, he might have mistaken them for regular good-for-nothings loitering around backyards, listening to hip-hop and smoking weed.

'Don't worry, Mr Pietruczuk!' One of them leaned over the handrail and waved at Asia's father gleefully. 'We'll protect her! She'll be fine.'

Pietruczuk recognised one of Krajnów's kids – one of his indoctrinated little soldiers. Now he was sure Asia would *not* be fine. If she went with the nationalists to town hall, the whole family would be in trouble. He spun on his heel and bumped into his wife. She aimed a finger at him, pinning him with a hateful glare.

'You encouraged her. This is your fault,' she hissed.

'Get dressed!' He threw her a trench coat from the hanger. She put it on over the dressing gown she was wearing and left the apartment, still in her slippers.

'If you can't talk some sense into her, I'll take her home by force,' Pietruczuk growled as they ran for the car. 'And then I'll spank the living hell out of her. Stupid girl and her imaginary war!'

The fingerprint collecting tent had been pitched an hour ago. They were supposed to use the cyanoacrylate method. Superglue, in a word. Uniformed constables were patrolling the area, followed by forensic technicians. There was a line of expensive black cars parked by the market square. Their licence plates suggested they were the property of the Ministry of Internal Affairs.

Doman commandeered one of the empty stalls and proceeded to set up his temporary command centre. Plastic chairs had been brought in and Doman was currently reporting to his immediate superior and the prosecutor. It looked like a kangaroo court, with a panel of judges listening to the confessions of someone already considered guilty. Shouts and hostile growls could be heard from the crowd of onlookers outside, behind the police tape.

Romanowska was doing her best not to pass out. Her headache had only got worse. He eye was twitching. The puking would come any time now. This had to be an effect of sleep deprivation. But she hadn't dared ask for a couple of hours off to sleep the pain away. She greeted the bigwigs coming in one by one. Most of them hadn't been to the region before and she was trying to make a good first impression. Apparently, the Chief Constable from Central HQ was on her way to personally oversee the crime scene. This was her future in the balance, right here. It could go either way. It was making Romanowska feel really queasy.

The market itself had been emptied of people and the police tape strung around the circumference of the square, along the street, so that no civilian could so much as catch a glimpse of the police work being done inside. There were more reporters and camera operators than during the last presidential elections, when Kwaśniewski himself had come to their little town looking for votes.

The local officers were given the worst part of the job. They had to do all the legwork, question all the potential witnesses, including 'tourists' from over the eastern border, who were now doing their best to disappear. None of them had a trade licence. Their goods had already been confiscated and were now being combed through for illegal substances, firearms and stolen items. They had their hands full and that wouldn't change for at least a week. Of course, they couldn't put each and every regular at the Ruble Mart in the hotseat. Looking for the killer would be like looking for a needle in a haystack.

Romanowska had ordered her officers to keep working non-stop, though officially shifts were supposed to change every eight hours. She had promised them they'd get bonuses for the overtime. She had even tried wooing them with special goodie packages for Christmas. Surprisingly, not even a single one had refused. They all knew the gravity of the situation.

Romanowska herself had the mayor, the starost and all the local businessmen calling her pretty much non-stop. They were shitting their pants. How would this murder affect their businesses, they all wanted to know. It was understandable; they had to protect their interests, and the victim was one of the town bigwigs: Piotr Bondaruk.

The news of the severed head found in a barrel of sauerkraut spread across the city instantly. The locals quickly put two and two together and within an hour everyone knew the director of the lumber mill had been murdered. The only thing the police managed to keep under the radar was what the technicians discovered when they toppled the barrel over and fished the pickled head out of the cabbage juice. The murderer had put a short letter in Bondaruk's mouth, having had the foresight to get it laminated beforehand. The paper was white, and the writing on it was in Belarusian. The commissioner was certain that if the police decided to reveal that, it would turn into a national sensation in no time. *Woś żyćcio kastrapataje. Choczam, kab nas kachali. Ale czamu? Hetaha nichto nie wiedaje.* 'This is our harsh life. We all want to be loved. But why? To that question, nobody knows the answer.'

They had to solve this case right away. Otherwise, heads would roll, and Romanowska couldn't have that. The deal she had been promised could be off the table now. And she had only just been told she could swap her job with the police for a cosy position at town hall.

A court pathologist passed her. The prosecutor, Anita Krawczyk, shook the man's hand and gestured for Romanowska to guard the entrance. Relieved, Romanowska retired to a spot by the police tape, and didn't even hold it against the prosecutor that she had treated her, the commissioner, like some low-ranking patrol cop. She whistled to Błażej, who was questioning another customer of the TO-MI-TO eager to put the blame on another 'suspect individual' they'd seen at the market. Romanowska looked at the woman and immediately saw through her bullshit. She had nothing of value to say.

'Stay here,' she ordered her son and turned to the witness. 'Please report to the station. The officer on duty will question you.'

'What about me?'

It was Anatol Pires. He was leading his AmStaff on a short leash. The dog, as always, wasn't muzzled.

'Good day, Principal,' Romanowska greeted the old creep, already thinking about how to ditch him. 'If you would be so kind, I'd like you to report to the station too. Unless this is really urgent.'

'It is.' Pires bobbed his head eagerly. He continued in Belarusian. 'Though you're probably not interested in what an old codger like me has to say.'

'Sir, I've a lot on my plate right now. Please cut to the chase. You see what's happening.'

Pires leaned in closer. His sleepy dog didn't move. It observed the goings-on apathetically.

'Does it bite?' The commissioner indicated the dog.

'*It* is a *she*,' the old man corrected her. 'She only bites bad people.'

'All right. What have you got for me?' Romanowska sighed.

'Oh, this and that.' Pires waved a hand dismissively with a playful wink. He wanted her to ask.

Romanowska rolled her eyes. 'Well, are you going to tell me? I'm in a bit of a hurry,' she lied.

'On the day of Bondaruk's wedding, his sons commissioned me to kill him,' the man said simply.

Romanowska stared at Pires, dumbfounded.

'They offered me money. All three of them chipped in. Fucking brothers Karamazov.'

'How much, if you don't mind me asking?'

'I don't know. I refused.'

Romanowska patted the old man on the shoulder. 'We'll check up on that lead. They're at the top of our list of suspects. All thanks to you.'

'Wait. That's not all.' He grabbed her by the lapel with his gnarly hand. 'I know who took the job.'

Romanowska didn't react and the old man seemed to deflate. The conversation was going nowhere; she thought him a crazy old fool, and he was certain the commissioner wouldn't believe him. He smiled gently and started to whistle. She didn't quite recognise the song. Some kind of anthem, maybe?

'Well, I'm all ears,' she prodded the man, seeing at the same time that a police van full of people was approaching.

The police had called in the six people who could have had anything to do with that barrel of sauerkraut. They were going to take a lot of fingerprints: from those warehouse workers and all the market vendors. They had to be clear about which prints had something to do with the case and which they could safely ignore.

'I can't tell you here.' Pires turned his back on the commissioner and began shuffling away.

'Hey! Sir!' she called and jogged after him. 'This isn't a good time to withhold information.'

'There are three possibilities,' he said without any more games. He suddenly looked in a hurry himself to spill whatever details he knew. 'The butcher, Nesteruk, for one. The father of that Bison girl is my second guess. And the third is that girl with the broken arm.'

'Załuska?' Romanowska was trying her best to keep from laughing.

'Don't know her name,' Pires grumbled. 'That redhead sniffing around town.'

'Why do you think she's behind this?'

'I saw them last night in the forest. At the burned-down cottage. You know, the one where they used to keep pigs and where the whisperer lives now. They were talking right by the unmarked grave at the weeping willow.'

'The birch tree, you mean?'

'There's a little birch copse over there, you're right. But the place is known as the weeping willow. I can see you're not from here. Anyway, they talked for a long, long time.'

'Does it matter if I'm local? If it does, why do you come to me? Why not report it officially?'

He grinned. 'I don't want to be in any records. But I need you to know something. She's not an outsider.'

'Who?'

'The redhead. She's local, I tell you. She must have come to avenge Staszek's death.'

He leaned close to her and whispered, 'Maybe she's Stepan's daughter. Who knows. Don't be afraid of the dog that barks. Fear the one that growls.'

'Right. Thanks for that.' Romanowska offered the man a hand, but instead of shaking it, the old fool puffed out his chest and placed a wet kiss on her palm.

'You know where I live if you need me.' He winked at her and waddled away, his dog trailing in his wake.

The commissioner watched the pair until they rounded a corner. She stood rooted in place for a long while after they'd gone, even more confused than before.

'What did he want?' Jah-Jah had appeared from out of nowhere.

'He said he knows who murdered Piotr,' she replied.

'Is it me or you? Maybe someone at town hall? The guy likes his stories, you got to give him that.'

Romanowska didn't laugh. 'Listen, what exactly happened when the profiler from Gdańsk came to town? Where did you find her?'

'Not me,' Jah-Jah said. 'A patrol. They found her here, just wandering around, no documents or anything on her.'

'Are we one hundred per cent sure she is who she says she is?' Romanowska fastened her gaze on Jah-Jah.

'What are you suggesting?'

'Did we have her papers checked?'

Jah-Jah lowered his gaze and mumbled something vaguely.

'What if she's just impersonating a profiler? What if she's pretending?' Romanowska asked, growing agitated. 'Maybe she's just printed out some random doctoral thesis and forged the documents. And what about this cop she was calling over and over again?'

'The guy never showed up.'

'Isn't that weird?' The commissioner cocked her head. 'How can we be sure about who she is? There are no photos of a Sasza Załuska on the Internet. Or at HQ in Gdańsk.'

Jah-Jah produced a toothpick and stuck it in his mouth.

'You quit smoking?'

'Yup. Two hours clean,' he grunted. 'I got meat in my teeth.'

They were silent for a while.

'You think she's a fraud? A con artist?' Jah-Jah asked.

Romanowska shrugged. 'This whole shitshow started with her, didn't it? As soon as she came to town,' she paused, 'everything went to crap.'

'So who is she—' Suddenly, it dawned on him. He stared at Romanowska. 'You think *she's* back? Now? After all those years? Come to think of it, that would make sense. The media couldn't shut up about Bondaruk's wedding. Maybe she read about it on the Internet or heard it on TVP Polonia? She doesn't look like Stepan, though.'

'Yeah, sure, as if you would remember how her mother looked,' Romanowska scoffed.

She took a look around, making sure nobody was listening in on them.

'Sell it to the prosecutor. She'll buy anything now,' she said. 'And send a photo of Irma to that anthroposcopy magician. We might as well check up on that.'

Jah-Jah took out a pack of cigarettes. 'That would really make sense,' he said. 'If she really is Irma, she had motive to cut the fucker's head off. She might have done all the rest, too.'

'That would be a beautiful solution to all of our problems.' Romanowska beamed and headed towards the crime scene. She suddenly realised that her headache was gone.

'Where do you think you're going?'

'I want to see the show too,' she replied and assumed her official manner. 'Wait here, Officer. Nobody will disturb you. They wouldn't dare. And all they want to do is pester me.'

'All right. Go if you want. It's boring anyway. They're just scanning everything or something. The doc is recording, and the technicians are digging through the cabbage.'

'They found nothing apart from the head?'

He nodded, adding, 'I won't be eating *bigos* for years, though. If you don't want to feel the same, you might not want to go in there. Let the guys from central do their work. I'll deal with Irma's photo right away.'

Romanowska wasn't listening any more. She disappeared into the tent, only to rush back out and vomit all over the fence a moment later.

'What a bloody mess.' She glanced at Jah-Jah. He sent her a sympathetic look. 'It's hard to believe, but Four-Eyes finally really is dead.'

Jah-Jah didn't have a chance to reply; suddenly they found themselves surrounded by a crowd of police officers. The prosecutor stood at the front of the group.

'The head was severed post-mortem,' she said. 'The pathologist says it was done by a professional. Someone who knows a thing or two about butchery. Maybe someone working at the meat processing plant. Go and narrow down the list of suspects for me. You know the locals.'

'Iwona, the bride we found yesterday, used to work at Nesteruk's,' Doman offered.

'Just like half of the town. That doesn't tell us much,' the prosecutor retorted. 'But I agree that she had motive. Interrogate her. And check out the place where she hid. It would be easier if we found the murder weapon. And get me the rest of the body. We'll have the GPR in a couple of hours. Get me a list of other places where you could hide a body around here.'

'There's a big forest around town, if you hadn't noticed. That makes a murderer's job quite a bit easier.'

'How about the profiler? She's never around when we need her.'

Jah-Jah and Romanowska exchanged quick looks.

'Doman has this friend.' Jah-Jah took it on himself to speak. 'I saw him a while back. He's a famous profiler from Śląsk.'

'All right, we won't have the GPR for long,' the prosecutor cut in. 'So get back to work, everyone.'

'Yes, ma'am!' Jah-Jah saluted with a silly grin.

Romanowska frowned. She said, 'Murder, decapitation, laminated letter, sticking the head in a barrel, nailing it shut. Why complicate things so much? That's hard to pull off. Was it one person or a group?'

'Don't know,' Jah-Jah replied. 'But I don't think we'll get to the bottom of this for months.'

Anita Krawczyk bristled, but patted Jah-Jah's muscled back.

'We'll get them, man. Don't you worry about that. There are a lot of fingerprints around, and a whole lot of other traces. Enough of that, though. I'm feeling peckish. I'm popping in somewhere for a quick pierogi.'

A dog's severed head, wearing a white and red collar with a Belarusian Pahonia symbol, flew through the open window of the mayor's office. It bounced off the desk, rolled to the door of the secretary's office, hit the wall and tumbled under the cupboard.

Unfortunately the office was empty, the mayor being out on an appointment and the secretary having gone out for lunch and a manicure. So nobody witnessed this daring act of protest. The cleaning lady came across it when she arrived to mop the floor. The head didn't even leave bloody traces, as had been the plan – it had been intended to symbolise the impurity of the mayor's blood.

The young National Hajnówka members had waited outside town hall for the screams of horror in vain.

Nonetheless, they resolved to stay there until the town officials came out of their den, however long that took. They chanted, 'Down with the commies' and 'Glory to the Heroes', but aside from a few lower-rank clerks who pressed their noses to the windows, and one security guard who looked more curious than scared, they had no audience.

Suddenly, someone pointed and shouted. A police patrol car was visible, coming towards them. The activists exchanged brief looks. There were only a dozen of them. Their leader, who went by the alias Snowdrift and was part of the guerrilla group, saw in his young associates' faces that they were getting scared. They were only schoolkids, after all. He gestured to them to hold their positions. There would be no surrender. No retreat.

This was when an old Tarpan truck clattered into the car park. Leszek Krajnów and his assistant, the receptionist from the Bison Motel, stepped out and marched straight towards the group of protesters. Artur Mackiewicz remained inside the car, keeping his friends under surveillance.

'What do you think you're doing?' Krajnów roared.

'Have you read the article in the newspaper, sir? They're accusing you of fascism. And they've offended us.'

Krajnów raised his hand. Then his steely expression softened into a grin. 'They've finally started to recognise us as a genuine force,' he said. 'There's no need to be angry about that. Besides, being compared to Bury is a compliment. Don't you think?'

Snowdrift, confused, muttered something in response and, finally, he nodded in agreement. Krajnów stroked the burly boy's head, like he would a naughty child's. Then he plucked the banner Snowdrift was holding from his shaking hand and took a good look at it.

'Outstanding job, son.'

'Asia painted it.'

'I recognise her style.'

Krajnów managed to roll the banner up again just before the police car reached them, and gave a warm smile to the constable leaning out of the window.

'This is an illegal assembly. You haven't been given permission to demonstrate here,' the constable barked.

'What assembly are you talking about, Romek?' Krajnów feigned surprise. 'We've just finished our history lesson. Town hall took our classroom from us, so I teach in the park now. While the Belarusians get the whole cinema for their lousy documentary movies. And who's paying for that? We are. The taxpayers.'

'I don't care about your games, Lech. Disperse,' the constable ordered, though his voice was comradely. He shot out a finger, aiming it at Krajnów. He wasn't serious in the least and Krajnów knew it. 'I see you, man. I'll be keeping an eye on you.'

He stepped out of the car and leaned in closer to Krajnów.

'Listen, mate. Get those kids somewhere else or I'll have to report it. Don't do this to me today. It's been a hard day. We've got all kinds of outsiders in town.'

'All right, no problem, mate.' Krajnów and the constable high-fived.

Mackiewicz emerged from the old truck and joined the group.

'Ah, here's the commander himself,' the constable said. Then, he winked playfully, lowered his voice, contorted his face in a hostile grimace and growled: 'Get lost, you *katsap*.'

The kids burst out laughing.

The constable, Krajnów and Mackiewicz fist-bumped and then the constable returned to his car. As it drove off, Krajnów called after it, 'Have a nice day, officer. Don't get your hands too dirty.'

He turned to the young activists. 'We'll have to postpone the operation. Mr Bondaruk stole our show today.'

At that precise moment, Asia's father rounded the corner of the building, with his wife hot on his heels. The woman was shouting something, but Pietruczuk didn't listen. He stormed over to the group, snatched his daughter by the sleeve and slapped her round the face. Snowdrift immediately stepped between the girl and her father and swung at the older man, a left hook. There was a crack as his skull hit the ground, and blood gushed from his mouth. Asia's mother dropped to her knees and wailed. Krajnów and Mackiewicz motioned for the kids to run, tossed their banners into the boot of their truck and called an ambulance.

Mackiewicz's Tarpan truck burned out later that night. Krajnów was suspended from his duties at school. Asia was arrested, but permitted to leave the station after only four hours; Mackiewicz personally went to the judge, bailed her out and convinced him to change her punishment from incarceration to police supervision.

A month later, a video of Asia climbing the town hall wall and tossing the severed dog's head through the window went viral. She was expelled from the Belarusian high school. For years to come, people would say this was the beginning of the Polish–Belarusian war, even though in reality it had been the nationalists' least successful operation and a complete fiasco.

'We need to talk.' Sasza caught Doman on the steps leading to the police station. He looked exhausted, swaying on his feet. 'I think I'm the last person who saw Bondaruk before his death.'

He stopped.

'Why does that not surprise me,' he muttered. 'You know they're looking for you?'

'Who?'

He didn't reply, just opened the door for her and gestured to the guard to let them both through, and they went to his office.

'What a mess,' he sighed, running his fingers through his hair. He massaged his temples. His eyes were bloodshot. He stank of sweat. He offered Sasza a can of Coke.

'What is it this time?'

'Yesterday he told me his story and showed me Stepan's and the priest's grave. He must have died between two and six in the morning.'

'You a pathologist now?'

'He took me to the motel before two. Truth be told, he was drunk as hell. The market opens at six. And someone put the head in the barrel before it arrived at the Ruble Mart. At least that's what the papers say. I don't have Internet access on my phone.'

Doman remained silent.

'You don't want to see the place?' she asked. 'I believe he died because he showed it to me.'

The officer pushed a stack of papers to the side of Romanowska's desk.

'I could have made commissioner here just a few years ago,' he said. 'I'm so glad I didn't. I can't wrap my head around this.'

Before Sasza could say anything, the door opened.

'Here she is,' said Romanowska, entering with the prosecutor, Krawczyk, on her heels. Jah-Jah was right behind them. 'I hope you have a good lawyer.'

'You're under arrest for the murder of Piotr Bondaruk and Danuta Pietrasik, as well as complicity in the kidnapping of Iwona Bondaruk, née Bejnar.'

'Very funny,' Sasza snorted.

Krawczyk shook her head.

'Sasza.' She addressed the other woman patiently, as if talking to a child. 'We have your fingerprints and a witness. Not to mention a whole chain of traces leading to you regarding several other cases. We've had you under surveillance for some time. I can guarantee you a shorter sentence if you point us to your partner. Also, we need you to tell us where you hid the rest of Bondaruk's body.'

'What? What partner?' Sasza asked, confused. 'What are you talking about? For the last week I've been doing nothing but helping you. Are you all out of your goddamned minds? I didn't kill anyone!'

'Iwona recognised you. We also have a witness testifying that you buried something down at the weeping willow last night.'

'I haven't buried anything! I was checking out the place. The earth looked like it had been dug up. Bondaruk showed me the place where he buried the bodies in that old case back in seventy-seven. Stepan and the priest.' She produced the documents Piotr had given her. The files – copies; she had photocopied the originals at Ciszynia and sent them via courier to Robert Duchnowski. Just in case. 'I called Jah-Jah earlier. Romanowska too. Nobody showed up to get me and now you're making a show of it? Fuck you. Apology not accepted. Have a nice day.'

She turned to leave, but Jah-Jah barred her way.

Krawczyk sat down. Jah-Jah pushed Sasza into the chair opposite the prosecutor and the woman took Sasza's hands in her own. She was behaving like it was painful for her to give Sasza the bad news, but it was only an act.

'We checked the place you pointed us to a while ago,' she said slowly. 'The GPR finally came in handy. There is nothing there. No bodies. What we did find, though, was a headless corpse. We're running a DNA check on it as we speak, but Bondaruk's housekeeper has already identified it. She recognised the pyjama bottoms, you see.'

Sasza blinked, dumbfounded. She recalled Piotr leading her into the bushes, telling her to keep the documents to herself. She hugged them to her chest now . She wouldn't show those files to them. Not any more.

'I won't talk to you without my lawyer present,' she said.

Piotr Bondaruk was buried with honours in the Orthodox cemetery, though Dunia Orzechowska had emerged from her lair to ask the mayor to instead inter him in his family grave at the Catholic burial ground. More people attended the funeral than had come to the wedding party. The priest read a couple of solemn recollections of the director's life, and the mayor awarded him a posthumous medal, promising that at the next town council meeting one of the streets would be named after their dearly departed hero. Piotr's sons huddled in the church vestibule throughout the ceremony, sticking together like three dour crows.

None of them carried the casket either. And they had refused to spend a dime on a wake for the locals, instead only inviting a couple of close friends the following week to the Forest Palace, where they enjoyed a discount. The flowers, the ceremony and the priest's wage had been covered by Iwona, who had to use the money he had left her and Quack for their new life. After all the expenses, she was left with only a couple of grand in her account, not even enough to pay a lawyer to get the Bison brothers out of jail when they were incarcerated for faking their sister's kidnapping. So, Iwona pawned the engagement ring Piotr had given her, as well as her wedding ring. The lawyer, Artur Mackiewicz, took her money, agreeing to waive the VAT this one time.

The casket remained closed for the duration of the funeral; nobody had wanted to pay for embalming the body. The casket, which was the cheapest variety, made of MDF board, was lowered into the grave while the townsfolk lined up to throw handfuls of dirt on top of it. Their exaggerated cries pierced the air as they tossed in cheap little crosses, small Orthodox icons and coloured ribbons. The locals really did mourn Bondaruk. His closest business partners, trusted advisors and companions, on the other hand, were just waiting for the show to end.

Mikołaj Nesteruk didn't even enter the church, standing at the cemetery gate and watching the ceremony from afar. After the funeral, Dunia walked up to him, head bowed, and he embraced her. It seemed the woman had grown more emaciated lately. People weren't offering their condolences to Bondaruk's family; they approached him and Dunia instead.

Amid the throng of townsfolk, Iwona recognised her father. That was surprising, she thought wryly; Dawid was sober and wearing his best suit. Iwona nearly burst into tears, seeing her father like that. As she watched him, she was thinking about Quack, too. He was still missing.

She stood among the crowd while her husband was buried, completely numb, and disillusioned. With the help of Mackiewicz, Piotr's sons had managed to bring the inheritance proceedings to a halt. Iwona had no money for her own lawyer, and thinking about the future caused her nearly physical pain. She would have to go back to waitressing at the Forest Palace. At least for old times' sake, the owner had agreed to let her start working from next Tuesday, so she wouldn't have to handle all the VIPs at the wake.

In his last will, Piotr left all his property to the Danuta 'Inka' Siedzikówna Historical Association. The sole administrator of his estate was to be his only biological son – Jurek Orzechowski. Quack. The will had been pored over by a graphologist, and then a team of lawyers, and had finally been passed to the court. Quack hadn't showed up at the notary's office to hear the last will, though, meaning that Tomik, Wasyl and Fionik could for the time being dispose of their father's riches as they saw fit. They set to it with wild abandon. They drove his cars, took over his office, and declared publicly that they would run his business from now on. Then, after they found out that Bondaruk's flat had been stripped of all his belongings, they accused Iwona of theft and sued her. In the end, Marianna Mackiewicz – the lawyer's mother and Bondaruk's housekeeper – managed to talk her son out of bringing the case to court. All Iwona was left with to show for her marriage to Bondaruk was the humongous oven, a plasma TV, and a small strip of land that Piotr had given over to her brothers before the wedding. The Bejnars didn't have the means to build their dream house there, though. They remained in their cramped flat on Chemiczna Street and the land went unused.

Iwona looked down as Dunia joined her. The older woman was dressed in her dirty rags, as always, although today they looked a tone or two darker. It was a funeral, after all, Iwona thought. Dunia took Iwona by the hand and pushed something into her palm. It was an Orthodox cross. Aluminium. Worthless. It had an inscription in Belarusian on the back. *'Spasi i sokhrani'* – save and protect us.

When Iwona's father approached Bondaruk's grave, the crowd parted. Iwona watched him, worried. Dawid picked up a handful of dirt, but instead of throwing it on the casket, he tucked it into his pocket. Then he took out a small package wrapped in an old Belarusian kerchief, and an equally ancient notebook bound in oil-cloth, and threw those items into the hole. As soon as he was done, the gravediggers got to work and quickly filled the pit with earth. People dropped flowers onto the little cairn and dispersed. An hour later the cemetery was deserted again.

Four-Eyes' grave blazed with light for weeks after the funeral. Ordinary people, grateful to Bondaruk for the work, help and support he had offered them, kept coming in with candles and vigil lights to pray for the soul of their benefactor.

The room was small and cramped. A table stood in the middle, with an old-fashioned stool placed at each end. The room was stuffy and smelled of cigarette smoke. It was a classic line-up room, with a one-way mirror on one side.

Sasza was led inside as the first. She wore a striped T-shirt and jeans. She seemed thinner than she was. She sat down on one of the stools and stared into the mirror. They were watching her. How many times had she been on the other side of just such a mirror? She couldn't count. It was her first time on this side, though. She was cold, but there was nothing she could cover herself with. They had taken her leather jacket because of its metal elements – zippers, a few rivets, a detachable belt. Now her trousers were too loose and she had to pull them up every now and then. Her glasses had been taken too, as well as her phone, wallet and her money. It wasn't a hypothesis any more; she was the main suspect now. She could be sentenced for murder. What was worse, she had no idea what they had on her. The only certainties were that Bondaruk was dead, they had his body, and Sasza was the perfect scapegoat. She had been working for that honour long and hard, it seemed.

The door creaked and a handsome, dark-haired man entered the room. His bushy brows formed a nearly unbroken line over his eyes. He was tall and lanky. The kind of guy who sometimes makes you pull in your belly and puff out your chest on instinct, Sasza thought. The kind of guy you listen to, really drink in his words, even if what he says is arrogant and crass. The kind of guy you want to marry as soon as he so much as smiles at you. His eyes were steely, cold, and his stare piercing. He took off his black trench coat, too dapper for the occasion, and threw it on the floor. He wore blue jeans and a black T-shirt. Sasza immediately knew who she was dealing with; he didn't have to introduce himself. He did anyway.

'Hubert Meyer,' he said. The forensic psychologist. 'I'm sorry we couldn't meet in different circumstances.'

'Can't say I really share your regret. I've been wondering for some time now just how good you were.'

Meyer smiled. 'Are you trying to put me off guard by playing with my ego?'

'Can't think of anything else to do.'

'A typical reaction for a smart suspect. Defence by counter-attacking.'

'You charged me with murder. What do you have on me?'

'Oh, I'm only a guest here. Won't be here for long.'

'Same here.'

'All right. You really want to keep playing games?'

'Don't know.' Sasza fell silent.

'You don't have a lawyer, you don't confess to anything, but you asked to see me. Why?'

'Because you're an outsider and a profiler, just like me. I don't trust anyone who was born here, has family here or has even visited this place before. They're all one happy clique,' Sasza said, with a disgusted grimace. 'And I know how this sounds, believe me.'

He smiled again. 'So, you're innocent.'

She didn't respond, keeping her eyes on the ground.

'How is it possible that you were the first on the crime scene when Iwona Bejnar was kidnapped? And then you found Danuta Pietrasik's body, and were the last person to see Piotr Bondaruk alive. To make things worse, you were in a relationship with Łukasz Polak, wanted by the police. Can you explain this?'

'It's actually pretty simple. I'm better than the locals at my job,' she replied, and waited for a reaction. Meyer didn't even blink. He was good – she had to give him that.

'Or maybe I just wanted those cases solved,' she added.

'And the police don't?'

'No. They don't.'

'Why?'

She sighed heavily.

'That's a long story. I did some digging and discovered some things the locals didn't want known. I'd like you to take a look at the documents I received from Bondaruk before he died. We can talk when you're finished with them.'

She got up to leave the room. Meyer remained seated, following her with his eyes. She pushed at the door, but nothing happened. They were locked in. They weren't going to let her out until Meyer was finished with her. Great. She'd have to sit here until she broke. At least, that was what they were counting on. She swore under her breath, but went back to her chair.

'Right. I forgot my role in this,' she said with a smile. 'Back to the questioning. I left a cigarette pack wrapper at Bondaruk's house. It has my fingerprints on it. And the letter. It was written by the director himself, wasn't it?'

Meyer didn't react. Sasza continued.

'Only someone familiar with our work would be able to plant that kind of evidence. I called the lead investigator and the commissioner, as well as her ex-husband, on the night of the murder. None of them returned my calls. Nobody showed up at the place I pointed them to. And they were the only people who knew where I was meeting Bondaruk. They also knew who was buried in that grave. You can check my phone bills if you'd like confirmation.'

'Are you accusing the police? Oh, that's good.'

'Yeah?' Sasza inhaled. 'So why don't you tell me what motive I had to do all that? A profiler's first question should be "why". Then "how". You don't get to hypothesise before that.'

Meyer pushed himself to his feet. 'Could you wait a minute, please?'

'I'm can't exactly go anywhere,' Sasza grunted, running her fingers through her hair. She couldn't tie it in a ponytail; they had taken her hairband too. She hated her hair like this, making her look like some kind of wild *rusalka.*

A minute passed. Meyer came back.

'What documents did you mean earlier?' he asked, sitting back down.

Sasza started to laugh. 'Those were only copies. I sent the originals to someone I trust. An officer in Gdańsk. Since he hasn't called you back, I guess he hasn't got them yet.'

Meyer leaned over the table and said, 'Why don't you explain something to me? I was told why you came here, but I can't wrap my head around why you didn't just turn round and leave. Why would you stick your nose into those investigations? They broke your arm, for God's sake. Why would you stay after that?'

Sasza thought about it. When she finally replied, Meyer had already lit a cigarette and was passing her the pack of Marlboro reds. She took one reluctantly. They were too strong for her liking.

'Have you ever been afraid?'

He nodded.

'For yourself or for others?'

'Both, I guess.'

'Then you know that fear has a limit. When you pass that threshold, it only becomes fuel.'

'Is that so? Sounds like a rather pathological mechanism. Psychopaths often act like that, feeding on adrenaline.'

'Just so.' She nodded. 'Like an engine of a plane. The momentum keeps it going, lifts it into the air and leads it to its destination, though at first glance it seems impossible.'

'That only works when you have wings.'

'I do. I have a daughter. Eight years old.'

Meyer observed her for a while and flicked the ash from his cigarette to the floor.

'What were you looking for here?'

'I thought I needed to challenge Łukasz Polak. I needed to confront him. I was wrong. What I really needed was forgiveness. I wanted to find him and apologise. He nearly died because of me. But the closer I got to him, the more embroiled I got in this investigation.'

'Maybe you shouldn't have lied so much.'

'That ship sailed a while ago,' she growled.

Meyer got up again and knocked on the door. It opened slightly and someone passed two bottles of mineral water through the crack. Sasza noticed Meyer nodding and giving someone a discreet sign, hoping she wouldn't spot it.

'If they let you go, will you leave?' he asked when he sat back down. 'Or will you keep digging?'

She looked up. 'Is that what this is all about? I'll leave. Even if I have to walk all the way to Gdańsk.'

Then, she told him Four-Eyes' real story. She told him all about the main players and their roles over the years. They talked for hours. At the end, Meyer asked her about Doman. Was he in on this too? Was he a part of the conspiracy? When they were finished, Meyer rose and picked up his trench coat. He brushed it down quickly and put it on, then left the room.

'Let her out before you embarrass yourselves even more,' he told Doman. 'You might as well close Danuta Pietrasik's case. It was an emotionally motivated murder committed by the Red Spider copycat. Just as I said. The pathologist confirmed the dental profile. Check the perp isn't faking mental illness, but I doubt it.' He stopped speaking abruptly and left without another word.

KUBA

(2000)

When Kuba woke up, programming had ended for the night and the TV was hissing with white noise. He sat up, scratched his balls and went to the kitchen annexe to get something to eat. He was naked, save a pair of boxer shorts. He had had his last drink before midnight. His food supply consisted of only a pack of oatmeal and a jar of jam. He didn't feel like making porridge again. He had eaten nothing else for the last day or so. His aversion only strengthened when he noticed his roommate's stash of meat tucked at the bottom of the bread shelf. As he sliced the roast pork shoulder and stuffed his mouth with the delicious meat his roomie brought in from his mum's each week, he heard footsteps. He licked the knife and waited. Someone was walking down the steps to the basement. Kuba hid the rest of the meat and bread at the back of the fridge.

'Are we doing shots or what?' asked Andrzej, the owner of this dirty hovel.

Kuba sighed with relief. Andrzej was hiding his drinking from his wife. He would go downstairs at every opportunity to have a sip or two of his home-made concoction. It was pure spirit mixed with water, fifty-fifty.

Kuba took out two glasses. One of them was dirty. He passed it to Andrzej. The old boozer didn't even notice the dirty smudges. They drank in silence.

'One more?'

'If you insist,' Kuba agreed.

He poured another shot for them both. This time Andrzej broke the silence.

'What does a guy like you do in a place like this?'

Kuba grew suspicious. There was one simple rule – you don't ask, you don't answer. Everyone's happy. The fat bastard didn't care for rules, apparently. Kuba had seen the man observing him a couple of times before. There was nothing sexual in it, only a kind of unquenchable curiosity Andrzej could never quite rein in. People tended to open up to him, spilling their dirty little secrets. And he probably felt a bit safer knowing the stories of the human rats hiding in his underground hole. That wouldn't work with Kuba, though.

'I'm having a little holiday.' He smiled his studied smile – one of the more innocent and charismatic ones in his arsenal. Seven out of ten on the charm scale. This obese pig didn't deserve more.

'Cheers.' Andrzej poured another shot, gulped it down and stashed the bottle in the pantry. Then, huffing and puffing, he climbed the stairs and disappeared.

Kuba collapsed onto his bed and pulled an old *Playboy* from under the mattress. He knew it by heart by now. Squinting, he brought the page showing an attractive Ukrainian Playmate closer to his face. An instant later, he tossed it away. The paper stank of mould. Instead of growing hard, his prick had shrivelled. Kuba pulled the filthy blanket over his head. There was no washing machine in the basement and he had to wash everything by hand. That meant he didn't wash anything at all. He tried to go to sleep.

The fags in the room next door must have been asleep already. Normally he could hear all their movements. He got up and walked over to his roommate's PC. He bent over, switched on the machine and then flicked the monitor on. The screen remained dark for a long while but finally, it loaded. It was password protected. Kuba tried three times: 'Shaggy'; the birthdate of that stupid cunt (because the guy had told him the story of his life the first day they had spent in this shithole); and finally the area postcode and name of the city he had been born in: Siedlce. It was no use. Worse, the computer threatened that the next time he gave the wrong password, it would lock down. Immediately, Kuba switched the PC off and returned to his own half of the room. He picked up his English copy of *Wisdom of Psychopaths* and tried to read it. Within a couple of minutes he had dozed off.

He dreamed he was at an intercity bus station, wanting to go to Japan, but the woman behind the counter was refusing to sell him a ticket. He jerked her up by the scruff of the neck and pulled her out of her cubbyhole, and stole cash from the register. Then he took the first departing bus and packed the money into his rucksack. Stupid cunt, he thought. How thick do you have to be to keep the cash box on top of the counter, with the key inside. He felt good. Happy. He could feel the weight of the money in his backpack. The coins rang so gleefully. It sounded so joyful, he started laughing like a baby hearing a baby rattle. Then, all of a sudden, he was swimming in a natural pool, but instead of plants and fish he was surrounded by floating banknotes. He opened his backpack and stuffed them into it until it was close to bursting. He slid the zip up with difficulty, stuffed some more money into his pockets and ate a few of the notes for good measure. That was unexpected. They tasted like . . . paper. Whatever. It was just nice to chew them, waste all that money. He knew that when he surfaced he'd be able to live like he wanted, not caring about all the fucking shitheads around. He decided to swim upwards and look for some more containers in which to store all the cash. His foot caught on something. He squirmed and fought. His backpack finally burst and the money drifted away. He couldn't catch all the notes, however he tried. The water started flooding his lungs. He was drowning. Falling. Deeper and deeper.

'Kuba,' someone whispered.

He opened an eye, though he'd have known who it was with them closed. Shaggy was always sweaty and stinking to high heaven. Kuba could feel his reek as soon as the man opened the door. It was Shaggy who was trying to wake him up now. The dumb fuck had ruined his beautiful dream.

'I was having such a bloody nice dream,' Kuba muttered. 'What you want, knobhead?'

'Where's my meat?'

'Fuck off,' Kuba spat. 'Andrzej dropped by. I gave him some. Go complain to the fat pisshead if you want. Maybe he'll pay you back in booze.'

He heard giggling. He opened his other eye. There was a cross-eyed lass with huge boobs standing in the doorway. She wore her hair in a wild Afro. He shut his eyes again. *It's a fucking nightmare. It must be,* he thought.

'Leave him,' the woman said in a raspy voice. 'Let's grab something in town.'

Kuba didn't even lift his head.

'Maybe there's something wrong with him,' another voice else said. Delicate, quiet. Another woman.

Kuba thought frantically. This was some serious shit. The archivist never brought any women back but, all of a sudden, here were two. He rolled to the side so that he could study them from under his blanket.

'Andrzej gave him booze again,' Shaggy complained. 'He'll go blind drinking that much spirit. Do you know how strong that stuff is?'

'All right, let's go,' the cross-eyed girl ordered.

Kuba heard feet shuffling. He half-opened his eyes and saw a flash of a pair of slim legs. Well, maybe she was cross-eyed, but she had some legs on her. Kuba pushed himself up on one elbow, revealing his naked chest. Surprisingly, his dick, which he had thought had gone permanently flaccid through lack of use, suddenly hardened.

'Hi there.' Kuba smiled at the busty girl.

'Hi yourself, handsome,' Cross-Eye replied.

He turned his gaze to the other girl, who had a wide, cute, heart-shaped face. She was blushing like a schoolgirl. She was dressed like a schoolgirl too, with worn trainers on. He liked it. He jumped out of bed, counting on the good impression his naked body would make. No woman, he thought, could resist the godlike shape of his muscled calves. They were his best feature.

'I'm Marek,' he introduced himself, feigning shyness. He bent down to pick up his jeans and pulled them on over his toned butt. He didn't care that Shaggy was shaking his head at his innocent lie. He added: 'How and where did that shaggy dork find such treasures?'

Both women giggled at that.

'Oi, mate, where's my chow?' Shaggy asked again. 'I had a piece of meat stashed here.'

'Why would you care about meat when you have such lovely ladies here to keep you company?' Kuba assumed the stern voice of his dead father. Then he switched to his mother's scolding manner. She would have been proud of him. 'And you've dragged them to this shithole? Take them to a restaurant, man! You should be ashamed. You uncultured swine! Not to mention, I'm naked here. They shouldn't see me like this. Has the hair overgrown your brain too? Jesus Christ, man.'

'We found a dog on our way,' the girl in the trainers said. 'We wanted to feed it.'

Kuba said nothing. He had been eating fucking porridge for days and drinking Andrzej's toxic booze, and Shaggy wanted to feed his roast to a bloody mutt? He smiled pleasantly at the cute girl. He was ready to forgive her her fondness for homeless dogs if she was up for a quick shag. Come to think of it, he was a bit like a homeless dog himself. He wouldn't mind her taking care of him for a while.

'I've introduced myself – how about you? What's your name?'

She reached out a hand. There was a bandage round her forearm, but no ring on any of her fingers. Good.

'Monika.'

'Everybody calls her Jowita,' the other woman cut in.

'Not true,' Monika – Jowita – protested.

'I like both those names.' Kuba sent the girl his smile number one-oh-seven. This one was a ten out of ten. He hit the jackpot. 'You could be called the Mona Lisa, as long as you stay.'

'I'm Marzena,' interjected the cross-eyed girl. Kuba nodded and gave her a slightly lower-watt smile. He pulled on his tight-fitting bike shirt, which brought out his toned muscles. Then he slid his feet into a pair of brand new Nikes and put an old baseball cap on.

'So. Where are we going?'

'We?' Shaggy asked incredulously. 'I'm going to sleep. I got work at eight tomorrow.'

'What a bore,' Kuba sighed and assumed a grimace of disappointment. 'Why did I put my clothes on?'

'Let's have some fun right here, why don't we?' Marzena suggested, taking out a cigarette.

'It's not allowed,' Shaggy replied. 'Andrzej doesn't like it.'

'Having fun or smoking?' Marzena sent Shaggy a quick glance.

Kuba offered her a light. She responded with a smile and once again he had to admit she had a weird kind of appeal. She wasn't that bad after all. If she was rich, he could get used to her ugliness.

'You two figure something out and I'll wait in the car.' Jowita turned and headed to the door. 'My boy might wake up and he'll cry if I'm not there. And I'll check up on the dog, too.'

Kuba's smile vanished. Such a young girl, and she already had a kid. What a waste. She didn't wear a ring, so she was probably a single mother. That kind of thing wasn't for him. He didn't intend to nurse some brat. He was the one in need of some nursing.

'You got a driving licence, handsome?'

The cross-eyed one was getting on his nerves now, but he nodded.

'Come,' she said, pointing to the stairs. 'We'll have a smoke and a chat. You free tomorrow? And do you know the way to Hajnówka?'

'Not really,' he lied. 'But I'm always willing to help a lady. Depends on the job, though.'

'And the pay, eh?' Marzena saw through him. 'I know a thing or two about people.'

Shaggy tried protesting, but Marzena planted a kiss on his lips and went upstairs. Kuba and Jowita followed her.

'See ya, knobhead.' He waved at his roommate. 'Oh, and your PC might be down. I tried fixing it, but you didn't give me the password.'

A quick dodge saved Kuba from being hit by a flying boot. Marzena burst out laughing. 'Who lives in a hovel like that?' she asked as they climbed the stairs.

'Only rats, rogues and men who hate women.' He pointed at the next door and flicked his hand limply to show that it was occupied by a gay couple.

'You're funny.' Marzena started turning round but slipped, and her breasts rubbed against his cheek. He was finding it difficult to remain calm, and she wasn't making it any easier for him. She froze for an instant, letting her breasts stay in contact with Kuba's face. She whispered: 'I can see Jowita caught your eye. She's single, you know. But hurt her in any way and I'll rip your cock off and eat it.'

'Got it. I kind of like it, so I won't be taking any risks.'

They left the building. Kuba took the black perfumed cigarillo Marzena offered him.

'I got a job for you,' the woman said bluntly. She took a glance around, making sure Jowita was out of earshot. 'Someone hurt Jowita really badly. I got it on tape. That someone needs to pay now, and after they have, I need that someone eliminated.'

Kuba eyed her up and down and finally burst out laughing. 'You're a joker, aren't you?'

'Yeah,' Marzena replied coolly and stuck out a hand. 'It was nice meeting you. Ciao.'

Kuba shot out his arm but didn't go for her hand. Instead he grabbed her by the hair and yanked her towards him. She hissed in pain but freed herself nimbly. He was left with a handful of blond hair.

'That's an ambitious plan,' he said. 'How much?'

'I'm not the one paying, but you won't be living in this hovel. That, I can guarantee.'

'Let's go then.' He grabbed the handle of the back door of her car, a snow-white Mercedes E-class.

'What about your things? Aren't you going to pack them?'

Kuba looked puzzled.

'Everything I need is right here,' he said, patting his crotch.

'What an absolute nutter.'

'*You're* the nutter here. You barely know me.'

'I can smell a good hitman from a mile away.'

Flattery always worked on him. He wrapped an arm around her. 'So, you like bad boys, eh?'

Marzena giggled and passed him the car keys. 'It may be old, but it's still a good ride,' she said.

Kuba settled into the driver's seat. 'I got a sister in Hajnówka,' he said. 'Works in a hospital.'

Marzena, alert as always, sent him a suspicious glare. 'I need a name,' she said.

'Magda Prus. Mackiewicz now. She took her husband's name. Do you know her?'

She was quiet, clearly sorting through familiar faces in her head. He was sure Marzena knew his sister. He thought he'd seen her twitch slightly when he said the name. Besides, Hajnówka was a small town.

'We're going to her place.' Marzena broke her silence. 'Call her. Tell her to get a couple of beds ready. Two hours and she'll have guests. And we need some food, too. The kid hasn't had anything since we left.'

'She's a bit of a bore.' Kuba attempted to dissuade Marzena. 'And she kinda hates me. She's a lot older, you see. Twenty years, give or take.'

'Seriously?'

'She's adopted. My folks had me a lot later. Born with a silver spoon in me gob.' He grinned.

'Lucky Luke.'

'Fucking A.'

Magdalena looked through the peephole. Her wayward brother. She went rigid. Whenever he showed up, trouble soon followed. And he never called her if he didn't want something. If he had driven all the way down here, it meant she'd have to deal with his antics until she scrounged up enough cash to satisfy his needs. And as soon as she'd paid him off, he'd vanish. That was his speciality; he wandered around the country, changing homes like gloves. The authorities and his numerous creditors had a hard time finding him and he liked that just fine. He had perfected the art of covering his tracks. Well, almost; sometimes a court, a prosecutor or a debt collector did come knocking, trying to recover the money her brother hadn't paid back. She had asked him countless times to leave her out of his shady business. But she always took him in and helped him out. They were family, after all, and you don't turn away family.

Artur Mackiewicz, her husband, was asleep already, so she tiptoed out to the staircase. Kuba wasn't alone. One of the two women with him looked like a prostitute. The other one, who had a sleeping kid in her arms, looked okay. Maybe with a bit of work she could even be considered pretty. But if she was hanging out with a whore and Magdalena's unhinged little brother, she surely lacked in the instinct for self-preservation.

'I can't take you in. You should have called,' she scolded Kuba.

'My phone died,' he lied.

'You sold it or lost it, more likely.'

'Yeah, maybe so, sis.' He dropped his head apologetically. 'But where else were we to go? It's late.'

'This isn't some hamlet. There are hotels, you know.'

'Please, sis. The kid's starving.' Kuba made his most innocent face. 'I couldn't leave them like that.'

'Bugger off, you sot,' Magda hissed.

'We'll just sort out some business and we'll be gone by tomorrow. And you'll have a chance to fulfil your Hippocratic oath. Help out a bit, you know?'

'I can't believe it. Why must you always get yourself in a mess?'

'It's the last time, I promise,' he said. Magdalena knew this response by heart by now, as she did the humble tone Kuba always used to placate her. 'On my honour,' he added solemnly.

She gave in. 'Okay. Wait a minute.' She turned on her heel and retreated into her apartment.

They stood on the staircase, fooling around. Kuba cracked jokes, Marzena laughed her raspy laugh and Jowita stared at the handsome man, utterly spellbound.

Finally, Magda returned with a bunch of keys. She motioned for them to follow her and went down to her car. She drove slowly, carefully. Kuba overtook her in the E-class, speeding, showing off. When they finally reached the hospital, Magda led them to an unused room cluttered with clunky, decrepit hospital beds. She brought them blankets from the storage room, warning them to keep the lights off.

'Thank you for helping us and my little Tomek,' the nicer of the two girls said.

Magda didn't respond at first. She felt queasy. Kuba was getting into some new kind of trouble, and the only way she could deal with it was to not ask any questions. The less she knew, the better.

The kid – Tomek – was sleeping like a stone. She wondered how the boy would cope when he woke up in a completely unfamiliar place.

'You're welcome,' she said, finally. 'Rest now. Just don't make a mess.'

'A mess? Us?' Kuba exclaimed. 'Never!'

'I'm serious,' Magda growled and led her brother outside to the corridor. 'So, what brings you here this time?'

'Business.' He smiled.

'Don't you work at that telecom company any more?'

'That's way in the past, sis.'

'What do you do for a living, then?'

'Oh, you know, this and that,' he muttered. 'The usual. But I'm done with hacking and wiretaps, if that's what you're asking about. Don't worry.'

'They're looking for you. The police have been to my place. You were keeping stolen shoes in my basement. Do you have the slightest idea how much explaining I had to do on your behalf? You could have told me. I would have given you the keys to the garage in the hospital.'

'Sorry, sis. Really. That wasn't a good time for me.'

Magda fell for his innocent expression again. 'I'm such a poor boy', it said.

'I don't want any trouble this time, you hear? If you want to waste your life, be my guest. Just don't count on me bailing you out any more. I'm not your mother.'

'Ten-four, sis. I'm definitely not going back to prison. One time was enough.'

'I'm going to become the director at Ciszynia. Vice-director at least. Do you understand what that means?'

'What is there to understand? You're a successful woman.'

'Who are your companions?'

'Colleagues.'

'The cross-eyed one is a prostitute, isn't she? What about the other one?'

'It's nothing, really. Scout's honour!' He struck his chest. 'It's just business. By the way, I'm undercover. Call me Marek.'

Magda decided to drop it. 'All right. Do what you need to do, just don't get me involved.'

Kuba placed a hand on her shoulder. Just like their father used to when he wanted the kids to feel supported.

'You can count on me. Always.'

She hugged him. 'I'm just worried for you, is all.'

'Remember,' he said. 'I want you to know I'm there for you.'

'I know.'

Magda's eyes were tearing up. Kuba was struggling not to burst out in hysterical laughter, but he kept his most chivalric expression on. 'I'm the gallant knight. I am your *brother*', this one said. It always worked. This time was no exception. Magda reached into her pocket and shoved a couple of banknotes into his palm.

'Buy the kid some milk when he wakes up.'

'Sure thing, Mum.' He winked.

'Say goodbye to your ladies from me.' She patted him on the cheek and left quickly, without looking back.

Marzena got up first and woke the others. Jowita stretched out and yawned, but stayed in bed for some time playing with little Tomek, giggling. As if they had all the time in the world. There was work to do, and little time.

'Marek!' She shook the sleeping man. With his eyes closed and not spewing nonsense, he looked like an angel. Thick lips, long, straight nose, square jaw. He was just her type. She liked bad boys with boyish faces and dark pasts. She was still a bit angry with him, though. She had heard him trying to get into Jowita's bed during the night, when he thought she was asleep. How could he ignore her, the Wasp? It wasn't about jealousy per se. If he'd tried getting into *her* bed, she would have kicked him out. Sure as sure. This was no time to be fooling around. But tomorrow? Who knew. Now, he opened one eye.

'Don't say a thing.' She stopped him with a gesture.

'You angry with me?'

'I'm angry with everyone,' she grunted. 'We're going to meet someone.'

'Can't you go alone?'

'Look at him! So snowed under with work!' She cocked her head and laughed. 'You're here to do a job, not have a holiday, you lout. I need to collect some cash. To pay you, among other things. So get your arse out of bed and come on.'

That motivated him. He threw off the blanket and rubbed at his eyes. Seeing Jowita and the boy looking at his naked body, he blushed a bit and pulled on his clothes. He caught up with Marzena, who was waiting impatiently for him, counting money.

'You got any change?' she asked.

He pulled out the lining of his pocket, showing the big hole in it.

'You're an incurable case. End-stage terminal poverty. I had you figured out from the get-go.' She went to the car and rummaged in the glove compartment for a long time. She came out with a handful of coins and a phone card.

'Eureka!' She beamed. 'We're saved.'

There was a phone booth on the street. Kuba didn't understand why she needed him to keep his distance in the car and stand guard while she talked.

'Look out for anyone approaching,' she instructed. 'If anyone shows up, talk to them. Keep them away. Nobody can see me, do you understand?'

'Why the big mystery?' he moaned. 'I'm hungry.'

She crossed the distance between them and glared at him. 'I'm not your nanny, okay? Be a man. If you can't, fuck off.'

He raised his hands in defence. 'All right, all right,' he capitulated. 'But since I got us the beds, you get us some breakfast. Just not that vegan idiocy. I need meat.'

'If everything goes according to plan, we'll have a job set up today. For one of the bigwigs.'

She went back to the phone booth and talked, jotting things down, laughing. Finally, she dropped the receiver and marched back to the car.

'Done. We're going to the bank.'

'What about your friend?'

'She'll be okay.' Marzena settled into the back seat and barked: 'What are you waiting for? Go.'

He had to stay by the entrance to the bank, like a useless cunt again, killing time by counting the bollards lining the street and then the lamp posts outside the town hall. He couldn't even have a smoke; Marzena had taken the cigarettes with her. She had doled him out two, which he had smoked in a couple of minutes, listening to his stomach grumbling. He would have given everything for that last piece of pork shoulder he had left Shaggy yesterday.

Marzena was inside the bank for the better part of an hour. Finally, she appeared in the doorway with a satisfied smile on her face and a large, grey envelope under her arm. They bought so much food, alcohol and women's clothes at the local market that he could barely lift the bags. As he was throwing it all into the boot, he tore himself a piece of sweet challah bread and took a large swig of milk. He looked around. Marzena was heading to another phone booth. This time he overheard some of the conversation and, for the first time, he felt something approaching respect for the woman. She was talking like she was starring in a movie and someone really smart had written her lines.

'Four o'clock. Same place as always. Toss it into the rubbish bin by the bank. Grey envelope. I have it all with me. I have a copy at home and I'll keep it safe until you pay up, so no fucking around, you get it? And don't be late, or my rate goes up. I'll wait for twenty minutes. Then I go straight to the police. He'll pay up too, don't you worry. And I'm taking a quarter for myself.'

She put the receiver down and spun round. Kuba must have been making a funny face involuntarily; she mimicked him. Suddenly, she seemed to remember something and went back to the booth.

'He didn't try to bring the rate down, if you have to know,' she said into the phone.

Then she listened for a long time, nodding and trying to cut in. Apparently her interlocutor didn't give her the opportunity.

'My card's almost drained,' she managed to say at one point. 'Don't worry, I got the right man. Experienced. If you screw up, you'll end up the same. That's the reciprocity rule for you.'

She rasped out some laughter.

'No, I don't have any more copies of the video. Don't you worry.'

The card must have been spent; she threw the receiver down again. She scrabbled some coins from her pocket and slid them into the phone.

'We've got a problem, sweetheart,' she said, her voice turning genial and sweet. Kuba pricked up his ears. She must have been talking to someone else now.

'He made some demands. It'll cost you a bit more.'

She held the receiver away from her ear.

'I'll take care of it myself. I know where he lives. Stop yapping and start collecting the cash. I earned it.'

Suddenly, Kuba realised he was just a small cog in a very large and intricate machine. Marzena knew what she was doing. She could have run her own legitimate business if she wanted. Why she had found herself on the lowest rung of the social ladder, he didn't know. He didn't want to know. But it dawned on him that without him her grand plan would go to shit. He had the upper hand here.

'So, do you know how much I'll get paid?' he asked, innocently. He wasn't worried she wouldn't pay him, but if he was supposed to do the dirty work, he needed the best rate possible.

She offered him a cigarette and leaned against the car. 'We're going to visit someone. Everything's got a bit more complicated. Someone beat us to it and there might be some trouble ahead.'

'The fuck do I care?' Kuba was growing irritated. 'I'm a simple guy. You point me in the right direction and pay me my money, and I'll make sure things get done. You just make sure it's worth my while.'

'Thirty,' she said. 'Okay with you?'

He nodded.

'But you got to shoot two birds instead of one.'

'That's cool with me. One, two, three – no difference. As long as the plan's good.' He pretended he knew what he was talking about. In reality, he had no idea how to kill a man. But he was dutifully playing his part. The prospect of getting paid thirty grand immediately improved his mood. He was pretty much untraceable. A pilgrim, a vagabond, a free spirit. He'd do what he was asked and then fuck off overseas.

'And I could use some gear. I don't like working with bare hands,' he sighed theatrically.

Marzena took out her envelope and opened it. Kuba took a peek inside. It housed an old revolver with the barrel sawn off right at the cylinder.

'Do a good job and the sponsor might give us a bonus. I'll throw in ten grand more. I'd like to be done with it as soon as possible.'

She flicked the cigarette butt to the ground and stepped into the car.

'Time's ticking. Don't tell Jowita anything. She has to be safe.'

'Sure thing, oh queen.'

Bondaruk's housekeeper got given the day off as soon as Jowita, Marzena and Kuba showed up at the door. Kuba looked on as the older man greeted Jowita with a tender embrace. He could smell the money on the guy. As they were shown into Bondaruk's mansion he estimated the value of the audio and video equipment, adding the liquor cabinet, which was filled with all kinds of expensive booze.

'Get that stuff out. Everything on the table. Today, we celebrate,' Bondaruk said to Kuba, smiling widely. 'So, girls, how's life?'

'Everything has sort of gone back to normal,' Jowita replied, hugging Bondaruk again. Hiding in his arms. Her son had received a present. A great big toy excavator that Piotr had brought from his storage room.

'It's as good as new,' he'd said. 'My ex's son has a whole room of toys.'

'Ex.' Marzena smirked. 'I've heard that before. You and Łarysa keep breaking up and then getting right back together.'

'This time it's official,' Piotr explained, winking at her. 'Łarysa's found a good man. She's really in love with him. But we're still working together. We're friends. And me? I'm just living my best life, you know. Only I'm still alone.'

If Jowita were a dog, she would have pricked up her ears, Kuba thought. She was putting the food Marzena and Kuba had brought on plates, arranging them on the table, seemingly indifferent to the conversation – but she was drinking in his words. Having made tea and brought glasses from the kitchen, she went to the toilet and came back with a little make-up on.

'Where's the champagne? I bought three bottles of the Russian stuff, didn't I?' Marzena asked.

'I won't drink that shit, woman. Not when we have gin, whisky, and all that high-end booze,' Kuba scoffed.

Marzena wasn't listening. She sent Jowita for the Sovietskoye Igristoye.

'It ain't a party without caviar and champagne! Well, I didn't get any caviar, but I bought some smoked mackerel. It'll have to do.' She unwrapped the pungent fish from its paper cover and started to remove the skin with her bare fingers. Kuba cringed at the sight, but Piotr only laughed and joined her.

'Let's take a photo,' Jowita called out. 'We see each other so rarely.'

'I got a new Polaroid just for the occasion. It's in the drawer under the TV,' Bondaruk instructed Kuba, wrapping one arm around each of the women.

Kuba went to the cabinet and returned with the camera, giddy with excitement. He had never seen such a piece of hardware before.

'Bloody brilliant stuff, mate. You don't have to get the photos developed? Absolutely brilliant.'

'Take it. It's yours.' Piotr laughed. 'Just snap a couple of pics of us first.'

Kuba immediately got to work, ordering the others to move this way and that, fine-tuning the composition as if it was a cover photo for a trendy magazine. He complained that if they didn't do what he told them, all he'd get pictures of would be the mackerel and the Russian champagne. They didn't care though, laughing and hugging each other, not listening to his instructions. Kuba snapped a whole series of photos, passing some to all three of them.

They had a nice evening together. Jowita burst into tears as they were saying their goodbyes.

'When are you leaving?' Piotr asked.

'First thing in the morning,' Marzena said.

'Keep in touch. And call me if you need anything. I'll be there for you.'

'Oh, we're just great!' Marzena, tipsy, waved a hand at him dismissively. 'But I've been jobless since that last time, and you can't exactly whore around in Warsaw without paying protection money. I'd have to team up with someone and cut them in. I'm not getting any younger and the competition is fierce. Besides, cross-eyed whores aren't exactly in fashion.' She laughed bitterly and pointed at Jowita. 'Anyone would take her, no questions asked, but she's all into milking cows now.'

Jowita shot Marzena a hate-filled glare and blushed, hiding her calloused hands behind her back.

'I don't want to live like that any more,' she declared.

Piotr pulled out the keys to the car Marzena had returned to him earlier and tossed them to Jowita.

'Take it,' he said. 'It's a good start. Open a business. Everyone does now, even here.'

'But I can't even drive.'

'Your friend will teach you.' He pointed at Kuba. 'I don't need the car any more. It's only a few minutes' walk to the lumber mill from here. And they drive me everywhere in the limo anyway.'

Jowita shook her head. She gave him the keys back.

'We'll get the papers in order. Don't worry,' Piotr insisted. 'I can have it done by the end of the week.'

'I couldn't. This is too much.'

Bondaruk stared at her, baffled. Marzena chuckled.

'Stupid girl. It's free. Take it!'

Jowita stretched out her arms and hugged Piotr. She whispered something in his ear, at which he smiled and nodded.

'You can stay with me if you want. All four of you.'

'Silly girl fell in love,' Marzena spat. 'Don't get your hopes up, lass. He's got someone else and you can't do a thing about it.'

Tomek marched out onto the terrace where they stood, giggling gleefully, wielding his new excavator. But seeing his mother in Piotr's embrace, he stopped instantly and his lips started to tremble.

Piotr stroked Jowita's hair, gently pushed her arms away from him and winked at the boy. 'Mummy's yours, don't you worry, little buddy.' Then he turned to Kuba, who was feeling jealous, and barked an order: 'You take care of her.'

It started raining. The fat droplets were mixed with hailstones. Kuba swept a hand across the cloth he was laying on and wiggled on his belly to find a better position. He turned his baseball cap so that the peak didn't obscure his view. His hands were numb with the cold, but he didn't put his gloves on. It would be too much of a risk. What if his finger slipped on the trigger and he missed?

The road was deserted. Marzena had told him his target would exit the garage at exactly three thirty a.m. and the car would reach the road to Białystok fifteen minutes later. Kuba glanced at his watch. It was nearly four. He couldn't wait much longer. The sun would be up soon. And there wouldn't be another opportunity like this.

Suddenly, he saw the white Mercedes on the horizon. He recognised it at once. He had driven it himself a while ago, after all.

First, he shot at one of the tyres. He missed. His second shot was on target though, and the tyre deflated instantly. The driver struggled to keep the car on the road; the Mercedes swerved into the opposite lane, shot off the road and landed in the ditch. Kuba couldn't see his target. Instead he aimed for the head of the woman in the car. As soon as she leaned back and Bondaruk's face appeared, he squeezed the trigger, shooting a whole salvo of bullets. The car windows fogged over in a matter of seconds and Kuba couldn't see much. He sent the last few bullets on their way blind. The gun had grown red-hot; it was burning his hand badly. When the cylinder was empty he bundled up his things, hissing with pain, and jumped down from the roof of the low building. He might have cocked up the entire operation. The door on the driver's side was wide open. Bondaruk must have fled into the fields.

Lights were coming on in the windows of the nearby farmhouses. When the police arrived, they would be stopping all outbound cars, turning up every stone to find him. Fortunately, it was remote around here and it would take them some time to arrive. But Kuba didn't tarry. He scrambled to the vehicle, got in and managed to drive to the nearest clearing. There, he put on the spare tyre, hoisted up the dead woman – her name was Łarysa – and stuffed her into the boot before returning for Marzena and Jowita.

Marzena grabbed her things quickly and ran straight to the car, but Jowita was slowing them down. She was hysterical, crying and screaming. The bullet holes in the doors told her what she needed to know. She threw herself at Marzena, fists flailing, threatening to call the police. Kuba was finding it difficult to keep calm himself. This was taking ages. He could only think about the fact that his target had survived, and that the police would show up at Bondaruk's door any second. He swung at Jowita and knocked her out. With Marzena, he packed her into the car and drove off at speed.

They stopped some time later at an old pagan holy site in a town called Zbucz. Jowita had come to a while earlier, and now she struggled out of the car and straightened up, swaying slightly. Her speech was slurred, and she spoke slowly and lethargically. Kuba's hitting her must have given her a concussion. Then, suddenly, she realised her son wasn't with them. They had forgotten about little

Tomek. Jowita went to pieces all over again. This time Kuba didn't have to be instructed. He knew what needed to be done.

They buried the two women, Łarysa and Jowita, together in a single grave, covering it with an old, mossy stone.

They only got half of the agreed amount, the advance, as they didn't dare return to the meeting place to collect the rest. It didn't take them long to come to blows over how to share the spoils, although they managed to curb their tempers for a while with the carton of booze they had stolen from Bondaruk's liquor cabinet.

The next day Kuba woke up with the worst hangover he could remember, only to find himself alone in the car. The Wasp had vanished with all the money, and his brand new camera to boot. She had only left the pictures and the video cassette she had used to blackmail their employer. She must have forgotten them while she was collecting the cash and running from their hiding spot.

Kuba drove the car all the way to the car park at Warsaw's Chopin airport. He paid for as long as he could afford, which amounted to three days. Then he returned to his hovel, where he hunkered down with Shaggy, and went back to drinking moonshine with Andrzej.

He started reading the papers every day. Bondaruk had survived and been placed in a psychiatric hospital for observation. He had been charged with murdering Łarysa. Kuba found it funny.

He never saw Marzena again. One day, he finally watched the video she had left. It was a recording of the gang rape of Jowita. He went back to Hajnówka and got a job at Ciszynia psychiatric hospital, where his sister had become the vice-director. His job included driving an industrial-grade floor cleaning machine. For years, he would systematically collect data on and nurse grudges against all the men who had been involved in that horrific time in his and Jowita's lives, but he never did anything with that knowledge.

Bondaruk had left the hospital before Kuba started working there, but he came back to visit Krzysztof Saczko, the director, many times. Bondaruk never gave the impression of recognising the man who had come so close to killing him. Kuba thought about it often, finally concluding that he had simply been too insignificant for the lumber mill manager. That only increased his hate for Bondaruk.

Gdańsk, 2014

Robert 'Ghost' Duchnowski had just dropped off the kids with his ex-wife. He caught himself dreading the whole week of idleness he had ahead of him. Waligóra, the commissioner, had called him in yesterday and put him on obligatory leave. Apparently, the ministry wanted to know the figures for unpaid overtime at the station and the boss needed to sort out the statistics asap.

'Go fishing or something. Just don't show up at work until Monday,' he ordered.

Ghost was feeling sullen. He wasn't sure what he'd do with so much free time. Sasza had messed up, big time. She hadn't showed up for the exam and wasn't responding to his texts. He was afraid to call her by this stage. She must have taken offence at him not showing up in Hajnówka to collect her. But he really had told her the truth. His car was off the road, having died in the middle of a roundabout. Then he had got caught up with work.

He stepped into his flat. His fat ginger cat rubbed against his shins and he picked up a pack of the dried liver snacks the cat loved so much. Smelling the treats, the cat began its customary dance until Ghost put some on the floor for it. He pulled his shoes off and reclined in his armchair, pulling a low pouffe closer and resting his legs on it. For a while he just sat like some flaccid old fart, before finally reaching for man's best friend – the TV remote. He switched the TV on and the screen showed a rerun of the recent Poland–Germany football game.

'The Polish footballers play like they're sponsored by a heart disease drug manufacturer,' he told his cat, but the animal only turned its furry arse on him.

It was still too early for a live league game, there were no ski jumping contests in May, and he hated snooker with a passion, so he settled on channel-surfing. Soap operas, reality shows and idiotic commercials he knew by heart. Finally he found a news channel. But he despised politics and hadn't taken out a loan in Swiss francs lately, so he left the TV on and went to the kitchen to grab a beer.

'Who's got the worst day ever, kitty?' He meant the question for the cat, but the animal had disappeared, so Ghost answered his own question, with a loud chortle: 'A miner with a franc loan.'

He opened the fridge – which brought the treacherous little fur-ball back into the kitchen – opened a beer and took a large swig, and concluded that having some free time wasn't so bad after all. He would just need to drop by the supermarket and buy a crate of beer and another bag of those liver cat treats.

'If there's food, there isn't a place you wouldn't follow me to, eh?' he said to the ginger cat, which blinked.

'Listen, women are like this fridge,' Ghost continued. 'First they lure you in, and then *slam*, and it's closed again. Why isn't she call-ing back?'

He poured some milk for the cat.

'Quit fooling around, you know who I'm talking about. Red-haired and bitchy. Just like you. Me and my taste in com-panions . . .'

He had nearly finished his beer by now, so he took another can from the fridge. He took off his denim shirt. His hair was in dis-array and he tried patting it back into some order, which only made it worse. He couldn't look at himself like that. He took the shirt and hung it on the mirror.

'I won't have to look at my ugly mug for the next week. And you'll cope somehow, won't you? We'll sneak out at night. Buy you those snacks,' he whispered to the cat, winking. He couldn't keep going like this. Talking to himself like he was mental when the fat cat didn't understand a word he was saying.

Ghost went back to the living room, sat down in his armchair and let himself fall into the sweet embrace of hops, malt and alco-hol. He let the tirades of the politicos on the TV news enter one ear and flow right through his head and out from the other. Bliss.

'Dear nationalists: I am neither an activist, nor do I associate with the left wing,' someone on the TV was saying. 'I simply know that wearing Nazi symbols and writing "Bury should have eradicated all Belarusians. Pity he didn't have the time" on the National Hajnówka website is unacceptable.'

Ghost half-shut his eyes. An activist. He wasn't really paying attention. He drifted off a bit.

'Poles and Belarusians of Hajnówka had been living in peace for generations, until a group of Polish pseudo-patriots started inciting nationality-based conflicts. But Belarusians have the same right to live on this land as Poles.'

The reporter took over. She was standing in front of Hajnówka town hall, where, she said solemnly, staff had found a dog's severed head with a collar in the colours of the Belarusian flag. Then the TV flashed with a fast-paced montage reminding the viewers that Hajnówka, a quiet town by the Białowieża Forest, had already been the talk of the nation for the past couple of days, awash with rumours of a murderous cannibal stalking its streets.

'The rumours were being denied by the prosecutor's office and the police until yesterday,' the reporter was saying. 'But this morning, the disembodied head of the town's richest and most influential citizen was found in a sauerkraut barrel at the town market. The body has not been found yet.'

Ghost's eyes snapped open.

'That monster ate him!' A passer-by was shaking a fist at the camera.

'We're scared!' Another passer-by called out, a woman, hiding her small child behind her.

'What a farce,' Ghost snorted, but his expression quickly turned sour as the TV showed a picture of the last victim – an elegant elderly man with a charismatic face. Ghost recognised him at once. They had talked just three days ago. He had been supposed to drive Piotr Bondaruk to Hajnówka, but had had other things to do. His car was in the garage, for one. And his daughter had had an English exam in town and he wouldn't like her to stay with her crazy grandfather alone.

'No comment.' A quick shot of a prosecutor, wearing trainers, entering the station building.

Then the reporter's face filled the screen again.

'The police cannot write off the hypotheses about dealings between criminal organisations or the workings of radical nationalist groups. Piotr Bondaruk was a local VIP and businessman. A promoter of Belarusian culture, patron of a local sports club, and an ethnic minority rights activist. Though it has to be said that those minorities actually form the majority of the local populace.'

'How can a minority be a majority?' Ghost scoffed. 'Go learn some Polish, stupid girl. How did you even pass your exams?'

He shut his mouth, struck dumb by another realisation – he was talking to the TV now. He was just about to switch the channels when a voiceover came on.

'Our sources say that one of the suspects is one Aleksandra Z., an ex-police officer, currently a profiler living in the UK, who has been detained by the police this morning. A famous criminologist, Huber Meyer, has also arrived in Hajnówka to interrogate his colleague and help the investigators in solving the mysterious kidnappings and murders. What will be the result of his work? Will Hajnówka become the Polish Twin Peaks?'

The report ended with a short fragment of the *Twin Peaks* theme tune. Ghost muted the TV and crumpled his beer can in one hand. He tried calling Sasza. No answer. He tried calling Romanowska. She wasn't picking up either. He found the number for the local police HQ and asked to speak to the commissioner.

'The commissioner is currently leading investigative operations,' the voice said. 'Please contact the spokesman.'

'I'm not a fucking reporter!' Ghost burst out, but reined himself in immediately. 'My name is Chief Inspector Robert Duchnowski from the Central Police Station in Gdańsk, criminal division. I need to speak to a high-ranking officer at your station.'

He recited his mobile number and hung up. Almost immediately, his phone rang. He waited a good long while before picking up. 'You got to treat those provincial twats the way they deserve,' he explained to the ginger cat. 'Otherwise, they won't respect you.'

He put the phone to his ear. It was Zosia, Commissioner Waligóra's secretary.

'You want to call me back to work? No way.' He played the tough guy. 'You throw me out, you've got to ask me back nicely. Tell Wally to call me himself.'

She laughed and lowered her voice to a whisper. 'Something arrived for you. A big package. Letters from some kind of hospital.

They're all addressed to you personally, so I didn't open any of them.'

'Leave them on my desk.'

'Hey,' she began and hesitated, 'have you seen the news?'

'No,' he lied. 'I'm on holiday, Zosia. I'm keeping away from the news. It's not good for you, you know? Messes with your head . . . So, tell me what I've missed.'

'People are saying,' she breathed, 'that the suspect in that town over in the east, the one where that famous provider went . . .'

'Profiler.'

'Right. Anyhow, that the woman's our Sasza.' She giggled nervously.

'I don't know anything about that,' he kept lying. He was feeling worse and worse about it.

'And that's important, I think,' Zosia went on, 'because those letters are from Sasza. Only they have a stamp on them saying "Ciszynia psychiatric hospital". Maybe they locked her up in there? And the boss has already seen them and as soon as he's back from dinner he'll tell me to open them. You know him! He won't pass that opportunity up.'

Ghost was nearly exploding with anxiety, but he kept pretending nonchalance.

'All right, I'll pop by. I'll bring the cat for a walk. He might like a break. He's been pretty busy lately, you know.'

He hung up, put on his clothes, picked the ginger cat up and put a collar round its neck. It was brand new. One of his kids had given it to him for Christmas.

'It's your big day, little fellow. You can do it,' he said as he led the cat out of the door. 'We can do it. Or not. We'll see.'

He closed the door, still talking to the cat. One of the neighbours, outside their own door, shot him a worried look. A few more years living alone and that might become his thing for good. He couldn't resist though; he added, 'What has that witch got us into this time?'

Hajnówka, 2014

Sasza left the station building and picked up her things: a suitcase and car documents. The blue Uno was still at the police car park. She headed out. The bus stop was nearby, and she could use a walk. She didn't want to spend another minute in that godforsaken place. Immersed in her thoughts, she didn't notice a car trailing her for some time. An unremarkable navy blue VW Passat. It had no taxi light on its roof, but its doors were covered with stickers reading 'passenger transport'.

A man wearing a baseball cap sat behind the steering wheel. The window on the driver's side was rolled down and the man's elbow stuck out.

She finally noticed it. 'You free?' she asked the driver. She leaned closer to the window and for an instant, dark spots whirled across her field of vision and she felt dizzy. She was exhausted.

'How much to Białystok?' she asked.

'Hundred and fifty złoty. Maybe two hundred. We'll figure something out,' the driver replied.

Sasza didn't think twice. She put her suitcase in the rear seat and said, 'To the train station, then, please.'

'Got it.'

Sasza closed her eyes and got lost in her thoughts again. There were hundreds of them vying for her attention. The last one was: how the hell would she pay the fare? She didn't have any cash on her. But that wasn't the most pressing thought. She'd think of something on the way. Maybe they'd stop at a bank. Would the staff let her withdraw the money from her account with just her ID?

One thing was certain – she couldn't stay in Hajnówka. The stress was slowly dissipating, and the only thing she felt now was fatigue. She was on the brink of breaking down in tears in front of

the cab driver. The only thing that was stopping her was embar-
rassment. She was determined to get a grip on herself for now and
only allow herself to cry on the train back to Gdańsk. With a bit of
luck, she'd be home by the evening. She relaxed, thinking about the
long walk along the seafront she'd take barefoot, the cigarette she'd
have at the pier in Sopot, and the peaceful view of the sunset. That
view always soothed her. It was the only thing she had been missing
while in England.

Sasza took out her phone and turned it on. There were a few
missed calls, including one from Ghost from two hours ago. She
smiled. She had been thinking about him, especially when she was
at the station. She had it all figured out now. Her pathological bel-
licosity was one of her biggest flaws. She had to overcome it; either
she changed her modus operandi or, she was convinced, her life
would end in catastrophe. This went for both her professional and
personal life.

I'll be gentle, delicate, helpless and as agreeable as it gets, Sasza
decided.

She called Ghost's mobile with a clear plan as to what she'd tell
him: 'I'm going back. Let's grab dinner together.' At least, that's
what she would tell him if he picked up. She made a couple more
attempts, but the number was still busy. A moment later, she got a
text saying that he was available. She called again, but the call was
rejected after one ring.

Furious, she smashed her mobile into her suitcase. It looked like
she'd have to remain bellicose for a while yet.

They were like fire and ice, the two of them. It would never work
out. She leaned back and half-closed her eyes again. It looked like
the driver was staring at her through the rear-view mirror. She lifted
an eyelid a fraction more and it confirmed her suspicion. Instead
of looking at the road he was staring at her, his eyes never leaving
her. Sasza straightened up and leaned forward, meeting the man's
eyes with her own angry stare. He smiled slightly. She caught a
glimpse of his gloved right hand. The two smallest fingers seemed
shorter, shrivelled. The cap had fooled her at first, but now she
knew who he really was. Had he caught the glint of recognition in
her eyes? She looked around and realised they weren't on the way

to Białystok at all. After all the time she'd spent in Hajnówka, she could tell – they were going to the forest.

She shot out an arm and grabbed the door handle, but the man was quicker. He hit the central lock button, locking all doors.

'What are you doing?' she asked grimly.

Her eyes never wavered, pinning the man's own in the mirror. She grabbed her mobile and texted Ghost without looking, her fingers frantically hitting what she hoped were the right buttons. 'Help me. I need rescue. Please.' A moment later, she saw they were nearing the Ciszynia hospital. She texted Ghost that too. The car entered through the hospital's back gate.

'Someone asked me to bring you here,' the driver said.

Kuba took his cap off and turned round, looking at Sasza. His head was cleanly shaven now. Right in the middle of his scalp was an old scar. She felt shivers running down her spine. Then she took another look at his hands and a memory returned in a flash: he had been the one to attack her in the forest. It all fell into place. He had kidnapped Iwona Bejnar. And it had been his work clothes in which she had found the wedding outfit. Not Łukasz Polak's.

'You're kidnapping me,' she breathed. Her hands slowly reached for her suitcase and started unlocking it. Unfortunately, her Beretta was wrapped in an evidence bag and so was the ammo. If she pulled it out, Kuba would hear it.

'If the conversation we are about to have goes according to expectations, I'll take you to Białystok,' he assured her. But then he added, his face utterly impassive, 'My word is worth more than money.'

He parked the car. Right in front of the entrance where she had left her bag that last time. This was like *Groundhog Day*. Except that every time she showed up here, things got a bit worse.

'I won't go,' she declared stubbornly. 'If someone wants to see me, let them come here.'

'I'd rather not take you by force. Believe me.'

Her phone rang. As she went to pick it up she also quickly snatched the evidence bag out of her suitcase and stuck it down inside her belt. But before she could pick up the call, Ghost had hung up.

'Even a suspect gets one call, isn't that right?' she asked.

He nodded reluctantly and stepped out of the car. His eyes remained focused on her the whole time.

'How are you, honeybuns?' Ghost picked up at once this time.

She said nothing at first, only staring at the man in the baseball cap. She was beginning to understand, finally. But the direness of her current circumstances was paralysing her.

'Hey, Sasza?' Ghost said, concern creeping into his voice. 'You there?'

'Come for me,' she whispered. 'I'll explain everything. I'm neck deep in shit here. Please, take me away. Help me.'

Then it happened. She broke down, sobbing.

'Where are you? What's happening? Talk to me!'

'I can't explain now. There's no time. I've been kidnapped. Ciszynia,' she breathed. 'I don't know what's going to happen. I might not be able to talk. I'm scared.'

Kuba knocked at the window. 'Let's go,' he ordered.

'I'm so scared,' Sasza sobbed. 'If something happens, tell my daughter . . .'

Her voice broke. The clichéd movie line sounded so cheesy when she said it.

'I love her. And I . . . really like you. Kinda,' she stammered.

Ghost was silent. She knew he understood.

'I'm not crazy,' she said quickly, her voice slowly going back to normal. 'I'm not drunk. He's looking at me. I can't talk any more.'

'Don't hang up!' Ghost cried. 'Put it on silent and hide it in your underwear. That's how I'll track you. Don't be afraid. You'll get through this. What the bloody hell is going on?'

The car door opened and Sasza broke the connection at once. Kuba reached for her mobile. She shook her head, turned it off and showed him the screen was dark. He shrugged and waited for her to step out of the car.

'You'll be all right,' he assured her with a wide smile.

'I believe you,' she lied.

He led her into the hospital, to the reception desk, which was empty now, leaned over the counter and took a key. With it he unlocked the door to one of the rooms.

'Suitcase,' he said, holding out his hand. She complied in silence.

'Mobile,' he barked, sticking out the hand not holding the suit-case.

'Am I going to prison?' she tried joking.

'We have some dangerous patients here. It's for your own good.'

She looked around. She needed to keep him talking and switch her mobile on again.

'Business must be going pretty badly, eh? I can't see any patients.'

'They're having dinner. The canteen is in another wing.'

After a pause, she decided to give him her phone. If she refused, he'd just search her and take it anyway, and he'd find the gun too. She was afraid to lose that now. It offered her a shadow of a chance, at least. Fortunately, Kuba wasn't looking at her any more. He just took the phone and tossed it into her suitcase. He zipped it up, then put the case on the floor of the room and locked the door. He was very precise in his movements. Like a machine. Or someone with extensive experience, who had done such things dozens of times before.

They set off down a long corridor to the area she had seen the first time she had visited. The information board, the little fern, the wall. Kuba took the board off the wall. There was a high-tech digit-al panel underneath. He punched in the code too fast for Sasza to memorise; she only got the sound the buttons made. They formed a melody from a popular song. She wouldn't be able to get out of here without that code. And nobody would be able to get in to help her. Everything was in her hands. The only tools she had were her psychological knowledge and the hard data she had worked so hard to collect. And she had the gun.

This other part of the hospital, the secret part, was a lot more run-down. The walls were bare brick. Pipes stuck out from the ceil-ing, their insulation rotted and peeling off. The floors were cobbled with antique clinker bricks, crumbling and so worn with time that patches of ground could be seen under them. It all made Sasza think of castle dungeons, or maze-like passages in old factories. No health protection officials had ever been here, she would wager.

The surroundings changed dramatically when they turned a corner. Everything was newer, and immaculately clean. The semi-circular corridor wall was broken up every few metres by solid metal room doors. Sasza suspected there was another entrance to this wing, perhaps through one of the offices, an operating theatre or a treatment room, and that Kuba was taking her via this route to keep the other exit a secret.

Suddenly, the lights went out. Sasza jumped and took a step away from her guide. She cursed that she didn't have time to grab her gun. A few seconds later, the ceiling strip lights buzzed and the corridor was awash with the greenish light again.

'Our special effects,' Kuba joked, but Sasza couldn't bring herself to so much as smirk.

They reached an old service lift, its shaft leading down. Producing a key, Kuba opened the cage and pulled a lever. Sasza saw that the lift only served one floor. They descended for a long time, though. The thick lines the mechanism was suspended from creaked horribly, like reanimated skeletons rising from their graves in old horror flicks.

'We're here.' Kuba slid the metal doors open and, when they'd left the lift, closed them again, locking the cage's heavy padlock. 'As you can see, your phone wouldn't be of any use here. There's no reception.'

'I should have known,' Sasza replied with a grimace. 'You're going to lock me up in a dungeon. And there's no other exit.'

'You're not all wrong,' he said, surprising her. 'Not everyone leaves this place. But there are people who pay good money to be brought here. Regrettably, I'm not at liberty to tell you more. My sister will explain everything much better.'

'I see,' Sasza grunted.

They walked for a dozen more metres or so, before Kuba stopped abruptly. He opened a door and led Sasza into a large operating theatre. Its floor and walls were lined with sterile white tiles. The equipment was modern. State-of-the-art. In the middle of the room stood Magdalena Prus, her back to the door, looking like the Snow Queen receiving little Gerda in her icy palace.

'I am aware we started off on the wrong foot, but that may yet change,' she said.

'Should I feel honoured for being granted this audience?' Sasza scanned the room with her eyes. 'I can't think of a reason why I should be chosen to learn your little secret. Am I going to die for that?'

The psychiatrist smirked and bowed slightly, mistaking the irony for a compliment. She spread her arms. 'Welcome to my rejuvenation facility.'

'Rejuvenation what?' Sasza laughed, despite the gravity of the situation. Prus grimaced, losing her good humour. Sasza grew serious at once, recalling that the only reason she had lost in their last encounter was her own arrogance and derision. This time would be different. Sasza intended to outsmart her adversary. And if she failed, she'd just kill everyone. That foolish thought cheered her up. Suddenly it seemed silly to have broken down during her conversation with Ghost. They wouldn't just kill her, would they? That was impossible. People would look for her. Ghost wouldn't leave a stone unturned. At the same time, she thought, she had seen enough in this little town to believe anything was possible.

'I'm sorry.' Sasza clasped her hands, as if preparing for prayer. 'I'll stay serious this time. I promise.'

Prus seemed confused. She shot Sasza a distrustful look.

'If you would be so good as to explain why I'm here and what this place is,' Sasza said slowly, carefully.

Prus swallowed the bait. She walked over to Sasza, stopping just a few inches away, and pinched her on the cheek. Hard. Sasza hissed with pain. It seemed to bring the psychiatrist at least some little pleasure. She grinned.

'There's a lot to improve. Quite a lot. The fatty layer is practically non-existent.'

Now it was Sasza's turn to feel confused. She stared at Prus, waiting for some kind of explanation. Suddenly the psychiatrist spun round. Cheap theatrics. She was pretentious, showy, a Disneyesque villain. Professor Abrams would have a great time analysing her. Classic psychopath.

'How old am I? Take a guess.'

Sasza immediately realised she had to be careful here, that it was a sensitive subject.

'Eighteen?' She grinned lopsidedly.

Prus closed on her, touching her face again. This time at least she didn't pinch it, but lifted the skin on Sasza's cheek between her fingers, checking how far it would stretch.

'No, not non-existent after all. Thirty per cent, give or take,' she estimated, patting Sasza on the cheek and then rubbing the skin roughly. 'So, you can be polite if you want. But enough with the pleasantries. How old do you really think I am?'

Sasza scrutinised the psychiatrist's figure. It was immaculate. The woman had to work out daily. She probably had an open pass to the local gym or was an avid practitioner of Nordic walking. Then she studied the woman's face for lines. There was almost nothing. Only the beginnings of a vertical wrinkle on her forehead, between the eyebrows. The rest was perfectly smooth. That had to be botox. Sasza herself had 'thinker's wrinkles', as she liked to call them, on her forehead from the constant grimacing she did when she thought hard about her cases.

'I've had no surgery,' Prus said. 'Nothing. Not even botox. And I must admit I have an atavistic loathing of all sports. Which, I deduce from your shape, we share.'

'Thirty-three,' Sasza said, though if she was being truthful she probably would have gone with thirty-eight – her own age.

'Wrong.' Prus chuckled.

'Thirty-five?'

'You flatterer, you.' The psychiatrist wagged a finger at Sasza.

'I really don't know,' Sasza capitulated. 'I'll have one last guess. Forty and a half.'

Prus looked gleeful. She was clearly waiting for Sasza to continue guessing, but Sasza only spread her arms helplessly.

'I was born in nineteen sixty,' Prus announced with pride. 'Would you believe it?'

Sasza had never been good at maths, so it took her a while to calculate the woman's true age.

'Fifty-four? No way,' she blurted out. She didn't have to fake her astonishment.

'I'm living proof that my method works,' Prus explained, adding, 'You haven't seen me naked. I have tits any supermodel would kill for.'

'I can only imagine,' Sasza muttered. 'It's a pity I don't.'

'And that is exactly my point!' Prus beamed. 'We can change that!'

'Thanks, but I'm good.' Sasza was getting scared again. Really scared. 'I simply can't wait to be old. Why would I want to stay the same all the time? Changing is good. It's natural.'

That was not the right answer. The psychiatrist frowned.

'Ah. Your view on that is a bit of a complication. I'm afraid you're rather unusual in your attitude. My clients are very important people. Celebrities. Stars. And not only Polish. Not only second-rate, soap opera stars either,' she said with emphasis.

'Sorry, but I know as much about celebrities as about Chinese grammar.'

Prus made another attempt to bring Sasza over to her side. 'You don't look as old as some forty-year-olds,' she said. 'We've dealt with bigger bags than yours, as my little brother likes to say.' She was getting emotional, excited.

'I'm not forty yet,' Sasza retorted.

'And you're lucky!' Prus smiled. 'After forty, forty-five maybe, I guarantee there are going to be irreversible changes in your appearance. Men start ageing later. Their skin is thicker. More fatty tissue. So the age-reversal process is simpler and less costly for them. So you see, you should really make the right decision as early as possible. If it were up to me, every woman should start thinking about preserving their youth as early as in their mid-twenties.'

Sasza was quickly losing her patience. She still wasn't sure what this was all about and the psychiatrist's theatrics were getting on her nerves. She wasn't sure how much more she could bear before she snapped.

'So how do you do your magic, exactly? Dieting, quitting alcohol and cigarettes, lots of sleep, sex, pretty clothes, or something else?'

'Blood.'

Sasza froze.

'Pure, young blood,' Prus repeated. Her lips stretched into a predatory smile. She looked like a vampire. 'I bathe in it once a month. The fresher, the better, but frozen blood keeps most of its properties. Or you can drink it, of course, like Elizabeth Báthory, but believe me – I've tried it and it's not worth it. Unless you actually like the taste. Some people find drinking blood sexually arousing. At least that's what they tell me, and I choose to believe them. Sexual vampirism is something of a hobby to me. But hedonism aside, when it comes to rejuvenation, the only effective method is full transfusion. Replacing old blood with new. Or rather, blood plasma. Of course, you need to use appropriate blood types. But if you're AB, we could use any other type. People with type O blood are unlucky – they can only use their own blood type. You have to pay the most for that.'

'We've found a portable refrigerator filled with blood in Bond-aruk's car. Was it yours?'

'Mine. My personal blood.' Prus nodded. 'I happen to be type O. Fortunately, I managed to get that last transfusion. What you found was my own, old blood.'

Sasza looked around.

'Why aren't the police all over this place?' she asked. 'They should have checked this place right at the start. They must have checked the DNA in those samples! It's procedure. It has to be, even in this wretched town.'

Prus poured herself a glass of water from a carafe standing on a metal table. 'It's a lucky coincidence that the commissioner is one of our regular clients.'

'It was Białystok's case. She can't be that influential.'

The psychiatrist turned back to Sasza. 'Actually, I think we swapped the fridges. We have a lot of spare blood. It must have been one of our Jane Does.'

'Excuse me?'

'Some people never leave this place,' Prus explained impassively. 'My brother must have already told you.'

Sasza didn't know what to say to that. Prus grabbed a small dagger and pinched the tip of her index finger with it. A small droplet of blood appeared on her skin. The psychiatrist put the finger in her mouth and sucked it clean of blood.

'I never kill anyone,' she said. 'That would be too simple. If you drain the blood little by little, the patient can survive. That's how blood donating works. Only we need a lot more of it. And we never offer chocolate bars in return – we pay in hard cash. And most of our donors are twenty-five or under. The younger the better.'

'Was it really the blood of a single person?'

'Yes. Otherwise it doesn't work. Who do you think I am? I can't risk an infection. I'd lose my clients.'

'But there was close to six litres. That person couldn't have survived.'

'You're joking, aren't you?' Prus scoffed. 'Of course they didn't. But it took time. And we all die someday. You can't live for too long when your blood is drained for a protracted period of time. You get oxygen deficiency, malnourishment, heart conditions. Psychosis, too. Those are the side effects. But some people are just greedy. I pay them a lot for their blood, so they skip the occupational health and safety part of the deal.'

'Occupational health and . . . what are you talking about?'

'We have regular donors. I pay them for their blood and their silence. You didn't think I just sat here with a needle and drained all kinds of people of all their blood without checking them for HIV and other diseases? This is a highly complex business. Our rejuvenation facility may be small, but our brand is very strong.'

'I can't believe it.'

'The trend came from the west, of course. You can even buy blood plasma on the Internet nowadays. Sure, it's not for the faint of heart. I like to think that you have to be really brave to try this. But anyway, in the west you don't have to hide underground to buy blood. But, as with most other things, blood here is a lot cheaper, so a lot of our clients come from abroad. Even with the costs of coming all the way here, it still works out more afford-able. And you can get your teeth done while you're at it. Do you understand now?'

'How many transfusions do you do each month?'

'I'm not greedy and I like discretion. I never accept any new clients without a written recommendation and up-to-date medical test results. We check them again in our clinic, just in case. The results may differ from the last ones for all kinds of reasons. Unpro-tected sex and such. So, to answer your question – twenty, thirty procedures a year.'

'That's not many.' Sasza couldn't quite believe she was saying that in the circumstances.

'With our equipment, we could do as much as three hundred, you know. We just choose not to. We need the prestige.'

'Who exactly are "we"?'

'If we can come to an understanding, I'll introduce you to all our members. You've met one already. Regrettably, he's dead now.'

Sasza looked at the psychiatrist, raising her brows.

'Oh yes, Piotr was our customer too. Why are you surprised? He was vain.' She paused. 'But we had nothing to do with his death. It wouldn't suit our goals. We don't want our secret to be found out, you see.'

'What are you? Some kind of foundation?'

'Officially, we deal with helping people with mental issues, eating disorders, and other such trivialities. We *do* do all those things, of course, but all the money comes from our main line of business.'

Sasza shook her head, still unable to process what she was hearing.

'But, does it really work? Do people even really believe it?'

'Such impudence!' Prus exclaimed. 'I'm not a fraud. You told me I looked thirty-three yourself! I assure you – when I turn eighty, I'll still be in perfect condition. Besides, young blood treats all kinds of other diseases. It's especially good for your heart. Scientists have been working on that since the sixties, and humanity has been searching for the elixir of youth for millennia. You must have heard about that experiment scientists from Harvard and Stanford did once. They discovered growth differentiation factor eleven – GDF 11. Its concentration in the blood of young mice is significantly higher than in older specimens. In short, it rejuvenates the heart muscle, and the younger the heart, the better access to nutrients and oxygen. Recent research has proven the same goes for skeletal muscles and the brain. But I've known this for quite a while anyway, through my own empirical research.'

'I'm not really into medicine,' Sasza said.

'The method will soon be used in treating Alzheimer's disease. And in a hundred years rejuvenation facilities such as this one will be commonplace. Want to go to a spa or visit a dentist? Why not drop by for a rejuvenation session too? It'll become as legitimate as any other kind of clinic. But even today everybody knows you don't have to gorge on drugs to stop some diseases, even if you're old. To put it as simply as I can, a blood transfusion rewinds your clock.'

'But has this method been officially tested on humans yet?' Sasza asked.

'Well, not *officially*, but there are facilities like ours all around the world.'

Sasza swept the room with her eyes. There weren't any chairs. Only a metal table that reminded her of those slabs used for post-mortem examinations.

'But enough idle chit-chat!' Prus clapped her hands. 'Let's talk business.'

'What can I do for you?' Sasza pursed her lips.

'I offer you eternal youth and guarantee good health. Also, until one of us passes away, I won't charge you for my services. It's all completely free. Isn't that a good offer? Bear in mind that a single session would normally cost you around ten thousand dollars. And it goes without saying, I guarantee complete discretion.'

'You're the devil himself,' Sasza said, shaking her head. 'Doctor Faustus would have fallen for it, but I'm pausing for thought.'

'You can call me whatever you want,' the psychiatrist retorted. 'I simply don't like unfinished business. If I do something, I give my best. It had led me to where I am today. You like danger, and I like blood. To each their own.'

'What do you expect in return?'

Prus smiled again. 'A small favour is all I ask.'

'Don't keep me on tenterhooks. I can feel my GD 11 falling.'

'It's nothing really.' Prus shrugged. 'You just leave town and forget. Erase everything you've heard here from your memory. Every little thing that you thought strange or hard to explain. And, for the love of God, you finally quit this nosing around.'

'Nosing around is in my job description.'

'If you promise to keep everything you saw here to yourself, Kuba will lead you to the preparation room. We'll make the transfusion today.'

'Wait a second,' Sasza cut in, taking a step back. 'I can't believe I'm even entertaining this conversation, but – why would I trust you to inject me with the right blood type? This is ridiculous.'

Prus started to laugh.

'You underestimate me. We've already tested you. You have the same blood type as I do. Which, as I see it, is rather convenient as well as a pleasant surprise, as I have a stock I keep for myself. Remember, you've been in our town hospital. I have access to all the patient data.'

'You seriously want to hook me up to an IV,' Sasza exclaimed, 'or put me to sleep. Or whatever your crazy procedure consists of. I wouldn't trust you to wake me up! I think it's you who is underestimating me. I might have acted without thinking once or twice, but I'm not an idiot!'

'I never said you were.' Prus tried placating her. 'On the contrary. I've explained everything to you precisely so you feel safe.'

'Why should I agree?' Sasza was still playing along.

Prus gestured at the door. It opened, and Kuba entered. He must have been waiting on the other side, like the loyal lapdog he was. He approached a steel roller-blind and pulled a lever, making it rise, very slowly and completely soundlessly.

First Sasza saw two feet in trainers, tied at the ankle to a chair with duct tape. Then the blind rolled all the way up, and she recognised the bound man. It was Łukasz Polak. He was gagged, and his hands were tied behind his back. He was trying to shout, but only wasting his air supply; he coughed and gagged before falling silent again. His eyes looked at Sasza pleadingly.

She swallowed loudly. She couldn't understand how this man could once have elicited such animalistic fear in her. What had she been so afraid of for all these years? Why had she allowed herself to become so terrified?

'Why are you showing me this?' she asked, her voice breaking. 'He means nothing to me any more. I don't care what you do with him. I'd gladly watch him die.'

That was just the answer Prus had been waiting for.

'Your wish is my command,' she said sweetly. 'We'll drain him as inhumanely as possible, so you can see how the procedure works.'

'Great,' Sasza barked, her voice returning to normal. 'May I go now?'

Prus seemed to find her words funny. She grinned and wagged a finger at her. Kuba walked over to the profiler and pushed her towards his sister and the bound man. Sasza had no choice. She had to walk right by Polak. As she was passing him, she saw the device they'd use to drain his blood. It looked like a modernised version of something a medieval torturer would use. It was a roughly person-sized cabinet with translucent doors, its inner walls covered with long, thin needles. The rest of the space inside was filled with countless tubes, all leading from the needles to a hermetically sealed container outside. Like a colossal coffee machine,

Sasza thought. There was also a steel rack inside, which reminded her of a cross.

'Here is where the patient steps in,' Prus explained. 'The donor is kept standing thanks to the rack. The principle is quite similar to that adopted during Christ's crucifixion, although in our device, the donor isn't nailed down, of course, only held in place by means of those silicone straps you see over here. Normally the procedure takes three series of thirty-minute sessions over a period of eight days. Each day we push the doors a bit further closed, so the needles penetrate the tissue a bit deeper. During a regular exsanguination the lesions are kept to a bare minimum and the donor is kept under anaesthesia, which stops all pain.'

Prus turned round. Sasza clamped a hand over her mouth, desperately trying to keep herself from vomiting. She had been here before, she realised. She had already had some of her blood drained. That was where those little bloody dots on her body had come from the morning when she had woken up thinking she was hungover.

'It's all right. Don't be alarmed. This is a perfectly natural reaction,' Prus said, seeing Sasza's state, and calmly went to pour her a glass of water. On her way back she took a plastic bag from a hook on the wall, probably kept there for just such an occasion. Sasza vomited into it as soon as Prus handed it to her. The psychiatrist patted her on the back gently.

'Most patients feel nauseous at the beginning of the therapy. I remember university. Half of my group dropped out. They couldn't bear the sight of blood. Obviously, I have no such qualms. I like blood. It's a matter of experience, I believe.'

Sasza raised her head. She flushed her mouth and drank some of the water. Standing straight unassisted was still difficult though. Magdalena Prus closed the torture device and said, 'I have but one question. It's a matter of ideology, you might say. Are you Polish?'

Sasza didn't hesitate. She nodded.

'Because, you see,' Prus hesitated, 'I have been told it isn't certain. And if you do have eastern roots, if you're really one of us, I couldn't pump you full of impure blood.'

Sasza shot her a puzzled glance. 'You're insane.'

'Insanity is the source of all wisdom.'

'I'm one hundred per cent Polish,' Sasza said.

'Really? What about your name? Is that your husband's? Or your family name? Please forgive my prying.'

Sasza couldn't stand this digging. 'My family name,' she growled. 'I know where this is going. The peasants murdered during Bury's pogroms. There were two Załuski brothers among the victims. I hate to disappoint you, but I've already asked my mother about that. My family has been living in the north for generations.'

That was clearly enough for Prus: she clapped her hands with glee. Then she passed Sasza a crumpled envelope. 'This is just a little incentive.'

Sasza recognised Łukasz Polak's handwriting at once. 'He never actually sent it?'

Prus smiled triumphantly. 'You didn't want to read it, did you? Anyway, everything is ready. Can we proceed?'

'No,' Sasza breathed. She wasn't able to say anything more.

'No?' Prus raised her eyebrows. 'No?'

Kuba suddenly loomed over Sasza, and stuck a needle into her arm faster than she could react.

'Take her to Quack,' Prus barked. 'She'll come round faster when she sees him.' Then she pointed to Polak, still squirming on his chair. 'We begin in an hour. I'm going to make some preparations first. You've been here much too long, my dear. You're all nervous now. This will surely impact the coagulation factor. You're not that young, but sometimes we offer discounts and older blood is just perfect for such occasions. Regular customers don't even notice. But even if yours turns out useless, I'll be delighted to use it for a bath.'

Meanwhile, Kuba hauled the unconscious Sasza to a cramped storage room filled with more of those torture devices. The vast majority were open. Aside from one, by the back wall.

When Sasza came to, she was bound by both ankles and one hand; but the hand with the cast on was free. Kuba apparently hadn't been able to think of any way to tie her down effectively and had settled on taking away her sling. He had tied her other hand painfully tightly to the chair standing exactly opposite the only occupied exsanguination cabinet.

Sasza lifted her throbbing head and saw . . . Jesus on the cross. No. It was Quack. Naked, lethargic, covered in countless bloody gashes. He must have spent hours, if not days, here, judging by the amount of blood he had already lost. His eyes were unfocused, and every now and then he moaned softly. He was clearly clinging to life by the barest scrap of willpower.

Iwona was sitting in front of her gigantic TV, which was turned off. She stared apathetically at her own reflection on the dark screen. She wasn't reacting to her mother's pleading. No threats, demands or requests to get a grip and start living again were having any effect on her. The young widow said nothing, didn't eat, and barely slept. She spent all her days sitting, staring blindly at the flat-screen TV Bondaruk had given her mother. It was always blank – yesterday they had had the power cut off after another month of skipping bill payments.

Since Bondaruk's head had been found, the Bison brothers were bingeing on booze, having the time of their lives, and celebrating Iwona's husband's untimely death. They had even called her a couple of times to offer congratulations. They hadn't got the memo, it seemed, and were still imagining that their family would soon become impossibly rich; but another 'last will' had been found. This time it had to be the real thing, was the thinking; but Iwona knew better. This new last testament said that Piotr gave a substantial portion of his fortune to Iwona and her future children, whoever she decided to have them with. It left his sons his house, his cars, and a small share in the lumber mill. Most of his assets were meant for Dunia Orzechowska's son, but he hadn't signed the papers and collected his due. Nobody knew why, or where he was. That part of the inheritance would instead go to Iwona, too.

An hour ago, a whole police unit had barged into the Bejnars' slum on Chemiczna Street to arrest the entire family, but their lawyer, Artur Mackiewicz, had turned up out of the blue and negotiated a lesser penalty. They were supposed to be under constant police surveillance from now on. Mackiewicz magnanimously agreed to collect his fee only after the family came into its inheritance. Iwona couldn't wrap her head around it all. How could a man become such a spineless cocksucker? A few days ago, the lawyer wouldn't so much as look her way, and now she was his most valued customer. Anyway, the Bison boys were bingeing their arses off on drink, and anyone who had ever said a bad word about their family was trembling with fear now. The Bejnars were suddenly one of the most influential families in town.

Bożena offered her daughter a plate of peeled apples, cut into bite-sized chunks.

'Come on, eat a bit.'

She poured Iwona a glass of orange soda. Iwona had always loved it, though her mother was sure that from a strictly health-related point of view, she would be better off drinking paint water instead. 'Here, I've bought you some of this soda you like so much. Have some, won't you?'

No reaction. Iwona would get up for three things only: when she needed to go to the toilet, to charge her mobile, and when she heard the roar of a motorbike passing by.

'Sweetie, you have to accept it. He's not going to come,' Bożena tried reasoning with her. 'Unless he gets wind of the new last will – but maybe not even then. He might think he'd lose his honour, accepting giveaways like that. Men are monsters.'

Iwona hid her face in her hands and sobbed. 'It's not like that, Mum,' she said. It was the first thing that had come out of her mouth since she had come out of hiding. 'He loves me. I know it. Something must have happened to him. I can feel it in my bones. My soul aches!'

Bożena walked over to her daughter and hugged her.

'Don't be naive,' she said. 'You'll find someone else. You can live the way you want now. Sell the lumber mill. You'll be rich. And when you have money, love will come a-knocking in no time. You'll see. There'll be a line of men at your door. And love always remains the same, no matter who you offer it to.'

Iwona disentangled herself from the embrace and stormed out of the flat. She ran across the street and kept on running until she had exhausted all her strength. She propped her hands on her thighs and tried to calm her breathing. The sprint had dried her tears. She went the rest of the way to Quack's mother's house at a brisk marching pace. She had never walked so far in her life.

As she knocked on the door of the old shack by the forest, Dunia was treating an alcoholic. Iwona sat down in the doorway, leaning her back against its frame, and observed the ritual. The whisperer paused in her prayers and approached her daughter-in-law. She poured some poppy seeds into Iwona's hand, clamping her fingers around the girl's palm, making sure not even a single seed fell out. Then she handed her a laminated photo of some sacred relics.

'Keep holding it and pray,' she said in Belarusian. 'Any way you think will do. Your heart will tell you what to say. Pray in Polish, Russian, English, whatever. But be sincere.'

Iwona stared at the picture of bones arranged on a decorative tablecloth and realised with surprise that the photo was pleasantly warm to the touch. At first she just felt some warmth in the leg on which she had rested the holy picture, but then her sadness and pain started subsiding. She felt dizzy. She slipped into a light trance. She closed her eyes and listened to the droning of Dunia's prayers. When she opened her eyes again, she was lying in bed, covered with a thick duvet. There was a glass of cold tea in an old-school wire basket standing by the bed. Dunia was crocheting a beret. As soon as she realised the girl's eyes were open, she said, 'You've been asleep for close to thirty hours, daughter. I don't have a phone here, and your mother must be worried sick. Call her.'

Iwona stood up. She felt fresh, cheerful.

'Will you help me like you helped that man?'

'What bothers you, girl?' The whisperer shot out an arm and held Iwona's chin between her fingers, lifting it slightly. The younger woman broke eye contact first. 'What is it that really bothers you? I can keep a secret. You have to tell the truth, girl, otherwise God won't help you.'

Iwona sobbed loudly and cuddled against the elderly woman.

'I'm pregnant. And he's gone!'

Dunia stroked her hair and turned towards the kitchen table. The room was small. She could reach anything in it from her chair. She took a carton of sugar from the cabinet and started pouring little cairns of the white stuff on the paper she had spread out on the table. She counted in Belarusian until she decided there were enough mounds.

'Do you love him? Do you want that child?' she asked.

Iwona nodded eagerly. She wiped away her tears.

'*Sorok tochek*,' the whisperer explained. 'Forty spots. Pray over each one. Recite "Our Father", the "Apostles' Creed" and the "Cherubic Hymn". In Polish, if you don't know them in our own language. When you're finished, press your finger into one of the sugar cairns. When you're done with them all, collect the sugar and sweeten a cup of tea with it.'

Dunia tore a small square from a newspaper and poured some poppy seeds onto it.

'Sprinkle some of these into each of your pockets. After you wash your clothes, remember to pour more poppy seeds into them. When you're out of seeds, buy some more and ask a priest to bless them. Or come to me with them. That will get rid of your fear. You'll still be left with the healthy fear. The one that prods you to act and protects you against danger. But there will be no panic.'

Then the whisperer offered Iwona a slice of stale bread and poured some water from a bucket into an old Coke bottle. She prayed a while over these things and crossed herself.

'Drink one or two swigs a day. No more. Think about your beloved. Break the bread and eat it like it is. Dry. It's prosphora. Do not lose even a single crumb. If you do all that, Jurek will return to you.'

She hesitated and glanced at a holy icon hanging on the wall below a richly embroidered wall rug. She crossed herself again. Iwona copied her movements on instinct.

'If he's alive,' Dunia added. 'If he's alive, he'll come back to us.'

'He asked me, so I did it. We were friends, after all.'

Romanowska was looking at the old man with disbelief. He was standing by the metal table, wearing a rubber apron, cutting meat into small chunks and throwing it into the mincer. The police had turned Nesteruk's meat processing plant upside down, but hadn't found anything suspicious. They had checked the meat itself, too, to make sure he wasn't the violent cannibal prowling the streets of Hajnówka.

'No human meat here,' the lab assistant had told Romanowska, summarising the test results. 'Pork, beef and a bit of lamb. Everything certified and legit.'

Nesteruk left the table and went to a wood-panelled wall. Dozens of hooks were screwed into the wood. They served as hangers for various saws, cleavers, knives and spikes. He took down a small, unassuming serrated blade and attached it to an electric saw. It reminded Romanowska of the saws forensic pathologists used to cut open skulls during post-mortems.

'Hamet 54. Turbo-charged. Best to cut through bones. If you keep it in good condition and sharpen the blades once a month, it'll last decades,' Nesteruk explained and added, seeing the commissioner's disgust, 'Death is inevitable, and God told humans to eat meat. It wouldn't be right to challenge God's will. In the Bible, meat is always the best sacrifice. That was the case here too.'

Romanowska turned as she heard someone entering the room. The young man bowed slightly on seeing her, but he didn't look even the slightest bit worried, despite the fact that she had her full uniform on. The man passed Nesteruk a briefcase, probably filled with tools judging by the old man's stoop and silent hiss as he tried to lift the heavy thing.

'May we arrange the payments tomorrow?' he asked the younger man, pointing his chin at Romanowska. 'As you can see, I have a guest.'

'No problem,' the man replied. The commissioner noticed that one of his palms had an ugly burn scar. 'Though, if it's not too much, I'd like you to pay me before Wednesday. I'm going on holiday and I need to do some shopping before I leave.'

'I might as well pay you right now, then' Nesteruk said. 'Wait a second.'

He walked round the counter and opened the lowest shelf of an armoured cabinet. It was full of grey folders. The old butcher had more case files than Romanowska's old boss at the station had ever managed to amass. Nesteruk pulled out a fat envelope, counted out banknotes and passed the wad to the younger man. He said a polite goodbye and left, and Nesteruk turned to Romanowska, saying, 'He's a very talented lad. Not a knife grinder by trade, but he always supplies me with exceptionally good blades. He doesn't charge too much and his wares are a lot better than the ones you buy on the market.'

If that's supposed to be cheap, I picked the wrong profession, Romanowska thought.

'I don't know him,' she said out loud.

'He's a relative of Doctor Prus, I think,' Nesteruk continued. 'He's been working at the clinic for a few years now. He drives those floor cleaning machines and keeps the equipment in good condition. A handyman, doing a bit of everything. I've tried convincing him to start his own business, but the lad hasn't got the balls to sail the high waters. He's a good boy, though. Quiet. And he has a knack for working with metal. You wouldn't believe me if I told you how good he was with computers too. When my system went down once, he just came in and repaired it without breaking a sweat. I know nothing of those things. He's friends with your son too, I think. I remember seeing them together.'

Romanowska indicated the equipment hanging on the wall. 'So, you used that Hamet of yours to cut Bondaruk's head off?'

'I've already told you, dear.' Nesteruk shook his head. 'I did it with a Hamet, but not this one. That one broke down after I did it. I've sent it for sharpening.'

'To that lad who just left?' She gestured at the door.

Nesteruk hesitated. 'Maybe it's actually still somewhere here. Do you need it?'

'It's the murder weapon.' She sighed. 'My people will find it if it's around. And if you've moved it somewhere else, please tell me. I'm counting on your honesty.'

Nesteruk didn't respond, just went on with his mincing.

'You do realise you'll have to come with us?' she said.

'Let me just finish this first,' he said. 'I didn't call you to try to avoid responsibility now.'

'Are you sure Mr Bondaruk didn't leave a letter? Any kind of message?' Romanowska asked. 'Anything that would confirm your version? It would go in your favour.'

'Maybe he did, but I don't know where,' the old man replied stubbornly. 'I won't go and dig through his trash, if that's what you're saying. If there was a message, his sons have it. Or the housekeeper. Him and I, we didn't really talk a lot those last years.'

'You had a falling-out?'

'Oh, no. Nothing of the sort.' He shook his head vigorously. 'We didn't even meet at first. He just called me and asked me to come over. He wanted me to take possession of some kind of documents he had been keeping for years. Said he'd send a car for me, but I refused. I was afraid he'd want to pin something on me. I have a lot of problems of my own, you see.' He cleared his throat. 'Then, in the middle of the night, he came here and told me he wanted to say goodbye.'

'To say goodbye?'

'The bride's father was with him. They looked like they knew each other.'

'Dawid?' Romanowska raised her brows. 'That old drunk?'

'He might be a drunk now, but in the old days he used to be an officer. Security Service operative "Hangdog". He recruited Piotr. Then he got it into his head that it was Piotr who got him booted out of the force. But it wasn't true. Dawid was quarrelsome and liked to drink a lot, right from the start. He got on the wrong side of some powerful people and abused his own power. Then, for years he stalked Bondaruk. Threatened him. To be honest, I think he just couldn't find a place for himself in the new reality. He hated capitalism. He wanted it all to be like in the good old days.'

'When he was young and held the power, you mean?'

'Exactly. When they gave him the boot, he couldn't harm Piotr. Didn't have the resources. And Bondaruk wasn't stupid. He kept files on Hangdog. He kept dirt on everyone. Me, the starost, all members of the Council. You too,' Nesteruk said. His voice was monotonous and impassive. 'I didn't condone it. When Łarysa disappeared, he told me everything. The starost and the previous commissioner swept it under the rug, because they were afraid Piotr would dig up some of their dirty secrets.'

'Okay, but what exactly did he tell you?' Romanowska said impatiently. 'I need the details.'

'Hangdog used to frequent Nikolai's . . . escort agency. Nikolai was a good, proper Ukrainian, although he was a whoremonger. God bless his soul. Dawid met Iwona's mother there. Bożena Bejnar. His previous wife had left him as soon as he told her they'd fired him from the force. She didn't want to have a freeloader around. So he came to Hajnówka, telling those fancy stories about being an engineer. They were lies, although he genuinely had finished university. He never really worked though. He just pushed paper, keeping tabs on people and interrogating them. His whole job revolved around denouncing others. But it seems he must have said one thing too many about someone a bit too powerful – they kicked him out of Ełk. He wanted to find a job with the local police, but nobody wanted him around. He was an outsider, after all. Bożena fell in love with him. Allowed him to live with her and even tolerated his drinking for a while. Dawid stuck to her like a leech. Gave her a baby. That lass, Iwona. But in the end, Bożena couldn't take it any more. Maybe she discovered he liked other women a bit too much. I don't know. So he hunkered down in some hovel. The starost gave him a council flat in Judzianka, right next to where the prison stands today. So Hangdog made friends with Anatol Pires and they lived like two vagrants, drinking themselves into a stupor on a daily basis. Only Dawid couldn't hold his liquor like Pires could. He hit rock bottom soon enough. Anyway, he had his favourite girl at Nikolai's. Her name was Jowita. She disappeared right after Łarysa. Piotr thought it was Hangdog's doing. The man had always known how to get things done, after all. He hired some young hotshot from Warsaw and eliminated the girl.'

'And the commissioner made sure the case hit a dead end.'

'Just so. It was easier in this case,' Nesteruk agreed, shaking his head sadly. 'Nobody even looked for her and the body was never found.'

'What about Mariola? She used to work for Bondaruk too.'

'Can't help you there.' He grew silent. He was losing his calm, breathing heavily. The case of the disappearance of his own daughter was clearly still an open wound for him. 'When I learned that Piotr had had an affair with my Mariola, I was livid. I couldn't take it. And then she vanished. Just like the other two. I was devastated. How does a man cope with something like that? To lose a beloved daughter through the sins of a friend. Why did I have to rescue him in the first place? That's why we stopped talking to each other.'

'Why didn't you say any of that during your questioning way back when? I remember that day. I was the one who wrote down your statement.'

Nesteruk shrugged. 'Damned if I know. I must have been afraid,' he replied. 'In this place you could be offed just for the blood that flows in your veins. It's just one of those places.'

'And that fear was greater than the need to find your daughter?'

'Well, at first I didn't believe she was still alive. I asked Piotr to talk to Hangdog. I offered him money. I promised we'd keep the secret. He told me he'd help. But the trace quickly went cold.'

They kept silent for a long while. Nesteruk left his meat mincing station, washed his hands in a bucket of water and put a kettle on the stove. Then he returned to the table where Romanowska was waiting and sat down heavily, catching his breath.

'That's why I understand Hangdog. He must have been furious when he learned that Bondaruk took his daughter and was offering money to Bożena instead of him. I understood it and I kept my mouth shut. If you ask me, I think he was the one who kidnapped Iwona in the forest. I can't be sure, though.'

'How did Piotr die?'

'When Hangdog came to my house that night, I thought I was about to meet the same end Bondaruk had. Dawid pulled a gun on me and made me lead him to the slaughterhouse. I prepared a taser and switched the lights on. It would be a quick death. Humanitarian. Then, he returned with Piotr, all tied up. Petya asked me to do it myself. He didn't want to die by Hangdog's hand. At first, I refused. I couldn't do it.' Nesteruk dropped his head. 'I didn't want to have a human life on my conscience. His least of all.'

'You didn't try to object? Fight?'

'I'm Belarusian. We suffer in silence. I watched it and thought I'd be next,' he said with emphasis. 'I've lived through the war, survived the *russkies*, Bury's pogrom, the Polish bands. This was no different. An execution just like the ones from during and after the war. Dawid made me choose a saw, so I chose the Hamet. Afterwards, he took Piotr's head and left. And I was saved by a Pole for the second time in my life. This time Piotr was the sacrifice. The first time, I survived because of his father. He took Bury's soldiers' attention off me when he cut that cross into the tree just after the war. It was near Puchały, when we were all to be shot in the head. Executed. I took the opportunity and ran. That was the reason why me and Bondaruk had always been so close. Why I always defended him. His father was a traitor, but he had a heart. He might have sent all those people to their deaths, but he saved me. Piotr never hurt anyone. Well, at least he never hurt anyone innocent. Both of those he did do for were pure-blood Belarusians, but they had it coming.'

Romanowska nodded. She didn't have to ask. He was talking about Stepan and the priest.

'What happened to the rest of Piotr's body?'

'I buried it under the weeping willow. By that cross I tended to all those years. But you should know that already.'

'Were you alone?'

He nodded.

'Why are you lying?'

'Nobody else was there,' he repeated, too hastily.

'Do you know that Hangdog did not confirm your version? He denied everything.'

'I can believe that. It's the only line of defence he has left.'

'Why would he leave a witness? Why didn't he attack you?'

'He was sure I wouldn't rat him out. He thought I would be his ally. I kept quiet when Stepan, Larysa, and even my own Mariola died. So I'm sure he thought I'd keep quiet this time too.'

'Where are the bodies of those women?'

'Somewhere in the forest. I didn't bury them.'

'Are you sure they're even dead?'

'I know it as I know we'll all leave this miserable world in the end.'

'You'll have to repeat all this to the prosecutor.' Romanowska stood up, turned to the door and called in a constable. Nesteruk didn't protest when they cuffed him and led him out of the building.

'Stop!' A middle-aged woman appeared in the door of a room with a sign on the door reading 'No trespassing'. She was plump and wore a peplum dress that was severely out of fashion and only made her look fatter and older. 'My father is lying.'

Krystyna motioned for the officers to stop.

'He told you he's guilty to protect me.'

'Mariola!' Nesteruk protested. 'Go to your room right now!'

'I can't keep living like a rat, Dad,' the woman replied without raising her voice. 'I can't keep hiding any more. My name is Mariola Nesteruk. I have been listed as missing since two thousand and four. Now Piotr is finally dead, I won't have to be afraid someone will see me as I sneak out to meet my son. Living in the back of a slaughterhouse is worse than prison. It's hell. I know you were doing your best, Dad, and I'm grateful, but I've had enough.'

Carefully hiding her surprise, Romanowska pulled out an old school photo from a file she was carrying.

'Do you recognise this woman? She's Stepan's daughter. She went missing aged seventeen. Do you know anything about it?'

Mariola eyed the picture carefully and nodded.

'Yes. She looks a lot better now, though.'

Romanowska called another officer over. He passed her a plastic file containing an age progression photo they had received an hour ago from the Central Forensic Laboratory. If you used a bit of imagination, you would see a similarity to Magdalena Prus, vice-director of the Ciszynia hospital.

DAWID

(2014)

Piotr parked the car in the garage and walked to his flat. It wasn't yet dawn, but he didn't switch the lights on. He looked out of the large hallway window. There was a dog outside. An old AmStaff. Piotr remembered it as a pup, fetching a rubber ball he had thrown it. Anatol Pires appeared a moment later. Approaching the window, he flattened his nose against the glass, looking in. Piotr retreated deeper into the hallway. His mobile chimed. He didn't pick up at once, instead going to the liquor cabinet to pour himself a glass of vodka.

When he did pick up his phone and take the call: 'Open the door,' a voice said. 'You have guests.'

Piotr selected a bottle from the cabinet, then went to open the door. Pires and his old dog were already waiting outside. Dawid – Hangdog – Iwona's father was with them. He smiled a crooked smile and stepped over the threshold like he owned the place.

'What about the rest?' Piotr asked hesitantly.

'Only two of us left,' Pires replied. '"Giewont" ran and the rest are dead. Nesteruk isn't going to show up. We've decided he'll take the blame.'

Piotr swallowed loudly. 'Who did you choose in my place?'

'Not so fast.' Pires chortled. 'You messed up, and you'll have to pay. But first, we have to clear up a few things. Don't you want to know what you're charged with?'

'Close the door behind you,' Bondaruk said, and went to the kitchen to fetch some glasses.

When he returned, alongside Pires and Dawid in the living room he saw Magdalena Prus, Artur Mackiewicz, Leszek Krajnów and Mariusz Korcz, the leader of the Podlasie Autonomy Movement.

The group parted, letting the last member of the Council step ahead. Alla, Piotr's old friend took centre stage. She said in flawless Polish: 'And thus, life has come full circle. You asked who will take your place.' The elderly woman wrapped her arm around Magdalena Prus' shoulders, then handed Dawid the old Bulldog revolver that she and Pires had fished out of the well by the house Iwona and Quack had been hiding in. 'Would you believe it still works? We won't need it, though. Take it apart and throw it into the river,' she barked.

Prus swept the room with her gaze, clearly unimpressed. 'I don't like it here. You have no taste. I'd like you to do one thing for me, Piotr – when you get to the other side, tell my father I've avenged him.'

Anatol made a barely noticeable gesture to his dog and the AmStaff pounced on Piotr, but only to scare him and distract his attention from the real danger. Dawid did the rest. A pair of meat shears, freshly sharpened by Kuba, glinted in his hand. Piotr didn't have a chance to protest before the blade sliced across his neck, rending a deep gash in his voice box. A torrent of blood gushed down his clean shirt.

'Don't be afraid of the dog that barks,' Pires drawled, helping himself to a sip of vodka and giving Magdalena Prus a cold stare. 'Fear the one that growls.' Then he raised his voice and pointed at Dawid. 'And my dog attacks without warning. In perfect silence. And silence is what he leaves behind him.'

The new Council of the Righteous left Piotr's house one by one. Dawid cleaned up the crime scene and then searched for Bondaruk's files.

Sasza tried freeing herself, but the tape had been wrapped around her arm and legs too tightly. She had to think fast. She was alone. They hadn't taken her gun; the Beretta was digging into her skin through the fabric of her pocket. It was the one thing that still gave her some courage. Suddenly, she heard footsteps. Someone was trying to sneak towards her. Then there was a muffled clicking sound, each click followed by a tone. Combined, they formed a melody she had heard before. The entrance code to all the doors was the same, it seemed. The door opened slowly and Łukasz Polak stood in the entrance. His hair was a mess and his clothes were torn. He was dirty and his skin was cut and scratched in numerous places. Without saying a word, he walked over to Sasza and started to tear the duct tape from her hand and legs. He ripped off the piece of tape that had been plastered over her mouth with a sudden, sharp jerk. The pain was paralysing. Sasza gasped in air.

'Run!' Łukasz hissed as soon as her ties were off. He pushed her towards the door.

'What about him?' She pointed at Quack.

'We can't save him. They'll notice I escaped soon. We don't have time.'

Sasza didn't listen. She ran back to the cabinet where Quack was imprisoned and pulled at the doors. They didn't budge. She tried the control panel, pressing buttons at random. She smashed her cast into the plexiglas cover. It was no use. Finally, she looked back at Polak.

'Enter the code.'

He hesitated, but stepped up and keyed in the numbers. The machine emitted a short, loud beep and its lights went out. It was off. Sasza started unbuckling the straps holding Quack in place, but with only one hand, it was taking too long. Łukasz added his own efforts to hers, and after some time they pulled the blood-covered man out of the torture device. He moaned as they lifted him, the action pulling the needles out of his flesh. They had been embedded deeply, a good few inches into the tissue. Blood spurted from the disconnected tubes. Quack fell limply into Polak's arms.

They were of equal height and build, but Quack seemed at least twice as heavy as he should be. He was completely slack, unwieldy, like a sack of potatoes. Łukasz threw him over his shoulder and headed towards the corridor before stopping and leaning against the wall.

'I can't do it,' he gasped. His breath was laboured. 'We have to leave him.'

With her good hand, Sasza tried propping the listless man up. She knew Polak was right. 'He's still alive,' she said. 'But he won't survive unless we get help. Would you be able to live with that?'

Łukasz arranged his face into an expression of despair. 'They'll find us,' he whispered.

'So go,' she snapped, unable to keep the fury out of her voice. 'You've just failed the psycho test! The train and the man strapped to the rails. If you had no other choice and you had to steer the train towards the other guy to save yourself, would you do it?'

Łukasz didn't reply, just slumped against the wall and sank to the floor, exhausted.

'I think I like the other version better. A woman keeps meeting a handsome guy at funerals. So to see him again, she murders her own sister.'

Sasza couldn't help herself. She burst out laughing.

'Right,' Polak grunted, but his gaze was sympathetic. 'It'll be better if we all die.'

'Shut up and let me think,' she ordered. 'We need to find some kind of wheelchair. Or a stretcher. Anything. They have to get all those bodies moved somehow. That bloody vampire can't carry them all on her own back, can she?'

Łukasz jumped to his feet and scrambled to find something they could lay the wounded man on, but most of the rooms were locked. Finally, he stumbled on a lift, its entrance obscured by cartons and

protected with a padlock. He and Sasza began moving the obstacles out of the way.

'It's no use,' Łukasz tried reasoning with her. 'We don't have a
key. And it's probably out of order.'

Sasza didn't stop.

'Go and fetch Quack,' she barked, breathing heavily. 'And get a sheet
from one of the rooms. Wrap him in it. We need to stop the bleeding.'

Łukasz looked at Quack. The other man's lips were chapped, his
eyes closed. He was mumbling something, delirious.

'Give him some water!' Sasza called after Polak, not stopping
what she was doing.

A short while later, Łukasz was back with a clean sheet and water
in a bucket, which he simply poured over the wounded man. The
entrance to the lift was clear now and Sasza was standing in front
of it, legs wide, aiming a gun at the padlock. Two shots reverberated
through the corridor. Both missed. A third broke the padlock. The
roar of the discharge was shockingly loud. The bangs echoed across
the entire facility and the silence that fell afterwards seemed to last
for an eternity. Sasza came to her senses first. She slid the barred
lift door open and stepped towards the old, corroded switchboard.
Meanwhile, Polak dragged Quack closer. The man was slipping in
and out of consciousness. Together, Łukasz and Sasza managed
to slide the rusty lever upwards. The lift jerked and slowly started
ascending.

'They're probably waiting for us at the door, you know,' Łukasz
muttered.

'I'll kill them all,' Sasza hissed in response, her eyes wide and
wild. But she smiled. 'You saved me again.'

'It wasn't me. I haven't killed anyone,' he whispered.

'I know. I saw the painting.' Sasza took out the letter Prus had
given her from her pocket. 'I'll read it later.'

They said nothing for a while.

'I'm so sorry,' she broke the silence finally.

Łukasz froze, looking at her.

'I . . . I needed to see you so badly,' he breathed. 'To see her. You
named her Karolina?'

Quack moaned softly. Sasza placed a hand on his forehead. He
was burning up, still only semi-conscious.

'We'll talk later,' she said. 'Okay?'

He nodded. His eyes were still fixed on her. She could see that he wanted to say something more, that he had questions for her but didn't dare challenge her. A moment later, the lift stopped abruptly. Through the barred door, they could see that the corridor was deserted.

'There's a back exit by the canteen. Let's hope it isn't locked,' he said and added, 'You're a genius!'

'I know,' she replied and smiled at him. She couldn't believe they'd done it. 'So reception is over there?'

He nodded.

'But you have to punch in the code.'

'What is it?'

'No idea.'

'What code did you use to free me?'

'Two-five-zero-six-one-nine-seven-seven. It's the date of death of Prus's father. I don't know if it will work here, though.'

'Run,' she told him, pulling out her gun again. 'I'll cover you until you're out.'

He started moving. Slowly. Quack had passed out again and was limp and unwieldy. Sasza stood and covered them until they reached the door and turned the opposite way.

'What about you?' she heard Łukasz calling.

He stood looking her way, trying desperately to stay upright with the unconscious man over his shoulder.

'I need my phone back. We need backup!' she called back. 'Stop the first car you see and get him to the hospital. I'll find you.'

Sasza managed to find her way to the corridor with the room where Kuba had locked up her things. She found the right number key and inserted it. Surprisingly, the door wasn't locked. Carefully, she pushed it open. It was completely dark inside. She stepped over the threshold. A hand shot out of the gloom, wrapping around her neck and plastering a gauze smelling of ether over her mouth. All that she noticed before she blacked out was that her assailant's other hand was crippled, some of the fingers crooked and useless. That other hand was holding her files on the Załuski brothers. And she saw her suitcase, open on the floor. Then she collapsed.

The day was beautiful, hot and sunny. A group of young travellers was spilling out of a bus with Warsaw licence plates. The boys wore large rucksacks, sturdy boots and military green parkas. The girls had their hair tied in buns on the tops of their heads. The girls went straight to a market stall selling local wares and bought traditional headscarves, tying them around their waists. Meanwhile, the boys headed to the liquor store.

The locals seemed friendly. As the entire group, reconvened, headed down the main street, passers-by smiled at them, making way for the youngsters.

'You sure we'll be able to hitch a ride here?' the oldest of the boys asked another.

'Sure thing. I got to France that way,' his friend replied calmingly. 'Why wouldn't it work here?'

As they passed a group of people crowding around another market stall, someone called, 'Fuck the Poles!'

And then a dozen young men dressed in uniforms sprinted towards four civilians with clearly hostile intent. The police arrived out of nowhere and broke up the two groups. All this was recorded on cameras.

'They're probably shooting a movie or something,' one of the girls commented. 'I'm hungry. Let's go to that place over there. Forest Palace. Looks local enough.'

They did as she suggested and a couple of minutes later the whole group was sitting at a table, waiting for their orders. The restaurant was practically empty. Only a weird-looking man with a large unmuzzled dog sat in one corner of the room. He was completely drunk and was mumbling something about a clique holding the town in an iron grip. None of the staff were paying him any attention. The man started hooting and shouting, singing songs in Belarusian. He grew so loud that the group couldn't hold a conversation. The waitress warned him that he'd have to leave if he didn't pipe down.

'It's okay. He doesn't bother us,' the travellers chimed in. 'He's kinda funny, actually.'

Hearing this, Anatol Pires pushed himself up and headed towards them. The dog plodded slowly behind him. They brought him a chair. When the waitress brought their food, they ordered the man another beer. Pires shook his head, saying that he didn't drink piss. He ordered Stolichnaya vodka instead. They sat there, feasting, for another hour, and then more people started arriving. The waitress led them down some stairs.

'There's a party,' Pires explained in a whisper. Leaning close to the ear of the girl sitting next to him, he started naming the people flooding in: the mayor, the commissioner, the lawyer, the priest, the starost, the high-school principal, the owner of the local TV station and various other town officials. After about half an hour, chatter and sounds of festivity started floating up from the room downstairs.

'And what do you do for a living?' one of the girls asked him.

'Me?' Pires smirked. 'I'm the dirty work expert, though everyone thinks I'm a spy.'

The whole group erupted in laughter at that. Pires, meanwhile, grew sullen.

'I dug up two bodies in the forest last night, and buried three more. The new grave is a lot better. There's space enough for a couple more people in there, though it won't be needed. I'm the last one alive,' he said. His face was serious, but the only response he got was more laughter.

He smiled widely as he realised they wouldn't believe anything he said. So he decided to just tell them everything about what had been happening in town for the last two weeks. He told them about the skulls, the kidnapping of the bride, the dog's head and the scandal with the mural on the renovated water tower. They listened, drinking their beer, laughing more with his every word. As he talked about the cannibal who had nearly bitten a Belarusian girl's arm off, the boy with the beard nearly choked on his dumpling.

'You have quite the imagination, Grandad.'

'I sure do,' Pires replied, nodding. 'I've been living in this fairy-tale land for close to eighty years.'

He took out a cigarette. Some of the youngsters felt like having a smoke after dinner too. They followed the old man out to the terrace.

'Have you read *American Gods*?' Pires asked the oldest of the boys.

'Yeah. I don't remember much of it, though. It was a long time ago.'

'There is one very wise thing in it: "Three may keep a secret, if two of them are dead",' Pires said. Nobody laughed this time. Suddenly, they felt like maybe the old tramp wasn't making all those things up. 'There were seven of us,' he went on. 'The magnificent seven. We've held the power around here since the war. Me, Mikołaj and Piotr were the last of the old guard. One of us joined his ancestors yesterday. Another will have to take a long holiday. And I can keep my mouth shut. And I will. The rest? All the rest have abdicated and the power has been passed to the younger generation. That's just the way it is.'

He pushed himself up slowly, clipped a lead to his dog's collar and left without another word. They followed him with uncertain stares. Their eyes widened as the old man turned towards one of the cars in the car park. He got into the driver's seat of the old black Mercedes and its four headlights lit up. The dog sat next to him, on the front passenger seat. The door had three holes in it, with smudges of anti-rust paste around them. The whole car had countless dents and scratches on its body. The four-eyed clunker was the perfect fit for its owner.

'What a weird guy,' one of the girls mused. 'I'm glad he's gone.'

'I kinda like it here though, you know? The peace and quiet,' another one said. 'It was a great idea to come here. Everyone probably knows each other and nobody has to call first before they go round for a coffee. I always wanted to live in a small town like this.'

Sasza was alone; her attacker must have gone to confer with his sister. This time she wasn't gagged, but the place was deserted; nobody would hear her if she cried out. She hoped Łukasz had managed to call for backup and that they'd arrive before Kuba and Magdalena crucified her on one of their torture devices.

She looked around, her eyes slowly growing accustomed to the darkness. There were work clothes hanging on the walls. A Coke bottle was sticking out of the pocket of one of them. Slowly, trying to make as little noise as possible, Sasza started to swing on her chair until she managed to slip off the seat. She hissed in pain as the chair toppled over and the plastic tie-wrap bit deeply into her wrist. Her hand was quickly turning numb.

She lowered the backrest to the floor carefully and stuck a hand underneath it so it didn't make a noise as she crawled towards the cleaning machine, pulling the chair behind her.

She had noticed a loose metal slat on the thing as soon as Kuba had locked her in the room. Its steel surface gleamed with the reflected light of the street lamps. She couldn't be sure it was sharp enough, but there was nothing else in the room that she could use as a knife. The chair slipped out of her hand and slammed to the floor with a dry smack. She flinched, but nobody came. She must have been alone on this floor. She knew she didn't have much time; she decided to risk making some noise so she could free herself quicker.

Sasza slammed her broken arm into the metal slat again and again until the cast broke, revealing the skin underneath. She didn't feel any pain; she had too much fury inside her and was utterly focused on her task. She managed to detach the slat after only a dozen or so strikes. She grabbed it and started to rub its sharpest part against the tie-wrap binding her other arm. Her breath was raspy. Her nose was running. Her eyes stung and the pain, which had suddenly flooded in, radiated all the way from her arm to her left ankle. It didn't stop her, though. The survival instinct took over. She felt her Beretta chafing at her groin. It took a conscious effort not to think about the fact that it was loaded and cocked. Sasza kept sawing through the tie-wrap until her hands were bleeding. It was nearly broken. Last three jerks and it snapped.

Sasza freed her hand and pushed the chair away. There were brownish stains all over the backrest. Probably bearing her finger-prints. She didn't care. She shook and squeezed life back into her healthy hand, then started to remove the remains of her cast. It stuck to her skin but finally she managed to smash it against the floor, howling in pain. As soon as both hands were free, she started working on her legs, taking her shoes off to make her task simpler. She was lucky she had settled on a pair today with no laces to untie. The gun slipped down her trousers and fell to the floor. Sasza snatched it up and checked the clip. Four bullets remaining. One was bent and she flicked it to the floor. She couldn't risk the Beretta jamming and giving her tormentors a chance. So, three bullets. Only three chances. That was enough. Sasza tightened her grip on the handle and practised aiming the gun, but her broken arm hurt and was swelling, and was shaking badly. Still too weak. She put the gun down and pulled the chair closer, propping herself up on the elbow of her bad hand. That made her too visible from the door. She felt her eyes tearing up. She tried again. Her fingers balled into a fist and then stretched out again. She got up, but standing upright was too difficult. She collapsed back to the floor, trying to gather her strength. What were her options? She took a careful look around the storage room.

It was no larger than fifteen square metres. The windows were narrow and didn't open. They were also barred. Even a cat wouldn't sneak out that way. There was also nowhere to hide. Sasza would be out in the open. But, she told herself, nobody was coming. The building was deathly quiet. There was still time to come up with a plan.

She peeked through the window. There was someone skulking between the trees. She could see legs wearing blue jeans and military boots. Whoever it was was running from the direction of the park, trying to remain unseen. A moment later, Sasza heard music. The beginning of her favourite song – 'Jism' by the Tindersticks. She froze. It was her mobile. The room the murderer had locked her things in must be next to this one. She was so close. And yet she couldn't get out . . . She pulled herself together. There had to be a way.

Sasza rubbed at her eyes, pressing fingers to her temples. Her broken hand was itching something awful. She scratched it, leaving bloody welts in the skin, and then crawled towards the door. Just as she suspected, it was locked. There wasn't even a handle to grab. For a few moments she tried prying it open, but in vain. Next, she tried punching in the code Łukasz had given her, though she wasn't sure she remembered it right. The small panel bleeped in protest. She tried again. It was no use. She slid down onto her knees. Either the code she had was wrong or it had been changed. She wouldn't be able to get out without forcing the door open, but she was nearly drained by now and besides, she had nothing to use as a battering ram. *The floor cleaning machine,* she thought.

She went over to it and tried moving it. It was easier than she had anticipated; the wheels meant she could move it without too much exertion. Sasza positioned the machine so that its front faced the door, and crouched behind it. Then she leaned her back against it and tested aiming her gun at the entrance and slipping back behind the cover of the machine. She leaned to the side, pointing the gun, and then pushed with her legs, jumping straight at the door, counting the time it took her to cross the space. A few attempts later, she was drenched in sweat and panting heavily. If the murderer opened the door, she wouldn't aim at his legs. She'd go straight for the torso. One of the three shots she had needed to take him down. She wouldn't get another chance. He would put her out of her misery for good.

Her mobile went off again. A single short chime. Somebody had just left her a voice message. She had no idea how long she had been here or how long they planned to keep her. The stress slowly left her muscles. She was growing sleepy. It would be so easy to retreat into slumber, to finally stop feeling that throbbing pain. Her broken arm hung limply by her side, swollen like a balloon and completely useless. Sasza tried not to think about it but couldn't focus on anything else. She got to her feet and took one of the aprons hanging by the cleaning staff's outfits, and started tying it into a makeshift sling. Before she was finished, she heard clicking and the short melody of the door's key panel. Someone was punching in the code.

Sasza scrambled back behind the cleaning machine and adopted the shooter's position behind it an instant before the door swung open. As soon as the man barged in, Sasza leaned over the side of the machine and shot. She missed. The man lunged at her. She shot again, panicking. She wasn't sure if she was aiming at the head or the torso but she was quick. Too quick for him. Her assailant made a gurgling sound and toppled to the ground, hitting his head on the floor with a crack.

Sasza didn't hesitate. She sprang up and moved to the door, limping. Her aim never wavered. She kept the gun pointed at the man as she passed him, but he didn't move. The fight had gone out of him. The light from the corridor blinded her and she had to shut her eyes briefly.

'Sasza.' She heard a rasp from the floor.

She spun round. The man lying on the floor in a spreading pool of blood was Robert Duchnowski. Ghost.

'I knew you couldn't see shit without those glasses,' he croaked weakly. 'You've killed me.'

Sasza dropped to her knees with a yelp. She shook her dying friend.

'It's going to be okay, Ghost!' She tried to stem the blood flowing from his wound with her one good hand. She wasn't doing a good job. She couldn't speak. She broke down crying.

'You haven't practised.' Ghost's lips made a grimace that, in different circumstances, would probably have been as a smile. 'Shit, it hurts so much.'

'Don't die! Please, don't die,' Sasza sobbed, hugging the man and snuggling her face against his cheek. 'Don't do this to me.'

'I'm only sorry about that bed, Sasza. That we never had a chance,' Ghost rasped, then blacked out.

END OF BOOK II

Afterword

I have chosen to locate the events of this book in my home town. Hajnówka is a small place on the outskirts of the Białowieża Forest – green, calm and very atmospheric. When I first announced my decision, many people reacted with surprise. A backwater in the middle of nowhere? Why? Because the history of the place is amazing, I responded. I haven't changed my mind.

The history of Hajnówka is a little like the accounts from the first settlements in the Wild West. The only thing that's different is the scale. A long time ago, it was a place where wanderers from the entire world thronged in search of a new life, success and money. Instead of gold, though, at first they were seeking game. It was mercilessly decimated. Then lumber, which used to be even more valuable than the gleaming ore. The forest covers the shifting border of the country, and there are many places nearby where the blood of innocents has been spilled. Nevertheless, Hajnówka and its surroundings are still not a popular topic in the media.

This book also touches on my own family's story. Since I was a child, I have been hearing various accounts of the life of my grandmother, the mother of my mother, who died during the Second World War. She was seven months pregnant at the time and, according to the stories, she was shot by a German tank. Her name was Katarzyna. I was named after her. My mother was orphaned aged six. When I was researching a certain wartime story for the purposes of this book, I stumbled on the files concerning the pogrom of the Orthodox villages near Hajnówka in the archives of the Polish IPN (Institute of National Remembrance). It was a massacre perpetrated by a unit under the command of one of the so called 'Cursed Soldiers' – Romuald Rajs, aka 'Bury'. The headstrong soldiers of the radical anti-communist underground resistance killed and maimed more than a hundred people. They were civilians, women and children among them. Fifty carters were abducted, thirty of whom, all of the Orthodox creed, were executed. Their bodies were not found until 1994. They were immortalised on a monument only in 1997, after their second exhumation. For nearly half a century the local community remained silent out of fear, though everyone had known the location of the mass grave.

It wasn't the only offence committed by the anti-communist underground resistance against innocent people, who had to die only because they refused to emigrate, as the communist regime had suggested, and because of the Polish guerrillas' dream of a 'Poland for Poles'. Those locals who still remember those difficult times claim that the number of victims was significantly higher – at least a few hundred. Numerous Belarusian villages were wiped off the map. Many bodies have never been found, and people were simply too afraid to even mention this old tragedy in conversation. My grandmother was one of the victims of the pogrom. I would like to dedicate this book to her and to my mother.

When I read those documents at the IPN, I felt shivers running down my spine. Every word in the files touched me personally. Sometimes I like to say it is not the author who comes up with a story, but the story that chooses the author as the only person who can tell it. It was like that in this case. We never talked about matters of national origin at home. Nationalism and radical political views were anathema to my parents. They are well educated, well read and cool-headed people. They wanted to protect their children from the past by simply forgetting it, keeping it tucked safely behind a veil of silence. It was safer than reopening old wounds. When I first went to a Belarusian high school, I didn't even know the Cyrillic alphabet. We've always talked in Polish at home.

I do remember protesting vocally when they told me at school that I had Belarusian roots. I was too young to understand. I didn't grasp the importance of the notion of land, or that the psychological memory of our ancestors, the history we've grown out of, which still shines over our cultural and social heritage as well as our thought processes themselves, is part of us, trailing us like a shadow. It's impossible to run from it. It needs to be known and understood, not only to grant future generations a degree of peace of mind but also so we can learn about ourselves. Maybe I write the books I write because of the bloody psychological genome of my ancestors (as I learned about my roots, psychologically speaking, I uncovered even more tragedies and misfortunes that my forefathers had endured). But that is a topic for another story altogether. Maybe I'll write it down someday.

The blood of the people of Hajnówka is a mix of Polish, Belarusian, Ukrainian, Lithuanian and Russian, but there is also French, German and Jewish heritage; and that is not even counting the numerous other nationalities that have settled in the region. The cultural melting pot that is Hajnówka, however, dominated by Belarusians, still constitutes a fascinating mix. I recommend that all my readers come and visit this place and learn about the secrets of the 'locals'.

But as I grew up in Hajnówka, attending primary and high school here, working on this book was all the more difficult for me. I had to cut myself off from my childhood memories – idealised, naïve and unrealistic by their very nature. They don't help in the process of constructing the plot, which requires cold judgement instead of literary onanism or excessive sugar-coating. I've visited Hajnówka 'for work' countless times in order to be able to finally perceive the place as a setting for my book and not just 'Baćkaŭščyna', or Fatherland.

The subject of the pogrom and the issues of national origin are still sensitive matters here. During my work on this book I experienced open hostility as well as distorting or manipulative approaches to historical facts. I feel like I need to say this with great emphasis – this is a work of fiction, a crime novel, not a documentary or a historical tract. All events described here are wholly fictional, though of course inspired by reality. From the very beginning of the town's existence – 1951, or the year when Hajnówka was granted city rights – there probably haven't been as many murders here as I've described in this book. All of you who are interested in the topic of the pogroms should have a read through the IPN documents, and talk to people who still remember those horrendous events.

It is also not true that Hajnówka is inhabited only by the evil and deceitful people so characteristic of all my crime novels. I like to believe that the Orthodox and the Catholics live here in peace and respect for each other. Mixed families are nothing out of the ordinary. That just makes our holidays and religious rituals last twice as long. Besides, the melting pot of cultures and religions as well as local traditions can only really still be found in the east of Poland, though globalisation and commercialism have triumphantly entered this world too, and are enjoying great success. Maybe you'd have a bit more of a problem if you wanted to pay for something by credit card, but at the same time, the east is a place where the old adage '*Gość w dom, Bóg w dom*' (literally 'hosting a guest is like hosting God himself') is still very much alive.

And nowhere else in the whole wide world have I had better potato *babka*, smoked pork lard, or *pelmeni* generously stuffed with garlic. It's the perfect place to visit for a weekend. It's also a great starting point for hiking across the forest. There is no other place inhabited by so many species of birds and other animals you can observe at arm's length. You can sometimes glimpse a bison, an elk or a deer crossing the road. Old holy matrons, *whisperers*, are still a thing. Superstition is part of reality. I myself still believe in some old wives' tales!

I don't know who really holds the power in town, and whether Hajnówka is full of ex-communists. I'm not the one to judge that, and it is definitely not the aim of this book. I despise politics. Unless it ruins the peace and quiet of the ordinary man, barging into the domain of emotion, when it becomes of interest to me, but only professionally. It is true, though, that in such a small town the power of rumour is enormous. A lot greater than online chat about celebrities and morning shows on the TV. The reality of the media holds little sway over the locals. It is a place of contrasts, soaked with the stench of a dilapidated backwater, poverty and slums, but also home to modern guerrillas and radical nationalists – on both sides of the conflict.

Nature is what you get in return for Hajnówka's numerous social shortcomings. There is no other place steeped in such complete silence, and you'd be hard pressed to find another spot with so many different shades of green. The land – both literally and metaphorically speaking – holds a special place in the hearts of the locals. People here are close-mouthed and discreet, and keep their secrets hidden deep below the surface. There are things you'll never learn about them. But that is a truth characteristic of any small, close-knit community.

I'm proud that I come from Hajnówka. I'm sure that my roots, the cultural wealth in my genes and the courage that I acquired in those most crucial years for any individual – youth and adolescence – have affected who I am today and who I will be in the future. Unlike my parents with me, I don't keep those things from my daughter, speaking openly with her about her origins and history. That is what I wholeheartedly recommend you do too. Silence isn't golden. The truth is always better than an elusive peace of mind. We should know where we come from and where the land of our ancestors lies.

That is why I also dedicate this book to my fellow countrymen – the past, the present, and the future ones.

Acknowledgements

For the tours, hiding the bodies of the imaginary victims, and a new way to look at my hometown: Jauhien Jańczuk and Alicja Gryc, who opened the doors to the town library for me, allowing me to unearth the town's history. I would also like to thank all the librarians there, especially Ewa Litwiniec.

For telling me the story of his father, closely intertwined with the tale of Bury – the owner of the Sioło Budy restaurant and resort. I dug into the details of the story later in the Białystok division of the Institute of National Remembrance, collecting and reading various books, local press archives, and old photo albums. I wouldn't be able to remember all the titles now.

I would also like to thank Sebastian Kaczmarek from the Central Police Headquarters; Dariusz Zajdel from the Central Forensic Laboratory of the Police; Professor Rafał Pankowski from Collegium Civitas; Karol Supryczyński – the master and commander of electricity; sociologist Tomasz Sulima; town councilman Bogusław Łabędzki; Barbara Poleszuk; Jacek Prokopiuk – journalist at the *Głos Siemiatycz* and other local papers; Łukasz Stepaniuk from Ratsiya Radio; Anna Bondaruk – an authentic whisperer from the village of Rutka; Irena Kuptel and Adam Bondaruk from the Poviat Police Headquarters in Hajnówka; Roman Sacharczuk; Włodzimierz Poskrobko – retired director of the HPPD (Hajnówka Lumber Industry Company); Filip Łobodziński, who wrote the limerick about the cannibal on his way to Ełk (that's why I decided to make it Hangdog's hometown) and it only took him a minute or so; Leszek Koźmiński and Paweł Leśniewski from the Police Academy in Piła and Inspector Robert Duchnowski – a retired criminology expert; public prosecutor Paweł Kaliszczak – a member of the Board of the Public Prosecutors' and Prosecutor's Office Employees Foundation (Rada Fundacji Prokuratorów i Pracowników Prokuratury im.

Ireny Babińskiej), an ex-academic staff member at the Department of Forensic Science of the Jagiellonian University in Kraków under the academic supervision of Professor Tadeusz Hanausek; Jacek Cichowski – movie director, documentarist – for all the tales about the forest and taking me to the shooting range; Paulina Wilk for the inspiring conversations about the 1956–89 history of Poland; the part about the butcher – Ivan Marchenko – was inspired by an article by Arkariusz Panasiuk published in the *Reporter*.

Furthermore, I would like to thank Robert Gromek and the 'Wąbrzeźno Electrician'; the director and staff of the Żubrówka Hotel for being gracious hosts throughout my stay. I have to whole-heartedly recommend the food their restaurant serves. Kinga Kosiek and Iwona Bejnar who allowed me to use their names, though there is nothing of their own lives in the stories of the characters in this book. The same goes for all the other characters; all the names and stories in this book are fictional and are by no means intended to correspond to any real-life names or people. A big hug for Marcin Wroński, a writer and an obsessive fan of the Eastern Hinterland, or Kresy, as it's called in Polish, for finally convincing me that the people of Hajnówka deserve their own book.

Hats off to Irma Iwaszko, who stoically suffers my lack of math-ematical talent, boorish jokes, and constant cussing unbefitting her refined tastes, while analysing every detail of my novels and finding all the fragments that need rewriting or improving. Such an editor is a treasure. Thank you, Irma. I hope we will enjoy a long and fruitful relationship.

Special thanks to:

Małgorzata Młodzian, my long-time friend who always has my back, for helping out with all kinds of logistical, technical and fac-tual issues – as with all my other books. This time she also provided me with knowledge about methods of farm animal slaughter and the rituals related thereto.

And

Mariusz Czubaj, who has been there since the beginning of my fight for the book, when the novel was still only my *idée fixe*. For helping me out, scrutinising my numerous plans and verifying my ideas as well as motivating me to find the courage to cut myself off from my childhood memories and write a story about Hajnówka as if it wasn't my hometown. After all, monuments of bronze grow old too fast. Mariusz was also my first reader and, as an 'experienced crime writer', my greatest advisor. I haven't used all of your advice, Mario, but please don't hold it against me.

My mum – for the family stories and praying that I finish the book before it finished me off.

My daughter – for putting up with a mother with a job as weird as this.

Grandma Jasia Purzycka – for her invaluable help and the treats she fed me when, near the end of the writing process, I was starting to lose my grip on reality.

My brother – for the leads with the 'Sunday tracksuit', *Wisdom of Psychopaths* and his collection of chauvinist jokes.

My publisher – especially Małgorzata Czarzasty and Małgorzata Burakiewicz for their staunch support, infinite patience and for believing in this book before it was even finished.

Thank you
Katarzyna Bonda

THRILLINGLY GOOD BOOKS FROM CRIMINALLY GOOD WRITERS

CRIME FILES BRINGS YOU THE LATEST RELEASES FROM TOP CRIME AND THRILLER AUTHORS.

SIGN UP ONLINE FOR OUR MONTHLY NEWSLETTER AND BE THE FIRST TO KNOW ABOUT OUR COMPETITIONS, NEW BOOKS AND MORE.

VISIT OUR WEBSITE: WWW.CRIMEFILES.CO.UK
LIKE US ON FACEBOOK: FACEBOOK.COM/CRIMEFILES
FOLLOW US ON TWITTER: @CRIMEFILESBOOKS